CAUTION: THESE STORIES CONTAIN VERY STRONG LANGUAGE WITH GRAPHIC & EXPLICIT SEXUAL REFERENCES. THEY ARE SUITABLE FOR ADULT AUDIENCES ONLY! – YOU HAVE BEEN WARNED.

Visit the **'Alexandra'** website: scan this code:

Or type: https://**xxxalexandra.blogspot.com**
[Bing or Firefox recommended.]

"THE ADVENTURES OF ALEXANDRA."

SERIES 1

By STEPHEN J. WILLIAMS

Based on the original internet adventure series:"The amazing adventures of Alexandra" by Stephen J. Williams writing as 'William Alexander Stephens.'

THESE ARE THE ALTERNATIVE ADULT VERSIONS FROM 'THE TEMPORAL DETECTIVES' SERIES. THEY WILL DIFFER FROM THE ORIGINAL STORIES - AS PREVIOUSLY PUBLISHED - IN THAT SERIES. THEY ARE ONLY SUITABLE FOR ADULT AUDIENCES!

Series 1 contains TEN selected episodes of those adventures from the Internet site. The series is also known as the 'THROUGH THE KEYHOLE' collection in some territories.

IT WOULD GREATLY ASSIST THE READER TO ENJOY THESE STORIES, IF THEY ARE FAMILIAR WITH THE BOOK SERIES: 'THE TEMPORAL DETECTIVES' BY THE SAME AUTHOR.

ISBN-SBN: 9781738487561

NOTE: Cover and illustrations on pages 1, 3 & 6 found in the Public Domain with no copyright details apparent. Illustrations on pages 99 & 388 and pages 488 & 489 are copyrighted by the author. All silhouette drawings were found in the Public Domain.

AUTHORS NOTE:

"INTRODUCTION TO THE TEMPORAL DETECTIVES and DETECTIVE ALEXANDRA CAPPANNI."

Jericho lives in Stark Island's Lighthouse on Heaven's Edge bay, in the North of Scotland. A wild and desolate place, the now disused lighthouse is his home and office. You see, Jericho actually works for God! Well, his direct Boss is, for now, Angel Margret who is the current Duty Death Angel and runs the Temporal Detectives Department.

The Temporal Detectives police the current Timeline of Humanity on the lookout for people who, for whatever reason, have appeared in the wrong time and place in human history. Their mission is protecting the current human Timeline from unwanted changes.

Jericho is the Inspector currently in charge of TEAM 74. He has three full time assistants to help him: Temporal Detective Sergeant Wilson Franklyn, Temporal Detective Constable Alexandra Cappanni and trainee Temporal Detective Constable Owen Jones. The team has a full support staff at hand [as all Teams have]. The Support Staff provide anything - and I mean anything - that the Team may require to complete a mission successfully.

They can provide 'extras', period clothing, money, carriages and cars. For one mission to Ancient Egypt in 2300BC, they provided camels, servants and gold - but no sunglasses! Another Department the Temporal Detectives have many dealings with is 'Collections'. These men and women collect the recently deceased souls for processing in the afterlife. They often call upon the detectives when they find no soul to collect and upon occasion; pass on a story that a soul has described to them that may require investigation.

They really are the 'front line' of the afterlife process! The 'Guardian's' Department specialise in vanquishing minor demons of the 'Dark Prince' and are waiting for the call from any of the temporal detectives at any time. Armed with a 'Staff of Mosses' they fearlessly tackle the demons of the underworld. Oscar Le Farge is such a Guardian and is well known to TEAM 74; he was Jericho's sergeant at one time and just loves returning to the lighthouse for dinner with his old colleagues and good friends.

But for the major demons and 'Dark Angels', there are the 'Knights of God' - these are the elite of the afterlife and are handpicked by the 'Boss' himself [God]. Bestowed with special powers they are referred to as 'little angels' and can cross over into the world of living humans [both Dark Angels and Angels of Light are prohibited to enter the realm of living humans by agreement between the 'Boss' and the 'Dark Prince'.]

These are the naughty adventures of Temporal Detective Constable Alexandra Mary Cappanni [Nee Featherstone] who was born in 1871 in London. She was one of the few qualified female Doctors at the time. Alex worked at the Whitechapel Hospital in London's East End. Her father – Arthur – and her older brother – Charles – were also surgeons. Her younger sister Elizabeth was an aspiring actress on the London stage and married to a young lawyer, a certain Mister Jericho Tibbs!

But in 1901, Alexandra suddenly vanished and no trace of her was ever found, in that time period. But in 1790 there appeared in Italy; an English Countess of Cappanni; newly married to the dashing and handsome young Count of Cappanni; Henri the 16th Count.

Henri was a 'time traveler' and had persuaded Alex to abscond with him back to Cappanni in the 1790's.

In 1801; tragedy struck the seemingly happy couple when Alex –
in childbirth – almost died. Henri in a desperate bid to save her
life; returned her to 1901 and sought her father and brothers
assistance. He also knew that – if she died out of her ordained
time period – her soul would be lost to the darkness of real
death.

Alex could not be saved and died February 28th, 1901. But her
soul was collected and processed. Temporal Detective Inspector
Jericho Tibbs persuaded the Duty Death Angel – Margret – that
she would be a valuable asset to the Department and so Alex
joined the temporal detectives.

Having experienced death; Alex decided to grab this chance at
'living' again with both hands.

She certainly did that!"

SJW.

IMPORTANT DISCLAIMER:

"All incidents and dialogue, and all characters with the exception of some well-known historical figures, are products of the author's imagination and are not to be construed as real. Where real-life historical figures appear, the situations, incidents, and dialogues concerning those persons are entirely fictional and are not intended to depict actual events or to change the entirely fictional nature of the work. In all other respects, any resemblance to actual persons, living or dead, events, or locales is entirely coincidental."

CAUTION:

"SOME OF THESE EPISODES CONTAIN VERY STRONG LANGUAGE, VIOLENCE, HORROR AND GRAPHIC SEXUAL REFERENCES. They are RECOMMENDED suitable for persons aged 18+ years only."

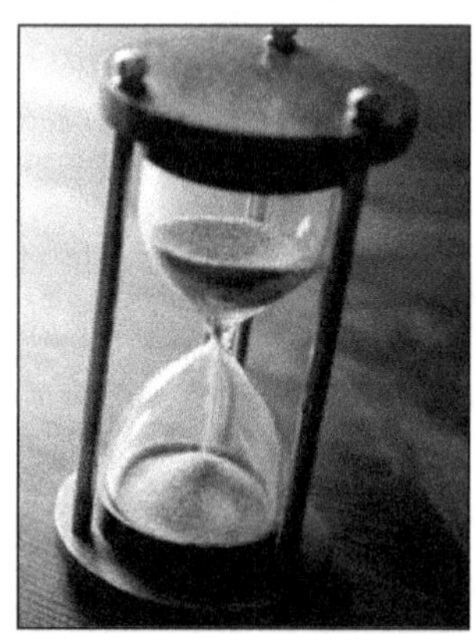

"Countless as the sands of the sea are human passions."
Nikolai Gogol

SERIES 1 EPISODES:

NOTE: 'TRIGGER' WARNINGS ARE SHOWN ON THE START PAGE OF EACH EPISODE.

1. ALEXANDRA AND THE OLD QUEEN ELEANOR MYSTERY.
Start page: 12

PROLOGUE: "In the summer 0f 1969, the old tramp steamer The Queen Eleanor leaves it home port for the final time; she headed for the scrap yards of India. But Alex and the team are on board because the old ship will founder, and the crew souls go missing. She becomes interested in her young cabin steward and the rugged captain [of course!] but things don't quite go to plan with pirates, storms and unexplained deaths distracting her."

The original version of this story is published and appears in the **TEMPORAL DETECTIVES:** Series 2 – Episode 2 entitled: **"QUEEN ELEANOR'S LAST VOYAGE TO THE DARKNESS."**

2. ALEXANDRA GETS THE JUNGLE FEVER.
Start page: 57

PROLOGUE: "The year 2010 is the 100th anniversary of the mysterious disappearance of the famous Edwardian Archaeologist and explorer; Professor Jack Dawes. He and his entire team simply vanished, whilst travelling up the Amazon to find the fabled lost city of Noah. Now, a hundred years later, Doctor Amber Bellman is going to retrace his journey with a team of her students in an effort to discover the Professor's fate - what she discovers is a whole new world! Alex gets a bad case of 'jungle fever' with some young men..."

The original version of this story is published and appears in the **TEMPORAL DETECTIVES:** Series 2 – Episode 3 entitled: **"PROFESSOR JACK DAWES LOST EXPEDITION TO THE AMAZON'S SUBTERRANEAN WORLD."**

This is a special EXTENDED episode of the original story.

3. **ALEXANDRA: THE RELUCTANT FRENCH MAID.**
Start page: 100

PROLOGUE: "On a wet afternoon in East London, workmen are clearing the basement rooms of a large Victorian Villa; the old house will become a private rest home for affluent pensioners. But they discover two small skeletons in shallow graves and all work is halted whilst the police investigate. Local stories and tales about the 'French House' particularly about its owner of a hundred years ago, make Jericho travel back to the 1880's in search of lost souls. But Alexandra and Owen are stranded and have to survive until rescue. This means that Alexandra has to become a naughty 'French Maid' in Sir Edward Coleville's London house, and she encounters some very horny Victorians who certainly are not sexually repressed!"

The original version of this story is published and appears in the **TEMPORAL DETECTIVES:** Series 4 – Episode 3 entitled; **"SIR EDWARD COLEVILLE'S FRENCH HOUSE."**

This is a special EXTENDED episode of the original story.

4. **ALEXANDRA AND THE AZTECS.**
Start page: 167

PROLOGUE: "There are strange happenings with the conquest of Mexico. The Timeline is under threat, and it appears to centre on a Spanish Captain who doesn't follow the historical norm - Captain Hernando De Plaza, who is a very different Spanish Conquistador, appears to have gone native! - Mr. Tibbs must investigate before the history of South America changes and with it, the modern world. Alex encounters an Aztec Prince and a young Spanish Knight; she's playing a Nun....a very naughty Nun!"

The original version of this story is published and appears in the **TEMPORAL DETECTIVES:** Series 2 – Episode 6 entitled: **"THE LEGEND OF CAPTAIN HERNANDO DE PLAZA."**

5. **ALEXANDRA GRABS A SECOND CHANCE AT HAPPINESS.**

Start page: 205

PROLOGUE: "Hyde Park London; in 1898. Doctor Reginald Dickens and his lovely wife, with the happy children are having a picnic in Hyde Park, London. It's 1898 and Queen Victoria is on the throne and the South African war has started. But on this warm summer day something very strange happens. The family and two of their servants are simply snatched by someti8ng or someone and disappear. The only witness is so traumatized by what he saw; he's now in an asylum. Jericho is sent to investigate the disappearance of six souls from the current human timeline. Alex realizes that she has been given a second chance to do something about what she bitterly regretted not doing her entire life. She and Owen share a secret and he finds out who he might be."

The original version of this story is published and appears in the **TEMPORAL DETECTIVES:** Series 2 – Episode 1 entitled: **"FRACTURES IN TIME."**

6. **ALEXANDRA AND THE PIRATES.**

Start page: 252

PROLOGUE: "A strange pirate ship is attacking craft around the islands of the West Indies, robbing ships and sinking them. The islands are British Colonies and so the British Government dispatches the frigate HMS Steadfast to investigate and put an end to the pirate raids. So, Lt. Commander Jeb Parker and his crew arrive at the islands in pursuit of the pirates. There is one slight problem; the year is 1954 and there have been no pirates around the islands for almost a century! Jericho and Team 74 are on scene because the pirate ship [The Bathsheba] is from the 1700's! Alex has some fun with the British navy and an 'Errol Flynn' lookalike!"

THE Original version of this story is published and appears in the **TEMPORAL DETECTIVES:** Series 2 – Episode 4 entitled: **"THE PECULIAR PIRATES OF PARADISE BAY."**

This is a special EXTENDED episode of the original story.

7. ALEXANDRA GOES BEYOND THE JERUSALEM MIRROR.

Start page: 306

PROLOGUE: "Whilst investigating mysterious disappearances from an old house on the Yorkshire Moors in 1974, Alex accidently stumbles through a 'Jerusalem Mirror' and finds herself a mysterious lover in 1735. She also finds that she has to perform a service for the old King, to free the feisty Mr. Parker from the bloody Bastille! She also has a memorable encounter with the Kings 'Black Stallion that will give her some food for thought..."

The original version of this story is published and appears in the **TEMPORAL DETECTIVES:** Series 3 – Episode 1 entitled: **"THE JERUSALEM MIRROR."**

This is a special EXTENDED episode of the original story.

8. ALEXANDRA AND CHRISTMAS WAR IN SINGAPORE.

Start page: 358

PROLOGUE: "On December 18th, 1941, the Imperial Japanese Army invaded the British Crown colony of Hong Kong. On Christmas Eve, a small band of English soldiers, accompanied by three army nurses escaped into the jungle to rendezvous with an Australian submarine off the coast. A condemned prisoner was also taken with them; Private John Hook faced the death penalty for killing his officer during the fighting. Jericho and his team are dispatched because what John Hook did on that desperate journey, should never have happened! Alex gets involved with the soldiers and natives and certainly lifts morale!"

THE Original version of this story is published and appears in the **TEMPORAL DETECTIVES:** Series 2 – Episode 13 entitled: **"THE REDEMPTION (ALMOST) OF PRIVATE JOHN HOOK."**

PROLOGUE: "Britain is in turmoil and civil war in 1985 as Scotland fights for independence after the discovery of the 'Scottish Ascension Document' and Alex and the team is there to discover who's behind it. But she discovers there are a lot of horny Scots there and back in the 1780's. Alex discovers that some men will simply not take no for an answer!"

The original version of this story is published and appears in the **TEMPORAL DETECTIVES:** Series 1 – Episode 8 entitled: **"CORDLESS, CORDLESS & FRASER (SOLICITORS)."**

This is a special EXTENDED episode of the original story.

PROLOGUE: "Someone or something is trying to change the outcome of the American Civil War and Mr. Tibbs must prevent the Time-Line from being altered; so it's back to 1863 and the forthcoming Battle of Gettysburg. Jericho must discover the plot and who's behind it and quickly, for he also knows that someone is about to betray the temporal detectives - is it a spy, time-traveller or something more sinister? Alex has her moments at Midnight - twice! - and persuades the local old Sheriff not to lock her up!"

THE Original version of this story is published and appears in the **TEMPORAL DETECTIVES:** Series 1 – Episode 6 entitled: **"BETRAYAL AT GETTYSBURG."**

EPISODE 1: "ALEXANDRA AND THE OLD QUEEN ELEANOR MYSTERY."

EPISODE PROLOGUE: "In the summer 0f 1969, the old tramp steamer The Queen Eleanor leaves it home port for the final time; she headed for the scrap yards of India. But Alex and the team are on board because the old ship will founder, and the crew souls go missing. She becomes interested in her young cabin steward and the rugged captain [of course!] but things don't quite go to plan with pirates, storms and unexplained deaths distracting her."

60 Minutes approx. **Episode Warnings:** Smoking – Alcohol – Strong language – Violence [including sexual violence, BDSM] – Strong graphic sexual references – Mild horror – References to death & cannibalism.

NOTES: This is the ADULT version of the original version of this story is published and appears in the **"TEMPORAL DETECTIVES"** Book Series 2 – Episode 2 entitled: **"QUEEN ELEANOR'S LAST VOYAGE TO THE DARKNESS."**

CAUTION: Recommended for 18+ only.

1. THE PRESENT [1969] APPARENTLY....

The little boat had been drifting for some days upon the slow current of the warm Indian Ocean. The stern had a loose and flapping piece of dirty canvas slung across it, shielding the sole occupant a little from the hot sun.

Well, that wasn't quite accurate; whilst ship's cook Franklyn Moneypenny was apparently the sole human survivor from the wreck of the Queen Eleanor, there was someone else sharing the small boat with him: 'Nelson' the old Queen's ships cat lay sleeping under the canvas too – curled up by Frankie's head – the pair had served on several ships, over the years they had been shipmates and now lay sleeping under the salt encrusted canvas together.

Frankie stirred slowly and lifted the canvas just enough to peer at the skyline – nothing but blue sky and green sea; no birds, planes or ships in sight. He fumbled in his trousers pockets and found the little fob-watch, which had been given to him by his father, the day young Frankie left for sea. He blinked several times as he focused upon the time: 6.35, he wondered if that was PM or AM. He groaned and turned upon his back, staring up at the filthy grey canvas and wondered how many days the pair had drifted.

The fat ginger cat also stirred and pushed himself against Frankie's outstretched hand, as if saying 'Hello'. Frankie managed a grin and stroked his little friend gently. "Time for a little water my old friend." He whispered with cracked and dry lips. He pulled the large china flagon from the old crate stored under the seat and pulled the cork, sniffing at the spout and gently swirling the jug. The little splashing noise made Frankie smile; they still had some water left – not much now, after drifting for about a week he quickly reasoned – then lifted a shallow saucer from the crate and with great care poured a little water onto it.

"He we go; share and share a like shipmate." He spoke softly and watched the cat lapping up his ration of the precious liquid. Frankie took a shallow swing from the jug and rubbed a little upon his lips. "Good job I was re-stocking this fucker when the storm hit. Now, that was a piece or luck - or was it?"

He now faced the real awful prospect of dying very slowly of starvation and/or perishing of terrible thirst. He eased himself up a little and stared at the horizon; nothing but sky and sea. His prospects for survival didn't look good.

He stared at the gently rippling waves and knew when the time comes, that he would slip quietly over side and let the ocean wash away his misery, for eternity. He shook the thoughts away and tried to think positive and happy thoughts. He actually smiled and said to Nelson the cat; "Still, do you remember that lady who always patted you? Christ, if I'm about to die - quite horribly - then I'll just think about her and the fucking ladder!"

Franklyn leaned back and recalled that wonderful moment, when he left the galley to throw the 'slopes' bucket over the side and stepped out on deck, just in time to see the gorgeous lady passenger climbing a ladder up to the Fore deck [where the passengers took their recreation] and he watched her go up the ladder. She was wearing a tight-fitting t-shirt and small blue mini skirt. He watched and thoroughly enjoyed the view of her small panties, bum and crotch. But the best bit was when she looked down at his happy face and just smiled, saying quietly; "You get some wonderful views from up here."

He actually laughed, as he recalled removing his hat and replying: "You get some bloody terrific ones from down here as well!" Franklyn ran both hands over his face and spoke to the cat; "What a fucking woman. She knew exactly what I meant and just smiled. Then she climbed the ladder real slow; like she was letting me have a real good look at heaven on earth. She stopped at the top and shouted down for me to tell young Hugh to bring her some cold lemonade. Her bloody panties couldn't hide her big fanny and there it was staring at me as I looked up. For fuck sake, her old man is one lucky bastard!"

Franklyn was still smiling when he noticed the sun was low on the horizon and now knew his old watch was showing 6.35 PM. "Bake during the day and shiver through the night!" He muttered and cussed several times, searching in the crate for a full tin of anything; he found beans [again!] and started to open it with the short little knife that he always carried in his boot.

"Good job you're not fussy Nelson; otherwise, you'd go hungry around here." Frankie grinned at the cat sitting at his feet, who watched him break open the tin and place a spoonful on the saucer – which Nelson scoffed down leaving not a trace of beans or sauce.

Frankie ate from the tin and stared across the gently moving waves at the sunset. "Some fuckers would pay a small fortune to see this - bloody tosser's - I'd sooner have the lady and the ladder any day!" He chuckled and lifted his leg slightly and farted loudly, adding; "Fucking beans!" The cat moved back under the tarpaulin and napped, well away from Frankie's rancid arse.

Frankie chuckled and sat back, staring at the tin. "Life's a funny old game Nelson. What if I hadn't been refilling the lifeboat stores when that storm struck?" He sighed and spun the tin with both hands. He stared at the horizon and licked his dry lips. He couldn't get the bloody woman out of his thoughts!

"Rescue or rain." He said softly and washed the empty tin with seawater and placed it, upturned, with several others in the bow; they were all bone dry.

 "Rain or fucking rescue." He repeated and pulled the other piece of dirty canvas about his shoulders and watched the sun sink. Frankie smiled at the big cat, which now curled into a ball by his legs and drifted off to sleep. Leaning back against the stern's rudder-handle, Frankie again slipped into thoughts and half-dreams about old Queen Eleanor's demise. But the ladder and the woman's panties and peach shaped bum soon dominated his dreams and he really didn't mind a bit. He dozed quietly with only the noise of the sea for company; apart from the cat of course!

2. FOUR WEEKS EARLIER....AND DEFINATELY 1969.

Captain Cole Ward read the instructions from Head Office with some amusement and frankly, a little amazement, "Three bloody passengers on a wrecking job; are they nuts?" He asked the grinning Boson who shook his head and wiped his face with a rag, then placed his cap back on. "Don't know about that Skipper, but the buggers have turned up and young Robert's is escorting them from Gate 4. They're a husband and wife with her young brother in tow."

"What the fuck are they travelling with us for?" Captain Ward re-read his instructions, then shoved the paper into his shirt pocket and sighed loudly. "Fuck." He added and pulled a packet of Marlboro from the same pocket and pushed a cigarette into his mouth. He offered the Boson one, which was gratefully accepted and they shared the same match. They both stood in silence for a minute or the so, with the captain shaking his head in disbelieve; "Fucking passengers on a wrecking job. Fucking unbelievable."

"According to Doris in the office, the wife is recovering from some major illness and can't fly. She didn't like the idea of the people and fuss of a passenger ship and so we're the next best bet. Apparently, his brother owns plantations in India and she's going to convalesce there. The young brother is along for the ride, I guess." The Boson shrugged his shoulders and puffed on his cigarette, adding; "I let cookie know and he's pulled extra rations from the Chandlers. I also borrowed that mangy cat of his and let it run around the passenger accommodation. It came up with three of the little bastards in thirty minutes; at least we won't have a mouse problem on this bloody trip with that furry fucker on board!"

The captain nodded his approval and peered down the gangway at the three passengers who came aboard with young Mr. Roberts [the Second Officer] who was now taking them to their cabins. "Fuck; it's bad enough having a woman on board without her looking like that." He muttered and the Boson had to agree; "She's a fucking stunner alright." The Boson smiled to himself and returned to the engine room, whilst the captain paced the bridge and cursed; that's what this shitty trip really needed: a bloody woman on board for bad luck he told himself; several times but could do nothing about it now.

Still, the lady was a doctor and that may prove very useful on a trip like this. The old Queen (against Board of Trade regulations) wasn't carrying a MO (Medical Officer) on this trip to save money. The shipping company liked to be frugal - or tight-fisted bastards - as the Boson would say. Still, the crew couldn't moan too much; they were being paid 'wrecking' rates for this trip. That made Captain Cole smile a little and he started to shout orders for the ship to get underway to his deck crew through a megaphone.

They would catch the evening tide and be underway before dark. Cole actually smiled too himself; he would certainly dine with the passengers tonight to get a good look at the woman. A captain had to have some bloody perks!

The Queen Eleanor left her home port for the last time on the evening tide. No fanfares or well-wishers saw her off from the Dockside: but a couple of burly dockworkers did wave and shout. "Goodbye and good luck!" Some of the deck crew waved back; actually, a little sad that it was the old Queen's last departure from her home port. The captain watched from the bridge and wondered which ship the company would give him next. He hoped it was the new cargo and the American routes.

"We're underway." Jericho said simply, feeling the movement of the ship beneath him and peered through the porthole at the rolling sea. "The weather will be good until we pass the African coast, then it becomes a bit playful. I pulled the weather charts for this time period and area." He sat on the cabins sofa and pulled a brown paper file from his valise.

Owen stuck his head out from the bathroom and asked if the water was safe to drink. That made Alex laugh and she nodded affirmative; "It's quite safe Owen; for bathing, cleaning your teeth and flushing the toilet."

"I'll stick to alcohol." He muttered and tipped the glass he had filled into the cracked and worn sink. "I wonder how the big man's doing." He asked Alex and dropped onto the threadbare armchair, by the cabin door. She grinned; "As long as Wilson passes the damn Inspectors Exam, he should get his promotion - that's right Jericho?"

Jericho nodded, then slightly smiled; "Ah, but who will we get as his replacement, that's the big question." Owen groaned; "As long as it's not bloody 'Jumbo'. I can't understand a bloody word that mad Scot says."

Alex threw her hands up in mock despair; "God no, please tell us it's not him!" She spoke to Jericho with real concern in her voice - but Jericho just chuckled and relaxed back on the sofa.

Alex relaxed into the other large, upholstered chair and looked about the room. "Actually, this is quite pleasant, a lot better than I imagined." She spoke to Jericho who smiled and tapped the file. "In just over three weeks this ship will simply disappear with her crew somewhere in the Indian ocean. But most importantly, there was not a single Soul collected. They vanished in June 1969 and sadly, no Souls were recovered from that incident. We know that at the time, there was an intrusion in the Timeline for this area of quite a large magnitude. But nothing apparently changed since this ship was due to flounder and her crew pass-over; except no Souls were collected. That's the real mystery here, so we'll enjoy a pleasant sea voyage and solve that damn mystery." He smiled broadly and then someone knocked on the cabin door.

"I'll get that." Owen pulled open the door and Hugh Dougal stood smiling but looking a little ill-at-ease in the Stewards outfit that the Boson told him to wear. "Good evening, Madam & gentlemen. I will show you to the Dining Room as Dinner is scheduled for six PM. You will, of course, be dining with the ship's Captain and Officers." Hugh gestured down the brightly lit corridor and both Alex and Jericho rose together with Owen following.

"Who's that?" Alex asked the young man, pointing to the large ginger cat sitting at the foot of the stairs, who appeared to be watching them with his sole good eye. "That's Nelson, the ship's cat. He is a very good mouser."

They walked to the stairs and young Hugh stopped; "Well he's the Cook's cat actually, they both joined us together at Liverpool. Apparently, they have been on several ships over the time they have been at sea." He pointed up the stairs and added; "Please follow me, the Dining Room for Officers is located in the Officer's corridor."

The Dining Room was surprisingly spacious, and the table well set with cutlery, glasses and plates. Owen lifted the Menu Card from his napkin and smiled; "Lamb with mint sauce, Chateau potatoes and green peas. That'll do me."

Alex sipped her water glass and tapped the Menu card; "I am impressed; a choice of two main course's. I'm going with Sirloin of Beef, new potatoes, green peas and creamed carrots, followed by a Chocolate & Vanilla Éclair."

Young Mr. Robert's joined the table and ordered the Lamb & Mint sauce with a can of 'Long-life' beer. That caught Owens interest and he also ordered a can of the beer. Jericho had the Beef with no desert and did enjoy his meal. They sent their compliments about the meals to the cook. Mr. Roberts apologized that the captain and the chief Engineer [the only other officers on board] couldn't join them for dinner. They were sorting out a minor problem in the engine room.

That made Jericho smile: on an old ship like this, any 'minor' problems with the damn engines were actually a major problem! He kept those thoughts to himself. But Mr. Roberts was a congenial host and made light conversation, especially with Alex. The young man really couldn't hide his interest in her. That also made Jericho smile.

The dinner was quite pleasant, with Alex and Owen impressed by the decent brandy that was served afterwards by their Steward, Hugh. He also clearly had an interest in Alex and hung about the table, smiling at her. Mr. Roberts had to actually send him away at one point. Owen grinned and whispered to Jericho; "Add two more moths to her long list."

In their cabin, Owen sipped his after-dinner beer and smiled; "The big man would have loved that meal. I hope he's enjoying his training course; does this mean he'll get promoted to Inspector soon?" Jericho shook his head; "Not quite straight away, but he needs to pass this course to be considered for promotion."

"I think he would have loved a nice sea voyage." Murmured Alex and swallowed down her glass of brandy. Owen chuckled; "What; on a tramp steamer about to flounder and bump off the entire crew?" Alex shrugged; "You know what I Mean."

The team retired for the night, with Owen disappearing into the adjoining cabin and Alex slipping into her gaudy, red silk pajama's in the bathroom. "Are you decent hubby dear?" She shouted and waited for Jericho's mumbled reply of 'yes'. She stepped out the bathroom, placing her clothes on the nearby chair and just had to smile at Jericho's plain stripped pajamas. "The height of bedroom fashion in bloody 1910." She muttered and climbed into the big bed and settled down for the night.

Jericho was under a blanket on the sofa. That always amazed Alex, when they had to play husband and wife that Jericho could sleep soundly on any old sofa, couch or chair.

She had to smile to herself about her Inspector; in all they times they 'slept' together on missions as a married couple, she had never worried once about him making sexual advances to her.

Alex knew full well, that she certainly wouldn't feel that safe with many other men. "He's a bloody true, old English gentleman; right down to his pajamas." She whispered to herself and dropped off to sleep; smiling.

3. STRANGE STORIES AFTER DINNER.

The following day had glorious weather and the team relaxed on the deck. Jericho sat in a deck chair under a drab grey umbrella and read "War & Peace' in the original Russian language. He sipped a glass of cold white wine and occasionally looked up from his book and watched the calm sea. He spoke quietly to Owen, who was dossed in the deckchair next to him; "Almost like a bloody cruise ship holiday; pity about the sinking and deaths that will unfold soon."

Owen just grunted; he had a small transistor radio next to his head; listening to 'pop' music, which being an ex Medieval Monk, actually made no sense to him. But he did enjoy it.

The pair looked up to see Alex join them. She was carrying a blanket, a pillow, a towel and some sun tan lotion.

Owen sighed loudly; "Christ sake Alex! Couldn't you find a swimsuit that covered a little bit more?" Alex was wearing the height of ladies bathing fashion for 1969: the bikini. She just waved his words away and laid her blanket and pillow down.

Even Jericho had to take a second look; the little black bikini barely hid her ample charms - and as usual - she looked absolutely stunning. She sat on her blanket and rubbed the lotion over herself. A couple of sailors stood by the rail and just stared as they rubbed the rail with a couple of dirty cloths.

Alex held up the bottle and said quietly; "Can someone please rub this on back and shoulders?" Directing her request to Jericho, but both sailors raised their hands to volunteer and was very disappointed when Jericho nodded and took the bottle. The team heard the two sailors groan loudly and really did start to rub the rails with some vigor.

Jericho slapped some lotion on Alex's back and began rubbing – not as vigorously as the two staring sailors were rubbing the bloody old railings – he sighed and slapped on more lotion. He carried out his arduous duty with a small smile. He rubbed the lotion into her shoulders and back and then did the back of her legs. He stopped short of rubbing it on the bare cheeks of her arse. But Alex turned and gestured to her bum; "Rub it on please hubby dear, I don't want a sunburned bottom. I'll have to stand through dinner."

Jericho sighed and nodded. "Some of the bloody duties we poor Inspectors have to carry out." He said quietly and Owen just groaned; he would have happily thrown his dear mother overboard to get that 'duty'.

The two sailors stopped rubbing the rail and just stared as Jericho applied the lotion to Alex's bum. The older man wiped his face with the dirty rag and said softly; "I've never had the urge or need to marry, but for sweet Jesus' sake I would happily marry that bitch without a second thought." He then realised he had rubbed rusting paintwork all over his face. His younger companion just smiled; his bloody erection was killing him.

Owen sat clutching the small radio and wondered how long before he made Inspector and could rub his female Detective Constables back too. He grunted to himself; "I suppose with all the serious responsibilities that Inspectors have, they must have to get some perks." With that, he closed his eyes and laid back; the music didn't seem that entertaining now.

Captain Ward stood on the bridge and peered through his binoculars; he wasn't watching the sea. He lowered them and shook his head; "Those two have been rubbing that bloody rail for at least twenty minutes. Mr. Roberts, go down and move them on, that bloody rail is gleaming." He turned to see that the young officer had already gone. Now that did make him chuckle, adding; "That's the fastest he's ever obeyed an order of mine." The old sailor at the wheel just laughed outright. The captain stared at him with some disapproval; then laughed too.

The old Chief stood arms folded, grinning from ear to ear. "Skipper, this little trip could be very entertaining and pleasurable with that lady on board. I will pray that the sunny weather holds, so that she can sunbath as much as she likes."

The captain nodded and whispered; "Fucking Amen to that." He went back to his binoculars and was rewarded by Alex turning over. He groaned a little and studied her arse with some determination and real pleasure.

Owen and Jericho just had to laugh. That little piece of railing was rubbed down by several sailors over the time Alex lay sunbathing. At one point, a fight almost broke about, when there were no less than six crewmen all trying to rub down the same piece of rail. Mr. Roberts finally managed to send the unhappy men away. But stood for some minutes himself, just looking at Alex. It was the captain; shouting through a megaphone from the bridge that made the reluctant young officer return to his duties.

Hugh appeared with more drinks and took over ten minutes to serve two glasses of wine and some cold lemonade [for Alex]. He returned several times, to see if more drinks or snacks were needed. For once, he really did enjoy playing the Cabin Steward to the passengers!

That night, Alex wore a stunning black cocktail dress which was quite low cut and several sailors gathered at the end of the officer's corridor to watch her walk to dinner.

They could see that, with the short dress and black high heels, she was clearly wearing stockings under the thin dress. Some actually took to crossing themselves and were ordered away and back to their duties by the captain. He watched Alex go into the dining room and with some real reluctance, decided to speak to her husband about the lady dressing more appropriately with so many men on board and only one woman.

"But what a fucking woman!" He muttered to himself as he followed Alex into the dining room. He simply couldn't take his eyes off her backside as it swung gently with her little walk. He groaned several times and for once, was looking forward to dining with the bloody passengers that the shipping company normally fostered on him.

There was social chatting about the table when Captain Cole Ward joined the diners. He was very polite and sociable and clearly interested in Alex as most males were! That made Jericho smile to himself; he wondered if the captain would be so keen, if he knew Alex [if still alive] would be nearly a hundred human years old or two hundred years, if you believed the rumours about her!

Alex skillfully turned the conversation around to her 'husbands' hobby, the study of the Paranormal. That made Mr. Roberts really interested in the table talk and he declared that the old Queen Eleanor had several strange stories circulating about her. Jericho asked the young officer to elaborate, and he did with some enthusiasm.

It appears that weird happenings had plagued the ship since her launch in 1933. On her maiden voyage to Casablanca, several crew members reported seeing a woman about the decks: a very beautiful apparition by all accounts. There were no women on board, not even amongst the few passengers she carried. She was to make several appearances over the years to both crew and passengers – the crew gave her the nickname 'Eleanor'.

Then, just before the War {World War II] on a trip to India, the ship encountered a lifeboat drifting on the current. When recovered, they were horrified to find a skeleton, wrapped in canvas with the clothes just rags and had clearly been dead for many years.

The little boat was so old and damaged that no one could read the name of her mother ship. They buried the unknown sailor at sea and recorded everything in the log.

Then in 1943, during a hot summer's night on a journey to South Africa, the ships log recorded a strange weather phenomenon; it snowed, and the sea and air temperatures dropped dramatically. There were snowball fights on deck and then suddenly, the hot weather was back. The Queen Eleanor survived the War and in 1948, on a journey to India, she collided with an old colliery ship; The SS Frank Jones in thick fog and two sailors sleeping in their quarters located in the bow; were killed. The old coal boat floundered and sank, taking nine of twenty-six crew members to the bottom of the sea.

The Queen managed to limp into port and was patched up. The Board of Trade Enquiry exonerated the Queen's Captain of any blame. The two crew members who died had a small plaque fixed to the bar in the crew mess room. Within several weeks, the crew was reporting sightings of their former colleagues about the ship

– particularly near the bow storeroom [which was the old sleeping quarters - converted into a store during her repairs] The pair would also make appearances over the years; like 'Eleanor' but never at the same time.

Nothing of note was recorded for several years. But in 1955, her wireless room received an SOS late one winter's night, on a rare Atlantic trip to New York. The wireless operator rushed to the captain's cabin and woke him from a deep sleep, brandishing the call written in his log. A certain RMS Titanic was sinking after striking an ice-berg – unfortunately for the hapless operator, he had been secretly drinking and was promptly thrown in the brig!

But he never changed his story and even repeated it at his discipline hearing; he was removed from sea duties and later dismissed. He maintained the story was true for the remainder of his life.

The final story retold by Mr. Roberts had happened just six years ago, a few days after the Kennedy assassination and so, was largely overlooked by the media at the time. A body fell from the sky and landed in the sea just yards from the ship; it was recovered and created a mystery still unsolved to this day [1969]. The young man was badly burnt, as if killed in an explosion and carried no identity papers. His clothes were so burnt they yielded no clues to his name, only his strange shoes may have solved the mystery [but they didn't] they appear to have been made of plastic and rubber, looking like running shoes without the spikes.

At first, it was believed to be a body from an aircraft that exploded in mid-air, but where the ship was; there were no flight paths, and this was the middle of the Indian Ocean. No planes had been reported missing and so the body was buried at sea; yet another mystery disappeared under the waves.

The dinner party broke up and the passengers took a turn around the decks before returning to their cabins and the Queen Eleanor steamed on. The captain never did speak to Jericho about his 'wife's' clothes; He enjoyed the views too much! The days and nights passed slowly, but skirting the African coast, she encountered a tropical storm, and the crew was impressed by their passenger's resilience to stormy waters.

4. ALEX GETS FIRST CLASS SERVICE!

The captain didn't know whether to smile or be angry, when he found out that the crew held a raffle each morning for cleaning duties in the Officer's corridor of an evening. The Boson wasn't puzzled by it and explained [with a big smile, gripping his ticket tightly] that each evening two men were selected to clean the officers corridor and because nearly every member of the crew now volunteered; the raffle was the best way to select the lucky fellows.

The captain just sighed. He knew why; Alexandra walked from her cabin to the dining room each evening. Her evening and cocktail dresses were [of course] the height of 1960's fashion; normally miniskirts or short dresses.

He watched every night himself and - rather unusually for him - never missed dining with the passengers. He had the privilege of sitting opposite her and the real pleasure of catching her crossing her long legs or bending forward over the table in those low-cut dresses.

He explained to the Chief and the Boson that it helped 'crew morale' and gave the men something to look forward too. No one in the crew disagreed with that!

The cook was in demand [and not just for his excellent food] but had to recount the 'ladder incident' nearly every night to a packed audience in his small kitchen. But he never revealed the whole story: the crafty cook waited each morning by the ladder, pretending to throw the 'slopes' overboard. For two days he was disappointed; Alex wore shorts. But on the third day his patience was rewarded.

She appeared saying; "Good morning cookie!" with a big smile and wearing short denim skirt. As she started to climb the ladder, he grabbed inside the empty bucket and discretely pulled his little Japanese camera out. He managed to take several pictures as Alex climbed. When she disappeared at the top of the ladder, he hurriedly hid the camera and walked back to the Galley with a huge smile on his face, but a little puzzled and intrigued.

He had been treated to Alex wearing the tiniest pair of red panties he had ever seen; they hid nothing. Franklyn had no idea they made woman's knickers' that small. He had also found out, that the woman must shave her private parts. "What a fucking shaven haven!" He said to himself and wondered how he could get the damn pictures developed.

Hugh was also besieged to tell his story of how he knocked [with a tray of drinks] at the Tibbs cabin and walked in to find her standing in just a small towel, drying her hair. "If I die tomorrow, I'd die a happy man." He confessed, not realising how prophetic his words - sadly - would be. Like the crafty cook, he didn't tell the whole story.

He had placed the tray down very slowly; his eyes never leaving her and noticed that she wasn't angry about him catching her in just a small towel. She smiled and asked what's on the lunch menu. He had spluttered out a few items and just stood smiling, both hands covering his very apparent erection.

Alex stared down at the bulging lump in his white trousers and grinned; "Well, he's a good looking and well-built young man; why not? He won't be around for long when the damn ship goes down. I suppose I could give him a little treat before that happens." She muttered to herself and 'accidently' dropped her towel as she picked up the glass of lemonade.

She heard him groan loudly and she stood stark naked before the trembling young man and sipped her lemonade. She smiled broadly; "Oops! How careless of me." and stepped forward, placing her glass down. She ran both hands down his uniform jacket and pressed a finger against his lips. "Now if you say nothing about this, then neither will I." She whispered, pulling open his trousers' zipper with eager fingers. She was well pleased with what she pulled from those immaculate white trousers.

She knelt slowly and ran a finger over the swollen head of his big cock; "Ah, wet already. Good boy." She whispered and enclosed the cock's end with her wet, warm mouth and began to suck. 'I don't think he'll last long. I do hope he can recover quickly, or I may be a little disappointed here.' She thought, as she slowly ran her tongue around the throbbing cock's top and swallowed a little. 'Tastes good, bloody good.' she told herself.

Young Hugh was pulling off his jacket and breathing heavily. He had heard about this happening to young stewards on the Company's cruise ships, but simply couldn't believe it was happening to him.

He managed to remove his trousers and kick off his shoes as Alex sucked hard on his cock. She pulled off his shorts with one hand and didn't stop licking and sucking. She was right; poor Hugh exploded into her mouth and she gulped down the hot sour liquid with some relish. Alex continued to suck and lick the young man's cock until she decided that some cold lemonade would be nice to wash her early 'lunch' down.

Still holding his cock, she guided the panting young man towards the bed, stopping only to gulp down some lemonade. With nothing said between the pair, she pushed the naked young man onto the bed and started again on his cock. He lay on his back staring in disbelieve [of his luck!] as Alex worked his cock with her mouth and hands, until it erected again. Still gently jerking his cock, she reached into the bedside drawers and pulled some 'KY' jelly - in a plain tube - from it.

She let him watch - eyes wide - as she smeared his cock thoroughly with the gel. Then with a small smile, she climbed on top and inserted his cock into her welcoming vagina. Hugh groaned as Alex began to push herself up and down on him. Her hands gripped his and the love making started.

The young man may have been inexperienced with women; but he sure learnt quickly what Alex wanted him to do. After she had ridden him for a few minutes, she pulled him on top of her and he started to fuck Alex real hard. They both groaned and cussed a little as they entwined, filling their mouths with eager tongues. She pushed up and gripped his thrusting arse with both hands. He didn't care that her nails dug into his bum cheeks. Leaning on one hand, he gripped a breast and with the other, squeezed hard and sucked on the big red nipple.

Young Hugh certainly had stamina; he fucked Alex hard for some minutes and then felt her vagina contracting tightly against his cock. She groaned loudly and really gripped his arse. That's when she had her first of several small orgasms and he felt every drop; it splattered his belly and down his thighs. 'For Christ sake, it's like a tap being turned on' he thought as she wiggled and moaned under him, not that he was complaining.

Then he realised - quite suddenly - that he was ejaculating too. He shouted out and emptied his second load into her. They lay together panting, exchanging long wet kisses, their tongues in each other's mouths. Alex lay back panting; she certainly hadn't been disappointed with the young man's performance, despite his obvious inexperience with women. They must have lain together for some minutes and then Alex ran her hands over his face and kissed him. She giggled; "I think I need another shower. You probably need one too. Do you want to join me?" He nodded and gently pulled his cock from inside her and lay back, breathing heavily.

He watched as Alex slid from the bed and pushed the small towel between her legs and made for the bathroom. She smiled and threw the towel down; "Come on before someone realises your missing." She held out her hand and Hugh leapt from the bed and gripped it tightly. "You can scrub my back...and other parts." She whispered and the happy pair disappeared into the small bathroom, laughing together.

Hugh stood in the corridor and adjusted his jacket. He still really couldn't believe what had happened. The old sailor George Parish came down the corridor and smiled at him; "You alright boy?" He asked and Hugh nodded.

George sighed; "You look like you've just won the bloody 'pools', what's up?" [He's referring to the 'Football Pools', where you could win thousands of pounds by predicting football results - it was big in the 1960's and 1970's - before the National lottery took over]. Hugh just smiled and muttered about being late for the lunch sittings.

He strode up the corridor with a big smile on his face. It would be the happiest day of his short young life.

5. DEATH AND TIME.

The strange death of young Hugh Dougal, during the night of 'white light' soon followed those words. On a quiet warm evening, a strange cloud formation began to appear above the ship, so both crew and passengers gathered on the deck to view the odd phenomena - the dark clouds appear to be riddled with flashing bright lights and with a suddenness that even surprised the very experienced officers and crew; a new, strange storm swept over the old Queen. With rolling waves and torrential rain, the ship was tossed about like a plastic toy. Jericho, with Alex and Owen following, headed for the bridge and joined Captain Ward who was struggling to control the rolling ship. The bridge was suddenly illuminated by a burst of bright light, so intense that you simply had to close your eyes until it passed. The storm abated quickly, and it was the Boson bursting through the deck hatchway onto the bridge shouting that actually shocked everyone; he looked and sounded totally distraught.

"Hugh Dougal is dead! The boy is fucking dead!" The Boson grabbed the captain by the arm, still shouting; "The boy is dead!" Captain Ward pulled away from the Boson and tried to calm the old man. Alex thrust her hipflask under the Boson's nose and told him to drink; he gulped down a couple of swigs and appeared to calm down.

"He just dropped in front of me; stone fucking dead." He whispered with some disbelieve in his voice and wiped his face with a dirty hankie.

Captain Cole turned to Alex and quite firmly, told her to look at the young man's body - then added a little 'please' afterwards. Alex agreed and the Boson guided her, with Owen and Jericho following, down to the Engine Room corridor, where the lifeless body of the late Hugh Dougal lay sprawled upon the dirty floor.

Alex took a few minutes examining the body; "There's not a mark on him that I can see at the moment. But we need to get him to the medical bay, so I can examine him properly. Did he have any history of heart conditions?" The Boson shook his head; "He loved to play football; he was only twenty-two for Christ sake." Alex sighed; "Well, can you get some men to move him to the Medical Bay please." The Boson shouted down the corridor and two burly and filthy men appeared from the engine room - coal stokers for the engines.

The Boson told them to take young Hugh to the medical Bay and be gentle about it. They grunted and easily lifted the boy's body between them. Slowly the little group made for the old Medical Officers cabin which doubled as his surgery.

Jericho held Alex and Owen back for a few seconds, he sounded quite grim; "No Collector appeared, this death was unscheduled and that's nearly impossible. The only explanation is that the boy was out of his natural time period. Now that is interesting." His mirror buzzed gently, and he discretely read the message without smiling. Jericho sighed; "We've been assigned the case of the boy's missing soul." Owen grunted; "One down; twenty-one to go."

Alex was surprised that she felt really sad about the young man's death; especially since no collector had appeared. It meant that the boy was out of his pre-ordained time or had sold his soul to the dark Prince. For once she hoped he was a follower of the Dark prince, and his soul wasn't lost in the darkness of real death.

The three followed the others quietly down the dark corridor until they reached the medical Room. Captain Cole was waiting for them, looking really concerned, he turned to the Boson and spoke quietly; "The radio is dead. Nothing, not even static."

The body was placed on the Doctors large table and Alex switched on the two lamps that hung above it. Owen helped her strip the body and cover it with a clean white sheet. The captain thanked her and dismissed the other men, then returned to the bridge to try the radio again.

Jericho gathered the three together and closed the door; "Check your mirrors people and you may be a little surprised." He held up his mirror and they could see the current date and time: 14th September 1757 at four o'clock in the afternoon. "According to my mirror, we're now in the Pacific Ocean off the Midway Atoll." Owen lowered his mirror and looked down at the late Hugh Dougal and added; "He's not alone being out of time; everybody is!"

Alex could not find a single mark upon the body of Hugh Dougal; "It has to be a massive heart failure, yet he's rather too young, to suffer from undiagnosed heart problems." She had no proper equipment to perform a post-mortem and thus, could only make a guess at the cause of his sudden death. They all knew that the young man's soul had been lost to the darkness of real death.

Jericho stood quietly in the corner, arms folded, deep in thought. Finally, he sighed loudly; "Members of the crew who die while we're in the wrong time period, will not have their flipping souls collected. That explains nicely why no souls were collected when the Queen Eleanor disappeared in 1969. The whole bloody ship was in the wrong time. It must have been hit by a rogue time portal of massive energy."

The door opened slowly, and young Mr. Roberts stuck his head around the door; "The Captain wants to see you on the bridge.... there's been a couple of strange developments that you should really know about." Jericho waved the officer in and Mr. Roberts pulled off his hat and stood by the table staring at the body of Hugh; covered with the white sheet. Jericho smiled and tapped the young man's arm; "What strange developments?"

Mr. Roberts coughed - he looked a little distraught actually - and nervously rubbed his hands together. "The small lifeboat that was kept at the stern has gone and..... with it the bloody cook and his mangy cat." He pulled a hankie from his trouser pocket and wiped his face; "According to old man Parish [an elderly seaman of many years experience] the bloody cook was replacing the stores in the lifeboats with new provisions and stuff, when the storm struck, and the boat just flew over the side - complete with the cook and his damn cat - the old man has only just told the captain. This was the first opportunity he had, you know with Hugh dropping dead and all that...."

"You said developments, what else has happened?" Jericho asked quietly. Young Mr. Roberts looked out into the corridor and slowly closed the door; "The captain used the sexton to fix our position and it wasn't right." Owen, Alex and Jericho all exchanged a knowing glance. "Why wasn't it right?" Jericho asked and folded his arms. Mr. Roberts took a deep breath and looked quite grim; "We're about a thousand miles off course, we're somewhere in the Pacific Ocean which is bloody impossible!" He wiped his face again and re-checked the corridor.

"The Captain and the Chief have both checked the ship's clocks; every one of them has stopped at 6.10pm." He held up his wristwatch; "Every single watch has stopped at that time; the exact time when the strange storm struck."

He walked to the door and turned slightly; "The captain has to turn around and go after the bloody cook; can't leave the poor bugger drifting out there." He managed a smile and replaced his cap; "So don't worry when you feel the old Queen turning one eighty." He added and disappeared through the door.

Owen shrugged his shoulders; "No bloody dinner then." Alex and Jericho just stared at him and then smiled. "Well, we can do something about that." Alex said and rolled up her sleeves.

6. THE ISLAND.

With no cook, Alex and Owen knocked up a curry for the evening meal; for themselves and the crew - that went down really well with the men, and the captain thanked the pair with real gratitude. "You're a bloody lucky man Mr. Tibbs, your wife is intelligent, brave and beautiful and can knock up a bloody decent curry!" The captain smiled and Alex demurely acknowledged his compliment. Owen grinned and gave the thumbs up; for a young monk from Medieval England, he was an excellent curry cook!

Mr. Robert's rose from the table and fixed a white apron on; the captain stared at him. The young man grinned; "I'm going to help with the washing up." He spluttered out and started to collect dishes from the table. Captain Cole waved him back into his chair and leaned close to him; "Mr. Roberts, you're a bloody officer, not a bloody galley boy. Just order a couple of the youngsters to do it."

Mr. Roberts slowly removed the apron and nodded; "Sorry Sir... I just thought..." The captain waved his words away and grunted; "Go and relieve the Chief on the bridge, so he can get his bloody dinner." Mr. Roberts said nothing more and headed for the bridge - suitably rebuked. The captain slumped back in his chair and sighed; "He's actually going to make a good officer - in a few more years - I take it, he's told you about our.... unusual situation?" Jericho nodded. The phone on the wall buzzed and the captain jumped up and answered it. He replaced the receiver with some puzzlement on his face.

"What is it?" Jericho asked, though he had a good idea what the call was about. The captain ran a hand over his face; "There's a bloody Island off starboard." He said simply and headed for the bridge. The team left the table for the deck with Owen muttering; "Which bleeding side is starboard?" Alex grinned; "Just follow us."

They stood by the railings and could just make out the island in the gathering gloom of night. It was the little flickering lights in two separate locations that caught their attention. "Fires, large bonfires on the beach probably." Jericho said and pulled his mirror out.

"It's inhabited then." Owen stated and stared hard at the dim lights. He couldn't make anything out despite the vivid blazes. The boson appeared behind the team and coughed; causing Jericho to plunge his mirror back into his pocket. "Sorry, to disturb you people, but the captains made a decision about young Dougal." Jericho smiled; "What about young Hugh?" The boson wiped his face and did not smile; "We've no way to store the body. I mean we don't have a fridge big enough to hold a body, so the captain's decided to bury the boy on the island. At least that way, it could be retrieved later by his family or someone. There would be no chance of that, if we bury him at sea."

Jericho nodded at the good sense of that and obviously said nothing about the fact, that the year was 1757 and his family or friends could never recover the body in 1969.

The boson turned to go and added; "We'll do it tomorrow morning. You're welcome to come and pay your respects - if you wish." He walked back down the deck towards the bridge ladder and disappeared. "I think he saw your mirror." Alex said quietly to Jericho, who just nodded and pulled his mirror back out; "I was just reading that in 1757, this island was inhabited by two fierce tribes who attacked and killed each other on a regular basis. They were also cannibals and cooked up their victims on the beaches; some sort of primitive ritual I suppose."

Alex grimaced, and Owen sighed; "Charming. I take it they won't be interested in my curry recipes." Alex and Jericho just groaned, and the team headed back to their cabins. "This bloody old tub does carry some guns? - doesn't it?" Owen muttered. No one answered because they didn't know.

The following morning after a light breakfast, the landing/burial party gathered on the foredeck. The body of young Hugh had been carefully wrapped in white bed sheets and then placed in a canvas bag which had been sewed together by his friends, a real old tradition of the sea. Everyone watched in silence as his body was lowered into the lifeboat.

The captain had opened the ships armoury [on Jericho's suggestion] and issued two of his mature men with rifles. He carried a pistol and a bible - for the burial service. Owen managed to persuade the captain to issue him with a rifle; he really did smile at that; much to the dismay of Alex, who told him that she didn't approve of guns; especially in the hands of youth. Owen just smiled and clutched the rifle with some reverence. "Probably thinks he's bloody Ale Capone." Alex muttered to Jericho as they climbed into the small boat, and it was lowered away.

The little outboard motor powered the boat towards the shore. As they approached, they could make out a blackened pile of stones near the tree line, still with a little whispery grey smoke rising. They beached a few minutes later and heaved the boat up onto the sand - to prevent the tide dragging it back out. Cole, Jericho and Owen left the boat and headed for the stones - the remainder waited by the boat with Alex - rifles at the ready.

Cole wiped a hand across his face and stared down at the bones sprawled across the stones; a smashed and burnt skull lay nearby. There were numerous, older bones and skulls littered around the grim site - including quite small ones - "Probably women or children's." Jericho spoke to Cole, who admitted he wanted to vomit.

"Sweet fucking Jesus, fucking cannibals in the late 20th century don't make sense. How is that possible?" The captain said quietly; Jericho and Owen didn't answer because they knew the year was really 1757 and the people of these islands had not yet been civilized or introduced to Christianity, by some very brave Missionaries.

Owen tapped Jericho on the shoulder and pointed towards the small mountain that dominated this part of the island. "Near the top of the hill, there appears to be some kind of wooden stockade and it doesn't look that overgrown." Both Jericho and Cole Ward stared up at the small structure. "Well, there's been or is, some civilized fuckers around here." The captain muttered and looked back down at the bones.

"I really don't think this is the proper place to bury young Hugh; do you?" The captain asked Jericho, who had to agree with him; the bloody savages would probably did the body up and feast on it. That really did turn Owens's guts. He pointed – again - to the mysterious structure; "That's a bloody flag hanging from the tower - at the end - isn't it?"

Jericho nodded; "It's an old Spanish flag I think."

That's when a shot rang out, followed quickly by a couple more. The sailors with the lifeboat were firing at the tree line and with good reason; at least twenty natives had appeared. An arrow bounced off the stones and another slapped the sand next to Owens's boots. He pulled back the bolt on his rifle and pushed it forward, raising the rife and then fired. One native dropped to the ground and the remainder charged. A spear went past Jericho's head, and the three men ran back to the boat.

With much shouting and swearing, they pushed the boat out and started the engine. Old John Ebbs was hit in the shoulder with an arrow and had to be pulled aboard. They just made it, crouching low in the boat and firing when they could take a shot. The natives stood at the water's edge and watched the little boat depart in urgent haste. They danced and screamed, waving their spears.

As the lifeboat approached the 'Queen Eleanor' Alex wrapped part of her ripped petticoat around Ebb's shoulder to stop the bleeding and she shouted to Jericho; "Did you see who was with those bastards?" He shook his head; "A bloody white man appeared to be leading them!" She panted.

Jericho stared back at the now crowded beach and could clearly see a big white male standing, arms folded, watching them. He was dressed like the natives except for a magnificent, feathered bonnet and curved sword.

He made a gesture with his arm and the native warriors fell silent and he turned away, disappearing back into the jungle; the natives quietly following. Old John Ebbs was taken to the medical room and Alex managed to remove the arrowhead and stitch him up. He was given some brandy and antibiotics. He confessed that he preferred the brandy, rather than the damn needles.

"He'll be fine." Alex told Captain Cole, who gave the old man a couple of cold bottles of beer. The captain thanked her and headed for the door, he stopped and said quietly; "We'll move out to sea, where the currents are strong and running away from that murderous shithole. Then we'll bury young Hugh properly; a sailors funeral." Alex nodded and took a swig from the brandy bottle that she had been feeding John Ebb's from, adding; "You've got my vote on that plan." Cole Ward chuckled and headed for the bridge; he really did have a growing passion for that woman and smiled to himself.

7. THE CAPTAIN'S TABLE.

It was just after midnight and Captain Cole Ward sat in the Officer's dining room alone and sipped coffee. The Chief had just relieved him on the bridge, and everyone was in bed - except the night watch - which would be on the bridge with the Chief and one of the Stokers in the engine room. He rolled the cup in his hands and thought about Alex. He sighed and shook his head; she had really climbed under his skin, and he couldn't shake thoughts of her from his mind. He admitted to himself that he ached for her, like no other woman before. That worried him because she was another man's wife. But he couldn't escape from thinking about her.

"That's some big sigh, what's up?" He jumped a little at the voice and looked up. Alex was standing by the table, arms wrapped around her short pink bed jacket. She had matched pink slippers and her hair tied back in a white ribbon. She still looked stunning.

He smiled; "Sorry, i was miles away there. What brings you here at this time of night?" Alex smiled and gestured to the coffee urn; "Needed a hot drink. I couldn't ring for young poor Hugh could I." The captain nodded and gestured to the empty chair; "Grab your coffee and sit down. No point both of us drinking alone."

He watched her walk over to the urn and groaned inside; the night coat was short enough to give a little glimpse of her perfect bum cheeks as she walked. He smiled; she was clearly not wearing any panties. He felt his cock shift in his pants and realised that he was getting an erection. He sipped his coffee and watched as she poured herself a cup and turned, smiling at him; "Want a refill?" He shook his head, adding; "No thanks or I'll be awake all night."

Alex smiled and walked back - slowly - and he caught a glimpse of her inner thighs and knew that she had nothing on under the damn coat. She sat on the chair, her legs a little open and he gulped. He was getting a little glimpse of heaven; but did this mean it was on offer? He had to find out; never mind the consequences. He smiled broadly and placed his cup down. There was silence between the pair for a minute or so and finally the captain gestured to Alex's leg's and said quietly; "Is that an invitation Alex?"

She opened her legs and rubbed one against his, under the table and simply smiled, placing her cup down. The captain didn't need it in writing. He stood and walked around the small table and standing behind Alex, he took hold of her and easily lifted her onto the table. He pulled the cord on her bed jacket, and it fell open. He ran both hands up her soft, yielding body and gently caressed her big breasts. Nothing was said between the pair and Alex pulled open his trousers and staring into his eyes, pulled his erect cock out; gently squeezing and tugging it with both hands.

She leaned forward and they kissed passionately until she whispered into his ear; "My jacket pocket." was all she said. With one hand still on her apple breasts, he plunged his hand in to the right-hand pocket and pulled the tube of 'KY' jelly from it and laughed. "You came prepared darling." Alex nodded and caressed his cock. Then she lay back, placing her hands above her head.

"I'm yours." She whispered and opened her legs, so that he could stand closely between them. His trousers and underpants hit the floor and he squeezed a little gel onto his erection. Alex sighed a little; it wasn't as big as young Hugh's, but he should know how to please a woman at his age. Alex was certainly wrong about that. Cole shoved his cock into her with some force and holding down her shoulders, thrust hard and fast for a few minutes.

Alex actually said to him at one point; to slow down a little and make it last. He clearly didn't hear. He fucked her so hard that she almost screamed a couple of times. The old table was creaking and groaning under their weight, as he held her down and suddenly groaned loudly as he came inside of her. It was all over in just a few short minutes.

He lay across her - panting. Alex ran a hand over her face and was about to say something, then realized the captain probably wasn't the sort of man that a woman could criticize, for his sexual performance, especially to his face. He pulled from her and grabbed some serviettes from the table and wiped his cock. "That was fucking great!" He exclaimed and started to pull up his trousers and shorts. Alex slipped quickly from the table and wrapped her bed jacket around herself. To say she was utterly disappointed was a very big understatement. She headed for the door without a word. But Cole grabbed her arm and grinned. She realised that he wasn't the man she had thought he was. She now felt a little stupid and strangely; a little vulnerable and frightened.

Cole pulled her back into his arms and kissed her with some strength. More anger that passion she thought. "Your fucking mine now." He said and kissed her again. She pulled away and managed a smile, whispering that she had to go. He shook his head and took hold of her arm and started to walk her to the door, saying; "No my darling. You're fucking mine now and with me your going to stay." She could see that he actually meant those words. She shuddered and tried to pull away. He held on tight and with his free hand slapped her hard across the arse. Alex yelped and he pulled her back to the table and chairs.

She was yelling for him to let her go. But Cole dropped onto the chair and pushed the struggling Alex across his lap. "Like most fucking dirty little whores, you need to be kept in check and taught how to behave with your man!"

He pulled up her bed jacket, then holding her firmly and with some strength; proceeded to spank her arse. He must have slapped both bum cheeks three or four times before stopping and grabbing her hair, lifting her tear-stained face up. She was sobbing and lying quite still. "You'll get punished every time you defy me, do you understand?" When he got no answer, he repeated it and slapped her bum one more time; really hard.

Alex nodded and sobbed loudly. The captain released his grip and dumped her on the floor. He straightened his jacket and pushed both hands through his hair. The phone buzzed and he walked over and lifted the receiver. It was the bridge; there was a problem in the engine room and the Chief couldn't leave the bridge until Cole relieved him. He turned back and saw Alex disappearing through the door; she was actually running, having kicked off her slippers. He folded his arms and stared at his feet.

It was some minutes before he left the dining room and made his way to the bridge. He was cursing himself; it had happened a fucking again. This time with a woman that he really was passionate about. He stopped outside the bridge door and stared out at the dark shifting sea; his ex-wife had been right about him. He wiped his face and pushed the terrible memories of that short marriage out of his mind. "Never again; I can't let it happen again. What if I overdo it and...." He whispered to himself and with great sadness, guilt and self pity, pushed the door and stepped on his bridge. He was the captain after all.

Alex made her cabin in record time. Only stopping to compose herself before opening the door. Jericho was on the sofa, snoring a little. She crept past him to the bathroom and slipped inside. It took a few minutes to clean herself up. She washed her vagina twice and massaged her bruised arse with cold water. She fixed what little make up she wore at night and taking a couple of deep breaths, quietly crept back into the bedroom. She checked that the door was locked and slipped into bed. Her sleep was shallow [when it finally came] and plagued by some dark dreams.

She awoke in the morning to find Jericho had gone. She quickly showered and dressed; in a loose shirt and jeans, then made for the dining room. She was relieved to find Jericho and Owen were the only people there.

They didn't ask why she stood to eat her toast and sip her morning coffee. Alex almost ran from the room when the captain entered with Mr. Roberts. But she stood her ground and didn't even say good morning. The captain was all charm and outlined the funeral details to them. He smiled at Alex and sipped his coffee. It wasn't the same man that had abused her last night.

She watched him go and sighed with relief.

Jericho rose from his chair and smiled at Alex. "Let's get this done." He said and walked to the door. But Alex stopped him and said nothing until Owen had left. The pair sat at the captain's table and Alex unburdened herself to the only person she could really talk to - with the exception of Wilson probably – and Jericho listened without judgment. They talked for some minutes and then the pair left for the decks together.

Alex knew that whatever she said to Jericho remained with him.

She would stick really close to her Inspector now. But it was the captain's behavior after the incident that actually shocked and puzzled Alex; it was like the whole thing never happened!
For him, anyway - But Alex kept well clear of the man whenever she could. She had resolved not to let the incident change her or her lifestyle; "Chalk that one up to experience and I best get back on the damn horse as soon as possible." She told herself and meant it.

8. BACK ON THE DAMN HORSE!

Alex changed into shorts, a clinging white T-shirt and deck shoes; and little else. She wandered down the Engineering service corridor and stopped suddenly; she could hear a stunning voice singing! She stood and smiled at the words, they were quite ripe, possibly an old sea shanty. She found herself chuckling as the singer belted out his naughty song.

"A priest in Austria thought one day
Ho ho ho, He'd go to France without delay.

Halla-ralla-ray, halla-ralla-rah.
He'd go to France without delay.
Halla-ralla-ray ho ho!

And when the father came to France
Ho ho etc.
'Twas seven sick nuns he found by chance
Halla-ralla-ray etc.

He saw these nuns in the convent yard
All lying down on benches hard.

To one he said, "What can I do?
I'm priest as well as doctor, too."

The sick nun made a quick reply,
"Oh treat me, Father, ere I die."

He took in hand his mighty prick
And he fucked that nun so very quick.

The others ran that they might see,
And they asked the priest what could it be.

"A medicine stick in my hand I hold
To cure all sick nuns in my fold"

Another nun who lay close by
Cried, "Father, none so sick as I!"

He fucked each nun with all his might
And said he'd come another night.

Their pleasure gone they looked in vain
For the priest who carried the medicine cane."

She walked slowly up to the open doorway and peered in. There was a big man, stripped to the waist, shoveling coal into the furnace. He was sweaty and had dark patches of coal dust everywhere. She noticed his muscles and sinewy back and arms. There wasn't an ounce of fat on him. He had just a pair of blue shorts on and safety boots. Alex reckoned he must be in his early thirties; he wasn't that handsome but had a nice smile as he sang.

He must have sensed that he wasn't alone and suddenly stopped feeding the blazing furnace and turned around. He smiled broadly at her and leaned on his shovel. "Can I help you missus?" He spoke softly and wiped his forehead with the back of his big hand. Alex smiled back and said, "Yes, you certainly bloody can help me!" She pulled the door and closed it behind her. The big man grinned and laid the shovel down; he didn't need any explanation as to what help he could give her.

She stepped up to him and ran a gentle hand down his heaving sweaty chest; it was rock hard. He simply took hold of her t-shirt and with both hands pulled it off, over her head. Her magnificent breasts spilled out and he grabbed them slowly and lowered his head. His hot mouth worked her nipples whilst those hands squeezed and caressed. It was hot in the damn room, but Alex's nipples were standing up; soft, yet firm and yielding to his mouth and tongue.

His big rough hands slid down and took hold of her shorts and tugged them down with just one pull. A small tube of 'KY' jelly tumbled to the floor. He just grinned and Alex's hands were on the waistband of his grubby shorts, and she reciprocated by pushing them down. Her eager hands gripped his cock, and she was well pleased. It grew rapidly to her gentle caress and just kept growing. Both kicked off their shorts and Alex slowly squatted down and eased the monster into her mouth. The big man groaned as she licked, sucked and stroked his cock.

This went on for several minutes before he gently pushed her to the floor and knelt between her legs. His tongue and mouth found her clitoris instantly and he began to work on her like a true professional. Alex shifted on the dirty floor and groaned loudly. She gripped his big shoulders and watched through half closed eyes as he worked her fanny with his mouth, tongue and fingers. If he knew how to play the damn piano; he could play at bloody concerts! She thought and ran her hands over his head.

The big man, now satisfied, that Alex was lubricated enough, gently mounted her, pushing his cock slowly into her. He fucked her on the coal dust covered floor with some skill. Their mouths came together, and their tongues explored each other with real urgency. She threw her arms around his big neck and shoulders and pushed her bum up to meet his downward thrusts.

The pair fucked hard on the dirty floor for some minutes and then changed position; Alex was now on top riding the big man in an ecstatic frenzy, he gripped her big swinging tits with some determination and occasionally slapped her dirty arse, leaving wonderful black handprints. She pulled herself up, squatting over him and pushed down hard, then slowly up. He groaned and pulled her down to him and they kissed with some passion.

They changed positions again and he knelt behind her and fucked her hard; Alex had an enormous orgasm which made her legs tremble and her bum cheeks wobble. She groaned loudly and gasped as he gripped her shoulders and thrusted deeper and harder. He cussed loudly and came inside her. They lay together for some minutes and Alex eased herself from under him and gently pushed his big cock into her mouth. She worked the shaft with mouth, tongue and hands.

It took just minutes for his new erection to appear under that gentle caressing. He picked Alex up like a rag doll and she grabbed up the KY jelly tube at the same time. He carried her to the big, rough dirty chair that the stokers rested on between feeding the furnace. He sat on the chair and Alex smothered his cock in with the jelly and then pushed the rest of the tube's contents up her open bum hole. Carefully and slowly she - facing away from him – lowered herself onto his lap. His big cock slowly eased into her bum hole and Alex settled on it, cursing a little. Slowly at first, she began to ride his cock. He gripped her around the waist with one hand whilst the other probed her open wert fanny. Alex groaned; his fingers worked her vagina beautifully and she squirted again.

She was now riding his cock with some determination and skill. Her stomach felt hard, and another monster climax shot from her fanny and splashed on the floor. She screamed and bounced up and down on the big cock with some real passion. They changed position and he fucked Alex deep up her bum hole as she bent over the chair, hands gripping the rocking chairs back.

He slapped her dirty pink arse and finally managed to say; "For fuck sake, where do you want it missus?" She quickly slipped off his cock and pushed it into her mouth, sucking hard. He cussed and groaned and spurted into her mouth. She swallowed down every drop and then proceeded to thoroughly clean his twitching dick.

The pair collapsed on the floor and watched as the old chair fell apart before their eyes. They both laughed loud and long. Alex pulled herself up and pulled on her t-shirt and shorts. She blew the big man a kiss and slipped out the door, walking a little awkwardly back to her cabin. The big man pulled on his shorts and threw the chair – piece by piece – into the furnace. He would have to find another, or his two fellow stokers would moan.

Alex stood under the lukewarm shower and watched patches of coal dust disappear down the plug hole. She had already decided to seek out the big man again and then realized that she didn't even know his bloody name!

Drying herself in the cabin, she sorted through her chest of drawers and lifted out a thick, black suspender belt. "I have a feeling that these, black stocking and lacy black bra will do the trick." She muttered to herself with a really big smile; give the man a little treat for his efforts; that's if she could find out where his cabin was!

9. NOT WHERE MATTERS; BUT WHEN.

Captain Cole had posted an armed watch on both the bridge and the stern. He had moved the old 'Queen Eleanor' some miles out to sea and stopped. That warm afternoon, he conducted a burial at sea for young Hugh Dougal which everyone attended. Hugh's body was placed under ship's flag [the Red Ensign] and part of the railings was removed. The large table from the medical Room was used to slide his body over the side. It had been weighed down with pieces of metal and chain; anything that was heavy.

The captain stood by the rail - cap removed - and the crew and passengers stood in silence. He lifted his face up and spoke; "Unto Almighty God we commend the soul of our brother Hugh Dougal departed, and we commit his body to the deep; in sure and certain hope of the Resurrection unto eternal life, through our Lord Jesus Christ; at whose coming in glorious majesty to judge the world, the sea shall give up her dead; and the corruptible bodies of those who sleep in him shall be changed, and made like unto his glorious body; according to the mighty working whereby he is able to subdue all things unto himself."

They all said the 'Lord's Prayer' and stood in silence for a minute. Alex was actually moved to a few tears which didn't go un-noticed by the crew or her colleagues. Owen gripped her arm and whispered; "We can't do anything for poor Hugh now, but we can recover the other's souls." Alex nodded and blew her nose into Owens's hankie, which he had offered. She handed it back to him and smiled; "Cheer's." He muttered and pulled a face.

"The bar's open to everybody." Cole announced and that afternoon the passengers and crew sat in the small bar and quietly enjoyed a much-needed drink. The 'wake' broke up after a couple of hours and Jericho and the team retired to their cabins. Alex was in the small bathroom, enjoying a hot bath and heard Jericho open the door to Captain Cole. She quietly listened and didn't smile.

Apparently, both the Captain and the Chief had taken Sexton readings; where the ship was, wasn't right; impossibly not right. The radio was dead, and radar showed no shipping for miles; except a small unidentified blip, some miles astern. He had also identified the island; he hadn't recognised it at first; there were no docks or town or busy population or traffic. He had docked here only two years ago, when he commanded the cargo ship; 'The Sea Princess'. Apparently, there had been an old, derelict whitewashed church standing where they saw the stockade. He asked Jericho outright if he knew 'what the fuck' was going on.

Alex heard Jericho explaining that was impossible, but the captain insisted he answer, come up with something; anything. Finally, Jericho managed to get Cole to accept a brandy and sit.

Alex slipped from her bath and wrapped a bath robe about her. She quietly opened the door and smiled, greeting the captain with some warmth. His aggressive mood changed immediately. Jericho did smile to himself; Alex would be the best Magicians Assistant - ever [all magicians' assistants were used for distraction].

Alex settled on the sofa with a brandy; the robe didn't cover much of her long legs and the captain couldn't look away. She had certainly taken the heat out of the discussion. They sat chatting more reasonably now and finally Captain Cole Ward answered his own question; "I may be going nuts, but I think we've slipped back in time, and it was that bloody strange storm that did it."

Jericho agreed with that possibility and Alex mentioned the story of Moberly & Jourdain, two ladies who had, in 1901, apparently slipped back in time to the Palace of Versailles, just before the French Revolution of 1789. Cole nodded his head; even he had heard that story.

"They did return to their own time; eventually." Alex added and Jericho re-filled her glass. There was a knock and young Mr. Robert's stuck his head around the door; "Sorry Captain, but there's a sailing ship some fifteen miles south of us. She has three masts and is under full sail towards us. The Chief thinks it's quite bonkers." Captain Cole stood up and placed his empty glass down. "Why does the Chief think a barque is bonkers?" He asked Mr. Robert's who was staring at Alex's legs.

The young officer half smiled; "Well, it's flying the 'Skull & Crossbones' Sir." Cole and Jericho exchanged a strange look and followed Mr. Roberts to the bridge. Alex quickly finished drying herself and dressed. She banged on Owens's door, and he joined her; then they also made their way to the bridge.

The Chief was watching through binoculars and shook his head in disbelief; "It's a fucking pirate ship! - Sorry about the language Miss - it does actually appear to have bloody cannons poking out the sides." He nearly laughed; "What the fuck is going on? Sorry Miss."

Alex just smiled and raised the binoculars that Mr. Robert's had given her. "I can make out the name, I think. It's the...'The Boudicca'. Must be an English ship." She said softly and lowered the lasses. Owen slipped into the bridge's chart room and consulted his mirror. He gestured for Alex to join him. They both looked hard at his mirror. "She belongs to a notorious 18th Century pirate called Joseph Deadlegg - an Englishman apparently - who was noted for his cruelty, murder, rape and of course; piracy."

He looked around and added; "It was believed that the ship was lost at sea in 1756 because, after he departed his home port in the August of that year, the damn ship was never seen or heard of again. It disappeared; assumed sunk with all hands in some storm or another."

"She's certainly gaining on us; almost bloody flying." The Chief sounded like he actually admired the little wooden ship. That's when they saw the puffs of smoke appear from the starboard side of the ship and heard the bangs. Something slammed against the metal hull of the old Queen.

"They're fucking firing at us!" exclaimed Mr. Roberts.

"No shit Sherlock." The Chief said and turned to the captain; "All we have are a couple of rifles and some flares." The captain lowered his glasses; "Get the men ready chief, soon as she's close enough, fire a couple of flares into her. Get Simm's to do that - he could knock the wings off a fly."

The Chief disappeared from the bridge, shouting to his men.

There were a couple of more hits; one pierced a small hole in the funnel. "Turn her about Mr. Robert's." The captain shouted and picked up the bridge phone. "Engine room; get full steam up." Mr. Robert's stared at the captain; "Are you going to fucking ram her?" He asked with some amazement in his voice. The captain nodded and quite calmly added; "They are bloody firing at us Mr. Robert's and that gives us the right to defend ourselves; by any means necessary." He told the helmsman to swing the old Queen around; hard, bloody hard.

Another shot from 'The Boudicca' smashed through the forward store and set the place alight. Captain Cole Ward sounded the ship's alarm and ordered the fire-fighting party forward. He gripped the ship's wheel with the helmsman and said with some authority; "Find something to hang onto, but this will hurt them more than it does us." He turned the 'Queen Eleanor' hard into the Pirate ship.

Simm's lived up to his reputation and fired two flares perfectly into the pirate ship; everyone could see the dense smoke and some flame on her deck and rear mast. But the pirates were now close enough to fire their muskets and pistols.

Two bullets shattered the big window of the bridge: sending glass everywhere. But young Tony Groves was struck by a musket ball that took part of his head off; he was dead before hitting the deck. No Collector appeared. He would be buried that evening at sea; there was no-where to keep the body refrigerated and the heat was intense.

The two ships collided with frightening noise and the Queen shuddered from bow to stern. Wood and sail mixed with steel and for just a few seconds, there was almost an eerie silence. Then firing could be heard; the pirates still had some fight left in them.

The Chief appeared in the hatchway - rifle in hand - and shouted; "They're trying to board!" Captain Cole: a picture of calm authority nodded; "Turn the fire hoses on the bastards." The Chief grinned and disappeared.

Captain Cole turned the Queen again and increased speed. The pirate ship was now sinking by the bow and ablaze; but the pirates were still firing, and musket balls slammed into the woodwork of the old bridge.

 "The bastards are abandoning ship!" yelled Jim Grieves - the Helmsmen - as a bullet shattered the swinging lamp by his head. Jericho could see a small boat being rowed away from the pirate ship with about a dozen men aboard. They were heading for the Queen and still firing.

"Let's get the fuck out of here." Muttered the Captain and the Queen started to pull away from the scene. Owen rose slowly from the floor and with head low, stared out the shattered window. "They have only one place to go now; that bloody island." He said quietly and smiled. The Queen was moving further away from the little boat full of hate with every minute.

10. S.O.S. - LITERALY: SAVE OUR SOULS!

Owen and Alex had attended the wounded; they had been lucky. The pirate attack had cost them one dead and three injured: not seriously. Jericho sat in his cabin and called up the Duty Controller; she listened to his request and nodded her full agreement. Souls were being lost and more could fall into the darkness unless some drastic action was taken. A Knight of God was on their way; and apparently, Wilson was keen to join his colleagues. Even the normally dour Controller smiled at Jericho's audacious plan to get them aboard.

Alex had found the mysterious stoker's cabin and knocked gently on the door; "Come!" was her reply and she recongised that singing voice. She opened the door and slipped in. The big man was standing by the bunk bed, pulling on a clean shirt; he had showered and changed now his shift was over. He really did grin as Alex slipped her long summer coat off. She was wearing a half-cut bra, suspender belt, black stockings and panties with low black heels. He nodded his approval; "I see you need some more help missus." He whispered and gathered her up in his big arms.

She ran her hand down and pulled open his zipper and took hold of his growing erection. That's when the little man in the bottom bunk bed chuckled; Alex just stared at him. The big man grinned; "It's ok love, it's only Snorkle, the other stoker." Alex gripped his cock and asked why he was called 'Snorkel'. The big man chuckled and said," Show her why Snorkle."

Alex's eyes widened as the little man threw back the covers and gripped his own erection with both hands. It was huge. The big man smiled; "If it was a real snorkel, the bugger would never drown, would he?" They all laughed at that and Alex sighed; "Well, if you don't mind, it would be a shame to waste it." The big man nodded, and his colleague jumped from the bed and grabbed Alex from behind; his big cock pushing against her bum. "I'll take her arse and you can have her happy hole." Was all the big man said to his well-equipped friend.

The little man gripped a tit and his other hand disappeared into Alex's panties. The big man leaned forward and flipped open the small, mirrored cabinet on the wall opposite. He pulled a tube of KY jelly out and said quietly; "My turn to provide the lube." Alex smiled as she felt the other man tugging down her lacy panties.

Alex lay on the floor, her back against several pillow, with her legs open and the two men took turns fucking her: hard. She loved it and had a couple of small orgasms. They changed position and Alex climbed on the eager little man and pushed his monster into her wet and gaping vagina. She lifted her arse to the big man, and he mounted her as well. Both men fucked her hard and she a huge climax, spraying cum everywhere while groaning, panting and screaming.

They fucked for some minutes before both men cussed and shouted as they came inside of her. The three collapsed on the floor, laughing and panting. Alex grabbed the little man's big cock and sucked it hard. The big man slapped her pink bum and sighed; "I think we'll go again. Let's swap happy holes Snorkle!"

And they did; Alex struggled for a few minutes to get 'Snorkel's' cock into her already gaping and well lubricated bum hole, but she managed it. She lay back and made herself as comfortable as she could, facing the big man and his swollen cock. He pulled up her legs and carefully mounted her and the fucking started again. The little man reached around and gripped her big swinging tits as he thrusted up and his friend thrusted down. Alex had another huge climax and groaned loudly.

She threw one arm about the big man's shoulders, and he kissed her passionately. They were fucking with some vigour when there was a knock on the cabin door and a loud voice shouted; "Come on or be late for bloody dinner!" The big man groaned and yelled back; "I'm coming!" and he did.

Alex left the two men lying on the floor clutching their flaccid cocks and headed back to her cabin. She smiled to herself; people are right about sea cruises; they certainly are invigorating!

Jericho joined Captain Cole on the bridge as night was falling, bringing him a welcome cup of coffee. The captain accepted it with real gratitude and sipped it quietly. Finally, he said to Jericho; "We are ok for fuel and drinking water, the ships stores are carrying provisions for a full crew. So, we're fine for a while, but we need to get back to our own time. Any suggestions would be gratefully received." Jericho nodded and handed the other cup to the helmsman - Jim Grieves - who almost downed it in one go. "Well, this is some story to tell my grandson." He muttered and gripped the wheel with his spare hand.

The captain placed his cup down; "Time to take a few readings of the stars, I think." He pulled his old sexton from the cupboard in the chart room and headed for the deck. Jericho watched him go; Captain Cole was every inch a sea captain, clam under extreme pressure and not afraid to make decisions. He was also an excellent sailor. But he had a real, growing fixation for Alexandra and that could prove a problem. Jericho found himself smiling at that thought; why was he surprised by the man's passion for Alexandra!

Owen had bought a plate for the bridge crew and Jim Grieves thanked brandy with him; the stuff that's left on board is like paint in the ships small bar and now only had the 'dregs' left [as Owen called it]. Alex slapped his back; "Yes, but it's better than no bloody brandy!" Everyone agreed on that.

"Here we go, right on time." Jericho muttered and their attention was turned to the Queen's slow-moving stern. A little white light was flashing. The bridge phone buzzed, and Owen took the helm, whilst Jim answered it. "This is great; I'm driving the damn ship." He said to Alex, who just sighed and whispered; "Boys and their bloody big toys." Jim looked quite puzzled; "There's a little boat a stern of us, a small motor launch. What the fuck - sorry miss - is it doing out here, in the middle of nowhere?"

Jericho smiled at him; "After what happened today; I wouldn't be surprised by anything." Jim had to agree with that observation. The captain had returned to the bridge and was watching his stern. "It can't be the bloody pirates; it's a motor launch." He said to Jericho, who wiped his face and smiled; "More lost souls in this mad place?" The captain nodded. "Tell Mr. Roberts to bring our visitors to the bridge." He instructed Jim and then stared at Owen, happily gripping the ship's wheel and just sighed.

Captain Cole had a good long look at Alex talking to her 'husband' and wasn't happy. He couldn't take his eyes off her bum in those tight trousers and the shirt she was wearing couldn't hide her magnificent breasts; he particularly watched them moving up and down as she breathed. He had decided to take another chance with her. He had to; it was as simple as that. It was Jim speaking in his ear that finally pulled his attention from her. "Jesus, that's the two biggest blokes I've seen in a long time."

Captain Cole had to agree with him as he shook hands with the pair. Jericho and his team had to pretend - very hard - that they didn't know Wilson and James. James was explaining about the mysterious storm and strange lights when the bridge phone buzzed. Jim answered it and said to the captain; "It's the chief - there's a problem with the engines skipper. He wants you down there." Captain Cole nodded and apologised to his two new guests; leaving them in the care of Jericho and his wife.

The team assembled on the fore-deck - after a very reluctant Owen had to be nearly prised from the ships wheel - and James explained what he had in mind. Jericho nodded his agreement with it; they would have to cut their losses - three souls had already been lost - they needed to save the remaining nineteen.

That's when they realised the old Queen had stopped. Jericho touched the nearest railing and could feel no vibration; that was not good. Young Mr. Robert's appeared and looked anxious and distraught; "The bloody engines have failed. The Chief reckons that's it. The pumps have failed and we've no spares on board. We're adrift with no control over her."

"How long will we have power for the lights and air conditioning?" Jericho asked the young officer, who continually wiped his face. "About twelve hours before we run out of bloody diesel for the emergency generators; the tight-fisted bastards - sorry miss - at company HQ had decided that since the ship is being scrapped, we didn't need too much of the stuff; and no real spare parts either." He walked slowly away; head bowed a little. James sighed; "Well, that's that. We have to go with the plan now."

Just after midnight, in dull moonlight, Jericho and the team climbed carefully down the wet rope ladder into the motor launch. Owen chuckled and said to Alex; "Someone in Supplies has a bloody weird sense of humour, look at the name." Alex glanced down and did smile; the little boat was called 'The Celeste.'

They settled in the small cabin and Owen asked Alex why she was suddenly so moody. She sighed; "That bloody captain Cole made a pass at me. It took me quite by surprise. The things he said to me were very flattering, but totally inappropriate. I told him I was a very happily married woman, and do you know what he said?" Owen grinned and said 'no' quietly. She never finished her story; Wilson appeared in the small hatchway and said simply; "We're underway. This should be some show."

The motor launch pulled away and rocked and pitched in the swelling sea. "This may get rough, so hang onto something." James shouted above the rising winds and waves. Owen wiped spray from his face and pointed to the sky; "The storms back." They crowded into the cabin and stared through the windows; they could see the old Queen in the distance; her lights flickering, and she seemed to be lifting up and down. "Poor bastards." Was all Wilson said, as he gripped the fixed table.

The storm must have lasted less than fifteen minutes and then the sea was quiet again. Jericho and James watched through binoculars as the old ship appeared stationary, but at a strange angle, in the distance. Wilson pulled out his mirror; "It's 1969 again." Owen leaned forward and screwed up his face; "Do you know, I think she's sinking." James lowered his binoculars and said quietly; "She is, they are getting in the two remaining lifeboats." Jericho placed his glasses down and asked Wilson for the bottle of brandy, he had in his old canvas bag. Owen fetched some plastic cups and Wilson poured everyone some brandy.

"There she goes." James muttered as the old Queen Eleanor slipped from sight. "Did they make the lifeboats?" Alex asked with some real concern in her voice. Jericho nodded - he looked quite grim; this was one part of the job; he really couldn't stomach sometimes. "It won't do them any good; we're miles from the normal shipping lanes. They don't get picked up." He said quietly and sipped his brandy.

She nodded and slipped back into the small cabinet; mostly to hide her tears from her colleagues. That was the first real time she had witnessed the power of the Knights; little wonder 'THE

BOSS' picked his Knights with great care: they were just short of being angels. Now, they had to just let the poor bastards die in the lifeboats; so that their souls could be saved from the darkness of real death. That thought did not comfort Alex.

11. INTERVIEW WITH THE ANGEL.

The team sat in relative silence outside the angel's office and Jericho pressed back against the wall; if he had another lifetime, for all the time he spent sitting, waiting and being bored outside Angel Margret's office; he would be well over a million years old! [Slight exaggeration there] He glanced at Alexandra, sitting next to him, and really couldn't refrain from smiling; she certainly knew how to surprise people - even her colleagues - who thought they knew her well.

Wilson sighed and placed his hand on Alex's; "Well, I've always said you had a soft spot for the living, but that was a blinder." He chuckled and leaned back on the marble bench. He slapped Owen with his free hand; "Stop chewing your bloody nails. When did you start that?" He asked and Owen just shrugged his shoulders. "Maybe we could make up some sort of story...or something." He said to Wilson, who shook his head; "If you hadn't noticed; you can't lie to a bloody angel. It's impossible." Owen grunted and went back to sucking his fingers.

"Sorry boys." Was all Alex said softly and received chuckles and smiles in return. "Using 'The Celeste's' radio to call for help wasn't in the plan my girl. That bloody German freighter was off course by nearly eighty miles, and they picked it up. They should never have been there, but they were. Nineteen men got a second chance at life and that doesn't happen every day. You know damn well that we'll stand with you. Like those bloody over dressed tosser's - the three Musketeers - it's one for all and all for one." Wilson chuckled again and slapped Owens's hand - again.

The team was happy about one thing; Wilson had passed his Inspectors Course with flying colours and now had to wait for the next sitting of the Promotions Board. Jericho had dug about the 'Afterlife Offices' and found that it was planned to make up four new Inspectors. He also discovered that eleven sergeants had passed the course with five returned, having failed to complete the course successfully - this time. Wilson stood a good chance of promotion with just eleven trying for an Inspectors position. Should he be promoted, he would have to work as a 'Locum' and stand in for existing Inspectors until a team became available. Jericho was relieved that Wilson wouldn't be leaving the team; yet. He had a pretty good idea which sergeant would replace the big man and that made him smile; Alex and Owen wouldn't be happy with the replacement!

Mr. Colgate [the angels personal secretary] appeared in the doorway and gestured for them to enter. They rose slowly and walked into Angel Margret's private office. "Let Jericho do the bloody talking girl." Wilson whispered to Alex as they lined up in front of the angel's large, ornate desk. She was sitting reading a piece of thin glass and glanced up at Team 74. "Nineteen living humans have been returned to the current timeline. By any measure, that must be a good thing; except they all should have passed over. That's bit of a problem, isn't it?" She asked no one in particular.

Jericho looked up and didn't smile; "If I could just explain Ma'am..." But the angel interrupted her Inspector. "Jericho, you're not under investigation here, nor is Mr. Wilson or young Owen." She didn't smile, adding; "Just our feisty Alexandra who does seem to have a problem with following instructions." She sighed and placed the glass sheet down and peered at Alex. "Do you have any explanation whatsoever why you did what you did?" Alex nodded. "Excellent. Let's hear it." The angel smiled a little and Jericho noticed that; he actually relaxed some.

"Well, you see Ma'am; I thought that if the ship had been taken by a rogue time portal, then the crew of that old ship wasn't intended to die, they were just...eh, misplaced. So, when James returned them to their own time; they should still be living. So they can face their own destiny in the correct time and they couldn't do that if they were all dead. If you see what I mean Ma'am?" Alex almost smiled; but stopped herself. She saw the look on Jericho's and Wilson's faces; Wilson actually ran a hand across his and muttered something under his breath.

The angel stared at Alex and clasped both hands together on her desk; there was no expression on her face. Finally, she said quietly; "Misplaced? They were misplaced?" Alex nodded and did smile - a little; "Yes Ma'am. Misplaced and we found them and returned them to where they should be." Jericho joined Wilson in running his hand over his face. Owen just chewed his fingers and tried not to grin, due to nerves. "Stop that Owen and don't do it again." She waved a hand at him, and he stopped immediately - and for good!

"Misplaced? Now why didn't I think of that?" The angel sat back in her chair and stared at Team 74. She picked up the glass sheet and then replaced it. "Misplaced?" She said quietly and relaxed in her chair. "So, nineteen souls who were lost - sorry - misplaced - were returned to the current Human Timeline and that caused some changes - agreed?" She asked the team, who all nodded their agreement. "Good, I'm glad we can agree on that at least."

The angel sighed and then smiled; "You should have taken your misplaced idea and ran it past your Inspector, before acting Temporal Constable Cappanni - do you agree?" Alex nodded and said nothing. The angel turned to Jericho; "The changes can be absorbed in the current timeline. I am of the opinion, that had the rouge time portal not taken the ship, then the crew would have lived out their pre-ordained lives. So, I accept that Constable Cappanni acted in the best interests of the Department."

Angel Margret sat back in her chair and waved to the doorway; "Off you go, I understand that Mrs. Harris has prepared Alex's favourite; Treacle pudding. That's what it's apparently called. But I need to see you Jericho."

The Team - all smiles - shuffled out the office, except Jericho of course. They waited outside and each of them would have sworn, they heard Jericho and the Angel laughing. Owen grunted; "Do angels laugh?" staring at his nails; now back to their pre-chewed condition. Wilson just sighed and didn't bother to answer. Alex folded her arms and almost smiled; "I was a bit annoyed when Hugh walked in on me wearing just that small towel. But the huge smile on his young face made me forgive him. I'm sort of glad that he got to see something he really enjoyed before he died." She also sighed adding; "Lost in the darkness is no place for such a young man." Owen nodded and then rubbed his chin; "I'm younger than he was. Does that mean I can see you in just a towel...Please?"

Alex slapped his arm and said firmly; "No." Wilson laughed at seeing Owens's disappointed face and the team members disappeared back to the lighthouse for dinner. Alex and Owen walked behind Wilson, who was reading his mirror – arm in arm – and smiled at each other. Owen whispered; "Maybe we should take up acting as a career. If we weren't already dead!"

Jericho followed some minutes later; clutching a Mission File and chuckling to himself; "Alex will go nuts with this one. A bloody trek through the Amazon jungle will not make her happy. There are no proper toilets!"

EPISODE PROLOGUE: "The year 2010 is the 100th anniversary of the mysterious disappearance of the famous Edwardian Archaeologist and explorer; Professor Jack Dawes. He and his entire team simply vanished, whilst travelling up the Amazon to find the fabled lost city of Noah. Now, a hundred years later, Doctor Amber Bellman is going to retrace his journey with a team of her students in an effort to discover the Professor's fate - what she discovers is a whole new world! Alex gets a bad case of 'jungle fever' with some young men..."

 **75 Minutes approx.** **Episode Warnings:** Smoking – Alcohol – Strong language – Violence [including sexual violence] – Strong graphic sexual references – Mild horror.

 NOTES: The original version of this story is published and appears in the **TEMPORAL DETECTIVES:** Book Series 2 – Episode 3 entitled: **"PROFESSOR JACK DAWES LOST EXPEDITION TO THE AMAZON'S SUBTERRANEAN WORLD. "** This is a special EXTENDED episode of the original story.

CAUTION: Recommended for 18+ only.

1. IN THE FOOTSTEPS OF PROFESSOR JACK DAWES.

The Helicopter swung left, dipped a little and then listed right as the winds rose and dropped. The rain cascaded down the small window and Dr. Amber Bellman struggled to see anything outside as the gathering gloom of nightfall started to descend over the thick dark jungle. Her companion and assistant, Anzio Parker dropped back into his seat next to her and tried to shout above the noise of the engine and blades; "According to the Pilot, we have another fifteen minutes of this before we reach Telos." He smiled and shrugged his shoulders, then sighed; "Mind you, he said the same thing ten minutes ago!" Anzio grinned and pulled a packet of mints from his shirt pocket and offered them around.

The Doctor declined, despite her dry mouth; she had a pretty good feeling that if she placed anything on her tongue, her troubled stomach would react with a little violent eruption – the air-sickness pills were reaching the end of their effectiveness. She prayed hard for a quick and safe landing with her eyes closed tight.

The good Doctors other student-assistant; Yoke Azzurri leaned across the pair and pointed at the little window, shouting; "Look, there's lights down by the river!" Everyone peered through the rain swept windows and could clearly see the lights below; and they were coming up quite fast.

"I'm really looking forward to a hot bath and some 'Jack Daniels'." Muttered Anzio and wiped his mouth in anticipation of his favourite beverage - apart from coffee. Everyone was jerked about in their seats as the helicopter started to descend towards the helicopter pad attached to 'The Emerald Forest Hotel'.

"Hold on to your hats - and everything else!" Anzio shouted and gripped the arms of his seat quite tightly. He glanced at Doctor Bellman and grinned; her eyes were firmly closed, and she gripped her old leather briefcase with both hands.

"Not long now!" Yoke said to no one in particular and gripped her seat's armrests with hidden strength. She also smiled at the good Doctor and actually would be seriously relieved to be on land again - even if it was the bloody jungle!

The 'copter landed with a bounce and Doctor Bellman's party

departed the craft - with some relief - for the comfort of 'Emerald Forest Hotel'. Anzio pointed out the flat-bottomed river boat, the 'Madre de Deus' moored against the nearest river jetty. "That's our ride tomorrow." He said simply and Yoke grinned broadly; "At least it can't drop out the sky and it comes with a bloody lifeboat." They both chuckled, but the tired Doctor said nothing, and they headed for reception.

They were a little surprised to be greeted by the Hotel Manager; his name badge boasted ' Miguel Joao Murphy'. Yoke smiled at Anzio; "Murphy. The Managers name is bloody Murphy!" Anzio shook his hand and asked where the Irish name came from. The happy man informed the party that his Great, great grandfather was from Wexford and that's why the hotel logo is a shamrock and was called the 'Emerald'. In good English he also announced that the hotel sold the best Guinness in Brazil and kept a good stock of Irish whisky.

After they booked in, Miguel showed them the rooms he had allocated, telling them several times they were the best in the hotel; "Very few insects and snakes." He smiled broadly and Doctor Bellman asked if their guide had arrived and the look upon the Managers face was priceless when she named their guide.

The smile was gone, he rubbed his hands together and shuffled his feet; "You have hired Senhor Crawford?" Miguel rolled his eyes and nodded with some apprehension; "A most excellent man in the forest, but no good around whisky and girls." He shrugged his shoulders and told them dinner would be served at six; he left muttering to himself, and it wasn't flattering about 'Senhor Crawford'.

Doctor Bellman threw her case upon the big bed and slumped next to it; "Well, I didn't hire the fellow - I've never met him - he was hired by the Geographical Society's office in Brasilia." She told herself and closed her eyes, drifting off to sleep.

In the small bar, Anzio and Yoke were enjoying 'Jack Daniels' after a couple of very cold bottles of beer. The little barman's English wasn't great, but he knew his beers and spirits and always had a broad smile on his face - especially for Yoke who he called 'Angel lady'. The smile faded from his happy face when a tall, strapping white man approached the bar.

Yoke prodded Anzio and whispered; "Now that's a good-looking man who looks like he knows his way around the jungle." Anzio nodded and said quietly; "He's probably an office clerk!" They both chuckled and then noticed the barman didn't pour him a whisky but placed the bottle on the bar with a clean glass.

"São esses dois com a festa dos médicos ingleses?" he spoke directly to Carlos, the barman and jerked his thumb towards Anzio and Yoke; then smiled and poured himself a large whisky. The Barman nodded and refilled their glasses without comment or introduction of the stranger. The big man turned to Anzio and Yoke with his hand held out; "I'm Jack Crawford." He said simply and grinned broadly. Both Anzio and Yoke had a strange feeling that Jack Crawford seemed strangely familiar to them, but those thoughts soon disappeared as the drinks started to flow.

It was just before midnight when Anzio and Yoke made it to their respective bedrooms - they had enjoyed the evening immensely; Jack Crawford certainly knew how to recount tales, stories and legends of the Amazon with much humour and whisky. Anzio loved his story about the cannibal tribe that worshipped a giant Anaconda and made human sacrifices to the creature, which was part myth and part bar story telling.

But he became really interested, when Yoke mentioned the ill fated 1910 expedition of Professor Jack Dawes. Both Anzio and Yoke were actually impressed and a little amazed, that he knew about the professor's total disappearance, whilst searching for the fabled city of Noah.

He had the pair almost crying with laughter, when he likened their expedition to a very, very late rescue mission. "I can see the old professor sitting on a wooden crate, chewing on some half-cooked lizard, with a long white beard wondering if they will back pay his old age pension!"

The drinks flowed and they only stopped to eat salt beef sandwiches and some fruit, Yoke also had a bottle of cold water to accompany her 'Jack Daniels' and coke. Anzio noted that Jack Crawford was running up a 'tab' behind the bar, despite the notice that said this wasn't allowed. When jack went to the toilet, Anzio asked the barman about that; Carlos shrugged his shoulders and whispered in broken English that Senhor Crawford was good for any credit offered; "He very wealthy man I think.

Manager say it ok." Carlos said and refilled the drinks, adding; "He say your money no good here. All on him."

But it was the arrival of the three strangers in the bar at about nine o'clock that Anzio remembered clearly: a well dressed young white man, in a resplendent cream 'safari suit' complete with straw hat, caught Yoke's attention. But Anzio's and Jacks eyes were immediately drawn to the young woman that accompanied him - she was a real beauty in a stunning silk jacket and dress.

The big African drew stares all round; he looked the sort of man you didn't mess with. "Probably their bloody bodyguard or something." Whispered Yoke and they watched the Hotel Manager falling over himself to greet and serve them.

The three sat at a corner table drinking and talking very quietly amongst themselves and Anzio also noted they spoke in fluent Portuguese to the waiter and other staff they dealt with. "Rich tourists." was all jack commented but didn't take his eyes off the woman. The party broke up and Jack left the bar, heading for the river boat, where he was staying the night with his friend; Captain Carlos Henrique Garcia.

Anzio made his bed with some difficulty and slept soundly until his watch alarm woke him up at seven o'clock. He couldn't shake the image of the young woman from his mind; a real beauty he mused as he showered and shaved. The hangover had kicked in and paracetamol was necessary to get him down the stairs to breakfast.

Doctor Bellman was quite amused by the subdued behaviour of her young colleagues at their breakfast. The pair was drinking bottle after bottle of cold water and only managed some toast to eat. But they did recount their encounter with Senhor Jack Crawford in some detail. Anzio informed the Doctor that Crawford and his assistant would meet them at the river boat after breakfast.

A very subdued Yoke whispered across the table to her companions; "Apparently the gorgeous couple are a couple of rich tourists, travelling with an old friend from New York - they're from Scotland. Carlos the barman says the woman has 'Dr.' on her luggage - a medical doctor I suppose. But her husband is stinking rich, probably owns a bloody castle in the Highlands or something. Maybe he keeps the Loch Ness monster as a pet for her."

Doctor Bellman smiled; "Miguel told me that they're travelling on the river boat with us until the township at San Marco. A real doctor on board could be really useful." She gathered her papers together and pushed them into her old briefcase, adding; "If you're finished, let's get going."

2. THE 'MADRE de DEUS' RIVER BOAT.

Captain Carlos watched his passengers arrive with a fixed smile; he was glad that the good Doctor's party had hired a guide who actually knew what he was doing in the jungle - they don't travel cheap then. He slapped jack Crawford on the shoulder and actually grinned; "The other party - the Scottish group - his Lordship paid in American dollars and in advance. I like them." Jack laughed then fell silent and pointed out Doctor Alex Tibbs to Carlos.

Both men watched as the lady came aboard on the arm of her husband, they also noticed that most of the men on the jetty were also watching. "isso é beleza real e uma mulher real. "Carlos muttered and returned to the bridge, shaking his head and drawing heavily on his fat cigar. He hoped that his friend would behave himself around such a woman - then sighed; "o papa é casado?"

Alex was quite impressed by the cabin; "Not bad, toss you for the bed!" She gestured to the big double bed and smiled. Jericho just grunted and dropped his travelling suitcase on the small table by the door. He nodded and smiled a little; "Ladies first for the bed, you know I sleep well in chairs or on sofas." Alex was more than happy with that decision and sat on the bed - bouncing up and down until Wilson appeared, drinking a cold bottle of beer and chuckling to himself.

"What's so funny?" Alex asked the big man, who handed her and Jericho a cold beer. He grinned and jerked a thumb down the corridor; "The little native steward - Paulo, I think - is telling everyone, all he can hear is the god damn bed springs in here!" That did make the little group laugh.

Jericho closed the door, with a smile and checked the window was closed despite the heat. "Right, this boat will reach the small township of San Marco in a couple of days, where the good Doctor Amber Bellman will start to trace the journey of Professor Jack Dawes. It should take her to the ruins of the old silver mining town [at the time named Para'.] on the edge of the jungle. The place has been practically abandoned since the 1960's - but in 1910 it was a booming frontier town. It was from there that the professor disappeared into the jungle and was never seen again." Jericho eased into the armchair by the window and sipped his beer.

Wilson pulled out a brown paper file and read parts from it: "There was the professor and two assistants; a young American man called Gordon Grant and an Englishman, who was a railway surveyor from Manchester, and went by the impossible name of Colgate Standround! They had several native bearers, and their guide was a strange white man called Lewis Ludlow, who actually knew the jungle well - he had worked for a couple of mining companies, protecting their staff exploring the jungle for oil, gold or other minerals. They were well armed and well equipped, with experience of the jungle and yet they simply vanished - no stories or sightings emerged about them until just after the Second World War - 1948 I think - when some American oil men returned from the jungle mountains near here, with an old English 'Lee-Enfield' rifle inscribed with the letters; 'LL'. It remains the only item found, that could be linked to the ill-fated expedition."

Wilson dropped on the bed and passed Alex the brown paper file. "When does Owen join us?" She asked the deep-thinking Jericho, and he waved a hand; "At San Marco - I sent him ahead to poke about."

Wilson chuckled again and gripped Alex's arm; "He's gonna love his undercover disguise!" Alex grinned and asked why. "He's father Owen Jones - he's been promoted from a Monk at last!" Wilson really did laugh to himself at that. Alex just shook her head; but she did smile broadly - as did Jericho.

"Not a single soul has ever been recovered from the expedition; which means they didn't meet a natural end. Now after a hundred human years not one can still be living. So we need to discover what exactly happened to them - why no souls, if they came to a normal human death?" Jericho stood by the window and stared out across the river. "We'll tag along with Doctor Bellman and see what happens." he added and finished his beer.

Everyone went silent, as they could hear shouting and the ships whistle sounded several times - the movement of the boat told them they were underway.

"Up the bloody Amazon without a paddle!" Yoke laughed to herself as the boat pulled away from the jetty, heading upriver. She couldn't help but keep glancing at Essa, jack Crawford's assistant; the little native sat cross legged at the stern, pulling thin rope through his teeth and winding it around long arrows, that he was making by hand. Essa was from the mountain-jungle tribe of the 'Shimsac' - they had been renowned as fierce warriors, before the arrival of Christianity had subdued them slightly.

But it was their immediate neighbours that caused concern; the 'Tahain' were a mountain people, brave warriors who still indulged in the odd bit of cannibalism, human sacrifice and giant snake worship! Anzio had been deeply shocked to find that the people he had laughed about, in the bar with Yoke and Jack, did actually exist.

Wilson had made friends with the boat's old cook and the pair sat drinking cold beer in the small dining room. The cook, who was half French European and half native [his mother had been a local girl] had a quite few tales to impart about the good Captain Carlos, jack Crawford and the river itself.

Miguel the cook was actually quite good at what he did; the food was simple and definitely edible - and plenty of it. He fussed over Alex; when she mentioned that tomato soup was a favourite - it appeared the very next meal. For three days and nights the 'Madre de Deus' moved slowly upriver; heading towards the heart of the jungle and further away from civilization with every kilometer.

Jack Crawford had desperately tried to get Alex interested in him, with little success and his ego was greatly bruised, but it amused Captain Carlos to see his friend's sexual ambitions thwarted by a beautiful woman: who didn't stand any nonsense from preening men! Alex – unusually – hadn't taken a likening to the man and so, sex wise, that was that.

But Jericho and Alex had cultivated a shipboard friendship with Doctor Bellman and her two young assistants; finding out about the ill-fated expedition of Professor Jack Dawes back in 1910.

After a few shots of Vodka, Amber Bellman opened up about the purpose of the expedition; to gain closure for the family: the missing Professor Dawes was her Maternal Great, great, grandfather. So, the background story of the expedition was common knowledge to Amber Bellman and she seemed quite happy to tell the two very friendly strangers, who wouldn't allow anyone to buy a drink - including the sulking Jack Crawford – who drank his in almost silence.

That night, the three temporal detectives met up in Jericho's and Alex's suite to swap information and make a few decisions. Wilson had discovered that Jack Crawford was a former Mining Guard, who had quit his well-paid job because he really didn't like shooting natives, protesting about their land being stolen!

"Least he has some sort of morale's." Alex sighed and smiled broadly, thinking about his futile attempts to seduce her; his ego would make Mount Everest look like a hillock, she mused.

But everyone one agreed on one thing; apparently he knew his way around the jungle.

It appears that the Dawes expedition had left 'San Marco' in the spring of 1910 and headed for Para - which was booming at the time - he departed from there and travelled north towards the Jungle Mountains and vanished completely.

3. ALEX SAYS THANK YOU!

Dressed in a loose white blouse - with no bra [to annoy the frustrated Mr. Crawford]- very small shorts, cotton panties, socks, and little ankle boots because of the damp heat. She certainly drew the attention of the boat's males and so young Yoke dressed the same. A touch jealous, but she actually fancied Alex a little herself!

Alex went exploring the old boat and found herself in the crew corridor. The old cook passed her, lifting his hat and saying good morning. He was a lovely old man who spoilt Alex with anything [where possible] that she wanted for dinner, lunch or breakfast.

He disappeared up the stairs, struggling for breath. Alex sighed and wondered if she should give the nice old man a little treat, so she headed for the galley and found him amongst his pots and pans, listening to an old transistor radio. He had just a vest and shorts under his striped apron because of the heat in the kitchen. She stood in the doorway and smiled, asking about the forthcoming meals and how he was keeping.

He gripped his ladle and smiled telling her that she was his princess and what she wanted she could have. Alex smiled again and closed the door behind her. "You're so generous and kind to me I would like to thank you properly; as long as you can keep it a secret between us." He slowly grinned and tossed the ladle into the full sink with a splash; "Oh, my little darling I could keep any secret you wanted me too." Alex drew close to him and picked up a large cucumber from a pile of vegetables on the packed table and ran her hands around its girth. "This reminds me of an old friend; the incredible Hulk!" She said quietly and the cook laughed, lifting his apron; "My darling, you don't need that when you could have the real thing and it's not bloody green!"

Alex slowly lowered the cucumber as the cook dropped his shorts and she whistled; "Cookie, you must be the best equipped chef on the bloody Amazon!" and tossed the cucumber back onto the table. She was quickly on her knees, sucking hard. Her hands gently and firmly, caressing his swollen cock as she licked his sweaty balls. He groaned and stroked her hair, muttering in Spanish about the how God was indeed generous and merciful.

She worked his cock for a few minutes, sucking and jerking, and noticed that it was already leaking, which she licked up with her darting tongue. He managed to warn her about his imminent ejaculation, and she just smiled, as best she could with her mouth full of his cock. He groaned and cussed – in Spanish – and spurted, filling her mouth and throat with cum. She noisily gulped it down and continued to suck as he shuddered and moaned in sheer delight. He reluctantly pulled away and wiped his cock on the apron as Alex rose, wiping her mouth and she smiled broadly. "That was the starter cookie, would you like the main course or the desert next?"

The old man whispered something again in Spanish as Alex slowly pulled down her shorts and panties in one move: revealing her shaven fanny to him. He wiped his face with the apron and again praised God for his generosity. Alex slipped out of her fallen clothes and ran a hand between her legs, patting her vagina. She said softly; "That's the main course and this could be the desert." She turned a little and pulled open a bum cheek, revealing her cute brown anus. She giggled; "So what do you fancy?" The Cook wiped his face again and gripped his flaccid cock, jerking it hard. "My little darling, I have a sweet tooth!" he declared and grabbed a bottle of virgin olive oil from the table.

Alex bent over the table, both hands holding her arse cheeks apart as he applied the oil with shaking hands and fingers. She looked over her shoulder to see him smearing his new erection with the oil. He mounted her with some urgency, pushing his cock into her arse slowly and gently. Once settled in her welcoming back passage, he gripped her shoulders and started to push deeper and with more speed. She groaned as he thrusted with some strength and the old cook fucked her arse like that for several minutes before praising God [again] and emptying his balls fully. Alex guessed he was quite a religious man!

Sitting on a small stool, wiping his cock on his apron, the old man confessed that he couldn't manage a main course just right now. Alex just smiled and kissed his sweaty, red face and pulled up her panties and shorts. He made her promise to deliver his next meal soon and Alex left the happy old man singing God's praises amongst his pots and pans.

But she was now really sexually aroused and needed a good fucking. She wandered down the corridor and knew that the next man she came across could really be a lucky bastard. She needed cock and urgently. Then saw a slightly open door and couldn't help herself; she peered in.

She quickly slapped a hand against her mouth to stop gasping loudly. Essa, Jack Crawford's young native assistant was standing by the sink, washing his dark body down with warm water and a little oil. He could have posed for art classes; he had a real toughened body with not a ounce of fat from living and surviving in the jungle. He was really fit and could easily run for miles.

But what really caught her attention was what hung between his short strong legs. His cock was flaccid, but still reached just above his knees. Even when not erected; Alex reckoned that she couldn't get her fingers around the girth of the damn thing. "A black bleeding Anaconda." She whispered and chuckled.

He turned suddenly and saw her. Alex smiled and spluttered; "Just exploring the old ship." He nodded and pushed his flannel over his shaven head, making no attempt to cover himself. Alex tried desperately to maintain 'eye contact' as she rambled on about the little boat. But her eyes were drawn back to that stunning cock. She just stood and stared as it twitched, moving a little from side to side, lifting a little. Sweet Jesus, it's awake; the bloody black anaconda had sensed prey and she knew the prey was her!

Essa said nothing and pushed the flannel under his armpits and threw it casually into the sink. He did smile. Alex wiped her face; his teeth could be used in a bloody toothpaste advert. He clearly hadn't been spoilt with sweets as a child.

Essa folded his arms and Alex watched with widening eyes as the cock grew more and more; the young man was erecting right in front of her! This time she did let out a little gasp. The tip almost reached his bloody belly button. She looked up and down the deserted corridor and stepped in the room, drawn by that black beauty that seemed to hypnotize her with its grace and size. She quietly closed the door behind her.

4. ALEX GOES NATIVE!

He watched her strip quickly without saying a word; his smiling expression didn't change. Alex, with trembling fingers, unbuttoned her blouse and pulled it off. Her magnificent breasts rose and fell with her deep breaths. She pulled down her shorts and panties in one go and dropped them on her discarded blouse and walked over to him. With real anticipation, she knelt and took hold of his cock and pushed it into her mouth. He gently stroked her hair and face as she sucked hard, but softly licked and caressed him.

She pleased him for a good ten minutes and rubbed her crotch with some vigour; she was already very wet and her vagina was coming open more and more. He reached across and opened the small bathroom cabinet and pulled something out. He handed it to her; it was a bloody tube of 'KY' jelly. She just had to smile at that.

Alex coated her vagina with lots of the cream and then thoroughly smeared his cock, making sure to cover it as much as possible. Then she laid back and opened her legs fully and held her arms up to him, throwing the tube on the small bunk bed. He reached behind him and produced a fat little stick, which surprised Alex until she saw the teeth marks on it. She had to smile again. He pushed it into her open mouth, and she gripped it tightly with her teeth. Essa knelt between her legs and pushed his huge cock into her welcoming fanny.

Slow and gentle at first, then Essa speeded up and went deeper; he started to thrust with some power and skill. Alex bit down hard on the stick and groaned. The young man fucked like a human road drill and Alex was soon having some quite large orgasms; the little stick helping to bite off her screams of passion. He totally dominated her, and she loved it. Her juice was flooding down her thighs as her body convulsed with passion; this was certainly some incredible fucking she was receiving at the little man's hands.

Her arse rose and fell, slapping the cold floor and Alex struggled to cope with the unbelievable fucking she was getting at his hands. They fucked for a good twenty minutes, then he gave a little groan and flooded her already filled fanny with his cum. He smiled and patted her belly and then sucked her nipples really hard for another few minutes.

Alex just lay on the floor; groaning, moaning and wiping happy tears from her face. Finally, he gently pulled his cock from her and stood up. Alex raised herself on her elbows and spat the stick out. She was panting and had difficulty catching her breath. He sat on the bed and wiped his cock with a soft towel. She stared between her quivering legs and saw her vagina was leaking a small puddle of cum onto the floor, then had to chuckle; the cum just kept coming!

She pulled herself up and accepted the towel from Essa. But first, she just had to taste that wonderful native juice. She knelt and slowly licked up the cum, off the dirty floor without hesitation. Now that made Essa grin. She wiped her mouth with the towel and stood up; her legs were still shaking, and he pulled her to him and she sat on his lap, arms around his shoulders. His head went down, and his strong hands gripped her big breasts. His mouth found a nipple and he went to work with his tongue and fingers. She groaned and stroked his face and head, then realised that something big and hard was prodding her bum. He was fully erect again and when he had enjoyed her breasts, he pushed her onto the small bed, shoving pillows behind her back and shoulders. He mounted her without saying anything and took up where he had left off, fucking her hard, deep and fast.

She grabbed a small scabbard from the bedside cabinet and shoved the leather pouch into her mouth. If she hadn't then the room would soon have been filled with everyone on board; wondering who the hell was being murdered! The little bed creaked and rattled under the furious fucking taking place on it. Alex had another huge orgasm and lay back, shaking and crying, gripping the young man's shoulders as he, as some would colloquially put it 'Fucked her brains out'. She was left dazed and confused as he came in her again and they lay together without a word being said.

Finally, managed to summon up the strength to slip from under him and with legs shaking; dressed slowly. Alex kissed him on the forehead and slipped quietly from the room and realised that the young man had not said a damn word, the whole fucking time! She walked back to her cabin with some difficulty and cleaned herself up; lunch would soon be served. She giggled, at the thought; that she wouldn't need a 'starter' today!

5. JUNGLE FEVER IS CATCHING!

Alex diagnosed herself as having 'Jungle fever'. She came to that conclusion laying in the bath and decided that she needed no pills. The only treatment was the injection of more native cock by young Essa. She eased from the bath and dried herself carefully, planning her 'treatment' as she rubbed herself with the soft towel.

Early that evening, Alex made for the crew corridor again and was glad to find it empty. She made straight for Essa's cabin. She was wearing a little dress, no bra [again] white frilly panties and small heels. Her hair tied up with a blue ribbon. She was also wearing a small thin black collar. She had seen plenty of interracial porn films and the white bitches normally wore a black collar to signify they were 'black cock sluts'. "I'm certainly one of those now!" She told herself and pushed open his cabin door and slipped in. She just had to grin.

The bunk bed was already busy. Yoke lay on her back that infamous little stick jammed in her mouth. Essa was on top thrusting hard, his tight arse gripped by Yoke as he pounded her with real expertise. He looked up at Alex, nodded and smiled. Yoke pulled the stick from her mouth and gasped; "It's not what it looks like Alex! He's not forcing me or anything.... Oh, fucking shit...."She rammed the stick back in, to cut off another scream as she had a big orgasm - again - then cried a little.

Alex quietly slipped out of her dress and slowly pulled her panties down; she was already wet. She noticed the discarded - and empty - tube of 'KY' jelly on the floor and sighed. Then saw the bathroom cabinet was open. She chuckled and shook her head; it was filled with tubes of 'KY' jelly!

She took a tube and placed it on the small bedside cabinet and waited patiently for her turn with the Amazon bull. She slowly and carefully lubricated her crotch thoroughly and wiped her hands on a discarded towel and watched the pair fucking with some real interest.

Yoke's legs were kicking in the air, and she had her little ankle boots and socks still on. Her shorts and t-shirt lay on the floor, next to her matching white bra and panties. Finally, Essa stopped and pulled from Yoke, kissing her forehead as a thank you. He slipped off the bed and gestured to the panting Yoke, who now had a hand clutching her crotch. She spat out the stick and gasped; "I'm bloody full of cum. He wouldn't use a bloody condom."

Alex just nodded and knelt between her open shaking legs and pulled her hand away. The cum oozed onto her eager tongue and into her mouth. Alex cleaned Yoke up whilst Essa gently prepared her fanny with more 'KY' Jelly.

Yoke had another little orgasm under Alex's hard licking and groaned loudly, slapping a hand over her mouth. Alex eyes really did widen as she felt Essa mounting her with another full erection. She groaned and snatched up the stick and pushed it into her mouth. Yoke slipped from the bed and turned round, sliding back under Alex and started to work on her fanny, now gorged with Essa's big dark cock.

The bed was creaking, Alex was moaning - biting the stick - and

Yoke was slobbering over Alex's cock filled fanny. While Essa pumped Alex hard, the two girls now kissed passionately; the stick discarded. Yoke pulled herself up against the headboard, legs open and Alex went down on her again, using tongue and fingers. She couldn't believe that Yoke still had some cum inside her, but it did add to the flavour. Essa gripped her waist and fucked with the precision of an engine running at full tilt.

Alex had a couple of big ejaculations, which Yoke quickly and passionately cleaned up. Finally, Essa came inside of Alex and Yoke cleaned that up too. They sat on the bed, Essa between the two girls, an arm around each and a hand cupping a breast. The girls passed a cold bottle of beer between them and chatted like old friends. Yoke laughed and ran a hand down Essa's tight chest and gripped his cock. "He really doesn't say much Alex; does he?"

Alex sipped the most welcome beer and sighed; "Yoke, he bloody doesn't need too!" They both laughed at that. Yoke ran a hand over her stomach and didn't smile; "You don't think I'll be full of black baby soon, do you?" Alex just shrugged her shoulders; "I don't know Yoke."

The girls dressed and left the young man sleeping off his exertions. They had both been well satisfied by 'The Amazon Bull'. Yoke's words were to prove prophetic. Some months later she found her belly and breasts swollen and the following year gave birth to a little dark baby boy. Her new husband - a young white man - was not impressed and walked out the door.

Finally, with her struggling career and alienated from her disproving parents, a desperate Yoke gave the boy up for adoption. She regretted that for the rest of her life, despite marrying well and having another two children: both girls. All that would unfold if the current timeline remained unchanged.

6. FATHER PATRICK COOK'S JOURNAL.

The 'Madre de Deus' docked the following morning and Captain Carlos was a little sad to see his very friendly - and generous - passengers depart. 'Father' Owen Jones greeted his friends at the dockside, accompanied by a gaggle of ragged children, some clung to his robes and Alex could see they were outcast orphans; there were few social services in the jungle.

A very sheepish Owen tried to explain to Jericho how he became involved with the starving, homeless children who now lived in his part ruined church. Jericho said nothing as he watched Alex and Wilson take the children's hands and walk with them to the old church. Owen whispered to Alex; "I don't think Jericho is too pleased, but I just sort of acquired them. I gave some food to one little girl and treated her cut feet. Then suddenly I had a dozen of them!" Alex just smiled broadly and gripped Owens's arm; "Well you are playing a priest after-all."

"I'm going to give them the once over, see what their medical conditions need." Alex stated and Jericho, strangely enough, didn't argue. The team was a little embarrassed when hoards of local natives, cheered and clapped them as they walked through the poverty-stricken streets of San Marco. Many pushed coins into their hands for the children; coins many couldn't actually afford to give away.

"I did make one major discovery that will interest everyone." Owen said, carrying a little girl who had bloodied rags tied about her feet. Jericho nodded his approval; "We'll get together after the children are settled in and Alex's had a look at them." Wilson smiled broadly and whispered to Alex; "I really think that our boss does actually have a heart hidden somewhere in that old coat of his." Alex chuckled and then noticed that Amber Bellman and her team were approaching - with Jack Crawford and his native assistant in tow - carrying what appears to be bags of shopping!

"When Captain Carlos told us about what Father Jones had been doing for the street children, we raided the two local shops for some supplies the children may need and Yoke can assist Dr. Alex, she's a second-year medical student - when not exploring the jungle!" Amber Bellman smiled broadly and then everyone entered the church buildings, laughing and chatting.

Alex and Yoke worked tirelessly through the day, examining each of the dozen street children, whose ages ranged from three years to eleven. All were suffering from malnutrition, worms and lice. Two clearly needed urgent medical care for injuries to feet and arms - Alex arranged for a local native woman to take the pair on the river boat, back to Telos, for hospital treatment and paid for it herself. The two older girls [aged eight and nine] reduced Alex and Yoke to tears; they had been working as prostitutes to earn money for food. The stories they told made Yoke very upset and she had to walk around the old churchyard to compose herself. Alex cleared up her own tears and got back to work with the other children - she was clearly made of sterner stuff than poor young Yoke.

That night, when the children had been settled down, Wilson produced a brandy bottle and, in the Priest's, small rooms, Jericho and his team listened to what Owen had discovered. Owen produced from his robes a faded and fragile old notebook; he held it up; "The Journal of Father Patrick Cook who was the Parish Priest here from 1905 to 1921. There are several pages that cover the arrival of Professor Jack Dawes in the spring of 1910."

It became apparent that Father Patrick disliked Dawes, referring to him as 'an arrogant Godless man' of little charity or mercy, with an ego that could rival Mount Everest! Alex actually chuckled; "Christ! I said that about our current gentleman Jack." Wilson nodded and poured more brandy into the small plastic cup that Alex was using; "It appears Crawford and Dawes have a lot in common." He noticed that Jericho was consulting his mirror and rubbing his chin in thought.

Owen continued; "Dawes and his team stayed for just two days before heading into the jungle. But he did impart some important information to Father Patrick; Dawes told him that he had a map, an ancient map, that showed the fabled city of gold [Noah] in the jungle mountain range called "Montanha de almas perturbadas" or 'Mountain of troubled souls' - apparently, even the local tribes avoided the mountain like the plague, he had to pay his bearers extra wages, or they wouldn't go near the place. Two simply refused and deserted into the jungle the night before - after being told their destination - and none of the local natives would go, so he left two men short. Father Patrick did note one strange thing about Dawes guide Ludlow; he couldn't speak any Spanish or Portuguese!"

Wilson grunted in real puzzlement; "If he was an experienced guide around these parts, how could he operate without knowing the bloody language?"

Alex sipped her brandy and said quietly; "Even our Jack speaks the language quite fluently, so how the hell did Ludlow cope?"

Owen turned a couple of faded pages and tapped the notebook; "There's an entry for Christmas 1913 that you might find interesting. Two German explorers arrived in Para and sought out anyone who had dealings with Dawes. They questioned Father Cook and repeatedly asked him if Dawes had an old map and rather strangely; a square compass!" Wilson chuckled, refilling everyone's cup; "A bloody square compass; what use would that be?"

Owen shrugged his shoulders; "Dunno, but according to Father Patrick the pair left on Boxing Day and he never saw them again - and he actually notes that the four bearers they employed in Para, never did return to their families."

Everyone sat in silence until Owen turned a few more pages and read out; "March 7th, 1919, news arrived today that the Great European war is over and contained with the same mail, came news that my dear brother Joseph was killed in France in 1917. God rest his soul. I also received a letter from a Richard Dawes saying he will be arriving after the rainy season and urgently needed to speak with me." Owen closed the fragile book carefully and added; "The last entry was written by Father Patrick's curate, saying that the dear father had been gathered unto God - it's dated August 1921. You can still make out his name on a weathered tombstone in the derelict churchyard."

"Richard Dawes." Jericho spoke quietly and finished his brandy but accepted a refill from Wilson who tapped his cup and asked directly; "Jericho, what are we doing here in 2010, when we could just jump back to 1910 and deal with everything as it happened?"

Owen chuckled; "I've wanted to ask that since we bloody started!"

Jericho sighed but smiled; "Angel Margret gave pretty implicit instructions that we work this case backwards - I have no idea why." Everyone exchanges puzzled glances, until Alex drained her cup and said, "I'm going to check the children, then get some sleep. If Angel Margret insisted that we work this mission backwards, then she will have a bloody good reason for doing so." Owen nodded at that and joined Alex in checking the sleeping children. "You actually make a really good Priest Owen; you did miss your true vocation." Alex patted Owens's shoulder with some real pride in her young colleague.

7. INTO THE JUNGLE.

Jack Crawford checked his small shoulder haversack for essentials and grunted in satisfaction, it contained; two bottles of whisky, four packets of tobacco and papers, a large bag of humbugs and two packets of condoms; in case he got lucky with Dr. Bellman and/or her assistant Yoke.

"Preparation is everything." He muttered to Issa, who simply nodded; he had worked with Jack Crawford long enough to know the man well. They watched as the little expedition assembled with last minute checking of supplies and equipment until, finally Dr. Bellman was happy and gave the nod to Jack to get underway. Anzio shouldered his camera and started to film the leaving of San Marco for Para, when he noticed, only briefly, two natives standing in the tree line.

Yoke saw them too and whispered to him; "Essa [who spoke good English when needed] told me they are scouts from that mountain tribe, he said they'll probably shadow us for the journey to their mountain home. Apparently our Jack has already visited their Chief's village on the lower slopes, to get permission for us to cross their sacred land - something Dawes didn't bother to do and look how that turned out!"

The pair picked up their equipment and signaled the eight bearers to load their burdens and everyone moved into the forest, behind Jack and the good Doctor - Essa had already gone ahead and he simply vanished from sight.

"I have several fully charged batteries for my satellite phone and our expedition office in Brasilia can track our movement into the jungle via GPS, using the phone. We won't ever be out of contact with civilization." She smiled at Jack as the pair led the expedition, deep into the dark green forest.

Watching from the part ruined church, Jericho and Wilson exchanged looks and both consulted their mirrors; "He should arrive in a couple of minutes, and he'll easily pick up their trail. You best get Owen and Alexandra ready. Make sure they have good boots on." Jericho smiled at Wilson and pushed the mirror into his dark green shirt and wiped his face - placing his jungle hat on completed his jungle designed uniform. Wilson was dressed the same; they looked like soldiers without any rank insignia.

Watching from the part ruined church, Jericho and Wilson exchanged looks and both consulted their mirrors; "He should arrive in a couple of minutes, and he'll easily pick up their trail. You best get Owen and Alexandra ready. Make sure they have good boots on." Jericho smiled at Wilson and pushed the mirror into his dark green shirt and wiped his face - placing his jungle hat on completed his jungle designed uniform – and said, "Well, we look the part at least."

Wilson was dressed the same; they looked like soldiers without any rank insignia.

Jericho stared at the jungle in silence until Wilson returned with Alex and Owen; both suitably dressed for their adventure. "Young Miguel will oversee the children; he's applied to the local Bishop to join the church and according to Records, he ends up a bloody Bishop!" Owen chuckled as he spoke and pulled on his backpack. Alex just smiled and spoke to Wilson; "I didn't know the Brazilian army had boy soldiers." Wilson grinned and checked her pack straps, then handed Owen a rifle and slung his own, over his shoulder. "He's here." He said simply as a figure approached the church ruins.

Former Brazilian army Captain Hernando Santos raised his arm in salute and joined the little group, placing his rife and shoulder bag down. Alex noted that he was a big man, equal in statue to Wilson or Mr. Harris [Jericho's Butler] with bright blue eyes and brown hair with streaks of natural blond. Captain Santos had served in the army, training the men for jungle combat and survival. But on leave in Brasilia one summer in 1971, he contracted pneumonia and died several days later. He had worked as a Collector for a while and then joined Inspector Stella Longstreet's team as a Temporal Detective. He was a very happy man to be back in the jungle; even for this one mission.

He shook hands all round and the little group chatted for a while, then he re-checked everyone's packs and boots. "I'm glad to see you are all carrying two water bottles each; dehydration can be a soldier's downfall in the heat of the jungle." Wilson, rather sheepishly, had to admit that one bottle was full of brandy! The captain actually chuckled, while shaking his head in disapproval, then laughed out loud when Owen also admitted that one of his bottles contained brandy!

Alex said nothing and pushed one bottle around her belt; out of sight to the captain. Only Jericho, apparently, was actually carrying two water bottles. "We'll track the good doctor's party whilst we still have light, then camp near the river with the small waterfall, over night. If their guide is any good, he'll do something similar, so we may have to change our plans slightly. Do you know who their man is?" The captain turned to Jericho and adjusted his pack.

"I doubt if you'll know him coming from the 1970's; he's called Jack Crawford and he certainly has a reputation for knowing his way around the jungle." Alex accepted a mint from Owen who added; "He also has a reputation for women and whisky, oh, and tall tales of the jungle." The captain chuckled; "Sweet Jesus, that sounds like the civilian guide we [the Brazilian Army] use to hire sometimes, back in the sixties. he was excellent in the forest - there was none better. But he couldn't leave the damn women or whisky alone and some of the stories he came out with, would make your hair curl; if you believed them."

The captain scratched his chin; thinking, after a few moments, he snapped his fingers and smiled; "Jack London, bloody Jack London. He was a strapping English gentleman who could drink all night and appear totally sober for breakfast; normally with some young tart in tow!"

The group stood in silence, exchanging glances. The captain noticed the change in their demeanor and asked what bothered them. Jericho consulted his mirror and held it up to Hernando; "Is that your man Jack London?"

The captain smiled broadly; "Oh yes, that's the bugger!" Jericho showed the mirror around to everyone; it was a photo of Jack Crawford.

8. PARA.

"If he was in his late forties in the 1960's, then he should be nearly ninety now." Wilson spoke softly to Alex as the little group moved slowly through the thick vegetation, behind Captain

Hernando and Jericho. Owen grunted, his rife cradled in his arms; "He's not ageing because his not in his own time, so who exactly is Jack Crawford?"

Jericho turned about and smiled, wiping sweat from his face; "Our friend Jack must be unique in history - he's leading an expedition to trace himself." Wilson laughed out loud; "I'll update my last statement; he should be nearly 130 years old!" Owen shook his head in amazement; "So jack Crawford is really Jack Dawes!" Alex sipped from her water bottle and adjusted her pack; "Well, we know he's no time-traveler, so how is he staying the same age despite a century passing by? - now that's the real interesting question."

Jericho looked quite grim and said quietly; "Remember Professor Wolfgang Leitcher, that bastard was born in 1764 and he's still around - somewhere - and we all know who he serves." Wilson explained to Captain Hernando about the team's mission to Nazi Germany, as they progressed through the dark jungle.

The captain told the group; that they should make Para in about four days of jungle travel. "I warn you all, the place is like the bloody Wild West!" He added, unsmiling.

They camped by a small stream and Owen started the dinner over a reluctant fire, whilst Jericho and Alex raised the tents. Wilson and Hernando went ahead to scout out the other party. They returned just before nightfall and in time for dinner; Owen had knocked up curry and rice. It vanished off the plates in double quick time.

Hernando informed Jericho and the team that 'Jack Crawford' had indeed camped by the small waterfall and his native assistant was scouting ahead - he hadn't seen him yet. He also told them that two warriors from the mountain tribes were following Dr. Bellman's party. "Their bearer's are a surly lot and a little scared about approaching 'Montanha de almas perturbadas' - I think they'll disappear at the first sign of real trouble. We need to keep on our toes." Jericho nodded his agreement and the very tired group settled down for the night.

"Where is he taking the good doctor and perhaps more importantly; why?" Wilson threw the question out to everyone, as they carefully negotiated the old jungle trail towards the outskirts of Para. "I think we need to discover how he has survived - un-aged - for a century in a very hostile environment and what the hell happened back in 1910 to cause those changes." Jericho panted and adjusted his pack straps, swinging his machete at some thick bushes along the route, which made him feel better about the trek.

They were just hours away from Para and Alex had become subject to some humour from the team - especially Wilson - over her shrinking shorts and shirt. Four days in the hot steaming jungle, had strangely, made Alex's shorts much smaller than before and her shirt was now sleeveless and tied around her, with her bra showing. "Alex, my baby girl, you better hope we reach Para today because come tomorrow - at this rate of clothes loss - you'll be walking along stark naked - apart from your hat." Wilson managed to say between chuckles. He received a straight finger digit in reply and some words that a real lady shouldn't use - the jungle heat was really starting to get on her nerves.

"I'd sleep with the bloody devil himself for a shower or bath." She confided to Owen, who grinned, saying: "I'd bet he would take you up on that." They reached Para that afternoon and were told by a car mechanic, that Doctor Bellman's party had already left. He was a very generous man and upon hearing Alex's real need for a shower; offered Alex his shower-room. All she had to do was let him, his grandfather, brother and two sons watch; she declined his offer not very politely.

The local Madame of Para's best brothel came to her aid and allowed Alex to use its facilities - a tin bath in a room that actually could not be locked and boasted a large window that had no curtains. Apparently, the brothels incumbent girls' weekly bath day was a highlight in Para - there were no televisions or Internet. The Madame [a shrewd businesswoman] even offered to split the takings from Alex's performance - Alex politely declined her offer and paid for the facilities with brandy and some spare make-up.

Alex was determined to get her relaxing bath, without any worries about being disturbed by perverts; So, Wilson sat on a small stool outside the room - rifle in hand - whilst Owen pinned his ground sheet over the window - it worked.

"I could have made a small fortune; several men from the town offered me brides to drop the curtain at the right moment." he sighed, adding; "I've no real head for business." Wilson congratulated him on making the right decision, explaining that Alex would have probably used the rife on him - had he succumbed to those generous offers from the men.

He started to laugh until he realised that Wilson wasn't joking.

Jericho's party left the following morning - including a much more relaxed and agreeable Alex - plunging back into the jungle - heading for 'Montanha de almas perturbadas'.

Alex couldn't really understand why Jericho and Wilson laughed for some time, as they trudged through the forest. Neither of the pair had the courage to explain the joke. Wilson had confessed to Jericho; that Alex had taken every precaution not to be overlooked during her much-needed bath. "But she forgot to bung up the very large keyhole and I'm just a man." He admitted with a very big grin. Jericho really did laugh at that and said nothing to Alex; for the sake of a 'peaceful' mission.

9. THE TEMPLE RUINS.

They camped that night in a small clearing at the base of a waterfall that fell from a Cliffside into a fast-moving river. The tents were pitched close together; all facing the fire and Alex made and served up a respectable chili which proved popular.

Captain Hernando was impressed with Alex and spoke directly to Wilson; "Stunningly beautiful, can trek through a jungle without whining - well not too much - cook a decent chili and have a laugh." He smiled, as he received a second portion, Wilson just sighed; "Another moth to the flame."

Jericho took the first watch, sitting staring up at the bright stars and even brighter moon; he always enjoyed the heavens, and the clear jungle night made them shine like lamps against the darkness. That's when he noticed the strange grey clouds and suddenly could feel wind against his face and body. He woke Captain Hernando very quietly who came to the same conclusion as Jericho; a jungle storm was approaching; fast.

The rain was simply torrential, and the group had to abandon their camp and head for several large trees to seek shelter and some safety. The sky was streaked with red, orange and white lightening. The very earth seemed to shift and roll beneath the tree's, in which they clung for dear life. "It's like some fucker is tipping buckets down!" Owen shouted as he climbed a big tree, with Alex close behind. They both laughed; gripping the thick branches and watched Wilson struggle to climb a tree opposite as the rain poured down. Finally, the big man made it and sat – drenched – in the canopy of leaves and really didn't appreciate the pair laughing at his expense. He stuck up a single finger.

Jericho and Hernando sought refuge up a similar tree and stared in amazement at the force of the strange storm. The sky lit up with several brilliant flashes of white and by sunrise and lasted just minutes; the jungle was quiet again.

They managed to salvage most of their camp and the captain led them into the forest, stopping several times to check his compass. Finally, they halted about noon and Alex brewed coffee and they ate from tins directly. Hernando pulled Jericho to one side and showed him the compass. Both men watched, a little amazed, as the needle slowly swept round the face, very slowly and covered a full 360 degrees!

"It's been like that since this morning. Check your one." Captain Santos looked extremely worried; without a good compass they could walk in circles - not a good idea in a jungle. Jericho pulled his small pocket compass out and both men saw it was behaving exactly the same.

The little group assembled around Jericho, who explained the dilemma - they now faced - they could try and continue to follow the Bellman party, relying on the captains experience and skill or return to the lighthouse. They unanimously agreed to continue, which made the captain feel quite good about himself. "Thank you for your confidence in me..." He was saying when Essa - Jack Crawford's assistant - burst from the trees and ran towards the group. Hernando raised his rifle, which Jericho pushed gently down; explaining who the native was.

Essa was panting heavily and took several breaths before he could speak to them. Alex gave him a water bottle which he gratefully sipped from [not the brandy filled one, as Alex knew the little man didn't touch alcohol]. He handed the bottle back and spoke directly to Jericho and Hernando, but everyone stood in silence as Essa recounted what happened.

Essa had gone ahead of the main party by a mile or so and found the pig shaped rock formation that jack Crawford had told him to locate. But was trapped there for some hours while the storm raged; He returned slowly through the soaking wet jungle and found that the party had left where they had been camped.

Despite the heavy rainfall, Essa had the skill to track Dr. Bellman's party back into the jungle and received the surprise of his life; a ruined temple. All their tracks ended there and no tracks could be found heading away from the strange place. Captain Hernando asked Essa why he thought, the old, ruined temple was strange. Essa shrugged his dark shoulders; "I have passed that way many times and it was never there before!" "Then, that is certainly strange." Muttered Jericho and asked Essa if he could take them there. He agreed and they set off at once. It took four hours to come upon the Temple and they stood before it with real puzzlement; "It appears to be a jumble of Ancient Egyptian, Aztec and even Indian culture. It shouldn't exist." Jericho spoke out, consulting his mirror and that's when he shouted; "There it is!" Everyone stared at the ruins and could see nothing but forest and stones.

Jericho pointed to the rear of the Temple and an overgrown gateway with a dark inside; "Check your mirrors people and see what they are reporting." Alex tapped her screen and sighed; "It's a portal; hidden behind that cave entrance which has been carved like a doorway."

Wilson and Owen stood a few feet from the doorway; "its pitch black in there, does anyone's mirror show where it is linked too?" Wilson asked; reading his own mirror with some real intent.

Alex lowered her mirror; "You don't think our Jack has disappeared in there with the good doctor and her party?"

"Well, there's only one way to find out." Muttered Jericho and disappeared into the darkness, Captain Hernando advised Essa to remain here at the cave entrance, in case the any of the good Doctor's party should turn up and then he too; disappeared into the cave.

Wilson, Owen and Alex made no comment and followed Jericho

and Hernando into the darkness.

10. ANOTHER TIME; SAME PLACE.

Jericho and his team stood on the small ridge and stared down onto the valley, which was thick with jungle and two small waterfalls, a few kilometers apart, at the far end. Wilson then looked up and simply couldn't believe what he saw in the sky; there was no sky!

"We're in some subterranean world that can only be accessed when the Temple appears above and that doesn't happen every day, I suspect." Jericho pulled his water Bottle out and took a couple of mouthfuls; the heat was damp and oppressive.

Alex pointed out the pools of 'silver or glass' that appear to be part of the grey, rocky ceiling. "That's where the light and heat is coming from." She said and sipped her water bottle. Owen coughed, he had a dry mouth; "My mirror tells me that the current Human Earth Time is minus eighty-three million...or thereabouts."

"Well, keep a bloody eye out for dinosaurs then." Wilson took a long swig from his water bottle and stared up at the roof again; that's when he saw old wooden plane approaching slowly, almost struggling to keep aloft. "What the fuck...." He yelled and everybody looked up. The bullets hit the trees around them, and they dived for cover below the edge of the ridge. They watched as the single propeller pulled the two-winged plane upwards. It carried two persons, and one was firing a machine gun from the rear of the cockpit.

"That's from the First World War!" Captain Hernando shouted as they made their way deeper into the dark forest. Jericho watched the plane disappear out of sight and consulted his mirror; "The number painted on the tail tells me that it shouldn't exist; it has never existed - odd that."

Alex shook her head and dumped her pack and promptly sat on it; "This place doesn't make any sense, our mirrors tell us the correct time is: minus eighty-three million years, but they have planes from the bloody First World War; what next?"

"One of them, I suppose." Owen calmly pointed down the valley, towards the fierce looking Dinosaur with three horns upon its head. It was lumbering slowly through the forest, pushing small trees over and crushing thick bushes beneath its huge grey and green feet. They could hear its voice, even from where they were standing, some distance away.

"Always did like dinosaurs but not this up close," Alex spoke with some amazement in her voice. "Now, who the fuck are they?" Wilson asked, jerking up his rifle in anticipation of trouble.

Three ragged figures, holding each other up were making their way towards Jericho's team from the small ridge above. Alex stared hard at the threesome struggling through the thick grass and bushes. "Sweet Jesus; its Doctor Bellman with Yoke and Anzio!" No-one could believe these three skinny, dirty people dressed in rags were the same people who left San Marco just days ago.

Doctor Bellman collapsed upon her knees in front of Jericho and grabbed the water bottle he offered and gulped it down. Wilson handed out biscuits and apples. Anzio swallowed some water and grabbed hold of Owens's arm; "You have to get the fuck out of here, this place is fucking crazy and dangerous!" He slumped upon the grass and wept.

Owen gripped his shoulders and offered him some brandy from his hipflask, which was gratefully accepted; "Crawford just abandoned us, he disappeared a few hours after we came here and we are only still alive due to luck - the bastard." Anzio cursed and swigged the brandy.

Doctor Bellman had recovered her composure and spoke to Jericho; "This place seems to be a jumble of time zones from Earth's history. Dinosaurs roam the great forest whilst there's a city on that far mountain. You've already seen one of their patrol planes; they are not a friendly people." Doctor Bellman drank some more water and sighed loudly; "The bloody satellite phone stopped working after the storm, it was like the satellite wasn't there anymore - a useless piece of junk that didn't work when you really needed the bloody thing!"

Jericho nodded and stared at the ragged threesome and knew he had to make a hard decision. He also knew that this temporal mess would need some serious sorting out and that bloody jack

Crawford/Dawes was the cause for all what was happening. He sighed and called everyone together. They gathered around and Jericho outlined his plan.

Owen and Alexandra would take Doctor Bellman and her distressed party back through the portal, whilst he, Captain Hernando and Wilson would try to find the elusive 'Jack Crawford'. Jericho gave clear and concise instructions to Alex and Owen; "Take those sorry looking souls back to where the storm started, that way they will not have suffered all this and will remember nothing about the temple ruins or the damn time portal it hides. I strongly suspect that our Jack will not join them again. He won't return to that time for a while yet. We can rely on Essa to take them back to Para."

Alex and her little group left a few minutes later and Captain Hernando, Jericho and Wilson headed for the city that could be seen on the mountain opposite. Warm rain tumbled down as they passed beneath the huge and ancient trees, occasionally hearing the calls and roars of the odd dinosaur within the depths of the jungle.

They stopped briefly by a beautiful little waterfall which was escaping from a crack in the ridge that towered above them. They ate some cheese and apples, sipping their canteens. That's when the flickering lights caught Wilson's eyes and he stared hard at the waterfall, Wilson tapped Jericho upon the arm; "Unless I'm seeing things, there are some lights behind that waterfall." Jericho and Hernando stood and watched the waterfall - sure enough - there were lights flickering behind the cascading water.

Jericho rubbed his chin and then pointed towards the falling water; "Well, let's get our feet wet." Wilson and Hernando nodded their agreement and the curious group disappeared into the falling water.

11. A LITTLE RELIEF IN THE JUNGLE.

Dr. Bellman was still a little angry about the apparent disappearance of Jack Crawford. She confided to Alex that she and the guide had 'hot words' over his attempted seduction of her and young Yoke. "He's gone because he couldn't get his bloody end away with us." She sounded quite aggrieved.

Alex just nodded; she had returned the Bellman party back to before the storm changed everything. She knew that Jack had to go; he could only pass through the portal when the storm hit and couldn't chance waiting for another. Alex had explained that Wilson and Jericho was looking for him with their guide; who knew the jungle well. That seemed to cover the missing members of the team; for now.

They camped where the temple ruins would appear [if another storm came] and Essa smiled at Yoke and Alex in equal measure; he knew full well that he would be probably fucking the pair again - if the chance occurred - and settled down for the night, under a large tree, away from the camp and waited.

After a decent dinner knocked up by Yoke and Owen, the small group settled down for the night. Alex was restless; all she could think of was Essa fucking her. That's when she noticed that Yoke was missing, and she smiled to herself; the damn girl had already gone after Essa. She crept from her little tent and found the tree where Essa had made camp. Sure enough, Essa was fucking Yoke up against that tree.

Alex had to chuckle; Yoke had a piece of wood stuffed in her mouth. "I bet Essa has a pack of 'KY' jelly with him." She said to herself, then jumped. Anzio stood next to her and pushed a hand through his hair, "You think you know someone and then you see that." He grunted and turned back, taking hold of Alex's arm. "Come on before they see us, it'll embarrass Yoke to know that we've seen them."

They walked slowly back to camp, Anzio still holding Alex's arm. Alex stopped by a small stream and a big tree, She smiled at Anzio and he smiled back. "I think they have the right idea. A little relief in the jungle is always welcome." Alex was soon sucking young Anzio's cock; it wasn't as big as Essa's, but it was certainly adequate, and she found out that the young man knew how to use it.

They fucked doggy style on the floor of the jungle. Anzio had a good technique and Alex had a little orgasm under his thrusting. That really seemed to make the young man happy. He gripped her big swinging tits and thoroughly enjoyed himself. He had been quite concerned about 'making love' without a condom, in case Alex fell pregnant by him. But she had pointed out, that she was a married woman and having his baby wouldn't really matter. That also made him happy, and he fucked her good and hard. Not the most skilled lover Alex ever had but she wasn't complaining!

He really liked the idea of fucking a married woman and giving her a baby for her dumb husband to raise. He shot his load into her, and they lay back on the grass and Alex sucked his cock until he was ready again. They fucked in the Missionary Position, and he lasted a bit longer this time. He had asked to fuck her arse, but without proper lubricant, Alex had to turn him down.

But he was happy when Alex agreed to let him cum in her mouth, which he did with a lot of moaning and cussing. He contently watched as she swallowed down his load and then licked his cock clean. Alex really didn't fill satisfied by the brief sex [to her] but she consulted herself with the thought, that it was better than no sex!

They walked back to camp and Anzio really upset her with an off the cuff remark, probably meant as some sort of joke. He chuckled; "The way you gulped down my cum and smiled; I bet you've swallowed more semen than the bloody Pacific Ocean!" He didn't even notice the look she gave him and the dreadful silence afterwards.

'Fucking twat.' Was the thought that crept through Alex's mind; she already was regretted letting him fuck her.

At least he said nothing to 'Father' Jones about his 'conquest' in the jungle. He may not know how to really handle a woman and her feelings; but he could – at least – keep such indiscretions to himself.

Alex groaned to herself; Anzio wouldn't be the first man that she had fucked; then regretted it afterwards [just a little] and he certainly wouldn't be the last!

What did really bother Alex, was not getting another chance to fuck with Essa, before the mission was over. Now that could be a real disappointment. She wondered how Jericho and Wilson was getting on, in their search for the elusive Jack Crawford aka Professor Jack Dawes aka Jack London and any other name he's used over the years in the jungle!

12. THE SELF-IMPOSED CASTAWAY.

They followed the rugged little tunnel, which was lit with small bulkhead lamps, for some minutes until they came upon a large wooden door, braced with steel bands. It looked quite knew but must have stood for some time.

An amused Jericho pointed out the small camera fixed above it. "Someone takes his security seriously." Wilson was examining the door carefully; "No keyhole or lock apparent, how do they open the damn thing?" Jericho smiled and waved at the camera; "I think it can only be opened from the inside, which means there must be at least two people in there."

Hernando looked puzzled; "How can you know that?" Jericho grinned; "If it cannot be opened from the outside, then someone must always remain behind, when the others are out, to open the damn thing from the inside, so there must be at least two people involved, logical really."

"Hello, can I help you?" A woman's voice made the three men fall silent until Jericho pointed to the camera; "Probably has a two-way microphone connected to it." He looked up and said loudly; "We're here to see Jack, thank you."

There was silence for a short while and then a man's voice was heard; "Is that Mister Jericho Tibbs?" Jericho shouted back: yes. Everyone heard the door locks clicking behind the door and the heavy door swung open a few inches. Wilson gripped the door and pulled it open enough for each one of them to squeeze through. They were in a wood paneled hallway, complete with ornate mirror, umbrella stand and coat pegs which carried black oil skins. Several pairs of green wellingtons lay neatly placed beneath the coats.

The large door slowly closed behind them, and they heard the locks come on. "Yep, they certainly do take their security seriously." muttered Wilson. Captain Hernando pointed out a portrait of the English King Edward the Seventh on the opposite wall; "The crazy English always did love their royalty." and relaxed a little - but still with rifle in hand. That's when he noticed the portrait of the beautiful young woman opposite the King's picture. "I don't think that's Queen Alexandra," He added and stared at the artist's signature and date.

"Lady Charlotte; 1952." Wilson peered over his shoulder and read the details out to Jericho, who checked his mirror and grunted with some satisfaction.

The door at the end of the hall came open slowly and a young man stood, rifle in hand. Jericho smiled and removed his hat; "Richard, we've come to speak to your father." Wilson nodded to Hernando and said softly; "Like two pea's in a pod." They were staring at a younger version of Jack Crawford/Jack Dawes. The young man didn't lower the gun or smile; "Why did you come here Mr. Tibbs?" He asked softly and then they saw the young girl standing behind him - with an oversized pistol clutched in both hands – and looking nervous and unsmiling.

"Daddy did say he could trust the man." She said quietly and lowered her big pistol and stepped back. Richard nodded and lowered the rifle, clicking the safety catch on. "You best come in and have a whisky." He cradled the gun and actually smiled a little. Jericho nodded his thanks and the three dumped the packs and rifles in the hallway.

The girl placed her pistol back in the holster hanging next to the door and showed them into a beautifully furnished room; then produced a tray with a whisky bottle and several glasses.

The young girl was very pretty by anyone's standard of beauty; she was wearing a check shirt and clean white shorts with ankle boots. Wilson certainly admired her long legs and smiled back at her, when she handed him a glass and filled it with whisky - very good whisky.

"You look like your mother, the lady in the hall portrait." Captain Hernando said, sipping his whisky and easing himself upon the large leather sofa and looking about the room. Richard half smiled; "Yeah, Charlotte does look a lot like her mum."

Charlotte sat on a chair by the fireplace and smiled; "Thank you. That was painted the year mum and dad was married. I was born a couple of years later." She was drinking a bottle of coke-cola with a straw and looked the picture of young innocence from a very different world. Wilson stared at the young woman; she should be nearly sixty years old now and her stepbrother would be over a hundred. The passing of human time apparently did not happen in this strange place. It was a lost world; lost from the of human time and various periods of the earth's past were still present in the place; including the people and animals.

Jericho drank some whisky and sat upon a chair opposite the grand fireplace. "Your mother was Lady Charlotte Wells-Gordon, who according to history was a painter and photographer. She disappeared in the jungle in 1952, whilst working as a freelance photographer for a Zoological expedition along the Amazon River. She was never seen again by any living person and can I assume she is, sadly, no longer with us?"

The young girl nodded; but said nothing. She jumped to her feet when a deep voice came over the door intercom; it was her father: Professor Jack Dawes. Jericho placed his glass down and rose from his seat, the look on Jacks face was priceless as he heaved his pack and rifle against the wall. "Hello Hernando, it's been a long time." He spoke softly, accepting a glass of whisky from his son.

Hernando nodded; "Over fifty years Jack and you look like you haven't aged a day." Jack smiled; "I did go to your funeral; the piss up afterwards almost became a legend." Hernando chuckled at that and raised his glass in salute.

Jericho picked up his glass and sipped his whisky, he said simply; "What happened in 1910 Jack?"

Jack slumped into his favourite armchair and rolled his glass between his hands and stared up at the ceiling, he sighed loudly, and half smiled; "Bloody disaster Jericho; a real bloody disaster."

13. THE STORY OF JACK DAWES.

"I had obtained the map from two old natives who owed me more than any money could repay; I had rescued their young granddaughter from the clutches of sex traffickers, who tried to sell the abducted girl to a brothel ran by a bloody big mining corporation." Jack shifted uncomfortably in his chair and his attentive daughter refilled his glass.

"The map was very old and written in Portuguese; but the city's name was clear enough; Noah - the fabled city of gold. I picked my team, as best I could, given where I was and the time constraints; I wanted to get underway straight away. That was my first big mistake, a real whopper actually." He grunted and sipped his whisky.

"The guide was no guide, right?" Jack chuckled; "Spot on, you're a clever man Jericho. He couldn't guide a pen to paper. I caught on after a few days, but it was too late by then, we were in uncharted jungle and frankly; quite lost." He rose from his chair and walked to the big desk in the corner and rummaged in the top drawer. He handed Jericho a well-worn leather pouch.

Jericho slowly opened the pouch and stared at the old map. Wilson leaned over him and held his mirror above the paper. "Jesus Jericho, it's about four hundred years old." Jack chuckled and gestured to the paper; "Take it and get rid of it; it's caused more deaths that smallpox, I think." Jericho nodded; "What happened to the rest of them?" Jack slumped back in his armchair and his daughter sat at his feet. He affectionately touched her hair.

"There was a fierce and strange storm that washed away most of our equipment and made our compasses go nuts. All our watches had stopped. The native bearers simply disappeared over night; we were really in a bad way. Then we came across the temple. I knew it wasn't right, but we camped down for the night."

"Lewis Ludlow was a liar and a con man; the only true part of his story was that he had, in fact, worked for a Mining Company - a small outfit - and they were after him because he took off with a lot of their money. A small venomous snake got the stupid bugger, he didn't even know to shake his boots out in the morning." Jack smiled at that.

"They found his rife some years later." Wilson said and finished his whisky. Jack nodded; "We marked his grave with that. It was no point keeping the damn thing; the brains of Brittan had only brought enough ammunition for one clip!" His smile dropped; "Cole got it next [Colegate Standround]. He started with a fever and vomiting blood, less than a day later, we buried him. I had never seen fever like it. It took him like that." Jack snapped his fingers; "He was actually a good man, pretty loyal and decent compared to most."

"It was Gordon that found the portal and I followed him in. The bastards in the city got him. They chased us through the forests, and he slipped and fell down a small ravine. It was unlike him to be so clumsy, and he certainly paid for that slip up. He was still alive; I could hear him calling for help. Those bastards climbed down the ravine on ropes. I was hidden, watching from a tree. They beat him to death with the butts of their old rifles - muskets actually - and then, in utter horror, I watched them dismember his naked body and shove it in canvas bags. I was actually sick. The bastards ate human flesh."

Jack's face betrayed what he was thinking, but he spelled it out clearly; "After that, whenever I - we - encountered anyone from the city; we killed them. Man, woman or child, we killed them like the fucking vermin they are."

Wilson showed Jericho his mirror; "Those three are all missing souls; like jack is. No Collector appeared because they were clearly out of their ordained time. Their souls are lost." Jericho gestured around the room; "Where did all this come from?"

Jack smiled; "A very nice old Frenchman called Jean De Floret, he was trapped here in the 1680's and spent years constructing this little fortress. He took me in, and it was with some incredible realisation, as we spoke together - he spoke quite good English - that he was nearly three hundred years old! Time here doesn't affect us humans from above. We simply don't age, but we can be killed." He sighed loudly, adding; "We learnt that the hard way."

Jack sipped his whisky and continued; " He was careless one morning, filling water caskets by the waterfall, one of the really big bloody snakes got him. They make anaconda's look like nasty worms. I really did miss him. He was a good man; for a Frenchman!"

Jericho eased from his chair and rubbed his chin; "You can't stay here Jack. Doctor Bellman was a descendant of yours and she wanted to know what happened to you. Other expeditions have been lost or killed trying to find you and that damn map. It has to stop; is that a yes Jack?"

Jack slowly nodded; he knew only too well that it had to stop. He ran a hand over his face; "But how Jericho?" He asked and glanced at his young daughter, who in the world above, would now be nearly 56 years old. His son would be over 112 years old and Jack, himself, would be near 150 years old!

Jericho smiled; "Leave that to us Jack, but if you give me your word, I'll return you 1910 and you can stop yourself ending up in this nightmare. It's also your son's time period and he can join you. It will be both your ordained time period. You can live out your natural lives, but more importantly; when the time comes, your souls can be collected and processed properly. Your three companions that died will have never met you and so won't die on the expedition. That means their souls can be recovered by the natural process of death in their own time periods."

Jack nodded and gestured at his daughter; "And..." He muttered and looked quite sad. Jericho smiled again; "We can make a little exception for her Jack - if you co-operate with us - I can guarantee that the young lady will have a good life in the modern world, and of course, she will die within her ordained time period and have her soul collected properly, when the time comes. She will be allocated a new body; just born in the current time and live her life there. Her soul now exists and must be looked after."

Jack nodded slowly; he knew what he had to do; for himself and especially for his two children. They deserved better than this.

Jericho continued: "The good doctor and her team will have never come on this expedition to discover your fate, since you never disappeared. None of you will – obviously - remember any of this; since it never now happened!"

Hernando gripped Jericho's shoulder and smiled; "I think Inspector, we should allow them a little time together; to say goodbye; yes?"

Jericho nodded and he and Wilson waited on the other side of the big door. Wilson managed to chuckle; "Now I see why Angel Margret insisted we work this case backwards. We would have missed the young girl's soul and it would have been lost. Angels are really clever buggers- aren't they?" Jericho just laughed and nodded; "Ain't they just." He murmured.

14. BACK TO CIVILASTION.

Jericho's little party re-joined the Bellman party the following morning. They explained that they had 'rescued' young Charlotte from some natives, she had foolishly become detached from her party of visiting students; studying the jungle flora and animals. The explanation was accepted without real comment, and she was taken in by Dr. Bellman and her team; especially Anzio. Alex and Yoke shared a tent and both moaned about not seeing Essa again, when they returned to civilization. Alex - with a very Naughty grin - said quietly; "Well, we're not back there yet!" and after dark, when everyone was sleeping, they slipped from the camp and found Essa's tree.

To their delight, he was there, but unfortunately [for them] he wasn't alone. They squatted down behind some bushes and really had to restrain outright laughter. Essa was doing what he does best, fuck. They both stared - a little envious - and watched Doctor Amber Bellman get a good hard fucking at his skilled hands. They both giggled as they saw the stick jammed into her mouth. Alex - laughing softly - pointed out the discarded tube of 'KY' jelly on the jungle floor, next to the good Doctor's panties and shorts. "He must have been an Amazon boy scout; he's always prepared." chuckled Yoke.

They watched as the pair was now fucking on all fours and Yoke really leaned forward and almost gasped with amazement and some real respect for the Doctor. "For Christ sake, he's buried in her bloody arse!" Alex stared and nodded; "That is some brave woman; to take that anaconda up her bloody bum." Yoke sighed; "Shall we watch to the finish or go back. Maybe another opportunity will arise."

Alex watched Essa's tight arse thrusting away and nodded; then touched Yoke's face with a gentle hand. "There are plenty of tree's around here sweetie." Yoke smiled and took her hand, then pushed it into her shirt. "I really do like eating you out darling." The pair kissed with some real desire, urgent desire. They made for another tree and went at it.

The pair rolled around having hard rough, lesbian sex. Yoke even fisted Alex to a subdued [for noise only] climax and Alex reciprocated. Eager mouths found each other, while fingers probed willing vaginas and bum holes, with real passion and urgency. When they had finished, Yoke kissed Alex and whispered in her ear.

The request actually shocked Alex - and that didn't happen often

- and she simply couldn't believe what Yoke wanted her to do. She was a little reluctant, but Yoke pleaded with her and finally she gave in. She squatted over Yoke's face and open mouth, then with a real sigh; pissed on her. Yoke gasped and gurgled, drinking down the warm liquid with ease and unrestrained enjoyment. She had certainly indulged in this before. There was more to young Yoke - sexually - that anyone could imagine!

After cleaning themselves up, as best they could, they headed back to their tent and sleep soundly. The following morning, they both insisted on a dip under the waterfall before the party moved off and were joined by Dr. Bellman, The three naked women splashed and bathed in the cold water. Alex really had to restrain from laughing when the good doctor - still stark naked - bent over her clothes. Her anus was almost glowing and still much gaped from the fucking she had received.

Yoke saw where Alex was staring and chuckled, whispering; "She could use that poor bloody thing as torch around here now." Both women laughed and they all returned - suitably refreshed - to the camp.

Yoke further surprised Alex as they walked the jungle trail, being cut by Jericho and Captain Hernando, who were following Essa. The women stopped briefly, and Yoke pulled down her shorts and damp panties. Alex just had to smile; Yoke had stuffed her moist pink vagina with bloody native beads! She guided Alex's hand down to rub her fanny, now gorged with the little wooden balls.

"I'll be ready for your or Essa tonight; preferably both of you." She said quietly, grinning. Yoke really had caught 'Jungle fever'. The pair followed the other with Yoke pushing her arm through Alex's; smiling in real anticipation of what the night could bring. Alex patted her arm and knew damn well that she would be pulling those beads from Yoke's pouting fanny; with her teeth, preferably whilst Essa poked her willing arse.

The sight of the doctors open anus had given her a real tight feeling in her stomach. She hoped that Essa still had plenty of 'KY' jelly left. Alex and Yoke were both a little disappointed; Essa was serving the good doctor again in a small clearing near the camp. But the pair did see young Anzio - also hiding - watching Essa and the doctor and masturbating frantically in some bushes. Now that did make them happy. Yoke whispered; "I won't let that creep near me. He's a total arsehole when it comes to women." Alex could - ruefully - only agree. Yoke also sighed; "'I'd jump on Father Jones if he wasn't a bloody priest. He's cute."

That bought a smile back to Alex's face, as did Yoke's next soft-spoken comment; "Come on, these bloody beads need to come out and I'm really thirsty for a proper drink. So don't pee yet; please!" Alex sighed and knew that talking to young Yoke about her odd sexual appetite wouldn't do much good. Alex patted her belly: "My bloody bladder will be full for you darling, so don't worry." Giggling quietly, the two women made their way back to their tent.

Yoke surprised Alex - yet again - by producing a tin cup after their heated lesbian session and Alex filled it up with piss [much to her bladder's relief] and Yoke sat sipping it like fine wine, whilst Alex enjoyed some brandy. Yoke really wanted to meet again after the jungle adventure was over; but Alex knew that was impossible. But she didn't mention that and the pair sleep soundly; again.

The jungle party broke up when they reached Para. Dr. Bellman would continue on with Essa guiding; back to meet the river boat. Alex grinned; with the doctor and Yoke in the party, he would be well rewarded for his efforts and we're not talking about money and jungle trading trinkets!

The Tibb's party would apparently continue on with their 'holiday' trip. There were lots of farewells and waves as they parted - and some tears from the girls - Alex watched Essa wave from the jungle edge and disappear with some real regret. But he had given Alex a little keep sake of their time together; the bloody well chewed stick!

Jericho waited until they had all gone before calling the Senior Time Controller – Mr. Albian – on his mirror. The team was always amazed to see the changing ripple of time, as it spread across the jungle and the events which had unfolded on the jungle adventure were gone.

Professor Jack Dawes had been returned to his own time and never did follow the map. Doctor Bellman – consequently – didn't follow in the steps of her 'interesting' ancestor and neither did her assistants take the Amazon trip. The Human Timeline returned to its original state in most respects, with few changes and those minor alterations were deemed acceptable by Angel Margret.

But this wouldn't be only time, the team would meet Professor Jack Dawes; he only went and lost his soul again on another expedition to the Sudan!

Alex smiled as they walked back to the lighthouse and slowly pushed the well chewed little stick into her pocket.

"MISS DOROTHY HADDEN: Series 1. The early Edwardian adventures - Part 1."

AVAILABLE FROM 'AMAZON.COM' and all good bookshops!

Scan QR code to visit website.

AGE RECOMMENDATION:

"These stories contain mild adult erotica which is recommended only suitable for persons aged 18 years and over."

EPISODE 3: "ALEXANDRA: THE RELUCTANT FRENCH MAID."

EPISODE PROLOGUE: "On a wet afternoon in East London, workmen are clearing the basement rooms of a large Victorian Villa; the old house will become a private rest home for affluent pensioners. But they discover two small skeletons in shallow graves and all work is halted whilst the police investigate. Local stories and tales about the 'French House' particularly about its owner of a hundred years ago, make Jericho travel back to the 1880's in search of lost souls. This means that Alexandra has to become a naughty 'French Maid' in Sir Edward Coleville's London house, and she encounters some very horny Victorians who certainly are not sexually repressed!"

75 Minutes approx. Episode Warnings: Smoking – Alcohol – Strong language – Violence [including sexual violence] – Strong graphic sexual references – Mild horror.

NOTES: The original version of this story is published and appears in the **TEMPORAL DETECTIVES:** Book Series 4 – Episode 3 entitled:**"SIR EDWARD COLEVILLE'S FRENCH HOUSE."** This is a special EXTENDED episode of the original story.

CAUTION: Recommended for 18+ only.

1. THE CELLARS.

Doctor Ben Roberts was sweating - badly - because of the portable lights and the heat they generated in this small space. He stood up and stretched and began to scribble notes into his little red notebook. Inspector Thomas March sighed and wiped his face, he glanced at Sergeant Dave Soames and rolled his eyes in mock despair. "When you're ready doc." He muttered and stared at the two newly exposed small skeletons. "Do I need to summon CID and forensics for this one?" He added, wiping his face again with his gaudy red hankie.

The doctor looked around and almost smiled; "No Tom, these little bones have been in the ground for at least a hundred years. But I will confirm that with some tests, when they're at the morgue. I can see no signs of physical violence, but I'll know more when Lloyd James [the local pathologist] has taken a look." He snapped his notebook shut and picked up his old leather bag that he always carried and headed for the ladder. "You can get them moved now." He added, and climbed up, into the relative cool of the kitchens above.

The Inspector pushed a fresh stick of chewing gum into his mouth and tapped his sergeants arm; "Come on Dave, there's no mileage in this. Even if they were done in, there's certainly no suspects to arrest, everyone who actually knew who they were, are long dead - along with any killer. Let's get them moved." He gripped the ladder and ascended to the kitchens; the sergeant following closely behind. There were several other uniformed police officers in the spacious kitchen area and also several workman from the builders, who were refurbishing the big old London villa called the 'French House'.

Dave brushed some dust from his uniform jacket and told a nearby PC to inform the station; to contact the local morgue and get the bones moved there. "I can't see this getting the bloody royal wedding off the front pages." He spoke quietly to his old friend and colleague PC Paul Marshal, who nodded; "Yeah, that would take a bloody nuclear war or something similar." They both chuckled and followed the Inspector out into the gardens. They gathered under a large oak tree, out of the persistent drizzle. Dave and Paul lit up cigarettes, whilst the Inspector wrote in his notebook. They watched as Doctor Benjamin 'Ben' Roberts pulled away in his brand-new Metro.

Paul chuckled; "You know that Lady Di has one just like it. Not that she'll be doing much driving, once she marries Chas." Dave smoked slowly and nodded, He was glad to be out the cellars; something down there gave him the creeps and it wasn't just the two pathetic small skeletons, lying in the dirt. "You're from around these parts, any strange and creepy tales about this place?" He asked Paul, who shrugged his shoulders and flicked his ash onto the wet grass.

"Born just five streets away. My old granny could tell you about this place alright. But she passed away six years ago. Nan always said that the original owner; a certain Lord Coleville was a strange, eccentric young man. Rich as shit apparently. He had the house built to resemble a Paris Villa, but that's not why the local's called it the 'French House' - they knew fuck all about Paris Villa's or what they looked like - the house got the name because of the bloody house maids." Paul finished his cigarette and tossed the butt away.

Dave was now intrigued and interested; "How do you mean, because of the house maids?" He asked, finishing his cigarette and stamping slowly on the butt. Paul smiled; "Apparently the rich young sod liked women. He paid his house maids a really good wage to dress like proper French maids. You know, little black skirts, stockings and frilly pants. Rumour has it; they served his meals topless; an invitation to one of his dinner parties was really sought after!"

Paul leaned against the big tree and smiled; "Apparently it was quite a scandal in its day. But the dirty sod had lots of powerful friends, even a couple of bloody government ministers came for dinners. Girls were always trying to get work there because he paid good wages. You imagine, if they worked sixty hours in a bloody east end sweatshop, they would earn about two quid. My Nan said girls were making twice that doing just a little light housework and parading around in their outfits for him and his guests. There was no shortage of girls willing to do that kind of work for that sort of money."

"Dirty lucky bastard." Muttered Dave and watched the black, private ambulance arrive at the gates, from the local Funeral Directors. He stared back at the dark, brooding old house and thought about the two little skeletons, lying in the dirt, a hundred years and now no one would give a toss about what had happened to them. He scratched his chin, well, maybe a local Historian or reporter would be interested in their untold story.

He would make a few telephone calls when he got back to the nick. The two dour faced undertakers were walking up the path, carrying black hold alls. "Oh, it's fucking Laurel and Hardy from old man's Shubert's corpse parlor." Paul muttered and carefully straightened his jacket, putting his cap back on. "Show them where to go." Inspector March said to him and walked down the gravel path to his car. Dave slapped Paul on the back; "Leave it up to you then, mate." and followed his Inspector down the same path.

"That Inspector is a real strange character and no mistake about that." Paul muttered to himself. No bloody friends at the nick and kept he's own counsel. Yep, a real strange one. Paul gestured to the two undertakers to follow him and stared up at the old house. His Nan had always said that something sinister, something really evil went on in there and the authorities did nothing. Young Lord Coleville had really powerful friends and his family had money, power and position. Then, of course, there was the mystery of the vanishing lady in white and the dreadful death of Sir Edward's valet. Now that scandal did bring the fun and sex games, at the French House, to an apparent stop.

It was rumoured that Sir Edward had to flee the country, ending up France and apparently, dying just before the First World War; still in disgrace and exile.

"Pity my inept colleagues back there hadn't discovered the little bodies then, the dirty bastard may have been brought to justice." He muttered to himself, showing the undertakers the neat hole made in the floor. The original entrance and staircase to the cellars had been closed up years ago. The Architect, designing the old people's home had decided on a new opening and placement of boilers in the cellars. That simple decision had revealed the tragedy of the bones, hidden away for years.

He watched the pair descend down into the cellar and squatted down to watch. Suddenly he felt the hair go up on his neck and he actually shivered a little, as they were carefully placing the bones from each skeleton into a separate hold all. He stood up and took a deep breath, he had seen plenty of dead bodies - most a lot worse than this pair - so why the strange, uneasy feeling? The old workman standing next to him; filling his small pipe, smiled; "You felt it too?" He whispered and placed the unlit pipe in his mouth. Paul nodded and folded his arms. The old man gestured towards the ceiling. "Me and little 'arry were clearing up the bedrooms and we felt it there too. I would swear on my grand kid's life, that I could hear people talking above us, up in the bloody attics. To be honest, it sounded like children. So, we went up there and nobody was there, just dust and cobwebs. But 'arry found a sketch book behind the wall cabinet, when we pulled it down - rotten it was, the cabinet I mean - but you want to see the bloody sketches. Just tell 'arry I said so; especially the one of the maid."

He turned and walked into the gardens; to enjoy his pipe. Paul soon found young Harry, sitting on a box in one of the big reception rooms. He told him what the old man had said, that he should have a look at the sketch book. Harry sighed and carefully pulled the faded A4 book from his lunch bag. Paul carefully and gently turned the pages; all young girls and women, mostly naked and posing on furniture. The unknown artist clearly had real talent. Then he saw the one with the French maid, standing by a dinner table, holding a small tray of drinks in one hand. She was topless and almost smiling. She was really beautiful. Paul imagined that the woman must have been quite a stunner in her day.

Harry smiled; "Bet you're looking at the tart in the maids outfit. I would love to have been there when the lucky artist drew that. She was a fucking cracker." He carefully took the fragile book and placed it back into his bag, adding; "I'm going to photocopy that one and then see, if any antique shop wants the book. The drawings are really good; they must be worth a few quid."

Paul nodded; the sketch of the maid had been dated July 29th, 1881. That made him smile; that's exactly a hundred years ago to the day, of the forthcoming royal wedding. He made his way back downstairs and watched the undertaker's van leave. He would head back to the nick, for a very welcome cup of tea.

2. WOULD YOU CALL IT A CO-INCIDENCE?

Eric Smalls stood over the hole and stared down into the cellars. He was a little annoyed, but the Project Manager had said that the company would co-operate with the local newspaper and historical society over the two skeletons. Thus, he was waiting for their arrival. He looked out the window and watched the rain coming down. It wouldn't be dark for another couple of hours, then it was home for the evening news and some dinner with the missus and kids. He heard the loud knocking and made his way to the temporary front door and pulled it open.

The little group wandered slowly in and stood, looking around the grand hallway. The very well-dressed young man introduced himself to Eric with a handshake. "Jerry Tibbs from the Evening Standard; I spoke to inspector March on the 'phone, and he said it was fine to check out the cellars. I understand that your boss; Mr. Jarvis has cleared it with your good self?"

Eric nodded and stared at the others; Christ, that was the biggest black fella he had seen in a lifetime. The boy gripping his notepad looked a little dumb, but the young woman was a stunner. 'Jerry Tibbs' introduced his team; Mr. Wilson was a colleague from the paper and would take a few pictures. Wilson held up a really expensive camera and flash. He smiled; "Have camera will snap." Mr. Owen Jones was part of the local Historical Society and assisted Miss Alexandra Cappanni, who was from the same group.

Eric just nodded and kept staring at Alex, finally he had to ask; "Does your family come from around here?" Alex smiled and nodded; "Well, from the East End. Whitechapel, my father and brother are doctors, but the family has been around here since the 1850's. Why do you ask?"

Eric rubbed his face and smiled a little; "Well, because I looked at your double earlier today. If the sketch wasn't over a hundred years old, I would have sworn blind that he sketched you." It appears that young 'arry had shown the sketch book to more than just PC Marshall and his old friend, Stan. Such was the demand for the old drawing, 'arry had to make several photocopies for his colleagues!

Alex smiled and shrugged her shoulders; "Now you have really intrigued me, Eric. I must see it." Eric walked over to his bag and pulled the photocopy out. He held it up; "It's only black & white the photocopy machine didn't do colour. But you'll see what I mean. It is a bit naughty miss." He handed it over with a small smile.

He couldn't wait to tell the other lads that he had met the bloody model in the flesh; well, a really close look-a-like. The team gathered about her, and Owen whistled through his teeth; "Christ Alex, it is you. I would recognize those magnificent bres..." Wilson slowly crushing his foot stopped Owen in mid sentence and he fell silent, wincing a little. Alex nodded, clearly a little perplexed to be looking at her reflection. "My, my, the face does seem pretty similar."

Eric chuckled; "Not similar young lady; blooming identical I would say, If that wasn't drawn exactly a hundred years ago. I would swear that it was you!" Jericho stared at the picture and noted the date; that could prove quite useful. Wilson causally took a snap of the sketch and smiled. Jericho coughed; "The artist was certainly talented; he caught all the young lady's obvious charms."

That made Owen look again; real hard. He smiled, when he realised what Jericho was saying; the artist had drawn the lace panties as being quite transparent. Rather unusually, the model was shaved for that era. Jericho certainly noted that and smiled at Alex; she really would go the extra mile to get a case solved. He now, knew how to crack the mystery of the French House. They had done it before!

Eric took the picture back and gestured towards the kitchens; "There's a hole in the floor that goes down to the cellars. The original door and staircase down were apparently bricked up years ago. The cellars will hold the boilers for the new, old people's home."

They followed him into the quiet kitchens and stared down the hole. Eric pulled a switch down and the cellars were lit up. "Be careful going down the ladder." He muttered and Jericho descended first, and Alex was next and Eric smiled; now that's my kind of women; doesn't bat an eyelid about going down a ladder in a short skirt. That fucker 'Jerry' must be getting an eyeful; the lucky bastard.

Owen and Wilson followed them down and Eric returned to his bag, he still had some coffee left in his flask. He pulled the photocopy back out and looked at it closely; if he wasn't a sane man, then that young woman down the cellar was the girl in the picture! He looked at the date on the drawing and shook his head. It must be an ancestor of the young woman, there could be no other logical explanation for it. He unscrewed his flask and poured some lukewarm coffee into the lid that served as a cup. Suddenly a cold shiver ran up his spine, so bad that he dropped a little coffee on the floor. He stared about the quiet rooms and sighed; this fucking place was starting to get at him.

Wilson took a picture of the broken staircase that ended against a solid brick wall and noted that the cellar had been divided up, at some point in the past. He could still see the remains of the brick wall on the floor, despite the dirt and dust. Owen stood watching the hole in case Eric returned unannounced. Jericho pulled his orb from a pocket in his jacket and held it up. Nothing coloured its circumference. "No demonic activity." He said quietly and pulled out his mirror, replacing the orb carefully.

Alex sighed; "They've removed the bones. Now we have to attend the bloody morgue to run our mirrors over them and discover who they were." Jericho nodded; "No collector has attended this place [the cellars] at any time. So, what the hell happened to their souls?"

Wilson grunted; "Bit of a co-incidence that Alex is dressed up as one of the maids here, back in 1881. That means we've been here before; so why don't we have any recollection of it?" Jericho smiled; "That's because we haven't gone back yet. Well, not 'Us' as we are now. But at some time, we do. That sketch of Alex proves that. Rather unusually, we're already part of this. For instance, there's a picture of me - in the background - back in 1916 at an Army field hospital." He rubbed chin and continued. "I nearly fell off my seat, when I saw it in a book about the medical service of the First World War. I was researching the time and place for a mission back there. It happened, when we investigated that doctor who was saving lives with a machine he had invented. I had become part of the history for that event, so it does happen."

Alex sighed; "So, yet again, I'm dressed as a tart. This time showing off my crotch and boobs for some dirty, young Victorian pervert." Owen grinned; "I cannot wait to see you in that outfit in the flesh. Much better that just a damn drawing."

Alex slapped his arm hard and said nothing more. He got the

message that Alex wasn't happy and started to read his mirror. "Heads up people, Herbie [the Collector] has just informed control that, he has just collected a soul from this very location. He's a real good man; he knew we're on a case here. I really don't know why he doesn't join the Department." Jericho rubbed his face; "What are the details?"

"He has just collected a certain Miss Jessica Rowling's soul. She died at 22 years old with Type 1 diabetes in the year 1881, in April. She was a maid. Here's the really interesting part; she confessed to Herbie that she was a naughty French maid for her master, a certain Sir Edward Coleville. Apparently, he paid for doctors and had her nursed until she died. She's singing his praises as a very good man - for the time - he simply didn't abandon her, when she became too ill to work. That doesn't sound like the man as current history records him." Owen shrugged his shoulders, adding; "Strange that. She also said that he never laid a hand on her or the other girls who were naughty maids here. Now that doesn't make sense."

Wilson looked about the dismal little cellars and sighed; "Well, someone buried two young children down here for some reason. Maybe our Sir Edward only liked really young girls or boys. Any girl or boy over nine or ten was safe." Alex shuddered at that thought and pushed her fingers through her loose dark hair. "Sooner we run our mirror over those bones the better."

Jericho nodded at that and gestured towards the ladder; "Let's go. I'll make arrangements to see the bones." They followed him up the ladder; Alex going last. She stopped halfway up and looked about the cellar, yet again.

"What is it?" Wilson asked, holding out his hand. Alex didn't smile; "I just thought - for a second or so - that I could hear a child talking. Saying something about his missing mother; I don't know; I can't be sure." She continued up the ladder and Wilson helped her out the hole. Everyone stared back down into the cellar and jumped a little, as Eric appeared and switched off the lights down there. "You're not the only one who has heard the kid's voices around this dump Miss. Old Stan and young Harry Fellows swear they heard kid's voices up in the attics. That's where Harry found the sketch book with your drawing in." He smiled a little.

Alex brushed down her jacket and skirt, muttering; "You mean my double." Eric nodded and showed the team out.

The team stood on the pavement and stared at the old house in the persistent drizzle. Alex put up her umbrella and walked towards their white van. That's when PC Paul Marshal appeared from his 'Panda' car, throwing his unfinished cigarette down. He stared really hard at Alex, but spoke to Jericho; "You Jerry Tibbs the reporter?" He asked, pulling on his short raincoat. Jericho nodded and PC Marshal gestured to his police car; "My Inspector wants to see you Sir, down the station." Wilson interrupted; "We can follow you there in our van officer." Paul nodded and jumped back in his car.

"Now what?" Owen asked and the team clambered into their van and followed the police car to Brick Lane Police Station.

3. OTHER STORIES ABOUT THE FRENCH HOUSE.

 "It's certainly changed some since I was last here." Jericho said quietly to Alex. They were waiting outside Inspector March's office. "They must have just kept the façade. This is all new." He muttered and started to stand as the door to the Inspectors office opened. Inspector Thomas March was a big man. Owen pointed out that he had hands 'like shovels'. He smiled at Jericho and especially Alex, who stood next to him. He actually looked Alex up and down; slowly. Alex glanced at the floor; she knew very well that he was undressing her with his eyes. Jericho introduced the team, and the Inspector invited him and Alex into his office.

"Charming." Was all Owen said, as he and Wilson sat back down and waited outside. Wilson chuckled; "We can't compete with Alex when there are other men around. She'll get the invitation every time, baby brother." He sat and stared down the bare corridor, then grinned. A tall policeman smiled at him - who was another 'brother' [as Wilson would say] the pair shook hands and the tall officer dropped onto the bench next to them. "You part of the group having a look at the bones from the old 'French House?" he asked, and Wilson nodded.

The tall officer chuckled; "You want to have a look at the Station's Occurrence Book's about the calls that were made to that place, back in the 1880's. That'll give you a story alright."

His radio bleeped and his number was being called. Constable 466H answered, apologized and walked off; he had a call to attend to.

Owen smiled; "Occurrence Books had summaries about all incidents that took place on the station's patch. If the police were called to the place [the French House] then, there would be a record of it written up in them."

Wilson ran a hand over his face; "Now that could be a real source of information. But how do we get to see them?" Owen sighed and tapped his jacket pocket; "That's what we have mirrors for big man." Wilson grunted and slapped Owens's shoulder, murmuring; "Spot on baby brother. I wondered when you would spot that." Owen just rolled his eyes in mock despair and stood slowly, as the Inspector's door opened.

The team sat quietly in the van and watched the people and police officers, coming and going from Brick Lane Police Station. Wilson sat behind the wheel and stared up at the falling rain. He turned to Jericho, who was sitting next to him and said quietly; "So the bloody bones are about seven thousand years old, and the two kids were from the bloody stone-age?"

Jericho nodded and eased back in his seat; "They must have been buried there, thousands of years ago. I'm waiting for Dispatches to pull up the details. A collector would have attended way back then. They must have only been disturbed with the current work at the house. How the builders of the damn house missed them back in 1878 [when the house was constructed], I don't know."

"So, we don't really have a mission. If the kid's bones are that old, Sir Edward clearly had nothing to do with them; except they were buried in his cellar thousands of years before he or his cellars ever existed!" Alex spoke softly, resting her chin on her hand, watching out the windows. Jericho shrugged his shoulders and folded his arms; "Yes, but that is definitely you in that drawing from 1881, so we were definitely on the case there, at that time; unless you're moonlighting as a naughty French maid in another time period." He smiled, adding; "But why the hell are we there, now the bones have been cleared up?"

Owen looked up from his mirror and grinned; "That young officer was right Wilson. There is certainly a story about the old French House that would interest us and it's in the Occurrence Book for Brick Lane Station in 1881. There's an entry about police being called to the house because Sir Edward Coleville's young bride had vanished, minutes after arriving back from church. She just vanished from a locked room with several people standing outside. The only window was nailed down and the glass wasn't broken. There was no explanation possible for her disappearance. The police practically took the room apart looking for trap doors; secret openings etc. and found nothing. The young bride was never seen or heard of again."

Wilson shifted in his seat; "Sounds good, but was a human soul reported as disappearing from the timeline, at the time?" Owen shook his head; "There's no breaches of the timeline for that date and time. She was no time traveler, so where the hell did, she go?" Wilson shrugged his shoulders; he didn't know.

Owen continued; "Not five weeks after his bride disappeared, Sir Edward's Valet, a certain Michael Good was found at the bottom of the stairs with his neck broken and five stab wounds. He told the collector, that Sir Edward had stabbed him repeatedly and thrown him down the stairs. He actually didn't say why Sir Edward did that. Now that's a bit strange. But Michael's soul was placed in quarantine for one hundred years, so the Duty Death Angel [Francis at the time] thought he deserved it for something he did."

"Was Sir Edward arrested or charged with the killing?" Jericho asked and Owen shook his head; "No he wasn't. He claimed that Michael was killed by a burglar that he had apparently disturbed and with his power and position; that was that." Alex sighed and stretched her long legs out. "What happened to Sir Edward's soul, when he died? If had murdered someone, then he would have done time in quarantine too?"

Owen tapped at his mirror and sat up straight; "Sweet fanny Adam's! His soul is listed as missing!" He read on and held his mirror up; "According to Human Records and Dispatches, Sir Edward Coleville has never died. He missed his dispatch date in 1914. He didn't show up. Inspector Stella Longstreet and Team 35 have been assigned the case; there's no resolution yet."
"Well those bones have - unintentionally - opened a real tin of worms here." Jericho said and consulted his mirror, turning to

Owen and smiling; "By the way, that was an excellent little piece of research Owen. Well done." Owen grinned broadly and rewarded himself, by staring at Alex's long legs stretched out next to him. She just slapped his arm and pulled the hem of her skirt down and muttered; "Bloody monastery."

Wilson turned around in his seat and was about to speak to Alex, when he noticed she was deep in thought; he asked her what she was thinking. Alex sat up and started to tie her loose dark hair in a ribbon. "I wonder if Sir Edward is related to the famous Victorian Archaeologist; Lord John Coleville?" He was noted for excavations around Mesopotamia and the near East back then."

Owen was already on to that. "He was Lord John's second son. Does that help?" He answered and Alex just shook her head. "When I was the trainee on Stella's team, we dealt with an incident in ancient Mesopotamia, and I recall that Lord John Coleville was one of the archaeologists involved. Nothing untoward, it's just I remember the name."

Jericho slapped the seat armrest, pushing his mirror back into his jacket pocket and smiled; "Operational Control has given to go ahead to investigate further. They have stood Stella's team down since we're already on scene. So, Alex, you're about to get your dream job; a topless French maid in a horny young Victorian gentleman's naughty household!"

Alex just sighed; very loudly and Wilson - chuckling - started the van and pulled away. They would find a quiet spot to jump, and Supplies could collect the van. Owen rubbed his hands together; "This is going to make my day, seeing you in that outfit for real." He said to Alex who just ignored him and stared out the window.

She didn't notice the young man standing behind the bus stop, under his plain black umbrella, who watched the van pass by with some real interest. Sir Edward Coleville [currently Edward Kemp; a Stockbroker of some note] walked slowly back to his large black Bentley motor car and told the chauffeur to take him home. He really did smile. What a bloody woman and I let her go! He now knew that Alex and Owen had been temporal detectives, probably on his case. But what else had they uncovered at the old house?

4. LONDON - SUMMER 1881.

"At least it's not bloody raining." Muttered Owen as he carefully placed the worn bowler hat on and then adjusted his jacket and braces. Wilson stood by the carriage and smiled; "You look poor and well-worn baby brother. The holes in the shoes are a nice touch. Costumes have done well."

He turned to Alex who was straightening her old jacket and smoothing down the skirt that had seen better days. Her hair was loose and unwashed; the little bonnet she wore was old and a little threadbare. She had very little makeup on. Wilson sighed; she still looked fucking gorgeous!

Jericho sat in the carriage with the door open and pushed his mirror back into his coat pocket. "The tradesmen entrance is at the side of the house. I've checked my mirror and the old Housekeeper; a certain Mrs. Kathleen Gamble is in the kitchen's sitting room. She should come to the door. Impress her Alex and you're in." He leaned back and smiled; "Apparently, she hired young Sir Coleville's girls and looked after his 'special maids'. They never answered the door or did any of the hard work. Just pretend you're desperate for work and a place to stay. But don't lay it on too thick."

Alex nodded; "My sister Liz would be better at this." Jericho chuckled and gestured to the 'French House'. "Off you go and bloody well keep in touch." Alex and Owen walked up the path and past the grand front doors, they stood before the simple door marked' Trade only' and Alex knocked loudly on the door. It was a minute or so before Mrs. Gamble pulled open the door and stared at the roughly dressed pair standing on her step.

"What do you want?" She asked and folded her arms but looking closely at the young woman. Under the street dirt and unwashed hair, she really could see something special. The boy didn't interest her in the slightest; he looked dumb and a little pathetic.

Alex curtsied and said quietly; "Good morning Ma'am. My brother and I are looking for work. I'm a trained House maid and my young brother here would make an excellent Footman. I understand that your master hires girls who..." She deliberately hesitated and looked at the floor, very demurely and then continued; "That don't mind doing some things that please him. Dressing for him, I mean. I'm not a street girl Ma'am. My old employer died, and his heir has sold the house. My brother and I find ourselves in hard times and we're desperate for a position, Ma'am." She gripped her small case with both hands and tried to look as pathetic as Owen already did, without acting!

Kate [the housekeeper] grunted and was about to close the door on the pair, when she stopped and didn't smile; "Undo you coat girl." She said and Alex placed her case down and unbuttoned her coat. She held it open and didn't smile or say anything. Kate rubbed her face; on the surface this girl had a really good figure, and her face was quite beautiful; despite the street dirt. She folded her arms; "We may have a position for you girl. But your brother is of no use. His Lordship has two young footmen already, who do bugger all."

Alex nodded and gripped Owens's arm; "Please Ma'am, we can't be separated. He's all I have. I'm sure the master would be generous and hire the pair of us. Please Ma'am, we're hard working and must stay together." Kate just sighed; "I'll take a look at you and if your something special, I'll see what the young master says about the boy." She gestured for them to enter and follow her up the back stairs.

They sat in a quiet upstairs study. The walls were lined with shelves that contained numerous books and there were glass cabinets scattered around containing small, ancient sculptures. "I bet there from Mesopotamia, objects his father dug up." Alex whispered to Owen, who sat clutching his hat with both hands. It was some minutes before Kate returned and the pair stood. She told Owen to sit and wait, but Alex was to follow her. They went up another flight of back stairs to Kate's private parlour and Kate dropped into a high-backed chair and pointed to an empty chair. "Put your clothes on that. I want you to strip down and I mean everything. I need to see you nude. Do you understand that girl?"

Alex nodded and hesitated as she removed her hat; "I'm not a street girl Ma'am. I just desperately need a job." Kate actually smiled; "Believe me child, you'll be safer here than on the streets, even stark naked." She then chuckled and gestured for Alex to get on with it. Alex removed her clothes and stood naked. hands covering her private bits. Kate made her turn several times and told her twice to drop her hands. Finally, Alex did so. Kate pointed down to her thighs; "Why are you shaved girl?" She seemed most puzzled, and Alex blustered out; "I caught some lice sleeping on the streets and that was the only way I could get rid of them." Some small tears fell down her face.

Old Kate chuckled; "Well, you won't get lice here, so grow the damn thing out. The master loves a good bush in see through knickers. Now wait here, the master will take a look at you and decide. It's alright girl, he won't hurt you."

Alex stood naked in the little room for a minute or so and the door reopened as Kate wandered in talking to the young man that followed her. Sir Edward Coleville was a strikingly handsome man for the period - or any period - he was smoking a small cigar and he stood and stared at Alex, who lowered her head and looked at the floor. He walked around her, stopping to study her bum.

"As I said sir, lovely arse and a fine pair of milkers. She's also very pretty as a bonus. Those big nipples and round arse are worth her wages on their own." Kate smiled and told Alex to bend over a little so that the master could view her arse properly. Alex did so and Sir Edward grunted in satisfaction.

"Alright, I'll take the bloody brother on as well. You don't get quality like this turn up every day. Put her on duty tonight. There are some important guests for dinner and the young lady can show us, if she can do the job. See to it please Mrs. Gamble." He simply turned and walked from the room. Alex was a little astounded; he hadn't made a single move to touch her!

Kate chuckled and pointed to Alex's clothes piled on the chair; "I told you girl; you could walk stark naked around here and be perfectly safe with that one." She then rubbed her face and added; "But keep away from Michael, Sir Edwards's valet. I wouldn't trust him with a dead cat." And sat herself down and watched Alex hurriedly dressing herself.

"I'm not surprised that his lordship took your brother on; your worth his wages as well; easily. You're a real little beauty my girl. You behave yourself and train up well and there's four pounds a week wages in it. That's twice as much you'd get anywhere else and you would have to work bloody hard for it!" She laughed and relaxed in her chair. Yes, this one was quite a turn up for the books, they needed to replace the poor late Jessica and a real Venus knocks at the door. Of course, the master was going to snap her up, even if it meant taking on the dopy looking brother.

Alex re-joined Owen and she whispered to him what had happened, and they were both now employed in the French House. Jericho would be happy about that turn of events. Owen pulled out his mirror; "I'll let him know that we're in."

She immediately noticed his grim face and especially no comments about her stripping naked for the master. "What's up?" She said quietly and Owen ran a hand over his face. "The bloody mirrors are offline." Alex quickly - and discretely - checked her mirror; no signals; it was offline too. They both stared at each other; they were trapped until help arrived; but even if it did, would their mirrors be offline too?

The change in their circumstances, by the failure of their mirrors was enormous, the pair was now trapped. They had no money [being poor was part of their disguise!] and nowhere to run too. Late Victorian London was no place to be poor, destitute and homeless. They both knew that only minutes would pass for Wilson and Jericho, whilst days could go past here. "We fucked." Was all Owen said and Alex sighed; "And I may well be, unless we want to live on the streets and go hungry." Owen nodded; "For fuck sake, you have to play this for real Alex. We don't have a bloody choice anymore."

Alex leaned back on her chair and ran a hand over her face. The streets were no place for them. Death was all around and whilst she was 'safe' if she died here; young Owen was not. [This was part of Alex's ordained time period and so her soul could be collected] but Owen was from Medieval times and he's would be lost to the darkness; for good. She stared at him and sighed, like it or not, he was her responsibility. She would have to play the tart for real, just to stay here until rescue.

Owen sighed; "There must be a 'Judas Stone' somewhere in the house. Maybe Sir Edward's father dug it up in Mesopotamia. Now that's really a fucking crappy piece of luck; for us anyway." Alex agreed and clasped her hands together; this mission was turning rotten by the minute.

They would have to locate the bloody 'Judas Stone' as quickly as possible and get rid of it. But where the hell would they start in a house this size? It was probably the size of a man's thumb. Their thoughts were disturbed by Young William [a footman] who showed Alex her room and couldn't stop smiling at her. He told Owen that he was sharing with him and would show him, where to get his new uniform.

William grinned at Alex; "Looking forward to seeing you in costume girl. The master said you're a fucking stunner and he'll probably keep you for himself; he has plans for you I think - lucky beggar - he was quite sad at losing young Jessica after he spent so much money on her, with clothes and training." That didn't improve Alex's mood. She was trapped and needed to take real care from now on.

But something wasn't right; the late Jessica had said that Sir Edward hadn't put a hand on her or the other girls; so, what did the young footman mean by that? He showed them the maid's quarters and waited for Owen at the foot of the small, creaky staircase. Owen dropped Alex's small case upon the only chair and stared about the room; "I bet it's better than mine." He moaned but smiled. Alex sat on the bed and looked out the small window. The rear gardens were beautifully kept. "It's not too bad actually; i was expecting a lot worse and I really don't think this bedroom is for servants. Whatever, it's better than sleeping on a street corner." She murmured and removed her little hat and placed it on the bed.

"Well, that horny young sod was certainly interested in you. But I'm not surprised by that; showing your bits to him – stripping stark naked, just like that – he must think he's on a right winner." Owen dropped his voice and peered out into the upstairs corridor. Alex chuckled; "Well, he's going to be a disappointed young man." That's when they heard the footsteps outside and both fell silent. Young Lizzie appeared in the doorway and Owen removed his bowler hat and adjusted his necktie.

Lizzie was one of the 'upstairs' maids. Owen couldn't take his eyes off her and she smiled broadly at the pair. "Just come to say welcome and give you the uniform. There's only one for now, Mr. Babette will order you some more; if you prove satisfactory." She spoke to Alex but smiled at Owen. Lizzie was wearing her 'French maid' costume and Owen was enjoying it already. She placed the small bundle down on the bed, next to Alex, who thanked her and Owen really did smile, as she – quite slowly and deliberately – bent over the bed. Her short black skirt was already exposing her silk panties and her small round arse was pushed up for his benefit. She had black silk stockings and short high heels. That's when he realised the silk knickers were quite transparent in the light. She turned and smiled; her large breasts hardly restrained by her black bodice top. She adjusted her little frilly mop cap and by lifting her arms, raised the already short skirt. Owen was getting a real treat.

Lizzie patted Owen on the cheek; "We have our own little dining room up here. I'll ask Mr. Babette if you can serve us 'upstairs maids' tonight. That will give you something to look forward to." She turned back to Alex; "I'll collect you at six and show you the dining room and bathroom. Best slip into your costume, it's all new, nothing has been worn before. It should fit, but Kate will do any adjustments you may need, if she hasn't disappeared on some errand for the master - again. Sir Edward will want to see how you look in it." She stepped out the room and Owen watched her walk down the corridor, hips swinging and her peach like bum wobbling. Owen groaned and Alex managed a chuckle; "You've gone a little red my dear perverted brother."

Owen picked up his case and headed for the door; "Better find my room and brush my footman's uniform down." He turned and finally did smile; "I can't wait to see you in that outfit. Now that will make my bloody day. Well, possibly my bloody year if we still had them." He disappeared and Alex closed the door and locked it. The key was left in the lock, and she also left it there. She lay back on the bed and sighed; she was really playing the tart now!

5. DINNER & A SURPRISING PROPOSAL.

She sorted through the small bundle; the bodice wasn't quite her size and she would certainly be hanging out of it. "As long as I don't bend over too much or breathe deeply; it should do." She muttered to herself. At least there were three pairs of silk panties – all new and still wrapped in clean paper – she had to admit the uniform certainly wasn't cheap in any way. Just the stockings would have cost a working-class girl; a month's wages!

There was a soft knock at the door and she unlocked and opened it slowly. Kate stood outside, a sewing basket in her hands. She didn't smile; "Let's see how the uniform fits. I'll make any adjustments if needed. The Master wants to see how you look." She stepped in and Alex started to remove her jacket. The woman smiled; "Jesus, I can see why he hired you straight away, even if it meant taking on another footman, you're a right little cracker. He was quite taken by you girl and that hasn't happened before. He really loved the way; you didn't bat an eyelid about being stark naked in front of him." She saw the worried look on Alex's face and added; "It's alright girl. He knows you're not a prossie [prostitute] just down on your luck and he was most impressed that you stay with your brother; to look after the boy."

Alex watched her open the sewing basket and noticed the small tattoo's on the back of both hands. She knew that such tattoos were very unusual on women for this time and place. Kate saw her looking at the tattoo's and smiled a little. "I have others. I was a little wild in my younger days. Ran away from home at fourteen and joined a bloody circus. They were good days. Kept my dad's dirty fucking hands off me, anyway." She said and pulled a needle and thread out. "Come on girl, I have to see to the dinner for tonight." She said and smiled.

Kate made all the necessary adjustments and the pair of woman chatted like old friends. Kate had clearly taken to her new French Maid. She told Alex all about the goings on at the French House. She sang Sir Edwards praises; the young master was apparently immensely popular with his staff and friends. Kate also told Alex about the resident ghosts of the place; two children who could be heard laughing and talking. Kate was a little mystified by that, since the house was brand new and only just built.

Alex really wanted to tell her about the Stone Age bones in the cellars, but she wouldn't be able to explain, how she knows about them!

Alex stared at herself in the full-length mirror, fixed on the wall opposite the bed. No matter how she tried to pull the skirt down, even a little; her crotch was still exposed. Designed that way she thought to herself. The bodice certainly fitted better after Kate's adjustments, but still exposed a lot of her magnificent bosom. Kate had shown her the secret straps at each side; all she had to do was push her thumbs into each and the bodice folded neatly down, exposing her breasts fully.

"That's how you'll wear it, when serving dinner to the master and his guests. He'll going to try you out tonight; he has a couple of very important dinner guests and he'll want to show you off."

Kate had informed her as she left. Alex pulled on a cardigan and buttoned it up, but she couldn't do anything about the damn short skirt. Earlier, Kate had seemed quite surprised that Alex was shaved; women in this century really didn't shave their privates. Kate had chuckled; "I bet he'll [the master] tell you to grow that bush of yours. He likes that. A hairy fanny through silk knickers is quite a turn on for him."

Alex [and Owen!] had both noticed that young Lizzie certainly didn't trim her private parts, including her armpits. But then, that simply wasn't done in this era. She sighed; there was another knock at the door, and she opened it. Sir Edward stood smoking; he didn't attempt to enter the room and looked Alex straight in the eyes and slowly smiled.

"At dinner tonight, Lizzie and Emma will show you the ropes. They can earn extra money by being nice to the guests. I understand that Lizzie has made enough to buy herself a little place in the country. I don't know what Emma does with her extra money. But you, I understand from Kate, don't wish to take part in those...those types of games. So, i will inform the guests to keep their hands off you." He looked down at her legs and short skirt. "I'll speak to you later Alexandra. I have a proposal for you that you may be interested in. I have waited a long time for a woman with your qualities." He smiled and walked away, leaving Alex quite puzzled.

She was absolutely amazed that he hadn't tried anything on. He clearly wanted her, but was disciplined enough to keep his hands to himself; for now? She looked at herself in the mirror and wondered, where the hell could she keep her damn mirror in this outfit! - Even if the bloody thing was offline; she would hold onto it. She also had to find out where the bloody Judas stone was. But where the fuck could it be?

Alex was introduced to Emma – the other 'upstairs maid' - just before dinner. Emma was quite tall and had dark raven hair with long legs and a pair of breasts that easily matched Alex's. But she had an atrocious East End accent. Every other word she uttered was an obscenity, but not in front of the young master. She really became quite demure, when he was present.

Kate assembled the girls in the small parlour that was linked to the private upstairs dining room. She instructed the girls carefully about how the dinner would be served and told Lizzie to look after Alex.

The various courses were assembled by Mr. Babette and Kate. Alex could hear talking and a little laughter coming from the dining room. She was stunned to hear a woman's posh voice. She whispered to Lizzie about that, who just smiled; "That's Lady Gabby [Gabriella] she's the wife of the master's best friend; Lord Robert. She'll have her hands up your skirt before the second course. She plays both sides apparently, just don't scream or drop anything and you'll be fine. Just let her have a feel round with a smile on your face and everyone will be happy. But she does have bloody cold hands." Lizzie grinned and Mr. Babette called for the girl's attention.

There were seven courses' to be served and Mr. Babette would serve the drinks. Alex noted there were four open wine bottles on the serving table and brandy had been decanted into an exquisite – and very expensive – crystal decanter. She stared at it and really wished for a glass. But her attention was drawn back to Mr. Babette, who clapped his hands softly and said, "Covers down please."

Alex watched as Lizzie and Emma dropped their bodices and stood straight, like soldiers awaiting inspection. She slowly followed and stood a little straighter. Mr. Babette turned to Kate and actually smiled. "Now that's the best pair of knockers I've seen in years. The young master will be pleased." He turned back to the girls, each now holding two soup plates, whilst Alex carried only one. Mr. Babette had told her, that she would exclusively serve the master tonight. Emma and Lizzie would wait on the four other guests. He gestured for them to follow him. Mr. Babette pushed open the swing door and the girls followed him out into the dining room.

The master sat at the head of the table with Lady Gabby to his left and Lord Robert on his right. A very tall young man with a thick black, short beard and shoulder length hair [unusual for the period] sat opposite. Alex noted that he was a very handsome, strapping young man. In modern times, he would easily be referred to as a 'babe magnet'.

He smiled at Alex, and she couldn't stop herself smiling back. He sat next to Lady Gabby. Lord Robert had a much older man sitting next to him. He was short and plump with thin glasses; he must have been in his early fifties. The conversation appeared to centre around Edward; the Prince of Wales and his latest Mistress and then it turned to money.

The plump little man was moaning about the prince; he hadn't paid his gambling debts – again – and owed Howard [the plump man] nearly a hundred pounds now. [that would be thousands of pounds in today's money]. Alex had her soup plate filled by Mr. Babette from the silver soup tureen and placed it down on the master's table mat. Lady Gabby stared at her: "Colly, [short for Coleville?] I must say that your new girl is an absolute stunner. Where on earth did you get her? She could be a damn Hapsburg Princess!" The other guests all agreed with that statement, especially the young man with the beard. He waved his spoon about and pleaded with 'Colly' to let him sketch her after dinner.

The master agreed and ran his hand up Alex's leg and patted her bum. "If you offer her the right money Ross, I'm sure she'll pose for you. In fact, I'll pay you handsomely to paint her in oils." He gave Alex's bum cheek a little squeeze and smiled; well pleased that she was quite docile and submissive to his touch. He turned back to the 'artist' and sipped his soup, saying; "I would love you to paint her naked, sitting on the old bench in the gardens. I might even have her photographed in some very naughty poses." He squeezed her arse again and smiled at her – really smiled – and returned to his soup.

Alex was a little surprised by his groping; apparently, he had never 'laid a hand' on the other girls, so why was he touching her up? Ross the artist sketched Alex standing by the dining table holding a small silver tray with a couple of glasses on; just like in the sketch found in 1981.

The others watched, sipping their wine and chatting. When he had enough to complete the sketch later, Ross pulled a white five-pound note from his pocket and very slowly pushed it into Alex's panties, making sure he 'accidently' touched her vagina more than once. He smiled and said softly that there were more of those [the note] to come if she behaved herself, whilst he painted her for 'Colly later on. Alex suddenly realized - with a little shock - that she had enjoyed his gentle touch. Close up he really was a handsome man. But Alex was constantly 'touched up' by 'Colly and the guests throughout dinner. But then, so were the other girls. Lady Gabby had asked to feel her and Colly' agreed. Alex had to stand next to the woman while she felt round her bum and pushed her cold hands between Alex's legs. Gabby declared that she 'would suckle those big tits after dinner' and everyone laughed. She gently squeezed Alex's vagina through the thin silk panties and whispered to Alex that she would pay her ten pounds, for a couple of hours in bed. [That was serious money for a working-class girl in this era]. Alex said nothing.

Howard was the worse one out of them; he pushed his fingers into Alex's bum crack and tried to insert a finger into her bum hole, but Alex clenched her buttocks tightly and the little man failed miserably, in his efforts to finger her arse. He withdrew his hand in dismal failure and finished his desert. But he tried twice more before the evening ended.

But Alex was again, surprised by Ross touching her so intimately; Sir Edward had said; he would tell his guest that Alex didn't want to play that game. After dinner, the guests sat in the study and were served more drinks by Emma and Lizzie. 'Colly' pulled Alex upon his lap and sat with one arm about her waist. The other held a full glass of brandy. He occasionally took a sip and allowed Alex a little from the same glass. They were watching Lizzie and Emma giving Ross and Lord Robert a blow job, directly in front of them. Lady Gabby was instructing Emma how her groaning husband liked his small cock sucked.

Ross rested his hands on Lizzie's bobbing head and smiled directly at Alex, who watched Lizzie's performance closely; the young artist was certainly well equipped. It was in stark contrast to Lord Robert, who held Emma by the hair and pushed her onto his small cock and called her a slut and whore. He had quite an evil grin on his face and Lady Gabby slapped the girls arse on several occasions. Alex decided the pair was really quite a nasty couple. They were clearly made for each other.

Howard sat pulling his limp dick and repeatedly asked 'Colly' if he could have Alex. 'Colly' said no to each request and gently pulled Alex to him and held her quite tight. He sipped his brandy and made Alex do the same.

You're playing no part in this little game, tonight or any night. We have many bigger and better plans for you and your stunning charms, my dear." He placed the brandy glass down and started to kiss her neck and shoulder. She tried to pull away and was shocked by the scene unfolding in front of her. He pushed his hand into her thighs, and rubbed her crotch, "That's a good girl. Don't try and refuse me or I will beat your brains out and not think twice about doing it." He slapped Alex's bum cheek so hard, that she actually screamed and tried to jump from his lap. He held her tight and raised his hand again.

"I would really behave yourself girl. I won't just spank you for being naughty, next time." He formed his hand into a big fist and gently waved it under her chin. "You refuse me anything and I will use this, and it won't be pleasant; for you." He roughly turned her head and pushed his mouth over hers. He 'French kissed' her for some minutes; even sucking hard on her tongue at one point. She knew, she had to submit to this and closed her eyes and thought of...horse riding, for whatever reason!

her submit to his gropes. He sucked her nipples real hard and slapped her bum several times more; but not so hard. He repeatedly pushed his fingers into her crotch, under her panties and the terrible groping was only halted when the Butler whispered into his ear.

He kissed her bare shoulder slowly and whispered in her ear. "They [Lizzie & Emma] will fuck with them all - except Ross - as usual. He's normally happy with just a good sucking. But you can retire to bed my dear, after we finish our brandy. You must be tired after your first shift. I want you fresh tomorrow, for your portrait sitting and photographs. Then it's your big day on Saturday. That's when it will be explained, just what a wealthy and happy woman you are about to become." He laughed in a very unpleasant way and roughly squeezed her breasts, giving her a love bite on her back. "That's a little something to keep. When I do have you, you'll enjoy every bite."

The master was, apparently, not happy with what the Butler told him. Howard groaned as he masturbated into his hankie and asked 'Colly' for Alex yet again. The answer was 'no' - yet again. He even offered the incredible sum of a hundred pounds just for her to suck his cock. 'Colly' sighed and kissed the distressed Alex on the forehead; "No Howard; She's too precious for that. Lizzie or Emma will relieve you. This young lady has bigger fish to catch." He stood and pulled Alex to her feet and they walked to the door; he made Alex walk in front of him, so he could see her hips and bum swinging. He gave her bum another little slap and chuckled; "We are going to make a fortune together; my dear. An absolute fortune, But I now have to go and sort out a little problem; otherwise, you would be on your knees with my cock in your arse."

The pair [the master and Alex] left the modest little orgy that was getting under way and 'Colly' walked Alex to her room and kissed her strongly again. He - again - groped her private parts and almost bit her on the shoulder. But he sighed, turned and walked away, but stopped and looked back at her. "I've had the key left in the lock, so you'll feel safe my dear. Just keep an eye out for that bloody valet Michael; he really has a thing for beautiful things and your mine." He chuckled and disappeared down the small back stairs.

Alex dashed into her room and locked the door; also putting a chair under the door handle. She still couldn't believe what had happened to her.

Sir Edward was a dirty nasty, violent groper and sex predator, who wouldn't take no for an answer and certainly didn't keep his word about her not being touched by him or the guests. She sighed and wondered how Owen was getting on. But so much for Kate saying that she would be safe in the house with the young master; "Total bollocks!" Muttered Alex and slept on the bed - dressed - and slept badly.

6. THE PAINTER.

Alex stood in the morning room [selected because of the wonderful amount of light that came through the big window] and watched Ross set up his easel and position his paints. He moved gracefully - like a big cat - Alex thought and he turned and smiled; gesturing towards a white sheet, hung between two poles. "I had that erected for you. I know I'm about to paint you stark naked, But A lot of models like to undress in private. There's also a clean sheet behind there. So, you can cover yourself between sessions."

He pushed both hands through his thick, dark curly hair and sighed; "I just hope I have the skill to capture your beauty. You are simply the most beautiful model I have had the privilege to commit to oils. I know Eddy is paying me for this, but I do thank you - for my self - for allowing me to capture your beauty. I know I'm truly blessed with this fantastic piece of luck."

Alex nodded and said quietly; "Thank you for your kind considerations." She had already decided that she needed to 'get back on the horse after a fall'. And this young man could just be the answer to that little problem!

He turned to his easel and pulled off his jacket, rolling up his sleeves, like a worker about to dig roads. Alex sighed, that was the signal he was about to start. She walked over to the chair by the door and pulled her shoes off.

Ross stood and watched; slowly mixing a little paint onto his palette. He was impressed; she was going to strip in front of him. Alex sat on the chair and slowly rolled each stocking down and placed them on the small table by the chair. She stood and removed her frilly little white apron and then pulled down the short skirt. She stared straight at Ross, standing now, only in panties and top; she removed her top and dropped it on the chair next to the discarded skirt.

Ross carefully licked the end of his brush and really did smile at those magnificent breasts. He believed he could spend several days just sketching and painting them; never mind the rest of her, which in his eyes; was equally magnificent.

Alex very slowly pulled down her panties and threw them onto the chair, with her suspender belt. Finally, she reached up and removed her mop cap, allowing her long dark hair to fall about her face and shoulders. There was a good minute of silence between the pair. Ross holding was his brush and smiling.

Alex was standing, hands at her sides and yes, smiling a little. Ross gestured to the large couch, covered with a clean white bed cover and several pillows. Alex walked slowly past him, and he watched the swing of her hips and that gorgeous peach shaped bum moving gently. She sat quite straight; legs open a little and said softly; "How do you want to take me?"

The young painter said nothing but placed down his brush and walked over to Alex. He held up his big hands and said, "I need to touch you. To pose you the way I think best. Do you mind?"

Alex shook her head and Ross gently took hold of both shoulders and pushed her slowly back against the pillows. Alex quite deliberately opened her legs a little wider and Ross stared at her exposed vagina and really did smile. "Are you comfortable with this?" He whispered and again Alex nodded. She smiled and pushed back against the pillows, allowing her legs to fall open.

"My dear darling, does that mean what I think it does or am I just dreaming?" Alex leaned forward and said softly in his ear; "Neither of us are sleeping."

Ross had his loose shirt and baggy trousers off in an instant. Alex was a little surprised by the fact that he was wearing no underwear. She smiled at him and said, "No pants- quite Bohemian of you - or do you always paint so well prepared?" The young man just grinned and presented his erection to her, kicking off his shoes. She ran both hands down his taught chest and abdomen; she had been right; the young man was well built and didn't carry a single ounce of spare flesh. She gripped his cock with gentle fingers and felt it come alive under her touch. "What would you like?" She said and lowered her head as he knelt on the covers. "I'm literally in your hands darling. You do as you want." He replied.

Alex giggled a little and took him in her mouth; he groaned quietly and ran his hands over her hair. He was a big man and filled her mouth with just the tip of his cock. Her tongue licked and probed his cock with exquisite care. He removed one hand from her hair and pushed it gently between her legs. Her vagina was wet and open. He groaned in satisfaction at finding that. She was already moist enough. She sucked his cock for a few minutes and then he insisted in returning the compliment.

Alex lay back and actually loudly moaned, gripping the pillows tightly. The young man knew his way around a woman's clitoris and hers was certainly swollen and ready for lovemaking. He feasted on her for some minutes and Alex was truly surprised when she had a couple of small orgasms. She gripped his head and said loudly; "For fuck sake, fuck me, Fuck me hard."

The young man didn't need to be told twice. He mounted her immediately, having little difficulty pushing in his big cock. Alex was ready; very wet and now really wanting the love making to start properly. He didn't disappoint her as she lay back, her hands clutching his shoulders, pushing her hips up to meet his thrusts. Their tongues urgently explored each others willing mouths and they rolled about the covers; locked in a passionate embrace.

They changed position several times and Alex found herself on top, with his eager mouth on her breasts. She had an orgasm again which left her with a tight stomach and shaking legs. But she didn't stop riding her stallion. He pulled her down and the pair kissed again. He exploded in her and Alex felt every drop. It was like someone had shoved a soda siphon in her and let it go. She had, yet another orgasm and collapsed on top of her skilled lover.

They lay panting together, swapping hot passionate wet kisses. Their tongues really didn't want to part. Finally, Alex broke the spell and gently rolled off the young man and laid back, pulling a pillow behind her head. He leaned over and gently ran a hand down her neck and stomach. They both stared into each other's eyes and knew they didn't have to speak. He slowly turned her back to him and passionately kissed her. She responded to his probing tongue, and they lay together in each other's arms for some time. Whispering to each other and kissing.

Ross sat up, Alex cradled in his arms, and laughed; "Sweet Jesus darling, we've been at it for over an hour." He pointed to the clock on the mantel piece and chuckled, squeezing her tightly, kissing her neck and shoulders. Alex pulled down his head and kissed his lips. She waved a hand across her face and smiled; "I'm practically glowing. That was the best bloody sex I've had in a very long time." She really did kiss her lover and she meant what she said.

He pulled a sheet across the love-struck pair and stroked her hair and face. For a big man he was gentle in his touch. Alex turned in his arms and the pair embraced and kissed. He ran a finger down her lips and sighed; "I can't give you up Alex. I know that Eddy can offer you money, clothes, carriages, servants, world travel and everything you could wish for. I barely earn a living as a bloody painter. For Christ sake, I can't even afford bloody underwear or decent clothes. All the money I have is what Eddy gives me." He ran his hands over her hair and face again. His hands were trembling. He stared into her eyes and said softly; "All I can offer is me. I have nothing else to give you and you deserve every good thing this damn world can give." He wiped his face and stared at the window. He knew that it was probably all the pair would have; together.

"For god sake, a real man shouldn't blub, should he?" He said quietly. Alex wiped a tear from her own face and pulled him to her breasts. "Maybe you're all I want." She whispered and kissed his face and mouth. The pair fell back and the love making started again, with real unbridled passion. They made love until - finally exhausted - they lay back - under the sheet and held each other tight. Alex hadn't had such feelings about a man like this, for a very long time.

Ross pulled from her embrace and slipped from the couch and curled up on the floor, clutching himself tightly. He was crying, Alex jumped from the couch and went to comfort him, but he held up a hand and said angrily; "Don't touch me Alex. I'm not the man you think I am....I'm not really a man." He sobbed and Alex, now totally confused just chuckled; "After what you did to me, you're a real man alright."

Ross shook his head and wiped his face. He took a couple of deep breaths and stared at her - unsmiling - he rose slowly, still naked and sighed, deep and loud. He hesitated for a while and then confessed fully.

 Alex staggered a little and sat on the edge of the couch and ran both hands over her face. Young Ross - the skilled painter and lover - was an undeclared homosexual. He went with women as a cover; to be a homosexual in these times was a serious criminal offence; punishable by prison and punished by society with the stigma of a social outcast. No one would ever buy his pictures and he wouldn't be invited anywhere by anyone in polite society. His 'life' would be over. There was no 'coming out' in Victorian Society. As a homosexual, he would only be allowed to exist in the shadows.

Acceptance of such a talented and decent young man would come far too late for young Ross and certainly never in his lifetime. Pulling herself together, Alex walked slowly over to him and held the sobbing young man in her arms. There was nothing said between the pair. She cried a little as he wept in her arms.

Alex knew the reality of both their situations; she also knew that this day was all the pair would have. She cried softly and cursed her fate and his.

That evening, Alex sat in the deserted kitchen and cradled her teacup with both hands. She felt terribly tired and couldn't stop herself feeling sad, thinking about the young painter, his touch and hidden strength; those big hands on her body and that mouth over hers. She sighed and placed the cup down. Few men had really touched her soul like that. Now she wondered - frequently - just how much was a covering game for Ross.

She jumped a little as Owen came through the door and sat down. He shrugged his shoulders; there was still no luck in finding the damn 'Judas Stone'. The only place he hadn't thoroughly searched was Sir Edwards study and that was always locked, when Sir Edward wasn't actually in there. They would have to come up with a plan to get in and search. Even the Butler or Housekeeper didn't have a spare key.

Alex nodded but was only half listening. Owen smiled and tapped the table; "Hello, I'm Owen. What have you done with our Alex?" She smiled and whispered sorry. Owen leaned back in his chair; "Alex, you were a long time with that Ross character, are you OK?"

Alex nodded; "Well, he was painting me. It's not like a photograph - snap and it's done - I had to sit really still for ages and it was bloody cold with no clothes on." Owen chuckled; "That's more like our Alex. Is he any good?" Alex stared at the empty cup and really did smile; "Yes. He was very good. One of he best. He could easily be very famous one day and people will pay a fortune for my picture."

Owen just sighed; "Yeah, that's the day that really hot place turns to snow." The little bell on the 'Call Board' tinkled and Owen looked up. "The front door; I best get going. Both the other boys [the footmen] are off tonight; gone to the bloody Music Hall." He rose from his chair and disappeared, leaving Alex to her very sad and private thoughts.

Alex knew one certainty; she wouldn't check Human records and find out the eventual fate of the young painter. She really didn't want to know. She obviously knew he would be dead and his soul would have moved on - hopefully - and that's all she wished to know about the young man who had touched her so suddenly, so unexpectedly and so deeply; only to find that it could have been just a façade.

7. THE OUTRAGED HUSBAND SCAM.

Alex carried the breakfast tray into the Sir Edward's private study. She was nervous and a little afraid; she knocked on the door and a soft voice called out for her to enter. Sir Edward must have a visitor; there were two cups on the tray.

Alex sighed; someone is about to get an eyeful. At least she wasn't bloody topless. She opened the door and entered, curtsying. Sir Edward stood up and walked over; Alex actually took a step back, feeling really vulnerable in the maids outfit and especially after the dreadful groping and threats, she had endured last night at his hands.

But Sir Edward took the tray from her and placed it on his desk. He was alone in the study - well, apart from Alex - he walked back to his desk and gestured for her to sit on the chair in front of his desk. Alex very carefully and slowly eased herself down. She sat with her knees closed tight together; she certainly wouldn't be crossing her legs in front of him; in this bloody short skirt and wearing panties that were practically transparent.

He poured two coffees and handed one to Alex. He smiled and sat back. "I have a little proposition for you Alex - may I call you Alex? - That you may be interested in. It means money, plenty of it, travel abroad and around Britain, as a lady of quality. You'll have your own maid and a very generous clothes allowance. All you have to do is what you're doing now, showing yourself off in private. Now, does that interest you?"

Alex sipped the hot coffee and nodded; what the fuck is he up too? Playing Mr. Nice guy now and what for, what is he after? She shuddered a little; she bloody knew what he was after; her. She nodded that she was interested.

Sir Edward smiled and nodded to himself; "That's good Alex. My brother Harold and I have a little scheme, which is not quite legal or moral. But it will produce lots of money and I mean loads of the stuff." He leaned back in the chair and sighed; "You see, our father has squandered most of the family fortune digging up

bloody ruins in the desert; and finding little of real value.
Harold and I will rectify that with your help. All you have to do is
tease and lure men - rich married men - to your rooms and we
will do the rest. There is no violence involved and you will be
perfectly safe. Are you still interested?"

Alex nodded again; the bloody pervert must have had acting
lessons! He was now playing a charming, supposedly straight
forward young man, trying to interest her in some bloody scam;
probably blackmail by the sound of it.

Sir Edward smiled and slapped his hands together with joy. That
made Alex jump a little; after last night she believed he could be
capable of violence; especially towards women who didn't submit
to his carnal desires.

"That's excellent; we have waited a long time for a young lady
like you. Beautiful, she had to be a living, Venus. But she also
had to capable of taking her clothes off in front of strange men.
That's why we had you painted; to see if you could perform. You
fit the bill perfectly. You look demure, obedient and you don't
mind stripping naked for a stranger; like I was yesterday. Alex,
my dear, you are about to become a very wealthy young lady."

He offered her the plate with the biscuits on and she took one.
Sir Edward was now smiling; Jesus, she thought, he really can
play Mister bloody charming when he wants to. "How does this
work?" She asked quietly and nibbled at her biscuit. She
refrained from 'dunking' the biscuit in her tea; that wasn't very
lady like. He grinned and held up several photographs: all mature
men in expensive suits.

He tapped one picture; "Lord George Campbell-Tate; married,
wealthy - very wealthy - and a real hound dog for beautiful
young woman who are married. He is our current target. We
believe he is good for five hundred pounds to keep his name out
of the papers and the divorce courts. He'll be easy pickings for
you."

Alex leaned forward and stared at the picture; "So I lure him to
my rooms, and you leapt out as the outraged husband and after
a little heated discussion; agree not to divorce your unfaithful
wife, if he pays up. Do I have that right?"

Sir Edwards slapped his hands together again and grinned; "I bloody well knew I had picked the right girl!" Alex nodded then sighed; "Just one fly in the ointment; we're not married, and everyone knows that your single."

Sir Edward smiled; "Well, we can soon rectify that particular fly. We'll marry tomorrow at St. Thomas's. It will be in all the papers. A quick honeymoon and then bang; we hit the first victim at a House party that Lord Campbell-Tate is holding at his Kent house country estate, early next month."

"I took the liberty of already making the arrangements, in anticipation that I was quite correct in my assessment of your character. Mrs. Gamble will adjust the dress that was delivered this morning. It's very nice and Lizzie & Emma will be your bridesmaids. I can even find a father to give you away."

Alex was surprised by that; he had already made the bloody arrangements. Probably would have threatened real violence, if she had said no. There was soft knock at the door and Mr. Babette entered; he smiled at Alex and spoke softly into Sir Edwards's ear. Alex finished her coffee and biscuit. Sir Edward didn't look happy - again - with his Butler's message.

Sir Edward nodded and spoke quietly to Mr. Babette; "I'll deal with that myself. Harold knows the plan. He can stand in for me. Wake him up - gently - and tell him to get his act together." Mr. Babette nodded and left the room. Sir Edward smiled at Alex and stood; she rose carefully from her seat and tugged a little at the short hem of her skirt; it didn't help. Sir Edward was getting a very close up view of her charms. He smiled and gestured to her short skirt and stocking tops. "You'll be wearing far better and classier clothes that that my dear. You will be attired as a lady - a naughty lady - but a lady." He pulled open the door for her and she slipped past him; really waiting for him to grab her or something. He didn't and she found herself in the corridor, totally puzzled by his change in behaviour. She needed to find Owen and discuss what had been discovered about Sir Edward; he was a blackmailer and probably trafficked young women for sex.

Yet Lizzie and Emma wouldn't have a word said against Sir Edward. The bloody man was practically a Saint to them. She shook her head and headed for Owens's room. He wasn't there, so she made her way back to the kitchens.

Mrs. Gamble stared at her and sighed; "Alex get your head together, where's the bloody coffee tray from the study?" She sighed but smiled.

Alex also smiled and held up her hands; "I forgot, sorry Ma'am." She was about to ask the whereabouts of Owen, when she noticed the two young footmen - sitting at the table with tea and toast - blatantly staring at her crotch. She dropped her hands and clasped them over her private parts that she knew could be seen through her thin panties. "Do you want to take a bloody photograph or something?" She asked with plenty of sarcasm in her voice.

They both giggled and William sipped his tea and smiled; "Nah, we've seen the sketch that Mr. Ross has done, Buts' it's nothing like the real thing. 'Colly' will be well pleased with that. But he'll soon have his hands on the real thing. You're in for a bloody good poking my girl. He wants you up in his bedroom with some morning tea. We don't expect to see you until lunch time."

The other footman laughed; "We'll know if he's enjoyed his favourite pastime. You'll be walking funny and won't poo right for a week!" They both laughed until Mrs. Gamble shouted at them to get back to work. They reluctantly left, with William whispering to Alex; "Take up plenty of butter on his breakfast tray. He'll need some for both his toast and his cock; otherwise, you'll be screaming the bloody house down as he pokes your bum hole."

Mrs. Gamble again told the boys to leave and sighed. She smiled at the look on Alex's face. "Don't worry girl. I've already sent Lizzie up there. She couldn't care less what 'Colly' shoves in her bum. Now, Sir Edward wants you fresh and looking lovely for tomorrow."

Alex actually sighed with relief at those words and asked where her 'brother' was. Mrs. Gamble smiled; "I've sent the boy to fetch the flowers for tomorrow. He seemed quite surprised by your arranged marriage. But was happy about it; after all, his big sister is about to become a wealthy young woman." She grinned and returned to slapping pasty around; beef Wellington was on the dinner menu tonight and it was Sir Edward's favourite.

Alex sat at the table and picked up the paper. It was all print and no pictures. She sighed and turned the pages without real interest. One article caught her eye; the brutal murder of a street prostitute who had been badly cut up. Alex rubbed her chin; it couldn't be bloody 'jack the Ripper', he didn't start until 1888.

That's when she noticed the thick brown envelope on the small table by the door, where the post usually went. She stood up and wandered over; the handwriting was really neat and addressed to Sir Edward. It was heavily sealed. Mrs. Gamble looked up from beating up the pastry and sighed; "My bloody head wouldn't save my legs. Could you place that on the small table outside Sir Edwards study my dear?"

Alex nodded and picked the envelope up. If he was in bed with the very willing Lizzie, then she was safe to return to his study. Alex stood outside and tapped the envelope; she gripped the door handle and turned it. The door was unlocked! She couldn't believe her luck and pushed open the study door and a surprised Sir Edward looked up. Now that was a shock and she apologized for not knocking and handed the envelope over. He waved her apology aside and smiled, opening the envelope immediately. He looked up at Alex; "Anything else you want my dear?"

Alex saw the legal looking papers spill out on his desk. She shook her head and apologized again. He just smiled and started to read the papers. He muttered to himself; "Damn, I will need to deal with this myself. I need to speak to Harold." Alex left quietly and stood in the corridor outside and rubbed her chin; what the fuck was going on?

8. ALEX GETS A PLEASANT & SATISFYING SURPRISE.

Alex decided to find out more about young Sir Edward and knew one person who would have some answers about him: Mr. Babette. Butlers always knew the secret stuff about their employers. She knew that Kate would keep such matters to herself; like all the girls here in the French House, she adored the 'Master'. So, when Kate asked for someone to take Mr. Babette his morning tea in the Butler's pantry; Alex volunteered. She knocked gently and received no answer, she called out that it was Alex with his morning tea. She - with some surprise - heard a woman's voice and recognized it at once; it was Emma.

She was telling Mr. Babette that is was alright; it was Alex, and she was told to enter by an apparently panting Butler.

Alex stepped in and closed the door; the tea tray shook a little as she desperately tried to restrain from laughing. Emma was bent over the big chair by the fireplace; her silk panties around one ankle and Mr. Babette - trousers around his ankles - was poking her bum hole!

She turned her head and smiled at Alex, seeing the look on Alex's face. "Put the bloody tray down and join in for fuck sake; he's the best equipped Butler in fucking London!" Alex placed the tray on the small table and walked slowly over and stood by the slowly thrusting Butler. Her eyes widened a little; Mr. Fredrick James Babette [Freddie to his friends] was hung like a horse and he clearly knew how to use it.

Emma groaned and was vigorously rubbing her fanny with a free hand - the other gripped the back of the chair - and she was pushing back on that well lubricated cock that was stuck up her willing back passage. "Don't worry my dear; I'll have more than enough for you." He panted and concentrated on his thrust.

Emma gasped; "He has the fucking stamina of a bull, he's fucked me and Lizzie in one afternoon; both of us twice!" Mr. Babette removed one hand from Emma's heaving bum cheeks and ran it up Alex's leg and gripped the cheek of her arse.

"Are you game my dear?" He grunted and smiled. He may be in his early fifties, but he was certainly in good shape. Alex found herself nodding and the Butler grinned; "Good girl. On the mantelpiece is a plate with some unsalted butter. Pop some up your bum and vagina - if you need it - and I shall arse fuck the pair of you together."

Freddie turned to Alex and said quietly; "I'm going to fuck Emma and suck your big titties. Come closer." Alex shuffled forward and presented her big breasts to him; her nipples were erect, and he loved the size and colour of them. His hot mouth was on a nipple in an instant and Freddie sucked hard; really hard and he poked Emma arse with some determination. He kept one hand on Emma's bum, whilst the other squeezed Alex's big tit, almost like he was trying to milk the damn thing. Alex winced in a little pain, but did nothing to stop him. He did this for some minutes then dropped Alex's tit and pushed his hand between her legs and asked her politely to open her legs, so he could get a couple of fingers into her moist vagina.

Freddie chuckled and smiled; "You're wet as hell girl. That's bloody fantastic. Come close." With fingers in her fanny, beneath her panties, he pulled her a little closer and his tongue probed her mouth. He sucked her twitching tongue, and this went on for a few minutes. Alex could feel some real strange sensations in her stomach already and she couldn't stop herself from responding to his fantastic French kissing. She placed an arm around his shoulders and the pair kissed passionately which surprised both of them.

Alex was now very wet between the legs and had strange feelings in her stomach and thighs. The sight of Emma being fucked in her arse, right before her eyes and his fingers working her vagina, with his tongue cleaning her mouth was seriously exciting her. Freddie groaned, breaking the kiss and pulled his hand from Alex's crotch. He had shot his load into Emma's receptive bum and Emma loved it!

Staying inside her, he pulled Alex closer and the pair continued to kiss; staring into each other's eyes and Alex felt a little orgasm escape which stunned her; 'What the fuck was happening?'

 His hands gripped her tits and arse, and she loved his touch. After a few minutes of this, he reluctantly let Alex go and patted Emma's bum cheeks. "Good girl. Stay like that whilst Alex cleans you up. You can clean my cock." He ran his hand over Alex's tits and smiled; "I want you to clean Emma's bum up with your tongue and eat all that wonderful cum of mine. Get straight down when I pull my cock out; do you understand?" Alex nodded and knelt by Emma's trembling bum.

Freddie slowly pulled his cock from the girls arse and pushed it into Emma's waiting open mouth. She sucked and cleaned without hesitation. Alex pushed her tongue between Emma's cheeks and her tongue pressed against the gaped and red hole. A little creamy cum oozed from it and Alex licked it up with her flicking tongue. Freddie groaned with sheer delight and real satisfaction. He watched carefully as more cum trickled onto Alex's probing tongue and she swallowed each drop slowly and carefully, making sure that none escaped. "For fuck sake girl; I'm going to fuck your brains out." He muttered, his cock already starting to stiffen under the sight of Alex's tongue deep in Emma's bum and the girl licking and sucking his dirty cock.

When Alex had finished cleaning, he pulled her to her feet and with both hands tugged down her little silk panties and threw them on the chair under Emma, who continued to suck his now fully erect cock. He patted Emma on the head and said quietly; "Good girl Emma. Now swap over and Alex; get your fucking arse up in the air. I'm going to have it." He slapped Emma on the bum and she eased herself up and stood by the chair, whilst Alex now took up the same position. Freddie slapped her arse and Told Emma to hand him the butter dish. With some butter on his fingers, he pushed two, then three into Alex's little bum hole; it yielded without any problem. He eased his cock in and started to thrust. Emma pushed a hand between Alex's legs and rubbed her vagina with some passion. "Fucking Christ, she's already soaking!" Emma muttered.

Freddie fucked Alex's arse hard and fast, occasionally giving her bum cheeks a good slap with each hand. Emma giggled as she felt the groaning Alex cum over her probing fingers. The old

butler certainly knew how to give good service and pounded Alex's bum hole with great skill and determination. Alex actually yelled at one point and had a huge orgasm, which surprised her and Emma. It poured over Emma's fingers and dropped on the chair, running down a leg onto the floor. Alex was trembling with her legs shaking uncontrollably, gripping the back of the chair tightly; it was one of her best orgasms ever. Freddie groaned loudly and cussed. He shot his second load into Alex and collapsed over her. "For fuck sake girl, I've never cum that quick on the second run!" He gasped and then stood straight, still buried in her gaped back passage. Everyone stood still; Someone was knocking at the door!

It was William the Footman; "Mr. Babette, Sir Edward wants you in his study at once Sir. he said to come at once." The butler groaned and cussed softly, finally shouting; "I'll be right there, thank you William." He slapped Alex's very red cheeks for a final time and gently pulled his cock from her. "Thank you, ladies; now please clean up this mess and get about your duties." He wiped his cock on Alex's discarded panties and pulled up his trousers and secured them with his black braces. He straightened his clothes and carefully pulled on his jacket and walked to the door. "Come on girls, look lively, we'll continue this tonight if we can. Now get about your duties."

Mr. Babette gestured Alex over to him and pulled her close; they kissed passionately by the door and Alex actually trembled under his caresses and was now truly stunned by how she felt about the old butler. She simply wanted him to fuck her again; as many times as he could.

He opened the door, making sure that William couldn't peer in and left for Sir Edwards study. Alex sat on the chair breathing heavily and wiped her face with the little towel offered by a grinning Emma. "I told you Alex, he's the best equipped fucking butler in London and he'll fuck us again tonight - if he can find the time - and probably do Lizzie as well." She giggled and handed Alex her soiled panties, while pulling her own up.

Alex just nodded and was really looking forward to another session with the butler; if he could fit her in with all the other girls he had to service around the damn house! She hadn't felt jealous like this for some time.

The girls cleaned up the room to the butler's exacting standards and Emma grabbed the butter dish and smiled; "I'll drop this off in old Babette's room, he'll probably want it tonight. Wait until he fucks your honey pot, if you came like that with him up your fucking arse; you'll drown the old bugger when he pokes you there." She laughed when Alex asked if she - and Lizzie, of course - wouldn't mind if she had the old stud to herself, tonight - If he can find the time - and she would do favours for the girls in return. Emma thought for a few seconds then grinned; "Yeah, sure. Both me and Lizzie like touching a little velvet now and again. She really does want to taste you."

Alex knew that 'touching the velvet' was a Victorian expression for lesbian sex. She nodded her agreement with a little smile of anticipation. Both girls left the Butler's pantry, walking a little awkwardly it must be said. Alex didn't like putting her panties back on, but she had no choice - she couldn't walk around the damn house without them, people might suspect something - and made for her room and thoroughly cleaned her private parts. She couldn't do much about her glowing red bum cheeks and just sighed. She put on fresh silk knickers and went about her duties;

but she couldn't get the butler out of her thoughts - delicious thoughts - if she was honest with herself. "I really hope the old boy finds the bloody time." She muttered to herself and grinned broadly.

Then realised she had found out sod all about Sir Edward. "Some bloody detective I am." She said to herself and went to find Owen; hopefully he's found that bloody 'Judas Stone'. Still, she may be able to find something out tonight if the bloody butler finds the time and smiled.

9. THE FRENCH HOUSE HAS MANY SURPRISES.

Sir Edward dined alone that night and Alex served him with just Mr. Babette in attendance. Sir Edward spoke with both with real affection and apparent friendship. Alex grunted her disgust at that, after her treatment at his hands last night. Soon as he was gone, Alex approached Mr. Babette and told him about her little arrangement with the other girls.

Mr. Babette nodded and didn't look surprised or aggrieved by the idea, he patted her arse and smiled; "I do hope you don't get too tired or sore quickly my girl. I do like to take my time if there's

only one in my bed." He told her to report to his room after everyone had gone to bed; naked and just wearing her long bed coat. "That saves time my girl." He added and went about his duties.

No sooner had everyone retired for the night; Alex made her way quickly to the Butlers rooms and knocked gently. She was stark naked under the long woolen bed coat and was already a little wet in anticipation of what may happen. "Come on in my dear." Mr. Babette called out and Alex hesitated for a moment then slowly entered the room. Mr. Babette was standing by the big double bed - stark naked and fully erect - he lifted a full wine glass saying softly; "Come and have a glass of wine my dear." Alex walked over to him and accepted a full glass of red wine; it was delicious. Mr. Babette grinned; "From 'Colly's' private stock."

They both chuckled and Alex pulled off her bed coat and placed the wine glass down. "I best start with some of this." She whispered, quickly kneeling and her eager mouth soon covered his big hard cock.

Freddie smiled and patted her head, as it moved up and down on his penis. "Good girl, I like plenty of tongue and suck hard; like you're trying to pull a pea up a straw." That made Alex chuckle and she set to work following the butler's instructions, who stood sipping his wine and watching quietly.

After some minutes, he too placed his wine down and pulled Alex to her feet and the pair kissed. Alex was impressed; he had a tongue like a lizard and it probed her mouth better than a dentist on steroids! He pushed her on to the bed and whispered; "Time to reciprocate, my dear." and gently pulled open her legs and he too, set to work on her wet vagina. It took just six or seven minutes before Alex gripped his head and screamed; she had one hell of an organism. He was that good, she almost cried with delight.

He mounted her and the fucking started in earnest, beginning with the good old fashioned 'Missionary position'. Alex simply couldn't believe the old man's incredible stamina and technique. He was trusting deep and hard yet was gentle about it. He was a highly skilled lover - no doubt about that - they locked in a passionate embrace, tongues in each other's mouths and both were surprised by the intensity of their love making.

They rolled about the bed, groaning, whispering, panting and fucking. At one point, Alex was face down on the pillows, clutching the blankets with both hands and moaning as he fucked her doggy style. Then she was astride him, riding hard as they clutched hands. Alex had another huge orgasm which made her collapse on top of Freddie. He simply turned her over and continued to fuck her hard, back in the missionary position.

"For God sake; cum!" She whispered, sweating and panting with her exertions. Mr. Babette just smiled and wiped sweat from his face and continued to thrust deep and hard. Alex found herself crawling about the big bed on all fours with Freddie fucking her hard like a dog. She buried herself in pillows and sheets, legs shaking, her entire body quivering under his unbelievable fucking. He still didn't stop, and they changed position again; Alex back on top, almost jumping up and down on that still rock hard cock. She came again and splattered him with her cum. That was it for Alex; for the first time - in a very long time - she was 'tapped out' and lay on top of him gasping and crying a little. He wiped her face and kissed it. "Roll over sweet one and I'll try to finish." Alex groaned loudly but did as she was asked. Back in the Missionary Position, Alex simply lay back and let the old Butler finish in her. He fucked her for some minutes and Alex was now crying a little; she hadn't been fucked like this; ever.

He came deep and hard inside and also collapsed. They lay gripped tightly in each other's arms; totally exhausted from the vigor of their love making. They managed some really passionate kissing and Alex raised her head and looked at the mantel piece clock.

"Holy fucking shit! We've been at it for two hours solid!" The old butler just chuckled and kissed her face and lips; "Don't worry my dear, with your help and lovely mouth, I'll soon be up and ready again. I always last longer the second or third time." Alex just stared at him and realized that he meant it!

She pulled him to her and they kissed and caressed, whispering to each other. Alex and Freddie became one on that creaking old bed. They fell asleep, cradled in each other's arms and Alex slept better than she had done in a very long time. She had a strange dream about a young mister Babette standing in her surgery office at the Whitechapel Hospital in army uniform. As the pair left her office – in the dream – Alex noticed that her name board on the door read; DR.A.M BABETTE.

Alex woke suddenly and sat up a little. The clock was reading almost four o'clock [in the morning] she groaned; she was getting 'married' today to Sir Edward. Freddie shifted and sat up next to her and she pushed into his arms. He kissed the back of her neck and shoulders, cupping her breasts from behind.

Alex whispered to him about the 'wedding' and he simply smiled and they French kissed. He ran a hand between her legs and chuckled; "Your still quite wet my dear. That's good." He gently pushed her onto the pillows and mounted her again.

Alex groaned out loud and the love making started again. She made him promise to come quickly and he nodded; "I do sometime come too quick with my early morning riser." She gripped his shoulders and whispered; "Thank fuck for that." and let him fuck her again; she had another two orgasms during this second session. They were still at it when young John the footman knocked at the door and told Mr. Babette it was six o'clock and time to rise. Alex, face down on the pillows and being hard fucked - yet again - managed to groan softly; "He's already fucking risen!" They both chuckled at that, and he finally came in her for a second time in over four hours of hard fucking.

Alex really struggled to get out of bed and follow him into the small bathroom to clean each other up. She actually walked strangely as she made for the kitchens and breakfast. They held hands until William the footman appeared in the top corridor and asked Mr. Babette about the wedding arrangement. He stared at the look on Alex's face and her funny walk but said nothing.

Alex sat alone at the kitchen table and sipped her tea. She hadn't quite recovered from the marathon sex session with Mr. Babette and was sitting with her legs slightly open. He had actually made her gape and that hadn't happened in some time. His incredible fucking had left her a little tender, but fully satisfied. She ran a hand over her face and cursed her bloody luck; he was the first man to match her sexual appetite in a very long time. He was an incredibly skilled lover with the stamina of a breeding beef bull. But was old enough to be her father!

"Never thought I would get a 'Daddy' complex." She chuckled, but what troubled her, was her reaction to his touch and kisses. They had set her body alight and she didn't give a damn about his age. She was already really anticipating the next session and wanted to see and be near him. They were totally compatible together; sexually. She sighed; what the fuck was going on with these feelings for the old man?

She then realized that she hadn't asked the Butler one single question about Sir Edward - again. She couldn't get thoughts of Mr. Babette from her head. She even seriously considered his request, that she move her things into his rooms, so they could be together at night.

He had confessed that, he was easily prepared to give up the other girls and only have her, if that's what she wanted. She was astonished to find that she would actually agree to his request and allow him sole access to her. She almost dropped the damn cup in surprise at those thoughts!

Alex had already made up her mind about one thing; she wasn't about to let this man disappear from her life; even if it meant sneaking back in time to see him. That thought struck a chord with her and she smiled broadly. Despite being exhausted from the love making; they had laid together in each other's arms and talked - really talked - about all sorts of things and he made her laugh out loud on several occasions. Under that prim and proper Butler's exterior was a warm, funny, charming sexual God. Sweet Jesus, she thought; if she had met him twenty years ago, she would have been Mrs. Babette - the butler's wife - and not Countess of bloody Cappanni. And would be really happy about that!

10. THE RELUCTANT BRIDE.

Alex sat in the warm ornate bathtub and sipped her mid-morning tea, thinking about the dress hanging in her room, which Kate was making final adjustments to. Lizzie and Emma's voices could be heard coming from the room; they actually sounded quite excited. They would jump in the tub after her., 'Colly insisted they were properly clean and presentable, after having sex with Lord Robert, Ross, Howard and Lady Gabby the night before.

She placed the cup on the small table near her bath and splashed a little water over her face and laid back in the soothing warm water. Sir Edward had quite an audacious plan to make his own fortune [and Alex's with him - apparently] by exploiting very rich men's weaknesses, their passion for a woman like Alex. But she couldn't just be some tart that could be bought for a few pounds, no, she had to be something special and apparently out of reach.

In the sexually restrained and oppressed Victorian society, one thing would lure them to Sir Edward; the opportunity to fuck his beautiful young, and seemingly innocent, new wife; Lady Alexandra! They would chase her, thinking they were the predators and Alex the prey, not realizing until too late, that they were the prey, and she was the huntress. They would not only be sexually disappointed; they would be seriously out of pocket too!

The plain was a simple and an audacious one; Alex would lure the man with a little flirting, ending up in a very compromising situation, where her outraged and wronged husband, would appear and demand a divorce, with all the horrendous scandal that would bring on the cheating husband. They would all pay 'compensation' to Edward to avoid that sort of scandal. None would want their names in the papers and the possibly, of their wives bringing divorce action themselves. It would certainly have them, rushing to hand over hundreds of pounds, and for the 'bigger fish', it could run to thousands. Even Alex had to admit it was an incredibly good scam.

Thus Kate was making final adjustments to Alex's wedding gown and the two bridesmaid's dresses for Lizzie and Emma. Her and Sir Edward would marry that very afternoon in St. Thomas's church and after a brief honeymoon, would hit the first 'sucker' upon their return to London. The 'Mark' was already set up for the sting. A very, very rich married man whose wife, apparently, really didn't 'understand' him. Eddy believed he could be worth at least five hundred pounds in 'compensation'. [That is incredibly serious money for the time; equivalent of the purchase price for a modern London house!].

Alex had queried how they could marry so quickly, without 'bands' being called for the obligatory two weeks before the ceremony. Edward just grinned; he had simply paid the bent priest, a large sum of money and had also paid off the two young boys, who had threatened the 'good' father, with their intentions to tell the police; about the little games he played with them. He had even arranged an old actor to play the part of her father!

They would 'honeymoon' in Paris for five days and upon their return, have a grand party at his father's house [Lord John Coleville] where the poor, gullible married mark' would be invited and appropriately; fleeced. She had asked about his father and his reaction, to his son, marrying a woman who had no family or money. Sir Edward had just laughed; "My dear, my father will only have to take a look at you and he'll damn well know why, I married you! You never know, the dirty old sod could end up paying me some of my inheritance early." That thought made him really chuckle, but Alex grimaced at the thought.

Edward knew that his father, who was digging around some ruins in bloody Persia, wouldn't be too bothered about missing the surprise wedding. The dirty bastard would drool over his new daughter-in-law, especially, when she would be made to parade around in her underwear, for his approval and to get her share of the allowances that he would award her, for good behavior. Edward's brother: Harold, was already setting up the wedding. They would meet up and Harold could keep his dirty hands-off Alex.

Alex's current thoughts were disturbed by Owen sticking his head around the door. He had his hand over his eyes and almost smiled; "Kate says to get your arse out the bath. The dress is ready to be fitted." He dropped his voice and did not smile, adding; "No bloody sign of the damn thing. [The Judas stone] But I'll keep searching."

Alex just sighed and said "OK" quietly. Owen disappeared and she eased herself from the bath and dried herself slowly and carefully with a towel and wrapped it around her body. She headed for her room and was just about to pull the door open, when Michael Good - unpleasant valet - jumped from the corner of the stairwell and shouted, rather strangely; "What's mine is his and what's his is mine!" He grabbed the hem of Alex's towel and pulled it down.

Alex was standing at the top of the stairs stark naked and Michael threw the towel back at her with real anger; "You best cover your fucking self, you bitch. If I get the chance, you're gone." He turned on his heels and walked away. Alex jumped into the room, trying to cover herself with the towel; she was actually shaking. Kate grabbed her and stroked her hair; "Never mind that bloody arsehole, he's been eaten up with jealously since Sir Edward told him about the marriage plans." Lizzie and Emma were already in their bridesmaid dresses, in a wonderful shade of blue. They were already tippling gin and they offered Alex a glass. She took it and knocked it back in one hit.

Kate grinned; "I knew his lordship had picked the right girl."

Lizzie and Emma laughed at that and refilled Alex's glass; and heir own. The young photographer had set up his cumbersome camera, at the foot of the grand staircase and stood idle, next to it. He sipped his glass of whisky and watched the bride appear at the top of the stairs; Kate and the two bridesmaids were getting her ready. Despite being much younger, than first Alex had met him, Bartholomew Blackberry was recognized immediately by Alex. But she knew that he would not know her - yet - that would come years later and in very similar circumstances, working a blackmail scam. "Bloody typical that he would turn up here." She muttered to herself; but was not surprised by his appearance.

'Colly' joined the photographer; he was now resplendent in his morning suit, with a subdued and glum looking Valet in tow. The master called up to Alex; "Just some pictures for me first. Now do as I tell you, you really don't want me to have to discipline you; like a good husband should. Thank you my dear." Kate chuckled; "See, he has that nasty little dog under control. Now lift your skirts darling and let Bart take some lovely intimate pictures for your new husband to treasure." Alex sighed, she stared at 'Colly' and remembered the threats of violence, he had made against her, if she refused him anything. She had already had a small sample of what he was capable of. She didn't want a good hiding just because she wouldn't pose for some mildly pornographic pictures.

Alex with Lizzie's help rearranged her beautiful silk and lace wedding dress. Bart actually whistled, as he dived under the dark cloth behind the camera. "That is some bloody piece of cake 'Colly'. She's bloody perfect for the job." 'Colly' just nodded, smiling broadly; "I know Bart. Oh, I really do know. We know

how to pick them." Yes, this young dirty filthy tart would make them some really good money and if she didn't do as she was told; well, he would always enjoy 'correcting' her error on that score. 'Colly' chuckled to himself and enjoyed the views on offer.

Alex stood with her dress pulled up, exposing her white silk stockings and panties. Lizzie and Emma did the same, except they also exposed their ample breasts. Bart and his assistant worked the camera for some minutes. With Alex and the girls in various, very naughty positions. Bart really did shout some encouragement, finally, he asked [with some anticipation] 'Colly' if he could take some real photographs. 'Colly' rubbed his chin and smiled; "Alex, my dear, 'Black Bart' would really like to take some truly intimate pictures. Please take down your panties. That's a good girl."

Before Alex could even reply, Kate had tugged down her lace panties and pulled them from her. "Show yourself properly. There's good little wife." She said and held up the panties for all to see. Everyone applauded and "Carry on." The master said, smiling broadly. Lizzie and Emma quickly followed, and Kate helped Alex pull her magnificent breasts out. "See, now your being a good little girl. He's a lot easier to handle, if you just obey him; saves a lot of fucking bruises and tears." Alex just stared at her. So much for him not touching the girls; he was a bloody vicious animal around women.

The three young footmen were all enjoying the show, happening at the top of the stairs. Especially Owen, who cursed his mirror - under his breath - for being out of service, He would have given anything to capture the sight above him. Young William tugged his sleeve and whispered; "Your sister's a right one. She's going to make a fucking fortune. No wonder his lordship, already thinks the sun shines out of her bum." He then chuckled adding; "It's a real shame, that's all he'll stick his dick into." The other footman laughed quietly, and Owen rubbed his chin; there was something not quite right about Sir Edward and his attitude to women. He stared across at Michael Good, who was unsmiling and staring at Alex with some real hatred. "Oh Fuck!" was all Owen muttered. He now knew that finding the stone was paramount and urgent.

Owen stood back in the doorway and thought hard; they [he and Alex] really needed to get the fuck out of here before she gets dragged off on honeymoon. That's when a light bulb went on inside his head. He hurriedly left the scene and made for the back stairs, running up them, two at a time, and found himself in Sir Edward's study, where he and Alex, had first been placed by Kate. He carefully went from cabinet to cabinet and then heard all the noise downstairs. The wedding party was leaving. He hesitated; he couldn't go to the church and miss this great opportunity to find the damn Judas Stone. He knew Alex wouldn't mind him missing her 'wedding' and so continued searching, slowly and methodically. Owen knew he must find the damn stone, or the current timeline would change, and not in the best interests of Alex.

11. JEKYLL & HYDE.

Father Grenville Digby wiped his sweaty hands on his cassock and picked up his bible. He carefully removed the thirty pounds that Sir Edward had placed in it and sighed. He could easily forge the dates of the 'bands' being called and marry the insistent Lord to his young bride. Her 'father' waited by the font; a little worse for whisky but was dressed appropriately. He stared out the vestibule window and watched 'Colly' walking up the path with his best man, Lord Robert. They were laughing together. The priest half smiled; if the devil could cast his net here, he certainly could fill a few corners of hell. He chuckled at his own humour and then realized; the net would scoop him up too. He crossed himself and headed for the altar.

The bride arrived a few minutes after the small congregation had settled in. She looked absolutely stunning; Lizzie and Emma looked clean & wholesome [for once]. She stood before Father Digby and her 'father' stood by her; he did sway a little and even managed to slur his words. When the priest asked; "Who gives this woman to be married to this man?" Everyone waited for a minute or two before he realized he was on; he threw an arm into the air and shouted; "I...does...I did.. I do...bollocks!." He was a lousy actor, but cheap enough for this performance.

'Colly' gave his full name; Edward Albert Scarborough Coleville and Alex muttered hers [for this show only] as Alexandra Mary Jones. That would make Owen happy, then realized that the pair was using Owens's real name; they were brother and sister after all. So Miss Jones married Mister Coleville and became 'Lady Coleville; for a very short time only, it was hoped.

'Colly' gripped Alex by the hands and smiled, as he said; "I do." Loud and clear. Alex practically whispered her reply and when the priest said, "You may kiss the bride." 'Colly' really did. The congregation actually started to talk amongst themselves as 'Colly' explored his new wife's mouth; He was more thorough than an orally obsessed dentist. Finally, Alex managed to get his tongue out of her mouth and gasp for breath. She had to forcibly pull his hand from under her dress; another couple of inches and 'Colly' would have hit the jackpot. He gripped her arm and with a broad smile, almost frog marched her back down the aisle, as the audience applauded the performance. Especially the glimpse of Alex's stocking tops, as she extracted his hand from her crotch. They posed for some minutes outside the small church as 'Black Bart' took some 'boring' wedding photographs. Alex refused point blank to 'get her tits out' for the wedding album and Bart was a little disappointed by that. Still, he would be in Paris for the honeymoon, and he really smiled in anticipation of that little assignment. Rice was thrown and the 'happy' couple jumped into their carriage and set off for the French House and a modest reception; then onto Paris by the night ferry.

Alex really had to struggle; her 'husband' had apparently grown more hands. He was back exploring her mouth and thighs - again. She really tried to push him away, but he was having none of that. He gripped her chin, quite hard, and said very quietly and firmly; "You will obey your husband my dear. In all things and you will be submissive when I want to take pleasure from you." He was a very strong man and Alex soon had bruises on her arms and around her thighs; he just would not take 'NO' for an answer. Finally, she just had to let him grope her or face some hard slaps, which could do real damage to her because of his strength and size.

They arrived at the house and a very distraught Alex was pulled from the carriage; her dress was pushed up and her panties had been ripped from her with some force. 'Colly' had placed them in his pocket. He allowed her a minute or so, to put her breasts back in the bodice and straighten her clothes. She wept openly and he raised his hand to her; "Stop the tears my dear. We don't want to embarrass the guests, now do we?" Alex took a couple of deep breaths and tried to arrange her clothes. She had hand marks on her neck, legs and bum, with finger-marks on her breasts and thighs. Her right shoulder had a bloodied red mark; caused by the 'love bite' that her new husband had inflicted upon her during the one-sided struggle.

With a firm grip on her arm, he marched her back into the house past Owen who was standing at the bottom of the stairs. The guests from the church had returned and were joined by other well wishers. Still gripping the silent and tear-stained Alex, 'Colly' told everyone to enjoy the wedding party. Alex looked at Owen and he mouthed; "I found it. They're working again." He repeated it as 'Colly' released Alex, to shake hands and accept a glass of champagne. Alex whispered to her new husband, that she really needed the bathroom; urgently.

'Colly' grinned; "Of course my darling." and leaned close to her and whispered; "Make sure you clean yourself properly, I've booked a sleeper on the trains, and I WILL enjoy your tight little arse and fanny tonight. You have five minutes before I come and get you out." They walked to the side corridor and 'Colly' and whispered; "Make sure you clean yourself properly, I've booked a sleeper on the trains, and I WILL enjoy your tight little arse and fanny tonight. You have five minutes before I come and get you out." They walked to the side corridor and 'Colly' unlocked the small toilet door and pushed Alex in. He locked it behind her and said simply; "Five minutes girl."

He stood there; arms folded talking to Lord Robert and Ross the artist. They both informed him, that they couldn't find Alex's dopy brother anywhere. 'Colly' just grunted and smiled; "I'm going to have him wed young Lizzie, keep it in the family, so as to speak. He won't get a choice in the matter if he really loves his sister." They all chuckled and finally Sir Edward banged loudly on the toilet door; "Cone on darling. Don't keep our guests waiting. We need to cut the cake, my dear." But there was no answer. He knocked again and there was still no answer. Cursing under his breath, he pulled out the keys and fumbled with the lock, finally opening it. The little room was empty.

'Colly' went a little berserk, at one point he actually pushed over the toilet, causing a minor flood. The window was still intact and had been previously nailed down to hinder any would be burglars. He pulled some of the ceiling down before his friends managed to drag him out. His young bride had simply vanished, from a completely enclosed and secured space. He had the only key and the little room had only one door, which he had stood outside of - the whole time - after pushing his new wife inside.

He collapsed at the foot of the stairs and accepted a large whisky from Ross and cursed loudly. Then slowly rose up and dashed from the house, yelling for a cab. Everyone stood in silence and Michael Good raised his glass; "To a marriage made in fucking heaven." and laughed. Lord Robert sighed and turned to his amazed wife; "Here we go... a fucking again! What is wrong with him? He's fucking nothing like his brother." Lady Gabby nodded and sipped her champagne.

Alex and Owen walked slowly towards the lighthouse in silence. Owen could see that Alex was bruised and upset, so he said nothing, waiting for her to speak. Finally, she stopped at the foot of the steps and stood with both hands-on hips and shook her head - with some disbelief - at what had transpired between her and Sir Edward. "A full blown, bloody Jekyll and Hyde. There's no other way to describe the bastard. All nice and then bang! He was like a bloody animal in the carriage back from the church. If we weren't on a public road in an open carriage; the bastard would have raped me - there and then - and he would have really slapped me about, if I hadn't let him grope me; the bastard."

Owen sighed; "I don't think this is the time, but his bloody Valet was more than just a Valet...if you get what I mean." Alex sighed; "That would explain why Mister Michael Good hated my guts, without really knowing me. The first time I encountered him, he called me a bitch and snatched by towel; leaving me bloody stark naked at the top of the stairs." Owen nodded and smiled to himself; he had missed that cracker! But didn't say anything about it. "I think he swung both ways and Michael Good saw you as real serious rival for his lover's affections." Owen said quietly and took hold of her hand, adding; "Let's get you cleaned up. Some brandy will do the trick."

Alex nodded and composed herself as Mr. Harris appeared at the door and stared at the pair. Alex in a wedding dress and Mister Owen in a morning suit; complete with white buttonhole. Alex saw the look on the big man's face and managed a smile; "It's alright Mr. Harris, we are not hitched. I might be a little crazy, but I'm not insane." She marched up the steps and headed for her rooms, telling Owen that a hot bath and some bloody brandy was in order. Owen dived into the study and found Wilson and Jericho reading. "You won't believe what the fuck happened to us..." He shouted and grabbed the brandy decanter and poured himself a large one.

The dinner conversation was a little subdued and Alex picked at her food. Jericho leaned back in his seat and sipped his wine; "There was a breach of the timeline from London, 1881 to London 1981 and I suspect it was Sir Edward. I believe he may be residing in that time period. So, he must have a time portal linked between those years. The first place to start would be the French House, but Wilson and I checked it and it's clean of time portals. So the portal must be elsewhere. We need to find it and close the damn thing." Wilson nodded; "It has to be somewhere he visits - regularly - in both time periods."

Alex slapped her spoon down and picked up her wine glass - she didn't smile - and sipped for a few seconds, then placed the glass down. "He's father's house in North London. I bet it still exists in 1981, and probably well into the 21st century. His father was an Archaeologist, and it was him that dug up the bloody Judas Stone in Mesopotamia and maybe the time portal object. Owen was clever enough to find the stone in a display cabinet at the French House. I don't believe that the Bastard knew its real power. That's where we should start; Lord John Coleville's house."

Everyone nodded their agreement at that.

Jericho smiled at Alex; "So, I think a visit to the Archaeologists

house is our next job. We really need to find and close that time
That's where we should start; Lord John Coleville's house."
Everyone nodded their agreement at that.

Jericho smiled at Alex; "So, I think a visit to the Archaeologists
house is our next job. We really need to find and close that time
portal. Stop young Mister Jekyll & Hyde from travelling and make
him face his fate, in his own time." Alex raised her glass and said
quietly; "I demand the first kick; in the bastards nuts, when we
catch up with him." Everyone chuckled raising their glasses and
said together; "Bloody Amen to that."

12. THE JOHN COLEVILLE MUSEUM.

"Five bloody pounds each. It's not exactly, the bloody Victoria &
Albert is it." Owen moaned and stared hard at the small booklet
he had been given. Jericho just sighed and the small party
walked into the first set of rooms. The place was full of artifacts
from ancient Mesopotamia and the near east. Hanging alone at
the far end of the room was a huge portrait of Lord John
Coleville. Alex stood under it and folded her arms; "He looks
exactly like an older version of the bastard." She said softly.
Wilson chuckled; "I take it when you say 'the bastard', you're
always referring to Sir Edward?" Alex just smiled and the team
walked on.

Owen had his mirror discretely tucked under his booklet.
"Nothing yet." He said and stopped before yet another portrait.
He called Alex over and pointed up to the picture; "Who the fuck
does that look like?" Alex really did smile; it was her!

Wilson and Jericho joined them and Wilson grinned; "Sweet Jesus
Alex; that's the best arse on a Victorian reclining nude I've seen.
Will you marry me immediately?" Alex gave him a single digit
salute but smiled; "That young artist must have finished the job -
despite me running off - and he gave me ten pounds for posing
naked. Well, naked apart from a white sheet. The bastard must
have still paid him for it."

Alex stared at the painting and remembered the day it was
painted. She had promised never to look up the young man in
Human Records; but something inside of her wanted to know -
really know - and either way, knowing or not knowing; she would
be sad. Jericho peered at the little brass plaque beneath the

picture and chuckled; "Lady Alexandra Coleville circa 1881. I must say Alexandra; you do pose well." Owen looked up from his guidebook and smiled; "Says here, she's the famous 'vanishing lady in white' of the Coleville family and quite a legend. Was married to Sir Edward Coleville for approximately forty minutes before disappearing totally and was never seen or heard of again. Her true identity remains a total mystery and has been subject to much speculation, as to whom she really was."

"Mystery bloody solved." Alex muttered and the little group moved on. There was a portrait of Lord John's son 'The bastard'. Alex had to be restrained from picking up an ancient vase and slinging it at the smiling Sir Edward. "Now young lady; your best behaviour please." Jericho patted Alex's arm and gently pulled the vase from her grip and replaced it on the pedestal; the group moved on again. They were the only people in the bloody place [as Owen put it] and caught the attention of the young woman, who was the staff member, on duty today.

Ms Jane Holiness wandered over and tried to make herself available for questions, any bloody questions. She was bored out of her mind and suddenly having four people, who really appeared interested in the dull old place, was a real challenge. She asked - twice - if she could help anyone. Wilson switched on his charm and asked the keen young woman about Sir Edward. Now she really did smile; "Oh, quite a handsome man for the period - or any period - dashing and charming. A real gent apparently. He was sadly, married to the infamous 'vanishing lady in white' for a very short time. He's portrait is real magnet for women and girls, who come here. Those lovely blue eyes seem to follow you around. "

"Charming and a gentleman, my bloody arse..." Alex didn't finish her sentence because Jericho gently pulled her to one side and just smiled at her. She shrugged her shoulders and said quietly; "just saying. You can't judge someone from a bloody picture; stupid tart." Luckily young Ms Jane hadn't heard what Alex said and continued; "The daft woman left him broken hearted, running off on their wedding day. My opinion is that she was ashamed about her dirty past."

Everyone was suddenly interested in that statement. Jericho pressed her for details. Ms Jane looked about and lowered her voice; "The painting is not the only image we have of the woman in white. But it's the only picture that can be displayed that's - frankly - not pornographic." Ms Jane really did have their undivided attention; especially a shocked Alex.

"Please do tell." Wilson said, smiling - no, he was grinning - and Ms Jane gestured towards the stairs marked 'Staff Only'; "In the attic archives, there are a collection of photographs, sketches and drawings of the woman, all from 1881, the year of the failed marriage. They are quite explicit for the time. She was clearly some kind of 'lady of the night' [Victorian for prostitute] who managed to snare the dashing young Sir Edward with her obvious evil charms."

"Keep it shut." Was all Jericho said to Alex and she folded her arms in silence. "They are - obviously - not for public view. The Museum Curator has been asked on numerous occasions to display them. But he will only let true, accredited academics view them. Even members of staff cannot view them." Alex sighed; that's why the daft woman, hasn't recognized her from them and she was relieved, that the images weren't on public display. She couldn't actually believe that they still existed!

Jericho asked very nicely, who the current Curator was. Ms Jane smiled and - again - gestured towards the staff only door. "Why its Doctor Michael Good; he's only been here a few months. He replaced Mr. Warrington - who sadly died - and he's very popular with staff and visitors." She clasped her hands together; "At least the family was spared the scandal and disgrace of the woman's departure. Nothing was said about her disappearance in any of the newspapers or magazines at the time. They just reported the marriage. The secret was kept by the family until the late 1950's and by then; no one was really interested because the Coleville line had died out."

Owen grunted; "If the line died out, who set the museum up?" Ms Jane smiled; at last, some really interested people. "Why it was a Mrs. Kathleen Gamble, a rich widow by all accounts and a family friend. It was due to her patronage that the Coleville Collection survives intact. She's bit of a mystery herself; nothing is really known about her. She died in America during the 1960's apparently. But her trust fund keeps the museum afloat, even to this day." She finished speaking and smiled broadly.

Alex opened her mouth in total surprise and Jericho hurried her away to a big glass cabinet that contained large, ancient clay pots. "Keep a lid on it Alexandra. This could be the lead we're looking for." Alex calmed down and nodded. "The portal must be here." She said quietly and Jericho agreed. The problem was finding the damn thing in a place like this. Alex couldn't believe that old Kate had been a time traveler too! It appears that the team had really only scratched the surface, of the goings on at the 'French House'.

Wilson asked the woman about 'Doctor Good' and was he in today. Ms Jane nodded; "The Doctor is in his office." She gestured - for a third time - to the staff door and Wilson thanked Ms Jane for all her assistance. They gathered around the huge ornate doorway and held a brief conference. All Owen added to the discussion was 'How the hell, do we get to see the pictures of Alex in those pornographic poses?' That was greeted by silence and a really nasty look from Alex. Owen just shrugged his shoulders, muttering; "I only asked for Christ sake."

It was decided to continue their tour of the museum; the place was now the centre of their investigation. Jericho made the decision, that the time was right to employ a drastic measure; he would stop time [for the maximum amount allowed to a Temporal Inspector] and explain to the Duty Time Controller later. They dashed past the still Ms Jane and up the 'Staff only' stairs to the attic's, which now served as archives and offices. They easily found the door marked 'Curator' and pushed in. Alex was gently restrained by Wilson from throwing a punch at the frozen 'Doctor Michael Good'. Jericho smiled at her; "I take it that's Sir Edward's Valet from 1881?" Alex nodded; "The other bastard." She said and Wilson chuckled; "There was certainly a lot of bastards back then."

"Apart from that bloody stupid little beard, which makes him look like the tosser he is: that's him." Alex said, with a little anger in her voice, that didn't go un-noticed by her colleagues. "Remind me never to get on your bad side, baby sister." Wilson murmured, smiling. Jericho leaned over the 'Doctor' and tapped the ledger he was reading. "There are some interesting dates here, with amounts of money in English pounds. Do you know any of these names from back then Alex?" Jericho asked and Alex picked up the ledger and rubbed her chin, thinking. "None of the names jump out to me." She turned the page and stopped; "Sweet Jesus, take a look at who paid a thousand pounds to Sir

Edward in August 1884...and what the fuck!" She looked up and shook her head; "That's bloody impossible, it's dated 1884 and I was gone in 1881."

Wilson looked over her shoulder and whistled. He read out the entry; "The Prince of Wales; one thousand pounds. 9th August 1884. Alex had to submit to anal sex before I managed to get there. She moaned about that but was happy with the necklace I bought her. Eddy." They all stared at Alex, who turned another page and Wilson read out the next entry; "Lord Wallace Cumberland; Five hundred pounds. 3rd October 1884. Straight forward trick, Alex happy, she only had to let the old bugger feel her up. She wanted and received a diamond ring for that performance. Eddy."

Wilson took the ledger from a shocked and almost speechless Alex and flicked through the pages; "There are loads of entries, amounting to some serious money for the time and nearly everyone mentions Alex being paid to perform." He read the last entry and didn't smile; "Sir Norman Juppe-House; 7th February 1885. The trick went badly wrong, and Alex was badly injured. I think she will not make it. Eddy." He dropped the ledger back on the desk. Jericho tapped the book; "It doesn't make sense; Alex could not have been there; on any of those dates. It's impossible, so what the hell is happening here?"

Owen grinned broadly and slapped his hand down on the big wooden chest of office drawers by the stationery cupboard door. "Found them!" He gleefully pulled the thick brown envelope out and unwound the red string that sealed it. "It's marked Alexandra Coleville - 1881. This must be the pictures." He tipped the contents onto the desk, and everyone picked up a picture, even Alex. Wilson smiled; "The one on the top of the stairs is pretty good. Nice pose, squatting down with your legs wide open, holding your panties in one hand." He tapped the picture and smiled; broadly; "Pity it's not you. That definitely takes something away from it."

The team checked every picture and drawing; it was a very pretty young woman, in some very naughty poses; but it certainly wasn't Alex. Owen groaned in utter disappointment and received a slap on the hand from a very relieved Alex.

"Same bloody name; different girl." muttered Wilson. "He must have found a substitute girl and used my name - his wife's name - to lure the punters in. That makes sense; the papers would have carried the story of the wedding and so, he had to let the girl use my name, or the punters would be suspicious." Alex reasoned and picked up the photos again. "Poor bloody bitch, if she's under that bastard's control."

Jericho jerked a thumb to the door; "Let's go. We need to find that bloody portal. Owen, you've your mirror out, anything in here?" Owen checked his mirror and shook his head. "Nothing, except that the good doctor has a bloody time portal in his top pocket!" Wilson laughed outright; "This bloody case has more twists and turns than a snake with the shits." Everyone agreed with that, laughing.

Jericho searched Michael Good and gently pulled a small female figurine from his pocket; it was very ancient. "Lord John must have found it during his excavations in Mesopotamia." Jericho searched further and pulled a copy of the local paper dated 1981. [The current year] and in the same pocket; an engraved cigarette case inscribed 'to Eddy, Christmas 1881 from Harold.'

Jericho held both up; "The paper for onward travel to 1981 and the cigarette case for return to 1881. Put one with the figurine and you're off. Simple." He pushed everything into his coat pocket. "Now, Wilson, you take our time travelling friend back to 1881 and dump him outside the 'French House'. That will put an end to his travelling out of his own time. Take Owen with you. Alex and I will try and locate Sir Edward - sorry, the bastard - in this time period."

Wilson nodded and operated his mirror; he, Michael Good and Owen disappeared. Alex and Jericho walked back down the stairs and into the museum. Alex stopped and stared at the all the portraits and pictures displayed about the place. "That's funny, Ican't see any painting or picture of the Bastards brother, Harold. That's strange, isn't it? There's several of HIM, but not the brother. Jericho chuckled; "Perhaps he was the black sheep of the family!" Alex sighed; "For Christ sake, then he would make Jack the bloody ripper look like the Pope."

Jericho restarted time and they left the museum and jumped into their van. Alex was happy to drive and pulled away. The small, expensive sports car also pulled out the car park and followed.

Sir Edward had been right in his deductions that Alex would eventually go to his father's old house.

13. THE LUCKIEST WOMAN ALIVE?

The van was parked opposite the French House and Jericho sat reading his mirror and grunted with satisfaction; "According to Human Records, Michael Good was murdered in 1881, just weeks after we returned him to that time; so no changes to the Time Line." Alex leaned over the steering wheel and stared at the old house; it really didn't hold any pleasant memories for her. Well, except one maybe.

Now all they had to find was Sir Edward himself and return him to his own time. The team had had closed his time portal and taken possession of the time portal object, the figurine. He was trapped in this era.

Jericho grunted and tapped his mirror; "I did a check on Sir Edward's brother; he died in 1889 in London. No cause of death recorded, and his soul was quarantined for three hundred years! That's a serious penalty, what the fuck did he do..."

He never finished because Alex slapped his arm; "The little sports car, parked at the entrance to the next street, guess whose sitting in it, bold as bloody brass!" Jericho stared across and didn't smile; "It's the Bastard."

Alex nodded and switched off the engine. She jumped in her seat as Owen stuck his head in the window; she hadn't seen him, and Wilson appear. "Guess who's sitting in that little..." Owen said and jerked a thumb towards the little sports car. "I bloody know." Was all Alex replied with some anger.

Alex and Jericho jumped from the van and joined Wilson and Owen on the pavement. "Come on, let's get this done and home for dinner." Muttered Jericho and walked directly over to Sir Edward's car, followed by the team.

Edward jumped from the sports car and stood, arms folded leaning against it. "For fuck sake don't smile." Wilson said quietly, but Sir Edward grinned and held out his hand to Alex; "I am so glad to see you again my dear...." He never finished the sentence because Alex - without a word being said - kicked him straight in his testicles. He collapsed upon the damp pavement and vomited. Alex stood over him and booted him hard in the back, then kicked him hard up the arse. She walked back to the van; not saying a word.

Owen stared down at the young man rolling and crying in his own vomit and said quietly to Wilson; "Remind me never, ever to upset our Alex." Wilson nodded; "Spot on baby brother." Jericho just sighed and gestured to Sir Edward; "Get him up and drop him off back in 1881. Tell him that his time travelling days are over and he got what he deserved for treating our Alex that way."

Wilson and Owen smiled and hauled the babbling young man to his feet. "Come on my dear; time to go home; for good." Wilson chuckled and they were gone.

Jericho walked back to the van and jumped in; "Find a nice empty stretch of road and I call Supplies to pick up the van." He patted Alex's hand on the steering wheel; "Feel better for that?" He asked. Alex shook her head; "No, not really. I'm not a violent person." She smiled at Jericho who just laughed outright; "Not a violent person my arse!" Alex started the engine and the van pulled away, leaving the French House behind.

Alex was in a good mood at dinner and really enjoyed the Chicken in white wine sauce. Wilson and Owen sat quietly opposite her and exchanged glances, finally they tossed a coin and Owen called 'heads', It was tails much to Wilson's relief and amusement. "Go on you lost. You tell her." Owen sighed and pushed the useless coin back into his pocket. "Tell HER what?" Alex asked, sipping her wine. Owen smiled and lifted his wine glass; "Did you notice something funny about Sir Edward and what the staff said about him?"

Owen actually started to chuckle, and Alex stared at him. She sipped her drink and didn't smile. Alex leaned back in her chair; "Oh yeah, I noticed something funny about the bastard; he knocked me about and tried to rape me. I had to walk about showing my crotch and just for a treat, at dinner time I had to get my bloody boobs out. Yeah, I had a real hysterical time. What's your point?" Alex spoke with a little anger and some real sarcasm in her voice.

Owen just nodded and sipped his wine. Wilson leaned across the table; "Since numb nuts here is incapable of recounting the story properly I will." Alex nodded; now a little intrigued.

Wilson sighed; "It wasn't Sir Edward that knocked you about and tried to have sex with you against your will. He actually never did lay a hand or anything else on the girls in the French House. He was straight forward and honest with you, when you met and spoke together. He would have kept his word - he always did - and you would have had a fare share of the blackmail money. It was his twin brother; Harold that assaulted you groped you in the wedding coach and at the dinner party. He and Harold are identical twins; no-one could tell them apart."

"So, you kicked the wrong bloody man in the balls my girl." Owen said and finished his wine, adding; "That's what we never caught on to; why the staff referred to 'the master' as Sir Edward or 'Colly' which was Harold's childhood nickname and short for Coleville. We never caught on that everyone was talking about two different men; Sir Edward and Sir Harold."

Alex slumped back in her seat; "I thought he had a Jekyll and Hyde character; a real bad case of it." She said softly. "So it was Harold that ..." She stopped and sipped her drink, finishing her words; "He was the bastard that tried to rape me. Sir Edward never did actually lay a hand on me; just like the other girls. Poor young Jessica was right about him after all."

Owen didn't smile and topped up his and Alex's glass; "You haven't heard the best or worse; bit yet. Sir Edward died in France in 1914, just before the First World War and his soul was collected. He was allowed to jump immediately with no quarantine imposed."

Alex was a little confused by that; "But he murdered Michael Good - his valet - he should have received some kind of quarantine for that?"

Owen didn't smile and topped up his and Alex's glass; he shook his head; "Again, that was evil Harold. The twins were so alike that even Michael, who I suspect loved Sir Edward, couldn't tell them apart. But, of course, Dispatches knew the truth."

Alex sighed and almost smiled; "So his twin brother Harold was bit of an evil bugger. His picture and portrait were hanging at the Museum, except I thought they were all of Sir Edward." She actually chuckled. Wilson re-filled his wine glass and handed the bottle to Jericho. He gestured to Alex's glass; "You best refill that. You will need it or maybe even a brandy." Alex smiled; "I always need a brandy. Go on, what is it?" Wilson tapped his glass with a finger; "Harold died in 1889. His father Lord John poisoned his brandy and the family Doctor signed off the death as suspected Pneumonia. He was buried very quietly and with little fuss. You'll understand that when I tell you just how lucky you were to escape from him. Really lucky to escape with your life and avoid a horrendous death. "

Alex folded her arms and stared at Wilson, who sipped his wine; "The killings ended in 1889 because Sir Harold - who was a failed medical student - died at his distraught and desperate father's hands. You see, his father knew that Harold was Jack the Ripper." Wilson raised his glass; "To the luckiest lady alive - well, sort of alive!" Alex raised her glass in stunned silence; the horrendous 'What if's' crowding into her mind. She realized that Sir Edward was supposed to marry her, but was called away and so Harold - 'Colly' - stepped in; no one would notice the switch, and it didn't really matter who married Alex as long as she was 'Lady Coleville' for the purposes of the 'Outraged Husband Scam'. The thought of a 'honeymoon' with bloody Jack the Ripper made Alex shudder and she really did need a brandy.

"I should really apologize to poor Sir Edward. He really did treat me like a lady; like he said he would." Alex sighed and sipped her brandy that Mr. Harris had handed her. She grimaced a little, thinking about her foot crashing into his testicles, then booting him up the arse for good measure. "Oh dear; what a terrible mistake." She said and Wilson chuckled; "Now that was some bad case of mistaken identity girl!"

Everyone laughed at that; except Alex, who felt a little guilty and sad about poor Sir Edward. His only fault was having a murdering, sexually perverted psychopath for a twin brother!

14. JUST A MOMENT IN ENDLESS TIME.

Alex sat up in bed and slowly ate the warm, well buttered toast, then sipped her tea. She chuckled at Freddie - standing naked by the small paraffin stove - turning his slice of bread constantly.

"So, toast takes five minutes a bloody side." He turned and smiled; "My brother has the best skill at making toast. He seems to get it done far quicker than me darling." Alex nodded and looked about the shabby room that Freddie's brother - Eric - had loaned them for the day. He would be back at five o'clock and they would have to depart.

But they almost had the whole day to themselves; and that was a start. Freddie apologized - again - for not picking up anything better to eat other than some bread, cheese and apples. Alex waved that aside and slowly pulled the sheet down and off her, she was quite naked. Freddie watched with a growing smile and erection, as she pushed back against the pillow and opened her legs fully. She placed the cup down and wiped her mouth. "I bet you could find a better use for that damn butter, if you tried darling." And giggled, gesturing with both hands for him to come to her.

Freddie blew out the small stove and tossed the half-burnt slice away. "Your wish is my command, Mrs. Babette." He walked over and slowly climbed on the bed and they embraced with some real urgent passion. Alex gripped his big cock and whispered in his ear; "Well, my darling hubby, since we're on honeymoon, I think your new young wife should let you have a little treat." He chuckled as she turned over and knelt on all fours. She released his twitching cock and slowly pulled the cheeks of her arse apart. He laughed outright; she had already well buttered her bum hole in anticipation of pleasing her husband with his little 'treat'.

"Thank you so much my darling." He muttered and slowly inserted his cock into her arse, gently at first, then a little deeper and with more strength. Alex groaned and reached round with both hands; gripping his thrusting thighs. He fucked her slow and hard. Occasionally, slapping her pale arse until her cheeks reddened and she moaned loudly with a little pain and much pleasure.

The old bed creaked and shook as they fucked. Soon they were on their sides, with Alex's arm around his neck, his hands on both breasts and his darting, probing tongue in her hot mouth. Alex came quickly, in little spurts, as he poked her bum hole, steadily getting faster. "Thank fuck for unsalted butter!" She moaned and old Freddie suddenly groaned and emptied his load into Alex's all too welcoming back passage. She giggled and stroked his face with some affection and satisfaction. He gasped and they kissed passionately. He remained in her bum for some minutes before gently extracting his cock and lay back on the pillows, panting.

Alex turned and the pair embraced with passion equal to the love making that had just taken place. Quickly, she went down on his big cock without even cleaning it first. He groaned and cursed; he was still sensitive from his ejaculation, but really didn't care or mind; inside her mouth was absolute heaven for him.

She spent some minutes cleaning his rapidly swelling cock and he pushed her onto the pillows, and they renewed their love making in their favourite position, the missionary. Alex had her knees under his arms, and they fucked furiously and passionately. She had one hell of an orgasm and had to place a hand over her mouth to stop the bloody neighbours complaining about the noise. He was fucking her hard and fast, when they heard an ominous cracking noise and were both surprised when the old bed collapsed under them.

They lay amongst the ruins of the bed and laughed hard, Alex almost crying with laughter. "Fuck it." was all Freddie said and continued to shaft Alex with some renewed determination and they both climaxed together. They stayed locked together for time until Freddie withdrew from her - very reluctantly - and lay together; still laughing softly.

Alex sat on the chair and watched her 'husband' examining the ruins of the bed; wondering what the hell he could tell his brother. Finally, he just sighed and shrugged his shoulders. "I'll get the kettle on darling. Hopefully, that bloody thing won't blow up or something." They laughed together - again. He stood in front of Alex, and she saw that his was erect.

"Bloody hell darling. We'll have to use the bloody floor. I really do hope that doesn't bloody collapse under us!" She said and they giggled together. Freddie fucked her doggy style on the floor and then on the chair. This was followed by sex against a wall, until a fucking picture of the old Queen fell down, just missing the gasping and groaning pair.

Freddie whispered; "Poor Eric will simply not believe what happened, so I won't embarrass you my love, by telling the silly bugger." They now fucked against the front door, Alex's legs around his waist, hands gripping his shoulders, as he drove his big cock into her soaking fanny. The door was - thankfully - sold and he finally came inside of her. They slid down and lay on the floor, kissing with real passion.

They lay on the floor in each other's arms, in silence for a while until Freddie softly kissed Alex's eyes, nose and lips. They stared at each other, then Freddie finally whispered; "I utterly adore and love you my darling." Alex pulled him to her and whispered; "I love you." and nothing further was said as they kissed slowly with overwhelming affection and unbridled passion. He may be old enough to be her father, but she had finally found the right man and she cried a little with real bloody happiness.

Freddie was on duty at the French House that afternoon and so the pair cleaned up the room as best they could and parted - very reluctantly and Alex waved Freddie off at the tram stop, after they had kissed and held hands, to the amazement of the other passengers, waiting at the stop. Alex watched and waved until the tram disappeared out of sight. She walked down the street with a huge smile on her face. She wasn't happy for long.

Jericho stepped from a shop doorway and pushed his arm through hers and they walked together in silence, until Jericho spoke very quietly; "I was quite surprised when I checked my mirror and found my Detective Constable had - with no authorization - returned here. I called up your Duty tape and was further surprised to find you having quite passionate sex with old Mr. Babette."

Alex said nothing but stared ahead. Her heart was sinking rapidly, she had a good idea where this impromptu conversation was headed. Jericho gripped her arm and didn't smile. Then He discretely checked his mirror and continued; "Finding that a certain Miss Alexandra Mary Jones had married a Mr. Frederick James Babette, in a local Registry Office, was quite disturbing. He used his brother's address on the marriage license, so it was easy to find you. I take it; he couldn't put his residence down as the French House that would have raised too many questions. Luckily enough, you have the sense to stop this before the Timeline changes and would be in real serious trouble. I can cover your little illegal journey this time, but I won't be able to do that again. Do you understand what I'm saying Alexandra?"

Alex nodded, her smile was gone, and she knew that her time with Mr. Babette was also gone; for good apparently. She pulled out a little hankie and wiped the tears away. Jericho sighed and they slipped down a quiet alley and Jericho operated his mirror and the pair disappeared.

Walking back to the lighthouse together Jericho said, "The matter is over, and I will not mention it again; to anyone. You have my word on that Alexandra as your Inspector and more importantly; as your friend." She just nodded and Mr. Harris met them at the door and informed Jericho that 'little Ivan' had delivered a Mission file and it was waiting in his study.

Jericho went there and Alex walked to her rooms and wept bitterly, sobbing into her pillows.

EPISODE 4: "ALEXANDRA AND THE AZTECS."

EPISODE PROLOGUE: "There are strange happenings with the conquest of Mexico. The Timeline is under threat, and it appears to centre on a Spanish Captain who doesn't follow the historical norm - Captain Hernando De Plaza, a very different Spanish Conquistador, appears to have gone native! - Mr. Tibbs must investigate before the history of South America changes and with it, the modern world. Alex encounters an Aztec Prince and a young Spanish Knight; she was playing a Nun....a very naughty Nun!"

60 Minutes approx. **Episode Warnings:** Alcohol – Strong language [including racial slurs] – Violence [including sexual violence & combat violence] – Strong graphic sexual references – Mild horror.

NOTES: The original version of this story is published and appears in the **TEMPORAL DETECTIVES**: Book Series 2 – Episode 6 entitled: **"THE LEGEND OF CAPTAIN HERNANDO DE PLAZA."**

CAUTION: Recommended for 18+ only.

1. THE PRESENT TIME.

"People never noticed that small changes had taken place. Most put it down to their memory or old age etc. It wasn't until the 'Information Age' arrived with people chatting together, on Social media, that some suddenly realized, they weren't the only ones that thought the past was different than its reported today." Alex explained to Owen and shifted her Castle across the board four spaces.

Owen nodded; "So until it became known as the 'Mandela Effect' most people thought it was just their memory playing tricks on them." He moved his Bishop, hesitated a few seconds before removing his fingers from the piece. "They have no idea, that these were small changes to the Human Time-Line that couldn't be undone?"

Alex smiled and captured his Knight with her Castle, continuing she added; "Sometimes the little changes cannot be undone despite our best efforts and some humans do realize that the present time has changed. But sometimes those 'little' changes create big change later down the Timeline."

Owen sat back considering his next move; "You mean like what happened with that strange Spanish Conquistador?" he asked and realized that Alex could check-mate him in another couple of moves, if he didn't really start to concentrate on the game.

Alex nodded and sipped her brandy; "South America and the world generally would have been so different, if that Spanish Captain hadn't fallen in love and nearly changed everything." She sighed to herself and remembered that adventure with great fondness and a little horror, if she was really honest.

2. BEFORE THE CHESS GAME....

Jericho returned to the lighthouse just as evening was moving in; his boots crunching upon the gravel as he walked slowly up to the large double, black doors. Mr. Harris pulled them open and slightly bowed; "Everyone has just left for the Dining Room Sir."

Jericho nodded and handed the big man his coat and hat, whilst the delicious smell of hot food wafted around the Hallway.

"Has our guest arrived? I asked Wilson to host him whilst I was with Angel Margret this afternoon." Mr. Harris nodded affirmative and opened the Dining Room door for Jericho. All conversation ceased for a few seconds, then Alex rose from her chair and waved at their guest, saying quietly; "Sir, this is Temporal Detective Inspector Jericho Tibbs." The little man stood and extended his hand to Jericho, who clasped it firmly; "Always a pleasure to greet a Senior Time Controller Mr. Albain, but we're all totally fascinated that you would call upon simple temporal detectives."

The little man smiled and adjusted his pebble glasses, then returned to his seat. He accepted a plate of hot soup from young Ruth and dropped his napkin upon his lap, lifting his spoon, Mr. Albain grinned; "I've heard the stories about your House-keepers cooking and well, I finally couldn't resist; especially when all your guests speak so highly of it!"

Everyone chuckled and Mr. Harris smiled, he was always pleased to hear compliments about his wife's wonderful cooking. Jericho dropped into his chair and Harris placed soup before him; "Brown Windsor, your favourite Sir." He said quietly and continued around the table, carrying the soup tureen, whilst Ruth dished the hot liquid up. Everyone noticed the large portion poured into young Owens's plate by the smiling young girl, but nobody commented upon it; they just smiled to themselves.

"I have a feeling that your visit is not entirely a social function Sir." Jericho sipped his soup and smiled a little. Mr. Albain nodded and placed his spoon down; "Well, Mr. Tibbs you are quite right about that, you see, with have a slight problem with the Aztecs, which left to fester may create unwanted changes to the Human Timeline further down its history." The little man clasped his hands together and sighed; the smile had gone.

"The problem centre's around a certain Spanish Conquistador; he's just not behaving as he should do!" The little man sounded quite frustrated and picked his spoon up, then placed it back down. Everyone chuckled and Mr. Albain continued; "He's being influenced by a young Native man who appears to exercise some sort of control over the man. Before his appearance, Captain Hernando De Plaza was quite normal for the time." He sighed.

"He killed and tortured, raped and stole from the local people without any regard for anything. Now, suddenly he's forgiving people and feeding the starving widows and children. He won't even burn heretics against the Catholic faith; which is quite unbelievable for that time period!" The frustration of the situation could be felt in the little man's voice.

"You mean he's gone native." Wilson said and slurped his soup. "Yes, yes; that's quite right Sergeant." Mr. Albain nodded and resumed his soup, relaxing a little. "If this is allowed to continue the Human Timeline will change and 'the BOSS' has ordered that it will not." He rolled his eyes towards the ceiling and sighed. Everyone knew exactly what he meant.

"What do we know about the young native man?" Asked Alex; sprinkling some salt into her soup. The little man placed his spoon down yet again and stared up at the ceiling, then turned to Alex; "His Spanish given name is Mafias, his original name is quite unpronounceable, and his behavior has changed too. Originally, he sold his fellow natives out to the Spanish conquerors because he can speak their language; the Spaniards paid him well for his much-needed talents. Then, suddenly he has become St. Mafias!"

Mr. Albain slumped back in his chair and gestured towards the ceiling; "He wants an end put to it and the line restored – by any means that achieves that end. Do you understand what that means Mr. Tibbs?"

Jericho nodded and sat back in his chair; direct interference with the natural progression of the Human Timeline, but what bothered Jericho was the change in personalities of the leading pair: Mafias and the Captain. He had an inkling that the 'Dark Prince' could be lurking in the shadows of this one and quite a neat job he has done already!

The change to upstanding "Christian's" by the two men would be a slap in 'the Bosses' face alright – using such tactics would not be received too well upstairs – That made Jericho smile a little. But then, 'the BOSS' didn't have much time for the religions that Humanity had saddled itself with, over the centuries of Human existence. Everyone knew that his sister had argued; that he should take a more proactive role with their creation – but 'the BOSS' had followed their Grand-father's approach and kept a 'hands off' policy in force – unlike their father. The BOSSES father had interfered with the fledgling humanity on several occasions: making headlines in the early religious books with thunderbolts, Angels, nuclear type blasts and turning people to sand; which were just some, of his more memorable forays, into the early life of mankind. But his son had other ideas about the creatures inherited from his Grandfather, who had first created them; they were unique from all other living entities: they could think and reason because they had been granted 'Free-will'.

So the 'BOSS' always stated the same answer to his sister's question; they [Humanity] had been given the privilege of 'Free Will' and how they exercised that, were up to them!

So he only ordered direct interference with Human affairs when it was absolutely necessary, like on the occasions that his wayward brother [Prince David who was known as the Dark Prince] stuck his nose in – maybe this was one of those?

Jericho had enjoyed his soup and dabbed his mouth with a napkin. He had discussed this very topic with Angel Margret that afternoon. His team would initially reconnoiter the problem and then report back to her. Then, undoubtedly, she would get a decision and subsequent authority to change the current time-line; from THE BOSS directly.

The dinner party broke up a couple of hours later with Mr. Albain thanking his hosts for a superb evening and taking some of Mrs. Harris delicious rhubarb pie home in a 'doggy bag'.

3. ALEX CULTIVATES A FRIEND TO HELP HER FUTURE PLANS.

Alex had hatched the plan and knew that the visit of Mr. Albain could prove most fortuitous to her; she just needed to convince him to help her when the time came. She smiled to herself and insisted in seeing the gentleman out. They stood on the steps of the lighthouse and chatted together. It was clear to Alex that the little man was interested in her. She smiled and laughed at his lousy attempts at humour and at one point pushed her arm through his and really smiled at him.

Finally, he asked if she wanted to see his office which overlooked the control desks of the duty Time Controllers. She nodded vigorously and clutched his arm with apparent joy and real anticipation. The little man didn't hesitate in whisking Alex to his office complex which was situated in an Austrian clockmaker's shop in 1860. Like temporal Inspectors, he had the privilege of choosing where he lived and worked. And like Jericho's lighthouse the place was enormous inside and existed in less than a tenth of a human second. His 'office' was plush and very well furnished including a big four poster bed in the main bedroom. They stood drinking very expensive brandy by the large open fireplace and Alex ensured that she laughed enough at his remarks and flirted with the man. Finally, he removed his spectacles and placed his brandy glass on the mantelpiece. "I'm not a very attractive man to women Miss Alexandra and a beautiful young woman like yourself showing me so much attention concerns me. Please be honest with me and speak about your intentions; they will go no further than this room. You know my word is solid and can be trusted, so please speak freely."

Now Alex did admire the little man's honesty [he was known for that] and straightforwardness, so she sat on the edge of the massive bed and patted it; gesturing for him to sit, which he did. She told him most candidly what she hoped for and asked earnestly for his help. He sat, hands in his lap, listening quite intently and finally said quietly; "Yes, I have the power to do that for you Miss Alexandra, but I must ask myself; why would I do it?" She smiled at him and ran a hand over his short curly hair and slowly placed her glass on the floor. "I can be very generous to those that help me and like yourself; I can keep little secrets. Do you want to see how much I would love you to help me?"

He slowly nodded and Alex stood and ran her hand down her blouse, popping the buttons and pulled it open; she wasn't wearing a bra. He slowly smiled as those magnificent breasts stood pert before him. She slipped off the blouse and slowly unzipped her little black dress, dropping it to the floor. She was wearing sheer black stockings and suspender belt with tiny, black lace panties. She dropped the skirt on the discarded blouse.

Alex knelt in front of him and gently jerked open the button on his flies. Nothing was said. He leaned a little backwards as she eased his cock out and pushed it into her mouth. Mr. Albain anticipated a 'blow job' to remember and that's what he got! Under Alex's expert sucking, licking and caressing he soon had an erection which Alex handled with great skill.

The little man striped his clothes off in less than a minute as she worked his cock with her hot moist mouth. He pulled her onto the bed and piled pillows under her head and shoulders; then knelt between her legs, slowly pulling down her panties. He pulled them off and held them to his nose; "The best perfume in the world." He whispered and set to work on her open vagina with his own mouth, tongue and fingers. Alex watched with real satisfaction as he found her clitoris and they both enjoyed his efforts. Satisfied that she wet enough; he mounted her with some unbridled lust and passion. He wasn't the biggest man to have her; but what he lacked in size, he certainly made up for in skill.

With her legs wide open and waving, Alex gripped his shoulders as he fucked her hard and fast. She groaned a little as he reached under her heaving arse and inserted his fingers into her bum and worked her anus with some determination. After five or six minutes of this frenzied fucking, they changed position, and he fucked her 'doggy-style' gripping her big tits with both hands as he buried his cock deep into her. She could feel his thighs slapping against her bum cheeks with some force. She groaned quietly as a couple of little orgasm's escaped. They quickly changed position again with Alex riding him as they gripped hands. She bounced up and down groaning and moaning as he thrusted upwards. She had another little squirt, and he dropped her hands to grip her swinging tits. He pulled her down and feasted on them with his eager mouth.

They fucked for a few more minutes and she felt him ejaculate inside her with just a little moaning. They lay together saying nothing and finally he eased from her and lay back, wiping his sweaty face with part of a sheet. He smiled and slipped from under her and gently turned her onto her back. He pulled open her legs and knelt between them and set to work cleaning her open fanny with some relish. Alex wanted to giggle, but she restrained herself as he cleaned up his own cum. 'Now that's different' she said under her breath and watched the little man working on her vagina.

They sat on the bed, their backs against the small mountain of pillows and shared a glass of brandy. He sighed as she finished the glass and ran a hand over face. "Now Miss Alexandra, may I ask for a special favour?" Alex nodded, thinking; 'Straight up my bum next, I expect' and was glad that she had a tube of the magic 'KY' jelly in her bag. He leaned into her ear and whispered. She nodded her head and sighed to herself. 'Oh well, I've gone this far, so here goes'. He knelt on the bed, bent over, gripping some pillows as Alex probed his tight bum hole with her fingers and tongue. He told her to get her tongue right in which she did and he groaned with pleasure as she tugged his flaccid cock with her free hand.

After that, he walked her to the bathroom and climbed into the big tub and lay down. Alex stood over him, gripping the sides and pissed on him. He laughed and splashed her hot piss about, like he was having a shower. When she had emptied her bladder over him, he sat up and asked if she needed to poo. She just stared at him and muttered that she didn't. He nodded and smiled; "I'm sure you could manage it Miss Alexandra. I love playing a toilet and you do really want my help." She sighed loudly and quickly squatted over him. It took a few minutes but the sick, perverted little man was well pleased with the result.

Alex walked up the lighthouse steps and finally managed to smile, her future plans now a solid start. All she had to do was keep the strange, sexually perverted Mr. Albain happy now and again.

The following morning the team gathered for a light breakfast and final briefing before heading to the Light Room and onward travel to Mexico in the year 1521.

4. A DYING EMPIRE.

The four young natives carried the litter with great skill over the broken path which rose continuously from the steaming jungle. Sister Serenity peered between the curtains and smiled; riding ahead, the young Bishop would be sweating profusely, despite having the privilege of a horse to carry him; from wearing that armour, jerkin and leather boots in this oppressive heat. She waved the delicate fan across her face; it didn't improve matters much and she fondly remembered the heat of Southern Italy.

The summers in Cappanni had always been gloriously warm and clean; not like this sweaty heat of the jungle, followed by the freezing cold of bare mountains at nightfall.

"Apparently another thirty leagues before we reach the outskirts of the encampment; this is slow going indeed my lady." Diego wiped his face with a soft cloth which was already drenched in sweat, but smiled and adjusted his shirt, which was wet with perspiration, flapping the cloth to allow air around his chest. Sister Serenity grinned; she thought Wilson would be comfortable with such heat; coming from Africa; then realized that he had resided in New York City, the entire time he was alive!

Glancing behind, she could see the long column of Spanish soldiers, in single file, following at a slow pace. Some men already laid upon rough wooden litters, inflicted by heat and fevers, being dragged by donkey's or their friends.

"Clean water, salt and Paracetamol would work wonders here." She muttered and then noticed the lone horseman approaching the convoy, the Spanish messenger from Captain Hernando De Plaza no doubt. Sister Serenity and Diego exchanged glances; Diego tapped young Santiago on the shoulder and pointed out the rider; "A visitor from our forthcoming hosts."

Santiago nodded wearily; he hated being back in a Monk's habit again, especially in weather like this, and the large wooden crucifix he carried was a real pain in the arse. He heaved the bloody thing upon his shoulder again, like slinging a rifle.

"Why couldn't he be nailed to a bloody fridge filled with cold beer!" he groaned and that made Diego laugh, then he noticed the strange looks being passed amongst the soldiers nearest to the palanquin. "Stick to old Spanish!" He whispered to Santiago and smiled at the soldiers, some of whom crossed themselves in unspoken fear. The strange, big black man made them really uneasy.

But he was the bishop's personal servant and the Bishop carried the King's word and that carried the power of life and death; the soldiers kept their thoughts and fears quiet.

The bishop lifted his right hand, and the column of struggling men and beasts came to a slow stop in the shimmering heat. Sister Serenity indicated to her carriers that they may rest, and the men gratefully lowered her gently to the rough ground. She stepped from the litter and stretched a little in the hot sunshine, covering her eyes, she viewed the Spanish Knight that saluted her 'brother' and bowed a little from the saddle. After a little conversation, the bishop turned and ordered the column to rest for thirty minutes whilst he and the Knight dismounted and continued talking. Diego, Sister Serenity and bother Santiago joined them – as did Lord Sebastian Garcia – the Bishop's Commander of cavalry and his Deputy.

The Commander had no time for fools, he turned to Sister Serenity and grinned broadly; "Has that idiot become normal again and started burning these heretics and collecting the tax owed to the King?" he slapped a hand upon his sword hilt and added; "If he's not capable, your brother and I will certainly carry out the King and his holiness the Pope's orders!"

Sister Serenity nodded her agreement, but sighed; she knew exactly what Lord Sebastian had in mind: fire and the sword. He removed his steel helmet and wiped his face and neck; Lord Sebastian was a big man - in size and appetite; he loved women and gold - in any order. He had already made plan his feelings about Sister Serenity's vows as a 'bride of Christ'.

"Fucking terrible waste; now the real fucking sin against God is that a beautiful young woman like you is fucking wasted. You should be in a man's bed and bringing children into this world - not on your knee's praying. The only time you would be on your knees, if I was your husband, would be when you're sucking..."

Sister Serenity had walked away at that point. He did apologise a little later - most grudgingly - it should be noted, for he felt he was still right in all he said. It was no surprise that most of the soldiers agreed with him!

"He has an ego the size of a mountain and talks far too plain. What he thinks he just says - a terrible habit." Father Alfredo had explained to Sister Serenity upon hearing the rumours of what Lord Sebastian had said to the young Nun. Father Alfredo was an educated man for a Priest; he had an interest in Astronomy and the habits of plants. There was another rumour that he had been questioned [as a young man] by the Holy Inquisition over his idea's that the earth and all other planets actually revolved around the sun.

It was considered heresy at the time to question anything that the Bible stated. It was said that after torture, the young man recanted and was made to join the priesthood. The choice between being burnt at the state after further torture or becoming a priest; was actually a hard decision for the young man to make. His dear mother's pleadings helped sway him to the Priesthood. Thus thirty years older and far much wiser in the ways of the Church and men; Father Alfredo was in the lands of the pagan Aztec's to convert them to the true path and like him; they faced a similar decision - convert to Christianity or be killed - quite unpleasantly it was promised.

But the good father was actually one of the better Christians for the age and was popular with the common soldiers because he was pious and kind, with an unusual sense of humour for a priest; in that he actually had a sense of humour!

Upon meeting Sister Serenity, he offered the young Nun his litter and native bearers for the journey. At first, she refused, saying the elderly priest would benefit from the ride more than a young person would. She stated that her legs were strong and could do the walking required. The old Father had crossed himself and lifted his eyes to heaven; "Forgive me for talking about a sister's legs; strong or otherwise!"

Everyone - especially the soldiers - laughed at that and Sister Serenity had accepted his offer of the litter; with a small smile upon her face and the convoy set forth to the world of the Aztec's. The journey north was far more brutal than the Conquistadors could ever have imagined.

The jungle trails they travelled were unforgiving with damp heat during the day and cruel cold at night; especially when the expedition crossed the mountain paths.

Several days into the adventure, the bishop had almost a third of his fighting men suffering from fevers and sickness. Some died and were given decent burials by Father Alfredo and Sister Serenity. At one point they had so many sick that Sister Serenity gave up her litter to the worse cases and walked at their side; attending to the dying men's need for comfort and care. That did not go un-noticed by the common soldiers [and many of the officers] and whenever they encountered the Nun, they would bow and cross themselves "Nestra pequena madre de amor" would be whispered. The young nun was gaining respect with each day of the torturous walk.

Now the column of weary and sick men rested in the hazy sunshine as the bishop held his officers conference with the Spanish knight sent by the now infamous Captain Hernando De Plaza - appointed Governor of this region; for the present.

"So the madman lays dying, truly the Lord works his will into the lives of men." Lord Sebastian grunted and crossed himself. The little conference broke up and everyone returned to the column - including the young Knight; Rodrigo Silvia De Rodriguez; the captain's messenger. He would lead the convoy tomorrow into the city that was now under Spanish control. The bishop, his sister, the monk Santiago and the Bishop's servant all gathered by the nun's litter and spoke quietly.

Captain Hernando apparently lay dying; stricken with a strange fever that caused hallucinations and visions of Christ and the Devil. The fevered captain had risen from his sick bed on two occasions; announcing the arrival of the 'Queen of Heaven' [the Virgin Mary] and collapsed back into his hammock.

Jericho [the bishop] didn't smile at the news but admitted that the demise of the captain would conclude the mission quite early and very satisfactorily. Owen particularly liked that idea; "No more humping that bleeding cross about." He smiled and wiped his face and neck - again.

Wilson pointed out - quite discreetly - that little Rosa, the collector - was back amongst the expedition and yet another man had died.

"Which reminds me; it's time for my rounds." Alex said softly and rolled up her sleeves. Jericho pulled her to one side and pointed out she was not here to save lives that should pass over; but she could help those who will survive anyway, as much as she wants. With that little reminder apparently taken on board; Alex went about her mission with the sick. Father Alfredo helping out where possible. Wilson watched the pair and said quietly to Jericho; "Hopefully, our baby sister will heed your words this time, remember what happened in that bloody hospital in that big fucking war?"

Jericho nodded; but he did smile; Alex was Alex after all.

5. THE CAPTAIN.

Captain Hernando turned in his hammock and groaned; Diego - his man servant- dipped the cloth into the bowl of cold water and wiped it around the captain's sweating face. Diego turned to Mafias and sadly shook his head; "He is not better Sir; he's still burning with fever."

Mafias, a young, tall native man, wrung his hands and stared at the old man turning slowly in his hammock, racked with fever and insatiable thirst. "I have asked Sir Rodrigo to meet the Lord Bishop, inform him of our master's plight. Hopefully they will have a surgeon with them, by the grace of God." Both men crossed themselves. Captain Hernando groaned loudly and suddenly sat up, eyes rolling and hands shaking violently; "Our Lady! Our Lady! Have mercy upon this poor soul; send your daughter to care for my soul!" He collapsed back in the hammock and struggled to sleep.

Diego sighed; "It's the same vision all the time Sir; the Virgin Mary." Mafias said nothing further but returned to his simple quarters and drank some wine. If his friend the captain died, then the bishop has the authority to appoint a new Governor and Mafias shuddered at the thought of Lord Sebastian Garcia.

The bishops Deputy would be the obvious choice; Mafias knew he would have nightmares about that selection and so would most of the native population of the city and surrounding countryside.

The convoy started to enter the city just as night was falling. The bishop and his officers made straight for the rooms of the stricken captain, with a concerned Mafias dashing from his quarters to join them. He walked quietly at the rear of the group and encountered Sister Serenity and Father Alfredo. He was not happy to discover that there was no surgeon with the convoy, but Father Alfredo championed the healing skills of the young nun. Mafias pleaded with Sister Serenity to attend his master; the captain. She, of course, agreed.

The group gathered around the hammock and the bishop called for the captain to explain himself. The captain half sat up with rolling eyes and contorted face; "I see you for what you are; minions of the Dark One! You do the bidding of the wrong one!" He collapsed back into his hammock and fell silent. Father Alfredo and Sister Serenity rushed to his aid. But Lord Sebastian grunted; "He's as mad as a bat wearing a hat. The sickness has corrupted his mind and soul. Amen." He crossed himself, as did everyone else; except Mafias.

Sister Serenity held his head gently and ran her hand down his face and neck. She almost smiled; but didn't. She stood back and spoke to his faithful servant; "Keep him doused with cold water and make him drink plenty; water that is. He will recover most of his senses within a day or so." Mafias just stared at the young nun; how could she male such a pronouncement? What Mafias didn't know, was that Alex had seen quite a few cases of Malaria and this was a mild bout of the infection. It had almost run its course. A dose of quinine would reduce it considerably.

She turned and spoke quietly with her 'brother' the bishop. "He would have recovered with or without us." and smiled a little. Jericho nodded and turned to Lord Sebastian; "Take over from him until he recovers. Let us get the King's and the Holy Father's orders underway."

Lord Sebastian actually grinned at that instruction. "Yes, your Grace!" He shouted with tremendous enthusiasm and walked to the door, only stopping to say softly to Sister Serenity; "See, your brother is blessed with good sense for one so young. I truly see why our King and Cardinals love him so." Sister Serenity did not reply or smile at his heartfelt compliment.

The sister and Father Alfredo would sit with the captain through the night. Mafias fetched a chair and blanket; he sat outside the room all night, catching sleep whenever he could. It was the Captain's servant shouting that woke him suddenly. He leapt from the chair, clutching the blanket like a child. Diego [the captain's servant] stood in the doorway and gestured for him to come. He pushed into the sick room and found Sister Serenity feeding the captain from a wooden bowl with a large spoon. This time he did cross himself.

"It's a miracle Mafias, a miracle!" Diego gripped his shoulder and smiled, saying softly; "They say she performs miracles in the name of the Blessed Virgin Mary." He rushed from the room to inform the other staff and soldiers of the garrison; of the good news. Mafias approached his old friend and took his hand. He could feel the difference. The fever had broken. He turned to Sister Serenity; "Thank you Sister. God bless you." He whispered and gripped his friend's hand.

"Don't thank me Mafias. Thank God for his mercy." Was all she said and ladled another spoon of warm gruel into the captain's mouth. Father Alfredo was kneeling at the foot of the bed, praying. Mafias joined him. The news did not please Lord Sebastian - strangely enough - and he grunted; "Sister Serenity is too close to the blessed Virgin for my taste." He had already managed to torture and hang a couple of natives. He had many more lined up for the same fate.

Lord Sebastian left his quarters and walked to the makeshift prison; he had another long day of torturing and hanging heretic dogs to come. He passed the servant Diego, standing in the doorway of the kitchens; "He was near death, and he called out for the Blessed Virgin to help him. Sister Serenity nursed him all night and now he lives, It is a miracle, for she is a daughter of Blessed Mary!"

Diego was happily speaking to the kitchen staff, who stood a little shocked; they were expecting very different news. Lord Sebastian sighed and gripped Diego by his shirt and flung him across the corridor. Diego slapped against the wall and groaned. "Sister Serenity is no closer to the Virgin Queen, than my arse is. If I hear you spreading such stories again; I'll have your tongue struck from your mouth. Do you understand?" He kicked Diego and headed for the prison.

The native servants in the kitchens all crossed themselves - quite vigorously - and many had realized that the 'Gods' of the white demons were far more powerful than the images they had worshipped. Even their feeble women could call the dead back from the 'afterlife'. Diego rose from the floor and dusted himself down. The rumours he had heard about Lord Sebastian certainly were not exaggerations!

The team came together in Jericho's rooms, and he explained that; should Captain De Plaza continue on his present course, the future of South America would be very different. As would be the present day. Jericho sighed; "I don't like saying it, but his death would have suited our mission. Now, he is not scheduled to die for another two years and that would be enough time for the changes to alter the future."

Alex sat on a stiff chair and rubbed her feet. "He would have recovered from the fever without us or anyone else's help." She said and accepted a cup of brandy from Owen; he had bought a couple of bottles with him; decanted into wine skins. He smiled at Alex; "Would you like me to do that?" She stuck up a single finger and pulled her boots back on.

Wilson stood by the doorway, arms folded, watching the corridor. "So what do we do now?" He asked and then waved everyone into silence. Mafias was walking slowly down the corridor with two other men: both natives. The older of the pair walked slowly; his legs bent from a childhood disease. But the other man was a strapping young fellow with a determined look about him.

Jericho rubbed his face and said softly; "Here we go." Mafias stood in the doorway and bowed; "My Lord Bishop; Patkin the elder and his son Astrin would like words with you. Patkin was chief of this city under 'the Aztec' and his son was the War chief, of the city for the same King."

Jericho gestured for both to enter; he asked Mafias to translate for him [even though Jericho and all other detectives had the ability to speak and understand any human language; well, except Scottish probably!]. He nodded for the old man to speak. Patkin bowed and spoke for about a minute, then stopped and folded his arms. Mafias clasped his hands together and nervously smiled; "The old Chief asks, if you will allow the natives to keep more of the harvest than last year. What the Spanish took, caused much hardship and some starvation amongst the people, especially the children. Some died."

Everyone glanced at each other and only Owen couldn't restrain a smile. The Chief had declared his hatred of the white demons and had cursed them back to hell. Jericho smiled a little; he had a pretty good idea what game Mafias was playing. He nodded and told Mafias to tell the old chief that more corn and vegetables would be put aside for them. Mafias spoke to the chief and the old man nodded. He turned his back on Jericho and walked from the room. His son stood staring at Sister Serenity, then turned and followed his father.

Mafias thanked the bishop and went after the pair. They had all heard Mafias tell the chief; "That the white demons would take what they wanted, any food or women they needed, and he should be grateful, that the white Lord hasn't taken his tongue for his words."

Everyone started to chuckle. Wilson picked up his cup and swallowed some brandy; "I think our young friend is either a con artist or a very good diplomat." He smiled and turned to Alex, adding; "I think a native moth has felt the warmth of your flame." Everyone laughed at that.

That's when they heard the striking of the big drums on the wall of their enclosure. An old trooper of Lord Sebastian's Cavalry appeared and bowed, saying quickly; "My Lord Bishop, the scouts have returned. There is a large native army about five hours away. The scouts said they watched them, for nearly a full half day, and still could not count their number in total."

Jericho told the old soldier to inform Lord Sebastian. He turned to the others and shrugged his shoulders; "This could be in our favour. If this fortress falls and all the whites are massacred, then the current timeline will roll on." Alex sighed; "Bloody charming. Loads of people have to die for us to succeed." No one could argue with that deduction.

6. A PRINCE OF THE AZTECS.

Alex sat in her quarters and checked her mirror; the handsome young Astrin was indeed a Prince of the Aztecs. She smiled to herself; he was a rugged, physically fit young man who would certainly turn women's heads - in any time - and he had certainly turned hers. That's when she heard a soft knock at the door and hid her mirror away. If any of the Spaniards saw it; they would be shouting witchcraft. Alex pulled open the door and couldn't stop herself smiling; young Astrin stood in the corridor and bowed a little.

"May I speak with you Sister?" He asked softly. Alex was surprised; he spoke English. He looked about the corridor and said; "Mafias did not speak the words of my father. But I understand why. Lord Sebastian has a reputation for killing first and then not bothering to ask anything later." Alex nodded and gestured for him to enter. She closed the door quietly and really did smile. The young man was clearly a little upset and she should really comfort him in his time of trouble. That's what Nuns are for, comforting the upset. Especially the naughty ones!

They spoke for a few minutes and then the pair fell silent; they were both just staring at each other. She placed a finger on his lips and whispered; "Can you keep a secret?" The young man took her finger and kissed it - very slowly - and nodded. Alex took his hand and guided him to the big bed, and she sat on the edge and very slowly pulled up her habit and opened her legs. His eyes widened, but not as much as his smile.

He quickly pulled off his exquisitely embroidered lion cloth and it was Alex's turn to smile broadly. She sighed with some real pleasure and expectation. She gripped his large erect cock and lowered her mouth onto it. He groaned a little as she went to work, while he pushed a trembling hand between her legs and slowly caressed her already wet vagina.

Astrin soon joined her on the bed with Alex pushed up against the pillows, her long legs wrapped around his back, as he mounted her. She moaned as he entered her slowly and then gently started to thrust, she quickly pulled at the buttons on her loose bodice and offered him her soft plump breasts. His mouth soon found the stiff nipples and sucked hard, thrusting harder and faster into her willing body.

Alex's hands ran down his strong back and gripped his thrusting arse, pulling him closer and deeper into her. Their mouths found each other, and the pair was now fucking hard and passionately, as the old bed creaked under the strain of their love making. She groaned loudly, pushing a hand over her mouth as his moist tongue now caressed her neck and shoulders.

Her first orgasm came hard and fast. Astrin, sensing what was happening, fucked her harder and another one quickly followed. Alex's legs were kicking in the air, trembling and shaking with lust and passion. She would have been screaming, but her hand clamped over own mouth cut them off. The young man pulled himself up on his elbows and whispered if it he could pour his seed into her; it sounded urgent. Alex nodded her head vigorously.

Astrin groaned and said something in his native language and filled her with cum. Alex had another orgasm and released her mouth; the pair kissed with some real passion, as they lay in each other's arms. Finally, the young man raised his head and drew a deep breath. He grinned and said softly; "If this is the new faith, then I'm becoming a bloody Christian!"

Alex laughed out loud and pulled him back to her mouth, whispering; "Bless you my son." which made Astrin laugh and plunge his tongue back into her delicious mouth.

They lay together for some minutes, kissing and whispering. Alex grinned and groaned a little; she could feel the young man's big cock growing inside her. He smiled and holding her firmly, but gently, turned her over and she sat on him. "I suppose it's my turn to do all the bloody work." She said and started to ride him with real strength and vigor. He groaned loudly and Alex placed a hand over his mouth, adding; "Keep it down. Our neighbours will be calling the bloody Spanish Inquisition!"

Astrin grinned and gently took hold of her big swinging tits and feasted on them. That should keep him quiet, she thought and arched her back and really bounced up and down with grim determination. She gripped his shoulders and pushed down hard, rotating her hips and felt the tightness in her stomach; she muffled a little scream. She had another shuddering climax and collapsed on her lover. The pair lay kissing frantically and passionately. He gripped her tightly and still locked together, rose slowly from the bed; he was a lot stronger than he looked. He stood by the bed and jerked her up and down. Alex had her legs wrapped around his waist and arms across his shoulders. She groaned loudly and he came inside of her and the pair fell on the bed, exhausted from their love making. She ran her fingers through his long black hair and they kissed like newlyweds.

They lay together for some time, talking softly and caressing each other. Then Alex realized, she had to attend the 'Officer's Conference' called by her 'brother' the bishop. They parted – very reluctantly - and Alex dipped a soft cloth into the bowl of water on her bedside table and cleaned her gaping vagina and wet thighs.

She had a strange, wonderful feeling in her stomach, and she smiled broadly as she cleaned herself. Her lover had pumped so much cum into her, it took some time to clean up and she still felt that she had some left in her. "Now that's a bloody good souvenir of this little trip." She whispered and giggled, then straightened her habit and wimple. She tided the bed and made for the conference; still smiling.

7. THE WAR CONFERENCE.

All the Bishop's officers assembled in the small hall of the enclosure and Mafias produced a drawing of the city and laid it upon the floor. Some knelt and studied the drawing with great care. Captain Hernando de Plaza was sitting on a stool with Mafias now by his side. He sipped some water, clutching the cup with a feeble hand. He wouldn't be much use in the impending battle; he could just lift a cup, never mind a sword. He sat in silence as the discussions centered on the means of defense.

Lord Sebastian wanted to take his cavalry and some infantry and attack the natives as they appeared. The bishop shook his head; "Why give up huge stone walls for an open field swarming with natives? Their two artillery pieces would cause havoc amongst the primitive solders of the 'Aztec'. We must fight with our strengths, gunpowder and stone walls. In such a small area, horses charging forward would be nearly useless. But if we make a killing courtyard and lure the natives in; we can cut them down in droves."

The young Bishop tapped the two walls which ran to the steps of the enclosure. "To reach us, they must take the entrance of our enclosure. But if these two walls have cannon placed upon each and good musket fire, then we can funnel them in and kill them in their hundreds. The cannons would be incredibly effective in such a small space; they will cut them up and drive fear into the hearts of those that witness such a terrible sight."

Every officer nodded their agreement - except Lord Sebastian, who just grunted and scratched his lice ridden crotch - Rodrigo Silvia De Rodriguez tapped the drawing with his dagger tip and smiled; "The Bishop is right. If we kill hundreds with cannon fire and muskets in such a small place, they will have to fight standing on the bodies of their friends!" The officers chuckled at that thought. Jericho glanced at Alex and smiled. He didn't even have to ask; what she was thinking!

Captain Hernando coughed and ran a hand across his damp face; "Should we not find out, what they want first. I mean before we start butchering them?" He handed the cup to Mafias and leaned upon his sword; "What harm could a little talking do?" He added and wiped his face again. Lord Sebastian shook his head; "You can't reason with these heretic dogs; they only respect the sword. So, I say let then savior it." A couple of officers nodded their agreement with that statement. But Captain Hernando just chuckled; "Don't you mean that only we know and respect the sword, my lord?" Alex actually smiled at that.

The Bishop held up his hand; "Let us consider all things, if a little talking with the natives buys us time to prepare our defenses, then so be it." Rodrigo Silvia De Rodriguez nodded his agreement; "The Bishop is right. Any delay strengthens us and weakens them." So, it was agreed to send an emissary to the native commander and find out his desires for the city and its inhabitants. Mafias would have to go - to translate - and Captain Hernando volunteered for the mission, which the bishop refused. Lord Sebastian would go.

The conference broke up and the officers headed to their assigned posts and duties. Lord Sebastian took hold of Mafias by the shirt and whispered close to his face; "Make sure you translate my words totally and completely. Do you understand that boy?" Mafias nodded and pulled away. He was shaking a little. "Yes of course my Lord." He muttered and bowed.

Captain Hernando rose - with some difficulty - from his seat and headed back to his rooms. Mafias rushed after him. Lord Sebastian turned to the bishop; "I suspect that there is a un-natural bond between those two. When I find it is so, I will kill the pair - with your permission of course, your Grace - and they can both rot in Hell for their perversions."

The bishop didn't reply; he was staring at the map, still laid upon the floor. He turned to Lord Sebastian and gripped his shoulder; "Find out their strength, their weapons and how much stores they carry. If they are expecting a quick victory, then a steadfast defense will not suit their purpose or planning, understand?" Lord Sebastian nodded and strode into the corridor, shouting for Mafias.

Rodrigo Silvia De Rodriguez slapped his hand against his sword hilt in salute; "For a man of God your Grace, I am so pleased that the King sent a Bishop who also understands war." He looked to the departing Lord Sebastian, adding - with a smile - "And men." He turned on his heels and went after Lord Sebastian.

With no one in the room but his team; Jericho pulled his mirror out and ran it over the drawing that Mafias had apparently drawn, just an hour before the conference. Wilson took up his position by the doorway and Owen asked; "What have you spotted Jericho?" Alex picked up the drawing and then noticed the look on Jericho's face. "What have you got?" She said and lowered the drawing. Jericho held up his mirror; the drawing was almost an exact copy of a drawing that illustrated a Spanish book on the conquest; except it was printed in 1798!

"Owen, can you run a check on young Mafias and do the same for the captain. I smell a time travelling rat here." Jericho smiled and thrust his mirror back into the folds of his jacket. Owen disappeared through the doorway and Alex folded her arms; "So, one or both are visitors here?" Jericho rubbed his face; "I strongly suspect that our dear Captain, didn't just change his spots overnight without good reason and the answer does, I believe, lay with Mafias."

Jericho walked to the doorway and stopped; "I suppose, I should tell you about the generous offer Lord Sebastian has made to me about you; should the city fall to the natives." Alex placed her hands on her hips and did not smile; "What bloody generous offer was that?" Jericho grinned; "He has offered to kill you - quite quickly - to spare you being raped by the native warriors. He said that you should go to God, untouched and pure, not ravaged by filthy heretic dogs. That was most kind of him, wasn't it?" He said that bit, with some real sarcasm in his voice.

Alex just sighed and said to Wilson; "I'm going to steer well clear of that mad bastard and watch my back." Wilson just smiled; "Believe me baby sister; I won't let the mad bastard get within ten feet of you; if this goes pair shaped." Alex patted his shoulder, smiling; "Thank you my gallant Knight." Wilson chuckled; "If that's the case, then I must be the very original black Knight!" They both laughed at that. Jericho just shook his head and made for the gateway of the enclosure; to see Lord Sebastian and Mafias depart.

Owen came back in the chamber and saw Alex and Wilson talking closely together; her hand on his shoulder. They both smiled at him. "I don't know how he does it. Jericho, I mean. Young Mafias is Philippe De Sousa. Human Records show him born in 1840 in Portugal. He should have died in 1902, but he missed his departure date; he's a missing soul." Wilson nodded; "What about the Captain?" Owen smiled; "Genuine, he belongs in this time period. He's due to die in just a couple of years. Killed by a rabid dog; not a pleasant death, rabies I mean."

"Remind me never to pat any bloody dogs running about here." Wilson grunted and turned back to Alex, who was staring at the window; she could hear voices and cheering, Lord Sebastian and Mafias were heading out to the Aztec army.

"Why on earth did Jericho send him?" She asked. Wilson adjusted his jacket and grinned; "Because the mad bastard is a good soldier and officer - despite being a total lunatic! - he'll get the information needed."

Owen sighed - unsmiling; "There's something that you should know - and Jericho, of course -that Mafias fled his home country for Spain in 1864. He was about to be arrested and tried for being a Homosexual. It was a crime in those days. Guess who else is of that inclination?" Wilson grunted; "The Captain?" Owen nodded. "That's why he is here. He was given the stark choice by his family; to get out of Spain or face the Holy Inquisition and we know what a really enlightened bunch of jokers, they were in 1521." Wilson gestured towards the door; "I think we should search young Mafias room for anything that doesn't belong in this time or place." Alex agreed with that; finding his time portal device - if one existed - would be a priority. If he had stumbled across a natural tear in the fabric of time, linked to this place, then they would have to try and find its location; and close it. Either way, searching his rooms would be a start.

They made for his small set of rooms and were not surprised to find Captain Hernando there; sitting slumped on a chair, clutching a shirt of Mafias with both hands. He clearly had been crying. Wilson stopped Owen from entering the room and said quietly; "I think this is best left for Alex."

8. THE 'AZTEC' HAS ARRIVED.

Captain Hernando De Plaza was utterly astonished that sister Serenity did not admonish him for his 'abominable sins' in the face of God's commandants. "I have only loved two people - truly loved them - in my life. Mafias are one and young Felipe was the other. He was caught and questioned by the Holy Inquisition. He was just nineteen years old, and they tortured him brutally. He betrayed all the men who had paid for his attention. But not me. I escaped all inquiry and watched him put to death; burnt in our town square. He had been tortured so badly, that he could not even scream in pain as the flames took him apart. I cannot - I will not - allow young Mafias to end that way." The Old Captain gripped Mafias' shirt and held it to his wet face.

Alex poured some wine and gave it to the distraught Captain. He accepted it with shaking hands and sipped slowly; "Never again." He whispered. Alex sat with her arm around his shoulder; little wonder he had changed. He would do anything to keep - and please - his young lover. Mafias - it appears - had persuaded him to change his administration of the natives. To stop the burnings and torture, stop the stealing of their precious crops and stop the rapes and violations of their women and girls.

She sighed and realized; they had been sent to ensure all those horrors continued. She felt a little sick inside. But the current human timeline had to be maintained; if only for all those souls that would cease to exist if it changed. She recalled what Jericho always said; "Humanity progresses over the dead bodies of fellow Humans." She now saw the terrible stark truth of his words.

Wilson knocked softly on the door and informed them, that Lord Sebastian was back, and the news wasn't good. Alex patted the old man and refilled his glass, without another word, she opened the door and joined Wilson and Owen on the other side, closing the door quietly. They made their way back to the bishop's quarters in silence; the corridors were packed with panicking native servants and their families. They clearly wanted to escape the city before the armies of the 'Aztec' arrived.

They stood in the room, drinking brandy poured from Owens's goatskins. Lord Sebastian had recounted that the 'Aztec' had about twenty thousand men under his command; but compared to the Spanish soldiers, they were lightly armed. They certainly had no muskets, cannon or horse. They would not 'parley' with the Spanish garrison; they were here to kill them all and take back the city. Any natives found to have 'co-operated' with the Spanish would be put to death - and their families - then, they would pick a hundred young men and sacrifice them at the temple.

Owen wiped his face; "They will hold each one down, over a stone alter, and rip their hearts out whilst still alive." Alex sipped her brandy; "These two sides are as bad as each other in reality."

She said softly and Wilson agreed with her. They could hear Spanish voices through the window and knew that the garrison was preparing for battle. "It's going to be a real fucking bloodbath with Cannons and muskets against clubs and spears. Jericho's plan is actually a real good one. I wonder where he gained his military skills from." Owen smiled and swallowed down his brandy.

"Just make sure that Alex is never alone with that mad bastard Lord Sebastian." Wilson told Owen, adding; "If you have too, use your bloody mirror. You can say that I ordered you. That will keep you in the clear." Owen nodded; "I fucking would; with or without your orders." Wilson slapped him on the back and grinned; "That's my baby brother!" Rodrigo Silvia De Rodriguez appeared in the doorway and told them to seek shelter in the inner rooms of the enclosure; the bishop's orders.

He took hold of Alex by the arm - which surprised her - and whispered into her ear; "If the time comes and those heathen dogs are going to overrun the city. I will kill you quickly. They will not lay a filthy hand upon you Sister. You have my word on that." He released her and headed for the walls of the courtyard. Alex sighed loudly; "Why do all these fuckers want to bump me off?" Wilson chuckled; "They certainly know how to sweet talk a lady." The three headed for the inner sanctuary of the enclosure. They were stopped by the young officer in charge of the cannon - hurrying to the walls - with his two old 'Bombardiers' in tow. He bowed to Sister Serenity and informed her, that should the 'Aztec' take the city, he would personally put her to death - quickly - he never finished his generous offer, because Sister Serenity just waved him aside; "Yes thank you so bloody much. Now clear off." He walked away, in some astonishment. Wilson and Owen really did laugh at that.

They found a passageway and it took them not to the inner rooms, but the East wall. The Spanish troops were lined along the wall top, crouching or laying, muskets ready. Behind them were some young natives, who really didn't love the 'Aztec'. They held spare muskets and were ready to reload. They would hand a fresh musket to their soldier and load the one he just discharged; that way they could keep up an almost constant fire upon the native warriors, who appeared in the courtyard below. They knew not to bother 'throwing themselves' on the 'Aztec's' mercy; he didn't have any.

On their hands and knees, the team crawled to the walls edge and peered down. Coming through the large gateway were about three hundred native warriors. It was quite a spectacle; they were dressed in vivid and colourful feathers, with shields to match. The men in front of the lines of warriors were dressed in jaguar skins and carried lethal looking wooden clubs studded with bone or metal spikes. The soldier next to Alex turned and asked her to bless him; he was about twenty years old and visibly shaking. She touched his shoulder; "God is at your side my son." He smiled and wiped his face.

He took her hand and kissed it; "I won't let them take you Sister; my dagger will do its duty and you will be..."He didn't finish. The look on Alex's face was enough to shut him up. He went back to staring at the natives.

"For Christ sake; they all want to bump me off. Why don't they just mind their own fu..."She didn't finish either, because Wilson tapped her shoulder and gestured to the other wall, the bishop [Jericho] was giving last minute orders to his officers, who rushed away. Lord Sebastian stood by his side; sword drawn. "We need to tell him about the captain and especially Mafias." He whispered and lay on his back, operating his mirror. The native sitting behind the young soldier, watched with some puzzlement. Why was the dark man talking into a piece of glass? White or black, these people were really strange.

Jericho stepped back from the wall's edge and read his mirror quite discretely. He looked up and waved at Wilson and Alex; Owen was still flat on the wall's floor. That wave started the battle. The Spanish open fire with everything they had. The noise was deafening, and smoke filled the enclosure. When the cannon fired from the East wall; it shook gently, and Alex held her hands over her ears.

"Jesus fucking Christ!" She said, as the young soldier and his native loader exchanged muskets. The soldier grinned at her; "That's the best blessing I've heard since joining the fucking army of Cortes!" He turned and fired again. The native was already finishing the reload. Alex crawled back to Owen, with Wilson right behind. "He certainly knows how to start a punch up!" She yelled to Wilson over the noise. The cannon fired again, and the wall actually shook this time. A dozen or more warriors Were mown down; heads and limbs flying, with blood splattering their struggling colleagues in the confined spaces of the courtyard. "They're stuffing all types of metal and crap in the cannon. Can you imagine what that's doing to the natives down there; they have no armour. No protection." Owen shouted as an arrow bounced off the floor next to his legs. It was quickly followed by another, then another and soon it was raining arrows. They found a gap in the stone wall, as it joined the building that it ran from, a small shelf. Wilson took hold of Alex and pushed her under it. "Keep your head down!" He shouted.

But she had seen the young soldier, struck by two arrows, lying still and prone. The native was now firing the musket down into the courtyard. She went to give aid, but Wilson physically pushed her back and shook his head; "Not this time baby sister, you are going to sit this one out!" Owen had pushed up against the buildings edge and checked his mirror. "Jericho says get to the fucking inner sanctuary and he'll join us there. They are taking the wounded there and you can help, if you want Alex." An arrow bounced off the wall, inches from his head. "To quote William Fucking Shakespeare; let's get the fuck outta here!" Wilson yelled and they left the wall; in a hurry.

9. THE DEVIL'S HOSPITAL.

They ran down the badly lit corridor and found their way blocked by the young artillery officer, they had met earlier. He had clearly been badly wounded. He had an arrow in one arm and one in a leg. But he held up his sword and panted; "Don't worry Sister, I'll do my duty...it will be quick..." He lifted his sword, but Wilson just grunted and decked him with a single punch. He and Owen then heaved the young man up and carried down to the rooms, which had been turned into a makeshift hospital; by the native women.

"That's the best pain relief he can get - in this time and place - Let me at him." Alex said quietly, as Wilson and Owen placed him on a pile of straw. A native woman handed Alex bandages and water. She also gave her an evil looking pair of thin tongs. Owen pointed to them; "What the fuck are they for?" Alex turned them in her hands; "Well, it will have to do. I should be able to get the arrow heads out with these."

More injured men were arriving. Alex now shouted her orders in the native tongue. That actually shocked the natives more than the terrible wounds on the men. How did the strange white woman suddenly pick up their language; and with such Fluency?

Some of the women crossed themselves but carried on tending the wounded. Owen stared into the big room next door; there were several dead bodies laid out and he knew that they would soon be joined by more of their comrades. "Where the fuck is Jericho?" Wilson muttered, then saw Mafias bending over a groaning soldier; his hands were coated with blood. He seemed to know his way around wounded men. The look on his face, when he heard Sister Serenity talking in his native tongue was priceless! A young native woman was assisting Alex. "I may be a simple woman of the 'Aztec', but you are gifted by the Gods Sister. You have the touch." She poured water over the gaping wound and the soldier groaned loudly. Alex was stitching him up with a rough needle and thread. The young officer opened his eyes and stared at her; "Sweet Jesus! The devil has arrived!" and collapsed back on the straw; groaning loudly.

"He's always been around. I know him personally; the bastard." Alex muttered and repeated her treatment on his leg. The native woman chuckled; Alex had forgotten she was still talking in the native tongue. She finished and moved on. Most injuries were caused by arrows. The real nasty - hand to hand - combat had not yet begun. The natives were a also little shocked, to see that, the Sister treated both native and Spaniards without favour to either. They had never seen that before and many crossed themselves in reverence to the nun.

The battle raged above for about an hour and then quiet descended on the enclosure. Owen and one of the young native boys went to find out what was now happening. The rooms of the underground chamber were now filled with injured and dying men. The temporary morgue now had about twenty corpses laid about the stone floor. They had to carry fresh bodies there with some care; the floor was running with blood.

Owen and the boy returned some minutes later; carrying buckets of water; which was gratefully received by everyone. Wilson and Alex pulled Owen to one side and asked about Jericho. "He's fine and so is Lord Sebastian - unfortunately - but a messenger managed to climb over the wall, he's from General Corte's army. He has taken Tenochtitlan and captured the Aztec King; the one here is a brother or uncle or something. They could have overwhelmed us, but they must have received the same news. They have stopped fighting and now are just sitting about."

The noise of fighting, screaming men and horses started to drift down the corridors and the team headed for the walls. They crept along the East wall; there many dead natives and Spanish soldiers sprawled long it. Alex actually turned away from the sight in the courtyard. It had been simply a slaughter; the bodies of the brave, young Aztec warriors were piled two or three deep, the entire length and breadth of the courtyard. The cannons and muskets had done their job with horrific efficiency. There were several Spanish soldiers climbing amongst the bodies, finishing off any wounded men with their swords and daggers.

Wilson stared through the gateway - from where all the noise was coming - and could see horses. Lord Sebastian's cavalry had charged the sitting Aztec's with the infantry behind him. Apparently, the native warriors offered little resistance and were slaughtered where they stood or sat. They Spanish were not taking prisoners.

The only thing that stopped the relentless killing of the natives, was the fall of night. It was too dark - and considered too dangerous - to continue in the darkness. Father Alfredo had arrived in the 'hospital' with boxes of fresh supplies and natives carrying much needed clean water and wine. He embraced Sister Serenity like a long-lost daughter. "Thank God for sending you, my Sister. The men say you are the blessed Virgin herself; returned to give aid and comfort to the Spanish soldiers. I am just a humble priest, but you fill my heart with such pride, that I have given myself a hundred 'Hail Mary's' for penitence!"

Alex just nodded at his praise and said quietly; "There must be burial parties arranged. The heat will soon make this entire city a rotting morgue and then disease and pestilence will soon follow, and the people of the city will become more victims."

The old priest nodded and tapped her arm; "I will speak to Lord Sebastian. He must see the sense of that." He turned to go, but Alex grabbed his arm; "Surely My brother - the bishop - is the man to speak too."

Father Alfredo shook his head; "The messenger that carried the incredible news of General Corte's victory also brought news that

that Lord Sebastian Garcia was to assume command of the region. Captain Hernando De Plaza has been arrested and imprisoned by Corte's order. Your brother - quite correctly - has stood aside." He made his way from the rooms, passing Rodrigo Silvia De Rodriguez, who stood and stared at the wounded. He bowed to Alex and smiled; "For all that Lord Sebastian claims victory here, everyone knows that your brother was the force behind it. But no one can take away your courage, dedication and skill with the wounded. May I kiss your hand?"

The young Knight bowed and held out his hand. Alex held out her hand and he kissed it with some passion and continued to hold for far longer than he should. She actually had to pull her hand away and wiped it on her habit. Rodrigo smiled and bowed again; "Should you ever have need of me; just call, my heart, soul and sword are yours." He turned away, not taking his eyes off her and then left. Wilson just sighed; "You know what I would say, so I'm not saying it!" He chuckled and gestured for them to follow him, adding; "Let's find Jericho and see what's next."

10. THE SPANISH KNIGHT.

Alex explained that she had to change her habit and apron; they were soaked with blood from the many wounded men she had attended. She ran to her room and began to undress. She was soon quite naked apart from her wimple and small black boots. That's when she realised she was not alone! Rodrigo Silvia De Rodriguez stepped from the shadows of the large curtains and bowed. "You are a real beauty, Sister; inside and out." Alex made no attempt to cover her nakedness.

Rodrigo threw down his sword belt and carefully placed his pistol on the bed. He pulled off his dirty blouse and threw that down too. He walked up to her and pulled Alex into his arms. "I will make you a real woman Sister and you will thank me for it." Alex said nothing, but just stared at him. His head went down and his mouth found her big breasts. He was not gentle and sucked hard and gripped them strongly. Alex groaned as a hand found her crotch and he pulled her onto the bed, roughly pulling down his trousers. He didn't bother to take off his black thigh boots.

Alex lay pressed against the pillows on her back and he pulled open her legs and mounted her without saying a word. She gripped the blankets and groaned; he wasn't gentle and started to thrust hard immediately. He fucked her like a bull in heat. He didn't attempt to kiss her and said nothing - except to praise God - and hold her firmly down as he took her quite brutally. "Not one for bloody foreplay then." She moaned and he slapped a hand across her mouth and continued to fuck her hard and fast. "Quiet woman while you please your man." He gasped and pushed her legs up, so that her knee's touched his shoulders. "I will teach you to submit as a woman should." He said, grinning.

Rodrigo fucked her hard for some minutes and Alex couldn't stop the bloody big orgasm that started in her stomach, ran down her shaking thighs and spurted from her cock filled cunt. She gripped the blankets tightly and groaned loudly. He chuckled; "That's right my little woman. Enjoy tour master's cock and pray for forgiveness afterwards." He fucked her for another couple of minutes and then cursed loudly as he came in her quivering fanny. He gasped and took several deep breaths, then pulled from her and stood stretching by the bed; like an athletic warming up. He pulled up his trousers and smiled at her.
 Alex lay against the pillow panting and wiping tears from her face.

"Now that's what a real woman does for her man and with God's grace, your belly will swell with my child and you will be a contented wife of a very rich man." He snatched up his sword belt and pistol and then tugged on his blouse. He walked to the door and said quietly; "Your brother will have to release you from your vows and accept my offer of marriage. No other man will want you now that I have poured my seed into you." He left, closing the door softly.

Alex lay crying and finally pulled herself together. If she was brutally honest with herself; she had really enjoyed the rough sex at his hands.He had taken her as he wished, dominating her and fucking her like a dog. She breathed deep a couple of times and slipped from the bed. She felt his cum running down her thighs and headed for the bowl of water and a soft cloth. She cleaned herself and then thought; she would [and the team] have to depart before Rodrigo approached her 'brother' and Jericho found out what had taken place between the pair. She didn't want him to know, especially after the incident with Mr. Babette. Those thoughts made her smile and ached for his caresses again. Alex sighed and dressed quickly. She headed out to join Owen and Wilson.

11. DARKNESS IN THE TEMPLE.

They made their way to the bishop's quarters; the corridors were filled with Spanish soldiers, drinking and singing. Many stood and bowed as Alex passed by them.

Many crossed themselves and a couple of much older men, called out to her; "Nestra pequena madre de amor!" The others all cheered. She just smiled at them. Owen chuckled; "I'll start taking names and maybe, a small subscription for your fan club." Wilson laughed at that.

They found Jericho in his quarters; sprawled in a hammock, with one leg hanging out, apparently reading a book. Owen noticed that a goatskin of brandy lay on the small rough table, near the swinging 'Bishop'. Jericho looked up and smiled; "Ah, my trusty troops. Everything OK?" Wilson eased himself onto the stiff backed chair near the window and held up a wooden cup, he gestured to the goatskin bag; "Any chance of some brandy?" Owen sighed and filled up two more cups with brandy; he re-filled Jericho's cup and eased himself down on the floor.

Alex accepted her cup and took a couple of sips. "What's going to happen to the captain now?" Jericho shrugged his shoulders; "His fate now lies with Lord Sebastian; the new Governor of this region. I doubt if Captain Hernando De Plaza will interfere with the human timeline anymore and that means our job here is done." He sipped his cup and swung his free leg back and forth, adding; "Our dear Lord 'let's murder everyone' Sebastian, will also deal with young Mafias. He suspects that the good captain and he [Mafias] are having a homosexual affair and that's punishable by death in this time and place. Since he now has total authority; his suspicions are good enough to have both condemned."

Wilson grunted his agreement; "But Mafias will be a lost soul and we shouldn't really allow that." Alex agreed with Wilson and stretched; she was quite stiff from bending over all those wounded men. Wilson grinned at her and jumped up from the old chair. "You better rest those legs of yours girl." Alex smiled and gently eased herself down on the seat. "Thank you, my gallant black knight." She whispered and drank some more brandy. Both her and Wilson chuckled. Owen just sighed; "Knight my arse."

Jericho leaned back in the hammock, thinking. He slapped the book down on the small table and rubbed his chin; "Wilson is right about that; if Mafias is put to death here; he's soul will be lost, and we certainly should prevent that - if we can - but the question is; how?"

Diego [the captain's loyal servant] appeared in the doorway; he didn't look happy - he looked terrified - and bowed, removing his hat. Jericho told him to speak.

"My Lord Bishop, they have taken the captain, to the temple and chained him up like a dog, in a room there. Please help him my lord. They say that he has been working for the devil and fornicating with young Mafias. Lord Sebastian has ordered his trial and they will find him guilty, even though he is innocent of worshipping the evil one. They say, that when he is found guilty of such crimes; they will garrote him on top of that accursed place which is forsaken by God and his angels."

"Good Spanish justice." muttered Owen with plenty of sarcasm in his voice. Jericho slipped from the hammock - most reluctantly - and straightened his jacket. "Where is Mafias now?" He asked the trembling man, who bowed yet again; "He has fled the city my lord. Gone. He has left the captain to face this alone." He wiped his face, he was crying for his good master.

Jericho sighed; "I'll see what can be done. Thank you. Your loyalty to your master is most admirable. Go now." Diego almost smiled and bowed again saying 'thank you' several times and was gone. "Well, that throws a spanner into the works. How can we help the twat [Mafias] if he's not bloody here?" Wilson said and sipped his brandy. That's when Father Alfredo appeared in the doorway looking terrified as well.

"Now what?" Owen whispered and finished his drink.

The old priest looked behind him several times and spoke quickly; there was total disbelief in his voice. "You must get her out of the city my Lord, even your position will not save her from the flames!" He gestured wildly at Alex, who rose slowly from her chair. He gasped a couple times and gripped his crucifix with both hands that trembled. "Lord Sebastian has heard that Sister

Serenity spoke in many tongues and performed surgery on the wounded men. A woman cannot do that; it's not allowed. He says that the devil must have given her such skills. He says a demon has taken her and she now serves the dark one and all of you will be tainted by her closeness to yourselves. You must go!"

Everyone was silent until Alex said quietly; "Ungrateful bastards." No one could argue with that sentiment!

Jericho calmed the old man down and said quietly; "The bastard is getting rid of anyone who witnessed that I commanded and won the battle. He's using Alex to for that end. It's actually me, he wants out the way." The priest pointed to Wilson; "The artillery captain, who she saved, has given testimony that your black servant struck him; knocking him to the floor. A black man cannot touch a white man. They will garrote him for that alone. You must flee; now!"

He ran to the door and called back; "Soldiers are coming. They come to arrest you all for witchcraft and devil worship, you must go...." He turned back and saw that the room was empty. He slowly kissed his crucifix and slid down the wall, the old priest had fainted. He clearly knew that he had been fooled by Satan himself and his minions, dressed up as members of the Church. Father Alfredo lay groaning on the floor, with a dozen, half drunk soldiers standing over him. They asked him several times about the 'Bishop' and the witch. He just lay moaning and so, they dragged him up and took him to Lord Sebastian.

"Ungrateful bunch of bastards." was all Alex said as they walked back to the lighthouse. That made Wilson chuckle. "Maybe in the future, you won't have such a soft spot for the living." Owen scratched his arse and swore blind that he had caught lice from some dirty bugger in that period. "They washed less than a desert scorpion." He muttered. Jericho walked ahead, swinging that book he had been reading, whilst laying in the hammock.

"What is that damn book about?" Alex asked - still a little angry at the treatment she had received from the Spanish - and it showed!

Jericho held the book up; it was an old leather-bound volume with no titles printed upon it. He shouted back; "It's a journal actually, written about 1537. It's in a mix of old Spanish and

Latin." He jumped up the steps and Mr. Harris took his coat and hat. Alex was intrigued, she turned to Wilson; "Where did he get hold of that? We were in the year 1521. That's some sixteen years before the bloody thing was written." Wilson shrugged his shoulders; he was now intrigued too.

Owen was too busy moaning about his arse to pay much attention to the conversation. But he did mutter: "How can it be from 1537 and yet, it's well worn and old? How can it be in that condition in 1521 [the year Jericho was reading it] It should be quite new; unless someone bought the damn book back with them from some future date." Wilson and Alex exchanged a glance; Young Owen may have his faults, but his mind was razor sharp!

They laid about the study; waiting for dinner to be called. Mr. Harris served everyone coffee and finally Alex had to ask: "What is the Significance of that damn book you were reading, whilst swinging in the hammock?" Jericho chuckled and placed the book on the coffee table and eased back in his chair.

"It's the rambling recollections of a young Spanish Nobleman who took part in the conquest of Mexico in the 1520's. It had been lost for many centuries, but was discovered in an old library in Madrid, about 1865. Then, just as authorities got all excited about its finding; the bloody thing disappeared. Some bugger had nicked it." Jericho picked the book back up and opened the first page; there was a self portrait of the writer. Everyone stared hard at the drawing.

Alex smiled: "Bloody Rodrigo Silvia De Rodriguez." She said simply and finished her coffee.

"Apparently he made more money from this, than he ever got by looting the Aztec Empire of its treasures." Jericho chuckled. He tapped the cover; "Your mentioned in it Alex, as is Wilson, Owen, me and Father Alfredo. They're all there; a real cast of characters. He makes it plain - without actually spelling it out - that you and he were lovers! In his 'recollections' you're not a nun, but a beautiful Spanish Courtesan [prostitute] and I'm a surgeon, who demands money from the wounded and sick before he does anything for them! Thus, history records Lord Sebastian as the victor of the battle and almost Saint like in character!"

"So it was a bloody big cover up and written to favour the victors." muttered Wilson, adding; "Winston Churchill always said that history was written by the bloody victors." Owen coughed; "Well, he may have quoted it, but no-one really knows who actually said it." Wilson shrugged his shoulders; "Don't matter who said it first; it's bloody true!"

Jericho chuckled; "That's why I said its fine to help the wounded Alex; you had already done so. Even if; in the book you were portrayed as a tart. The fact is that it happened. So you would have to help or the timeline would change because you didn't." He explained. Alex nodded; she had wondered why Jericho said it was ok.

They sat in silence for a few moments and then Alex exclaimed: "He's a bloody lying little shit bag!" She needed a brandy and walked over to the drinks cabinet. She knew that she didn't even have to ask the others, if they wanted one. Alex wouldn't mention her little fling with the book's writer and would sooner forget that incident now. She was always surprised that she was drawn to some real 'bad boys'. Little wonder he had written her up as he did, and she would keep that fact as her little secret. He [Rodrigo Silvia De Rodriguez] hadn't mentioned her encounter with the Aztec prince because he simply didn't know about it.

Alex smiled to herself remembering that young man who had now been dead for centuries; she hoped he found some kind of happiness in those dreadful times.

Jericho continued; "The big black man was a Christian Moor, who's favourite pastime was playing hangman for Lord Sebastian [the only character he represented almost accurately] and spent his leisure time raping native girls and praying for their heathen souls."

Wilson just shook his head; "What a fucking little shit!"

Jericho jerked a thumb at Owen; "Now, here's a classic. Owen was a brave young Spanish.....Accountant and Tax collector for the King!" He really laughed at that. "Apparently, you would have people tortured and mutilated, if they were a few pence short of the tax demand." Jericho added and finished his coffee.

Alex just shook her head; "So it's a pile of bollocks - a very old pile of bollocks - but bollocks nevertheless."

Wilson nodded; "Yeah, but there was probably no-one around to argue its dishonesty, when it was published. How many would have survived to return to Spain and tell the true story? Lord Sebastian certainly wouldn't have demanded he write the truth. He was now the all-conquering hero who served his King's will and collected taxes and served the holy church by torturing and hanging the so-called heretic natives. Oh yes, I can't see him denouncing the book as a pile of bollocks!"

Jericho smiled: "I found the book amongst young Mafias' possessions in his room. I knew he had brought the journal back from 1865 because of its condition. It may have come, as a bit of a surprise - no, shock - to find that we were not as recorded. He learnt a valuable lesson for a wannabe 'Time Lord' - History is never really how it is written or remembered!" Jericho chuckled, adding; "He [Rodrigo Silvia De Rodriguez] even did a hatchet job on poor old Father Alfredo, in the book, he is a fanatical Priest who wants all heretics burned. He described him as almost Pope like in his frenzy to bring Christianity to the natives. As for the good Captain De Plaza, well, he did a good job destroying his legacy. He's shown as a psychopath who thought he was Jesus Christ himself! The book claims he was seduced by a minion of the devil [Mafias] trying to drive the newly faithful away from the loving arms of Mother Church!" Jericho chuckled a little at that and leaned back, smiling broadly.

"Mafias clearly didn't recognize himself in the book otherwise – if he had any brains – he wouldn't have jumped back to his own time…or another pretty quickly. Maybe sometime in the 21st century, where life for such people was considerably better then the 16th century or the time he escaped from." Jericho sat up and grabbed the book from the coffee table smiling and held it up; "Anyone fancy a little bedtime story? The plot isn't much, but the characters are well drawn, even if, as Alexandra says, it's a big pile of bollocks!"

No-one took up Jericho's generous offer and he placed the book back on the coffee table, and then stared at it. He hadn't mentioned one chapter near the end of the book which was clearly written about a high paid Courtesan at the royal court of Spanish King Charles V. He smiled to himself; he had obviously recongnised Alex by her clear description and the author certainly described her clearly and had caught her manners and character really well. It appears she pleased whoever paid her what she commanded and Alex wouldn't be happy with that slur!

Jericho surmised that they must have a future mission there and Alex was playing the tart again! She wouldn't be happy about that, so best only tell her when that new mission file appears. Now that made the Temporal Inspector really smile and he wondered what Mrs. Harris had prepared for dinner. The conversation would certainly be lively and interesting tonight!

EPISODE 5: "ALEXANDRA GRABS A SECOND CHANCE AT HAPPINESS."

EPISODE PROLOGUE: "Hyde Park, London. In 1898, Queen Victoria is on the throne and the South African war has started. But on this lovely warm summer day something very strange happens. Alexandra who is on a case there meets her very first love and Fiancé who was killed that very year fighting in South Africa. She realizes that she has been given a second chance to do something about what she bitterly regretted not doing her entire life. She and Owen share a secret and he finds out just who he might be."

60 Minutes approx. Episode Warnings:
Alcohol – Smoking - Strong language – Violence [including sexual violence – Strong graphic sexual references [including references to prostitution] – Mild horror.

NOTES: The original version of this story is published and appears in the **TEMPORAL DETECTIVES:** Book Series 2 – Episode 1 entitled: **"FRACTURES IN TIME."**

CAUTION: Recommended for 18+ only.

1. HYDE PARK; LONDON - 4th AUGUST 1898.

Maude, the house maid, had laid the tablecloth upon the dry grass and started to lay the plates, cups and glasses. She smiled at Frank the young footman and wiped her face. The summer heat was quite troubling, but she was glad to be out of the house on such a day. Frank hauled the wicker picnic basket from the back of the carriage and placed it gently by the cloth. "Best get the seats; they're on their way back from the pond." She smiled at Frank, who just sighed and walked slowly back to the carriage.

Old Sam the groom was giving the horses water from the wooden bucket, that usually hung from the carriage and cussing under his breath; he really didn't like this heat. "They picked a right bloody day to have a picnic, not a drop of wind and no clouds well, except that strange dark one." He shielded his eyes and gestured towards the smoky grey cloud, floating above the tree line.

Frank stared at it; "Well, a drop of rain will be welcomed by the gardeners, the lawns are starting to turn brown." He pulled a couple of folding camp chairs from the carriages rear luggage box and wandered back to Maude.

"Old Sam is moaning about the weather; again." He spoke quietly to the maid and chuckled. He loved being out of the house and into the sunshine, especially on a day like this and having Maude all to himself; well, apart from old Sam and the family. He looked up at the strange cloud and wiped his face with his hankie. "I think it's going to rain; the cloud seems to be getter darker." Maude stared up at the cloud and sighed loudly; "Typical, just as we are getting the blooming food out." Frank smiled; "Best I get the big 'brolly out." He muttered and returned to the carriage.

He pulled the straw box out and checked the two wine bottles and then the children's glass bottles of lemonade. He fancied a swig of the lemonade, but reluctantly dismissed that thought; losing your job over a drop of bloody sugared water and lemons, simply wasn't worth it – never mind how thirsty he felt – and watched as Doctor Reginald Dickens, Mrs. Charlotte Dickens and the two children [Fanny & Robert] make their way to the picnic.

Frank grabbed up the big umbrella and pushed it under his already full arms and stared back at the strange cloud. Something inside him made him a little concerned; he had never seen such a strange cloud formation. Young Robert had his model boat clutched with both hands and Fanny was throwing her big red ball into the air and catching it. They were clearly enjoying a day away from 'Nanny' and the nursery. He watched Mrs. Dickens walking – on her husband's arm – and wiped his face again. He had a daydream about her; walking stark naked towards him, those wonderful big breasts of hers swinging and his hands slowly running over her bum.

Frank placed the straw box down and set up the umbrella, still watching the lovely Mrs. Dickens approaching. He thought - again - about those ample breasts, restrained under her pretty little summer jacket and smiled. But he was snapped from his delicious daydream by Maude speaking to him. "Penny for your thoughts; he [Doctor Dickens] would sack you with no notice, just for thinking about it." But she grinned and returned to the picnic hamper.

Frank sighed, not surprised by Maude's comments; she seemed to be able to read his bloody mind at times. But he smiled; good job the Doctor doesn't have that talent! Frank and young Peter [the other footman] both shared sexual fantasies over the good doctor's young wife. Maude was a pretty young girl, with quite a good figure, but Mrs. Dickens's was a real beauty and he regularly masturbated, whilst thinking about her. He would fuck her at the drop of a hat; if she signaled that such an arrangement was acceptable and wanted by her. Frank watched her carefully as she walked towards him, smiling under her colourful parasol that she twirled gently.

She had 'accidently' touched his hands a few times; when he served her at dinner and on the odd occasion, he had helped her into a coat. Mrs. Dickens's had always smiled demurely at him and said 'Thank you' quietly, with those stunning green eyes of hers, staring into his and blinking slowly. That was as far as the reality had gone; but his favourite fantasy was rushing into her bathroom. She would be shouting for help; there would a big spider in her bath. She would be standing naked, covered in soapy water and would fall into his arms. They would make passionate love – in various positions – until the water grew cold. Then they would part without a word being said. Then he remembered where he actually was and sighed.

He stared up at the cloud, now quite dark. There was no wind and a strange silence seemed to hang around this part of the park. He suddenly shivered; but there had been no drop in temperature and no wind had suddenly blown up. He walked slowly back to the little picnic and whispered to Maude; "Did you feel that? It felt really cold for a second or two." Maude shrugged her shoulders and muttered; "No." She was busy putting out the sandwiches, boiled eggs, pork pies and cold chicken. "Get a couple more blankets for the children please." She asked and gently placed the large, cooked ham down on a platter.

Frank started to walk back to the carriage, where old Sam was now checking the harnesses and still moaning about the sunshine. That's when the strangely dressed young man appeared in front of him, running full tilt and slammed into Frank, knocking him down and sprawling across the carefully laid out picnic. He rolled over the cloth and jumped to his feet. Frank eased himself up; a little shocked; the man had appeared from nowhere. "You dumb clot! What the hell are you doing?" Frank yelled, brushing himself down.

Frank stared at the young man; he was wearing dark trousers and a vivid pink shirt with what appeared to be a white doctor's coat. But the most remarkable – and very strange – fact about the stranger was that he appeared to be smoking hot. Frank could actually see smoke coming from his clothes, yet he certainly wasn't alight!

The man just stared at him and then pointed towards the sky; "For fuck sake! Run!" He shouted and turned, running as fast as he could from the scene. Frank turned and stared; there was nothing; just blackness. He could hear Maude screaming hysterically, but the darkness closed over him and he didn't see or hear anything more.

2. TWO WORLDS COLLIDE.

Professor Roger Phelps could hear his own breathing and adjusted the full-face mask and stared about the chamber. There were exposed cables and wrecked equipment strewn all across the small enclosure. He couldn't see much because the foam from the fire suppressant system was everywhere. The 'bomb proof' glass doors now resembled a frosted glass window on a large scale; but they had done their job. The explosion and fire and had been contained. He folded his arms and shook his head. There was no trace of his young assistants. They were both gone; apparently totally vaporized. No body parts, no blood, no pieces of clothes. There was nothing. Absolutely nothing left of the pair.

He left the desolate little room and ordered the doors boarded up and the foam pumped out. The Health & Safety vultures will have a field day with this one. He would be closed down for months; maybe for good. He was on the verge of a breakthrough and just needed more time, but that time had apparently run out. Then, what the hell would he tell the families? That Danny Graves and Barbara Hoops had simply disappeared? Gone without a trace. He walked slowly back to his office and slumped behind the desk. He could murder a whisky right now.

What the fuck where those two doing in the chamber when the machine was on? The pair had clearly defied standard operating procedures and paid for it with their young lives. What the fuck were they up to? So many questions and so few answers; yet. The Inquiry would jump all over him, despite the fact he wasn't even there. The project was his responsibility and now, he would face the inquisition. He sighed and stared at the ceiling. He recalled the arguments between himself and the pair; they wanted to try something new and recalibrate the machine. Danny had waved a thick wad of printouts under his nose, shouting about what the bloody computer had come up with. Barbara had – of course – agreed with Danny; she practically worshipped the ground he walked on. Well, not anymore. The pair had worked, lived, loved and now, died together.

Roger stared at his phone; nineteen missed calls. He sat, hands over his face and leaned back in his chair. He had been so close; so very close to success and now this. His office phone was lit up with unanswered calls. He grabbed it and threw it across the floor and then pulled open his bottom drawer, lifting the whisky bottle out. "Fuck it." Was all he said to himself.

Jericho held up the orb and turned to Wilson; "Nothing. No traces. So no bloody demons involved here." Wilson nodded and rubbed his chin; "It's a hell of a story. The papers have largely dismissed it as fairy tales or urban legend. They're full of the new war in South Africa. Least that damn war has pulled all the attention away from the incident." Jericho watched Owen and Alex walking back from the tree line and muttered; "Yeah, but we still have six souls missing from this time and place. So, something happened here."

Wilson consulted his mirror; "The only survivor was a certain Samuel Gassings, who was the Dickens's groom and he's now in an asylum, totally off his rocker apparently. Whatever he witnessed made his mind go walkabout." He pushed his mirror back into his coat pocket. He was quite happy to play the 'Colonial' gentleman on this mission. "Is it worth speaking to the poor old sod? I mean now that he's gone off his rocker." Jericho shrugged his shoulders; "He's the only witness we have at the moment."

Owen wiped his face with a hankie and smiled at Alex, who had her arm through his; she really was beautiful, especially up close. He glanced back towards the trees, as he pushed his hankie back into his jacket pocket. He caught sight of a young woman, who had her back to the pair and partially hidden below a bright red parasol. He almost stopped walking; despite not seeing her face; she seemed familiar to him. He shrugged his shoulders and thought no more about it.

Alex and Owen joined the pair and Owen moaned about the heat; "I never thought that bloody England could get so hot." He again, wiped his face and neck with his hankie. Alex was also moaning; not about the heat, but about the period clothes she was wearing. "I would have preferred to wear just shorts and a t-shirt. I had forgotten just how uncomfortable these damn clothes were, in warm weather. I think I'm bloody melting!"

Jericho chuckled; "If you walked around here in just shorts and a t-shirt, you would be arrested for indecency. Remember, these people use to cover bloody table legs, in case they caused men to have a sexual frenzy. We'll get you an ice cream." They walked slowly towards the Serpentine Road and a couple of ice-cream vendors that had set up there, under very colourful and large umbrellas.

Owen smiled at the thought of large cold ice cream, and he spoke to Jericho about what Operations Control had confirmed about the incident. "No rogue time portals. This was not a natural occurrence of a slip in time. So, we can tick that off the list. But what does that leave us?" They arrived at the ice cream stall and were greeted by a large Italian man who boasted a huge black moustache. He looked like an opera singer who had fallen on hard times. He dished up four ice cream cornets and one was huge. He gave that to Alex and promptly started to serenade her from the opera 'Nabucco' (1842) by Giuseppe Verdi; badly.

Jericho gave him two shillings and told him not to give up his day job. At least Alex thanked him with a big smile and he wasn't too disappointed. The team walked to the road's edge and watched the passing people and carriages. The ice creams were actually really good, though Owen moaned about the special treatment Alex received from the singing ice cream seller. Wilson just chuckled; the boy still hadn't learnt about the facts of life! A bloody big ice cream wasn't the only thing the ice cream man wanted to give Alex. He would have to explain the phenomena of sexual behaviour to Owen later – much later.

A troop of cavalry passed by, resplendent in their red and blue uniforms, mounted on dark horses. The young officer turned his head a couple of times, looking at the team. Well, at Alex actually [no surprise there] then stopped and turned his horse about. The troop halted at the Corporals command. The officer rode up and jumped, with some grace, from his horse and lifted his helmet. "My God, it is, it's you Alexandra!" He said with some unrestrained happiness in his voice. He was a strapping specimen and when he removed his helmet, everyone would agree that he had the looks too.

Alex just stared at him, totally surprised. Finally, she muttered; "David Shaw...David Shaw-Wilson. My word, you're in the army now?" He nodded and slapped his horse's neck, grinning. "This is 'Thunder', father bought him for me, when I received my commission into the regiment. How have you been? Vikki would go nuts to know that I bumped into you!" Alex was clearly looking shocked by this unscheduled and unforeseen meeting. She turned to the smiling team members and introduced them. Mr. Jericho Tibbs, an investigative lawyer, Mr. Wilson Franklyn, his associate from New York and finally; Mr. Owen Jones, Mr. Tibb's young research assistant and clerk.

David shook hands all round and slapped Wilson on the arm; "Sweet heaven's, are all you yanks this big? I wouldn't like to face you on the battlefield my friend. Are you enjoying your London visit?" Wilson was taken back a little by David's familiarity, but happy about it. "I'm enjoying it very much David." He replied slowly.

Alex said quietly to Owen; "David doesn't see colour in people, just people." She smiled and David said quickly, glancing back at his troop; "I must run. Duty calls, I have to get this bunch back for their lunch. But we must catch up, you and your friends come to 'Franco's' tonight at about seven, just tell them; you're the Shaw-Wilson party. It's all on me and I'll bring Vikki along, so you girls can chat and catch up on the gossip. See you then." He kissed Alex's hand - twice - and was most reluctant to let go.

Finally, he rode away - looking back at Alex several times - and the team watched the cavalry troop disappear from view. Jericho gently took hold of Alex's arm and pulled her close. Wilson and Owen just stared and then realized that Alex was crying; no, she was sobbing, and Jericho guided her to a bench and the pair sat down. Alex sobbed into Jericho's shoulder. Wilson and Owen were frankly shocked and puzzled by her behaviour; she wasn't a woman for crying over nothing. Owen slowly lowered his mirror and whispered what his mirror said about the young officer to Wilson who ran a hand over his face; "Poor bloody cow." was all he said.

3. FRACTURES OF THE HEART.

Alex was resting in her rooms. Ruth had taken her up some tea and sandwiches, but she hadn't touched them. Jericho stood by the fireplace, arms folded and unsmiling. Owen sat on the sofa, his mirror cradled in both hands. Wilson was slumped in his favourite chair, staring up at the ceiling.

Finally Jericho spoke quietly. "They were old friends; David was Alex's brother Charlie's, best friend. Apparently, they were quite mad about each other, but because they were so young, their families wouldn't let them marry at the time. So they had to wait. Alex went to medical school and graduated as a doctor in 1898 and David joined his father's regiment. They met again in Hyde Park the year she became a doctor. We, of course, weren't with her when that originally happened." Jericho slowly eased himself into his armchair and asked Owen to pass the brandies around.

Owen remembered the young woman in the park that had caught his eye and the realization came over him; that was bloody Alex, walking alone in the park, waiting to meet [unscheduled] the young man who would become her lover! But David had met the 'other' Alex instead and wondered if that would change anything between the two. Jericho was talking again and that pulled his attention back to the story.

"Well, they got engaged and the wedding was set for the following July. She would have become Mrs. or Doctor Alexandra Shaw-Wilson. But David was sent to South Africa with his regiment to fight the Boars. He was killed just weeks after arriving there. He went to help a wounded Boar soldier and the bastard pulled a pistol and shot him. Apparently, he told his men to take the Boar to the medical tent; with no further harm done to him. He made his sergeant promise to write to Alex, apologizing for letting her down. He died some minutes later."

Jericho accepted a glass of brandy from the silent Owen and knocked it back in one hit. The team sat in silence. No one could think of what to say to the grieving [yet again] Alex. The sudden meeting with her long-lost love had torn open the fractures of her heart that had taken so long to heal.

Owen sat on the sofa and quietly tapped his mirror and struggled with his thoughts, finally he came out with it [as usual!] he spoke directly to Jericho; "I'm sorry if this upsets anyone, but has Alex been lying to us? I mean, she always says that she married an Italian Count in the 1790's and died in 1801. How the hell could she get engaged to a bloody soldier in 1898 and become a doctor, working in Whitechapel Hospital in 1901? It doesn't make sense. Which is the true bloody story?"

Wilson stared at Jericho and sighed; he had really wanted to ask that question, but discretion and his growing feelings for Alex had stopped him. Jericho ran a hand over his face and almost smiled at the pair. "Both are true. Alex hasn't lied to you." Those words made Owen sit up in a little shock and some amazement. Wilson just smiled to himself. He had already figured that out, some time ago. Owen stared at the pair and said quietly; "But that means she must have travelled in time. I mean jumped back from the early 20th century or jumped forward to it?"

Jericho nodded; "She was born in 1871. The late Victorian and early Edwardian time period is her ordained time. She jumped back in time in 1790 to marry her Italian Count. He was the time traveler from the 1790's. She became very ill after a miscarriage in 1801 and would have died there, but Henri [her husband] bought her back to 1901 and Alex's father and brother tried to save her life. They were both surgeons as well. The only one of the family who wasn't a doctor was Alex's sister, Elizabeth. She was a stage actress." He finished his brandy and walked over to the tray. "Re-fill anyone?" he asked softly, then continued; "It was a scandal that the family hushed up. In 1901 Alex was unmarried [In that time period] and to die with a miscarriage was pure scandal. She was buried quietly, and Henri simply disappeared back in time. But, of course, the timeline had changed because she had given Henri a son and daughter; Philippe and Dorothy."

Owen sat in silence and shook his head, still confused; "How did she become a temporal detective? I mean she broke the rules, she should have been quarantined. How could she do that; you can't lie to an angel. The Duty Death Angel would have known her story." He sat back on the sofa and accepted another brandy from Jericho - who smiled broadly - and sipped his fresh brandy; "I convinced Angel Margret that she would make a good detective; after all, the best gamekeeper's were always former poachers!"

Owen stared at him - he could understand that - but why did Jericho help her? Jericho smiled again and slumped into his chair; "Oh, that was easy. I was married to her sister Elizabeth." The look on both Wilson's and Owens's face was totally priceless. Jericho was Alex's brother-in-law!

"Fuck me; I won't be ever more surprised in my life, not even if I live for a thousand years." Owen muttered and downed his brandy in one hit. "I know I can rely on the pair of you to keep this between us and Angel Margret." Jericho said and raised his glass; "To REAL friends." Was all he said. Owen and Wilson nodded at that sentiment.

"I don't think she should go to that dinner. That would be bloody awful for her." Wilson finally said and sipped his brandy; Owen had refilled all their glasses. The door swung open and a very sad, but composed Alex strode in. She was dressed in a beautiful dinner gown, wearing a stunning white necklace of pearls. She looked truly beautiful. She placed her hands on her hips and almost smiled; "Come on. He invited you as well. This will probably be the last time; I ever see and talk to the love of my entire life. So shift your bleeding bums!"

They all leapt to their feet, smiling broadly. "Whatever you say baby sister." Was all Wilson muttered and gave her shoulder a gentle squeeze. She grabbed his hand and held it tight for a few seconds. "First real love, do you understand that?" She whispered to him. Wilson nodded slowly; he certainly did. Jericho was pleased - and really impressed - that Owen kept his new knowledge about Alex's history to himself. The boy was really starting to grow up. He was about to impress Jericho even more, as they stood outside the posh restaurant in the warm evening sunshine. He had remembered about the other 'Alex' and spoke quietly to Jericho - who didn't smile - he had realized the serious ramifications that could happen with Owens's revelation. If the original Alex didn't show up tonight the current human timeline could change and with it; Alexandra's entire fate and destiny.

The team waited outside, whilst Owen was sent into the restaurant to see if the other 'Alex' was there. He came back grim faced; she wasn't. Jericho sighed and everyone headed for the pub opposite. There was no problem with Alex being in the pub; there were several ladies - with their escorts - already in the establishment; it catered for theatre crowds, which invariably had women amongst them. It was clearly considered a respectable place for women to be seen in.

Jericho summed up the situation, as they sipped drinks at a quiet table by the window, watching the restaurant opposite. They had basically cocked up and by 'their Alex' talking to young David and not her original self; there could be unwanted changes to the timeline and that wasn't good. Alex wiped a few tears from her face and could not smile, she desperately wanted a little chat with her lost love; she wanted that desperately. But she knew the danger she was now in. She was totally surprised and amazed - though pleased - that Wilson and Owen hadn't mentioned this little episode of her past; she couldn't explain it without more lies or half-truths, and she really didn't want to do that to them; they deserved far better.

Wilson checked his fob watch; only twenty minutes before young

David was due to arrive with his sister Vikki. For once, the temporal detectives were really running out of time! Jericho consulted his mirror discretely and ran a hand over his face; there was only one option left to them and he went for it. He would have some explaining to do with Angel Margret; but he really had no other choice.

Little Lillian, the barmaid stared across the pub, that was quickly filling with the usual theatre crowd and was confused and quite surprised; she would have sworn that table 7 had customers sitting around it. She had especially noticed the beautiful young women in a wonderful evening dress and of course, the big black fella. But there was no one sitting at table 7 now. How the hell did they depart without her seeing them go?

4. A TSUNAMI OF TIME.

Supplies had pulled out all stops and the team sat in the relative shade of their carriage, stationery on the Serpentine Road. Owen passed around a cold bottle of lemonade and everyone took a sip. Alex was constantly peering out the small window, on her side of the carriage, whilst Wilson did the same on his side.

Jericho consulted his mirror and sighed; "It's almost midday. That's about the time the papers record the strange event happening." He leaned across Alex and pointed to the trees, adding; "There's the Dickens's carriage and old Samuel. So that must be their picnic. I can see a maid; she was called Maude Manning and is eighteen. The young man must be the footman; Frank Holmes."

Owen took a swig from the lemonade bottle and pushed the cork back in. "I don't know who Mr. R. White was, but he made bloody good lemonade." and placed the bottle on the seat. Wilson chuckled; "Never mind the bloody lemonade, Angel Margret will go nuts, that we're taking this risk, by appearing at this time and place. She really doesn't like her teams being present when uncountable and unscheduled events occur in the timeline. Just by being here, we could change everything and make the situation far worse. Just one little action out of place and we're in the shit."

Alex nodded her agreement with that but smiled. She really did have friends and colleagues that would stand by her; regardless.

Jericho stared out the window on Alex's side and pulled out his mirror; it was flashing a warning. Something had occurred in 1984, in London and it was linked to here, at this time. "Some fucking idiot has fractured time!" He exclaimed and tapped at his mirror. "There's been a serious incident at a Research lab and two souls have been thrown into uncharted time…." He didn't finish because Owen interrupted him. He suddenly shouted; "For fuck sake! Look there! Some man has just appeared out of nowhere and he appears to be smoking hot!" Everyone squeezed near the window and watched in horror and fascination, as the huge black hole appeared. But it appeared to be moving like a wall of water. Wilson shouted; "A bloody Tsunami of time!"

They watched as it rolled over the family, then the young footman and finally the screaming maid. Everyone noted it had missed the young man in the doctor's coat and he was left hiding in a clump of trees. Jericho grunted; "Got it." He pushed open the carriage door and the team decamped, running up towards the picnic and the strange young man hiding in the bushes. They all noticed old Samuel staggering around, holding his head and screaming for his mother. He collapsed onto the grass, sobbing loudly.

"Leave him!" Was all Jericho shouted and they ran across to where the young man lay cowering. Owen helped him up. Jericho didn't waste any time, he told the man about the fracture in time in 1984 and what did he do, to cause the damn thing. Danny staggered a bit and sat back down; he held his head with both hands and breathed deeply. "We're almost had it. We knew with a few little adjustments we would succeed. How the hell did we fuck up?" He muttered.

Alex gripped his shoulder; "What were you about to succeed in Danny?" He looked up at her - he didn't smile - and sighed; "Moving physical objects from one place to another without the need for planes, trains, ships or vehicles. It would have been worth a fortune, not to mention the bloody fame and possibly Nobel prizes." He actually chuckled, adding; "What a bunch of bloody stupid bastards."

"Where the fuck is poor Barbara?" He asked and shook his head with great sadness. "She was right there, next to me when the bloody machine malfunctioned; she should be here now, shouldn't she?" He ran both hands over his face and looked quite distraught, adding; "We had checked the figures, the simulations, everything. But something went terribly wrong; like the bloody machine had been re-programmed without any bloody checks being done." He sighed and wrapped his arms about himself; "Where the fuck is she?" he said softly, and Alex patted his arm.

Jericho checked his mirror and shook his head; "There's no trace of Ms. Barbara Hoops in any timeline now..." He stopped talking and re-read his mirror and managed a smile; "According to Human Records, she popped up in this very park but in summer 1772. I hope she knows how to look after herself; this place was notorious - at the time - for prostitutes, cut throats, pimps and perverts."

Danny nodded; "She certainly can. She gave me a right hook just for insulting her crazy father." He rubbed his chin in memory of that unpleasant event. Alex grinned; "Now that sounds like the kind of woman; I would love to call a friend!" Wilson and Jericho chuckled, but Owen just pulled a face; "Another crazy feminist bitch that thinks it's a man." He muttered and then saw the look on Alex's face and added - with a smile - "That's what some very backward thinking men would say." He shrugged his shoulders as Wilson laughed at his wonderful piece of back peddling.

Jericho gestured to Alex and said quietly; "Jump back and pick her up please Alexandra and do it without changing the entire bloody world." Alex checked her mirror for the co-ordinates that Jericho had just sent her and operated her mirror. Danny staggered back in a little shock as Alex vanished. Jericho turned to him; "Don't worry Danny, Alexandra will pick her up. She'll be fine. Now let's sort this bloody mess out." Danny could only nod his head.

Jericho rubbed his chin; "They fractured the fabric of time. Somehow their bloody machine released a time portal of huge dimensions and power. It's rolling between time periods and sweeping up any living thing along with it. We could be standing here, and it could have dropped a bloody dinosaur on us...or send those poor people back to Jurassic times. My mirror clocked where it had come from and where it was now headed."

Wilson took a deep breath; "How do we stop the bloody thing?" Owen stood watching the skyline and said quietly; "That's a very good question big man and we need a answer fast; really fast." Wilson chuckled; "Why so fast baby brother?" Owen pointed to the tree line; "Because the fucking thing is back!" They all watched the gathering darkness and Jericho pulled out his mirror. "You're coming with us Danny; you started this nightmare, and you can help us stop it." He operated his mirror and the little group disappeared.

They stood in the slight drizzle and watched the traffic passing through the gates of the 'Klass Institute' with little interest until Danny quietly pointed out the big black BMW car that swept through the gates without being stopped by the several security guards.

"That's old man Klass himself. He came to visit the day before the machine went nuts. He was always pushing our boss; Professor Roger Phelps to get results - any bloody results - apparently the project had cost about 600 million dollars so far." Danny then looked a little puzzled; "I don't remember him visiting on the day of the accident."

Jericho checked his mirror; "We're here some two hours before the accident occurred. You're going to get us in there Danny, and we have to stop the accident happening." Danny nodded and stood thinking, hands on hips. Finally, he said; "They were expecting a medical team that morning - to give the staff a health check up - for insurance purposes. But it never turned up."

"How's that, we sent our only MD back to the crime centre of 1772, when we really could use her here." Wilson said and brushed rain from his face. Jericho just coughed; he was on his mirror contacting supplies. "I'll get us some costumes and stuff that a medical team would use in this time and place. Alexandra will be back soon."

He hadn't finishing speaking before Alex appeared with the distraught Ms. Barbara Hoops in tow. She and Danny really did say hello; they kissed and embraced so much that Jericho actually had to part the pair himself. Owen was telling Alex about the plan to gain access to the 'Klass Institute. Alex told him about Hyde Park of 1772. "There were people fucking everywhere, against trees, in bushes, you name it they were fucking on it or against it. Men together, women together!"

Alex smiled; "Well, I can answer the serious medical questions if asked; can you lot play nurses?" Wilson folded his arms; "I'm not wearing a bloody nurse's uniform; I too big and ugly." Owen chuckled; "I don't mind if I can wear suspenders and stockings." Then grinned; he stopped grinning when he saw the looks on everyone's faces. "Only bleeding joking!" He added hastily.

Wilson shook his head in despair and both he and Alex said together; "Bloody Monastery!" They didn't laugh.

Jericho just sighed and separated the amorous lovers - yet again - and gestured towards the white van parked outside 'The Queen's Head' pub; "There's old Joe from Supplies. Come on people." They walked over to the van and Owen suggested a 'quick one' in the pub, but - sadly - for the team and their guests; Jericho said NO.

5. THE KLASS INSTITUTE.

"What happens if we meet ourselves? Don't we just disappear or something terrible like that?" Danny asked Jericho with real concern in his voice, as he clutched Barbara's hand. Jericho patted his shoulder; "Don't worry about that. We'll take care of everything. Just get us to that damn machine."

Alex was now wearing a nice business suit with the obligatory white coat and stethoscope. Wilson had a white - male nurse's - coat on and uniform trousers, with a clipboard under his arm. Jericho was dressed as a senior doctor; a consultant of course, so he didn't actually have to do any work.

Wilson stood arms folded, waiting outside with everyone except Owen. "The little pervert MUST have the power of bloody prophecy." Alex just giggled; she really couldn't wait for this. Supplies could only provide one male nurses costume at such short notice, and it only fitted Wilson's big frame.

Nurse Owen [now Jacqueline] Jones stepped carefully from the van and straightened his uniform dress, there was silence from his fellow team members; young Owen actually looked stunning as a woman!

Alex couldn't bring herself to laugh, she just smiled and turned to Wilson; "He makes a bloody gorgeous woman, and he has a fantastic pair of legs!" She didn't even believe she said it - but she had - and Jackie held up her clipboard and said, "Well let's get it done people." Wilson just shook his head and groaned, while Alex really did smile to herself.

Jericho just slapped a hand over his face and shook his head; in all his centuries with the temporal department, he had never seen anything like this. But he had to agree with Alex; Owen really the looked the part. Wilson just looked 'Jacqueline' up and down and sighed loudly; very loudly!

The team headed for the security gates with Alex still having a little giggle to herself.

Wilson walked next to Owen and just had to ask; "I take it your wearing black tights?" Owen gave a girlish grin and said quietly; "Wouldn't you like to know big man." Then added; "Typical man, it's not proper to ask a lady about her underwear in the middle of the street." It was Wilson's turn to slap a hand over his face. Alex just fell about laughing but managed to compose herself at the security point.

Danny and Barbara did the talking and the team signed in. The two burly guards in the gatehouse smiled broadly at Alex and Owen. One was really interested in Owen - sorry, nurse Jacqueline Jones - and lingered around 'her; talking as she signed in.

The team gathered by the main doors and Owen folded his arms, talking quietly to Wilson; "You bloody men are all the same. That cheeky guard asked me if I had bloody stockings on and what was my phone number!" It was Alex's turn to 'full face palm'. But she really did smile; "Welcome to a woman's world." Was all she muttered. Danny gestured to the doors and the team followed him to the medical suite.

Owen walked next to Alex and finally Wilson asked him; "How did you learn to walk like a woman so bloody quickly?" Had the little pervert been practicing in secret? Owen just sighed; "I'm just copying how Alex walks." Wilson shook his head; "I wouldn't do that my girl. You'll have every male in the place following you about." Owen just smiled and walked on. Danny leaned over to Wilson; "I don't know about you, but she's got a bloody gorgeous arse." Wilson sighed; "You're not the first to say that about Alex."

Danny didn't smile; "No, I meant the little nurse." It was 'face palm' number two for Wilson. But he found himself staring at Owens's swinging hips and little walk. He shuddered; the 'little nurse' really did have a gorgeous arse!

He needed a brandy; urgently - or a woman - he really didn't mind which. He shook his head and walked on. They were shown into the medical suite by Danny.

They gathered in the bright clean rooms and Alex poked about the cupboards, looking for anything that may be useful in their little act. She found a huge box of suppositories' which surprised her. Owen held up a packet; "Christ. You would need to drink from a bucket to swallow these." Alex sighed and explained they were pushed up your bum. Owen dropped the packet and wiped his hands on a paper towel. Alex just had to say [giggling a little] "Dressed like that, that's not the only thing, some men would shove up your bum." Owen just stared at her.

Jericho and Wilson were talking quietly with Danny and Barbara about the machine, when the door opened and a big man in a superb suit walked in and shook hands all round [he lingered over Owens's handshake] it was John Klass himself. He would be first; "Always lead by example." He said, starting to undress.

Alex called for some privacy and the rest - apart from her nurse; Owen - moved into medical Reception and Wilson started to gather names and a brief medical history. No one noticed Jericho, Danny & Barbara slip away.

Kohn klass stood stark naked on the weighing scales and Owen measured him [his height!] and took notes. Mr. Klass - the multi-millionaire, hardnosed businessman - smiled at Owen; really smiled at him. Especially when Owen glanced at his large penis, which stared Owen in the face, as he knelt down to read the scale.

"You know, I was thinking of hiring a personal nurse to look after my daily medical needs. She wouldn't have to do much for her thirty thousand a year." He really did smile at Owen - again. [That sort of money, in 1984 was about 3 times' what a nurse would earn, working long and hard, on the wards].

Owen managed a smile and was very glad when Alex happily

pronounced Klass fit apart from some blood pressure problems and he could leave. Mr. Klass thanked her and with his dick swinging, walked over to Owen, who was getting his clothes ready.

Dressing, Mr. Klass had a private word with young Owen. Then whistling and smiling, walked happily from the room. Alex just had to ask and smiled at the red about Owens's cheeks.

Finally, Owen blurted out; "The dirty old sod is old enough to be my dad. But he asked me out. He said he was flying to a hotel in Paris that he owned and would I like to start my new job there." Alex really did laugh and patted his arm; she was about to say something when Owen continued; "He bloody told me that I'd needn't bring too many clothes. He would buy me anything I needed or wanted...especially lingerie!"

Alex sighed; "You'll get use to how men behave while you're dressed like that. The older they are the worse they are." Then with a really big grin added; "So what time is the flight? Is he sending a car? Yes, of course he would." Laughing, she walked to her desk and shouted "Next!" The big burly security guard, who propositioned Owen earlier, strolled in, grinning from ear to ear. He took his clothes off without even being asked. To keep up professional standards and appearances; Alex didn't laugh at the look on Owens's face. Well, she really tried hard not to.

They sat in staff canteen at lunch time and drank welcome coffee; Owen nibbled at a sandwich and picked up his banana and peeled it slowly. Wilson leaned forward and shook his head; "I wouldn't eat that my friend. Not here and now."

He nodded towards three young lads, in boiler suite, sitting at the table opposite. They hadn't taken their eyes of Alex and her nurse since they walked in. Owen just sighed and started on his banana. Alex nearly choked on her coffee as the three lads cheered, one shouted; "Go on girl. You've got my temperature up...and other things!" The oldest one grinned; "Christ, I'm running a temperature now. I had better see a nurse." The small one wasn't so sexually descriptive or forward; he just asked for Owens's phone number outright. Owen quickly put his half-eaten piece of fruit down and sipped his coffee.

"Great fun being a woman, isn't it?" Alex whispered to him. Owen stared down at his lunch; a hot dog wasn't the best thing to order today. He pushed the plate away and Wilson chuckled; "Not like you to miss food - any food - you best see a doctor."

Alex said softly; "Where's Jericho and the Frankenstein love birds?" Wilson finished his coffee and shrugged his shoulders; "I hope he's found that bloody machine. I've not heard a thing from my mirror."

Owen picked up his 'Mars bar' and then glanced - carefully - at the three lads, all leaning forward in anticipation and pushed it into his handbag. "Mine's quiet too." He muttered.

Jericho stood in the canteen doorway and gestured for them to come. They left their table and walked to the door. The 'girls' received wolf whistles and one lad shouted; "You got a gorgeous bum darling!" at Owen. Jericho just shook his head and they made for the medical centre, which seemed to be packed with men. Owen really groaned when the three lads from the canteen joined the throng: all smiling broadly.

They assembled in Alex's temporary office and Jericho outlined his plan and what had been discovered. "Someone has deliberately altered the machine's calibration. The new programmed changes contain lines of command that Danny or Barbara hadn't seen before. Pretty advanced stuff: it appears the machine was altered by someone who knew exactly what they were doing. Control advises me that the program is too far advanced to have been created in 1984 or any time close to this year."

Wilson nodded; "Someone from the future?" He asked and Jericho ran a hand over his face; "From about 2030 or thereabouts."

Alex folded her arms; "So we have a mad scientist from the future running around here somewhere and why the hell create a monster like that?" Owen stood in silence and then said softly; "That dirty old sod who offered me lots of naughty underwear said he was going to Paris, to meet a man who had convinced him to invest in the future of travel. And I mean 'future' travel. He said really special, expensive travel to places that you couldn't visit by plane, ship or car and the holiday would be totally unique."

Jericho was a little puzzled by the 'naughty underwear' remark, but pressed Owen further. "What sort of travel?" He asked; intrigued, as was Alex and Wilson.

Owen didn't smile; "The man said he would be able to send people back in time as holograms and they would be able to visit any period that took their fancy. Can you imagine that? People would pay a fortune for holidays like that."

Wilson grunted; "That's fucking brilliant actually. With holograms, there would be no causality, they couldn't actually effect the past; just visit it. A machine like that would be worth billions to the travel industry." They all nodded their agreement at that statement.

Jericho rubbed his chin and smiled at Owen; "Owen...sorry, Jacqueline, I'm going have to ask you to do something, we normally lumber Alex with." Then he grinned and Wilson sighed loudly; "I've heard it all now. Bloody Owen is now our 'honey trap'." Alex laughed outright and gripped Owens's arm; "Remember to take plenty of lubricant."

Owen just grimaced and pulled out his 'Mars bar' saying; "I need bloody chocolate." Alex - still laughing - nodded; "Spoken like a true woman." Everyone laughed at that, except Owen.

6. RENDEZVOUS IN PARIS.

Owen placed the phone down and really didn't smile, he turned to his colleagues and said quietly; "He's agreed that I can bring a girlfriend. I told him that my mum and dad wouldn't be happy if I went alone. He really seemed pleased that I wouldn't just up and go with him." Alex smiled; "You've a lot to learn about men and their sexual habits." Owen just stared at her; "No thank you. I'd sooner learn about women's sexual habits, thank you so very much."

Wilson gestured to the van and they walked back to where Jericho sat - in the front passenger seat - reading his mirror. He looked up as they climbed in; "Supplies have everything ready. They have some great outfits for you girls; especially you Owen...sorry, Jacqueline. You're going to look a million dollars according to Anna [the costume designer for the temporal teams] and that should keep our Mr. Klass happy."

Wilson sat in the driver's seat and started the van; "How did Harry and team 52 get on?" Jericho tapped his mirror; "As expected, young Harry has done well; he's recovered the family [the Dickens] from Roman Britain. Stella and her team recovered the maid and footman from some Native American Indians in the year 1482. That's ten years before bloody Columbus discovered the bloody place."

He grinned: "Oh and Specialist Team 153 returned that small dinosaur back to its own time. Our vets patched up its wounds and it will be fine." He actually chuckled; "No wonder there were so many stories floating about the Dark Ages, concerning a Knight fighting a bloody dragon; it appeared in 694 in Kent, England and a local Knight had a go at it. He [the Knight] was quite safe; it wouldn't have eaten him; it was a bloody herbivore."

Alex leaned over and asked; "Did Danny and Barbara manage to change the program back to its original settings?" Jericho nodded; "They're actually quite a clever pair of so and so's. But they don't succeed in making the parcel teleporter and end up working for a Spanish Company making next generation toys."

Wilson chuckled; "That's a lot damn safer than been hurdled through time and running from bloody Romans or dinosaurs."

The van pulled away; Owen and Alex had a private jet to catch, and Jericho and Wilson would be heading for Paris and booking in the same hotel. They needed to find out who the mysterious 'man' that Klass was dealing with; actually was. Jericho spoke quietly to his team, as they walked back to the lighthouse; "I think our Mr. Klass knows more about this, than we know at the moment. Remember Danny was puzzled that he turned up on the day of the accident. He didn't recall him being there, that day."

The big black limousine threaded through the traffic and arrived at Stanstead Airport in good time to catch the private jet of Mr. John Klass. They were welcomed at the plane steps by the captain, who welcomed the 'ladies' aboard. He told them that Mr. Klass would greet them at his hotel in Paris.

The captain settled them in their seats and back in the cockpit, said to his co-pilot; "What a fucking pair of crackers. Old Klass certainly has good taste in women. Apparently, it's the little dark haired beauty that he really wants. I can see why, She has a fucking gorgeous bum and long legs. Not as pretty as her friend, but I wouldn't say no to her." The young co-pilot chuckled and sighed; "What it is to be fucking rich!"

The plane took off just before nightfall. It was Owens's first flight, and he gripped the arm rests tightly. Alex just smiled and patted his hand.

She sipped her brandy and stared out the window at the beautiful, dark night sky, then turned to Owen, who sat nervously next to her. She patted his hand again; "You look bloody stunning Owen...sorry, Jacqueline, You really do make a lovely girl."

Owen just grunted in a very un-lady like manner; "It's not you he wants to fuck." He knocked his brandy back in one and refilled his glass, then topped up Alex's. Anna had really done a superb job on Owen; He was wearing a black cocktail dress, heels and matching short jacket, with a classic handbag.

Alex smiled; they were both wearing stockings and very expensive underwear. She was really impressed that Owen could walk in heels; as if he had done so for years. She had watched him carefully; he had a woman's mannerisms and stance already. She smiled to herself; he learns bloody quick or...She didn't follow that thought to its natural conclusion. But it was a very interesting one!

Alex thought about young David - her fiancé back in 1898 - and hoped she could get back to him. Jericho had persuaded the Senior Time Controller - with Angel Margret's authority - to hold that time for now. That was one date she really didn't want to miss.

Owen smoothed his dress down and pulled his mirror from the handbag and checked it. "Nothing from Jericho or Wilson." He said quietly and Alex peered out the window at the lights of Paris below. "We're here Jackie." Owen groaned; "I thought it would take longer than that. I'm a little nervous about this." Alex patted his arm; "You'll be fine. He's not likely to pounce on you, while I'm around. So, we'll stick together; like bloody sisters." Those words made 'Jacqueline' feel better. Not much better, but it was something.

Another limousine met them at 'Charles-De-Gaulle airport' and carried them to Mr. Klass's fabulous hotel. He greeted them in the exquisite foyer and embraced 'Jacqueline' with some real passion. Before Owen could even say anything, he kissed 'her' fully on the mouth - for some time - until 'she' managed to break away.

Klass gave Alex a peck on the cheek and had a Bellhop show them their suite of rooms. He was impressed that the pair were work colleagues and friends. He smiled broadly; "I now have two lovely ladies to entertain. I am in heaven already."

They would meet for dinner later; in the hotel restaurant - which had a 'Michelin' star - and so they jumped in the lift and were both impressed when the young lift operator announced; "Penthouse Suite." Alex gave Owens's hand a squeeze; "Your boyfriend really knows how to show a lady a good time."

Owen groaned softly; "I need mouthwash and toothpaste. His bloody tongue almost touched my Adam's apple." The suite was stunning. The 'girls' explored and found it had a master bedroom - that made Owen cringe - and two other superb bedrooms. There was a full bar - that made Owen happy - a bathroom with a tub the size of a swimming pool - and a Jacuzzi.

Their luggage was already waiting for them. Two maids appeared and unpacked for them, while they sat at the bar and stared out the huge French windows at Paris. "Let's have our drinks on the balcony." Alex suggested and they sat amongst a jungle of plants and small trees, watching the city below. They sipped their brandies and tried to relax. That's when they heard the door buzzer go. One of the maids answered it. She came onto the balcony and announced there was a gentleman here to see Mr. Klass.

Alex and Owen exchanged an inquisitive look and went to the reception room and found a very tall, good looking and middle aged man waiting for them. He bowed and ran a hand through his short goatee beard. He kissed 'Jacqueline's' hand and spoke softly. They couldn't identify the strange accent.

"You must be Miss Jacqueline; John said you were a little beauty, fresh and sweet. He's taste in everything is absolutely, truly marvelous." He kissed Alex's hand and nodded; "You should be painted by Michelangelo and hung in the Louvre. The painting that is!"

Apparently, he was joining them for dinner. "Just to make up the numbers, but now I see, I am blessed with beautiful, talented company. A pretty young doctor and her gorgeous nurse. John and I will be in good hands; medically speaking." He smiled and accepted a brandy from Alex.

Alex entertained him at the bar whilst Owen excused himself and disappeared into the toilet to check his mirror and inform Jericho that they may have made contact with their prey. He could hear Alex laughing; Monsignor Edwardo de Vance was clearly a witty and charming man.

Owen read his mirror and adjusted his annoying suspender belt; woman's clothes could be a real pain. He replaced his mirror after speaking quickly to Jericho. Monsignor De Vance was - apparently - from this time and place; another millionaire businessman who specialized in the travel industry and was known for his love of beautiful things, old buildings, antiques, food, wine and especially beautiful women. "Another bloody pussy hound." Owen muttered, checking his makeup and dress in the bathroom mirror. He joined them at the bar.

They were joined by a smiling John Klass, who swept 'Jacqueline' up in his arms and kissed her with some real unbridled passion. Alex just had to smile, and Mr. Edwardo de Vance tapped her hand; "He's absolutely taken by your sweet little friend. I've never seen him so open and passionate like that before. You're friend had better watch out or she'll be surprised to find she's quickly Mrs. Klass." Alex nodded and thought, the surprise wouldn't be Owens's!

Finally, Klass left her mouth, but keep a firm grip on her hand. The little group went to dinner and Mr. Klass snatched another passionate kiss from 'Jacqueline' in the damn lift. Edwardo spoke to Alex; "We're expecting our business partner to drop by. He won't stay for dinner - he never does - he's the real brains behind our latest adventure; travels to very unusual destinations." Now that did interest Alex.

The meal was superb - as expected - and John Klass dragged young Jacqueline onto the dance floor, when the band started.

They danced for some time and then returned to the table, with an annoyed looking Jacqueline straightening her dress. Alex rose and headed for the toilet.

Owen sat sipping a well-earned brandy; the dirty old sod had more arms than a bloody octopus. Still, what did he expect? That's what men were like, especially the older ones. He crossed his legs and found John's hand on his thigh.

The hand touched his stocking tops and He thought; 'Bloody stockings are a man magnet.' But smiled and John slapped a kiss on his lips; again.

That's when they were joined by Edwardo's and John's latest business partner. Jacqueline was introduced to him and he kissed her hand. Owen had a real tight feeling inside and quickly made the excuse that she needed the ladies room and walked with little rapid steps to the plush bathroom.

A bloody waiter winked at her as she passed him. He dived in the ladies and waited for a couple of elegant ladies to leave. One stopped and looked Jacqueline up and down; the lady smiled; "Quelle belle petite fille, une vraie beauté. Elle est magnifique." The other nodded her agreement. Soon as they left, Owen peered under each door; only one was occupied.

"Alex, is that you?" He shouted under the door and a voice - laced with sarcasm - answered; "No, it's bloody Santa Claus." He heard the toilet flush and Alex stepped out pulling down her dress. "The good thing with stockings is that only have to pull down your knickers; to have a pee." She washed her hands and saw the look on Owens's face. She carefully dried her hands.

Owen took a breath; "Klass'a and de Vance's other business partner has turned up." Alex nodded; "Yes, Edwardo told me, he would drop by. Apparently, he's the brains behind the whole 'let's have a bloody holiday during the Great Plague outbreak' travel scheme." Owen leaned closer and whispered; "It's fucking Wolfgang Leitcher."

"Little wonder he didn't recognise you dressed like that; your mum wouldn't know you. But he would have known me at once and know we're on his case. Bit of luck that my bladder needed to empty." Alex pulled her mirror out and contacted Jericho.

He told them what to do and they agreed. "Come on Jackie. The girls are on the case." Owen nodded; "Right on sister." Holding hands, they returned to the dinner table, to find their old adversary Wolfgang Leitcher had gone and John Klass had a special announcement to make; Alex and Jackie just stared at the large group of reporters and cameramen.

7. ROMANTIC PARIS.

The little party returned to the penthouse suite in good spirits, especially the men. John had his arm firmly around Jackie's waist and he stopped occasionally to kiss his young bride to be. Alex was holding hands with de Vance and knew damn well that he would be fucking her. She sighed as they pair behind stopped - again - and kissed.

The look on 'Jackie/Owens's face was priceless. Alex had to admit the ring was a stunner, probably worth the price of a house in London. They reached their room, and the foursome had a final drink at the bar in celebration. It was clear that both John and Edwardo wanted the girls in bed, as soon as possible; especially John. He really couldn't keep his tongue out of Jackie's mouth. de Vance raised his glass; "To the ladies that make life worth living." John agreed with that; "Especially the unique special girls."

De Vance kissed Alex and ran a hand down the back of her cocktail dress and took a firm grip on her arse cheek. His tongue was now exploring her mouth. She watched and saw Jackie was sitting on John's lap and John had a hand up her skirt. John was holding Jackie quite firmly and he too, was exploring that moist mouth he loved so much.

Alex felt Edwardo's hand between her legs, and he caressed her fanny gently. "Already nice and wet. Good girl." He slapped his drink down and called over to John; "Come on, the damn bed is getting cold." He chuckled and almost frog-marched Alex to the master bedroom. She watched as John, holding Jackie by the hand, followed. What the fuck is going on? He must know that 'Jacqueline' is not a bloody woman!

Edwardo tossed Alex on the bed and pulled off his clothes. He told her to undress; "Just leave your stockings and panties on." He pulled off his trousers and gripped his adequate erection. Alex was slipping out her dress and bra; watching John slowly undress Jackie. He tossed her dress away and pulled off her heels, slowly pushing her onto the bed.

Edwardo was now knelling in front of Alex on the same big bed and guided her mouth to his urgent erection. She slowly sucked and caressed the cock, all the time watching Jackie, who was pushed up against the mountain of pillow, just in stockings and panties. John had pushed his large cock into her mouth, and she was sucking hard. That really did make Alex's eyes widen. Both men had their cocks sucked, licked and stroked for some minutes.

Then, John - now naked - reached over and pulled a small tube from his bedside drawer. He groaned and patted Jackie's bobbing head; "This is good stuff darling. It's a lubricant and relaxant. It'll open your cute little brown button up for me."

He pulled his cock from her mouth and slowly pulled her panties down and tossed them to one side. Alex could see that Jackie had a full erection and really was quite big. John turned her over and made her kneel 'doggy style' and set about lubricating the anus offered to him. Alex was now on her belly, with Edwardo pulling her panties down. John turned and threw the tube to him. They had clearly done this before.

As Edwardo prepared her arse with careful fingers; Alex pulled herself up and now watched, mouth open as John slowly pushed his cock into Jacqueline's arse. She moaned loudly and gripped the pillows as the big man filled her tight arse hole with his throbbing cock. He gripped her hips and began to thrust; gentle and shallow at first. Alex yelped as Edwardo just shoved his cock into her back passage and started to fuck her hard straight away. He was on top of her, thrusting and talking to John.

The men were bloody comparing the arse's they were fucking!

Alex watched as John turned Jackie onto her side and placed her arm around his neck. He pushed his mouth over hers and kissed passionately, thrusting very gently into her arse. His other hand reached down and took hold of Jackie's erect cock and played with it. Stroking and gripping with his fingers; he was gently jerking her off. Edwardo was the opposite with Alex's bum; he was fucking her bum hole like a dog in heat. He gave her bum cheeks several hard slaps and groaned loudly; telling John just how good the woman's arse felt.

John didn't answer; he didn't want to remove his probing tongue from Jackie's mouth. He was now thrusting a little harder and Jackie was clearly crying; having her tight arsehole fully stretched out by John's big cock. She was jerking her own cock with some passion.

Jackie couldn't hold it anymore and ejaculated over the bed, that made John chuckle and he fucked her to a finish, shooting his large load into her already crammed back passage. He was moaning and groaning in-between passionate kisses. The pair lay panting and gasping against the pillows, with Jackie wiping away tears and having her tongue sucked by her fiancé. John was kissing and whispering to her, then both turned to Edwardo and Alex as she groaned; Edwardo had emptied his load into her back passage and collapsed on top of her, cussing about coming to quickly.

Alex watched as John lifted Jackie onto his lap, his back against the pillows and positioned her legs open, either side of his, with his cock still firmly implanted in her arse. He set about giving his young bride to be, a proper love bite on her neck and shoulders.

Jackie groaned as he bit and sucked with some skill. He's hands caressing Jackie's limp cock, gently but firmly. It started to grow in his skilful fingers. Alex stared at Edwardo, laying on his back and panting heavily. She crept across the bed and slowly pulled John's hands from Jackie's cock and pushed it into her mouth. She was about to give Jackie one hell of a blow job; and she did. John loved this little twist and encouraged her to suck like a 'fucking vacuum cleaner on steroids!'

Edwardo lifted up on his elbows and watched the scene playing out before him. He just groaned and cursed his limp dick. He staggered from the bed and headed for the bar with John calling after him to fetch brandies.

With John's mouth locked on hers, Jackie came in Alex's mouth and she gulped down every drop; to Johns delight - and Jackie's of course - and Alex sat back; smiling. Edwardo returned with four filled glasses and spoke to John. Alex and Jackie took their drinks and sipped slowly; Jackie groaned a little and whispered that John was bloody erecting again, still buried in her bum from the first session.

Edwardo asked John to let Jackie suck his cock whilst he arse fucked her again. To his surprise, John waved that request away, saying "I'll be the only man that has this sweet little thing now." But he didn't mind Alex joining in; they were good friends after all! [The girls that is].

Edwardo sat on the edge of the bed and tugged at his limp dick and drank his brandy without another word. John pulled Alex to him and said quietly; "Don't worry darling. Even after I've had my little princess again, I'll be ready to fuck your brains out and you'll come like a burst fire hydrant."

He was certainly a man of his word. After he fucked 'his little princess' - in the missionary position for some minutes - he wiped his big cock and fucked Alex real hard doggy style, in her wet fanny and she did squirt with some passion. Jackie lay against the pillows and groaned as Alex sucked her cock much to John's delight. The sex marathon continued for another half hour with John changing girls as he liked. He finally came over the pair as they knelt on the floor, shooting his load over their happy faces. They cleaned each other with fingers and tongues while John lay on the bed, panting and groaning. He told Alex that she would be bridesmaid at the wedding and continue her duties on the Honeymoon! They didn't even notice that Edwardo had fucked off, sulking a little. Both 'girls' finished cleaning each other up and the three slept soundly on the big bed until sunlight came through the windows.

8. SECRETS.

John slipped away just before dawn, whispering to a half-awake Alex about the day's activities. He slapped a credit card upon the bedside table and told her to take his 'princess' shopping and buy anything the pair wanted. He smiled and mentioned something about English schoolgirl costumes and Alex nodded her understanding and then dozed off again.

Alex woke Owen with some gentle kisses. She placed an arm around her neck and pulled her to him. Alex [and Owen] were both amazed and a little surprised by the passion of their kisses. Their tongues found each other, and they embraced, pushing back the sheets. Owen said softly; "I really need you Alex. I really need to have a woman... you know....because..." He never finished, Alex just grinned and whispered; "I know darling." She ran a hand down his sweat covered belly and took hold of his cock, which moved and twitched under her gentle caresses.

Owen looked about; "Where's John gone?" he whispered. Alex smiled as she eased his cock into mouth and sucked hard. John had showered and already gone for breakfast, leaving the 'girls' to sleep late. They had deserved it. He had told Alex that - tonight - it would just be the three of them. He had a business meeting straight after breakfast. But he would call his little princess after that.

When Owen was fully erect, Alex climbed on top of him and pushed his cock into her vagina. Nothing was said between the two as she rode him with some passion. He pulled her down to him, kissing and caressing those big swinging tits that he had loved for so long. Now he had them in his eager mouth and his big cock buried in that honey pot he had always dreamed of.

He quickly took control and Alex found herself in the reliable Missionary Position - legs pulled up to Owens's shoulders - being fucked hard. She had an early orgasm and gripped his shoulders as he thrusted with some real passion. They kissed and groaned; Alex couldn't believe how well Owen was fucking her. She tightly gripped his thrusting arse and moaned loudly; "Deeper! Fuck me hard!" and he did. They fucked hard for some minutes before Alex felt the big orgasm arrive; she screamed and cursed a little and spurted hard and fast. She lay bag gasping; her legs were shaking, and her stomach was tight. Owen groaned and came inside of her. They fell together, kissing passionately, hands and tongues everywhere.

Finally, Owen raised his head and smiled; "For fuck sake Alex, we should have done this a long time ago." Alex agreed and ran her tongue down his neck and kissed his heaving chest. Resting on his elbows and still firmly inside her; the pair whispered and kissed. Then Owen chuckled and pulled a face; "My bloody arse still hurts." That made Alex laugh and Owen groaned as his cock slipped from her soaked vagina. Alex kissed him and told to roll on his belly. She carefully examined his anus.

She slapped his arse; "Your well gaped from your husband's big cock. But he knew how to fuck your bum hole properly. You'll be fine. Your young and it will spring back."

They lay in each other's arms and kissed a little. She ran a finger down his lips and smiled, pushing back her dark hair which fell about her face. "He'll be straight back up your bum tonight; make no mistake about that. You're he's little princess now. I think he actually adores you." She kissed Owen, who sighed; "I could have married so well, lots of money, travel anywhere and be adored. What a bugger that I'm dead!"

They both laughed and embraced each other again. Alex kissed him quietly and gripped his cock; "If you can manage it. You can see why your husband loves to poke a bum hole."

Owen just grinned and Alex laughed as his cock erected in her hand. "Fucking right I want some of that." He said and Alex rolled on her belly and arched her back. "Find that bloody tube; it's good stuff." She pulled her bum cheeks apart and Owen just groaned, scrambling to find the elusive tube.

He was like a bloody bloodhound and found the damn thing quickly; coating Alex's bum hole with care and then mounted her with real urgency. He had wanted this for so long. "Fuck me how you like. Enjoy yourself darling." She said softly and Owen did as he was told. He fucked her arse hard, and Alex had another early morning ejaculation, spurting over the pillow clutched between her legs. He fucked her for some minutes before, he too, ejaculated in her back passage with some real passion. She lay in arms, still with his cock up her arse and the pair kissed and cuddled until Alex sighed and remembered they had a breakfast meeting with Jericho and Wilson.

She gave his bum a slap and they headed for the bathroom.

"The only thing that bugs me, is putting on war paint all the time." He held her hand and grinned. She just smiled; "I'll help you with that, just do as I say." Owen stopped and placed a right smacker on her lips and grinned; "I just thought I did." They both laughed and jumped in the bath together. They would be a little late for breakfast, but they really didn't care.

Alex – giggling a little – mentioned John's request about the schoolgirl outfits and Owen just sighed; "Did he say with stockings or socks?" Alex smiled; "With his money, both I expect." They both laughed and Owen carefully removed his large engagement ring and hid it. "Better not wear that to breakfast." Alex agreed with that. But what had happened must remain a secret between the pair; both knew and accepted that.

9. ON THE TRAIL OF OLD WOLFGANG.

Jericho and Wilson waited at the breakfast table for the 'girls' to appear. It was going to be a late one. "They've done a cracking job. I'm proud of our ladies." Jericho chuckled and sipped his excellent coffee. Wilson just sighed; "You mean our lady and our resident transvestite." Jericho smiled and looked up; "Their here. Go on; stand up when ladies join us. It's the done thing in posh places like this." Wilson and Jericho stood, and the 'girls' joined them.

A waiter appeared immediately, and they both ordered their breakfast. The pair was starving after their huge fucking session.

Wilson [and the waiter] was impressed; Owen/Jacqueline wanted full English. Alex had her usual, scrambled eggs on toast. "Hungry baby brother? Had a hard night, did you?" Owen stuck up a very un-lady like, single finger and accepted a coffee from Alex.

Alex and Jericho couldn't help but chuckle as a grinning Wilson held up the morning paper; the 'social' pages were very interesting. "I won't read it verbatim, but Mr. John Klass - multi millionaire business tycoon and one of Europe's most eligible Bachelors - has announced his surprise engagement to a young English Nurse, Mademoiselle Jacqueline Jones. The happy couple will marry in Rome and honeymoon in the Bahamas' at Mr. Klass's private island. They will divide their time between his English mansion in Surry and his villa in Italy. Their wedding will be a social highlight of the year." He slapped the paper down and added; "Congratulations my dear. The honeymoon should be a real cracker; full of surprises for the both of you."

Owen/Jacqueline just sipped his/her coffee and smiled at the waiter as the big breakfast was placed before him/her. Jericho admired Owens's calm demeanor and called the briefing to order.

He explained that old Wolfgang had the ability to travel in time;

so he must possess a time portal device. "That's how he hooked these two very rich men; he must have proved his 'machine' worked and they fell for it." Wilson said and finished his breakfast.

Owen leaned back and said softly; "It must a con. He's milking millions from them with a fake machine. Klass and de Vance are being scammed." Everyone nodded at that. Alex sighed; "But why?" Jericho smiled; "When we find that out, we will crack this case wide open, and Owen can go back to being a man; if he wants!" Now Wilson did laugh at that; Owen didn't but finished his breakfast in silence and helped himself to more hot buttered toast.

"The most important thing is that you and he never meet, until we are ready." Jericho told Alex who nodded. "That may be hard to do, Owens's enraptured fiancée is throwing a huge party here tonight, and I bet old Wolfgang will be invited."

"Now that could be a problem." muttered Wilson sipping his coffee. Jericho grunted; "Just come up with a way to avoid him for now. Our new girl has clearly fooled him, so she should be ok." Wilson wiped his mouth; "You mean our boy in drag." But he did smile at Owen, who again said nothing and finished his toast. His grapefruit was delivered, and he started on that. Wilson added; "At least his appetite is back to normal. Pity about the rest of him." On that note, the meeting broke up.

They walked to the lifts, the 'girls' in front chatting. Wilson found his eyes drawn to Jacqueline's swinging hips and firm bum. Christ, he thought, she really does have some kind of arse. "Makes a wonderful woman, doesn't he. Nice arse." Jericho chuckled, slapping Wilson on the arm, adding; "I think every male in the room is watching them." Wilson coughed; "I was looking at Alex's bum." Jericho smiled; "Yes, course you were."

Wilson started the plain white Renault Express car and followed the black van as it pulled from the hotel's underground car park and headed south. Jericho was consulting his mirror; "The driver is a Claude Vernon; a local petty thief and con man. The only passenger is our old friend Wolfgang."

Discretely and with great skill, Wilson followed the van unseen to a modest villa, on the outskirts of Paris. It sat in a few kilometers of woodland. A guard with a shotgun slung over his shoulder, opened the big gates and the van disappeared up the drive. Jericho checked his mirror; "There a five people in the place now, not counting the guard on the gates."

Wilson nodded and parked up a nearby gravel lane. "Anyone of interest?" Jericho shook his head; "Just more petty criminals and a young woman; unknown details. That's odd."

The pair jumped from the van and walked the crumbling brick wall that surrounded the place. They quickly found what they were looking for; a part of the wall had fallen, and they could climb over with ease. They walked slowly; the Villa's east side came in view. That's when they heard the barking. They both stopped and stared as three big dogs came bounding out the woods. Jericho just sighed and stopped time; they now had just half hour to reach the house and find out what's happening there. They ran, panting and swearing through the open front door and stood gasping and a little amazed.

At the foot of the stairs was a stark-naked young woman, wearing a big black collar and carrying a tray with several cups on. Jericho checked his mirror; "Caroline Burkeman, from 1890; went missing that year from the human timeline, she's reported as a lost soul." They exchanged a concerned glance and walked past her. "We'll deal with that later." Jericho muttered, noticing the stick marks across her back and buttocks.

"Bastards." Was all Wilson said and Jericho quietly agreed.

They found the 'machine' in the large back reception room. There were computers, cables and pipes everywhere. It looked like a giant bell jar; Jericho checked his mirror and grunted; "As suspected; no time portal there." Sitting at the desk was a huge man with an eye patch. His face was a mess; Wilson consulted his mirror; "Another petty criminal. This one use to make his living as an illegal bare-knuckle boxer."

The other man was much younger, wearing a smart suit. They both noticed the pistol and shoulder holster under his jacket. Jericho pulled his orb out and sighed with relief; "No demonic activity." He replaced the clear little ball and looked about. "Let's fix it." He said and Wilson grinned; he knew just how to do that.

The pair returned from 1890, after dropping the girl off - now suitably clothed by Supplies - and headed for the hotel. Old Wolfgang wasn't at the house; he must have suspected something and used his time portal device to get out.

Wilson stopped at the little gift shop in the hotel foyer and chuckled; the headlines of the afternoon edition [of the local paper] were about the mysterious fire at a modest villa in the suburbs of the city. It said there were no casualties or injuries, but its main reception rooms had been gutted. It did mention that the property was owned by a certain Monsignor Edwardo de Vance. That made him stop in his tracks and he called Jericho over. Jericho read the article and stared at the lifts. They walked quickly to the lift and told the young operator; "Penthouse Suite."

Jericho whispered; "de Vance is in this deeper than we suspected. Let's get to the girls." Wilson nodded and the operator opened the doors and they raced to the suite. Wilson called out for Alex and Owen, but there was no reply. Wilson pushed open the door to the master bedroom and shouted for Jericho. Alex was tied up on the floor; gagged and bound tightly; she was stark naked and very wet.

Wilson pulled the gag from her mouth and produced his pen knife and cut the ropes. "They took bloody Owen!" She shouted, sobbing. "I was in the bloody bath and heard all the shouting and suddenly Wolfgang and some big thug grabbed me. But they took Owen!" Jericho handed her the brandy bottle and she took a huge swig and then a deep breath. "They knocked John down; he's unconscious on the bedroom floor; he tried to stop them grabbing Owen. He needs an ambulance."

Wilson had pulled off his jacket and Alex wrapped it around herself. "They grabbed Owen." She repeated a lot calmer now. She took another deep breath; "Bloody de Vance was with them." Jericho and Wilson nodded.

"Did he have his mirror on him?" Jericho asked and Alex thought hard; "It's in his handbag. Yes, I think he had his handbag with him." Jericho pulled out his mirror and sighed; "The fucking thing is offline." Wilson was on the phone telling reception to call an ambulance. He replaced the receiver; "Police and ambulance are on the way. We best get the fuck out of here." Jericho nodded and operated his mirror and the team disappeared.

10. RESCUE THE 'DAMSAL' IN DISTRESS.

John Klass sat up in private hospital bed and just stared at Jericho, Wilson and Alex. Finally, he said; "Christ I didn't know that the medical profession stuck so bloody close together. Wish I could forge that sort of loyalty in my own bloody workforce."

Alex offered him some water and he sipped it slowly. Jericho asked him, if there was anywhere that de Vance would have taken 'Jacqueline'. Klass groaned; "My little Princess. I'll pay any bloody ransom to get her back. Anything." He gripped Alex's hand. Jericho and Wilson passed a strange look and Alex repeated Jericho's question. He stared up at the white ceiling and suddenly smiled, then groaned; his head hurt despite the painkillers. He nodded; "I always check out my new business partners and de Vance doesn't know that I know all about his little hobby."

Alex had to ask; "What hobby is that, John?" Mr. Klass leaned forward and said softly; "He keeps a basement apartment at his antique shop on the Rue St. Michel. He doesn't know that I know all about his little hobby." Alex asked again, this time with some real concern; her imagination was running wild, and it wasn't pleasant.

John Klass sighed; "He keeps exotic cats there. He loves cats." Alex really sighed with relief. Jericho thanked him and the team walked down the corridor and found a suitable linen closet to operate their mirrors in, without being seen. Wilson rubbed his chin; "Little princess? What the fuck is that all about?"

Alex shrugged her shoulders; "Just a pet name he has for Jacqu...Owen." Wilson sighed; "I've heard everything now. Bloody Little Princess my arse." They disappeared.

The big orderly placed his mop against the wall and wondered why the visiting English Consultant, Doctor and male nurse had gone in the cupboard. He shrugged his shoulders; the dumb English couldn't find a turd in a space suit. He walked over to the door and knocked; shouting in French, that the exit was at the bottom of the stairs. He got no answer and so pulled open the door; grinning. His smile disappeared and so did he, running down the corridor, yelling loudly for his supervisor.

They found the large and impressive shop, filled with antiques from around the world. The stock must have been worth millions. They trooped in and found a big man sitting reading a paper. It was the bare-knuckle fighter from the villa that Wilson and Jericho had committed a little arson on. He grinned at Alex and rose from his chair. Wilson smiled and swung a left hook that would have put a elephant to sleep. The big man stood there and rubbed his chin. He said something in French and just grinned. "Oh fuck," Was all Wilson said.

Alex sighed and pointed her mirror at the big thug and he flew back against the wall and slid down into a heap. But he was still grinning. Wilson rubbed his hand and just shrugged his shoulders. Jericho checked his mirror. "This way, the basement stairs are behind that door [which resembled a cupboard] it's picking up Owen."

They made their way down the stairs; Jericho's mirror hadn't located any other human on premises. Wolfgang and de Vance weren't there. "Slippery bastards." muttered Wilson and they pushed open the big door at the bottom of the stairs and stepped into the basement. It was a good job for the team that Alex still had her mirror out and set to stun. The lion stared at them and then jumped. It fell to the floor and lay silent. They stepped over the massive beast and walked to the cage.

Owen sat tied to a chair. A gag in his mouth and his beautiful dress torn a little; his stockings were torn and ripped; his shoes gone. Wilson had the lock on the cage open in just a few seconds and started to cut him free. Alex pulled the gag from his mouth and gave him a kiss. "You all right?" She asked. Owen nodded; "I wondered when you lot would be bothered to come and get me."

Wilson cut him free and he stood and stretched; "They didn't want to knock me about because they were about to get two million US dollars off Mr. Klass for my safe return and apparently, he wouldn't pay for damaged goods." He gestured to the big cat; "He's name is Sugar. Don't ask me why."

Everyone chuckled and Jericho operated his mirror. The big cat [and the big thug] would wake some minutes later, no worse for being stunned by Alex's mirror. But the big man had a small bruise on his chin and that hadn't happened for years from a punch and he taken quite a few in his time.

Alex sat in her favourite armchair by the fire and flicked through a magazine on shoes. Wilson was snoring happily in his big chair and Owen was sprawled on the sofa, stroking Mr. Parker. He said softly; "Now this is the sort of cat I don't mind." Alex grinned and put her magazine down. She walked to the drinks tray and poured the pair a brandy. Owen took it with a smile. That's when they heard Jericho come through the front door, talking to Mr. Harris. He came in and accepted the brandy offered by Alex, who poured herself another one. Jericho slumped in his chair and Wilson awoke and accepted the brandy from Alex, who returned to the tray muttering; "Maybe I'll get to drink this one."

Jericho called the impromptu briefing to order. He told them, that the Senior Time Controller had picked up a breech from Paris at the time they were there. It had to be Wolfgang. He had jumped to Moscow in the year 1881.

Monsignor Edwardo de Vane was on the run; not from the Gendarmes, but hordes of creditors. He was in debt up to his eyeballs. Little wonder he gone along with Wolfgang's plan to fleece Mr. Klass. Jericho sipped his drink and smiled; "Margret's given the go ahead to go after Wolfgang and find out what the fuck he's up to now. We'll be visiting English nobility; Alex will be Lady Tibb's [again!] Wilson would be an American Journalist from the Washington Post; there to cover the new Tsar's coronation [Tsar Alexander III] and Owen would be their travelling, Footman."

Jericho, would, of course, play Lord Tibbs [no surprise there!]

Alex sighed; "I can't travel without a proper ladies maid. Not in those times, it would really draw attention to us." Jericho nodded; "Ruth can play that. She love's going on a mission with you." Alex shook her head; "She's on the Collector's Entry Course. She's having a go at being a Collector." Jericho nodded; he had forgotten about that. "Well, I'll see if I can find someone." He said and sipped his brandy.

Then he smiled; "Oh, I've spoken to Angel Margret and she's quite happy for you to return to 1898 and say your piece with that ex- fiancé of yours. We'll leave for Moscow when you get back. Owen will accompany you. You're not going back alone." Alex smiled and said thank you quietly. Jericho could really surprise people with his compassion sometimes.

Owen sighed; "I could play Alex's maid. I fooled a lot of people last time and I should manage that again." Jericho chuckled, but Wilson groaned; "I told you he has gone strange. He wants to dress as a bloody woman again."

Alex smiled; "Miss Jacqueline Jones will make a lovely lady maid. I don't mind." Jericho grunted; "That's agreed then. Off you two go and have a good time, Alex." She grinned and headed upstairs with Owen behind. Wilson slumped back in his chair and shook his head; "He'll soon be wandering around the bloody lighthouse in a pretty frock." Groaning He added; "I need a bloody brandy." Jericho said nothing, but just smiled.

11. HYDE PARK; LONDON - 4th AUGUST 1898; REDUX.

Alex slowly twirled her parasol and looked - yet again - down the small roadway and sighed loudly. She really smiled at Owen, who looked utterly gorgeous in a late Victorian dress and bonnet.

"Sweet Jesus, you look lovely. You should have been born a woman. Little wonder old Klass went nuts over you." Alex said softly as Owen/Jacqueline smoothed down his summer dress and just smiled. Already several young - and not so young men - had tipped their hats to the 'ladies' waiting at the roadside.

Owen pointed to the ice cream seller and muttered; "I wonder if he will now give me a big one?" Alex laughed out loud and looked a little shocked until Owen just sighed; "Bloody ice cream. When I was plain old Owen, He gave me a small one and you a big one." Alex nodded; she had forgotten all about that.

"Dressed and looking like that; you'll get plenty of big ones and I'm not talking about just bloody ice creams." She chuckled. Owen smiled at her and said quietly. "That Calvary troop is coming up the road." Alex grinned and held his arm; "David is really going to take something with him to South Africa and it won't' just be my picture in a locket." Owen laughed at that and tipped his parasol back to get a better view. He noticed that the Dickens's family were packing up their picnic and going home.

They were totally oblivious of the fate that could have befallen them. The original timeline now played out; the only exception being Jacqueline accompanying Alex on that faithful day.

The troop of cavalry passed by, resplendent in their red and blue uniforms, mounted on dark horses. The young officer turned his head a couple of times, looking at the pair. Well, at Alex actually [no surprise there] then stopped and turned his horse about.

The troop halted at the Corporals command. The officer rode up and jumped, with some grace, from his horse and lifted his helmet. "My God, it is, it's you Alexandra!" He said with some unrestrained happiness in his voice. He was a strapping specimen and when he removed his helmet, Owen/Jackie saw that he had the looks too. He was looking at David quite differently now. Alex just stared at him, pretending to be totally surprised. Finally, she muttered; "David Shaw...David Shaw-Wilson. My word, you're in the army now?"

He nodded and slapped his horse's neck, grinning. "This is 'Thunder', father bought him for me, when I received my commission into the regiment. How have you been? Vikki would go nuts to know that I bumped into you!" Alex was pretending to be clearly shocked by this unscheduled and unforeseen meeting.

She turned to the smiling Miss Jacqueline Jones and introduced her. A good friend from the medical School that Alex had attended. David kissed Jackie's hand and really did smile at her. David said quickly, glancing back at his troop; "I must run. Duty calls, I have to get this bunch back for their lunch. But we must catch up, you and your friend come to 'Franco's' tonight at about seven, just tell them; you're the Shaw-Wilson party. See you then." He kissed Alex's hand - twice - and was most reluctant to let go. He also kissed Jackie's hand - twice - and told Alex to bring her friend tonight; for the second time.

Alex realized that the scene had changed; David had not mentioned about bringing his sister Victoria along. The pair of ladies walked to the top of the road and hailed a cab. Supplies had booked the pair into a very decent hotel; just around the corner from the restaurant that they would meet tonight.
The Maitre d escorted them to David's table. They were stunning, both wearing the height of ladies evening fashion with silver tiaras, white gloves and matching pearl choker necklaces. Every man's eyes were on the pair as they sat and smiled at David. He had stood for the ladies and now eased himself down and smiled.

"You both look absolutely stunning. Surely, all that effort wasn't just for me?" He whispered and downed his whisky in one hit. Alex leaned across the table and tapped a finger on his lips. "Everything is for you of course." Jackie lifted her wine glass and sipped very gracefully; "Alex really means that." She placed the wine glass down; "And I echo her sentiment."

Alex chuckled at the look on David's face and whispered to him; "Jacqueline is a very, very special lady. I bet you can't say no." and kissed his cheek.

David was totally bemused; what did Alex mean by that?

The young man found out after dinner at the ladies hotel room. He sat on the sofa and just stared, gripping his whisky with both hands. The girls stripped down to their exquisite underwear [for the time and place]. Both were wearing tight bodices with Alex's big breasts hanging over the top; nipples erect. Both were wearing matching black silk panties and stockings. Alex bounced over and with Jackie's help, soon had the young man standing naked.

They both knelt in front of him, and Alex took hold of his cock; it was an excellent size. The pair shared his erect cock for some minutes; their mouths working the tip and shaft with some expertise. David groaned and stroked both their heads.

While Jackie sucked his cock, Alex bent over in front of him, and he slowly slipped down her panties. They dropped around her ankles, and she opened her legs a little and ran a hand between them and opened her vagina. He could see that it was wet and ready. "I got prepared a little early." She giggled and knelt back down on the floor, lifting her bum to him. Jackie had stopped sucking his cock and gently guided him towards Alex's pouting fanny. "I really think that she wants you." Jackie chuckled and helped the young man insert his cock into Alex.

The pair was soon fucking hard on the floor as Jackie sipped some whisky and watched. Her erection was pushing at the tight little panties, and she really wanted to fuck. She was a little surprised by the thoughts of young David firmly buried in her bum hole, while Alex sucked her cock or....Jackie grinned at the idea of fucking Alex, while David fucked her. "This could be very, very interesting." she muttered.

That's when they heard the loud banging on the door and raised voices; it was the Hotel Detective with two uniformed constables apparently. They were after the two 'prostitutes' that the young officer was with.

David shouted; "I'm just coming!" and he did. Alex pulled from him, his cum running down her thighs and with Jackie following, ran into the bathroom. David grabbed his underpants and pulled them on. The detective had his pass key in the lock and they burst through the door.

The big man didn't smile and shouted; "No use hiding in the bloody bathroom you tarts, come out now!"

He received no answer. A uniform constable was already handcuffing the panting and distressed David. The other pulled open the bathroom door to find the small room empty. David just stared at the empty bathroom in total disbelief. Apparently the desk clerk had bought the matter of the two girls and young soldier to the detectives notice.

The detective stared at the women's clothes strewn about the place and sighed; "A fucking fine young gentleman and a Queen's officer, dressing up in bloody woman's clothes. What, did you pay the tarts to undress and fuck off so that you could wear them and wank?" They dragged the protesting young man away. His very influential father would soon put an end to the matter and David would disappear to South Africa. The detective would receive ten pounds [a great deal of money then] for his lapse of memory about the incident.

Owen and Alex hid behind the old boathouse and wondered how the hell they could get in without being seen. "At least you've still got your bloody knickers on!" Alex grunted and the pair just had to laugh. That's when they saw young Ruth appear and walk back towards the lighthouse, her Collectors Course work under her arm. Owen shrugged; "Leave this to me." Alex just sighed, Owen had a Sharpe mind and was quick witted, but this will top any story; he's come out with before.

Dinner was good - as usual - Owen and Alex shared a little smile. Ruth served them soup and just shook her head; the bloody lengths some Temporal Detectives will go too, in cracking a case. But she smiled at young Owen and carefully ladled his soup out.

He really did look good in women's clothes, well, women's underwear!

12. FAREWELL'S AND HELLO'S.

Alex and Jacqueline watched the big steamer pull away from the dock assisted by a small tugboat. David had flatly refused to meet Alex and he certainly didn't want to meet 'Jacqueline' again! He would keep their dirty little secret [since revealing it would also reveal his part in the unfinished orgy] and one had been a bloody transvestite.

He left for the war a little sad; but a wiser man now Miss Alexandra Featherstone was now forgotten and he would find a decent, respectable woman to marry on his return. He, of course, never did.

They walked back to their cab, as Alex wiped a tear away and Jackie gripped her arm. The young cabbie jumped down, pulled off his cap and opened the door for the ladies. "Said goodbye to a sweetheart have we Miss?" He asked Alex - noticing her tears - and took her hand, to assist her into the cab.

Alex smiled and nodded at the young man with rough, but gentle big hands. He smiled; "I waved off my younger brother Freddie last week. He's with the Warwick Regiment. I'll admit a few tears myself that day." Alex patted his arm and thanked him for his consideration and honesty about the tears. She stared at his big blue eyes and smiled at Jackie who slowly nodded.

"What's your name young man?" Jackie asked him as he helped her join her friend in the cab. He grinned; "Albert Ma'am. Albert Grimes." He replied and slowly closed the door. The cab pulled away, heading for a decent hotel away from the dock area. Jackie and Alex gripped each other's hands and whispered together. They both agreed that Albert Grimes - despite the terrible name - was a very good looking and fit young man.

They giggled as Alex kissed Jackie and the pair really did smile. "To quote the wonderful Sherlock Holmes; the games a foot." Jackie said and adjusted her little bonnet. The young cabbie was about to get a tip he would always remember!

He came through the hotel's tradesmen's entrance and up the

back stairs; he knocked softly on Room 7 and was told to enter. He stepped through and almost dropped his hat which he held with both hands. The two ladies were standing by the big double bed in nothing but stockings and panties holding hands. Alex gestured him over; "Me first and I bet you will not be able to refuse Jackie; she's a very special lady." Albert just smiled as the pair pulled off his clothes and both knelt before him, taking turns with his cock. They jerked and sucked it until it grew and stiffened; it was a good size and Albert tugged down Alex's panties and pushed her on the bed.

He fucked her with some skill and stamina whilst kissing and caressing Jackie. He seriously thought he had died and gone to heaven and wondered what Alex meant about a 'special Lady' – he couldn't wait to fuck Jackie!

Young Albert Grimes lay on the big bed, naked and panting. He had fucked Alex good and hard for at least twenty minutes before he came deep inside her fanny. Alex lay next to him, stroking and kissing his face. The young man had certainly given her a good orgasm and they both watched Jackie, bending over his cock, sucking gently, caressing it back into an erection. Alex pulled her tongue from his mouth and gestured to Jackie; "Yes, or no?" she giggled. Albert stared at Jackie's cock swaying as she worked his.

He groaned as her tongue rolled around his pulled back foreskin, then across the wet tip. He turned to Alex and whispered simply; "Yes."

Alex grinned and passionately kissed his mouth. She reached down and patted Jackie. That was the signal for her to stop sucking and mount the young man. "You're going to love this, Albert." Alex whispered, smiling.

He groaned as Jackie squatted over him, facing away and slowly pushed his cock into her willing arse. She lowered herself down and he really did groan, watching her bum consume his cock. Alex kissed his face and ran her fingers through his dark hair. "You're really going to enjoy this." He moaned and nodded vigorously. Jackie began to speed up, gripping his thighs and pushing down and lifting up quickly.

"Now you'll really enjoy this part." Alex grinned at him and slid down the bed and squatted in front of Jackie. She grabbed her erect cock and pushed it into her own bum. Jackie gripped her shoulders and co-ordinate the fucking with some skill. Young Albert groaned and cussed; his eyes widened at the sight, and he couldn't actually believe what he was seeing.

He rose up on his elbows and ran a hand down Jackie's back. "For fuck sake, this is just unbelievable, fucking great!" He had never fucked a woman in the arse - or another man for that matter - and loved it. Gwyn, his young wife certainly wouldn't let him anywhere near her bum. The girls were giggling, moaning and panting.

 The scene was Jackie in Alex's willing arse and young Albert in Jackie's equally willing back passage. The happy threesome fucked for several minutes until Jackie finally ejaculated deep into Alex's back passage and gripped her tight, frantically kissing her shoulders and neck. Albert let out one big groan and shot his lot up Jackie's bum. The girls collapsed on the bed, kissing each other and then turned back to Albert. They went to work together on his now flaccid cock. They sucked and cleaned it thoroughly, while Albert almost cried with sheer pleasure.

The lovers took a small break for some whisky and while Alex continued to suck Albert's cock, Jackie climbed on his chest and bent over his face, gripping the headboard with both hands. Albert didn't hesitate and pushed Jackie's cock into his mouth. He sucked clumsily, but Jackie couldn't care less. Alex laughed at the sight and went back to sucking his cock; hard and fast. She then mounted him, her arms around Jackie and rode the young man with some determination.

Alex felt the big one coming and groaned loudly as it started in her stomach and rolled down her to thighs. She lifted herself off and with shaking legs; squirted over Albert's erection and belly. Panting and moaning, she pushed herself down hard on his cock again and bounced up and down with real vigour. She clutched Jackie's waist and had another one hell of a climax and cried a little with pure satisfaction and delight. Jackie couldn't hold out either and came in Albert's mouth. She groaned with pleasure as he swallowed and continued to suck, until Jackie hoarsely whispered; "Enough darling."

Albert sat up against the pillows and sipped his well-deserved whisky and watched the girls rolling about the bed, fingers and tongues probing each other, kissing passionately, whispering and laughing. Much to Albert's amazement and pleasure they ended up in the '69' position licking and fingering each other's bum holes. He managed a smile, remembering Alex saying that Jackie was a very special woman. He had to agree with statement; fully. But he believed that both were certainly 'special ladies'. He fell asleep, the empty whisky glass falling from his hand. He woke with a start and looked about. The girls had gone. He rose slowly and dressed. He was normally honest with young Gwyn; but this was one secret that he would keep from her. He actually had troubling believing it himself.

The girls walked back to the lighthouse slowly; hand in hand until Mr. Harris appeared in the doorway. He announced that the team was in the study - they had received another mission file - and dinner would be served right on time; as usual. Alex sat at the dinner table and smiled at Owen. Then she recalled David. Alex had laid a ghost to rest and she was happy now.

EPISODE 6: "ALEXANDRA AND THE PIRATES."

EPISODE PROLOGUE: "A strange pirate ship is attacking craft around the islands of the West Indies, robbing ships and sinking them. The islands are British Colonies and so the British Government dispatches the frigate HMS Steadfast to investigate and put an end to the pirate raids. So, Lt. Commander Jeb Parker and his crew arrive at the islands in pursuit of the pirates. There is one slight problem; the year is 1954 and there have been no pirates around the islands for almost a century! Jericho and Team 74 are on scene because the pirate ship [THE BATHSHEBA] is from the 1700's! Alex has some fun with the British navy and an 'Errol Flynn' lookalike!"

75 Minutes approx. Episode Warnings: Alcohol – Smoking - Strong language – Violence [including sexual violence and murder – Strong graphic sexual references [including references to prostitution] – Mild horror.

NOTES: The original version of this story is published and appears in the **TEMPORAL DETECTIVES:** Book Series 2 – Episode 4 entitled: **"THE PECULIAR PIRATES OF PARADISE BAY."** This is a special EXTENDED episode of the original story.

CAUTION: Recommended for 18+ only.

1. HMS STEADFAST.

Lt. Commander Jeb Parker stared down at the docks and sighed; what a fucking shithole and this was the only dock that could take a ship the size of HMS Steadfast. The bloody islands were more suited to fancy yachts, and it had taken some careful maneuvering to get her in safely. Lt. Tom Hollis smiled at the expression on his skippers face.

"That was like trying to stuff a fist up a mouse's arse. Any closer and we would have to use bloody Vaseline." He chuckled and the bridge phone buzzed; he pulled it up and said simply; "Bridge Aye." He listened and groaned, replacing the receiver; "The old man [Admiral Foster-Jones] wants another bloody sit-rep." Jeb leaned back against the steel plates and sighed - again - the 'old man' was aboard HMS Courage - the flag ship of the small fleet- that was spread across the Caribbean and did love his bloody situation reports.

Jeb smiled at his friend; "Tell him, we parked her without any scratches and are reviewing the bloody situation, which I think is total bollocks." Tom chuckled; "I'll think of something to say without you losing a stripe." Jeb pushed his cap back and stared at the dockside and the jungles that loomed over the small town. The heat was sticky and oppressive; he was amazed that people paid a fortune to holiday here.

"That rich yank must be nuts. A fucking old pirate ship attacked his yacht and robbed him of everything, leaving him in a lifeboat in his underpants." Tom smiled; "With his third wife, much younger of course and his teenage daughter. Apparently, the yacht crew was dumped in a small rubber boat, five in that and three in the large lifeboat. American democracy and equality?"

Jeb smiled; "The bit I liked was the description of the pirate captain. For Christ Sake, an eye patch with large sword and fancy hat? The yank clearly had been smoking something."

Tom shrugged his shoulders; "Two other yachts that were attacked gave the same description. The captain looked like he stepped from a pirate movie." They turned to young Ensign Harold 'Harry' Kiddminster who jumped from the bridge ladder and saluted. Tom and Jeb returned the salute slowly. "What is it, Harry?" Tom asked. The young man smiled and rubbed his hands

together, he looked like a schoolboy on his summer holidays.
"I went through the reports Sir. Unbelievable!" and stood smiling.
There was a silence and Jeb sighed, folding his arms; "Apart from
being 'Unbelievable' what did they actually contain?" Harry stared
at him, then grinned; "Oh right yes Sir. Just all the women
interviewed by the Coastguard and Island Police said the same
thing about the pirate captain." He stood, nodding to himself.

Tom and Jeb exchanged a sad glance; Harry wasn't the brightest
prospect the Royal Navy had ever recruited. Tom said slowly;
"What did all the women say Harry?" It was like drawing blood
from a stone. Harry nodded again and said with real enthusiasm;
"They all said he was dashing, handsome and courteous to them.
A couple apparently said he looked a lot like Errol Flynn." He
rubbed his hands together and smiled broadly.

Jeb turned to Tom and said quietly; "Fucking great, now we're
chasing bloody Errol Flynn around this shithole: terrific." Tom
laughed and turned to Harry; "Anything else?" Harry nodded.
Tom really did sigh; "What is it Harry?" Harry shuffled his feet
and said quietly; "That team from home are flying into day. The
experts on Piracy; Historians I suppose."

Jeb laughed out loud; "That's exactly what we needed; a group of
old history teachers to tell us about piracy from hundreds of
bloody years' ago. Now that's bloody unbelievable!" Tom patted
his friends arm; "I'll get Farmer [the Boson] to arrange a pickup
for them. The Purser can arrange the cabins, when they actually
come aboard." Jeb just nodded and wiped his face. "Bloody
pirates my arse." He said softly, then added; "Bloody piracy
experts; my arse."

Tom left the bridge laughing, giving Simon 'Snakes' Simpson [the
Helmsman] an amused glance. 'Snakes' just smiled and stood by,
hands behind his back. This was a rum assignment he thought;
chasing an Errol Flynn look-a-like, so called pirate captain around
the bloody West Indies. If it wasn't so fucking serious to the top
brass, it would make a great comedy film. But given the captains
mood; he kept those thoughts to himself. The bridge phone
buzzed, and Jeb picked it up; "Bridge aye." He said and listened
to young Norman 'Nobby' Bannister, who was on communications
in the radio room.

"Just had a message from King George Airport Sir, the civilian experts are just going through customs. It will be about two hours before they arrive." Jeb wiped his face; "Inform Mr. Farmer please Nobby." Replacing the receiver, he turned to Simpson and said, "Bloody piracy experts my arse." Simpson did laugh this time.

Jeb really didn't laugh, standing on the bridge with Tom and the slow-witted Ensign watching the 'experts' arrive. They were coming up the gangplank with Mr. Farmer; the two seamen carrying their luggage were smiling. The officers could see why. Tom actually whistled and removed his cap, wiping his face and neck with his hankie. "Sweet Jesus, I'm in the wrong bloody profession. Do you think it's too late to become a history or piracy expert?" Jeb just stared at the woman, as she stepped onto the deck, quickly assisted by a very happy young seaman who offered his arm.

"That is the most fucking stunning woman I've seen in years." Tom muttered and Jeb really couldn't disagree. Harry held up the piece of paper and said, "It's a Professor J. Tibbs from York University with his assistant - a Mr. Owen Jones - the big man must be Wilson Franklyn, a Yank from Boston University apparently. The woman is a Doctor Alex Cappanni, also from York University. She sounds Italian to me."

Tom sighed; "With a name like Cappanni, that would be good guess Harry." Jeb smiled at Tom; "Brains and beauty in a bloody neat package."

 Alex was wearing a flowery summer dress and blue jacket, her dark hair tied with a blue ribbon and matching low blue heels. She was dressed in the height of women's fashion for 1954.

Tom grunted; "She looks like a bloody movie star with those dark glasses." They both watched as she walked down the deck, followed by her colleagues. Tom whistled again, watching her hips swinging gently with her little steps. He wiped his face again; "What a fucking gorgeous arse." Again, Jeb couldn't disagree with that observation.

The Ensign coughed and Tom turned to him but didn't take his eyes off Alex's bum. It seemed to fascinate him as it swung gently, the peach shape a little visible through the thin summer dress. He wiped his brow and spoke quietly to Harry.

"What is it Harry?" The Ensign gave him another piece of paper; "That Police Inspector will be here at six o'clock. He'll have dinner with us in the officer's mess. Apparently, there was another attack, yesterday morning; French owned motor yacht."

Tom stared at the paper and nodded; "Have the guests been told to eat in the Officer's Mess and what mealtimes are?" The Ensign nodded; "Mr. Farmer is seeing to that Sir." He hesitated, then said; "Just one problem with Doctor Cappanni, Mr. Farmer wants to know where and when she can use a shower." Jeb and Tom answered together; "She can use mine." Then the pair laughed and tossed a coin for it. The Commander - to his hidden delight - won.

Tom handed the paper to the happy Jeb and tapped it; "Do you see who authorized their assistance in this matter?" Jeb took the paper and stared at it; "You must be fucking joking!" Tom shook his head; "That's the real deal. That's the Prime Minister's signature." Harry grinned; "Do you mean our Prime Minster? The English one?"

They both stared at him, and Tom said quietly - the sarcasm in his voice went over Harry's head - "Well, it's not the bloody French one is it." Harry nodded and asked; "What times should I tell the Doctor that she can use your shower Sir?" Jeb grinned; "Any bloody time she likes." Harry really couldn't understand why the ship's two senior officers thought that really funny. When he informed Mr. Farmer, he was still no wiser as Mr. Farmer also just laughed.

2. SAMSON THE STEWARD.

Alex had unpacked and was quite impressed with her small cabin. It was clean and functional. She tried the single bed, bouncing up and down. She giggled and thought, not bad, obviously hasn't seen much action. But then this is a bloody warship full of men only'. Now that thought did make her smile. The only thing it lacked was a shower; but she had been told to use the one in the captain's cabin; any time she wished. The day had been warm and sticky, so Alex stripped naked and wrapped her long dressing gown around her and gathered shampoo, towels and scented soap together.

That's when she heard a soft knock and she shouted; "Come in."

The door opened and the Officer's Steward stepped in, holding a bundle of towels - freshly laundered - the young man smiled; "More towels for you Miss. I'm Samson, the Officer's Steward. I'll be looking after you this trip." He placed the bundle down.

Now Alex really did smile; Samson was a strapping African male with a gorgeous smile. He looked very smart in his 'Summer Whites' and asked if there was anything else the lady required. He was at her service. Alex grinned; a good service was just what she wanted and maybe this young man could provide it!

Alex sat on the bed stark naked with her legs open and held up with both her hands. Samson - now stripped down to his Navy regulation shorts - had his head between them; his big tongue working her open fanny and swollen clitoris in conjunction with his probing fingers. She groaned and threw back her head; he was really good and certainly knew his way around a woman's cunt. Her fanny was dribbling, and she moaned out loud.

She gently pushed his head away and slipped from the bed; kneeling in front of him as he stood. She frantically pulled down his shorts and actually gasped; her hands quickly grasping his huge erection. "Thank God for Vaseline." She whispered and began to devour the big cock with her eager mouth.

She licked, sucked and caressed the monster cock with some real expertise and passion. Samson groaned and stroked her hair, staring at those big tits; he couldn't wait to get his mouth and hands on them. Alex thoroughly enjoyed the taste and feel of his big black cock but wanted it inside of her; urgently. Her cunt was soaking in anticipation. She stood and guided his cock to the bed, stopping only to grab a small jar of the magic lubricant from her bedside table. He watched with a really big grin as she lay on the bed, her back pressed against the pillows and smeared lots of the cream in and around her fanny. She smiled and handed Samson the jar. She opened her legs and lay back, watching his big gentle hands coating his cock.

He mounted her slowly and gently. But soon the bed was creaking and shaking under his powerful thrusts. Alex had pulled her legs right up and gripped them tightly with both hands; the big man was pumping her hard; his mouth on her heaving breasts. He gripped each big nipple with his teeth and sucked hard. Alex groaned with pleasure at the little pain he was causing and ran her hands across his broad back.

They fucked for some minutes and Alex had a orgasm to match the big cock buried deep inside her. She groaned and cursed, squirting hard and fast. The big man didn't stop, and another climax quickly followed, and Alex slapped a hand over her mouth to prevent real loud screams escaping. The pair was so engrossed in their passionate fucking, they didn't see Owen slip into the room and sit on the small chair by the door; he really was grinning.

Alex looked over at him and smiled; whispering to Samson; "Can you handle my friend as well?" He glanced across to Owen; who was stripping down and was very surprised to see that he was wearing black stockings and suspenders, with matching little black panties under his trousers. Samson sighed; his mother always said that white people were a strange bunch. Alex's tongue was in his mouth and so he could only nod. Alex told him to lift her up and place her on the floor, which he did with no effort.

Owen joined the pair on the floor and Samson was surprised - again - to find the young man - who was very effeminate and actually quite pretty, probing his arse with his tongue. This could be a fucking interesting trip he thought.

After giving the groaning Alex another huge earth-shaking orgasm; Samson lay on his back on the floor and watched the pair taking turns with their mouths and hands on his cock. Alex left the big cock to Owen/Jacqueline and squatted over Samson's face; he greedily ate her soaking, quivering fanny with great relish and skill. He watched as Jackie applied more Vaseline to his throbbing cock and her own arse.

Samson groaned as Jackie - facing away from him - also squatted down and gently inserted the big cock into her yielding arse. Pushing down slowly and gently at first then started to thrust up and down with more speed. Ten minutes of Jackie riding him was enough for Samson; he groaned loudly and spurted his cum deep into her willing bum hole.

Samson sat on the floor watching Alex cleaning up Jackie's bum with her tongue and fingers. Mum was right; he thought and sipped a glass of well-earned water. The pair was soon back

working his cock with their mouths, taking turns and then both running their tongues up and down his hardening shaft.
Another erection quickly appeared. He fucked the pair again for at least twenty minutes and smiled as Alex sucked her friend off, while he fucked her doggy style on the floor. She clearly thoroughly enjoyed swallowing down Jackie's load. He came inside Alex and the happy threesome came to an end. Samson had to get to the officer's mess and lay out tea and coffees for the officers and visitors. He left the pair kissing passionately on the floor, swapping his cum from Alex's fanny.

He walked down the corridor and really couldn't stop smiling; yes, this could turn out to be a very interesting trip; his only regret was not fucking Alex's peach shaped, beautiful bum. But had a good idea that he would enjoy that before the trip was over; he reassured himself and headed for the Officer's mess.

3. THE POLICE AND THE EXPERTS.

Inspector John Johnson sat in the officer's mess and sipped his coffee, watching the team of piracy experts helping themselves to tea and coffee. In particular he watched Alex - no surprise there - and shook his head. If He wasn't happily married to Joyce....he dismissed the thoughts as the team sat at his table and Jericho introduced everyone. They shook hands all round and Jericho asked if there were any new developments.

The Inspector nodded and told the team about the latest attack. Again, the dashing pirate captain had treated his captives well; especially the two women on board. "A dead ringer for Mr. Errol Flynn apparently." He muttered and pushed the typed report to Jericho.

They were joined by Jeb and Tom [the bridge being manned by the 2nd Officer; Lester Caine] and the impromptu briefing and meeting started.

It was explained that the 'pirates' had now raided no less than five craft, from a large luxury steam yacht to smaller sail boats. They hadn't actually hurt anyone; just robbed them. The name of their old ship was 'The Bathsheba' and apparently had seven cannon on each side; old fashioned cannons that fired bloody big metal balls! Owen found that particularly interesting and informed the meeting of the only recorded ship with the name

'Bathsheba' was indeed a pirate ship, from about 1710, who was based on a small island called 'Paradise Bay' in the West Indies. It appears that the ship and relatively small crew disappeared - probably lost in a storm - around that year. The captain was a dashing fellow - apparently - who liked rum, women and piracy. He was called Captain Joshua 'Dagger' Jones or 'Captain Casanova'. His real name was Orville Suckles!

Jeb grunted and - with some sarcasm in his voice - asked how that was relevant to chasing pirates in 1954? That rebuke went right up Owens's nose; but he smiled and pointed out, that if the modern 'pirates' had named their ship after the old pirates, what else were they copying? Like, was their base on the small Paradise Bay Island? Tom nodded his approval at that; "He has a point skipper." Jeb just sighed and stared at Alex, sipping her coffee with some elegance. He really did want to fuck her.

Able seaman Jim Stanley appeared saluted and gave Jeb a message just received in the radio room. Jeb rose from his seat and smiled; "Well, it seems that our dashing pirate captain and his motley crew have been spotted by a Islands Coast Guard plane. About one hindered and fifty nautical miles south of..." He hesitated and lost his smile, adding dourly; "Some one hundred and fifty nautical miles south of Paradise Bay Island." Even the Police Inspector had to smile at that revelation. "We're getting underway immediately. Are you settled in your cabin Inspector?" John nodded; he was looking forward to a nice sea cruise; especially one that was free. He smiled at Alex; and something pleasant to look at.

Jeb and Tom headed for the bridge and HMS Steadfast was soon steaming from the docks into the open ocean. The weather was wonderfully clear and warm. The Inspector joined Alex and Owen on the deck, watching the Islands fading behind them. They chatted for a while and watched the sink sinking below the horizon and they returned to their cabins; dinner would be served at six o'clock.

Wilson commented to Alex and Owen that both the mess stewards were African. That was the only positions black men - regardless of their abilities - could obtain on Navy ships in this time period. Owen thought he was wrong on that point; the British Navy had employed black men since the times of Nelson and probably before even that. But he kept those thoughts to himself; maybe Wilson was thinking of the American Navy.

The meal was excellent, and everyone enjoyed the food and drinks; the British Navy certainly knew how to look after its crews; well, the officers anyway.

They were joined by the ships surgeon; a very big Scotsman called James Fergus. "The ship's doc with two first names." He quipped and drank whisky. He and Alex really got on; the doctor was impressed that Alex was a member of his profession and admitted that there should be more female doctors. Alex liked him for that and his sharp humour. Owen said quietly to her; "At least we can understand James; not like bloody 'Jumbo'."

Jeb was recalling some of his wartime adventures aboard the ships he served on during the last conflict [the Second World War]. He ruefully admitted he couldn't tell some of the more 'spicy' tales because there was a lady present. Owen made everyone laugh - including Alex - when he said, "Where?"

After more drinks and some smoking, the little party broke up and everyone retired to their cabins. Tom was standing the first half of the night watch on the bridge. He leaned against the shuddering wall [from vibrations of the engines] and watched the dark horizon. That's when the bridge phone buzzed, and he answered it quickly; it was the fore look out reporting small lights to their starboard. He walked to the window on that side and lifted his binoculars.

The lookout had sharp eyes; indeed, he could just make out the little lights flickering in the distance. They looked strange; not like ship's lights flickering in the darkness. He turned to the sailor next to him and gave him the glasses. "What do you make of that Pat?" The very experienced sailor took the binoculars and stared at the lights for a minute or so. He lowered the glasses and said quietly; "I think that's a craft on fire. That looks like flames."

Tom grabbed the phone and buzzed Jeb's quarters and woke him; explaining what was happening off starboard. Jeb was on the bridge some minutes later and the pair stood watching the flickering lights with their binoculars. Jeb ordered the helmsman to change course and the ship headed for the lights. He went to the chart room and worked out positions and speeds. "We should be there in about two hours." he muttered, and Tom told Pat to arouse some of the crew for action if necessary.

The rest of the men could sleep for now; there was no need to sound 'general Quarters' - just yet. A message was sent to the radio room [which was manned 24 hours] to call Navel operations and the Flag ship about the situation and change of course. Jeb also asked if any radio traffic had been picked up; that was a negative, apart from a couple of local fishing smack's chatting with each other.

HMS Steadfast made good headway on the quiet sea and reached the position just before midnight. A recovery crew - lead by Tom - was prepared and a small boat lowered in readiness. Jeb watched from the deck. It was a small lifeboat; he could make out the 'Mother Ships' name on the side; 'The Memphis Queen'.

There was wreckage still floating on the surface, a mast complete with brightly coloured sail caught his eye. There were bits of deck furniture and other stuff floating about. He ordered Tom's boat away and the boat headed for the other little boat.

Tom called him up on his 'walkie-talkie' - there were two people in the boat - a young boy and an old woman: probably the boys grandmother, by the look of things. Jeb told a sailor to rouse the surgeon and get the medical team ready.

Jeb also told the sailor to wake Dr. Cappanni; a woman doctor may be very useful in this situation. Tom called back to say that the old lady insisted that an old wooden ship flying the skull and bloody crossbones had attracted their yacht. The pirates had killed her daughter's husband and abducted the woman. She was the boy's mother. They [the pirates] had forced the old lady and her grandson into the small boat and set them adrift. She didn't know what happened to the other three crew members.

"So much for a dashing and charming pirate captain; he's just another lowlife murdering bastard." Jeb muttered and ordered 'Action stations'. A siren rang out about the ship, rousing the crew and its passengers.

4. 'COITUS INTERUPTUS'.

Alex was kneeling on the floor, groaning and panting as Samson thrust deep into her bum. He was gripping her quivering cheeks and groaning a little himself; thoroughly enjoying her gaping bum hole.

He loved fucking the woman wearing just her black stockings and matching heels. He looked across to his friend and fellow steward Solomon and grinned. He was fucking 'Jackie' in the Missionary Position on the bed. The pair was locked in a passionate embrace; their mouths firmly locked together. Jackie was also wearing black stockings and a matching Basque, gripping her well-built lover's shoulders with both hands.

Her long legs up and around the small of his back; the big African was also firmly buried in her arse, and they were having one hell of a fuck.

Samson was now on his back, with Alex riding him in the reverse 'cow-girl' position. He was thrusting up as she pushed down; groaning, cussing and panting from her exertions. She rubbed her wet fanny furiously with one hand as her big tits swung freely, her nipples standing up from the sexual passion being generated by the lovers. She stared at Jackie and Solomon, who had also changed position; they were now on the bed, lying on their sides, with Jackie's arm around his neck and her mouth firmly fixed on his. He was pumping her yielding arse with some real determination, and she loved every deep thrust.

Solomon slapped the pale arse several times and groaned loudly, when he could get his tongue out of Jackie's hot wet mouth. Alex had one hell of a shuddering orgasm, spurting down her thighs and making her groan loudly; Samson cussed loudly and came deep in Alex's arse, his whole-body trembling with passion.

He pulled her head to his and the pair kissed with unbridled joy. Solomon also finished, squirting his cum into Jackie's back passage with some frenzy. They both lay groaning and kissing on the bed. Samson asked the girls if they could do something a little special and Alex whispered; "I think we just did."

That made the boys laugh; Samson wanted Solomon to fuck Alex's arse - if she could take another big cock so soon - while he fucked her cunt. She could suck her friends cock at the same time. Alex loved the thought of a double penetration by the two big men.

Alex nodded her agreement; still panting. But first her and Jackie needed to suck their [the boys] cocks back to erections. The boys agreed with that, smiling broadly!

But their sexual plans were thwarted by a loud knocking on the cabin door. The sailor called out; "Sorry to disturb you Miss, but the captain wants you to assist the ships surgeon; we have survivors coming aboard. Shall I tell him your coming?" Alex sighed softly; "I just bloody well did!" Then she called out that she was on her way.

Samson and Solomon were well disappointed by this turn of events but had to accept the situation. Alex and Jackie kissed them both passionately and promised - if possible - that they would have more fun later. The two big Africans regretfully agreed and cleaned themselves up and dressed. Alex and Jackie quickly dressed and headed for the bridge. The two men gave each other a 'high five' and smiling broadly; returned to their cabins.

Solomon confessed to his friend that he had never had sex like it. He really wanted Jackie again; "She's fucking gorgeous, and I don't give a fuck that she has a big dick!" Samson just grinned and slapped his friend's shoulder; he felt the same about 'her'.

Owen whispered to Alex - as they walked awkwardly towards the bridge - that Solomon had whispered to him just how much he had enjoyed Jackie's arse and wanted to know her better; he definitely wanted more of her. Alex just smiled and really needed to clean up.

Her panties were already quite damp from Samson's cum running out and juices from her open fanny. He had shot his load quite deep inside her bum. "We'll try and arrange another little meeting and we can both enjoy them again." She said quietly and the pair arrived at the bridge.

5. A SURVIVORS'S TALE.

Alex and Owen stepped onto the bridge and found organised chaos. But Jeb was firmly in command of the situation, giving orders for the pursuit of the pirate vessel. "We should outrun the bastards easily, despite them having a four-hour head start." He was talking to Tom, who nodded and ordered the ships armoury opened and weapons issued to the assault party.

Jeb smiled at Alex and asked her to attend the medical suite; the old woman was in quite a state, she had seen her son-in-law murdered in front of her - and her daughter dragged away to suffer a terrible fate - at the hands of the evil bastards. The boy had a few cuts and bruises but seemed alright. He hadn't witnessed the murder of his father; thanks to his grandmother shielding him.

Alex nodded and left immediately. Owen joined Jericho and Wilson on the deck outside the bridge and the temporal Detectives spoke very quietly amongst themselves. Jericho told them what the old woman had said before being taken to the medical bay. "She says that the men [the pirates] called a big rough fellow who had a long black beard, 'Captain and Skipper'. She said he was clearly in charge. I think something has happened amongst the pirates; that are definitely not the previous descriptions of Captain Casanova."

Wilson nodded; "Maybe the dashing captain has been removed from command for some reason." Owen folded his arms; "On pirate ships, the captain could be replaced for various reasons; normally removed permanently from life as well. Something had certainly changed with them and not for the better." The other two agreed with that.

Tom stepped from the bridge and walked past them, turning to say - unsmiling - that the bastards had been picked up on the radar and Owen had been right; they were headed for Paradise Bay. He also said that he would be leading the assault on the pirate ship. They couldn't just let their big guns shatter the pirate ship with the woman prisoner on board. He stopped and asked Owen what would happen to her.

Owen sighed and ran a hand over his face; "Probably gang rape her, then throw her overboard. But if this was the 1700's, then they would have kept her alive and sold at her; at the white slave actions that were held around these Islands back then."

The officer grunted and walked away shouting for Jim Grieves, the ship's Chief Petty Officer. They had an assault party to get together. Wilson took a deep breath; "This has taken a really shit turn for the worse." Jericho and Owen couldn't argue with that assessment. Now the bridge was relatively quiet, they stepped in and saw Jeb bent over the radar scope.

Both hands were gripping the small cabinet. He really didn't look happy and was cussing under his breath. He grabbed the bridge phone and yelled down, that he wanted a bloody technician to the bridge; NOW. He turned to a young sailor and told him to find Tom and tell him to stand down - for now - the bloody pirate ship had simply disappeared from the radar.

The temporal team exchanged glances; they were all thinking the same thing; did the bloody pirates have access to a time controlling device? That would explain how they were here in the first place and how they avoided detection from the modern era ships and planes.

Jeb looked up at them and sighed; "I'm dropping off a small motor launch with three crew; to search for those missing three men from the yacht. I don't hold out much hope, but we must do it." Jericho nodded and asked what happens next. Jeb almost smiled; "We're going to pay a visit to Paradise Bay."

The team stood on deck and watched the small motor launch being lowered into the water. It disappeared into the darkness; two big, powerful search lights sweeping the dark waves. Owen grunted with some sadness as he discretely checked his mirror; "Little Raj the Collector has just reported collecting four souls from here. They all say, they were murdered by bloody pirates. The bastards ran them through with swords and threw them overboard like garbage." Jericho said nothing; they really couldn't tell Jeb that his search was totally useless; how would they explain how they knew?

"I need a fucking brandy." Owen muttered and they headed for the officers mess. He found Alex there, drinking a brandy and sitting alone. He sat down and asked how the old lady and the boy was.

Alex sighed; "She's sleeping - I hope - I gave her a sedative. Thankfully the boy didn't see his dad murdered, but I don't think he'll play pirates again." Owen nodded and sipped a most needed brandy. He then explained about the missing men and Jeb's decision to sail to Paradise Bay. Alex grunted; "He's a couple of hundred years too late."

Owen smiled; "But we can always pop back, can't we?"

Tom appeared and accepted a brandy from Samson; the big African Mess Steward and joined Owen and Alex. He was clearly disappointed at being stood down; for now. The three chatted and Tom admitted they [the captain and him] were mystified how the pirates had avoided detection these past few weeks. Owen and Alex exchanged a knowing glance, but obviously said nothing about the possibility of a time controlling device.

Tom gripped his glass and said softly; "That poor bloody woman." He sank his drink in one go and rose, bidding the pair goodnight.

They were joined by Jericho and Wilson, who both accepted brandy from Samson. Jericho's plan was simple; when the ship docked at Paradise Bay, the team would jump back to 1710, rescue the woman and find the time controller. "You make it sound so bloody simple Jericho." Owen said and smiled. Jericho nodded; "Supplies will meet us back there and kit us out. We're going to play pirates." Wilson smiled and sipped his drink; "Normally I would be delighted, there were many black pirates back then and they were treated as equals amongst the pirate community. But somehow, all this murder and abductions have taken the fun out of it." They all agreed with that.

Alex asked Owen if there were any pirate women. He nodded; "Yeah. There was and they were considered worse than the bloody men!" Now that revelation did make Alex smile. "No playing the bloody tart for me then." She said softly. The little briefing broke up and everyone returned to their cabins with Alex checking the old lady and the boy before retiring, well, after a little more unexpected fun.

6. DOCTOR CRIPPEN, I PRESUME?

Alex had washed herself in the small cabin sink; she couldn't use the captain's shower at this time of night and stood on a towel, quite naked, and washed her crotch, bum and thighs. That's when she heard a soft knock on her door. Wrapping her dressing gown around her naked body, she opened the door. It was a smiling Doctor James Fergus with a brandy bottle in his hand and two glasses. "I thought we could have a night cap and discuss our patients if it's not too late." Alex smiled and gestured the good doctor in. He sat on the only chair and Alex sprawled on her bunk, sipping a very decent brandy. They chatted about the poor woman and her grandson for a few minutes. Then James smiled broadly; "You're quite a woman Alex with no prejudices and apparently no inhibitions. I had a concerned young steward in my surgery wanting to know if he was mentally ill because he really enjoyed fucking a young white man in stockings. I reassured him he wasn't, but the act is illegal on his majesty's ships. He was quite graphic about yourself and your young friend. Who you fuck is your business and quite legal. But what the boys did wasn't. [At the time homosexual acts were a serious crime that could end in long imprisonment] You understand my problem here as an officer, never mind as a doctor." He sipped his brandy and Alex eased herself up, wondering which one had betrayed them, Samson or Solomon? But that didn't really matter now.

"What are you going to do James?" she asked, making sure that her dressing gown had fallen open a little. He shrugged his shoulders, carefully watching her exposed legs and a little glimpse of her magnificent breasts. "That's up to you. Do you want me to forget about your young friend?" He rolled the glass about in his hands and smiled a little. Alex finished her drink and sighed. "I would be very grateful if you forget the whole thing, James. I really would."

He smiled and placed his empty glass on the small table; "Now my dear, exactly how grateful is that?" She leaned back against some pillows and pulled off her dressing gown, letting it drop to the floor and slowly opened her legs, resting her hands on her knees. "This grateful." Was all she said.

There was no real foreplay, the horny blackmailing doctor kept his socks on and only stopped – after undressing – to slap a little KY jelly on his erection which was adequate, before mounting Alex. He eased his cock in and gripped the headboard with both hands. He fucked Alex hard with good, measured thrusts. He made no attempt to kiss her or make any kind of conversation; he simply fucked her as hard as he could in the missionary position. Alex leaned her head back and stared at the drab grey/white ceiling and comforted herself that poor Owen wouldn't be thrown in the brig and worse – possibly – Jericho and Wilson discover what went on.

At one point she stared at the small travel clock on the table and worked out that the doctor had been fucking her for some twenty minutes without any sign of finishing yet. She quietly asked him if he wanted to change position and he grunted a simple 'no' and continued to fuck her. She stretched her long legs a couple of times and James bluntly told her keep still and bloody keep her legs open. He fucked her for a few more minutes than groaned between gritted teeth; he had finally ejaculated. He leaned on his elbows and set about her breasts with his mouth, staying inside of her. He wasn't gentle and used his teeth on her nipples which she really didn't appreciate. But she said nothing and just endured his slobbering over her tits.

Finally, he appeared satisfied and pulled from her and sat on the bed, panting. He grabbed the discarded towel from the floor and carefully wiped his cock. Alex asked for the towel, but he just dropped it back on the floor and stood. He dressed without a word as Alex sat on the edge of the bed and stared at him.

He picked up his brandy bottle and the glasses and walked to the door. He turned and smiled a little; "I want to play with you some more. I have some nasty little games in mind that we can play. It involves some pain for you, but you won't mind if I keep your dirty little secret. So, when I've arranged to get some rope and weights, I'll invite you to my cabin. I really don't expect a refusal." He now really smiled, adding; "We'll start with a good spanking because you've been so naughty, then I'll tie your hands and breasts, hanging some decent weights from each big nipple and make you dance for me. That'll be the start. It will get more interesting and a little more painful for you, but I will really enjoy that."

He opened the door and checked the quiet corridor, then smiled again; "You know if I report you and your friend, you will be struck off and your young friend will go to prison, so I know you'll submit and play my games. I'm particularly anticipating hanging weights from your Labia Majora with crocodile clips and watch you crawl around the floor making dog noises. Oh, yet my dear, we'll have some fun." He disappeared through the door, closing it quietly behind him.

Alex stuck up a single digit and muttered; "In your fucking dreams you sick bastard." And knew that he would be disappointed in his perverted fantasies and stood by the small sink and cleaned herself; again. She would speak with Owen in the morning, then decided he should know immediately about the betrayal and the dirty doctor's demands. She called him on her mirror. He seriously wasn't impressed with this turn of events.

7. PARADISE BAY - PART 1.

HMS Steadfast dropped anchor at Paradise Bay in the late morning. The team stood on deck and took the stunning sight in. "It's bloody beautiful; totally Un-spoilt by tourism and untouched by commercialism. But in fifty years the place will be swarming with wealthy tourist and three huge hotels will dominate the beaches." Owen spoke to Alex, who could only agree - sadly – with his assessment of the little islands future. Tom would lead an armed party ashore - to reconnoiter - before the 'Experts' would be allowed to land. Alex - as usual - protested about that, but Tom just smiled at her; "Captains orders." And that was that; it wasn't up for discussion.

Wilson lowered the binoculars he had borrowed from Mr. Farmer and gestured towards the hill that dominated this side of the island. "There appears to be some kind of old fortification up there; looks well overgrown by jungle, but it's there all right." Owen took the binoculars and nodded; "It looks like a small 17th or 18th century fort. I think that could be worth a look when we get ashore."

Frustrated at not having any glasses, Alex stopped a passing young seaman and asked to borrow his glasses. He stared at her and grinned; Alex was just wearing a tight-fitting white t-shirt and shorts - short shorts - and slowly handed the binoculars over without a word. She really smiled at the boy and could have 'borrowed' his clothes, boots, watch and wallet - if she asked - and he wouldn't have hesitated handing them over!

She watched the landing party hit the beach, Tom and the Chief Petty Officer with six well armed ratings. They left one man guarding the boat and headed into the jungle without hesitation. Harry - the Ensign - joined the team; "The Executive Officer [Tom} was in the pacific Theatre of the last war; he knows about jungle fighting." Everyone just stared at the Ensign and really wanted to laugh; he was watching the deployment with a very old telescope. He grinned and held it up; "Old family heirloom. My family has been at sea for centuries. My Uncle Frederick is an Admiral." Wilson sighed; "That explains a lot."

It was almost noon before the 'experts' received the go ahead to land at Paradise Bay. They were escorted by Jim Grieves [The Chief Petty officer] and two ratings [the men were still armed] and made immediately for the old fort. It was a hard slog through the jungle and the Seamen were impressed by how easily Alex coped with it. They didn't know that Alex had already endured three adventures in steaming jungles already!

The little fort was in ruins, with crumbling walls and jungle vegetation growing over everything. Owen discretely consulted his mirror; "Built in 1705 by Spanish forces, who were driven from the island by a British Invasion in 1709; not the British navy but mainly British pirates and Buccaneers. The island became a pirate port until 1722 when the British navy did arrive - in force - and put an end to the piracy in these waters. That lasted for nearly two hundred years."

He looked about and pointed down towards the south walls; "There's a cemetery there. Let's check the graves." They walked carefully down to the old cemetery and Owen just sighed. You couldn't actually make out any graves; there were very few headstones and time and jungle had covered almost everything. Nevertheless, Owen walked the place, reading his mirror.

He stopped close to the fort's wall and waved a hand about; "All the remains can be identified with a mass 'Body Check'; all their souls were collected between 1705 and 1724; except this one." He gestured to the ground next to him. "These human remains belong to a missing soul; Caroline Harker who was born in 1919. What was the name of the woman taken?" He wiped his face and neck; the heat was sticky and oppressive.

Alex stood - hands on hips - and sighed; "Bloody Caroline Harker. Does it tell us when she died?" Owen shook his head; "No soul, so no date of death. But it has to be between the years the cemetery was in use; if that helps." Jericho grunted; "No, but it does confirm they have a time controlling device. That means we must go after them and close down their little operation, before we lose more souls to the darkness."

Jericho operated his mirror and sent a request to Supplies; the team would be jumping back to the Paradise Bay of the pirate era. Owen rubbed his hands together and practiced his pirate talk - well, his version of it - with phrases like; "Aye Jim lad! Splice

the main brace - whatever that fucking was! Aye, its buried
treasure lad! The others just stared at him and sighed. Wilson
slapped him on the back; "You crack on baby pirate brother!"
They did one last walk through of the old fort, looking about for
any clues.

Alex stopped by the doorway of a large room, by the gateway
and almost smiled; "Anyone else getting Déjà vu here? I certainly
am."

Wilson nodded and rubbed his chin; "You're right, I feel it too,
this gateway and that room. They're important to us in some
way." Owen tapped his mirror; "According to Historical Records
this was the South gateway and that was the powder store. They
stored gunpowder in there for their cannons and muskets."

Jericho chuckled; "Well, when we're back there, don't light a
lamp or strike a bloody match near the place; come on." They
met Joseph from Supplies at the rear of the fort; he shook hands
all round and smiled at Alex; "Anna [the teams regular costume
designer] has come up with a cracker. She loved your request for
a pirate lady's costume of the period." Alex smiled broadly; "No
playing the bloody tart for me this time." She told the others.

They watched Jericho - resplendent in his pirate Captain's outfit -
practicing with his sword. Wilson and Owen watched with real
interest and then smiled at Alex. She gave a little curtsey and
pushed her three-sided hat back on her head and gestured to her
blouse and trousers. Both men smiled; her magnificent breasts
were almost escaping from the loose silk blouse; pirate female
captains didn't wear bras or bodices. She tapped her sword,
dagger and pistol; "Well, I'm ready boys."

They all looked again at Jericho. Wilson gripped Alex's arm; "Is
he any good with that damn sword or is he just acting the part?"
Alex did smile; "He was a fencing champion at University, and I
know that he fought five duels with the sword; and won each
time. He's pretty good with a pistol too." Owen whistled; "The
bloody things we find out on these missions; Jericho fought
duels!"

It was time for Owen and Wilson to get into their costumes;
Wilson was particularly happy with his. He carried two pistols and
a huge cutlass sword, with thigh length boots and bright red

jacket and trousers. Even his big hat was red. He smiled at the others; "Red and black go together so well. I'm 'Bad Red; the feared African pirate'. Terror of the Spanish Main!" He turned and groaned upon seeing Owen. He was dressed as a 'buxom pirate wench' in a beautiful dress and small hat. Wilson rubbed his face and stared hard; "Are they real? They bloody look it."

He gestured to the fine bosom of the 'pirate wench' and was quite puzzled. Owen just grinned; "Wouldn't you like to know!" Alex gripped 'her' and waved the sword about; "Hands off my wench Bad Red! She's my girl!" She and Owen giggled.

Jericho just sighed deeply; sometimes he wished he had an office job. The team jumped back to 1710 and headed for the fort; the island was now a bustling pirate town with bars, brothels and a very good bakery that served delicate little French patisseries. Now that did surprise them; the cakes were excellent! They had to drag Owen…sorry, Jackie away after devouring half a dozen.

8. PARADISE BAY - PART 2.

"Bars are huge source of information; especially pirate bars." Jericho informed them and stopped at the first bar, just up from the beach. They stood outside and Alex shook her head and gestured to 'Jackie'. "She's not going in there!" Jericho shrugged his shoulders; the sign above this particular establishment declared 'The Rapist's Rest'. They quickly moved on with Wilson muttering; "Well, it is a bloody pirate hangout. It's not likely to be called the bloody 'Choir Boy's Bar and Grill."

The next bar had a name Alex didn't approve of either; 'Big Willy's bar and brothel.' They found a bar, just yards from the fort whose sign declared; 'The Queen's giving Head.' Wilson peered in and shook his head; "I think the patrons would like Owen too much dressed up like that. They all look like that 1980's pop singer; Allan Insect." Alex sighed; "You mean bloody Adam Ant." Jericho pointed to the establishment opposite; 'Blackbeard's Tavern'.

 Everyone nodded and they pushed through the doors; jumping aside as two burly men threw another screaming man past them. He landed in the sand and lay groaning. The two men stared at the team and the biggest one smiled at Jackie; he had no teeth and was missing fingers from both hands.

"Hello my darling. Are you out on business?" He said almost drooling. Alex just grabbed Jackie by the arm and almost frog marched her into the pub, saying; "Back off dog breath, that's my girl." The big man seemed quite upset by that remark but saw both Jericho and Wilson - sorry; Bad Red - had their pistols out. He grinned and bowed; "This way ma'am. Old Percival means no harm by it."

Jackie whispered; "Percival? A fucking pirate called Percival?" Alex told her to watch her mouth; she was a lady after all. "Dog breath?" Muttered Wilson and Jericho just sighed deeply - again. The place was packed with pirates and their women; all were drinking, some were singing, two couples were actually fucking over a table and one pirate looked suspiciously like he had died some time ago. The flies around him seemed to indicate that; oh, and the smell of course.

The team avoided that table. They sat down and a large lady came over, her huge breasts swinging freely; "What's you order luvvie's?" She asked and smiled at Wilson.

They ordered four jugs of beer and she demanded tuppence [two pence nowadays]. Jericho paid her and she bit each coin and nodded. She bought the beers back and stroked Wilson's arm; "I'm cheaper than the fucking beer my darling." Wilson just grunted and grabbed his beer. Disappointed, she wandered off - hand up her skirt - scratching her lice ridden arse. She returned and slapped four tankards down, grinning with her almost toothless mouth; "Four tankards of old Blackbeards surprise ale!" She announced.

Wilson stared into his jug and slowly inserted a couple of fingers, pulling out a large centipede and dropped it on the table; it appeared to stagger away despite having so many legs. Jericho leaned over the table and nodded towards the big table by the door; it was packed with, what seemed to be, a single ship's crew. The big man at the top of the table had caught his eye.

"Now doesn't that big ugly bugger match the old lady's description of the pirate captain?" They all nodded: he certainly did. Alex watched in horror, as a rat stuck its head out of his huge beard and was given some cheese by the big pirate.

"He keeps a fucking rat in his beard!" She gasped and took a sip of beer; she coughed violently. It tasted like warm horse piss.

Jackie just stared at her beer. "I think I have a dead snake in mine." and pushed the beer away. Wilson tapped Jericho's arm and both stared at the big man's chest, through his open filthy shirt. An Aztec emblem hung there. Wilson carefully checked his mirror; "Time portal device." He said simply. Jericho smiled; "That's our man." He was about to sip his beer but stopped and placed the jug down slowly. He didn't smile; "There appears to be an eyeball floating in mine. I think I know why it's called bleeding Blackbeards Surprise Ale: you don't know what the bloody hell is in it!"

"Here's looking at you kid!" Jackie giggled and then fell silent as the others just stared at her.

A skinny, ragged little man slid up to Jericho and whispered in his ear. Jericho nodded and slipped the man some coins. He spoke softly for a minute or so and slipped away. Jericho pulled the team closer and spoke softly; "That's our man. Now calls himself Captain Ratbeard and he commands 'The Bathsheba' since Captain Casanova's demise. According to the little man, he has a woman on board. So, our missing lady must still be alive; for now."

Jackie whispered; "What happened to our Errol Flynn look alike?"

Jericho rubbed his chin; "Apparently some of the crew mutinied over his gentle treatment of women prisoners. They demanded their right to rape them. So, there was a punch up and Casanova, with some loyal men; were thrown overboard. Luckily for them, the Bathsheba was docked in the bay, here at the time. That little man was one of the men that stayed loyal. They want their ship and Captain back."

"Where's the captain now?" whispered Alex.

"In the fort and guess who is the real big man around these parts and lives in the fort?" They all shrugged their shoulders. Jericho grinned'; "The big pirate himself, a man called Captain John Breholt. Strangely enough he simply vanished from history in 1711 - a year from now - and was never heard of again. He is a missing soul." Now that did impress the team.

Alex smiled; "Well, if Ratbeard and his scurvy crew are here, then who's guarding the woman on the ship? A really good time for a rescue don't you think?" That was quickly agreed upon and they left the tavern and looked for a rowboat. They found one on the beach - yes, actually on the beach - the sole occupant was trying to row back to his ship, but was so drunk, he couldn't launch the damn thing and was attempting to row in the sand. They quickly dumped him 'overboard' and stole the boat.
The sailor lay kicking in the sand; he couldn't even stand. He managed to raise his head and shout after the disappearing rowboat; "Fucking thieving Jews!" and collapsed back in the sand. Alex sounded puzzled; "We look bloody Jewish?" She asked. No one answered her.

There were three ships in the bay; the smallest was the Bathsheba. They quietly rowed past the 'Scallywag' and the 'Kraken'. Both sounded like they had parties going on. A couple of bodies fell from them splashing into the water dead or dead drunk. "Do you know that if you had lots of paracetamol; you could make a fortune around here with all the hangovers?" Jackie whispered, grinning. Everyone ignored her. They came up behind the stern and found a couple of ropes hanging down in the water.

"That's where the expression 'swinging the lead' comes from. They would throw measured ropes over the side, with a lead weight on the end; to measure the depth of the water, so the ship didn't run aground." Jericho explained; but only Jackie was interested in that.

That's when the other little rowboat bumped into them. The two sets of people stared at each other. The little skinny man lifted his weak lamp and sighed; "It's alright boys. It's those spies of the English Crown after fucking Ratbeard. They can be trusted; they're Jewish." The little group of men all nodded and waved.

The team exchanged glances of puzzlement and some amazement. Israel Feat [the little skinny man] grinned and grabbed a rope; he climbed like a monkey and disappeared onto the ship, with his men following. Jericho and the team did the same.

Alex was last up the rope, behind Jackie, she chuckled; "For Christ sake Jackie; you do have a gorgeous arse!" Jackie just sighed and climbed on board, helping Alex over the rail. The ship was deathly quiet; with only a strange grunting sound; they quickly found out what that was.

The two guards were both sprawled on the deck: drunk. Israel and his men slid them slowly over the side and took possession of their muskets and swords. He whispered to Jericho; "The woman is in the captain's cabin." He gestured down a hatchway and crept away, looking for any other 'guards'.

The team slipped quietly down the hatchway, swords and pistols ready. Alex whispered to Jackie; "Why does everyone think we're bloody Jewish?" Jackie didn't know, but would have a good look in her mirror, next time she did her makeup.

They burst into the captain's quarters and found a very pretty woman, possibly in her late thirties, sitting on the bunk bed, skirts pulled up, bodice loose, scratching an escaped tit; she was smoking a cob pipe.

She looked up and didn't smile; "Who the fuck are you?" She said and farted loudly adding; "The food is plentiful, but makes you fart and crap like a dog with fucking dysentery." Alex just stared at her, lowering her pistol; "Mrs. Carol Harker?" She asked in total amazement. The woman nodded; "Who the fuck wants to know?"

9. THE RELUCTANT RESCUE.

They sat where they could, drinking brandy. The captain kept a good supply of it. Mrs. Harker grunted; "It all belonged to young fancy pants - the previous captain? - He certainly had class. But old Ratbeard soon put an end to his game. The crew wanted to fuck me and he wouldn't let them. So, they quickly tossed him overboard. They're fucking pirates, not Choir boys on a church outing. I got through five of them before old Ratbeard shagged me. What a fucking man! Like a bloody road hammer. After that he kept me to himself; none of the crew argued with that. Best fucking sex I'd had in years. I came like a fucking burst fire hydrant." She refilled the glasses and sighed. "Is that old witch of a mother of mine still breathing?" Alex nodded; stunned and told her that the boy was fine.

"Fucking whining split little fucker. He's going to grow up to be a cock sucker like his pathetic dad. What happened to that tosser?" Mrs. Harker asked with no real concern whatsoever.

"I'm afraid they killed him and threw him overboard." Jackie said softly. Mrs. Harker just sighed; "That's probably the best thing that ever happened to the twat." and knocked her brandy back in one slug. She re-lit her pipe and smiled to herself. "Anyway, what the fuck do you want?"

Jericho explained quietly that they were here to rescue her. She laughed and actually wiped a tear from her eyes. "Rescue me?" She sounded incredulous at the thought. She smiled; "When I need fucking rescuing; I'll let you lovely Jewish people know. Now fuck off before old Ratbeard comes home and fucks all of you. And I mean fucks all of you." She laughed at that.

Israel Feat appeared in the doorway and pulled off his hat; "Evening Mistress Carol." He turned to Jericho and smiled; "The Bathsheba is ours. I've sent for the captain."

Carol Harker slumped on the bed, muttering; "Just when you find fucking true happiness, it's always snatched from you." She stared out the window and smiled; "I would fuck off quick; Old Ratbeard is back." They could see the two big row boats approaching the stern, the lamps on their stern and aft flickering in the darkness.

Jericho took command and told Israel to fire a cannon shot over Ratbeard and his crew; then get underway. Israel nodded and disappeared, followed by Jericho and Wilson.

Jericho shouted back; "Look after her." He told Alex and Jackie, adding; "Don't let her out of your sight." Carol sprawled on the bed and smoked her pipe. She gestured to Jackie, but spoke to Alex; "She your piece of skirt darling?" Alex found herself nodding.

Carol sighed; "I wouldn't mind some of that little peach myself. Probably has a tight fanny that tastes like honey." Alex just smiled; "Oh, she's definitely a special lady." Carol nodded; "I had a terrific lesbian experience with some basketball players, when I was at College. Then I met the twat and ended up rich and fucking unhappy. Such is life." She sighed, remembering her happy girlhood: the young women and the big strong black men.

They felt the ship move and cannon shot rang out. Carol leaned back on the bed. "He's not going to be happy about this. Your friends are going to die quite horribly and you two; had better love being fucked by a couple of dozen men every day. Though I might ask old Ratbeard if I can keep your little honey pot there; for myself." She puffed on her pipe and smiled at that thought. Alex asked her how long she had been on the boat. Carol waved the pipe about; "It's a fucking ship darling. I must have been enjoying myself now for a couple of months. Why do you ask?"

Alex turned to Jackie; "A Day for us and two months for her. Time travel can be a real bugger sometimes." Carol sat bolt upright on the bed and stared at the girls. She took a breath and grinned; "You're fucking temporal detectives. Old Ratbreard said you would turn up sooner or later. He told fancy pants that you would show up eventually, but he wouldn't listen."

Alex and Jackie both looked at each other; how the hell does 'old Ratbeard' know about Temporal Detectives? Alex rubbed her chin and knew that this was a real turn up and Jericho should know about it. Carol started to laugh; "Your so-called Captain knows shit about ships don't he?" Alex was about to defend Jericho's seamanship, when Carol laughed outright; "The fuckwit hasn't realized that the fucking tide is running inshore!"

Alex sighed; "Come on Jackie, let's secure the reluctant rescue and warn Jericho that he's spitting against the wind."

They left the protesting Carol tied against the bed and ran onto the deck. There was musket fire and men shouting; they found Jericho and Wilson by the capstan.

He just looked at them and grinned sheepishly; "I fucking know." was all he said.

They explained about Carol's revelation and Jericho grunted; "Time to retreat, I think. We're outgunned." Jackie sounded disappointed with herself; "I knew I should have run my mirror over old Ratbeard. I think the results would be interesting."

The team huddled by the sail locker and a couple of musket balls flew over their heads and splintered the mast. "Let's go people." Jericho shouted and operated his mirror; they were back at the fort. They watched the musket fire and uneven fight from the relative safety of their hill position. It was soon over. They turned to walk away when they saw him; leaned against a tree with one hand. Jackie actually grinned; "Sweet Jesus, he does actually look like Errol Flynn!" It was a somewhat distraught Captain Casanova or fancy pants as Carol called him. He was watching the fire fight too and wasn't happy with the outcome. He turned to the team and didn't smile; "Israel was a good and loyal man. He deserved better than to die at that pigs hands." He wiped his face and pushed his hat back on. Yes, he really did look like the dashing and handsome film star.

Jericho smiled at him; "Talking about Captain Ratbeard, can I ask you some questions about him?" Captain Casanova wiped his face and stared at them; "You're those detective people; aren't you? Norman kept telling me that you would show up."

Jackie said quietly; "Ratbeards real name is Norman?" Alex nodded; "His surname is probably bloody Smith or something." The young captain eased himself down under the tree and brushed dirt from his immaculately tailored jacket. "I accidently acquired the Aztec Emblem while running guns to Mexican bandits. Suddenly finding myself in Medieval Japan was bit of a surprise. Then I realized that my pocketknife was Japanese, I never did know just how old it was. So, I tried a musket ball from the American Civil war and found myself at Fredericksburg. That was some battle. Then, I was given an old pirate map to supposed buried treasure and found myself here."

He stared out at the bay and continued; "Then I met Norman; he was travelling in time too. His portal was an old Egyptian figurine. We joined forces and took over the Bathsheba. I thought it was just fun; playing pirates but found out that Norman wanted to play them for real. He took the emblem and now I'm stuck here."

Jericho rubbed his face; "Where or when or you originally from?" The captain sighed; "Australia actually. I was born in 1909." Jackie actually squeaked; "It's him! It's really him!" Wilson just patted her arm; "Keep your panties on darling, lots of people come from Australia and were born in 1909."

Jericho ignored Jackie and asked what year he left his own time? The captain stared up at the stars and said 1933. Alex whispered to Jackie; "That's two years before he became so famous;

playing a bloody pirate captain in that film: 'Captain Blood'. No wonder he was so good; he had been a real one!"

Jericho folded his arms and stared at the Bathsheba, swinging at anchor in Paradise Bay. "Now we have another bloody time traveler to stop; two bloody time portal devices to destroy and return a very reluctant woman back to her own time." He jerked a thumb at Captain Casanova; "Not forgetting to return him, so that he can become a huge bloody movie star." He sighed, he really wished sometimes; that he had stayed dead.

10. HOLLYWOOD 1933. (THE POOR END OF TOWN.)

The girls were dressed in period clothes and looked stunning. They really had pulled out all the stops. 'Captain Casanova' stopped outside a dingy apartment block and sighed; "This is it Ladies: the dump where I live. I do have some coffee if you want a cup?" He smiled and both Alex and Jackie exchanged a real smile and both nodded. "Coffee would be great Errol." Alex said softly and both put their arms through his and the threesome headed in.

His apartment was small, but strangely clean and tidy for a single man living on his own. Jackie - always curious - asked him about that as he put the coffee pot on the small stove and lit the gas. "I have a nice lady [Mrs. Iris Cope] that lives opposite; she and her daughter clean it for me. I can't pay them in cash, but they don't seem to mind."

Alex and Jackie really did exchange a smile at that. "Mother and daughter; you're a very naughty man Errol." Alex whispered, slipping out of her jacket. Jackie did the same. He stood staring as they dldn't stop at just slipping off their jackets. They stood in front of him, just in stockings, suspenders and panties. He leaned over the small stove and blew out the flame. "I guess the coffee can wait." He muttered and stripped down himself.

He slowly pulled down his shorts and both girls grinned - really grinned - and Jackie whispered; "The legends did say he was the best equipped actor in Hollywood." They walked towards him like lioness's stalking a gazelle.

He smiled; "Now, how can I assist you ladies?" Alex ran a finger over his lips; "By fucking our brains out darling." He grinned;

"Well, I certainly can do that; I not good at much else apparently. I work shit jobs just to pay for the rent on this dump."

Jackie knelt down and grasped his huge cock and eased it into her mouth. He groaned and ran a hand over her hair. The other hand gripped Alex's bum. "I do hope you like it up the bum. That's my favourite." He whispered, as his tongue disappeared into Alex's very willing mouth.

The former pirate captain fucked Alex first; doggy style, whilst she sucked Jackie's cock. He was a little surprised by Jackie's big secret, but thought 'what the hell, he would try anything new; especially when it came to sex.' Alex quickly had a couple of orgasms under his skilled thrusts, and they swapped over. He applied some of the magic cream to his throbbing cock - that's Vaseline - and fucked Jackie up the arse. Alex slowly sucked Jackie's cock, which suddenly exploded in her mouth. She didn't waste any. Jackie rode him in the 'reverse cowgirl position' while Alex squatted over his face, and he pleasured her quivering wet fanny with a very skilful tongue and mouth.

Finally, he moaned loudly and came in Jackie's back passage. He sipped some cheap Bourbon whisky while watching Alex clean that mess up. Both girls turned on him; sucking his cock together and it was soon Alex's turn to have her bum fucked. She lay across the edge of the bed with her arse in the air, gripping the blankets, knees on the floor. He poked her bum with some vigor, while exploring Jackie's mouth and tits. Then he put Jackie in the same position and fucked both up the arse, taking turns. The girls kissed passionately as he fucked them, groaning and panting together.

He came a second time, right up Alex's bum hole. Jackie cleaned that mess up with some relish. The happy lovers cuddled closely together on the small bed and shared the cheap Bourbon whisky. Alex pulled up her big bag and handed him her little present. It was a book. He took it and smiled; "Acting. I had never thought of trying that."

Jackie grinned; "Well, try it. What have you got to lose?" He shrugged his shoulders and placed it on the bedside cabinet, next to the Vaseline jar. He picked that up and smiled; "Up for more ladies?" The smiles on the girl's faces answered that question.

Alex was sandwiched between the two for some time and then Captain Casanova came up with a new idea; he mounted Alex whilst she knelt on the floor with him kneeling over her. Jackie then mounted him and the small tower of heaving lovers fucked hard and fast. To quote a colloquialism of the times [the 1930's] "he was a 'Saloon door" - he swung both ways - and clearly enjoyed doing so.

The three happy lovers fucked in various positions around the dingy apartment for about another half hour before Jackie and the captain came together over Alex's smiling face. The girls cleaned that up by kissing and licking each other on the floor, while the captain watched; panting and grinning. Alex discretely checked her mirror and whispered to Jackie; "Time to go."

The girls had just left his apartment and were walking towards the elevator, when a young woman passed them and knocked at the happy 'captains' door. They both watched as the door opened and he embraced the girl passionately. "Oh darling Orville." She said and he pulled her inside, grinning.

Jackie stood by the open lift doors and ran a hand across her face. "Orville. Bloody Orville Suckles." She had forgotten her own research in the frenzy of having sex with a legendary Hollywood star. They both stepped in and stared at each other; "Bloody Orville Suckles was Captain Casanova's real name!" Jackie whispered and as the lift descended; both girls roared with laughter and operated their mirrors, vanishing as the lift doors opened. Old Mrs. Cope [Orville's neighbour] stepped in a little puzzled: she would have sworn on her dead mother's grave that she had heard raucous laughter from the lift before the doors opened. "Oh fucking God, she was seeing and hearing bloody things again!" She mumbled and fumbled in her big bag and pulled a bottle Gin out and took an enormous swig; the fourth one of her hour long shopping trip today…..

11. CHASING NORMAN.

Jericho was standing by the old fort watching HMS Steadfast at anchor in the bay. Wilson joined him and handed him a water bottle. Jericho sipped and checked his mirror; "Alex and Owen should be back from 1933 any minute now." Wilson sighed; "That mad bastard is going to be famous, rich and popular. You know about his legendary sexual prowess? Two or three women in one

go. They say he was hung like a donkey. Lucky bastard."
Alex and Owen materialized, smiling. Owen just had to tell
Jericho and Wilson straight away; "We returned him 1933 and
bloody Alex just had to do it, didn't she?" Wilson grunted; "Do
what exactly?"

Owen laughed; "Give Mr. Errol - I'm a huge movie star - Flynn, a
bloody book entitled; 'How to be an Actor.' I laughed my socks
off." Jericho and Wilson chuckled at that. Alex just grinned.
"Well, he certainly must have read it."

Wilson nodded; "Lot of good it would do bloody Orville Suckles. I
just checked my mirror, and he ended up selling brushes door to
door for a living, selling to all those housewives, day after day.
Poor sod. I'm surprised that he didn't make a fortune being Errol
Flynn's double." He really couldn't understand why they laughed
so much.

"Never mind bleeding Errol Flynn's lookalike, we need to get after
bloody Norman before the timeline really starts to change."
Jericho grunted and pushed his mirror back in his jacket pocket.
He was sweating and not very happy; now he had to deal with
the officers of HMS Steadfast who could end up chasing a
'phantom' pirate ship in this time. Jericho scratched his head
thinking hard. "We need to jump back and deal with Norman, but
also keep Jeb and Tom off our backs, while we do it."

Owen grinned; "Let me and Alex convince Jeb that a beach party
would raise morale and we can slip away back to 1710, while
they're having a good time on this lovely beach." Everyone just
stared at him. He shrugged his shoulders; "Anyone got a better
idea, just bloody speak up."

The bonfire was soon ablaze, and the windup gramophone was
playing hits from the forties and early fifties. The crew was
dressed up in grass skirts with leaves on their heads. Everyone
from the ship wanted to dance with Alex, who was wearing a
stunning one-piece, black bathing costume with a flimsy grass
skirt.

Jeb grabbed Jericho and handed him a 'long life' beer "Fantastic
idea old boy! Just the bloody ticket!" He shouted over the noisy
and very happy party. Jericho just smiled and Owen grinned
broadly. "Come on people. Let's go." Jericho muttered to the

team who reluctantly followed him. They made their way back to the fort and jumped; they couldn't believe it: there was a big party in full swing!

Apparently, it was Captain Breholt's birthday, and the island was celebrating; or else! There were drunks everywhere. Alex soberly pointed out several new graves in the cemetery; "Probably old Israel and his men." She said sadly. Two drunken pirates tried to kiss Jackie, shouting "Merry Christmas!" to everyone. Jackie kneed one in the testicles and the other one wisely staggered off. "That's my girl." Alex smiled and they found themselves outside the gunpowder store.

The guard was slumped against the door, singing quite an obscene song about a certain ship called 'Venus'. Jericho stepped over him and pushed open the door, he peered in; it was stacked with muskets, swords and gunpowder barrels. He rubbed his chin and smiled.

"Heads up, isn't that our Norman?" Wilson said and everyone dived into the gunpowder store and watched through the half open door. Captain Ratbeard and Mrs. Harker were heading towards the party; hand in hand, surrounded by half a dozen crew members, dressed in their best. Well, they had washed their feet and hands. Jericho whispered to his group; "Now's the best time to end Ratbeard's jolly sea jaunts. Wilson and Owen... sorry Jackie, find us a couple of rowboats."

They both slipped away and headed for the beach. Jericho picked two barrels and with Alex's help, rolled them to the door. "Now for a bloody horse and cart." He smiled and they soon found one. They pulled the drunken driver from the seat and left him in a brothel doorway. When Wilson and Jackie returned giving the thumbs up, they loaded the barrels and set off for the beach.

Madame Claire sighed and with the help of 'big Betty' dragged the driver into the brothel hallway; they quickly took anything of value from the man and then carried him outside to the woodshed.

They tossed him onto a pile of about five or six men: still all quite drunk. All had been thoroughly robbed by the 'ladies of the night' - two were grinning with bloody mouths; they use to have a couple of gold teeth - and one was missing his wooden leg.

Madame Claire brushed herself down and smiled; "Come on girls, let's get to the party. There's money to be made."

She stopped and watched the cart disappearing through the gateway and rubbed her chin; "Where had I heard about four such strangers?" Madame Claire sighed and walked to the Garrison House of the fort, past a chalk board with four crude sketches and a notice declaring a Ten Pound reward for the capture of Captain Tibbs, Captain Alex Longlegs, Bad Red the African terror and a little dark-haired beauty called 'Salty Jack'. {Ten pounds Sterling would now be worth (in 2023) a shocking £352,300.00!!] Clearly Pirates were top earners in their day; a bit like professional footballers are nowadays.

It pointed out that she [Salty Jack] should be taken unharmed - Breholt himself wanted her - and that alone guaranteed that she would be unmolested by anyone; well, except the really stupid or those with a death wish.

Alex and Jericho followed Wilson and Jackie in the rowboat, which was carrying the two barrels. They came up under the stern of the 'Bathsheba' and Wilson secured the rowboat to the stern: really close and trailed a fuse down.

Jackie handed him the matches and he lit the slow burning rope. Wilson and Jackie quickly transferred to Jericho's and Alex's boat. They really did row away fast and headed for the beach. They stopped rowing and stared; there was a large group of people on the beach, firing - drunkenly - muskets and pistols at them. Madame Claire had just remembered and was now ten pounds better off.

Jericho cussed and pulled out his mirror; a musket ball knocked off his hat and he operated his mirror - just as the stern of the 'Bathsheba disappeared in a huge explosion - The team, complete with rowboat; vanished. Everyone on the beach had stopped partying and watched in amazement as the small rowboat landed on the shingle. The team jumped from their boat and bowed. Jeb walked up and stood in silence for a few seconds then burst out laughing; "Bloody good show! Dressing up as pirates to surprise everyone!" He thrust a beer into Jericho's hand and slapped his back. Everyone was now cheering and clapping in appreciation of the 'Pirate Experts' efforts to cheer everyone up. The party was quite a monster.

Tom sat next to Wilson - they were in deck chairs by the dying bonfire - and sipped their beers. Tom patted Wilson's arm; "You and your team are really pirate experts you know." Wilson smiled; "Glad to hear that, Tom." He said quietly. Tom sighed and finished his can, throwing it onto the fire. He scratched his head; "I still don't know, how you got your hands on a genuine 18th century 'jolly boat' on an uninhabited island. Did you have it in your luggage?" He smiled and walked back to the beach, gesturing for Wilson to follow; the last boat was leaving for the ship. Wilson just smiled to himself; 'you can't really fool an old sea dog'. The team met up in Jericho's cabin. Owen - now out of his 'party' costume - wasn't happy. Two sailors had asked him to their cabin with really big smiles on their faces. "Dirty old sods." Was all he said. Jericho pointed out that Ratbeard still had the time controllers and they really needed to disable them - but how? - The island back in 1710 would now be in uproar and everyone would be after the team. How could they return without being seen?

Alex sat on the bed and sipped her drink; she sat upright and smiled; "Only two of us can return to the island in 1710."
She jerked a thumb towards Owen and pointed to herself. "Owen can return as a pirate gentleman and I can accompany him as he's sister or wife or whatever. We simply swap sexes. They would never suspect that." Jericho did smile; "Alexandra my dear. You are worth your dress allowances." Owen grinned; "According to my research, even pirate towns welcomed preachers; especially the really rotten ones."

12. THE CAPTAINS CABIN.

Alex made her way to the captain's cabin, wrapped in her long bed jacket, holding her shampoo, soap and towels. She knocked gently on the door and was surprised to find Tom sitting at the captain's desk, writing up the days reports. He smiled and gestured to the bathroom door. "Help yourself; Jeb is on watch on the bridge. I'll relieve him a while." He pointed to the papers laid out before him; "The Executive Officer's duties include all the report writing that captains hate." Alex smiled and walked to the bathroom door, watched carefully by Tom and stepped into the small bathroom and closed the door slowly.

She stood naked and untied her hair, letting it fall about her shoulders. She grinned; wrapping a very small towel around herself and stuck her head out the door; "Tom, do Executive Officers duties extend to getting a bloody shower working. I can't get it to start." Tom rose slowly and walked over; he was about to explain about the two handles, when Alex gestured to the shower levers and asked if he could get them working. He grinned and leaned over the bath and pulled both handles in the proper sequence. Water splashed on his uniform shirt and trousers.

Alex leapt forward with a towel and rubbed the crotch of his trousers saying, "Tut Tut, so sorry, it's my fault entirely." The little towel she was wearing slipped to the floor. "Oops." was all she said, smiling.

His eager mouth was on Alex's in an instance, and she pulled at the buttons on his soaking shirt, as the pair groped each other under the shower. Her hands pulled at his trousers, and they fell down, with Tom kicking off his shoes. Alex took hold of a very erect large cock and she was certainly happy about the service that it gave. The navy was the senior service after all!

He fucked her hard doggy style on the floor of the shower cubicle; the lovers were now saturated and slippery. Tom pushed deep into her, gripping her hips with both hands, whilst Alex pushed back against his thrusts. She groaned loudly and slapped both hands against the wall; Tom was pumping her hard and fast. He reached up and pushed the shower levers; the bloody small room would soon flood if he didn't switch the damn thing off. He leaned back against the door, and it swung open.

Ensign Harry stood in the captain's cabin gripping a piece of paper and just stared at the pair fucking on the bathroom floor. The paper fluttered to the ground and young Harry really did grin. Alex looked up and smiled [Tom still fucking her with some passion] "Well. Don't just stand there boy; get in here!"

Harry maybe a little dumb but didn't need an offer like that twice. He was stripped down to his socks and underpants in seconds. Alex reached up and tugged down his crisp white shorts and both she and Tom said the same thing, at the same time; "Oh for fuck sake, that's unbelievable"

Young Harry was equipped with a cock that would make a stallion jealous. Tom didn't lose his rhythm as Alex shoved the stiffening monster into her mouth and sucked hard - really hard - and jerked it with some determination. It was a tight squeeze in the small bathroom and in Alex's open fanny as Harry pushed his cock inside of her. She was now on top of the young man, gripping his shoulders, whilst Tom mounted her arse with some urgency. The three lovers were groaning and cursing as they fucked each other hard. Alex had a leg trembling, cunt throbbing orgasm; twice and could only lay on the boy, gasping and tearful from sheer sexual ecstasy. She would have sworn that Harry's cock had reached the bottom of her bloody throat! It seemed to fill her entire body, never mind her gushing fanny.

Tom groaned loudly, slapping Alex's arse cheeks and squirted hard inside her back passage. Alex continued to ride young Harry and had yet another big spurt. Tom pulled from her arse and lay on the floor panting. Alex turned on her back and Harry really fucked her, gripping her slippery tits and sucking hard on her rock-hard nipples.

She held on tightly to his thrusting buttocks and screamed - yes, actually screamed, as he came inside of her. He just kept coming and collapsed on top, groaning loudly. Alex couldn't actually speak. She seemed to be full of cum. But she pulled Harry's mouth down to hers and the pair kissed passionately.

Tom rose from the wet floor and wiped his flaccid cock on Alex's little towel. "Shit!" He exclaimed, seeing the clock on the office wall. He should relieve Jeb on the bridge in just fifteen minutes. He grabbed up his wet uniform and headed from the bathroom very quickly. Alex was too busy sucking young Harrys tongue to notice his departure. Finally harry pulled from her and smiled; "Thank you Miss." Was all he said and gathered up his clothes and wearing just his underpants and vest; left Alex on the floor - still gasping - where she lay for some minutes.

Alex pulled herself up on still shaking legs and pulled the door shut. "Typical bloody men; cum and run." She muttered to herself and felt Harry's cum running down both thighs and legs; there was loads of the stuff. She slowly wiped her crotch and thighs with her towel and almost jumped as there was a loud knock on the door. She managed to shout "Hello, I'm in the shower!" Jeb laughed and shouted; "Yeah, Tom said you were in there. Everything OK? He said you had problems with the damn levers."

Alex gasped out; "Yes, but he sorted me out, thank you." She
smiled - he had certainly sorted her out in more ways than that -
she leaned against the wall and groaned. Any other time and she
would have dragged him in, but Harry's big cock had filled her up
and drained all her energy. Pity: she really did want to fuck him.
She could hear Jeb talking on the phone and she looked about
the bathroom; it was a bloody mess; with water everywhere.
She shrugged her shoulders and set about trying to clean the
damn place up. Alex wrapped her bed jacket around her still
damp body and gathered her things together. She slowly opened
the door and fixed a tired smile on her face; this would take a
little explaining as water seeped under the door onto the cabin
floor. Alex's eyes widened and she really did smile. Jeb was
sitting at his desk; stark naked, smoking a cigarette. He offered
her the packet and asked if she wanted one. She shook her head
and pulled off her bed jacket with a happy sigh.

13. 'COITUS INTERUPTUS' - YET A BLOODY AGAIN!

Alex was bent over the desk, hands gripping the edge with her
legs apart and her big boobs squashed against the hard wood.
Her head was down as Jeb fucked her hard from behind. He
inserted a thumb into her already open anus and asked - politely
- if he could fuck her up the arse later. Alex groaned and nodded;
he wouldn't need too much lubricant; Tom had filled her back
passage earlier with cum and she hadn't cleaned herself up
properly. Jeb chuckled and thrusted harder, gripping her
quivering arse with both hands.

They changed position, with Alex laying sideways on the desk
and Jeb thrusting like a road hammer. His hands now gripping
the edge of the desk for maximum effect. Alex had a little
orgasm - she was already really aroused from the threesome -
and groaned. She groaned really loudly when the bloody phone
buzzed, and Jeb casually answered it; still fucking her hard. He
spoke for about a minute and replaced the receiver.

"Bloody Sonar has picked up something in the bay, could be an
old wreck or something similar." He panted and turned Alex onto
her back, pushing the paperwork from the desk. "I'll have to go,
but not before I've come." He added with a little smile.

Alex just grunted as her gripped her big tits and squeezed hard,
pinching her nipples until she actually yelped. He cussed a couple

of times and came inside her. She just stared at him as he pulled his cock from her and started to gather his uniform together. He smiled; "We'll continue this another time my dear." He said simply and dressed quickly. He was gone a few minutes later.

Alex sat naked on the desk and folded her arms; she was really disappointed. She eased off the desk and picked up her towel and wiped her crotch. "Another typical fucking man who came and went." She muttered unhappily to herself and pulled on her bed jacket and yet again; gathered her things together.

Still, he was totally responsible for this big bloody ship, and he had to act accordantly, she told herself as she left the captain's cabin and headed back to her own. Owen was standing outside with a large bundle in his arms. He smiled and held them up; "Our new outfits are here. I'm going to be a good bad vicar." He said and pushed open her cabin door and followed her in.

Alex took the bundle from him and chucked it on the chair. "I need a man; NOW!" was all she said, and Owen sighed. They fucked on the small bed, on the floor, against the door and even on the small toilet. Owen's alter-ego may be Jacqueline, but he certainly knew how to fuck a woman who really needed sex. He was fucking Alex hard as she knelt on all fours and she spurted, groaning loudly and cussing. That's when Wilson banged on the door and said Jericho was waiting for them and was, they in their costumes yet.

Alex k leaned on her elbows and didn't smile; she felt Owen come inside of her and he muttered; "Not a bloody again. Is there no peace for me to enjoy a good fuck around here?" Owen patted her arse and said softly; "I don't know about you, but I enjoyed that." Alex just grunted; "I'm bloody well glad that someone did."

14. PARADISE BAY - PART 3.

Jericho really shrugged his shoulders and repeated he didn't know; he had no explanation about the old wreck lying at the bottom of the bay. Jeb just stared at him and tapped the scope again. "Well, Tom and I are pretty sure that the damn thing wasn't there yesterday." He walked to the window and gestured to the motor launch being lowered into the water. "It's in shallow water. Well, shallow enough for my team of divers to reach it safely. We'll find out what and who she was." He didn't smile.

Jericho managed a smile and wandered away. "Bloody Sonar." He muttered to himself and joined Wilson by the railings, who were watching the diving expedition get under way.

"Never thought of this; did we." He said softly to Jericho, who nodded. "Have our sex change companions gone?" Wilson chuckled; "that Owen looks like a bent preacher and Alex is dressed in widow's black, complete with veil." They walked to the officer's mess; they needed a drink, even if it was only ten o'clock in the morning!

Since her legs were still free, Alex kicked Owen's feet real hard. "Trust you to ask bloody Madame Claire. Oh, what's going on Madame? Oh, come this way Reverend and bring your sister! You bleeding twat!" She struggled against the ropes and failed. Owen couldn't answer; the gag in his mouth wouldn't let him.

The door to the woodshed sprung open and Madame Claire, accompanied by her loyal sidekick - big Betty - came in and smiled at the pair. She was a holding a small sack and held up Owens's mirror; "I'd love to know what this fucking thing does? What I do know, is that there is nothing on God's earth - if you excuse the use of the almighty's name Reverend - existing in this time and place and I mean the year of our Lord seventeen hundred and ten."

Big Betty knelt down next to Owen and held a rusty dagger against his neck; "Shall I cut his throat and dump him in the jungle?" Madame Claire shook her head. "No, he may be worth something to someone. A good-looking young boy like him is worth gold to some men who like their sex on the dark side."

She smiled and gestured to Alex; "I've already sold her holes to the big boss himself. He was very disappointed about not raping that little dark-haired tart. Now if I could get my hands on her, then I...we would be really in the money."

Alex just stared at her; "What fucking gives you the right to sell me you pox ridden bitch!" Madame Claire just grinned and produced a pistol from under her skirts and pointed it at Owen. "This does my lovely foul-mouthed slut." She expertly pulled the firing hammer back. Alex sighed; "Alright, alright you fucking trollop. I understand." Madame Claire smiled and snapped the hammer back. "See, you can learn things quickly. I hope you learnt enough from your dead husband to please a man like the boss. Your arse had better known a big dick my lovely. That's he's favourite."

The two women left laughing together and Alex leaned back against the wall and just sighed; "Thanks to you, you twat. I'm about to have my poor bloody bum hole stretched by a pox ridden pirate!" Owen just shrugged his shoulders and mumbled something. "Shut up." Was all Alex moaned and stared about the woodshed. That's when she saw the old axe sticking out of a log.

 They sneaked up to the back door of the brothel and peered in; young Delphi the African girl was stirring a big pot. They heard voices and crept under the window next door. They knelt in the dirt and listened; Madame Claire and Ratbeard were talking; about their bloody mirrors. Ratbeard paid her gold for them and walked away. The pair scurried into the jungle and hid in some bushes.

Owen sat knees under his chin and sighed; "Whoever Ratbeard is, he's knows what our mirrors are for. Who the hell is he?" Alex didn't know; "We need to get our mirrors back and close those bloody time portals. I know that much." She said and they pair made off; they wanted to put distance between the brothel and themselves.

They walked in the jungle for some time and found they were on the other side of the small island. It was dominated by the remains of a small volcano, long dead. They climbed and were rewarded by excellent views of the island, including Paradise Bay and the two ships in the small harbour.

Owen sat and wiped his neck and face; "Just out of interest; now what the fuck do we do?" Alex slumped next to him and rubbed her arms; "Bloody insects." She said and stared about. She tapped Owens's arm very slowly and didn't smile; "There's some crazy old man staring at us." Owen looked across at a thick clump of trees. The old man gestured for them to come. His clothes were almost rags and he had big leaves tied around his feet and on his head.

"It's bloody Ben Gunn." Owen groaned and the pair rose and

walked over. The old man grinned with a toothless mouth; he looked nearly a hundred years old but clearly fit as a Butcher's dog. He gripped Alex's arm; "You're not the lovely lady that old Breholt wants." He grinned at Owen and laughed - almost hysterically - to himself; "You're the lovely dark little girl he wants. Old Judea knows all these things. He watches and listens. The jungle has been his friend for thirty years." He gestured for them to follow him. They looked at each other and shrugged; then followed the strange little man into the dense jungle with Owen muttering about how the old man knew such things.

"I've been here since that bastard Captain Breholt dumped me here. Gave orders that no one should give me succour or be cut up like fish on a slab. The town's people all avoid me. Won't give me a cup of water or piece of bread. Bastards." He entered a rough hole behind a well grown bush, and they found themselves in a small cave. Judea chuckled; "Only old Israel Feat ever helped me. A good man."

Alex and Owen just stood; speechless and amazed. There was furniture stacked up, beds, tables and chests, Eastern carpets and tapestries. He pointed to a couple of royal looking chairs and produced a bucket of water and a ladle. He sipped and gargled; "Still fresh my lovelies." They sat and really enjoyed the water.

Old Judea dropped on the floor cross legged and smiled at the pair. "Old Redbeard know who you are." He laughed again and shook his head. "Old Judea knows who you are. God's people. "

Owen asked how he knew that. Old Judea laughed again and ran both hands over his bald head; "Old Judea knows what he knows. Redbeard and his new trollop know who you are. He's trying to buy passage on one of the other ships." He laughed hysterically, rolling about the cave floor. Finally, he sat up smiling; "Old Judea loved what you did to his ship. Old Judea loved it."

He jumped up and walked to a chest and pulled the lid up. Owen and Alex walked over and stared in; it was packed with gold cups, jewels, gold and silver coins. It was a fortune for the time. Judea dug deep amongst the treasures and pulled out a little black box.

He held it out to Alex and as she reached for it, snatched it back grinning. "Get nothing for nothing around here my darling." Alex just sighed; "I really don't need a little box thank you. You dirty old sod." Judea laughed again and whispered; "Not even one that will take you back from whence you came?"

Owen nodded; "How much would you bet that it contains a time portal?" Alex folded her arms and asked Judea what he wanted for it. He grinned and leapt around the place, then whispered in her ear. Alex just nodded; "Only if the bloody thing works." Judea nodded and jumped away from them; he slowly opened the lid and whispered into the box. He was gone. Alex and Owen stared at each other; a working time portal!

Judea was back, singing and dancing. he held out the box and snatched it away - again - when Owen reached for it. "Judea keeps his word if the lady keeps hers." Alex just sighed and pulled up her skirts. She squatted down and pissed. Owen just stood laughing. Judea watched with great interest and handed the box to Owen. "It only speaks Egyptian, the language of the Pharaoh's." He muttered and sat on the floor watching Alex brush down her skirts. "You're a dirty old pervert Judea." She admonished him but did chuckle.

Owen and Alex held hands and Owen flipped open the lid and Alex whispered into it. The pair were gone, and Judea lay back, laughing hysterically on the cave floor.

He leapt to his feet and walked to the big chest and pushed coins aside; he pulled up several little boxes and cuddled them to his thin chest. He smiled broadly, then sighed; "Old Judea is a clever old castaway from time and humans." He pushed the boxes back and flopped in his hammock and swung like a happy child. From a pocket in his ragged trousers, he pulled a little figurine of the Egyptian Goddess Isis and kissed it. He had fooled so many people over the years that it made him a little sad about the future of humans!

15. OLD JUDEA AND HIS MAGIC BOX.

Jericho and Wilson sat in the officer's mess and sipped brandies. Samson came over and spoke to Wilson; "Mr. Farmer is quite a navy historian. He thinks that the divers have found an old pirate ship from the 1700's. Apparently the stern is missing and there are some human bones scattered about the seabed. It must have sunk with the crew on board." Wilson thanked him and asked if they had identified the wreck. Samson shook his head and re-filled their glasses; "Not yet." He said and wandered back to the small bar and kitchen.

Wilson rubbed his chin; "That's funny, Owen in his research said that the 'Bathsheba' apparently sank around 1710. He thought it was lost in a storm at the time." Jericho nodded; he did remember the briefing when they first came on board. "Little did we realize that it was us that sank the bugger." He said quietly and sipped his drink. It wouldn't be the first time temporal detectives had to change things for the greater good. At least the original timeline would not be altered by the ship's loss.

Wilson discretely checked his mirror and looked concerned; "They should have been back by now or at least called in." Jericho stared out the window and grimaced. "My gut tells me that something is wrong." The pair rose and headed for their cabin; thanking Samson as they left.

They operated their mirrors and Jericho set his to find his missing detectives mirrors. They appeared in a bedroom and stood by the huge open window staring at the naked woman, face down on the bed, snoring.

It was Mrs. Carol Harker!

Wilson pointed to the bedside table and whispered; "The mirrors are in there." Jericho crept across and gently lifted the bag. He nodded at Mrs. Harker and smiled with real glee; "Shall we?" He said quietly and Wilson just grinned.

Mrs. Harker sat on the beach wrapped in just some leaves and watched the motor launch from HMS Steadfast approaching. She sighed. Those bastards. They know she can't say a thing about what happened to her - if she didn't want to end up in a loony bin - but on the bright side, she will inherit all the dead twats' money and there's bound to be plenty of horny sailors on board!

Jericho and Wilson were hiding in the jungle by the fort, watching the goings on. Redbeard had apparently fallen out of favour with Breholt and so had Madame Claire.

Jericho was patiently waiting on a call from Mr. Albian [a very Senior Time Controller] and finally his mirror buzzed. He answered it immediately and just sighed. He thanked Mr. Albian and turned to Wilson; "A breach of the timeline occurred here and now. Two people travelled back to the islands in the bloody year 68,510,241BC!" Wilson just groaned; "I hope they keep an eye out for bloody dinosaurs." Jericho shrugged his shoulders; "Let's go and find the pair of twats before they become lunch for some bloody big reptile." The Pair vanished.

They made their way through the steaming jungles, following Jericho's mirror which was set to search for two bodies: Alex and Owens's. They hoped their souls were still with them. Jericho stopped beneath a huge tree and slowly looked up. He laughed out loud and shouted; "Come down you pair of twats. Some bloody dinosaurs have very long necks!"

A very relieved Owen and Alex climbed down and were handed their mirrors. Wilson just laughed at the disheveled pair. Jericho said quietly; "Now let's close those time portals." Owen told them about old Judea and his big chest. "The old bugger never told us that it was one way." Jericho rubbed his chin and asked Owen to describe the old man, which he did. Jericho chuckled and turned to Alex; "Did he ask you to pee in front of him?" Alex was absolutely staggered and nodded slowly; actually, going a little red.

Jericho sighed; "Judea was a priest back in Ancient Egypt around the time the Great Pyramid was supposedly built. He's been time travelling for centuries. He likes to play a special little game with very pretty young women who find themselves in difficulty. Sounds like he's aged a bit, but that's not surprising for someone who has travelled in time so much. He must be nearly five thousand years old now." The team operated there mirrors had returned to Paradise Bay in 1710.

"So there was no time portal in that little box?" Owen sounded quite amazed as Jericho explained that Judea himself was the bloody time portal! "That one will only close when he dies." Jericho said, adding; "It's very rare. Temporal Intelligence believes the daft old bugger thinks a small figurine of the Goddess Isis is the device. But it's himself."

Wilson said quietly; "He's quite harmless really. Never changes anything of importance. He just likes to see pretty young women piss in front of him. Quite a harmless hobby really." He chuckled

when Alex retorted; "Not for bloody some big man." Jericho
waved them into some bushes and gestured down to the beach;
a big, bearded man was being put into a rowboat and set adrift.
He was stark naked; apparently, he had been stripped of
everything including his dignity.

Owen consulted his mirror and shrugged his shoulders; "It's a
certain Norman Dawson. A missing soul from 1891. Missing from
Scotland. He must be Ratbeard the pirate." Jericho nodded and
sighed; "Well, who the hell now has the time portals?" Wilson
pointed down to a big man standing by the shoreline. "That's
Breholt. I bet he has acquired the damn things." Jericho knelt
thinking; "We'll collect that twat later and return him to 1891.
But first, we need to get the bloody time portals off Breholt. Now
how do we go about that?"

Jericho really smiled at Owen, who just groaned. Alex patted his
arm; "Well, if it goes wrong, you'll either end up with your throat
cut or your bum hole stretched." She really grinned at that. "Oh,
what's going on Madame? Oh, come this way Reverend and bring
your sister!" She muttered with some sarcasm but smiling with a
little satisfaction.

16. CAPTAIN BREHOLT; GENTLEMAN PIRATE?

Madame Claire sat on the bucket and didn't smile. But the offer
from bloody Mr. Tibbs was a good one and; besides, she really
wanted to get back at Breholt. He had shut her brothel for ten
days. No one would come near the place until Breholt reopened
it. She would lose good money with another ship - full of horny
sailors - due in. She agreed to help, and Jericho had promised
her the two emblems that Ratbeard had owned - after he closed
the time portals - so that made her agreeable.

She really stared at 'Jackie'. Madame Claire asked Wilson if the
'Reverend' had a twin sister? Wilson just smiled. Alex helped
Jackie with her dress and make up; she really did look stunning.
They set off for the Garrison House in the fort. Madame Claire
knew all the little secret places to hide, and they soon appeared
at the back door; Jericho gave Claire an unloaded pistol and she
grabbed hold of Jackie and frog marched her into the kitchens.

The team hid in the pantry and followed events on their mirrors.
"Soon as we know that Breholt has the portals, we move in."

Jericho explained with a little smile as they gathered around the partly closed door and waited.

Captain Breholt smiled and scratched his beard. He really was a happy man now as he stared at Jackie who was pushed onto a chair by the windows. "You may re-open Madame Clare; you have done me a great service finding this girl." Madame Clare curtsied and stuffed her pistol back under her skirts. She left; also smiling to herself. Captain Breholt dropped into a chair opposite Jackie and adjusted his fine jacket and removed his sword belt; also placing a pistol on the small table next to his chair.

He gestured to the other table - which to Jackie's surprise – had been laid with tea pot, cups and delicate cakes - "I hope you enjoy Indian tea Miss Jackie, tea from China is quite difficult to get hold of in these troubled climes. It will be so pleasant and graceful to take tea with a proper lady. Shall I be mother?"

Somewhat amazed Jackie could only nod. Captain Breholt poured the tea with great pleasure and offered fresh milk and sugar. He sat back with his cup and sighed; "It's so nice to have good tea with the company of such a proper, beautiful young lady of quality." Again, Jackie just nodded. Now this was turn up for the books! Bloody drinking tea with a notorious pirate captain in his pirate stronghold.

Breholt finished his tea and rummaged in the old canvas sack that lay under the table. Jackie smiled; he pulled the two very emblems that the team was after from the bag. He slapped them on the table and ran fingers through his beard. "Worth a great deal of money my lady and I give them both to you." He smiled - again - and leaned forward, patting her hand. "These are just the start my dear. If you agree to my proposals, you will have much more gold. In fact, anything you wish, fine houses, servants, French gowns, anything."

Jackie placed her cup down and sighed; "And what are your proposals Sir?" She asked - not smiling - and the captain grinned. "Become my wife of course!" He exclaimed and chuckled, gripping her hand quite hard. "And if I don't agree Sir?" She said and found that she couldn't free her hand from his powerful grip. He lifted her hand and gently kissed it, smiling again.

He sighed; "Well. I don't think you're that stupid my lady. I would be forced by your refusal to fuck you quite brutally - in all your delicate orifices - and then give you to my men to do the same." He smiled broadly and released her hand. "So I thought a quiet wedding on Sunday morning would do nicely. I understand there's a young Reverend on the island with his pretty sister. I'm sure that I can persuade him to conduct the service." Now he grinned broadly.

Jackie sighed; now that would be interesting, conducting her own marriage service! It would certainly be a lively conversation piece over dinner. That's when she noticed - with some relief - that the captain had stopped in mid grin. She rose and grabbed the two emblems and headed for the door. It opened and Wilson stuck his head in and smiled; "Come on the almost future Mrs. 'I'm a big bad pirate' Breholt. Jericho wants to rescue naughty Norman's arse before he's bloody soul is lost." They headed to the pantry, passing several pirate men in the corridor; all frozen in time. Jackie stopped and prodded one with her finger; "Wilson, isn't this one supposed to be dead?"

Wilson nodded; it was Israel Feat! "I thought old Ratbeard had bumped him off. Now that's a turn up for the books." He grunted and shook his shoulders; "Come on, we'll let Jericho know." They joined the others in the kitchens and Jericho operated his mirror and the team disappeared.

Captain Breholt poured himself another cup of tea and enjoyed a moist little cake. He smiled and shouted for Israel Feat, who appeared in the doorway and pulled off his hat. "All done Sir?" He asked and Breholt nodded and enjoyed another cake.

Jericho stood on the beach and rubbed his chin; "Only one has a time portal. The Egyptian Figurine doesn't hold one." He said with a little surprise in his voice. He closed the portal in the Aztec emblem and handed the items back to Wilson; "Drop these off to the Madame Clare like I promised. I smell a rat here."

Alex stood with arms on hips and didn't smile. "If the figurine is not carrying a time portal, then how the hell did the naughty Norman get here?" Jericho smiled; "Let's ask the dumb sod." Jackie lowered the telescope and sighed; "Norman's rowboat is empty. He's bleeding gone."

Jericho consulted his mirror and cursed; "Breech of the time from this time and place, one human has crossed back to 1891, North Scotland." He lowered his mirror and rubbed his chin; "So Norman has jumped back to his own time. I don't think so."

The team glanced at each other. "What are you thinking?" Alex asked, knowing that look on Jericho's face. Jericho held up his mirror; "Norman Dawson is still shown as a missing soul. Had he jumped back to 1891 – he's own scheduled time period - he would no longer show as a missing soul. Someone else has used the portal. It must be locked to this year [1710] and 1891."

"So what the hell happed to naughty Norman?" Wilson asked, staring at the empty, drifting rowboat. Jericho shrugged his shoulders: "We were told by captain 'Fancy pants' that Norman's time portal was contained in an Egyptian figurine. He probably believed that. But we never saw the damn thing to check it with our mirrors." Wilson nodded; "But the Aztec emblem did carry one. I checked that with my mirror in the tavern. So, we assumed - wrongly - that both contained time portals." Jericho nodded; "Norman is a clever bastard. The figurine was just a fake to mask the real portal."

Alex sighed; "So where the damn thing is now and what form does it take?" Jericho shrugged his shoulders; he didn't know, but they had to find the damn thing and close it. They also had to find out who was now operating the bloody portal. He almost smiled; "I think I know a man who might assist in this matter."

17. A PUZZLE WITHIN A PUZZLE.

They stood outside old Judea's cave entrance and Jericho shouted for him. The old man appeared and grinned broadly; "Jericho my man! Long time, no see." He laughed and winked at Alex; "Hello my lovely." She stuck up a single finger; but did smile. He gestured for the team to follow him into his strange home. Judea leapt into his hammock and swung gently. "I know why you are here talking to old Judea. Old Judea knows you know." He smiled and slapped his hands together.

Jericho also smiled and folded his arms; "The Egyptian Figurine was the clue, my old mad friend. You've been using that bloody figurine as cover for years - centuries in fact - so I knew it was you behind all this."

Judea laughed loudly and swung vigorously; "You're clever young Jericho. Always said that. Old Doc always said that. [Doc is a reference to Doc Underhill; Jericho's old mentor in the Temporal Department] Knew you would figure it out. Judea knows these things." He stopped swinging and sighed loudly. "I dreamt badly one night and found myself in Scotland." He laughed and wrapped his thin arms about his equally thin torso. "Slept badly and woke up in Scotland. Soon made friends with young Norman. Sold him the figure for whisky and a little peek at his young sister having a pee." He giggled and smiled. "Sent him here and he soon joined up with fancy pants. But he knew that the figurine was fake. Knew that old Judea had fooled him. But fancy pants believed him, and Norman really wanted a real one. The one fancy pants had." He laughed with real madness in his voice.

He leapt from the hammock and did a little dance; "I've sent him somewhere nice and warm. He's back in ancient Rome. Arrived stark naked. He'll be alright!" He laughed again and went quiet. Jericho just sighed; "Who has jumped back to 1891? We know it wasn't Norman. He's soul is still missing, so being dumped in ancient Rome explains that. But who else fell for your little trick?"

The old man sat back on his hammock and smiled quite mischievously; "Breholt of course my inquisitive friend. Breholt the great pirate is now in old Scotland. I hope he likes snow and ice," He laughed again and swung his legs up and down with some joy.

Jericho ran a hand over his face and restrained from smiling. "That explains why he handed over the emblems so quickly and easily. He thought that would get us off his back. He knew that Jackie was one of us and used that to contact us. Telling everyone he wanted the girl, he knew we would come to him and he believed that could get a portal from old Judea, But fell for the mad old man's trick as we fell for his."

Wilson nodded; "He knew that we would be on his trail and so fobbed us off with one real portal and a fake. But didn't know that old Judea would be playing tricks on him - like he does everyone - and fell for it." Alex smiled a little; "I remember you saying [to Jericho] that Breholt just disappeared in 1711. Now we know why."

Jackie folded his arms; "I just checked my mirror and Breholt is classified as a missing soul. Yesterday was new Years Day in Western Europe. So, it's now 1711. He disappeared right on cue."

"Yeah, and old Israel Feat was the other player in all this. He probably told Breholt about the figurine and how he could get hold of the supposed real thing from old Judea. Little wonder that Breholt kept him from the clutches of Norman. That also explains why Breholt disgraced Norman after the loss of the ship." Jackie muttered and lowered her mirror. "We should have checked to see if Israel had actually died on that ship. Remember, we didn't see any collectors." She added and smiled a little.

Wilson stared at the mad old man, swinging on his hammock and said quietly; "So there never was a second time portal. Just this old nutter playing tricks with very gullible people." He smiled at Alex and Jackie, who said nothing, who were staring at the dirt floor. "Come on people. Let's get back to HMS bloody Steadfast." Was all Jericho said and the team disappeared. Judea lay back on his hammock and laughed hysterically, shouting; "Old Judea fools everyone. Even the great Jericho Tibbs!"

Inspector John Johnson stood at the railings and smiled as the little boat approached the warship. The 'pirate experts' were returning from the island. He walked down the deck and greeted them as they came up the swinging gangplank. He helped Alex aboard but spoke to Jericho; "Jeb wants you on the bridge. They have identified that old wreck, it appears..." He never finished the sentence; a sailor called to him about a message just received, in the radio room.

They walked slowly to the bridge and Owen stopped them under the bridge ladder; "Just for your information we are back to the very day we landed on the island for the first time. Everything from that moment has changed. There was no beach party, no arriving back in our costumes in that bloody old rowboat. It's all changed. The only fly in the ointment is that Breholt and Dawson [Norman] are still missing souls. There are no real pirates from the 1700's operating around here now." He grinned and slipped his mirror away. Jeb appeared and shouted down the ladder to the team; "We set sail for home people. The Inspector just received some good news about the bloody pirates." He turned and walked away.

The team all exchanged a glance and headed for the Officer's mess and ordered brandies from Samson - the mess steward - and sat quietly, there was no real conversation until Inspector John joined them, smiling broadly. Samson bought him a whisky and he sat down next to Alex. "Well, my friends, our little adventure is over. I just received a message that the Islands coastguard has picked up an old sailboat from the 1920's called the BATHSHEBA and found it stuffed with guns and stolen goods. They admit to a little piracy around these islands. So, we're heading home." He grinned and sipped his whisky. The team just smiled.

The Inspector gripped his glass and said quietly; "They [the current pirates?] admit to attacking boats around here, but not to murder and abduction. But I'm sure Mrs. Harker will identify the brutes as the bastards who murdered her husband and kidnapped her. After all, if they didn't; who the hell did?"

The team just nodded as one. They could answer that question easily, but the explanation of how they knew, could be a little complicated and somewhat awkward!

Jericho rose from the table and said softly; "Come on people, time to go." Alex and Owen stared at the doorway; Doctor James was standing smiling with a cardboard box in arms which rattled slightly. He grinned at Alex, and she walked over to him and peered in the box; there were ropes, padlocks, a couple of chains, some crocodile clips and several lead weights. Lying on top was masking tape and a cane. He gestured for her to following him which she did. "Must be a medical matter." Muttered Wilson as the remaining team headed for their cabins, but Owen wandered off down a different corridor. He was going to meet up with Alex before they jumped back to the lighthouse.

The confidential Navel Board of Inquiry convened in secret to pass judgment on Doctor James Fergus. The circumstances in which he was found in his surgery demanded that; they didn't want the newspapers all over the story.

The doctor – of previously good character – had been found in the Medical Bay in some pain; his cock tied up with tape to the table, weights hanging from his nipples and crocodile clips fixed to his testicles. There was a wooden cane jammed in his anus with a padlock hanging from it. The discipline committee concluded that he had been caught practicing some sadistic sexual act of utter perversion. His story that he had been forced was not accepted by the three admirals and they found him guilty on several counts. He was dismissed from the service and the punishment didn't stop there; the BMA [British Medical Association] struck him off to safeguard patient safety and he ended up working in a Liverpool bar.

Owen lay on the sofa and watched Mr. Parker [the lighthouse cat] chase his rubber ball about the study. He smiled and thought he would never cross Alex, under any circumstance!

The End

EPISODE 7. "ALEXANDRA GOES BEYOND THE JERUSALEM MIRROR."

EPISODE PROLOGUE: "Whilst investigating mysterious disappearances from an old house on the Yorkshire Moors in 1974, Alex accidently stumbles through a 'Jerusalem Mirror' and finds herself a mysterious lover in 1735. She also finds that she has to perform a service for the old King, to free the feisty Mr. Parker from the bloody Bastille! She also has a memorable encounter with the Kings 'Black stallion'.

75 Minutes approx. **Episode Warnings:** Alcohol – Smoking - Strong language – Violence [including sexual violence, BDSM & sexual torture and murder] – Strong graphic sexual references [including references to prostitution and sex trafficking] – Mild horror.

NOTES: The original version of this story is published and appears in the **TEMPORAL DETECTIVES:** Book Series 3 – Episode 1 entitled: **"THE JERUSALEM MIRROR."** This is a special EXTENDED episode of the original story.

CAUTION: Recommended for 18+ only.

1. 3rd MAY 1974 - A SOLICITOR CALLS.

Sally eased from the bed and pushed her long blond hair back whilst snatching up her dressing gown from the floor. The door bell sounded again and she muttered; "First bloody time we have a real lay in this week and someone is at the door." She looked back at Dave sprawled under the covers and shook her head; "Christ, You'd sleep through a bloody bomb going off." Sally wrapped her dressing gown around her naked body and made for the stairs.

She made her way down the stairs, passing the sleeping cat; Amy, on the top stair, who sat up and followed. "I'm coming!" She said loudly and reached the door, picking up several pieces of mail from the carpet. She tidied her hair and checked her dressing gown, then unlocked the front door and opened it a few inches. "Hello, can I help you. We're just having a lay in; we both do shift work you see," she said to the middle aged, well-dressed man standing on their step, clutching a leather briefcase. He smiled; "Does David Edward Fisher live here?" He asked and offered Sally a little white business card.

Sally took the card and read it slowly. "You're a lawyer from York?" She sounded quite surprised and held her dressing gown together quite tightly with the other hand. She didn't really want to flash a bloody solicitor at this time of the morning.

Patrick Well's nodded; "Yes, I'm here to speak to a David Edward Fisher, whose father was Norman David Fisher and Grand-father was Edward John Fisher; all from Sheffield." He rummaged around in his briefcase and pulled some papers out. "I'm here about his Great-Uncle Wesley's will."

"I didn't even know he had a Great-Uncle?" She was really surprised by that revelation; David's parents were both dead and he had no brothers or sisters. She slowly pulled the door chain off and opened the door. "You'd better come in and I'll get the idle bugger out of his pit." Sally smiled and gestured for Patrick Well's to go into the living room, whilst she headed back up the stairs and then cursed herself; the bloody man only had to glance up, to see her bare bum. She really should invest in a longer dressing gown, she mused. Sally didn't look back down the stairs to see if he was watching. She smiled to herself as she reached the bedroom door; still he was a good-looking well-groomed man at least - he probably wouldn't object to seeing a 22-year-old woman's private parts - especially one, most men considered 'pretty'. Well, non-one had complained, when she dances at the 'Blue Star Club' until the early hours of the morning. Her costume barely covered anything; but the money was good, and she really needed money.

She sighed and really didn't want to think about the debt they were in; it gave her enough sleepless days and nights already. Sally stared at the man snoring under the covers and had to smile; David had stood by her throughout the court cases and debt orders, the bailiffs and repossessions. She actually shuddered at the thoughts that crowded quickly into her head and now a bloody solicitor turns up at this time of the morning and she flashes her arse at him!

She shook David strongly and told him about the visitor, telling him to slip on a T-shirt and track bottoms and get downstairs. She would slip on some panties and her long padded house coat and told him to put the bloody kettle on!

Dave was mumbling about he hasn't got any fucking Uncles. He had never heard of a Great-Uncle bleeding Wesley. He stumbled down the stairs into the front room and greeted the solicitor - apologising for still being in bed - but he had finished night-shift at the local Meat Distribution Depot of Dewhurst the Butchers.

The solicitor waved his apology away with a smile; "I should be the one to apologise Mr. Fisher, I was in the area dealing with a complicated conveyance and I thought I would try my luck." Dave gestured for him to sit, and he would put the kettle on. The solicitor continued; "We have written several times and received no replies, so I thought a personal visit would be best." He sat and pulled more papers from his briefcase. "I'll make some tea." Dave muttered and headed for the kitchen, followed by Amy the cat who wanted her breakfast.

Dave switched the kettle on and sighed; "Great-Uncle Wesley?" He had never heard his parents speak of such a man; he couldn't ask them now; they had both passed on five years ago, after suffering a car accident on a dirt road in Spain, whilst on holiday. A tractor had pulled from a field, straight in front of them. Apparently, it took an ambulance nearly an hour to reach the accident site; it was in the foothills of some mountains. They were both dead upon arrival at the local hospital. He didn't want to be reminded of those dark days and pushed it from his mind as he made tea; yelling to the solicitor how he likes his; milk and two sugars came the reply. Sally appeared in the doorway and whispered; "What the fuck is this all about?" Dave shrugged his shoulders and whispered back; "I've never heard of a bloody Great-Uncle Wesley. He says that they have written to me several times, but I've never seen any bloody letters from them."

Sally looked down at the business card and covered her mouth with a hand; "Dave, I'm so sorry. I've seen letters with this Solicitors address on and panicked. I chucked them away. I'm so sorry. I thought they were after me for more money." Dave just shook his head; "Don't worry about it sweetheart; he's here now." He passed her a cup of tea and wandered into the living room with a cup for the solicitor.

Sally stood in the kitchen and sipped her tea; without Dave's steadfast support she really didn't know what would have happened to her. She had lost her flat, her car and even the bloody bank had closed her accounts. She had to leave a couple of steady jobs working in supermarkets because men had turned up at work, threatening her for money; even the Tax man was after his share and Sally found that she was paying a lot of her wages back to the Inland revenue. She struggled with that and finally had to find a job that paid cash in hand; the 'Blue Star Club' did that for her.

Now, four nights a week until the early hours; she danced and served drinks for money in her hand; that had helped greatly. But she really did feel ashamed, that she paraded around the club with a little silver tray and not much else. Her 'uniform' consisted of a little black mini skirt, high heels, frilly white apron, panties and stockings - nothing else - but a black dog collar around her neck with silver lettering showing ' Blue Star Club'. On certain nights she could earn really good tips by completing her duties without any panties on.

Then, there were the chances of earning really serious money by having sex with certain customers at the club. Leon came immediately to mind; he always gave her twenty pounds each time [good money for the era] when she called around his plush apartment in the city on her night off. But always when Dave was still on shift. The big African clearly liked small, blond, white girls

with ample breasts and he paid well for her company. He wanted
her for his full-time mistress and would keep her in comfort, at
one of the apartments he owned - if she agreed - she hadn't
done so because of what she owed Dave for his unswerving
support.

She sighed and then snapped from her thoughts as Dave called
her into the living room. She forced a smile and wandered in and
sat down. Amy jumped upon her lap and started cleaning herself.
Dave grinned broadly and gripped her hand; "You are never
going to believe what Patrick has just told me; I've inherited a
house near the Yorkshire Moors. Great-Uncle Wesley died without
a wife or any children and I'm his nearest blood relative still
living. He was my grandfather's youngest brother. I had never
heard Grandpa or dad ever talk about him."

Sally couldn't really absorb what Dave was saying for some
minutes and then realised this could be the answer to all her
problems. She cuddled him, pushing the cat from her lap; "I
really won't believe it until I see the place with my own eyes!"
She exclaimed and kissed him much to the amusement of the
solicitor who advised the pair to make an appointment with him
at his York offices; to receive the keys and sign for the property.
There was also a little cash to come.

"How much cash?" Sally asked straight away and was told that
Great-Uncle Wesley had left David about fifteen hundred pounds
- after Death Duties had been paid and - of course, some debts
owned by his late Great-Uncles estate; not to mention Solicitors
fee's.

So the happy couple made arrangement to visit 'Salem House as
soon as possible. Sally danced and served drinks that night, with
a smile on her face. But Dave worried about his inheritance and
what it would mean for the future of the pair. One thought
troubled him above the rest; why hadn't his father and
grandfather ever spoken about 'Great Uncle Wesley'?

2. 17th JUNE 1974, SALEM HOUSE - PART 1.

Dave jumped from the old Vauxhall Viva and stared at the old
house, a little amazed that he actually owned it. Sally grabbed
him around the waist and planted a big kiss on his lips. "I still
can't bloody believe it's yours." She kissed him again. Dave

grinned and held up the keys; "Ours." He said softly and the pair embraced in the overgrown driveway.

The removal lorry driver shook his head and stared up at the old house and turned to the other men in the cab; "I wouldn't have this fucking place if it came with gold beds." The younger man nodded and handed around the cigarettes; "I'd fuck his young tart, fantastic pair of tits." He muttered, quietly smoking. They watched as the young couple hugged and celebrated outside the old house.

Paddy the driver stared up at 'Salem House' and stopped smoking, very quietly he spoke to the other two men; "Look up at the attic on the right wing, the big window, can you see it?"

The other two men leaned forward and peered through the windscreen. "I see it." Whispered the younger man; his cigarette falling from his lips onto the cab floor. Terry gripped the dash and swore; "Fucking shit! Do you see her as well?"

All three men watched the figure standing at the dirty window in amazement; "Like something out of an old film." Paddy said softly and Terry agreed; "Like something in an old portrait you see in museums, or those big houses open to the public." Paddy crossed himself and kissed the little crucifix that hung around his neck; "I'd heard all the fucking stories about this shit hole, but never thought I'd see they were true." Terry wiped his face with the back of his hand - he was sweating without actually doing anything - The three exchanged concerned glances and made an unanimous decision; get the stuff into the fucking house as quick as possible and get the fuck out of here. They also decided it would be best - for the young couple - if they said nothing about the figure at the window.

All three men lapsed into a shocked silence as the figure disappeared. Paddy crossed himself again; he had not really prayed in some years; but he did now.

The young couple had unlocked the big double doors and were waving for the removal men to start unloading their possessions. Very reluctantly the men left the cab - all still staring at the upstairs window - and began to shift the boxes and items of furniture from their lorry in almost silence.
Dave and Sally were so engrossed in their happiness and relief

that they had escaped the dingy - and expensive - rented house; they didn't really notice the change in the removal men's mood. They were impressed with the speed that the men unloaded the lorry and piled their stuff in the house. They didn't even wait for the customary tips; disappearing down the drive without so much as a 'goodbye'.

Sally found a comfortable big bedroom on the first floor, near a bathroom and working toilet and made up the bed whilst Dave brewed tea in the small kitchen, that had been built on the same floor. He had found that cold tap worked, but the hot tap just made gurgling noises. They guessed correctly; this little suite of rooms had been occupied by Dave's great uncle Wesley, when he was alive.

It was Dave that pointed out the four locks on the bedroom door and as he looked about, he noticed the strange pattern woven into the old carpet. He studied it for some minutes before realising that it was a pentagon; what was the significance of that he wondered. Sally called him over to the large Gothic fireplace and both stared at the remains of a bird, burnt in the grate with withered flowers scattered about it. She made Dave clear that revolting mess up straight away.

Dave couldn't open the large window; it had been nailed shut and Sally pulled down the strings of rotted garlic from around the frame and they went in the bin with the dead bird. "He was one strange old fucker." She said quietly as she cleaned the window frame. Then giggling, she jumped on the bed and bounced up and down upon the large four poster bed until she looked up and saw the carving on the bed's canopy; it was Jesus on the Cross.

"Fucking charming; a religious nut as well as fucking strange and reclusive." She said to Dave, who just chuckled and headed back to the kitchen to see if the electricity meter was on and working. The gas certainly was; he had boiled the kettle on the small two ring stove that it contained.

The electricity only worked in this suite and he put fifty pence in the meter to start with. They sat on stools in the little kitchen and laughed together; the pair's relief that most of their problems were behind them now was palatable and obvious. For the first time in quite a while; they were actually happy.

Sally finally did mention about the strange behaviour of the removal men and Dave had to agree; he still had the five-pound note, he was going to give them as a tip. He pulled the crumpled note from his pocket as proof. Sally slowly eased it from his fingers with a big smile; "Well, I'll take it as a tip for being your hardworking girlfriend." Dave chuckled and nodded his head; "You're worth every penny." He spoke softly and kissed her again.

Sally released Amy from her cat basket and watched in amazement and surprise that the little creature ran back into her cage and refused to come out. Even food and treats wouldn't make the cat budge. "She just needs time to settle in; it's all new territory to her." Dave smiled and so they left the cage door open with food and water outside. The cat steadfastly remained inside. They worked for a couple of hours getting their rooms ready; the major disappointment was the little 'Bush' portable TV wouldn't pick a signal up. Dave sighed; "I can't find an aerial socket; old Wesley couldn't have had a TV. Strange that, but the solicitor said he was an odd old man." Sally's wireless radio wouldn't pick up a signal either. But her stereo record player worked alright; and so, they played Beatles records and a couple of singles by the 'Mama's and Papa's' as night gathered in.

After a supper of tinned vegetable soup and bread, they jumped into bed and celebrated their good fortune with passionate lovemaking. They were both soon asleep; but not for long.

Sally suddenly sat up and took a deep breath; what was that noise? She reached over to the ornate bedside cabinet and grabbed up her watch. She pressed the little button and the LCD display showed: '00.00'. Sally then realised - with some relief and some annoyance - that the grandfather clock in the downstairs hall was chiming Midnight. She glanced at Dave; he was still fast asleep. "A bloody bomb going off wouldn't wake you up." She muttered and flopped back on her pillows, pulling up the sheets again. She counted the chimes as they sounded in the quiet house.

For a second time, she sat straight up and breathed quickly and heavily; the bloody old clock had chimed thirteen times!

She also heard other noises coming from downstairs; it sounded like people having a muffled conversation amongst themselves.

She shook Dave quite violently and whispered that they had intruders in the house. He woke and pulled his trousers and shoes on, stopping only to pick up a large, heavy black poker from the fireplace. Sally climbed slowly from the bed and wrapped her long, padded coat around her naked body.

Sally noticed that the cat basket was empty; but the food and water appeared untouched. She scrambled about in a nearby cardboard box and found a torch. They quietly headed from the bedroom into the upper hall; both filled with a mix of fear and trepidation.

3. 24th JUNE 1974, SALEM HOUSE - PART 2.

Detective Inspector Roy Calms lit a cigarette and eased his large frame from the small car and headed to the uniform constable standing on the door - looking bored with his arms folded. He stood straight and saluted the Inspector. "Your sergeant is on the first floor with a couple more of your boys Sir." He greeted the Inspector who just nodded. A real queer one this; a young couple move into this old relic and simply disappear; he thought climbing the grand staircase.

Detective Sergeant Greg Chambers finished his cigarette and tossed the butt into the fireplace. He looked about the room and shook his head, speaking to the Detective Constable who was sorting through an open cardboard box on the floor; "Fisher's watch and wallet are still on the dresser and all his clothes still appear to be here. The bloody girl must have been naked; apart from a padded coat she always wore. Didn't take her purse, watch or shoes either. Bloody strange."

The constable nodded his agreement; "Uniform say that the place was all locked up when they arrived to investigate the missing person's report. They had to break in through a downstairs window, so how the fuck did they get out of the house?" He pulled a large black vibrator from the box and laughed; "Typical tart who danced half naked at that cesspit club and she owns this!" he waved the rubber penis about and switched it on; it didn't work. He laughed again; "She's worn the fucking batteries out and it takes four 'Duracell.'"

"She also wasn't averse, to sleeping with some of the customers, so her colleagues tell us." Inspector Calm's stood in the doorway and pulled his note book out. "The man was reliable as a Swiss watch according to his employers - never missed a shift in three years - then suddenly he doesn't turn up with no word; nothing. Right out of character. They all commented about the girl though, little better than a common prostitute. They really didn't know how such a good bloke got involved with a tart like her."

"She was an undischarged bankrupt, had no bank accounts and couldn't get credit anywhere. She was working at that club for 'cash in hand'. Even the bloody tax man was after her; a right one by the sounds of it." The Inspector added, looking around the room. Sergeant Chambers waved his hand about; "Most of their clothes and personal item are still here, they must have left practically naked and penniless." He pointed to the bedside cabinet and the little black diary laying there.

"That makes good reading Guv, payments from men who fucked her for twenty quid a time." The sergeant picked up the book and handed it to the Inspector. The constable whistled; "Twenty quid a time; she must have been a fucking good shag for that sort of money." The Inspector chuckled and tapped the book; "There are several references to someone called 'Leon'. I wonder if that's our old friend, the pimp and pornographer Leon Devine. I bet we could find a few films with our missing girl starring in them."

Sergeant Chambers folded his arms; "The last people we know, who saw the pair alive, were the three removal men from Baxter's removals. That was on the 17th of this month; no-one has seen them alive since that day. That's where it becomes really interesting; the youngest of the three men; a certain Robert Cornfield has quit his job and moved down south. All on the day he helped move the pair into this dump; and he made sure to leave no forwarding address. Odd co-incidence that."

The Inspector nodded and re-read his notebook; "Interesting threesome we have here; the driver, Patrick 'Paddy' O'Connor has previous for house breaking and some theft. But it was nearly fifteen years ago when he was much younger. His Driver's mate: Terry Jones has previous for sexual assault on young girls. Nothing is known about young Cornfield."

Detective Constable Matching's looked up from the cardboard box and chuckled; "When I spoke to that pair, they looked paler than a ginger birds arse. Claimed they dropped the gear and got the fuck outta the place because they saw a fucking ghost!" Everyone was amused by that. Then Detective Constable Harris stuck his head around the door; "Guv, uniform says you're wanted on the radio. The solicitor who dealt with the pair has finally turned up at the nick,"

The Inspector sighed and stared about the small rooms; "The old man who owned the place was found dead - at the foot of the stairs - some three years ago. His death was bloody queer too." the Inspector pushed his notebook away and headed for the door. "How was it queer Guv?" The sergeant asked.

The inspector didn't smile; "No marks upon the body, Doc Roberts believed the old man suffered a massive heart attack and died at the foot of the stairs. A PM confirmed that, but he was found stark naked clutching an old photograph which he had apparently written upon - in crayon - the words 'forgive me'. The picture had been taken about 1880 and showed a very young girl - a child - being abused by some creep. Some strait-laced Victorians really did enjoy child porn. We know he wrote the words because a red crayon was found clutched in his other hand; he must have written the words as he died."

The detective stopped searching the cupboard box and looked up; "How old was the old man Guv?" The Inspector grinned; "I know where you're heading with that Ken, Wesley Fisher was sixty-three years old when he died in 1971 and the photograph was taken in 1879 or 1880 according to the experts who took a look at it. It was shot long before the old man was even born. So why was he asking for forgiveness about something, he couldn't be remotely involved in?"

None of the Detectives present could answer that mystery and so the Inspector shrugged his shoulders and muttered; "Fucking queer all round." The sergeant rubbed his chin; "Shall I pull them removal men in Guv?" The Inspector said no. He wanted them to make voluntary statements for now but instructed the sergeant to issue a 'Person of Interest Notice' to all forces regarding young Cornfield. The Inspector looked about the room and shrugged his shoulders again; "No signs of burglary, no signs of a fight or any disturbance - except that poker and torch lying on top of the stairs - nothing really to go on."

Sergeant Chambers stared out the window and spoke directly to the Inspector; "We could pull in that dirty black bastard Leon and see what he knows about the tart?" The Inspector approved of that idea; "Yeah, sweat him for a few hours and see what jumps out." The Inspector chuckled and walked straight past the two Temporal Detectives standing in the top hall, both consulting their mirrors - he, of course, could not see or hear them - unless they wanted it so.

"Wesley Fisher's soul was collected and processed; he's now a motor mechanic in Mexico City. Nothing untoward was known about him. But he died in 1982 and in France! So, who was the stiff that the police were talking about?" Alex tapped her mirror, adding: "But this house has some real questions about it since it was built in 1767. Some of the previous owners have been devil worshippers, rapists and murders; you name something evil and its happened here over the centuries." Alex lowered her mirror and stared into the rooms where the other, living, detectives still worked.

"Find out who collected the soul of the dead body found here." Jericho rubbed his chin, something was wrong; if Wesley had been collected somewhere else, who the hell was the dead man? Alex nodded; "I'll get Owen onto it, that's right up his street."

"Here's an interesting thought; Wesley Fisher came from a poor working-class Sheffield family and had no real education or qualifications. In his early life he worked the steel mills for wages - poor wages - yet in his twilight years he could buy a house like this and have serious money in his bank accounts." Jericho gestured towards the grand staircase; "Some of the portraits, just on the bloody staircase could buy a decent house around here, so where did the money come from?"

Alex admitted she didn't know and pushed the mirror into her jacket pocket and watched the Inspector descending the stairs; "I don't think they have a clue about this place." She said quietly, but Jericho smiled; "Why should they? They're still amongst the living." Both looked up as Wilson and Owen appeared at the top of the attic stairs. Wilson gestured for them to join him. "Guess what we found in the attic." He jerked a thumb behind him and added; "A bloody Jerusalem Mirror."

Jericho rubbed his hands together and smiled; "Now that's more like it. We get the call that two souls have vanished - complete with their flesh suits still on - and there's a bloody Jerusalem mirror in the place." They made their way to the attic room and found the old, full-length mirror standing against a dirty wall, next to the window.

"Wonder which time and place it's linked to?" Asked Owen and started to re-read his mirror. Jericho was looking at the back of the mirror with a small torch. "It was made originally in France, at a place called 'la Masion des Tenebres' or that could be the company who manufactured it. The year shown is...." He leaned forward and strained to make out the writing; "In 1646."

"The House of Darkness." Alex sighed; "Charming name, must have had the customers queuing up outside." Owen interrupted everyone and tapped his mirror; "Says here, that one of the owners was a certain Marquis de Sade in 1765, in Paris."

"Now that is one interesting old French pervert; apparently." Wilson chuckled and then something on the floor caught his eye; a simple white rag that was too clean and laundered to have lain on the dusty floor for long. He walked over and picked it up; "A Lace hankie." He muttered and pulled it from his face; "It's being soaked in something very pungent and is still a little overpowering." He offered it to the others. Jericho took a slight sniff and nodded; "Old fashioned knock-out stuff and it's still quite fresh."

Jericho spoke to Owen; "Call into control and tell them we're going to use the mirror." Everyone watched as Jericho simply stepped into the 'glass' and disappeared. They all followed without question and the dirty little attic room was empty; again. Well, it wasn't quite empty; Amy the cat crept out from beneath a covered stool and ran towards the mirror and jumped through.

A dark shadow passed across the dirty floor and the man stood by the mirror; he stared down at his pocket watch and sighed. But he could now hear two of the living detectives approaching the attic rooms and without hesitation stepped through. So, all Detective Ken Lewis and his colleague found was a dirty room stuffed with old furniture. There was dust and cobwebs everywhere and so they concluded that no-one had been in the room for years.

They had a quick look around and then left, closing the door behind them. There was silence in the darkness until a weak white light appeared on the mirrors glass and the sound of footsteps could have been heard from the room; had the detectives stayed a little bit longer. But then; the time was now quite different.

The young woman gathered her dress about herself and listened intently at the door, then slowly approached the large window and peered down into the entrance of 'Salem House'. She saw the couple embracing by the ornate front doors and the removal van sitting on the gravel. She watched as the large black car swept into the drive and some people stepped from the car; they looked like Undertakers.

The woman groaned and cussed. "That old bastard; he must really hate me. He must have tipped them off." She whispered and headed for the mirror again.

4. 16th AUGUST 1767 - LA MASION DES TENEBRES (PARIS).

The carriage threaded slowly through the crowded streets and Alex waved her silk fan across her face; it didn't do much good in this heat. "I didn't think summer in Paris could be this hot." She muttered to Jericho who was wiping his face with a small hankie. He smiled and adjusted his powdered wig, causing little flakes of white chalk to fly about; "I think Owen has overdone the bloody powder on this thing." Alex managed a smile and eased her bosom beneath her thin cloak; "You only have to worry about chalk dust, this bloody corset has pushed my tits up and out so much, I'm practically topless."

Alex was dressed like a lady of the royal Court of King Louis XV, colloquially known as 'the beloved' and the ladies of his court were well known for their outrageous clothes and loose morals. Wilson, who was driving the ornate carriage leaned back and spoke through the small flap, covered with embroidered cloth, to Alex and Jericho; "I think we're here." Owen, who was standing upon the rear step [and gripping the leather straps with both hands] muttered; "Thank God for that, Wilson couldn't drive a greasy stick up a pig's arse."

The carriage stopped outside and a magnificent strapping African male in a stunning red and gold servants uniform, pulled open the door and bowed. Alex accepted his white gloved hand and stepped from the carriage, Jericho followed straightening his sword and blinking in the hot sunshine. He turned to Wilson; "Titus, wait for thirty minutes only." Wilson nodded; then it was Calvary time.

Owen stepped off the carriage and stretched his legs; he stared up at the black fronted building with little windows and bright red roof. The gold plate upon the wall declared; "'La Maison des Tenebres: Fonde 1689." Someone had scrawled beneath in white chalk: 'cher maison de pute'. Owen grinned at that and joined Wilson by the horses, with the water bucket that hung beneath the carriage. "They can have a drink." He said and patted the grey mare nearest to him.

The pair watched Alex and Jericho disappear into the dark building and the big servant resumed his position on the top of the stairs with no expression upon his face. "That's funny, I would have thought, he would have wanted to chat with a fellow African." Wilson murmured, but Owen smiled; "There are hundreds of African servants in Paris at this time, so he probably gets all the chat he could ever want." They both chuckled at that and Owen gave water to the other grey mare of the carriage's team.

Jericho and Alex were shown into a beautifully furnished sitting room by another resplendent African servant, he bowed and gestured towards two bright red upholstered chairs; "Ma'am and Sir, I will inform Madame Bella that you are here." He walked backwards and left the room. Alex slumped upon the chair and loosened her cloak: "In two hundred years, the contents of this room would fetch an absolute fortune, and this is just a bloody brothel."

Jericho nodded, and his sharp eyes had already seen the two spy holes set into the wall opposite; disguised as wall decorations of glass. He grunted; "Someone is already watching us; I wonder who that can be?" Alex didn't answer as the door opened and Madame Bella Varden strolled in. She was a tall, skinny woman in her late thirties, wearing thin white gloves with her long [and obviously expensive] gown. Around her neck was a gold chain, a snake and a circle. Jericho sat upright at the sight of her Satan worshipping necklace. Then stood and smiled, he bowed and kissed her outstretched hand.

"Madame Bella, may I present my Mistress; Mademoiselle Alexandra." Alex rose and curtsied but said nothing. Madame Bella ran her eyes up and down Alex and smiled; "Monsieur Tibbs, your friend is quite a beauty. Such a woman could earn a fortune here; probably in one night." Jericho also smiled; "Quite so, but I have come on a most urgent matter on behalf of an English friend. I seek the whereabouts of his missing mistress and I know the girl would make for such an establishment like that you command." Madame Bella nodded; her face expressionless; "Please sit." She spoke softly and her African servant placed a chair behind her, and she sat with some grace.

"My friend, quite foolishly in my opinion, mistreated the girl and she disappeared into the night. We know she made for France and most certainly to here; Paris I mean. There is a substantial reward for her recovery; quite substantial." Jericho pulled a small draawing from his pocket and offered it to Madame Bella; she took it very slowly and said quietly; "How substantial Monsieur Tibbs?" Jericho leaned forward and whispered into her ear. Alex caught the Madame's expression and smiled to herself; that little amount will put the cat amongst the pigeons; no doubt about that.

Madame Bella produced a beautiful blue fan and waved it about her face. "If your friend has that sort of money to throw after a...well, a....a young whore, then he is a fool. I'm sure that even good-looking harlots are cheap enough in England." She smiled and handed back the picture; Jericho knew she had recognised the likeness and the alarm in her eyes; which most would have missed, didn't go unnoticed by him or Alex.

Jericho chuckled and held up his hands; "I know Madame Bella, I know, but of all people you will understand the vagaries of the heart. He wants her back; it's as simple as that." Madame Bella stared at Alex; "Your young mistress is clearly well trained and obedient. Most girls like her would have endless useless chatter upon their tongues. She says nothing; but observes and hears everything. I am impressed. I would give you ten thousand Francs' right now for her; no questions asked."

Jericho shook his head; "I'm sorry Madame Bella, but it would probably cost me twice that to replace such a gem." Madame Bella smiled at that; "I'm afraid I cannot help you Monsieur Tibbs, I have never seen the girl in the likeness that you have offered. I'm sorry." She rose suddenly from her chair and pulled the rope cord to summon a servant. "Apollo will show you out." The big African appeared and gestured towards the door, bowing a little. "This way please." He said and waited for Jericho and Alex to rise and walk to the door.

Jericho turned to Madame Bella, smiled and bowed; "Please consider the reward; should you receive any information about the girl. I am staying with an old friend of my friend; He's called Louis." Madame Bella chuckled with some contempt in her voice; "Paris is a big city Monsieur, with many a Louis hanging about the place, which damn Louis would that be?"

Jericho hesitated in the doorway and smiled; "I am sorry Madame, my old friend's friend stays at Versailles; that's his home now." He took Alex by the hand and the pair left a clearly shocked Madame Bella, who stumbled across the room and slumped into her chair. She watched the pair go and wiped her face; could this pair be for real? The King would certainly have the kind of money mentioned for the English girl. But an old friend of the King who was from England? A name popped into her head, The Duke of Buckingham? She groaned quite loudly and shouted for Apollo to come.

She instructed him to attend Versailles and seek out an old friend of hers; Madame Aurelie who was an assistant Housekeeper there. She would certainly know about the visitors and gave Apollo some gold coins for the woman's help. He pocketed the coins, bowed and left. On horseback, he reached the palace quickly and found his contact instructing some footmen in her parlour. She was more than happy to accept the coins and spoke briefly with the quiet servant. He was particularly interested in Mademoiselle Alexandra [no surprise there!] and made his way to her rooms. A brief search of the huge bedroom yielded nothing. "She certainly travels light for a supposed lady of quality." He muttered to himself and then stood still as the bathroom door opened and Alex stepped through, wrapping a towel around her damp naked body. She had taken an afternoon bath because of the heat.

He bowed low and asked if he could be of assistance; he was here to check the drabs for Madame Aurelie who was going to have them replaced. Alex rea;;y smiled at him; he was a big, handsome, strapping young man with a gorgeous smile. She also remembered him from the brothel and knew this was an excellent opportunity to quiz him about his mistress, Madame Bella. She smiled broadly and waved her hand at the window telling him to carry on. Her towel slipped and fell around her ankles; she squeaked with 'shock' but didn't make any attempt to pick it up. She stood stark naked and didn't bother to hide anything. "Well, can you hand me my towel?" she said softly, and Apollo smiled and nodded; walking up to her and snatched up the towel, holding it out. Alex placed both hands on he's and said, "Thank you." He let the towel drop and pulled her close, his big hands running down her back and onto her buttocks. "Anything else I can assist you with Madame?" he asked quietly, and Alex whispered into his ear. He grinned and nodded; he certainly could do that.

Alex sat with a pile of pillows at her back, legs open and moaning softly on the big bed as Apollo – now equally naked – displayed his skill at pleasing a woman with his fingers, tongue and mouth. Alex ran her fingers through his short dark hair and quivered under the delicious assault on her fanny. She groped at the bedside cabinet and pulled a small jar from it and offered it to him as his head rose from her crotch. She watched with real anticipation as he spread some on his big cock and then around and into her vagina.

He mounted her with some urgency and started to thrust hard and deep immediately. Alex gripped his big shoulders and whispered for him to fuck her hard, which he did. His mouth found hers and they kissed passionately as she now threw her arms around him and pulled him close. Alex moaned loudly as he drove his cock home with some real power; he was like a human road drill [so she thought] and she quickly had a couple of orgasms under his incredible, relentless fucking. They changed position, with Alex on all fours and Apollo fucking her like a dog in heat. With a hand rubbing her crotch, feeling his big cock inside of her, she could feel a big orgasm coming and she shuddered and screamed as she squirted, soaking her hand and thighs. She collapsed on the bed, groaning and gasping, but Apollo continued to fuck her as she gripped the blankets, face down. He leaned over her and whispered; "Where do you want my seed?"

She raised her tear-stained face and said hoarsely; "Breed me! For God sake breed me!" He managed a soft laugh, then groaned

and cussed as he filled her with his seed. He lay on her, propped
up on his elbows and said quietly; "Madame, I think in a few
months you'll be carrying a black baby – my baby – and I hope
you have an understanding and sympathetic family." He cussed
again and rolled off her; now lying next to her, he ran a grateful
hand down her back and neck. "I think you should leave your
present master and move in with me so that I can service you
properly every night. I want to taste and explore every part of
you. You will be well satisfied Madame and I will fill you with
many babies."

Alex managed to raise her head and smile; "That's the best offer
I've had for some time." They both started to laugh and
embraced again. Kissing passionately; now with their tongues
doing the talking. They would make love again before Apollo had
to leave and make his report, while Alex had a team briefing and
dinner to attend. The King would be dinning with them. That
really impressed the young man as he dressed, while Alex sat on
the bed, legs open, watching him.

He gestured to her open crotch; "I s that an invitation for me to
return and fill it again?" he said softly, and Alex smiled; "It's
yours darling to use when you like." That made him chuckle and
they kissed again before he left. Alex lay on the bed and
suddenly groaned; she hadn't asked him one damn question
about bloody Madame Bella! She cursed and started to giggle.

That evening, 'La Masion des Tenebres was packed with
customers, but Madame Bella sat quietly in her study, sipping
wine and staring at fireplace. Her two gentlemen companions
also sat in silence, glasses of brandy in their hands.

Madame's maid servant Maria appeared and informed her
mistress that Apollo had returned. Everyone sat up as the big
African appeared, bowed and removed his hat. Madame Bella
gestured for him to speak. "I followed their carriage, and it did
indeed travel to Versailles. They entered the Palace through the
King's personal entrance and were met by Le Marquis Du Nantes;
the King's Private Secretary. I made some discrete inquiries
about the pair, and it appears that Monsieur Tibbs is some kind
of envoy for a very important and powerful Englishman. The
recovery of the girl seems to be a matter of personal honour for
the King now and as you would expect, he cannot take his eyes
off Mademoiselle Alexandra."

Madame Bella turned to the men and sighed; "It appears that Roland has fucked up with this one. He made the mistake; he can clear the mess up." She stood and headed for the door. The two men stood and nodded at each other; Madame was not a woman you cross easily. They placed their glasses down and followed her to the attics.

Madame Bella stood in the doorway and consulted her little blue notebook; the girl didn't stand her in too much money and that amount had been paid to Roland for her. She stared down at Sally; unconscious and totally naked upon the bed with her hands tied behind her back. She called for Madame Clare, who appeared from a room opposite, wiping her hands. The old woman was a little hunched over and had just a few yellow teeth left in her mouth. She grinned; "That one will be ready for work by tomorrow; she's already seen quite a few big cocks by my reckoning; her fanny's a little loose, but she's pretty enough for most of the bastards we get here. Besides, she does have a fine pair of big milk tits which all men like."

Madame Bella nodded and did not smile; "We may have been compromised by her or rather, by Monsieur Roland and I have sent a message to him to dispose of her without any links to my mansion." Monsieur Henri coughed and started pulling off his jacket; "Well, we may as well get some of our investment back." Monsieur Phillip agreed and started to remove his jacket. Madame Clare chuckled; "She won't come round for a few hours yet." Both men shrugged their shoulders and Monsieur Henri pulled open his lacy shirt; "I don't mind that, and I know Phillip enjoys a sleeper." The two Madame's both sighed and closed the door on the two men and Sally.

Madame Clare gripped Bella by the arm and spoke softly; "What about the man?" Madame Bella looked quite surprised by the admission that Roland had also acquired a man with the girl. But Bella had no idea what had happened to him. "Knowing Monsieur Roland, I would suspect that he sold him to Monsieur Franklyn."

Clare muttered and did grin to herself; Monsieur Franklyn ran the finest Homosexual brothel in Paris, and he always needed straight men for his 'dungeon' - which earns serious money from certain discerning clients.

Madame Bella returned to her customers, deep in thought and

instructed Apollo to fetch Monsieur Roland; at once. She collected a glass of brandy and sat in her drawing room alone. But Madame Bella was not alone in the beautiful room and jumped a little, when the large black cat pushed past her feet and disappeared behind a red and gold sofa. She stared at the sofa and wondered where the damn cat came from - they had some in the kitchens - for the rats and mice, but none were allowed upstairs. She hated cats.

Something in her memory was saying that this black cat belonged to Monsieur... She interrupted her thoughts and rose to ring the servant's bell and have the damn thing removed and killed, but never reached the bell pull. Madame Bella lay dead upon the floor with a large, gaping blood-filled wound to her throat, which had been slit wide open.

The figure left the room un-noticed despite the throngs of customers and girls. The cat followed it into the busy street and then into the plain black carriage that awaited them. It disappeared at speed into the gathering gloom of night.

The man stepped from the shadows opposite the grand doors of 'La Maison des Tenebres' and consulted his Italian pocket watch. With a broad smile, he lifted a hand and his handsome, dark red cab trundled towards him. He jumped in and settled down for the thirty-minute ride to Chateau Roi Charles. The big man sitting opposite said nothing and stared out the window - Paris was quite a grand city - but nothing could match the Palace of Versailles, that he was now privileged to attend with his new master. He smiled and adjusted his jacket which concealed both a pistol and dagger. Tomorrow could prove most interesting, he mused.

Apollo returned to the window and admired the countryside passing by. Then he smiled broadly as he thought about Mademoiselle Alexandra.

5. ALEX STUMBLES THROUGH A JERUSALEM MIRROR.

Alex held up the flickering little lamp and wandered down yet another corridor of the grand palace of Versailles and smiled to herself; she was lost. "I would have bloody sworn that this was the way to the team's rooms." She muttered and then noticed a heavily paneled door to her left was slightly open and a little yellowing light was escaping from it. She tapped on the door and stepped in; "Maybe someone here could direct me." But the room was empty despite being lit by several candles. It was bare of any furniture, except a large ornate mirror on the wall, opposite the window, which had the drapes pulled shut. She walked up to the mirror and held out a hand, gently touching the shimmering glass. The room was now empty again.

The room was now full of furniture and a smouldering fire in the fireplace. There was a truly magnificent Four Poster bed in the corner, hung with clearly expensive tapestries and silk curtains. But what caught Alex's eye was the gold-plated bathtub filled with hot water and the small table next to it, stacked with white towels. She jumped a little as the deep voice asked; "Are you lost mademoiselle?" She turned and standing in the doorway was a young man, maybe in his mid-twenties. He was a very good-looking young fellow who had a very pleasant smile. Alex had to giggle, and she held a hand up to her mouth, in a very ladylike fashion; the young man was stark naked!

He made no effort to cover his large cock and just stood; hands on hips: grinning. "I was about to bath young lady and never expected such a vision to appear in my room." He stared back at the main door and smiled again; "I did not even hear you enter. You must the soft walk of a young doe." He folded his arms and Alex noticed that his cock was moving and growing a little; he was getting an erection. She gracefully curtsied and said quietly; "Please forgive sir, I couldn't find my bed." He chuckled and walked over to the bathtub and dipped a hand in. "The water is wonderfully hot, and I must use its benefits before it cools."

"Then pray do so sir. I fear I have interrupted your nightly ablutions enough." Alex smiled and curtsied again. Her magnificent breasts barely restrained by her bodice. He certainly noticed that. The young man splashed water again and she could see he had a full erection now. He gestured to the bath with a wet hand and said softly; "Well my little apparition of Venus, you could always avail yourself of a hot bath and then settle down for the night in that bed."

She smiled at his sheer cheek and confidence, which she actually admired. She walked slowly over and dipped a hand into the scented water. It felt really good. "I wouldn't wish to deprive you of such a pleasure." He took her hand and dipped it back into the water. "You would not my lovely." and stepped into the bath, still holding her hand firmly. She smiled as he lowered himself down and gestured with his free hand; "Feel free to share, if you so wish. It would improve this particular immersion greatly."

Alex chucked and placed the lamp down. He released her hand - reluctantly - and she slowly removed her dress, bodice, long panties and shoes slowly. Now stark naked, she stepped into the wonderful hot water and sat facing him. He playfully splashed her with water, and she did the same. They came together almost instantly. Using a large pink sponge, they laughed, kissed and washed each other. He carefully washed her tits and vagina with a pink sponge and then she did the same to his impressive erection. They played in the bath for some minutes before he jumped from the tub and lifted her gently out. They didn't bother to use the towels and he carried her straight to the bed.

He lay back on the small mountain of pillows, hands behind head as Alex sucked and caressed his cock. He groaned several times as Alex ran her fingers down the length of his manhood. She was industrially sucking, when he sat up and pulled her to him, pushing her gently onto the pillows. She opened her legs, and he mounted her instantly. Their moths locked together and the love making started in earnest.

He was clearly a skilled lover and Alex had a couple of small organisms within a few minutes. He fucked her hard with long deep thrusts, his hands gently caressing her heaving body. She threw her arms about his shoulders, and they fucked hard for some time. She had another orgasm when she felt him cum inside of her. He stayed on top of her, and they kissed with real passion. He stroked her hair and face, whispering into her ear, which he also cleaned with his tongue. Alex groaned in pleasure and the pair finally separated some minutes later.

They lay in each other's arms, resting from the love making in silence. He slowly took her hand and guided it to his cock. She gently jerked it and felt the damn thing growing in her hand. She giggled and slid down his body and pushed his growing cock back into her mouth. She pleased him for some minutes before - again - he mounted her. They made love again for about twenty minutes, except this time, he pulled his cock from her willing vagina, and she accepted it back into her mouth. He came again and Alex enjoyed a little late snack.

The pair lay in each other's arms, and he stroked her face and hair, they kissed gently, and he stared into her eyes and whispered; "I cannot marry you, but I want you with me every day and night. You can have a little palace with servants, dresses and carriages. Anything you want because I want you and don't give a damn if you're the daughter of a pig farmer my lovely angel. I have been given everything a man could ask for and I thought I owned the world, but if you're not part of that world, then I own nothing." He passionately kissed her and gripped her tightly. "No, I can't give you away now that I have found you. Not for all of France. You have touched my soul my sweet darling and you're in my heart for good now."

Alex didn't quite know how to answer that and just smiled a little and he pulled her close and kissed her again with unbridled passion. He simply wouldn't let her go and so she fell asleep cradled in his arms until Alex woke and slipped from the bed. She very quietly tip-toed to her pile of clothes; discarded by the now cold bath and picked up her mirror.

She noticed that the mirror was showing the current time and date; July 9th, 1735. She looked back at the young man gently snoring on the big bed and quickly dressed. Alex left the room and operated the mirror, returning her to 1767. Walking down yet another corridor, she suddenly realised that she didn't even know the passionate young man's name!

6. 18th AUGUST 1767, THE PALACE OF VERSAILLES - PART 1.

"If this is the King's private dining room, can you imagine the bloody place they hold the State banquets in?" Owen stared around the plush chamber and counted no less than eight footmen and an under-Butler waiting behind the chairs. The huge table was laden with crockery, gold and silver cups and candle holders. The centre piece was a full-sized Peacock made of gold with its feathers encrusted with precious jewels and stones.

In one corner were several musicians who were warming up and they sounded good just practising. The young man at the harpsichord was particularly good and Owen enjoyed what he performed.

Wilson peered behind a bright red screen in one corner and

laughed. He walked back to the others and smiled; "There's a bucket behind there with a sponge and bowl on a stand. There are also several small towels. I think it's used if you're caught short." Jericho nodded; "You'll find them scattered all round the palace for guests to use; so they don't have to walk miles to the bloody privies. They certainly were not embarrassed about bodily functions at this time. It was common at dinner and during balls for women to nip behind a screen and piss, sometimes still keeping their place in the conversations that went on!"

Alex swept in and the team smiled as one; she looked stunning in a bright red dress with a very low-cut bodice. Her hair was piled up and held with a silver tiara and she wore a simple string of pearls around her neck with a small silver crucifix underneath [as was the custom] she actually looked like a royal princess and only Owen whispered that fact to her.

A footman appeared with a tray of glasses, and everyone took a glass. "Who else is invited tonight?" Wilson asked Jericho who was checking his mirror discretely. "Only one other, a certain Monsieur Henri Moreau who appears to be some close friend of the King, which is unusual because apparently, he has no title; Human records has no record of such a man and neither does history record his so called friendship with the King. But it could be just an alias which was common at the time. One of the powerful Dukes used the name Jean Voland on occasion to pass amongst the common people. I'll get Owen to run his mirror over him, bloody discretely I hope!"

Alex gestured with her glass to the wall opposite the big fireplace with a smile on her face; a full-sized portrait of a naked girl picking apples from a tree was opening. "The place is full of secret passages." Owen whispered to her, and everyone watched the young man step through, and he bowed a little. He was about six feet tall, with broad shoulders and the physical qualities of an athlete. He had long cascading dark hair tied in a black clasp, which was unusual for the time. He appeared to have light olive skin which probably indicated he was from southern France or Spain, somewhere around the Mediterranean anyway. Alex was truly impressed and whispered to Owen; "Now that's one bloody gorgeous man." Owen nodded, smiling broadly; "Jackie would absolutely agree with you there."

A footman offered him a glass which he waved away with a quiet

'Thank you' and walked straight up to the team and bowed again. "Monsieur Henri Moreau at your service my good lady and you gentleman. It is not an honour to dine with his Majesty, is it so?" He said quietly and Alex really smiled; to her, his voice was like chocolate being poured! Jericho, Owen and Wilson all bowed in reply, whilst Alex performed a pretty good imitation of a curtsey. Then a fat man in an elaborate blue uniform and huge hat suddenly appeared and banged a silver topped stick upon the floor and shouted; "THE KING!"

Everyone bowed low and Alex actually managed a good curtsey this time, but her breasts almost fell out. That's didn't go unnoticed by Monsieur Henri Moreau who smiled at her, and she had to wave her fan across her face, which actually reddened a little, like a shy schoolgirl falling in love for the first time. But it was the way the King greeted the young man that set Jericho's mind running. The King embraced him like a son and the pair spoke quietly together for a minute or so and the King, still gripping the young man's arm, gestured to the team and introduced them. He left Alex to last; "This beauty is Lady Alexandra of Cappanni. She is a Countess and has lit up the palace like a warm summer day." The young man bowed again, and Alex curtsied again; this time getting it perfect.

 Monsieur Henri Moreau took her hand and kissed it, lingering for a full half minute before releasing it. Wilson whispered to Owen; "Another moth." And Owen chuckled. The King sat at the head of the table and placed Alexandra to his left and Monsieur Henri Moreau to his right, so they faced each other. Jericho sat opposite Wilson and Owen faced no-one. The King didn't like that and told his butler to bring another guest to make the dinner party balance correctly. The Butler hurried away as the footman served the first course, lightly poached fish in an exquisite sauce.

The King spoke directly to his young friend and what he said made Jericho almost drop his fork in shock. "Monsieur Tibbs works for God and these good people are all members of his spectral team. They chase down naughty people who appear at the wrong time and place, not to mention the odd demon of Satan himself. It's all very complicated Henri, but with your mind and talent, you will understand those complexities easily. Oh, and apparently they have all been dead for some time. But they do look good for that little inconvenience, don't they?"

Henri placed down his fork and smiled; "They certainly do sir." There was absolute silence at the table as the King picked at his fish and smiled at everyone. It was broken by the Butler returning with a young lady who was very pretty and like Alex, hanging out of her Court dress. She eased herself down opposite Owen and smiled at everyone. The King grunted; "This is Agnes, one of my younger mistresses. She is a good choice because she knows small talk and knows when to keep her pretty little mouth closed. But she won't understand a word of the conversation we are having; pretty, but dumb as a doorknob." The young girl just smiled at everyone and started on her fish as soon as the footman placed it before her.

Henri turned to Jericho and dabbed his mouth with his napkin. "A most interesting and meritorious profession sir; I do hope our very indifferent God appreciates your efforts. Perhaps he would, upon occasion, lift a divine finger and assist his bewildered creation. But I suspect that's too much to ask; he's curriculum vitae indicates such apathy in our regard, that I will not hold my breath awaiting his action. Any action." He picked up his fork and continued with the fish.

Again, there was a silence until Alex started to clap and Owen followed her, Wilson just chuckled, and Jericho managed a smile and said nothing in reply. Agnes smiled broadly and clapped with Alex and Owen, then said; "What did Monsieur Moreau say?" Alex just groaned in mild despair, while Owen now laughed. The King sighed and said to Alex; "See, I told you; dumb as a doorknob."

Jericho said softly; "Many people believe he does act; through the actions of decent humans." Monsieur Moreau smiled; "Yes and many people still believe the earth is flat as a pancake and we both know that conclusion is a sad mistaken error. Our deity does nothing for humanity except to judge us when deceased and hand out cruel punishment for breaking his commandments. He sit's upon his omnipresent arse and does nothing. His silence is deafening my friend. Burning martyrs called out to him from the stake and he couldn't even be bothered to piss on the poor creatures to alleviate their suffering. Such is his utter contempt for us."

The King chuckled; "Now, now, Henri, let's not embarrass our very special guests and let's cease discussion on religion; it gives me bad indigestion." Henri smiled and nodded; "Yes, of course sir." Alex finished her fish and smiled at the strange young man. She was getting more impressed with him by the minute. Then as the second course arrived; Monsieur Moreau sat back and said quietly to the King: "Then maybe a story would entertain your guests." He clasped his hands together and smiled; "Many years ago, my dear father stayed in this very palace as a young man and one evening he was about to bathe. The bath was filled with delightful hot water and so quite naked he prepared to soak for some minutes. But suddenly, as if by magic, there appeared a stunning beautiful woman in the room and my father was taken by her charm and beauty and offered his tub to her; to share with his him. She accepted and soon they spent the night in exquisite lovemaking. He had never had a woman like this and desired to have only her, but alas, had been subject to an arranged marriage at the age of fifteen to a much older woman who he detested. So, he was brutally honest and told the woman he could only offer her himself. In the quiet of the night, she slipped away and he never saw her again. It simply broke his heart, he forgave her because he loved her so, but much as he tried; he couldn't forget her."

Alex was staring at her soup; her mind racing at the young man's strange story. She remembered the time on her mirror after leaving that young man who offered his bath and so much else; 1735. That was 32 years ago. The story had to be about her. She moved the spoon around in the bowl; her appetite had quickly diminished.

The young man continued; "About a year later, again he was here at the palace, soaking in his bathtub in the very same room when he a child crying. He snapped open his eyes and laid upon the floor in a small basket was an infant. All the doors and windows were locked so how did the mother gain entry. He held the child and realised that it had to be her; only she had the ability to walk through walls. The child was a boy and my father danced about the room for he always wanted a son. He thanked God and the woman and raised the boy as his son. His wife had been too old to provide a child but refused to acknowledge the boy as her son and thus the child could not, when grown, inherit his father's lands and titles. Nevertheless, the boy grew into a man under his devoted father's care and has a comfortable life. His father died last year, happy that he had a son to follow him, but distraught at never meeting the mother of his precious child again; for all the heartbreak and misery she gave the man, he

still loved her. He showed that by the tender care of her son."
Alex sat back and asked softly; "An amazing story Monsieur
Moreau, from which book did you gain it?" The young man did
not smile; "Madame, it was from no written text or storytellers
dribbling mouth. Nor from some over imaginative writers pen. I
know this because the man was my father, and I am that
woman's child grown to manhood."

Alex dropped her spoon and grabbed up her napkin, dabbing her
mouth. Her mind was in absolute turmoil; how the hell could this
story be true? She would have certainly remembered getting
pregnant, having a son and then giving the infant away to his
father! She carefully picked up her spoon and smiled a little; this
story is garbage, made up nonsense, but for what reason? But
how does he know about it if the man wasn't his father? There
was no-one else present; just me and the young man. She
wondered just who the hell was Monsieur Henri Moreau?

The little dinner party broke up an hour later and Alex couldn't
wait to grab Owen and ask what his mirror revealed about the
strange young man. The team gathered in Jericho's room and
Owen read out what had been revealed. "His name is Henri
Moreau born in 1736 so he belongs in this time and place.
Moreau being the family names of the Dukes of Perpignan, which
is located on the Mediterranean. His father Louis was 9th Duke
and he [Henri] would have been the tenth duke had his father's
wife accepted him as a son. But the two hated each other and so
that was that. Ah, now I understand the close connection with
the King; his father and the King were boyhood friends, the duke
was the King's closest confidante, and the King gave his friend a
state funeral when he died in 1761. Henri's scheduled departure
date is..." Alex griped his arm; "never mind that, who was his
mysterious mother?"

Owen rubbed his chin; "According to Human Records it was a
Mademoiselle Jacqueline Babette from.....shit! She was...is a
time traveller from the Edwardian Era. Born in 1882, she
vanished from the timeline in 1905 and is still shown as a
missing soul; if she has a time travel device that would explain
her mysterious comings and goings." Both Owen and Alex stared
at each other; they both remembered the last person they dealt
with called 'Babette' – the Butler at Sir Edward Coleville's 'French'
House – back in 1881. Jericho grunted and said that it's time to
retire. He smiled at Alex and walked away, chatting quietly with

Wilson. Owen whispered; "Must be a co-incidence. Babette is probably a common name in France." Alex folded her arms and said quietly; "You know what Jericho always says about co-incidence. Did she disappear from France or England?" Owen checked his mirror and sighed; "The breech in the timeline occurred in London in a place called Eastham in 1905." Alex didn't smile; "The east end, where the French house was, and Mr. Babette worked as the butler."

They walked to Alex's bedroom and Owen said goodnight. Alex didn't sleep well that night; her mind was in an utter turmoil.

7. 19th AUGUST 1767, CHATEAU ROI CHARLES (NEUILLY - SUR - SEINE).

Monsieur Roland watched the large grey crate unloaded from the cart with great care. He pointed towards the doors and told the men to take the grate to the cellar lift. They nodded and disappeared inside. He consulted his fob watch and stared down the driveway; a plain black cab was slowly making its way towards Chateau Roi Charles in the early morning sun.

He turned to Apollo and gestured towards the approaching cab; "By the time he arrives and enters my study, he will be exactly on time." Monsieur Roland chuckled and walked into his Chateau, telling Apollo to show Monsieur Le Chat into his study. He saw Madame Bridget standing by the foot of the main staircase; she bowed slightly but said nothing. He simply nodded and she disappeared towards the cellar stairs entrance; hidden in a grand stateroom cupboard, that stood in a quiet corner of the hallway.

Monsieur Roland eased himself behind his large ornate desk and stared at the open door. If it had been anyone else, he would have simply had the girl strangled and thrown into the Seine and they could go hang. But it was Monsieur Le Chat. A young maid entered and placed a tray of drinks upon a small table by the window, curtsied and left.

Apollo appeared, bowed a little and said simply; "Monsieur Le Chat." He stood to one side and the tall man, dressed in black, stepped slowly into the room, a few feet behind followed a large black cat, wearing a silver collar. Roland indicated to the chair placed in front of his desk. But Monsieur Le Chat shook his head and remained standing. He also refused a drink; the cat now sat at his feet and appeared to be watching Roland; carefully. "The story spreading around Paris is that Madam Bella was killed by an aggrieved customer who fled the scene. The local magistrate is only too happy to side with that tale." Monsieur Roland smiled and pulled a drawstring bag from his pocket and added; "One hundred gold pieces; good Spanish gold as you requested." He dropped the bag upon the desk and leaned back in his chair.

He almost jumped in surprise as the big cat leapt upon the desk and sniffed at the bag. He watched in utter amazement as the cat turned to its master and squeaked quietly. Monsieur Le Chat actually smiled; "One hundred Spanish gold pieces as agreed. The girl?" He asked and scooped the bag up, whilst the cat jumped from the desk.

Monsieur Roland wiped his face; "She only arrived minutes before you. I have Bridget cleaning her up and finding a cloak for her. Madame Clare delivered her in the same manner, that I delivered her to them; quite naked." Monsieur Le Chat nodded, his pale face expressionless. "And the young man?" Roland wiped his face again and really did force a smile; "I have sent a message to Monsieur Franklyn but have not received a reply yet."

Monsieur Le Chat almost sighed but dropped the money bag upon the desk. "That's for the young man's return; alive. Call it expenses." He bowed a little and walked to the door, the cat close behind him. He turned and said quietly; "Send Apollo with the message that you have retrieved him." He stood by the door and watched as Apollo carried the girl, bundled in a dark blue cloak down the steps to his carriage.

Roland rose from his chair and watched the strange man and his cat, disappear from view. Madame Bridget stood by the stairs and crossed herself - twice. "If you ever wished to see Mr. Death himself in person, then I have just witnessed it." She said softly and crossed herself - yet again. Roland wiped his sweaty face and couldn't disagree with her sentiments.

He returned to his study and poured himself a large class of brandy. Delivering the girl to Monsieur Le Chat and not to that man Tibbs had cost him dear. But when Monsieur Le Chat asks you for a 'favour' - you side with him every time - if you value being alive! And he certainly valued his. He sipped his brandy and watched through the window as the black carriage made it way down the drive. "Why the fuck is that little slut so important to so many powerful men?" He whispered. Roland had heard the stories circulating the dark underworld of Paris. That even the King was involved - apparently. He could understand it; if it was that Mademoiselle Alexandra; the English beauty that had turned the King's Mistresses green with envy. Now that was a female worthy of such endeavours and money.

He slumped back in his chair and drank some more brandy; those idiots had really fucked up this time, when they snatched the girl and her dumb boyfriend. Bloody laziness: they thought it would make their mission easy. He stared at the bag of coins upon the desk and wondered if that damn cat actually knew they were all there? Which they were of course; you didn't cheat Monsieur Le Chat. If you were stupid enough to do so; you may summon the undertaker at the same time. Roland actually shuddered and finished his brandy.

He would now have an irate Monsieur Franklyn to deal with. Fortunately, he was a shrewd businessman, and he certainly knew about Monsieur Le Chat's reputation; which should make this a lot easier than it could have been. He gripped his glass and closed his eyes and then they snapped open.

Madame Bridget had appeared in the doorway and curtsied; "That nasty little man of Monsieur Franklyn's has arrived." She walked away and Roland placed down his glass. He hoped that Monsieur Jarden had come with good news; the turnover of young men in Franklyn's dungeon didn't give him much hope for the man. He had been there some weeks, and most didn't survive that long.

Monsieur Jarden bowed a little and sat slowly on the chair; he smiled with a mouthful of yellow teeth. "What have you for me?" Roland asked and clasped both hands on the desk. Monsieur Jarden nodded; "The young man David has been removed and placed in the care of the sisters of Mercy at St. Maria's Convent. He will heal physically, but..." he tapped his head and didn't smile; "But in his head; he may not." he shrugged his shoulders and stared at the bag upon the desk.

Roland leaned back and ran a hand over his face. "Monsieur Le Chat said alive and nothing more. That is all that matters here."

He pushed the bag towards Jarden and said quietly; "Give that to your master as payment for the man and as thanks - personally - from me. It's a hundred Spanish Gold pieces." The look on Monsieur Jarden's face spoke volumes. He carefully picked up the bag and pushed it into his coat pocket. "All is well between your master and me?" Roland asked and smiled a little.

Monsieur Jarden nodded; "My master said that you don't discard a fine watch that has given many years of good service, just because it stops upon occasion. You have it repaired and it continues to serve you well." He rose from the chair and the two men shook hands. Roland noticed with distain, that the little man's hand was cold and clammy and weak. Monsieur Jarden stopped by the doorway and replaced his hat. "You will inform Monsieur Le Chat about the young man?"

Roland nodded, and Jarden turned and left. That went better than expected. He eased back onto his chair and his attention was drawn to the window. He rose and stared into the driveway. Apollo was greeting a fine carriage and Roland's heart sank. It was accompanied by a King's Officer and a troop of six cavalry.

He watched carefully as Mademoiselle Alexandra and Monsieur Tibbs stepped into the morning sunshine. "Putain de merde!" He exclaimed and returned to his chair, clutching another brandy. He then smiled a little; Monsieur Le Chat was now their problem and lifted his glass in a quiet salute and with some relief. His plan was carefully unfolding, and every little piece was coming together.

9. 22nd AUGUST 1767, THE PALACE OF VERSAILLES - PART 2.

The King eased down upon his gilded chair and groaned a little; his haemorrhoids were playing up again. He adjusted his fine tunic and stared at Monsieur Tibbs with a little mix of wonderment and fear. The man had not aged a single day since the King first saw him some thirty years ago. But then, that was a privilege of being a messenger of God. "Did it go well?" He asked quietly, gripping the arms of his chair.

"We now know that a certain Monsieur Le Chat has taken possession of the girl and has made arrangements for the recovery of the young man that was taken with her." Jericho bowed a little, standing with hat in hand. The King nodded but did not smile; "Monsieur Le Chat has a sinister, almost supernatural reputation for evil and total ruthlessness that is unequalled in France. He is a very dangerous man Jericho." The King shifted uneasily on his chair, despite the thick cushion placed upon it.

The audience with the King lasted another ten minutes and Jericho left the King's private apartments, walking quickly back to his rooms. Several couriers stood aside as he passed; a couple crossed themselves. Especially old Franco, the king's body servant; he had recognised Jericho from thirty years before, when he was a Hall boy here. He watched Jericho disappear down the magnificent corridor and crossed himself. No doubt his master would confide in him about the reason for such a creature's visit. Franco, of course, didn't know that only Jericho could have a King as a human agent!

The team assembled in Jericho's apartment and enjoyed the hospitality that Versailles offered. The first thing they all agreed upon was finding out who, exactly, was Monsieur Le Chat. Both the King and Monsieur Roland had told them that he was a very clever and dangerous man. The story about the stupid workman - fitting new doors to Monsieur Le Chat's chateau - had been told by both - the workman disliked cats and was seen kicking Le Chat's cat up its arse. He was found the following day on a quiet Paris street- He had been butchered, there was no other word for it.

"So he's a murdering psychopath, we've dealt with them before." muttered Owen who really did like the King's good quality brandy. They had decided that there must be some connection between Le Chat and the young couple and Salem House. "We need to check the fucker out with our mirrors; Human Records will be able to identify him." Owen added and refilled everyone's glasses. So, the priority was identifying Le Chat and retrieving Sally and Dave from his clutches.

Alex sipped brandy and was reading her mirror with real interest, she looked up and grinned broadly; "Well, we certainly know now who Monsieur Roland really is." She had everyone's attention with that statement. She tapped her mirror; "Monsieur Roland is a certain Sir Malcolm Grieves, whose soul is reported missing; he missed his departure date in February 1871. Guess what he did own and went missing from in 1870?" Wilson smiled; "Salem House." Alex nodded and continued; "I've just checked Dave Fisher's Great-Uncle Wesley and here's a real turn up for the books; his soul is missing, and he shouldn't even be dead in 1971 [the year the Police Inspector stated that his body had been found in Salem House] he's scheduled for 1982."

"So whose bloody body was found in 1971?" Owen asked and slumped down on the sofa, clutching his brandy. "Dispatches have no record of a collection on that date or at that place, whoever lay dead at the foot of the stairs wasn't old Great-Uncle Wesley Fisher." Alex said quietly and re-read her mirror.

"Well, either the fucker sold his soul to you-know-who, or he was out of his ordained time." Wilson grunted and relaxed in his chair. Jericho told Owen to check who dealt with the body in 1971; Temporal Detectives would have been called to a body without a soul being found, even if the death was unscheduled.

Owen nodded and started to read his mirror. "Holy shit!" He exclaimed and grinned broadly; "The body belonged to a Monsieur Louis Varden who should have died in 1777 in Paris, at the age of 65. He had a string of sexual offences against women and children. He would have been quarantined for some centuries, but obviously, never turned up at his departure date; his soul is officially missing."

"So it appears that Great Uncle Wesley Fisher is still alive and kicking and he has to be around this time and place; the 'Jerusalem Mirror' is locked here." Jericho said and rubbed his chin.

"There are more time travellers here than you can shake a stick at." Muttered Owen and finished his brandy. Alex sat bolt upright in her chair and clicked her fingers with a broad smile; "Varden was Madame Bella's surname!" Wilson nodded; "That would be stretching co-incidence if the pair are not related."

Jericho did the maths in his head; "If Louis should have died in 1777 at the age of 65, he would be 55 at this time and Madam Bella was 31; so either she married an old man or he was her father or Uncle or some kind of relative."

Owen re- read his mirror; "The Collector reported that Madame

Bella knew her killer - it was Monsieur Le Chat; with his bloody cat. Madame Bella had three husbands; two died and the third simply disappeared; he was called Louis." Wilson smiled; "Well, that solves who he was. Were the other husbands all older than her?" Owen nodded; "The first one was 61 and she was 18. The second husband was 52 when he married her at 24. The third we know about already."

"Clearly she liked a daddy figure." Alex said and relaxed back in her chair. Jericho actually grinned and nodded his head with some satisfaction. "People, we really need to know who the hell Monsieur Le Chat really is." Everyone agreed with that; but how?

"I have a cunning plan." Was all Jericho said and they gathered around.

9. 23rd AUGUST 1767, SALLE DES GRANDS DANSEURS [A PARIS THEATRE].

"I told Jericho that a visit to 18th century Paris would not be complete without a visit to the theatre and he is no philistine, so he agreed; as long as you came along." Alex spoke quietly to Jackie who just smiled; actually, happy to be back on scene and dressed so beautifully. She often considered 'Owen' as her 'alter-ego' and not the other way round. The two ladies joined the throng gathering outside the small theatre and admired the well-turned-out Parisians. Jackie whispered in her ear; "One of the star attractions here was a monkey named Turco who would lead parades along the boulevard to the theatre, then take the stage and enact current events. I do hope he puts in an appearance." Alex just sighed and ran a beautiful peacock fan over her face. The two ladies had already attracted the attention of two King's Officers, both resplendent in their uniforms and the bigger man immediately approached Alex and bowed.

"My lady, you and your lady maid should not be here without escorts. I have seen you at the palace and I offer you my protection for the evening." He kissed her outstretched hand and introduced his companion; John-Paul Casson, also a Kings Musketeer. Jackie smiled and curtsied; "Well, we have two of the three musketeers so we can't complain." that made Alex chuckle and she gracefully accepted Captain Andre Roulex's generous offer and they were escorted into the theatre.

The captain paid for seats near the stage which were quite expensive, and he was clearly a man of wealth and he certainly must have had some kind of reputation; for men took their hats off to him and ladies curtsied as he passed. Alex peered over her fan at him and smiled; he was a strapping, healthy looking individual with well-manicured hands and a tailored uniform. His friend was of a much slighter built but still handsome despite the small scar on the right side of his face. He told Jackie that it was a dueling scar. She touched it gently and asked if it hurt. He took her hand and kissed it with some passion, laughing that his opponent ended up far worse off; he [Jean-Paul] had removed three fingers from his left hand before the pair called the duel a draw and honour was satisfied.

The captain now had no interest in the acts that presented themselves on stage; his only interest was Alexandra and the pair talked and laughed quietly together over the noise of the crowds. Jean-Paul sat close to Jackie and smiled a lot; he seemed quite shy for a King's Musketeer and fighter of duels. Jackie loved that about him and did most of the 'chatting up' during the evening. The entertainment finished; the little group made their way to 'Bartholomew's Tavern' – a favourite haunt of wealthy Parisians who liked their drinking establishments on the rough side – and sat in a quiet corner drinking wine and brandy.

The fact that the girls were English drew some unwanted attention from the rowdy crowd drinking; especially amongst the women who were clearly jealous of the pair of beauties that the Musketeers were entertaining. Rumours about the English strangers staying at Versailles had gone around Paris and especially the English beauty called Alexandra. Now everyone could see that the rumours were true and that didn't go down well with some of the 'ladies' who frequented the tavern. The trouble started in less than half hour after they arrived.

A well-dressed woman with far too much make up on and her breasts almost hanging out her bodice made some remarks about 'English Trollope's' and the two men that accompanied her foolishly agreed with her. Captain Andre heard them and demanded they apologize for the foul tongue of their whore. Tables went over and tankards went flying as swords were drawn. Alex and Jackie dived behind the overturned table as the fight started. "I've never had a man actually fight over me before!" Jackie exclaimed as a tankard flew past her head.

The tavern was in uproar as other's joined in. The woman whose foul mouth had started the whole affair appeared and tried to drag Jackie to her feet; forcibly. Alex was having none of that and swung a right hook that would have dropped a donkey. The woman slid down the wall with a real look of surprise on her face. Captain Andre - sword in hand and grinning - grabbed Alex by the hand and the pair headed for the servant's door. She looked down to see the unconscious woman's escort lying dead, face upwards on the stone floor; sword still gripped in one hand. Jean-Paul grabbed Jackie and they followed Andre and Alex into the streets thronged with people who seemed to pay no interest to the massive fight that now spilled out into the thoroughfares of old Paris.

"Come on Mademoiselle Marcel Courdon! Let's find quieter habitation!" shouted Andre, not letting go of her hand. Alex turned to Jackie and asked; "Who the hell is Marcel Courdon?" It was a laughing Jean-Paul who answered, "He is a very famous and successful boxer Mademoiselle!" They ran past several of the city's guard rushing to the tavern; pikes and swords drawn. The young Lieutenant in charge just lifted his hat to Andre and smiled at Alex. "Good evening, Captain Roulex." Was all he said.

They made the captains rooms above the baker's in Le Rue de Vendeurs de Possion some minutes later and sat around laughing and panting. Jean-Paul fetched a beer jug, and everyone enjoyed the cool drinks. Andre and Alex were together on the large sofa by the window while Jackie was sitting on Jean-Paul's lap on the only other chair in the place. Andre finished his beer and tossed the tankard onto the floor and slowly pulled Alex to her feet; she smiled as they walked to the bedroom door; "See you at the barracks in the morning my friend." Andre said and gestured Alex into the small room, which was dominated by a huge bed, piled high with pillows.

Alex closed the door behind them, and they embraced with some passion; pulling at each other's clothes and kissing. They both stood naked in each other's arms; running their hands over each other and exchanging tongues. Andre lifted her easily and carried Alex to the bed, placing her on several pillows. She pulled him down to her with one hand behind his neck while the other gripped his erection. Alex opened her legs in invitation and Andre – smiling – accepted it. He mounted her with some urgency and pushed her legs up past his ears and gently thrusted a couple of times. Alex groaned and gripped his big arse with both hands as his mouth found her breasts and erect nipples. Leaning on both hands he started to push into her with more speed and force. She moaned with pleasure as he fucked her with some restrained passion for several minutes until they changed position without a word being said. Now on all fours, laid on a couple of pillows, Alex felt him inside of her with his big hands gripping her hips as he thrusted. She pushed a hand between her legs and rubbed her full vagina with some vigour and the first orgasm came easily. They rolled over again, and he fucked her propped against the pillows and headboard with her legs entwined around his waist and his arms around her; their tongues buried in each other's willing mouths. He heaved her up and carried her – still coupled – to the wall and fucked her hard against it with her arms gripping his powerful shoulders. She had one hell of a squirt and actually cried out in ecstasy as he fucked her with great skill.

They were soon back on the bed groaning and panting until he finally called out and came inside of her which made her scream and orgasm, frantically pulling him against her. They lay in the tight embrace for some minutes before he whispered; "Thank you my lady for that little trip to heaven. May I book another one please?" They both started to laugh and kiss again. "All aboard for heavens coach!" was all Alex managed to say. And Andre was more than happy to 'board' again!

Alex slipped from the bed, leaving the big man snoring gently, naked amongst the pillows. She quietly dressed and opened the door to find Jackie asleep on the sofa under a very coulourful blanket; there was no sign of Jean-Paul. Alex woke her gently and the pair crept down the stairs into the quiet Paris Street; it was almost midnight and so they used their mirrors to return to Versailles. They walked slowly and quietly to the rooms and Alex had to ask about young Jean-Paul. Jackie really did smile; "For a King's Musketeer and fighter of duels he didn't know much about women!"

Alex kissed her and demanded the full story which Jackie declined to tell at this time of night. All she said was; "He didn't know that men and some women are very similar, but he does now!" She kissed Alex and disappeared into her room, chuckling a little. Alex just sighed but smiled. She would get the full story in the morning but knowing Jackie she would have certainly enjoyed teaching the young man about sex. Alex slept soundly

that night and had a delicious dream about a certain King's
musketeer that left her a little wet in the morning!

10. 24th AUGUST 1767, THE PALACE OF VERSAILLES - PART 3.

Alex was a little annoyed; "Your original plan was fantastic but
trust the dirty old sod of a King to come up with this." She spoke
quietly to Jericho and stroked Mr. Parker with one hand, whilst
gripping her light summer cloak about her with the other. Jericho
just shrugged his shoulders and smiled; "He is the King and if he
wants a 'Tit and Pussy show' - then he gets one." Alex just
grunted and started to give Mr. Parker a final brush.

Mr. Parker' is Jericho's cat from the lighthouse and has been with
him since Jericho passed over and joined the Temporal
Detectives Department. He is a strange and mysterious creature,
like most cats!

Owen stood behind the table and giggled a little, drawing a stern
look from Alex. Wilson folded his arms; "Mr. Parker is a Maine
Coon cat - an American breed - the largest breed of domestic cat
there is. He will certainly be a sensation in this time and place.
Very few people in Europe would have seen one in the flesh."
Jericho agreed with that and watched as several other women
had arrived with their beloved cats. They were all topless and
didn't seem to mind a bit.

Owen was certainly enjoying the show; before it even started.

The King would be the judge; with the winning feline receiving a
fine silver collar and their owner a night with him. "He's going to
be disappointed if Alex wins." Wilson had to grin at Owens's
remarks. "Our girl and the damn cat are a winning combination.
Pity no-one is taking bets." He said softly, keeping a close eye on
the growing crowd in the magnificent Reception Room.

Madame Marie de Rouge [the King's newest and youngest
mistress] bounced over and stared at Mr. Parker, whilst Owen
stared at her magnificent bosom, adorned with golden nipple
caps in the shape of small swans. "My God! Is that really a
domestic cat?" She exclaimed and fluttered a silk fan across her
face.

Alex grinned and nodded, introducing 'Mr. Parker' to her. The cat bowed and Madame Marie squeaked with joy and ran her hand over his ears. "If he wasn't a bloody cat, I'd swear the bugger was smiling." Wilson said softly to Owen, who wasn't actually looking at the cat because Alex had removed her cloak. He just stared and groaned a little. Now that did make Wilson smile. "Steady lad, just remember that we're here to do a job."

"They're like a blind cobblers thumb!" Owen muttered and managed to look away. Alex had gold and silver snakes wrapped around her ample breasts and silver rings on each nipple; the circle and the snake; emblems of the Dark Prince's followers. "That will set the cat amongst the pigeons - if you pardon the pun - and will certainly attract our dark friend's followers here." Jericho spoke softly, his eyes darting about the crowd. Then a loud-mouthed servant banged a gold cane upon the floor and announced the arrival of the King.

The King sauntered in with some grace; well, as much as his haemorrhoids allowed him. He made straight for Madam de Rouge, who presented her cat - 'Duveteuse' - to him. He smiled and patted her arm, then saw Alex and Mr. Parker; the smile turned into a broad grin. "You have a wonderful big pussy Mademoiselle Alexandra.... and they are simply magnificent." He gestured to her exposed breasts. "Snakes and circles; very interesting my dear." He added and actually rubbed his hands together!

Alex curtsied and smiled; "Thank you your Majesty. He is such a lovely big cat." The King nodded and the Lord Chamberlain had to remind him twice, that there were several other cats to judge. Quite reluctantly, the King had to move on. Owen tapped Jericho's arm and said quietly; "Look who's turned up."

Standing in the doorway was Monsieur Le Chat and his cat. The conversation in the room slowly died away as people saw who had arrived. The King waved him over and greeted him with some warmth. He introduced the 'English' visitors to Monsieur Le Chat; whilst the two big cats eyed each other up in a very unfriendly manner. Alex had to pat Mr. Parker twice and tell him to behave himself; he didn't listen.

The team sat in Jericho's room - in silence - for a few minutes, then Alex, now suitably covered up; shook her head; "You can't imprison a bloody cat in the Bastille!" Everyone nodded at that, and Owen couldn't help himself, he chuckled; "Mr. Parker is probably now famous. The first bloody cat thrown into the Bastille for assaulting the King!" Even Jericho had to smile at that, he turned to Wilson; "What have we got?"

"Actually, no real surprise; Monsieur Le Chat is Great Uncle Wesley Fisher." He lowered his mirror and added; "There is now a real connection with Madame Bella; her old husband was found dead in Salem House and his nephew was taken from there with his girlfriend. Something must have gone wrong with his little arrangement of jumping between here and there."

Jericho nodded; "He must have lost the ability to jump forward to Salem House and could no longer access the power of the Jerusalem Mirror. But someone else did and snatched his great nephew and the girl." Owen jumped up from his chair and headed for the tray of drinks on a nearby ornate table.

He started to fill glasses and then stopped; "So where does that Monsieur Roland fit in all this?" Alex folded her arms; "Never mind that; how the hell do we get the King to release poor Mr. Parker?" Jericho sighed; "I'll leave that to you Alexandra. I'm sure your charm can easily persuade him to set free our troublesome and feisty colleague." Then smiled broadly; the King was not happy having his elaborate wig knocked off, by the big cat trying to get at Monsieur Le Chat's furry friend.

There had been total confusion and disorder in the Ballroom as the two big cats decided to fight it out; Mr. Parker won and Monsieur Le Chat's cat fled in ignominious defeat followed by its owner. But the king wasn't impressed and ordered Mr. Parker to the Bastille! Once he had his wig straight; apparently his new mistress - Madame de Rouge - won by default. At least the King would be happy with that result.

Jericho finished his drink and gestured towards the door; "While Alexandra gets the King to release our furry friend, we're heading for Monsieur Le Chat's chateau and have words about his nephew and the girl. He of all people must realise the importance of returning the pair to their own time." Alex sighed; "Time to play the bloody tart again." Wilson chuckled at that; "Yes, but you do it so well; it almost comes naturally." The look Alex gave the big man could have frozen peas, without the need for a freezer.

11. ALEX AND THE KING'S STALLION!

Alex sat in the King's bedchamber by the big fireplace and actually chuckled to herself. She ran fingers through her hair and stared at the big bed and sighed. She was dressed in red riding boots that came up to her knees and nothing else. She had a pretty good idea what she had to do; please the King and get the damn cat back!

The secret door behind the big painting of the King's Grandfather astride a white stallion, slid open and Louis wandered in. He smiled at Alex and sat down opposite her in an ornate chair [with a big cushion placed on it] he had something gripped in his hands. "I see Franco instructed you how to dress my dear?"

Alex nodded and stood, The King rubbed his face and sighed; "If only I was twenty years younger my girl, I could service you properly, as a young woman like you deserves." Alex curtsied and said nothing. She was surprised to see Franco appear with a large bowl of hot water and a towel. He looked her up and down with no expression on his face. The King grunted and Franco placed the bowl at the Kings feet and removed his master's shoes and socks. Franco accepted the big fur hat from the King and handed it to Alex, who placed it on her head. She really struggled not to laugh.

Franco gestured to the bowl and Alex knelt down before the King and he slowly immersed his feet. He groaned with simple pleasure. She stared at the pink sponge floating in the water, where had she seen that sponge before? She began to lather his feet, then looked up as the secret door was again opened. A big African male strolled in and stood by the King.

Alex stared hard at him as he folded his arms and said nothing. The man was naked - stark naked - and Alex could not take her eyes from the huge, erected cock that was just a couple of feet from her face.

The King grunted and gestured to the silent black man; "This is Alastor, my black stallion. He services all my mares [women] for me. He will take you and you will be well pleased by him." Franco stepped forward and handed Alastor a small jar. The big man unscrewed the lid and dipped a couple of fingers in. and then smeared the cream over his cock. The King sighed but smiled.

"Mount the mare Alastor and service her for me." The big black man nodded and walked behind the knelling Alex and knelt behind her. Alex gasped as she felt the big cock gently pushing inside her vagina. She was shaking a little, but continued to wash the King's feet. Who watched Alastor carefully as he started to thrust, gripping Alex's hips.

The big African lived up to his name and reputation; he fucked Alex hard for a good half hour. Franco topped up the Kings foot bowl with a little more hot water from a nearby jug, now and again. Alex was groaning loudly under Alastor's thrusts as he went a little deeper each time. Finally, she couldn't wash the Kings damn feet anymore; her organism exploded down her thighs and splattered onto the carpet. She had her head pressed against the floor and trembled as she came again.

The King leaned forward and patted her head like a favourite dog. "Alastor will release his impressive seed into you my girl. I believe my good stallion has fathered at least nineteen children over the years he has been in my service. In a few months your belly will swell with child. A black baby to remind you of your service to me. I hope you have an understanding husband and family." He chuckled and splashed his feet about in the bowl with some joy. Alex struggled to remember where she had heard that phrase before.

Alex had dropped the sponge and gripped the carpet with both hands as Alastor filled her with his 'seed' and didn't even speak or groan as he did so. She lay panting and gasping at the feet of the King and finally the big man pulled his cock from her throbbing vagina and some of his seed spilled onto the carpet. Alex groaned; he must produce the stuff in bloody pints. It ran from her like a little stream of opaque juice. She collapsed on the floor panting. Alastor stood and walked back to his master and stood next to him; still no expression on his face.

The King chuckled and patted his man's leg; "Well done Alastor." He turned to Alex who was slowly sitting up, some tears running down her face. The King gestured to Franco, who knelt and dried the Kings feet with a towel and replaced his shoes and socks.

The king stood and said to him; "Tell that idiot of a Governor of the Bastille to release her cat. She has just obtained its pardon." Franco nodded and he and Alastor followed the King through the secret door. The King stopped and scolded Franco; "Get my bloody sponge you idiot. You know I can't lose that." Franco nodded and bowed, he returned and retrieved the King's precious sponge and then left. Leaving Alex still sprawled on the floor trying to recover from the hard fucking she had just endured and her own orgasms; of course.

After a few minutes Alex managed to stand and rather awkwardly, walk to her chair and gather her clothes together. As she dressed, she was amazed to feel more of Alastor's seed run down her thighs. Alex noticed that her vagina was now well gaped, red and a little swollen. She didn't bother to wipe herself and made for the door. She really couldn't walk properly and that hadn't happened for some time after sex.

"Little wonder the King's Mistresses wander around the palace with bloody big smiles." She said to herself, then stopped suddenly and smiled; all she could think of was Wilson!

12. STILL THE 24th of AUGUST 1767. MONSINEUR LE CHAT'S CHATEAU.

Night was falling as the carriage waited in the stone gateway and everyone stared at the house. "Jesus, you could make a horror film here." Wilson lowered the reins and spoke through the small flap to Jericho, who was also staring at the house. Owen had to agree with the big man; "I'm waiting for Dracula or Frankenstein to open the bloody door." Wilson slapped the reins and the carriage rolled down the gravel driveway and stopped outside the dark entrance. They waited for a few minutes, but no servant appeared, and the doors remained closed to 'La Maison de le Nuit'.

Jericho jumped from the carriage and strode up to the big black doors and banged upon them with the hilt of his sword. Wilson and Owen joined him after securing the horses to the metal railings that formed part of the house's wall. There was no reply from inside. Jericho shouted several times in French, but again there was no answer and the doors remained shut. That's when Owen pushed at the left door and it creaked open. Everyone looked at each other and Jericho again shouted their arrival. Still no answer.

They stood in the grand hallway enveloped in an eerie silence.

"The place should be crawling with servants." Muttered Wilson and pulled out his mirror; "Sweet Jesus, there are no living humans recorded here." He added and lowered his mirror. Owen peered through a couple of open doors and rubbed his chin; "Do you know that this place looks like it hasn't had residents for years." There was dust and cobwebs everywhere and some of the furniture looked like it was starting to rot. The air was stale and heavy. "Nice place for a holiday." Wilson said softly and consulted his mirror again.

"La Maison de le Nuit was abandoned by its owners in 1731 after a major fire destroyed the rear of the building. All that remained was the exterior façade and some rooms at the front of the house. It was finally demolished in 1810 and a small villa and vineyard replaced it." Wilson said and Owen gripped his mirror and turned to his companions; "Maybe old Le Chat only uses it for a mail drop?"

"Or Monsieur Roland has fed us a load of bollocks about where Le Chat resides." Jericho said, a little annoyed with himself at taking what Roland said, at face value. "Why drag us out here?" Wilson asked and then grabbed up his mirror; "We have visitors." The team could see four humans approaching the house from the overgrown forest; two had muskets and two had pistols and swords.

"I don't think they're here to give us a warm French welcome." Muttered Owen and the team moved from the hall into an adjoining room. Wilson and Owen managed to close the door firmly and they stood in semi-darkness, in what was probably, the music room; it contained a derelict pianoforte and a large, string less harp. But it was the beautiful stone fireplace that caught Owens's attention.

"I think we should go into the fireplace." He said and held up his mirror, adding; "There's a time portal there, linked to this very place, but in the year 1980." They could hear raised, unfriendly voices in the hallway and so, the team disappeared into the fireplace.

They found themselves in the utility room cupboard, which was locked. But it didn't take Wilson long to sort that problem. "You were wasted as a cop." Owen muttered as they peered from the little room's door. "We're in the villa that replaced the old chateau, suitably modernized I expect." He added and they walked through the deserted kitchen. They saw Monsieur Le Chat's cat sitting in the doorway of a room off the hallway. It didn't move but squeaked loudly a couple of times. They walked past and saw Le Chat standing by the wood burning stove. He actually smiled.

"I knew you would get away from Malcolm's men [Roland's men] and find the portal. Welcome Jericho, please have a seat gentleman." His Yorkshire accent was quite noticeable. Jericho dropped on the sofa with Wilson, but Owen stood by the door, clutching his mirror. Jericho got straight to the point.

"You know we must take them back." He said simply and folded his arms; the matter was not up for negotiation. Le Chat nodded; "I know you must. My great nephew is in a bad way. I fear he has lost his sanity for good. But you can return him to 1974 and none of this would have taken place." Le Chat looked and sounded quite grim. He walked to the large window and stared out at the gardens. "The whore can remain back there. That time suits her talents quite well and David will be well rid of her." He sighed and opened the glass drinks cabinet.

"I'm afraid the girl must also return; we must not lose her soul in a time that's not been allocated to her. You know that." Jericho said, but Le Chat just chuckled; "She's outsmarted everyone Jericho. No sooner did I rescue her from Madame Bella and Roland's clutches, than she betrayed me to Monsieur Roland and escaped with him back to Salem House. They will alter your precious Time-line, probably as we are speaking now." He offered brandy all round and downed his own glass in a few sips.

"So Roland has the Jerusalem Mirror now?" Wilson asked, accepting a glass from Le Chat, who smiled; "Sir Malcolm Grieves always had the mirror and in reality, always owned Salem House. I was just a lodger, like Monsieur Varden. That filthy bastard liked little girls, had he stayed with his wife back in France, his crimes would have gained the notice of the King and he would have been hung. But Sir Malcolm protected him because of the business connections with his wife Bella. He was exiled to Salem House in Victorian times and continued his vile practises. He even took up photography to keep his new victims fresh in his mind. I hope no-one ever digs up the woodlands near the house."

"How do they intend to alter the time-line?" Wilson asked. Le Chat sighed; "They will return to the day that Dave and the slut moved into Salem House, Sir Malcolm will pretend to be me and the slut, will act as his new wife. They have carefully crafted a story that they have been abroad. That idiot solicitor believes Sir Malcolm IS me, since he has only dealt with Sir Malcolm AS me." He poured himself another glass and stared back out the window. "You know that those imbecilic policemen never asked the bloody solicitor to identify the body found at the foot of the stairs [Varden] and so it was obviously me."

"What no-one foresaw was that Varden would have a massive heart attack and die, clutching a photograph of him abusing another little victim back in the 1880's. Not one of those stupid police officers realised that the man dead on the floor was the same bastard in the picture!" Le Chat almost spate the words out.

"So, they intend to reclaim Salem House and Dave, with the other Sally would return to their previous lives; in debt and unhappy?" Owen said quietly and then smiled; "But surely, if the pair [Dave and Sally] was never to have Salem House and the money, then that IS the original time-line?" Jericho nodded at that deduction.

Le Chat slumped in a chair and smiled; "I understand that's it a prime directive of Temporal detectives to prevent two versions of the same person to inhabit the same timeline?" Jericho did not smile; "That's quite true, can I ask how you come to know so much about Temporal Detective duties?" Le Chat softly laughed; "Wouldn't you like to know. But more importantly, you need to return one of the versions of the whore back to 1767." Wilson grunted; "You seem to have forgotten, that if we return the pair to 1974, then nothing would have happened and so - like Owen said - the timeline would be back to its original state." He placed his glass down and did smile.

"That's true; but what will stop Sir Malcolm [Roland] from doing everything again?" Le Chat finished his brandy and fumbled in his pockets. He pulled a faded newspaper cutting from his pocket and unfolded it. He handed the paper to Jericho, who read it with some interest and pushed it into his pocket. "Let's go." Was all Jericho said.

13. 17th JUNE 1974, SALEM HOUSE - PART 3.

The big black car sat in the lay-by and Wilson relaxed in the driver's seat. He turned to Alex and smiled; "You haven't said, how you got old Mr. Parker out of the Bastille?" Alex shrugged her shoulders; "I can't claim that I did. It was Madame Le Rouge we have to thank for that." Owen lowered his mirror; "Madame Le Rouge had Mr. Parker freed?" Alex nodded; "She pleaded with the King that she would be really upset if her 'friend' didn't have her beloved pussy returned and the King agreed; didn't want to upset his new, young mistress I expect." Everyone turned to Jericho, who could be heard to chuckle at that comment. "Tut tut Alexandra." Was all he said.

Jericho grinned and stared down the road; "Yes, I'm sure that is how it happened." Everyone exchanged glances at that. Alex folded her arms; "What do you mean by that?" Jericho didn't answer but tapped Wilson's arm. The removal van was heading towards them and Salem House. They watched as the van passed by, followed by the old Vauxhall Viva containing Dave and Sally.

Wilson started the car and pulled out, staying well behind the little convoy. Jericho glanced over his shoulder a couple of times; "Owen, give 'Jumbo' a buzz and see how far behind us he is. Thanks." Owen checked his mirror and muttered; "The Scottish nutter should come into view about now." Wilson looked in the mirror and saw the van pull in behind them. Alex gave a little wave to Patricia (little Pat) Sabaskinski, the driver, who waved back. "Thank fuck Pat is driving; Jumbo couldn't drive a greasy stick...." Alex gave Owen a gentle slap; "Yes, that's enough. Thank you, we get the point."

Wilson slowed down and waited at the gates; everyone could see the young couple embracing in the driveway. "Do you see her at the attic window?" Wilson said quietly and everyone peered at the old house. "Yes, she's there alright." Owen lowered his mirror and placed it back into his pocket whilst Alex adjusted his tie. "Court appointed officers are always neat and tidy. That's why we all look like bloody undertakers." She grinned as the car and van pulled up behind the removal van. Jericho eased himself out and walked over to Dave and Sally, who stared, with a little fear and apprehension, at the team emerging from the car.

Paddy the removal van driver sighed; "I don't think anyone is moving today and our bloody company will have to wait for its fucking money." They watched as the 'Sherriff's Officer' pushed the Court Order into Dave's hand and took possession of Salem House. Dave got a little angry and was shouting that the debts were all Sally's, and his property couldn't be touched. Then he calmed down a little when Wilson walked up. Jericho patiently explained that, if the house was his 'sole' property, why did both he and Sally sign for the house?

Dave hung his head; that bloody Solicitor had told him not to give away part of the house to Sally. But Dave hadn't really listened. He cursed himself and threw down the paper and walked back to his old car and slumped across the wheel. Sally said nothing and walked over the Vauxhall and slowly eased in.

Jericho gestured to Wilson and Owen, who entered the house and made for the attic rooms. Alex walked over and tapped on Dave's driver window; he slowly wound it down. She explained that the house would be sold at auction and the proceeds used to pay off Sally's debts, which were now quite considerable because of the amount of interest accrued over the last couple of years. Dave simply stuck up two fingers and drove away.

The removal van followed the disappointed couple down the drive, and everyone turned to the old house as Wilson and Owen appeared with the Jerusalem Mirror, covered with some old bed sheets. "Get it in the van and then we'll search the house thoroughly for anything else that may interest us." Jericho smiled and the two teams disappeared into Salem House.

"If th' glaikit bugger hadn't added her bloody name tae th' deed, thay wid hae bben in th' clear." Jumbo spoke to Alex as they searched the ground floor rooms. She nodded and checked her mirror for any other nasty little time portals. After a couple of hours, the search was complete and everyone returned to the vehicles.

The team watched as the white van; with Jumbo, Patricia and the Jerusalem Mirror disappear down the lane. Owen passed his hipflask around; "What did that old piece of paper say?" He asked Jericho, who smiled and pulled the newspaper cutting from his pocket. Owen took it and began to read; "A notable Yorkshire property; Salem House, was today sold at auction for nearly twenty-two thousand pounds by order of the Court. The proceeds' of the sale will clear the previous part-owners debts and stop any further debt order proceedings against her. The new owner is a prominent Yorkshire businessman who plans to renovate the house and turn it into a luxury country hotel." Owen finished and asked Jericho; "Who bought the old place then?"

Jericho chuckled; "A certain Patrick Well's, through a third-party property company that he owns. That Solicitor wasn't really that dumb after all." Alex sighed; "No wonder he didn't object too strongly to Dave putting Sally on the deeds; the sneaky bugger."

Jericho accepted the hipflask and gestured towards the house; "It certainly suited our mission; it enabled us to close the portal, return two souls to their correct time and stop a couple of determined time travellers from carrying on their unsavoury occupations. Sir Malcolm [Roland] is now trapped in 1767 with no chance to go anywhere or continue his evil trade in human flesh."

"What about Le Chat?" Owen asked and Jericho sighed but had to smile; "He lives in comfort in 1980 with his bloody cat and can still pop back to 1767. So, he thinks." Wilson rubbed his face and really did grin; "I take it that his little time portal in the cupboard is now closed?" Jericho nodded; "I closed it up before we left. He'll be surprised by that." Owen still looked puzzled; "Why did he tip us off about the sale, that wasn't in his best interests was it?"

Wilson chuckled; "No it wasn't, but since Jericho insisted, we take the girl back - with his great nephew - that was the only way he could stop her benefiting from being with Dave. He must really hate her, but I suspect that he knew Dave would stand by her, but she wouldn't get any of the money this way. I think he's wrong about that too, since her debts are now paid off."

Jericho smiled; "The bonus is that Great Uncle Wesley is trapped in 1980, now his time portal is closed and since he was due to be dispatched [die] in 1982, he's in his own allocated time period and his soul can be collected."

Owen nodded, then turned again to Jericho; "What did you mean, when you said to Alex; 'Yes, I'm sure that is how it happened' earlier?" Jericho chuckled; "Over to you Alexandra. Honesty is always the best policy."

Alex pushed back in her seat and folded her arms; she didn't look happy. "Alright bloody alright. To get Mr. Parker back....I had to...I had to wash the old buggers feet. There, now you know." Wilson looked astounded; "Wash his feet! I mean just wash his feet?" Owen scratched his head; "I know the old King is a strange bugger but wash his feet?"

"Tut Tut Alexandra, half the truth is no truth really." Jericho said and grinned broadly. Alex sighed and threw up her hands in mock despair; "Alright, alright, the truth is, I had to wash his feet whilst stark naked. There, now are you satisfied?" Jericho gave Alex a knowing look and she finally added; "Alright, stark naked except a 'Davey Crockett' hat and red riding boots. That's all I did, and the old pervert pardoned the damn cat!"

There was silence for a few seconds, and everyone started to laugh; including Alex who could now see the funny side, despite her fanny still hanging open and aching a little from the fucking she had received from the King's 'black stallion'. That was a delicious memory that she would keep to herself. But the curious Monsieur Moreau intrigued her, and his mother fascinated – and troubled – her even more.

Jericho said quietly; "Honesty is always the best policy; sometimes." Then added; "Come on people, Alex and Owen need to jump to Scotland and reconnoitre a story that's surfaced there in the 1980's and I have an errant to run for Angel Margret. So, it looks like Wilson has some time off." Wilson just grunted; "Fat chance."

EPISODE PROLOGUE: "On December 18th, 1941, the Imperial Japanese Army invaded the British Crown colony of Hong Kong. On Christmas Eve, a small band of English soldiers, accompanied by three army nurses escaped into the jungle to rendezvous with an Australian submarine off the coast. A condemned prisoner was also taken with them; Private John Hook faced the death penalty for killing his officer during the fighting. Jericho and his team are dispatched because what John Hook did on that desperate journey, should never have happened! Alex gets involved with the soldiers and natives and certainly lifts morale!"

60 Minutes approx. **Episode Warnings:** Alcohol – Smoking - Strong language [including racial slurs] – Violence [including sexual violence & combat violence] – Strong graphic sexual references – Mild horror.

NOTES: The original version of this story is published and appears in the **TEMPORAL DETECTIVES:** Book Series 2 – Episode 13 entitled: **"THE REDEMPTION (ALMOST) OF PRIVATE JOHN HOOK."**

CAUTION: Recommended for 18+ only.

1. THE 'TENNIS CLUB' - A TEMPORARY MILITARY HOSPITAL.

The young nurse ran down the corridor, past the full stretchers of newly arrived wounded and her frantic colleagues, trying to cope with yet another influx of casualties. Nurse Ruth Chambers, newly arrived in Hong Kong, gripped the two small keys in her hand and stopped outside the private room. A hastily written note in chalk declared; 'POW - No Entry.' was hanging from the door. The guard was gone, now probably dead or wounded in the fighting that neared the makeshift hospital. She fumbled with the lock for a few seconds and finally managed to get the damn door open, bursting into the room. "You've got to run for it! The bloody Japanese are coming up the road; they'll be here in minutes."

Private John Devlin Hook, aged 23 years and under arrest for the apparent murder of his Platoon officer, jumped from the bed and held up his handcuffed wrist; "Sorry darling, I can't go anywhere unless I drag this bloody bed with me!" He shouted and shook his arm violently; the small metal bed rattled and slid across the floor a few inches. John Hook was quite a powerful man, fit from army life and boxing. The nurse didn't say anything but threw John the two keys and ran back out the door. John could now hear gunfire and small explosions; nearby and approaching.

He realised immediately that the small silver key, next to the door key would fit the handcuffs. He actually chuckled and muttered; "Fucking good on you Ruthie, you fucking came through for old Hooky boy!" The young nurse had been kind to the condemned man, bringing him extra portions of ice cream and paperback books.

She had dressed his wounded shoulder and gave him some painkillers. "A fucking good decent soul." He said softly; nothing like him. But there had been several 'good and decent' fuckers in his patrol that 2nd lieutenant Clifford Rees-Davis had abandoned to die, defending the small petrol dump. The bastard had simply ran away and John Hook had gone after him. He shot the cowardly fucker without hesitation and now faced death by hanging. He would have been hung tomorrow morning, but the invading Japanese Army, arriving suddenly, had thwarted that particular little show for the top brass, who John hated.

John hastily unlocked himself and grabbed up his shirt and small kitbag; then made for the hospital grounds. He ran past abandoned ambulances and blood-stained trucks, some still filled with wounded, who shouted at him for help and water. He ignored their pleas and dived into the small monsoon ditch. On his hands and knees, he made his way along the ditch, but stopped suddenly and pulled leaves and bushes down upon himself. He was hardly breathing, as he watched the Japanese officer and about two dozen men, approach the doors of the temporary hospital. They had their bayonets fixed and looked battle weary and a little angry. They had been fighting for years in China and now, they had the bloody British Empire to fight.

That made John smile a little; that's when he saw the two doctors with a large stick; a white pillow case tied to one end. They were waving it frantically, with their free hands in the air. They were shot dead where they stood, and two angry Japanese soldiers finished them off with bayonets. John Cussed under his breath and watched the soldiers enter the hospital. He cowed down as more and more shots rang out. He knew there was no fighting British soldiers in there, just patients, doctors, nurses and unarmed medical staff.

The shooting continued for a couple of minutes; then a really ominous silence came over the place. John eased himself up a little and thought about making a run for it, but three Japanese trucks had turned up with about six or seven soldiers scattered amongst them. John thought the empty trucks would be for prisoners and maybe, the wounded.

That's when he saw the two nurses being dragged from the hospital by half a dozen laughing and shouting Japanese soldiers. They ripped the nurse's uniforms off and left the two young women in just their army issue stockings. They were thrown to the ground and the rape party started. The screaming and sobbing made John clench and unclench his fists and curse repeatedly. Each girl was brutally, raped, punched and slapped by maybe six or seven men. When the soldiers had finished, two of the men pissed over the prostrate women; giggling loudly and slapping each other. The two girls were hauled up and thrown into the back of a truck; John could see little puddles of blood upon the gravel driveway.

 He watched, filled with useless and helpless anger, as another two young nurses were dragged out and the whole dreadful scene was repeated. Except one young woman tried to escape; she somehow managed to throw off the two soldiers who were holding her down for their colleagues to violate. She ran a few yards before being shot dead. A soldier ran up to the body and kicked it violently, then pulled his bayonet from his rifle and stabbed and chopped at the body for a few minutes. The other nurse, screaming hysterically was raped by nearly a dozen men and thrown, still and almost lifeless into the back of the truck, with her two friends.

 Another two women were dragged out and yet again, brutally raped and beaten before John's eyes, which were now filled with tears. He wasn't an emotional man by any means [except anger maybe] but the sights before him placed a large rock in his stomach and throat.

 This went on until nightfall; two girls each time including the grim-faced Sister, who the officer took first. Punching her and shouting, as he sodomised her in front of the other sobbing nurse and his cheering soldiers. After their ordeal, both women were thrown upon the truck with the other girls. When they had no new girls to rape, the Japanese and their trucks pulled away, with the bruised and battered nurses aboard and only about half a dozen soldiers remained to guard the silent buildings.

John lay in the ditch, head in hands, and slowly realised that he had not seen young 'Ruthie' amongst the violated women. He knew he had to find out about her, even if it caused more pain and anguish to him. He resolved to check out the hospital under the cover of darkness. But first he needed a weapon.

One Japanese soldier - probably a corporal - was drinking sake by the large ornamental flowerpots, near the hospital's side door. What caught John's eye was his pistol holster and belt. John flexed his fingers and quietly removed his leather belt. He made his way to the unsuspecting soldier, crawling on his belly. He was that close to the soldier that he could hear the man chuckling to himself. He had no idea that John Hook was behind him. John flexed his belt and struck. The soldier took about a minute to die, thrashing about and struggling in the gravel in almost silence. The belt had prevented any shouts for help as John strangled him.

John pulled the body behind the pots and stripped it of anything useful - especially the pistol - then noticed the specks of blood around the soldier's crotch. He grunted with satisfaction; "Hope you enjoyed those poor bitches my friend. You won't fuck anyone else." He muttered to himself and disappeared into the side door of the tennis Club, turned hospital.

There were bodies everywhere, on stretchers and in beds. The soldiers of Imperial Japan had butchered the sick and wounded with bullets and bayonets. He passed a young native nurse sprawled across a dead Australian soldier in his bed. She had clearly tried to protect the man and had been savagely bayoneted to death. John just shook his head and crept down the corridor and suddenly realised he could hear faint crying in the dark. With moonlight streaming through the windows, he could just make out the sign on the door; it was the morgue.

He quietly and slowly pushed on the door and crept in. In the far corner were huddled three nurses: all crying softly. To his immense relief, one was 'Ruthie'. She simply stared at John and then ran across the floor on her hands and knees, grabbing his legs. He ran his fingers through her long dark hair and whispered; "Your safe now, but we need to get the bloody hell out of here!"

 The three young nurses had actually hidden in the morgue drawers, along with cold dead bodies, as the soldiers searched the hospital. Lt. Ruth Chambers had managed to compose herself and her calm, had helped the other two nurses, to deal with the terrible situation they found themselves in. Lt. Patricia [Big Pat] Collins and Lt. Dawn Baines both gripped John by the shoulder and hand.

He could see the look of utter terror and fear upon their faces. They had seen what happened to their colleagues; through the small morgue window. Dawn gripped his hand and whispered;

"You will use that on me, if we're about to be captured by...by those...by those animals." She gestured to his pistol. John just nodded and told the women to follow him. They crept from the building and slipped into the Monsoon ditch after the girls removed their precious stockings [right in front of him, which made him smile a little]. The little group, in single file, crawled through the ditch, but stopped and watched the Japanese soldiers set fire to the hospital; they wanted to hide their evil deeds and fire could do that.

 The little group managed to avoid the many Japanese troops that were patrolling the small road, that lead up towards the mountains and by a derelict school they came upon a British Patrol; also trying to make the mountain road. John could not believe his bad luck; they were from his old Regiment and the young Captain certainly knew who he was.

2. THE BAND OF LITTLE HOPE.

Captain Frank Ames pointed his pistol at Private Hook and held out his other hand; "The gun you bastard or I'll shoot you down like the dog you are." John just stared at the young captain and shook his head. "The fucking Japanese are all over the place. Do you know what they did at the temporary hospital? You're going to need every man with a gun." The captain nodded, the pistol not moving from John; "I know what they did, and I know what you did; the gun now." He said and gestured for his sergeant to take John's pistol and holster. Sergeant Campbell walked over and held out his hand. John chuckled and pulled off the belt and handed it to the sergeant. "How are you, Donald?" He asked. The sergeant nodded and said softly; "Better for having you back, you mad bastard." and returned to the officer with the pistol belt.

The officer lowered his pistol and placed it back in his side holster. He threw John's gun to a young, skinny private who had no weapon. "Look after that Haines." The young soldier nodded and wiped his nose on the back of his hand. John turned to Ruth and said softly; "Most of these boys are no better than boy scouts; just arrived from England. There's only me, the sarge, big Alec Kent and little 'Spider' Murphy that's been in the jungle and had a set too with the bloody nips. The rest look like they couldn't fight their way out of a wet paper bag."

He sighed, adding; "Bloody cannon fodder." Ruth looked

concerned and whispered; "What about the captain?" John grunted; "Straight out of Sandhurst. He wasn't at the fight party. Sitting in battalion HQ sharpening his bloody pencils I expect."
 The captain smiled at the nurses' and asked if they would attend some of the men, they had minor injuries, but it would be nice to have them seen too. Ruth turned to the other girls, and they set about tending the boys with minor cuts and bruises. Captain Ames turned to John; "I can't lock you up. But you step out of line just once and I'll shoot you. Do you understand that you murdering bastard?" John just smiled at him and went over to some felled trees and sat down. The sergeant threw him a canteen of water and John asked him for a fag. The pair lit up a single cigarette and smoked it between them.

 "He's actually not bad for a green one; got us out of the depot when the japs paid us a visit. He kept his head, made the right decisions." He breathed out some smoke - not smiling - and added; "Besides, He's all we got and only he knows the call sign and radio code for that fucking Aussie sub."

 Now that did grab John's attention; "What fucking Aussie sub?" He asked with real interest. The sergeant smiled; "He managed to get hold of a Aussie sub, they'll pick us up - if we make Kanyo Point - in three days. That's going to be some feat, with Jap's crawling up our arse and towing three bloody women." John nodded; finishing the cigarette; "Don't worry about the girls, after what they witnessed; they'll crawl on their fucking bellies to get away from the nips." The sergeant chuckled and re-joined his men.

 The captain was getting everyone together. They were moving out. The captain shouted at John; "On your feet Hook and keep in front of me, where I can see you. I don't want you behind my bloody back." John smiled and slowly walked over to the little group of very desperate people. "It will be my pleasure to join your army of ragged arse jungle trained killers." The sarcasm in his voice was obvious. The captain just grunted, and the little band moved back into the jungle. The sergeant up front with John closes by.

John looked back at Ruth, helping a limping young soldier along and smiled. She had woken something in him that he had not felt for a long time about a woman. He cursed his bloody luck; it had to happen now, in the middle of war, chased by fucking evil murdering japs and facing the hangman's noose. He actually chuckled to himself; "Keep a grip hooky boy."

They made slow progress and night was falling fast. They had dived for cover several times as Japanese aircraft passed overhead. The jungle vanished into the darkness of night and the group had to stop; there would be no comforting fires, hot food or shelter. They huddled together beneath some really big trees and settled in for the night.

 The captain knelt under his pulled off jacket, with the sergeant and by weak torchlight, examined the map. The priority was reaching Kanyo Point and keeping the radio safe. The sergeant nodded; he had given that crucial job to big Alec. It was in safe hands. Then there was the officer murderer, Private John Hook. What was to be done with him? The sergeant sighed; "Sir, if there's a fucking fight in the jungle, then I want that murdering bastard right next to me." The officer nodded. The sergeant was a good man, experienced in the jungle and already had seen fierce fighting twice. That was good enough for him.

John and big Alec stood the first watch. They sat a little way from the camp and watched the jungle trail. Big Alec chuckled and whispered; "If you hadn't shot that bastard, I would have done it. But not in front of bloody witness's you mad bastard." John slapped his big shoulder and stared out into the darkness.

Just after midnight, john rubbed his tired eyes and then stiffened; his was now fully awake. He gently tapped big Alec. "I can hear something." He whispered. Alec shook his head and brushed off his tiredness. They lay hardly breathing and listened. John was right, someone was creeping through the jungle, heading right for their little camp. Alec raised his rifle and very slowly and quietly pulled the bolt back and forward. He was ready to shoot. John tapped his shoulder again and gestured to the jungle. "Let's not wake up the world until we know who that is." He whispered. Alec nodded and John slipped away.

He found the slight figure just yards from their position, carefully working its way through the thick, clinging vegetation. John smiled to himself; your good, but I'm better. He said to himself. A jap prisoner might be very useful. He had a pretty good idea that this jap was lost and didn't have a rifle. He crept forward, slowly and quietly. Then jumped, he had the figure on their back in an instant, hand across mouth and arm held tight. He grabbed the fellow's shirt and received quite a surprise; he was gripping a wonderful big breast, with the large nipple between his fingers. He stared hard and slowly moved his hand about to make sure; yes it was a woman's breast. The woman sighed; "You can remove your bloody hand from my tits now private." It was an Australian nurse!

They sat up and John stared hard at her; she adjusted her blouse and cussed; she had a couple of buttons missing. She gave him a very unpleasant look; "You realise, that thanks to you, I'll be walking around with my bloody boobs hanging out." She whispered and pulled down her dirty skirt. John caught a glimpse of white panties and really did smile. "Captain Alex Cappanni, 31st Australian Field Hospital. And who are you? My groping private?" John chuckled; "Ex-Private John Hook Ma'am. It's very nice to meet you."

She stared at him; "Ex Private?" She asked. He nodded; "Long story, we best get back to camp before big Alec starts shooting." He jumped up and held out his hand. She gripped it tightly and he pulled her up. He could see her magnificent breasts, barely hidden by her torn blouse in the moonlight. She saw where he was looking and held the blouse together with one hand. "When you've finished enjoying the view, shall we get moving?"

John chuckled; "What a fucking woman!" Then realised, he still had a firm grip on her hand. She gently pulled it from him and followed, as he headed for the camp; whispering for Alec to stand down.

3. REINFORCEMENTS; WELL, SORT OF.

The three young nurses were absolutely delighted to see the captain stride into camp, with John hook following and gathered around her with Captain Ames. Captain Cappanni explained that she and three men had escaped from the field hospital after it had been overrun by the Japanese. She took a deep breath and said simply; "They did not treat the prisoners well; especially the nurses." The girls nodded and held onto each other; they knew full well what the captain meant.

Young Ruth just had to ask; "Ma'am, what happened to your Bra?" The captain smiled, gripping her torn blouse; "I was advised by our jungle expert, that running about the jungle in basically, a strait jacket [her bra] wouldn't help me breath. So I ditched it; quite liberating really."

 The girls immediately agreed, with Dawn pushing her hands up her blouse, saying; "The Captain's bloody right. I've been struggling to breathe since we started." She pulled off her bra and stuffed it in her bag. The other two did the same. Captain Ames watched in astonishment - and a little pleasure - but didn't argue. This particular captain of Nurses clearly knew what she was about. She turned to Ames and asked; "Who's gone after my people?"

The captain smiled; "My sergeant and private Murphy. They both know their way around the jungle." Captain Cappanni nodded and pulled her blouse together again. Ruth smiled; "Ma'am, I've a needle and thread in my bag. We'll soon have that sewn up." Now that did make the Captain of Nurses smile and Ruth produced her sewing kit from her bag.

 Everyone settled back down and awaited the return of the sergeant with the 'reinforcements'. John Hook sipped the canteen offered to him by Private Chester Davis and said quietly; "Knew exactly what she was doing. Soon as I grabbed her, she went still as a rabbit in car headlights. Made bloody sure that I found out she was a woman. Lay with her legs up, showing her bloody panties with my hand gripping her big tit. She knew damn well that no man would kill that little honey." He grinned and kissed the hand that had handled that beautiful soft breast.

"What a fucking woman. I'd really go for her." He added. Chester smiled; "So would most of the men and they haven't groped those big tits or seen her crotch." John handed back the canteen and watched Captain Alex talking with the girls in the moonlight. Oh yes, he could really go for a woman like that. Preferably with young Ruth at the same time, smiling, he lay back against the tree and slept.

Alex sat with 'her' girls and sipped warm water from an enamel mug. She really wished it was bloody brandy. The girls spoke softly about what happened at the hospital. Ruth wiped her face; "If it wasn't for John, we would all probably be ...dead or worse. He killed a jap sentry and took us into the jungle. A couple of times, jap patrols passed within a few feet of us. I can't believe they would hang a man like that. "The other girls mumbled their agreement at that. Alex passed the mug around and Dawn topped it up from her water bottle. "He's a condemned man for killing that officer, regardless of the circumstances. The British Army doesn't take too kindly to privates killing their officers; whatever the bloody officer did." Alex said and glanced over at the sleeping private.

 She could fully understand he's reaction to the officer running away after telling his men to make 'a last stand'. She almost smiled to herself; he was a big strapping lad and his touch had made her feel good; even in the bloody jungle with Japanese troops crawling all over the place. "Maybe you could speak up for him Ma'am. I mean they might listen to an officer." Dawn said and sipped her cup; Alex shook her head; "I think they have already decided his fate. Besides, I don't think a British Court Marshal would pay much to an Australian Officer, a lowly Captain of Nurses and a woman as well." The girls all sighed, but they smiled when Alex said; "But I can try, I suppose. It must be worth a go; to save a man's life."

 The little gathering all broke up and the very tired girls tried to find a soft place to sleep. But the crawling bugs and nightmares about snakes and Japanese soldiers kept them awake until exhaustion took over and they slept badly on the dirty earth. Alex found a cosy bush and settled down. Captain Ames disturbed her; he offered her half of his chocolate bar, which she accepted. He spoke softly and grimly; he expected her to keep the girls going - whatever happened - pulling an army issue 'Smith & Weston' pistol from his canvas bag that he always carried.

He tapped it gently; "There's four rounds left Alex, should we be about to be over run and captured, I will use it on you and the other nurses. Do you agree?" Alex just stared at the pistol and found she was nodding. "Bloody good show." Was all he said and slipped away to find his bed for the night. Alex shuddered a little; she didn't know what frightened her more; him or the bloody Japanese!

Hook was aroused by his name being whispered; He looked up and saw Alex standing over him. "A word with you private in private please." She whispered, she had her legs slightly apart and he could see up her uniform skirt; the crotch of her damp panties looking straight at him. He rose quickly and nodded, gesturing for her to follow him. They slipped away from the camp; separately and met under a large tree.

John slowly ran his hands down her body and placed one on her bum. The other pushed into her blouse and their mouths came together. Alex groped in his shorts and was well pleased with what she discovered. "You are very well equipped private." She whispered as their tongues caressed each other. He grinned; "So are you Ma'am, you could easily make me like officers again."

His hand squeezed a breast, feeling the nipple harden under his touch. His other hand slipped beneath her panties and found quite a wet patch, which delighted him. She clearly wanted to fuck. They slowly sank down onto the grass and dirt. His hand tugged down her panties and she took them from him and stuffed them into her skirt pocket. They embraced for some time before she broke away and knelt over his cock. She pushed it into her mouth and set to work. John held a hand over his mouth to stifle his moans of pleasure. They both knew that sound carried far in the jungle at night.

John was on his back, his dirty shorts pulled down. Alex climbed on, squatting over his large cock and lowered her bum and fanny down, pushing it deep into her open, wet vagina. She also pushed a hand over her mouth and began to ride him. Slowly at first, then she gained speed as her vagina accepted him more fully. He took hold of her big heaving tits and squeezed and caressed them in equal measure. He pulled her down, until their mouths met - hands free - and the pair kissed passionately, exploring each other with some urgency. After some minutes, he carefully rolled Alex onto her back and began thrusting hard and fast. She gripped his shoulders and clenched her teeth; she dare not make a sound. John was having the same problem. But he really didn't want some fucking nip to stick a bayonet up his bum!

They quickly changed position; Alex was now on her knees, both hands over her mouth, as John drove his big cock into her. She endured a big orgasm in silence; well, apart from a little groan that escaped now and then.

John reached round and gripped those big tits he now loved so much. They were fucking hard and fast. He managed to whisper something and Alex felt him cum inside her. That triggered yet another orgasm and the pair collapsed onto the dirt, panting.

They lay together for some time, John kissing her neck and shoulders, caressing her, with his hands running over her limp body. Finally, he pulled his cock from her, and she quickly shoved a hand between her legs and allowed his cum to trickle on her hand. He watched with a real big smile, as she licked her fingers.

He chuckled quietly and Alex whispered – grinning – that 'one shouldn't waste good protein'. He pulled her to him, and pair kissed again. Alex stood by the tree and buttoned up her blouse and pulled up her panties. She straightened her skirt and hair, while he tugged up his shorts. "I could murder a bloody cigarette and a beer right now." He whispered and kissed her again, with real passion. She nodded; "Just a bloody brandy would do me." They made their way back to camp; holding hands, and then slipped in – hopefully un-noticed - like nothing had taken place.

The two natives watched from clearing's edge and exchanged an amused look. The older one gripped his bow and spoke into his comrade's ear. The young man restrained his laughter and slapped his friend on the shoulder. They both hoped and wished that the white woman would be as generous to native men. They made their way to the camp just after dawn.

4. NO CHRISTMAS HERE.

Captain Ames welcomed the pair with real warmth. He explained to his men – and women – that Sans and Retu were jungle men from the mountains, and they really hated the Japanese. "They're in bloody good company here." The sergeant muttered to the still smiling John, who simply couldn't stop looking at Alex. The captain had met the pair at Battalion HQ, and they had been hired as scouts. They would lead the small party through the jungle to Kanyo Point. They knew a short route through 'Diamond Valley' a narrow pass that was the only quick way to the submarine rendezvous point.

If, the Japanese did follow, they would have to go through the valley, which was an excellent place for an ambush. A small force could hold the much larger Japanese contingent there with ease. If the Japanese didn't go through, they would have to pass around the valley and that would add a day – at least – to their pursuit of the group. Retu, who spoke some English – taught to him by nun's at the missionary school he had attended on occasion – also told the captain about the Japanese that were now behind the group and following their trail. They could be in this very spot in maybe four or five hours. The captain nodded and the party immediately prepared to head out; they would be following the two natives. But not before Retu had slid up to Alex. Grinning and spoke quietly, so that he wasn't overheard. He asked the nice white lady if she would be 'generous' to him and Sans; like she was to the bad soldier who had killed his white brother for running away.

 Alex stared at the strong little man with large wooden hoops in both ears and smiled a little. She had no idea that she and John had been seen by the pair. She explained that she and John really didn't want the others know what happened in the jungle clearing. Retu grinned – again – and ran a finger across his lips; "You do us favour and we do you favour." He grinned – yet again – and joined his comrade. Alex sighed, she certainly didn't want Jericho and the other's to discover her little adventure. Besides the young man wasn't too bad looking and he was certainly fit. She wasn't too happy about letting the older one fuck her, but they seem to come as a pair. That made her chuckle; her unintended pun: 'cum' as a pair!

 The sergeant and private Murphy returned with Jericho, Wilson and Owen in tow, the team's cover story was simple; they had escaped when the Japanese had over run their Field Hospital. Jericho was playing a civilian supplier to the Australian Medical Corps - who had been caught up in the fighting - with Owen as his assistant. Wilson was a big South African soldier, who had been at the unit delivering supplies that had been swapped between the Field Hospital and his unit. They had all been caught out by the speed of the Japanese advance.

 Everyone commented on the big man. John Hook smiled and spoke to Donald [the sergeant] "Now that's one big bugger I want next to me in a pub fight." The sergeant agreed. The mood in the makeshift camp was sombre.

No one really wished anyone else' Merry Christmas!' But some morale was created when Owen handed around a packet of cigarettes and matches. He watched as the men shared one cigarette between a pair. They wanted their little Christmas treat to last for a while. They picked up the 'dogends' to leave no signs behind and hopefully; make up another cigarette from them.

 Big Patricia liked Owen and shared her chocolate bar with him and did wish him 'Merry Christmas'. Owen was really happy about that, and they chatted together for some time, until the other nurses dragged her away and the three walked together, laughing and talking. Wilson slapped Owen on the back; "She likes you baby brother." and smiled; "So do something bloody about it." Owen just grinned.

 They moved out at dawn and came across the smashed-up truck, halfway down a small ravine, just before mid-day. It was British and to their delight still had some equipment and supplies scattered about. They found some very welcome tins of 'Bully Beef' [corned beef] and peaches. But the captain was almost ecstatic at finding a 'Lewis' machine gun with ammunition boxes. Wilson and big Alec could easily manage it between them. They feasted on their wonderful find and the food caused morale to improve greatly; some even did wish 'Merry Christmas!' to each other. But they had to move on after the captain had stripped anything that the Japanese could use. They carried away the petrol cans and anything else of use.

 They camped just before nightfall and Captain Ames checked his position with a compass and map. They had actually - to his surprise - made good progress. At this rate, they should make the rendezvous point with a couple of hours to spare. But that wasn't much leeway, with the Japanese army right up their arses. The team assembled by the edge of the camp and held a discrete meeting about this mission. The mission was the man, John Hook. Wilson chuckled; "Didn't that famous Hollywood Director make a war film about that already?"

 Everyone chuckled at that. Jericho explained that in the original timeline, Hook deserts the group to save his own skin and the Japanese caught up with the little party, after following them through 'Diamond Valley'. There were only a couple of survivors left to tell the tale. He didn't say who.

 But something had changed - drastically - Hook became a bloody hero; killed holding off the Japanese forces, allowing the little group to escape. Their mission was to make sure that Hook runs off and the original timeline is recovered. Owen rubbed his face; "Why the hell did a man like Hook suddenly do that? I've pulled his life file from Human Records, and he was always in trouble as a civilian and as a soldier. He looked after himself and no one else; until now."

Alex said nothing; maybe her little encounter with the man had stirred something? She listened to the briefing in silence, thinking that she could well be the catalyst that caused the change, but that didn't make sense; she was only here because the damn timeline had changed already! But she couldn't get that thought from her mind. The team meeting broke up and Alex crept from camp towards a big tree.

5. THE NATIVES ARE FRIENDLY!

Alex waited at the agreed rendezvous point and sighed as Retu and Sans arrived, smiling in anticipation. "Oh well, they kept their word and said nothing." She stood and reached under her grubby skirt and pulled down her panties. She had already lubricated her fanny with some Vaseline from the medical kit. Retu gestured to her and Sans pulled off his loin cloth. "So, you must be first. Least they respect age around here." Alex stared at the little man with the big erect cock. It almost touched his belly button!

Alex groaned a little; "I wish I had used more bloody Vaseline." She lay back down and opened her legs. The little man knelt between them and spat on his cock. "Thank you for that." She said with some sarcasm, which – of course – wasn't understood by the men. He didn't waste any time pushing his cock into her and she groaned a little, lying back, as the old man thrust deep and quickly. Alex stared up at the stars and thought how beautiful the jungle night sky was, as Sans busied himself with her fanny. He didn't say anything as he fucked her like a sex doll.

Alex also said nothing but could feel every thrust of his big cock. She looked down at him a couple of times and sighed; the things she had to endure to keep her sex life secret!

She had too surprises, one was that he lasted almost twenty minutes; hard fucking her. The second was her two or three Orgasm's she had with him. They came quick and unexpected. Sans really did grin at that. He finally spurted deep inside of her and said nothing as he pulled out his cock. Alex stared between her legs, his cum was running from her open vagina and down her thighs; there was loads of the stuff. He stood and grinned, bowing a little. She took a deep breath as Retu pulled off his loin cloth and knelt between her legs. He wasn't wasting any time having his share of her slit. She groaned; he was even bigger than his friend!

Retu mounted her with urgency and fucked her deep and hard. Alex had to slap a hand over her mouth as she climaxed; really spurting hard. The little man grinned as her fluid splashed against his balls and thighs. He whispered; "It good for you most generous lady." Alex nodded and a couple of little groans escaped from under her hand. He fucked her hard, fast and constantly. She had yet another big squirt and lay back panting as he simply continued to fuck her. He finally came and Alex felt his hot liquid filling any spaces inside her cunt, which were not crammed with his big cock.

 She sat up on her elbows and watched as he pulled his cock out slowly and gently; the stream of cum flowed from her fanny and trickled into the dirt. Both men replaced their loin clothes and bowed. They turned, saying nothing and returned to camp. Alex staggered up and slowly pulled her panties up and straightened her clothes up. She walked back to camp a little awkwardly, her fanny was gaped, wet and a little tender. She stopped and just had to piss behind some thick bushes, squatting down, she groaned with relief as her hot piss, mixed with some of the men's cum, splashed into the dirt.

She stood and started to pull her soiled panties up, then stared at the Japanese soldier who was staring at her, mouth and eyes wide open. He wasn't even pointing his rifle at her. She stopped, with her knickers halfway up and for some reason; smiled. The young soldier grinned broadly and placed his rifle down and hurriedly began to unbutton his flies. "Oh, fucking hell." She whispered and knew she was about to be raped.

The figure came from the soldiers left and he was dead before falling to the ground, still clutching his small cock. The bayonet had been driven expertly through his throat, to cut off any screams. John smiled at her and wiped his knife on the dead soldier's shirt. "Pull your knickers up darling. If these bastards are this close, then we need to move and move bloody quickly."

Alex could only nod and tug up her panties. John grabbed her hand; "I wondered where you had gone. Next time you need to pee, bloody tell me and I'll come with you. There wouldn't be any unpleasant surprises that way." John said quietly, with no censor in his voice.

Alex nodded; he had clearly not seen the two natives fucking her brains out under the tree. She glanced back to see 'big Swen' the Collector talking to the young dead Japanese's soldier. Swen smiled and waved, the little soldier bowed to her with a big grin and followed Swen into the bright light. Now that did make Alex think; if a Collector had turned up for the dead soldier's soul, then his death was scheduled. But how could that be so? She practically caused it by being here and taking a piss and she certainly wouldn't have been in the original timeline! That's one for Jericho, she thought.

The group moved off quickly; the killing of the Japanese scout had galvanised everyone into rapid action. They made for the pass with Sans leading; Retu slid up to Alex and grinned; "We fuck you again. Then we keep big mouths shut." He said softly and actually winked. He ran and caught up with his friend. Alex just groaned and hoped that the little jar of Vaseline would be sufficient for another session with the two 'big' little men.

6. INTO 'DIAMOND VALLEY'.

Jericho admonished Alex about going into the jungle for a bloody pee and not telling anyone. "A bloody good job that Hook was there to save you're flipping butt." He muttered and Alex explained about the Collector being there. Jericho nodded, thinking hard; "That means the pair [Hook and the Japanese soldier] was scheduled to meet up and Hook kill him. Your right Alex, that's interesting and I wonder if Hook is telling the truth about going after you because he couldn't see you around the camp. What the hell was he doing out there?"

The team little meeting broke up and Alex caught Hook staring at her several times as the party progressed through the jungle. They would soon come upon the valley.

Owen was walking with Alex, and he smiled; "Our little native friends really like you. They say you're a most generous woman. In fact, they want to take you back to their village to be generous to all the men there." Alex sighed; she had forgotten that temporal detectives could understand and speak any human language of the time period they were in.

She chuckled; "How sweet, I treated their insect bites and they wanted to give me presents, which of course, I refused. So they think I'm generous, how nice." Owen grunted; "Their village men must suffer a lot of bloody insect bites." Alex smiled again but groaned inside; the thought of being 'generous' to a whole village of 'big' little men worried her. She would need a bloody barrel of Vaseline. Then she smiled at the thought!

Wilson turned and jerked a thumb behind them; "Our little native friend is back." They watched as Retu ran up to Captain Ames, who called for the party to halt. Wilson lowered the Lewis gun to the ground. He easily carried the big gun on his broad shoulders.

Owen shook his head; "I think we'll home in time for dinner. The Japanese have sent out a quick moving advance party. They're just hours behind us; the main body another couple of hours behind them." Wilson nodded; "Time for Hook to disappear, I think." Alex looked across at Hook, who was talking to Dawn and Ruth. The girls were smiling and laughing quietly with him. She watched as he patted Ruth's arm and spoke in her ear. The girl grinned and the two nurses wandered off to join their friend Patricia.

 But her attention was drawn back to Captain Ames, who had everyone gather closely around him. He explained just how dire their situation was. The Japanese advance party could be quickly on them. But he had a plan; it wasn't a very nice one. He wanted two volunteers to set up the Lewis gun in the valley and hold the Japs until the group could make the rendezvous point.

He made it clear that they would be killed or captured. Everyone stood in silence until finally the sergeant sighed; "I know how to use the fucking thing [the Lewis gun] I aren't married or anything. Got fuck all back home except my old dad, who regularly gave me a good kicking when I was a kid. I'll stay, but I'll need someone to the feed the bloody ammo."

The captain slapped the sergeant on the shoulder and asked; "Who's joining him boys?" There was silence for a second or two, then young Chester Davis stuck up his hand and sighed; "Me Sir.

I'm a Barnardo's boy. I ain't got anything or anyone back home. All the rest of the men are married or got sweethearts, a mum and dad at home, waiting for them to show up. There's only me and Hooky who ain't got anyone and he's a bloody prisoner. I'll stay sir."

Alex actually brushed a tear away and then noticed all her girls were doing the same. She swallowed hard; two bloody brave men who would never think of themselves as bloody heroes. That decided, the sergeant and young Davis would find a spot in the valley to set up the gun. Everyone shook their hands, and the girls kissed them; including Alex.

 Alex saw Hook standing away from the group, arms folded and staring at the ground. Then she remembered the sergeant telling Ruth about how he [Hook] had looked after young Chester, since he joined the Regiment. The sergeant had said, when Ruth asked why a man like Hook would do that. "Because he was like that Ma'am; young with nothing and no one, except, no one looked after young Hook. That's why he's the way he is. Only ever been him. But he did take to young Chester."

 The team gathered away from the rest and Jericho smiled; "Soon be home for dinner. Once our boy has departed, we'll do the same." Alex saw Hook talking to Sergeant Donald and wondered what their quiet conversation was about. Then Hook gestured to her. She walked slowly over as her colleagues stood talking amongst themselves. Hook whispered to Alex and gently touched her arm. He grinned and slapped a little kiss on her cheek; "Knew I could depend on a girl like you. Pity we hadn't met up when I was a bit younger. Probably got me self a job in some bloody factory to keep my missus and kids. Thank you for being a generous woman." He walked away with the sergeant, turned and smiled at Alex and the pair disappeared into some tree's, still talking.

Alex stood, arms folded and thought about what Hook had asked of her. She was to lure young Chester to a quite spot and let him fuck her, while Hook and the sergeant disappeared in the valley with the Lewis gun. He didn't want young Chester killed.

He had grinned, saying; it'll make a man of the boy. I just know you'll look after him, show him what women are really for. She now knew that Hook had changed the human timeline himself.

Some humans did that; they changed their Destiny in just an instant. It has happened before and will certainly do so again. This will not make Jericho - or Angel James - happy.

Then she thought - a little disturbed - what the hell did he mean by 'generous woman?' She groaned as she realised; he must have been watching her and certainly did see her being generous to the natives. No wonder he was out in the jungle at that time and could jump on the young Japanese solder!

 She watched as Hook, Donald and captain Ames checked the gun. Alex then wandered off to find young Chester and tell him about the change of plan. She found him under the tree that she and Hook had shared. She slapped a hand over her mouth to stop a surprised gasp escape. Young Chester was there with Ruth. They were embracing under the damn tree with some real passion. He had a hand up her skirt and his mouth firmly fixed on hers. Ruth broke the kiss and stared at Alex, who just smiled and walked up to the pair.

She glanced down at Chester's erection, which Ruth was grasping with one hand. It was certainly adequate. She grinned and asked Ruth if she had pleasured it properly, before lovemaking. Ruth confessed she didn't know what the captain meant. Alex smiled at her and said, "Just watch you'll get the idea." She knelt down and took hold of the shocked - but happy - private's private part.

She sucked his cock, gently caressing it. Chester lay on his back and groaned. Ruth knelt by Alex and watched; "He bloody loves it!" She whispered. Alex nodded, the young man's quivering cock in her mouth. After a few minutes of her wonderful mouth working his cock, the young man spurted, and Alex caught his load in her mouth. She leaned back and opened her mouth revealing a puddle of cum on her tongue.

Ruth really giggled and turned to Alex; "Did you really swallow all that cum?" Alex shook her head gently and with her free hand pulled Ruth to her. Ruth smiled as Alex guided her mouth to hers. The girls kissed with some passion, swapping the fresh cum between themselves and finally the pair did swallow their share of his cum.

Alex grinned; "Now a young man like Chester should be ready for more with a little encouragement and we can certainly encourage him." Alex pulled up Ruth's skirt and very slowly slipped her dirty damp panties down. Ruth groaned as Alex set to work on her fanny with her tongue and fingers. Chester sat up – wide eyed – and watched with real interest, gripping his flaccid cock.

Ruth lay back and clasped a hand over her mouth as Alex made her climax. Her legs kicked and trembled and her whole body appeared to convulse with sheer pleasure. Alex lifted her head and licked her lips; "Now I'll you show how to fuck your man properly." Ruth nodded enthusiastically.

They both set about raising Chester's flaccid cock with their mouths and hands; it worked. With a fresh erection to play with, Alex continued her sex lesson. She tugged down her grubby panties and climbed on Chester, pushing his cock into her. She rode him hard, and Ruth watched with wide eyes and open mouth; rubbing her cunt vigorously with one hand.

Alex pulled her close and her hand went between Ruth's willing thighs. The girls were now kissing with some real passion. Finally, Alex hoped off the young man and Ruth took her place. Chester's cock slipped in easily; Ruth's cunt was running like a leaking tap. She bounced up and down as the pair groaned and panted. Young Chester couldn't hold out and shot his second load into Ruth's welcoming fanny.

 Lying in each other's arms; the happy young couple thanked Alex, who pulled up her panties and wished the pair well. Alex walked back to the camp and discretely gave the thumbs up to Hook, who just nodded and slapped the sergeant's arm. The pair smiled and crept away, carrying the gun, some water canteens and spades to dig in.

 Alex then saw Owen smiling at her. He walked over and whispered to her; "For a minute there, I thought it was you that was young Chester's decoy. But he and Ruth are at it against a tree." Alex just nodded and whispered back; "They needed a bit of schooling, but they'll be fine."

Owen chuckled and discretely took her hand and pushed it against his crotch; he was stiff as a piece of wood. Alex sighed and nodded; "Come on, there must be plenty of tree's around here that are free." Alex didn't smile; "What; free of Jap soldiers or couples fucking?" Owen just shrugged his shoulders.

7. SOMETHING TO REMEMBER.

Alex was on all fours with Owen behind her, thrusting deep and slow. He knew how she liked to be fucked and speeded up a little, reaching around her and grabbing her big tits with both hands. She groaned a little and told him to fuck her harder. He did. He gave her quivering bum a hard slap and said quietly; "We have company." Alex looked up and saw Hook and Donald watching them. She gestured them over and said to Owen; "I think Jackie will be happy with Hook."

Donald leaned back against the tree with Alex on his lap, facing him. He wasn't a big man in the cock department, but he certainly knew how to use it. He loved sucking and squeezing those big tits of hers. "Now this is something fucking to remember about this shit patrol!" He gasped between mouthfuls of her tits and nipples. Alex glanced across at the other 'couple' and had to grin; she had been quite right in her suspicions about Hook and his sexual appetite.

'Jackie' was on all fours with Hook firmly buried up 'her' arse! Hook appreciated the anal sex he was getting by reaching around and jerking off Jackie's big cock. "I always guessed that Hooky swung both bleeding ways." Donald gasped; seemly unfazed by what was happening with his comrade.

Alex called the other pair over and leaned right over Donald with her arse in the air. Jackie mounted her slowly, still with Hook fucking her arse. The heap of humans groaned and cussed, fucking hard. Alex couldn't believe her luck; she was being DP'd in the middle of the bloody jungle in the middle of a bloody war!

They lay like sardines in a tin and continued to fuck. Alex had several little orgasms and Donald came inside of her with lots of swearing and groaning. That must have triggered Hook, for he came too. Jackie was last to shoot her load deep in Alex's willing arse. They all lay panting in the dirt and finally Alex eased off Donald and squatted down over Jackie's face. Who didn't hesitate in cleaning up her wet, open fanny.

Hook staggered up and stood in front of Alex and she cleaned his dirty cock with some gusto. Donald laid chuckling and muttering that he had never seen anything fucking like it. But he fucking loved it!

Under Alex's expert mouth and hands, Hook was soon erect again. He pushed Alex into the dirt and mounted her, pushing his cock deep into her cunt. They slowly rolled in the dirt kissing passionately and groaning together. Donald just shrugged his shoulders as Jackie gave him a blowjob that he would certainly remember. He realised that this could be his last day on fucking earth if the Japs had their way. He ran a hand down Jackie's back and then between the cheeks of her arse. He groaned as she probed under his foreskin with her tongue and gripped a bum cheek. He had never fucked a man before; but this one was something special; he was stunning as a women and Donald finally made his decision about fucking him/her and never mind that he had a big dick. He wanted 'her' arse and urgently.

"Fuck it!" was all Donald said and also pushed Jackie into the dirt – face down – and proceeded to fuck her arse very hard and quick. To his huge surprise, he became quite passionate with 'her' and turned Jackie on her side so they could kiss, and they went at it with real passion unleashed. Jackie had an arm around his neck and their tongues were enjoying each other. Donald admitted to himself that this was the best fucking sex he ever had, and he came inside her backside while enjoying her gorgeous soft mouth and tongue. Unusual for him; he continued to hold and kiss her for some time afterwards. The foursome had fucked for at least another twenty minutes and then Hook and Donald lay in the dirt watching Alex and Jackie in the sixty-nine positions; cleaning each other up.

Donald finally wiped his face and neck, then slapped Hook on the shoulder; "This was the best fucking patrol I've ever been on!" Hook could only chuckle and grip his flaccid cock. "We best get going." Was all he replied, and the two men gathered their discarded clothes and made off into the jungle. Donald wondered about Jackie; he already wanted her again and sighed to himself; was he now a fucking queer boy? He shook his head and decided that Jackie was a special case and was a woman, a real woman. Well, apart from her big cock of course. He chuckled to himself, and they made their way through the jungle.

Alex and Jackie lay hidden behind the big tree in a strong embrace. They were whispering and kissing each other. Alex lay back and sighed; "let's get back before we're missed." Owen nodded and the pair dressed, and both walked – a little awkwardly – back to the camp. They joined a very unhappy

Jericho, but a smiling Wilson. "The angel's accepted that human freewill has caused the changes, so that's that." He said quietly.

The team would stay with the party until they could find a suitable time and place to operate their mirrors. All Jericho said about the surprise changes was "Bloody human freewill." That made everyone else chuckle.

8. DEATH VALLEY.

The captain was annoyed about the change of plan. He admitted that he really wanted to see Hook 'swing' for killing his friend. But the pair had already disappeared into the jungle with the damn Lewis gun. He sighed; "Well, the sergeant got his wish; he always said that if he was in a jungle scrap, he wanted bloody Hook with him."

The party moved out and Alex noticed with some surprise that Retu and Sans had been joined by another two native men. One looked old enough to be Retu's damn grandfather. But the other was a strapping fellow with a shaved head and was wearing boots. He had a rifle slung over his shoulder; but still carried his bow and arrows. She sighed and hoped they would jump soon. She really didn't fancy being fucked by a man old enough to be someone's grandfather!

The little group moved with some speed through the jungle and soon they could hear gun fire coming from behind them. They stopped to listen, and young Chester said quietly; "That's the Lewis gun. I know what it sounds like." He stared at the ground and wiped his face. Big Alec grunted; "Hooky was always good with that bloody thing." They moved on as darkness started to fall. They could still hear the gunfire and now, small explosions; "Bloody grenades. Jap grenades, our boys didn't have any." Alec muttered. They watched the columns of smoke floating above the canopy of trees.

They made the beach about an hour later. Everyone was delighted to see the sea. They laughed and grabbed each other. The captain was setting up the radio. That's when everyone stopped and stood silent. There was no more shooting. Big Alec, bowed his head and crossed himself, saying softly; "The bastards got them." A sad ripple of agreement swept the little group and the young nurses wiped tears away.

Captain Ames told everyone to ditch everything; they may have to swim for it. He had made contact with the submarine and would be here in about an hour. Everyone turned back to the jungle and 'Diamond Valley'. Young Ruth, gripping Chester's hand whispered; "Thank you Hooky and sarge." She brushed tears away and joined the other nurses sitting amongst trees. Jericho brushed Alex's hand and nodded; "Time to go I think." He nodded towards the jungle. They would slip away, one at a time and meet up by two huge trees' that dominated the jungle near the beach. Alex nodded and then groaned a little; there were now nine native men, in a jungle clearing, some way off. They were all waving enthusiastically.

"They must have a plague of bloody insect bites in that village." Owen whispered into her ear and grinned. Alex just folded her arms and said nothing; she was thinking about John Hook. In a way, he had redeemed himself of the officer's murder. That's when Owen shouted, gesturing widely to the sky; "Jap planes! Take cover!" The two 'Zero's' dropped from the sky at speed. The bullets kicked up the sand and ripped pieces from trees. Young Andy Kent ran for the jungle and didn't make it. The big rounds - designed to bring down an enemy plane - tore through him, ripping off an arm and slicing a leg in two. The back of his skull shattered, and he was flung several feet across the sand, almost rolling into a grotesque ball.

Wilson grabbed the shocked Alex by the arm, and they jumped into a huge bush and Wilson pressed her down into the dirt. His body across her, she tried to look up, but he pushed her head down; "Keep down you daft cow!" He shouted above the gunfire and screaming planes, which turned and came back for a second run. Corporal Jack Haines staggered and fell in front of the bush; his hands desperately trying to push his exposed intestines back in. He seemed to stare at Wilson and the light disappeared from his eyes. The body kicked a few times and was still. The planes roared over the scattered little group and disappeared into the bright blue morning sky.

Wilson slowly rose and pulled Alex up; she embraced the big man tightly and stared at the body of Haines. All around was chaos; but one voice could be heard above the noise; Captain Ames. He told everyone to make for the two big trees [that the Temporal Detectives hoped to use for their disappearing act]. Panting, he ran past Wilson and Alex shouting; "Thank fuck the submarine wasn't fucking on the surface!" She with a great deal of relief, saw a sand covered Owen walking up to her. He brushed sand from his face and hair. "Jericho's already at the bloody trees. Bit useless now, everyone is heading there." He muttered.

Alex released Wilson and grabbed Owen and held him like a distraught mum. He chuckled; "Maybe I should get shot at more often." They all looked at the body of young Haines. Big Swen, the Collector was back; Kent and Haines nodded at them and walked to the light with him.

"I best see to my girls." Alex said and shouted for her nurses; all thankfully, uninjured, but in a real state of shock. Everyone gathered by the two big trees and Captain Ames told them that the submarine couldn't get close; it had to stay in deep water, especially with the nips flying around. They would ditch everything and swim for it - as soon as it surfaced - it would remain only for a few minutes on the surface.

When asked about the two dead men, the captain just shook his head; "No time to bury the poor bastards. The Japs will do that." He told everyone to strip down and asked with real urgency about non-swimmers. There were two, Private Parker and Nurse Ruth. But there were two very strong swimmers in the group, young Chester and Big Alec. They volunteered to help Parker and Ruth. Chester would - not surprisingly - take care of Ruth.

Amongst the confusion of shouting and stripping, Jericho nodded to his group, and they crept away into the jungle. No one apparently noticed. The girls tied their blouses up and pulled off their skirts; that really caught the notice of the men, who were only wearing their underpants and dog tags. Everyone wadded into the warm water and started to swim.

Owen whispered to Alex with a big grin; "Those three young ladies and us could have had quite an interesting time." Alex nodded with a smile; "Yes, but we may have needed some big toys to help out." Owen chuckled at that; the sight of the nurse's dirty panties had made his cock twitch.

As Alex disappeared into the trees, she could hear Ruth shouting her name. From the forest edge they watched the grey submarine rise slowly, sailors rushing to throw down ropes. They saw, with some smiles of relief, that little bedraggled and wet party, were all finally pulled aboard, and the submarine sank quickly below the surface. That's when Owen gestured to the jungle edge opposite; there were at least twenty Japanese soldiers and an officer. Jericho grunted and the team disappeared.

Watching from the clearing, Retu and Sans stared at each other; Retu said softly; "The generous lady is more than we know." Sans nodded and the little group of warriors faded into the trees before the Japanese spotted them.

9. DISCOVERIES.

They walked back to the lighthouse and all Alex could think of was a hot bath. Her crotch and panties were still sodden with sweat and some cum. She smiled, thinking about Retu and Sans; at least they bowed to her when they finished, most men don't even say 'goodbye'.

She then wondered about the sergeant and his sudden passion for Jackie; she had watched the pair and it definitely wasn't just sex. "Must have been quite a sexual wake-up call for the sergeant, but then Jackie is definitely a special lady!" she muttered under her breath and that made Alex chuckle. She gave Owen's hand a little squeeze and the pair smiled at each other, quickly releasing their grip when Wilson turned around.

"Well at least they made the damn submarine." Wilson said, still brushing sand from his clothes. Jericho was already making out his report to Angel James on his mirror. [Angel James was currently the Duty Death Angel, standing in for Margret, who was doing something for Archangel Michael] He grunted; "He can't moan too much; bloody human freewill and all that." He grinned.

Owen chuckled and whispered to Alex; "The mission was bit of a failure, wasn't it? We didn't restore the current Human Timeline and there are going to be changes. But what the hell, that happens. The bloody Angel can't blame us for that." Alex nodded and pushed her arm through his. "I hope Ruth and Chester make a real go of their marriage." Owen chuckled and gave her a little kiss on the forehead. "Well, with your marriage advice they should at least enjoy the honeymoon." The pair laughed together and said a big 'hello' to Mr. Harris standing in the doorway.

Alex sat in the study and flicked through her mirror, reading about the Christmas war in Singapore. She read about the atrocities committed by the invading Japanese forces; the killings and rapes, the torture, savage beheadings and beating of Allied POW's. She grimaced and then a little article caught her eye. She read it with some interest. A small story about the dramatic rescue of some British troops and three Army nurses from the beach at Kanyo point. She chuckled at that and tapped on related articles.

There was no mention of the mysterious three Australians and the South African soldier that were not rescued. History appears to be silent on their fate and that pleased Alex. But she read with some real shock that a Private John Hook had his death sentence commuted in 1946. He served nineteen years in prison and was released - on parole - in 1965. It stated that he worked in a Ford Car plant until his retirement and died at the age of 72.

She lowered the mirror in shock and amazement; how the hell did he survive? She was interrupted by Owen, who sprawled across his favourite sofa and smiled. "I bet I know who you're reading about?" She tapped her mirror; "How the hell did he get away and what happened to the sergeant?" Owen chuckled; "Young Chester said that Hook really knew about Lewis guns, as did the sarge. They set the bloody thing up to fire automatically and then set fire to the bleeding jungle with the petrol from that wrecked truck we came across. Do you remember that?"

Alex nodded and Owen continued; "They were later captured and sent to a Japanese POW camp. Unfortunately, the sergeant never survived the internment; he died of dysentery. But Hook survived to be liberated by Allied forces. Soon as they found out who he was; they slung him in prison, but he had a good lawyer, and the death sentence was set aside. Nineteen years later he walked free." Alex chuckled at that; one thing about John Hook; was he knew how to survive on his own.

"He did - almost - redeem himself for the murder of the cowardly Lieutenant." She said quietly to herself and raised her brandy glass in salute, then took a small sip. Owen jumped up and leaned over her, giving her forehead a little kiss; "Jacqueline really misses her girlfriend." He grinned and wandered off, but not before he stopped in the doorway and smiled; "Her friend is a most generous woman." Then was gone; Alex laughed out loud and slumped back in her chair. "Well, we can do something about that." There wasn't much that the sharp eyed Owen/Jackie missed; especially when it came to her!

BOOKS AVAILABLE IN THE "ADVENTURES OF ALEXANDRA" SERIES.

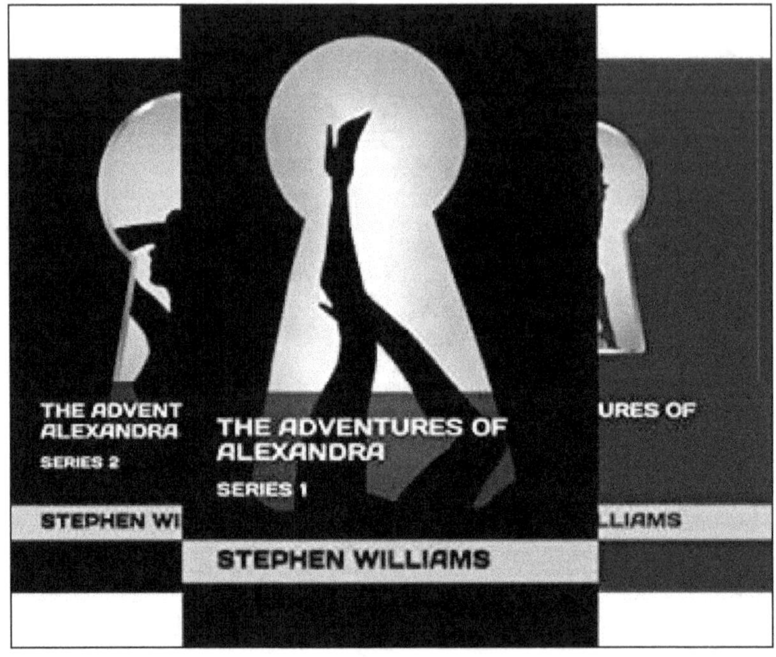

"The naughty adventures of **ALEXANDRA** - A character from The Temporal Detective series of books - follow Alexandra and her sexy & naughty adventures through time!

Warning: Contains content suitable for **ADULTS ONLY** with open and mature minds! These stories contain erotic scenes and graphic sexual descriptions, mixed with adventure, action, supernatural & paranormal activities: Not to mention time-travel!

These are the **ALTERNATIVE ADULT VERSIONS** of stores appearing in the series: **'THE TEMPORAL DETECTIVES'** by the same author. This series is also available on AMAZON and good bookshops everywhere."

REMEMEBR: 18+

EPISODE 9. "ALEXANDRA INVESTIGATES CORDLESS, CORDLESS & FRASER (SOLICITORS)."

EPISODE PROLOGUE: "The established family solicitors of Cordless, Cordless & Fraser have existed in the heart of Edinburgh's old city for over 200 years. In the summer of 1980, the young Clerk who looks after the basement archives of the firm, informs the Senior partner; Sir David Fraser, that it's time to deliver the old document pouch to the address marked upon it - except the pouch was lodged with the Solicitors way back in 1780, to be delivered on its Bicentennial year! - Mr. Tibbs is now on the case. But Alex discovers there are a lot of horny Scots there and back in the 1780's. Alex discovers that some men will simply not take no for an answer!"

75 Minutes approx. **Episode Warnings:** Smoking – Alcohol – Strong language – Violence [including sexual violence and references to combat deaths] – Strong graphic sexual references – Mild horror and Demonic references.

NOTES: The original version of this story is published and appears in the **TEMPORAL DETECTIVES:** Book Series 1 – Episode 8 entitled: **"CORDLESS, CORDLESS & FRASER (SOLICITORS)."** This is a special EXTENDED episode of the original story.

CAUTION: Recommended for 18+ only.

1. EDINBURGH CITY (LATE SEPTEMBER 1780)

The two horsemen entered through the old North gate amid little flurries of early winter snow. Several English soldiers manning the gate made no effort to stop or search the two old men; they could see no weapons, and both were wearing dirty breeches - weapons and kilts had been banned after the battle of Culloden in 1746 - there was talk that the ban would soon be lifted; but for now it was still in force.

The pair threaded through the busy traffic of people, horses and carriages looking for a specific street and set of offices. The taller one pointed down an alley and nodded. 'Cable Street' was their destination and they slowly passed down the narrow cobbled thoroughfare until stopping before a little wooden sign, hanging above a dark entrance, which declared in big letters: 'John Cordless - Solicitor'.

They exchanged smiles and dismounted, shaking snow from their long coats and the taller of the two old men, pulled a canvas sack from his saddle bag and patted it like a puppy dog. "John Cordless is young, hungry for business and won't ask too many questions." He grinned broadly, showing only a couple of remaining yellow teeth - most had been knocked out by an English musket stock; smashed into his face at the battle of Falkirk Muir. But Willy McKenzie knew that the injury he received had actually saved his life; because he missed the slaughter at Culloden Moor.

Whereas, old Danny Brown had fought on that dreadful Moor and lost an eye in the process - he escaped being shot by English soldiers, as he lay upon the battlefield, with nearly two thousand other dead and wounded Highlanders.

A woman camp follower called Edith Ross braved the bullets and bayonets of the English to drag him and her younger brother from that bloody field. Later that year he married the woman and had seven children by her - her young brother sadly died of his wounds, just days after the battle - he was sixteen.

The two battered old warriors stared at the sign hanging above their heads and nodded in agreement - they headed up the stairs to the office of young John Cordless, who greeted them with some enthusiasm, especially after they slapped the bag of

Spanish Doubloon coins upon his desk - they would be worth thousands upon thousands of pounds today. So impressed with his 'clients' was John Cordless, that he actually produced a bottle of whisky to seal the deal! With his eyes hardly leaving the sack of gold coins, they discussed what was required: Now that did make John sit up and take notice.

John Cordless sat sipping his whisky; watching the two old men throwing glass after glass of his precious whisky down their throats. Willy McKenzie leaned across John's polished [and quite empty] desk and pulled a large, leather document pouch from the canvas bag slung about his shoulders.

"You understand that no-one must open the pouch whilst it's in your care. That you'll care for it until it's delivered by hand to the addressee, who has been sewn onto the bag and it must be delivered on or after the day shown. This transaction between us and your company must remain totally confidential - we are paying you a good deal of money to EXACTLY carry out our instructions. Do you understand lad?"

John Cordless quietly accepted the bag which had little weight and nodded his agreement; he would draw up a contract, so that all the pair stipulated would be done under law. He stared at the address and coughed a little; "Wasn't Lord …."

Willy McKenzie stopped him in mid sentence and smiled; "Aye, we know the good Laird [Lord] was hung by the English at Fort William, but this fellow will..." Willy corrected himself and continued; "is a relative who will inherit his title."

John finished his whisky and scribbled more into his note book and looked up to see Danny Brown refilling the glasses. "Well, I have everything I need except the date you wish the commission enacted." He lifted his glass in salute and again watched the two men empty the glasses in one swallow.

Willy grinned; "By enacted, you mean delivered?" Both old men exchanged a glance and John nodded. He picked up his quill and waited to write in his notebook.

Danny wiped his mouth and nodded to the document pouch; "Your firm will deliver the pouch on 30th September nineteen hundred and eighty."

John started to write, but stopped suddenly; "Sorry Mr. Brown, but just for a second there, I thought you said nineteen hundred and eighty?" He chuckled: "That's my crazy hearing, you said...." Both men grinned and Willy McKenzie spoke softly; "Aye, you heard right lad, that's why your company has been given a big bag of Spanish gold; to pay for its rest in your hands until the year of our Lord nineteen hundred and eighty."

Everyone sat in silence for some seconds until John Cordless, staring at the bag of gold coins [yet again!] spoke; "All what you wish will be done as you specify gentlemen." The three men shook hands upon the deal and John told them to return in three days and sign the contract, which he would draw up himself. [He didn't have any assistants – he couldn't afford them – but he thought it sounded good to tell clients that he would perform the task himself.]

John stood at his small window and in the gathering gloom of snow and nightfall, watched the strange pair depart upon their plodding horses. They would stay at the 'Crown Hotel' until the contract was ready to be signed.

John Cordless poured himself another - large - whisky and started to laugh. With such an amount of money, he could now marry young Mary and set up a fine and proper household for her. He would also spend some on the offices and employ more clerks; John Cordless Solicitors would be a law firm of note in Edinburgh, in Scotland and quite possibly, the British Empire. All because two crazy old men wanted a pouch delivered in the hereafter!

He walked back to his desk and picked up the pouch; "Well gentlemen, thank you for your trust and whilst a Cordless runs this company, your wishes will be adhered too." He chuckled to himself and placed the pouch into the small safe, which was hidden inside a large and imposing set of drawers.

Sipping his whisky, John picked up his notebook and read again, the date specified by the pair; Nineteen hundred and eighty. That was exactly two hundred years hence - two hundred years!
He sat thinking about the bags contents; how relevant could anything written [he assumed it contains papers because of the weight - or rather lack of it] in the year seventeen hundred and eighty would be two hundred years later?

Still, he pushed the little mound of gold coins about his desk, feeling each in his hands and fingers, grinning broadly. He lifted his glass and said quietly; "Well Mister Brown and McKenzie, none of us will surely be around when the bloody thing is delivered!" Laughing, he gathered up the coins and secured them in a leather bag, which he placed in his frock coat. Jauntily, he slapped his hat on and wound a scarf around his neck against the chill of the night.

John Cordless walked home a happy man that night and now a rich one!

2. EDINBURGH CITY (LATE SEPTEMBER 1980)

Young Peter Davidson pushed his bike against the black iron railings and secured it with a large padlock and chain. He pulled his trousers from his bright red socks and clutching his holdall, headed for the offices of Cordless, Cordless & Fraser where he held the grand title of 'Archives Manager' - or filing clerk in the real world!

But today he had a task to fulfil that would take him to the very high offices of the Senior Partner of the firm; Sir David Fraser. Today he would inform Mr. Fraser that the old document pouch, held under lock and key, for two hundred years should now be delivered. It had actually put a spring in his step and with a cheery 'God Morning!' to the Security Guard sitting with Liz, the receptionist [who he really fancied] made for his basement office.

Peter sat at his desk, eating a strawberry yogurt with a small plastic spoon, reading a photocopy of the original agreement - he wondered who Daniel Brown and William McKenzie really were. They gave their joint address [at the time] as "Prospect House, Inverness." He had actually looked it up with no success, going right back to the 1690's. But the address sewn onto the old document pouch, well, that was a different matter!

The phone ringing made him jump and spill yogurt on his trousers, he lifted the receiver carefully, wiping strawberry yogurt from his knees. It was Sir David's Secretary; Margret, informing him that he was required in Sir David's office - with the pouch - at exactly midday. He mumbled his agreement and slowly replaced the phone.

Peter's assistant had arrived and slumped into his chair, blowing his nose and coughing; "I'm sure that bitch I snogged last night has given me the chill's." Carl wiped his face and grinned; "Today's the day my friend. After two hundred years of low paid, abused and bored filing clerks, you have been chosen, only you have the honour of delivering 'old crinkly' and getting your picture in the papers." He grinned broadly; "All the girls will think you're famous, you're bound to get laid once or twice!"

Peter just grunted; "Some fucking luck I don't think. SIR David will probably do the honour himself. I've already been summoned to his office at midday."

Carl shrugged his shoulders; "They probably know what's inside despite it remaining unsealed for all those bloody years, you've heard the legend about Sir David's Grandfather and Edinburgh Infirmary."

Peter nodded; he knew that story all too well. Sir David's grandfather: Sir Alistair Cordless, it was rumoured, had taken the pouch one night (in great secrecy) to an old friend at Edinburgh Infirmary and had it X-rayed. The legend tells that, all they could discover was the pouch contained several sheets of paper and what appeared to be a small ring. But it was just a story.

Peter sighed; "Pieces of paper are worth shit - unless they point to hidden treasure." He had also heard the legend of their founder's acquisition of old Spanish Gold - lots of it - apparently, because of the pouch.

"I dunno about that, look at the American Declaration of Independence; that little piece of paper changed the world." Carl pulled several files from his desk drawer and shuffled the contents about his desk.

"After that fixed referendum that's what we fucking need. A Scottish Declaration of Independence." Peter muttered and imagined himself dressed in a kilt, waving a broadsword at Mrs. bloody Thatcher! Peter could hear Carl laughing; "What the fuck are you doing mate?" Peter eased back into his chair after standing and waving his imaginary sword about; bloody Thatcher he repeated to himself and smiled.

"You taking that bird to 'Buster Browns' Saturday night?" Carl asked and threw a ball of screwed up paper at Peter, who grunted. The 'bird' Carl had mentioned was Liz the Receptionist and Peter still hadn't worked up the nerve to ask her out on Saturday night. "Maybe, maybe; I'll have to see." He said softly and the thought of Liz sitting naked behind her desk made the young man grin broadly.

Hamish, a young Junior Clerk from the third floor appeared in the doorway and jerked a thumb towards the ceiling; "The fucking press have turned up, there's a totally gorgeous tart reporter heading for Sir David's office with a cameraman. Jesus, she's all tits and long legs; fucking stunning." Peter and Carl exchanged looks; "Must be about 'old crinkly' - Sir David loves getting his name in the papers - he's a real tosser about publicity." Carl explained, looking over his shoulder and past Hamish in the doorway, who scratched his arse and added; "You on for 'Buster Browns' Saturday night?"

Both Carl and Peter nodded; "Fuck, I'll have to ask her now or be a fucking real lemon in front of these twats." Peter whispered, then sighed and chewed his pencil; then a wonderful idea came to him, and he shouted; "Yes!" punching a fist into the air. Carl and Hamish just chuckled; "What a knob." Hamish muttered and headed back upstairs, hoping to get another look at the reporter from the 'Scottish Record'.

Peter constantly looked at the office clock until it read eleven-thirty, then unlocked the wall key box and removed the old key for the basement safe. "Do you want me to make trumpet noses?" Carl giggled and stood; saluting.

Peter stuck up two fingers and headed for the safe.

With 'old crinkly' tucked safely under his arm, Peter slipped quietly into Reception and waved Liz over to him. His 'brilliant' idea actually worked, he showed Liz the package and managed to turn the conversation around to Saturday night. A very happy filing clerk headed for Sir David's office; Liz had said: yes.

Peter was shown into the outer office of Sir David's by Margret and stood waiting. He stared through the clear glass partition and grinned broadly; 'What a fucking piece of skirt!' he said to himself. Peter simply couldn't take his eyes of the female reporter who sat upright in a small office chair, with Sir David standing over her. The reporter had a short skirt, well above her knee and a matching blue jacket. Her white blouse simply couldn't hide her magnificent breasts. She was scribing notes and smiling at Sir David. She was simply stunning - in all respects.

Peter actually groaned a little, when she crossed her legs which seemed to go on forever. "Best put your tongue back in your mouth and do try to stop dribbling." Margret smiled at Peter and carried a tray with coffee into the main office. That's when he bothered to look at the cameraman and was well surprised, a big black man in a smart suit with a couple of expensive looking camera's hanging around his neck. "Jesus, that's a big man. You don't get many of him around here." He spoke softly and straightened his tie, as Margret indicated to join them.

He gripped the old document pouch with both hands and glanced down at the address, which had been hand sewn onto one side. "How the fuck did those two know, that there would still be a Lord Falkirk two hundred years later and still living in Falkirk Palace?" He whispered and smiling, walked with pretend purpose into the presence of Sir David and his gorgeous guest.

3. SIR DAVID FRASER.

Alex stood on the pavement outside the offices and pulled her short jacket about herself. She smiled as the sleek black BMW car rolled up to the kerbside and Sir David leaned across and pushed open the door. She gracefully slid into the front passenger seat and smiled.

Sir David was a very handsome man for his age. He had wisps of grey hair and some age lines about his face, but most women would still regard him as 'handsome'. Regular use of the company gym kept him in shape. Alex hadn't actually asked Sir David his age but guessed he was just short of fifty perhaps.

"Where we are going serves the most incredible Teriyaki Chicken; you'll love it." Alex slowly fixed her seat belt and said nothing about Sir David having a good long look at her legs. She made no effort to pull down her short skirt.

"Expensive restaurant, is it?" She asked and Sir David nodded; "But a lady of your quality should be dined properly. You wouldn't hang the Mona Lisa in a Miners Club Men's Room; would you?"

That made Alex chuckle: yes, Sir David was a witty and charming man, and his age really didn't matter to Alex; he treated her like a real lady [which in fact; she was!] and he certainly wasn't bloody decrepit.

They had a fabulous lunch at a very expensive city restaurant; the starter [soup] was fifteen quid a plate! They returned to the offices and the happy pair made for his personal suite. Only the security officers manning Reception were on site. Sir David unlocked his plush office and asked Alex if she wanted to freshen up, while he fixed brandies for the pair.

Alex nodded and to her surprise, Sir David pulled a small remote from his jacket pocket and pointed it to the ornate Bookcase against the opposite wall. She was utterly stunned to watch the bookcase slid open, revealing an entrance. She could see the lights come on automatically behind the moving bookcase. "Go on, it's my secret little place. The bathroom is first on the right." He said, pulling open the glass doors of the ornate drinks cabinet.

Alex walked through and stood smiling; it was superbly furnished with a four-poster bed, sofas, fireplace, large screen TV and mirrors on the ceiling. She pushed open the bathroom door and found a bathtub that could fit a football team in. She touched up her makeup and cleaned her teeth. She always carried a toothbrush and toothpaste in her handbag. That's when she heard Sir David call her. The drinks were ready.

She stepped out the bathroom and noticed the door had slid shut and Sir David was sprawled on the sofa; jacket and shoes thrown off. He handed her a large glass of brandy and she sat next to him, kicking off her heels.

"What do we drink to?" She asked him quietly and he sipped his brandy and ran a gentle hand down her face. "Just us meeting. Simple as that." He raised his glass, and they touched glasses, and he leaned forward and sipped Alex's brandy as she did his. They both placed the glasses down and he slowly pulled her to him, and they kissed with some real passion for a few minutes.

He whispered to Alex; asking if it was fine to touch her intimately. Now that did impress her, and she quietly said 'Yes'. He ran a hand up her short skirt and pushed it gently between her legs, which she opened a little. He smiled; she was wet already and clearly in the mood for love making. Alex ran a hand down to his crotch and was pleasantly surprised. His penis moved under her touch and was quite large. She pulled the zipper down and reached inside. She eased it out and slowly lowered her head.

Sir David groaned softly as Alex worked the top of his erection with her mouth and tongue whilst he quickly unbuttoned her blouse and had it off in seconds. Her bra was removed with one hand, and he took possession of her big breasts. She helped pull off his shirt and trousers. He reciprocated by pulling down her short skirt and Alex knelt on the floor and sucked his swollen cock with some determination. He stroked her hair and then slowly pulled her back onto the couch and gently tugged down her damp panties. He knew his way around a vagina and worked Alex's clitoris until she started to wiggle and gasp with pleasure.

He fingered her real hard and Alex [to her surprise] actually had a couple of small organisms. He mounted her gently and began to thrust as she pulled her legs up and her feet touched his shoulders. He fucked her hard and deep. She came several times; actually, screaming at one point from the really hard fucking she was getting.

They changed position a couple of times; he rammed her doggy style for several minutes, both hands gripping a swinging breast. He squeezed and pulled at her tits with real passion. Alex was to have small bruises and finger-marks on them for a few days after their love making sessions. Now on the carpeted floor, he fucked her hard in the 'Missionary Position' and they searched each other's mouths with eager tongues. Finally, he groaned and whispered to Alex where she wanted him to cum.

She gripped his arse and told him to unload into her. He did almost instantly. They lay on the floor gasping, panting and kissing. He stayed in her; pulling himself up on his elbows and gently kissed her face. They whispered together for some minutes. Alex had to sigh a little; he was a typical man. He had asked for a 'little treat'.

Sir David really wanted to fuck her in the arse. She kissed him and slowly nodded. He gently pulled from her and scooped her up in his arms and carried her to the expansive four poster bed. Alex knelt on the bed and pulled open her bum cheeks. She was amazed to see that he was already erect again. He pulled some lubricant from the bedside cabinet and applied it gently to her anus. He smeared some on his cock and very gently mounted her.

She actually gasped and cursed a little as he began to thrust, He was gentle and slow at first, but quickly began to thrust quite firmly and occasionally slapped her arse cheeks. He was spanking her with some force and Alex placed h a hand over her own mouth to stop screams from escaping. He rolled her onto her side and placed her arm around his neck. He could now suck a nipple and the pair could kiss as he arse fucked her quite hard. She would also have his handprints on her bum for some days.

The old-fashioned phone on the bedside cabinet suddenly buzzed and Sir David reached across and lifted the receiver. He didn't stop fucking her as he spoke on the phone. Alex simply couldn't believe what she was hearing; he was talking to his bloody wife whilst buried deep in her back passage!

He replaced the receiver and smiled; "Sorry about that darling. She can't make a bloody decision without me. You heard me tell her just to buy the damn three-piece suite. I didn't need to see it." He saw the expression on Alex's face and kissed her, adding; "I'll make it up to you darling." And held her quite tight and started to thrust again; like nothing had happened. Alex just lay there, bitterly disappointed in him; he should have let the damn phone just ring.

He came in her arse without even asking and then gave her a nasty little 'love bite' on the back of her neck. They lay together for few minutes; in silence this time and finally he pulled his cock from her arse and jumped from the bed and walked to the bathroom. Alex lay breathing hard and wiped some tears from her face. She could hear the shower turn on and he stuck his head through the door; "Come and join me darling. Don't worry about that damn phone call. Like I said, I'll make it up to you. I'll buy you a nice gold necklace or something. Whatever you want sweetheart. Your fucking arse alone is worth that." He grinned and went back inside.

Alex rose from the bed and awkwardly walked to her little pile of clothes and hurriedly dressed. She pulled her mirror from her handbag and operated the travel App.

She disappeared, leaving a very surprised and a little shocked, Sir David standing naked, wet and alone in his hidden rooms; mostly because the only exit [the door behind the bookcase] was locked and only he had the combination to open it from the inside.

Alex walked back to the lighthouse. She urgently needed the toilet and a hot bath. If she was really honest with herself; she felt a little disgusted at what had happened. She actually felt like a high-class call girl after his offer to buy her a 'necklace' for the anal sex. She wiped her face and took several deep breaths before entering the lighthouse and running up the stairs to her suite of room. She really couldn't face any of her colleagues or house staff at the moment.

4. WAR OF THE WHITE ROSE (FEBRUARY 1985)

Jericho wrapped his coat around and pointed down the quiet street towards the well-built barricade; "There are several rebels manning it, they're armed and clever, so be really careful in how you act and speak." He cautioned his team, who stood amid the snow flurries and shared a hipflask of brandy amongst themselves.

Alex adjusted her little woollen bonnet and allowed her long dark hair to fall about her shoulders. She pulled down her short skirt - again and straightened her coat. "They do know we're reporters and won't be trigger happy - will they?" Alex asked Jericho, who nodded and pushed his mirror back into the folds of his long coat.

"Baby sister, no man in his right mind would shoot a piece of cake like you - keep your coat open and show them legs; you'll be safe as houses." Wilson chuckled and then added, as an afterthought; "And they may not shoot at us either; just in case they hit you!"

Jericho raised his hand; "Best American accents now people." He said and the little party, very slowly, started to head towards the wall of overturned vehicles, paving stones and shop doors.

They were challenged by two large, red-faced men with rifles and kilts. They were wearing old army uniforms, covered with thick dark trench coats and black berets - each with a little white rose attached. Jericho pointed to a large plastic card around his neck, hanging from a red tape; "Hello boys, we're the press team from CNN as arranged by your Captain Davidson." Even Wilson was impressed with his 'New York' accent and muttered; "You really do sound like a damn Yankee." Owen chuckled at that and whispered to Alex; "And he should know!" They all showed their Press cards and smiled - broadly.

The two men lowered their rifles and one called over his shoulder for Captain Davidson. A small gap was made, and the little group squeezed through, bending low, and found themselves in a busy street. Several old army vehicles were parked down one side, including a Red Cross ambulance and two jeeps - both flying the Scottish flag. There must have been thirty soldiers milling around - including several women, a couple were wearing Red Cross arm bands - everyone seemed to stop and watch the reporters approach.

Alex received a couple of 'wolf-whistles' from two young soldiers sitting on the tailgate of a lorry. She smiled and pulled her coat around, as the snow seemed to be falling more quickly and increasing in density. That's when she saw the tired looking young Captain, emerge from a shattered shop doorway. She gripped Jericho by the arm; "Shit! That young man knows me and Wilson - he handed the pouch to his old boss back in 1980. Change of role I think." She nodded to Wilson, who had also recognised the former filing clerk.

"Hi, good to meet you! Jerry Tibbs from CNN." Jericho held out his hand, pulling the glove off. The captain gripped his hand firmly and smiled. Alex could see that the young man had changed some over the last five years; he seemed much older than his true age; but his eyes were still bright.

Jericho introduced his team in a wonderful 'New York' accent; Wilson his cameraman, Owen the production assistant and local liaison was Alexandra, a reporter from a national paper, who was assisting and guiding the team from New York.

Captain Peter Davidson of the SDF [Scottish Defence Force] smiled; "Hello Miss, I do remember you and your cameraman from the day the pouch was opened. I don't think any man could forget meeting you - or the big man." He indicated towards the shop doorway and added; "Follow me. Colonel McIves has his HQ in the basement of that shoe-shop; he's the one who authorised your Press visit. Like you Alex, I'm local liaison."

The little group exchanged glances at the mention of 'McIves'. "Is that Alexander McIves - from the Highlands?" Alex asked quietly and saw the look upon Jericho's face when the captain replied yes, and did she know the Colonel?

"By reputation only." She muttered and glanced at Jericho who had always described the persistent time traveller as an 'enigma'. Alexander McIves was well known to temporal detectives and was a thorn in their sides. He and team 74 had met previously and 'enigma' didn't quite do the strange man justice!

The group followed the captain into the shop doorway and descended some wooden stairs into the basement which was lit by candles. Colonel McIves was sitting at metal folding table, smoking a pipe and reading various pieces of paper. The big man was in army uniform and gripped a glass of whisky in one hand. The captain saluted and introduced the group. The Colonel looked up and smiled broadly; "Jerry Tibbs?" He said and stood, holding out his hand, telling the captain to check the radio room for messages.

Nothing was said between them until the captain left, then McIves indicated for them to seat. Several fold-up chairs, stacked in a dirty corner, were pulled out and everyone was seated. The Colonel passed several plastic cups around and produced a bottle of whisky from the canvas bag at his feet. "Jerry Tibbs." He repeated softly and chuckled. Then passed the bottle around.

There was a little silence as everyone filled their cups, then the Colonel scratched at his pipe with a small pen knife and refilled the bowl from a fat drawstring bag. He re-lit it slowly, peering over the top at Jericho. "I'm amazed that you let this slip by you Jericho, I'm sure Alex and Wilson reported back the contents of that pouch and what it could mean to the Scottish people - especially after that bent referendum that Thatcher concocted." He leaned back in his chair and puffed his pipe, smiling.

Jericho raised the plastic cup and shrugged; "Not my call McIves, I was running an errand for Angel Margret and the team were temporarily managed by Inspector Patrick O'Brien; who made the call; despite what Alexandra and Wilson reported. His decision has been called into question; that's why we're here."

"Ah, now I see. My faith in your abilities have been restored Jericho. But is your Mission to restore or damage limitation?" The Colonel sipped his whisky and placed his pipe down and shuffled some papers on his desk. Jericho sighed; "Neither really, our brief is to report the changes, so that Time-Control can run a few scenarios and see where it all ends up. Then the Boss will, apparently make the call himself."

"I think, we would all love to know how you did it McIves." Alex spoke softly and tapped her plastic cup with a finger; "We really would." The Colonel grinned and waved a hand into the air; "Jesus, I do love it when you use that Scottish accent Alex; makes the hairs rise on the back of my neck." He offered the bottle around for refills and slumped back in his chair. "I can't take all the credit for it. The real brain behind it was a certain French ship's captain; a Monsignor Francis de Ville - late of his French's Majesty's navy - a fellow who hailed from 1766, I believe."

Owen coughed; "He's a missing soul Jericho; his departure date is logged at 1787. He never appeared and is believed to have gained the ability to time travel." Owen replaced his mirror in a coat pocket and refilled his cup, adding; "The only Scottish connection shown, is that his mother; a certain Lady Alice MacKinnon was from Ayr. His father was a French merchant who traded with Scotland in the 1740's."

"That's not quite accurate Owen; his father was no French merchant, but the true King of Scotland." The Colonel smiled broadly; "All the proof needed was contained in that pouch; along with an incredible and iconic relic that tied everything up in nice fat ribbons." Jericho scratched his chin; "I don't understand that, the current Pretender [1985] to the Scottish Throne is some German Duke I believe - a direct descent of the Stuart's."

"Had it not been for the pouch and its incredible contents, you would be right." The Colonel re-lit his pipe and tapped the desk gently, adding; "The pouch had evidence, that the original line of Scottish Kings from Robert the Bruce were still in existence and that dear Francis de Ville, had a better and totally legitimate claim to the old Scottish Throne. He was a direct and legitimate male descendant of King Robert. That sole fact changed everything - Scotland had a real Scottish King in the form of the Earl of Falkirk - Francis direct descendant and heir."

"What was the relic that proved everything?" Wilson asked, quite intrigued and sipped his whisky. McIves chuckled; "Something that has been missing since 1329." He shifted on his chair and passed the whisky bottle around. "The pouch contained a simple gold ring inscribed with the word 'Fuimus', which was the Bruce clan motto. It was Robert the Bruce's coronation ring and had been missing for centuries. Experts examined the ring and declared it genuine. Then of course, there was the marriage contract between King David II [Robert the Bruce's son] and a certain Lady Mary Stratlain in 1363 and provisions for the King's son, another David, by that Lady. The Earl of Falkirk is his direct descendant and true King of Scotland by blood and Clan."

"I know my Scottish history is a little shaky, but wasn't King David married to Margaret Drummond who gave him no children?" Owen looked quite puzzled; his research was normally top-notch in these matters. McIves nodded his agreement and smiled - again; "Yes he did marry the woman. But in 1364; he desperately needed her family's support and so he simply hid his earlier marriage for political convenience and survival. It wasn't exactly uncommon in those days. Remember, in Scottish law, the earlier marriage would remain valid."

There was loud knocking at the door and a voice shouted; "An English patrol has been spotted east of the city Sir!" The Colonel jumped up, buttoning up his tunic and fixing his beret; "The captain will look after my guests until I return." He said to the young soldier who now appeared in the doorway - rifle in hand.

He patted Jericho on the shoulder and grinned; "Stay around Jerry and make yourself at home. I'm sure the great American public will love what you produce for CNN." He also winked and buckled his pistol belt on, disappearing up the staircase; shouting orders.

The group sat in silence for about a minute, considering what had been uncovered in that dark little cellar. "Shit, if that's all true, then Inspector O'Brien has made one of the greatest cock-ups in the history of the Temporal Department." Owen stated and shook his head, downing his whisky in one.

"No shit Sherlock." Muttered Wilson and slung the video camera back over his shoulder. Alex saw the concerned look on Jericho's face and whispered; "IF it is true, then surely the Boss will allow the new Time-Line to exist?" Jericho shook his head; "I don't really know, an independent Scottish Kingdom formed in the 1980's will cause major changes down the Timeline and could alter the history of humanity. Maybe not for the best either."

Jericho finished his whisky and eased from the uncomfortable little chair; "I think we need to take a closer look at this story." Alex replaced her mirror and looked quite grim; "People, the Time-Controller is holding this existence for twenty-four human hours. So we only have one human day to discover any truth about what's been discovered."

5. THE SIEGE OF EDINBURGH CASTLE.

Captain Davidson had found the team some reasonable accommodation in a looted town house, and they settled in. Alex found an armchair with a footrest and sat back, shoes off, massaging her feet. "If this snow gets any heavier, I'm going to need my wellingtons; these little ankle boots won't cope."She noticed that Owen was staring at her feet with a little smile on his face. "I'd swear young Owen is turning into a pervert." Wilson declared and chuckled, having noticed where Owen was staring. Alex sighed; "Owen, they are just feet. I'm not rubbing my breasts or anything like that." Owen grinned; "I know, but it's the way you're doing it." She rolled her eyes and sighed; forcing the boy into the Monastic life, at a young age, had done him no favours.

Wilson wandered over to the damaged table placed by the window and poked the plate of sandwiches, which had been provided by a very pleasant young women in uniform, wearing a Red Cross armband. "There's cheese or corned beef and a big pot of tea." He picked up a cheese sandwich and took a massive bite, adding; "Hey, they're not bad." Alex stared at the plate and asked Owen why the girl had called them 'pieces'. Owen explained that was Scottish for a sandwich. She shrugged and picked up a cheese one; "Who wants tea?"

They didn't get time to finish their 'pieces' or even try some tea. Captain Davidson burst through the broken door shouting; "They have broken our lines just south of the city and we've been ordered to reinforce the castle garrison - the castle can never fall into English hands - that would be a disaster."

A little calmer, he informed them that the unit was leaving Immediately for the castle; and the reporters would be coming with them. "What castle?" Wilson asked and Owen replied simply; "Edinburgh."

As they packed up the few items they carried, Owen spoke quietly to Jericho; "The papers and ring from that pouch are stored in the castle's archives, we won't get a better chance to examine then - given the time we have left." Jericho nodded his agreement, and the group quickly descended the stairs into the street which was in chaos; "You'll go in the ambulance. There's less chance that the bastards will shoot at it." Captain Davidson told them, and they jumped in, accompanied by the young female Medic, who slammed the doors shut.

"There's serious fighting to the south of the city and casualties have to be taken to the castle infirmary now, they've over run the hospital we've been using." She didn't smile and adjusted her beret adding; "Still, the poor sods in that hospital will get much better treatment from the English surgeons than we could ever provide." Everyone gripped something as the ambulance pulled away at speed, driven by the other girl, who shouted back; "Hold on - it's gonna be a bumpy ride!"

The little convoy arrived at the castle just before midday; amid a heavy snowstorm and the sound of fighting could now, actually be heard in the distance. The young medic helped Alex down and pointed to a dark doorway; "Apparently there are a couple of small rooms put aside for us, the boy's have one to themselves, but you have to share with me and Rosie." She indicated to the ambulance driver, who Wilson made laugh when he asked her; if she drove stock cars for a living.

Jericho gathered the team in the little dark room which was lit by two weak candles, stuck in egg cups. "There can be no better time to sneak around and get a look at the pouch's contents, everything is in chaos, and they won't pay too much attention to people already inside the castle. I've pulled up a map to the archives and where the pouch is stored." He tapped his mirror and checked the doorway; "Right, there's no time like the present - let's go!"

They carefully and quietly navigated the dark corridors, to the sound of gunfire and small explosions outside. "The castle is under siege." Owen said softly, lifting up his mirror to illuminate way. They found the Lower West corridor and stairs down to the archives. The room containing the pouch was just around the next turn, but Owen stopped suddenly and snapped the light out. "A guard outside the door, sitting on a stool; he is armed." He whispered, adding; "Looks very young, probably stuck him down here because of that."

"I doubt he'll just let us wander in and read the damn thing." Wilson muttered, lowering the video camera down and wiping his face. But Jericho smiled and tapped Alex on the shoulder; "Over to you, I think." Alex didn't look impressed but tidied up her hair and straightened her short skirt, pulling the hem up a few more inches; then opened some more buttons on her blouse. "Run your mirror over each page." Owen spoke softly and grinned. "I do know that." She muttered and took a few little breaths.

Alex switched her mirror light on and said loudly; "Hello, is anyone there?" They heard the young soldier jump up, his stool falling to the floor. "Halt, who goes there?" He shouted; quite nervously. Owen glanced at Wilson and said, "Do you think he'll fall for the oldest trick in the book?" Wilson grinned; "With our girl? - Hook, line and bloody sinker." They both nodded at that and even Jericho managed a smile.

Alex stepped around the corner with a big grin on her face, and with a little wave of her free hand, introduced herself. The remaining team waited in silence, but ready to spring if Alex needed assistance.

They could hear a conversation but couldn't actually make out what was being said. But they all grinned at each other, when after a few minutes; they heard a heavy door being unlocked. They heard it close, and they edged round to find the stool on the floor and the guard and Alex were gone.

"Hook, line and bloody sinker." Wilson whispered and they stood outside the door, waiting. After a while Owen glanced down at his mirror; "It's been almost ten minutes." He sounded a little concerned. The team stood quietly, and Jericho consulted his mirror; "Any longer and we'll have to go in." He said quietly.

But the door creaked open, and Alex stepped through and smiled; "Mission almost complete. But the ring is not there, apparently, the new Scottish King; Alexander, is wearing it." She pulled down her skirt to its original length and quickly buttoned her blouse up.

"Come on, back to those dismal rooms." Jericho said and nodded to Alex; "Well done." The team passed through the empty corridors and reached their 'dismal' rooms before anyone even realised they had disappeared. "You were right about why the boy was guarding that door, Owen." Alex said, checking her mirror; "Colonel McIves told him, that it was one of the most important tasks in the castle and that, he could depend upon young Colin from Aberdeen."

Wilson shrugged his shoulders and seemed quite surprised; "So the black hearted git does have a conscious." He turned to her and smiled; "It didn't take you long to achieve what we needed." Alex waved the compliment away, saying softly; "He's not much older than Owen and I told him that I really needed to see the papers for my newspaper and that I would be grateful - very grateful indeed - and would do really anything to get my story."

Wilson gave Alex a questioning look and said; "How grateful?"

Alex chuckled; "I slowly - very slowly - lifted my skirt so that he could have a good look at what's on offer and that done the trick. He had the door unlocked without a second thought." Owen actually groaned at the thought of that scene, which made Wilson and Jericho chuckle.

"He let me 'photograph' the papers because I promised him a little fun, when he came off duty in a couple of hours. But as down payment, I had to let feel round my bum, while I took the 'pictures'. He had very cold hands." Owen shook his head in a mix of frustration and disappointment that it wasn't his hands on Alex's bum. "I take it you won't keep that appointment?" Wilson muttered and Alex whispered; "I like men - real men - not boys. Sorry Owen." The look she gave Wilson didn't go unnoticed by the big man and he smiled to himself. Dancing naked around that dam tree stump did have it perks. Young Owen shrugged his shoulders and said quite sadly; "Lucky bastard."

Wilson passed around his hipflask and everyone enjoyed the brandy, whilst they waited for Human Records to analyse the papers. But loud sobbing from the room Alex shared with the medic's drew her attention - Jericho indicated she should investigate and Alex hurried out. It was some time before she returned - she had been clearly crying but was now quite composed. Wilson gripped her arm and asked what happened.

Alex drew a very heavy breath; "Young Rosie the ambulance driver went to help a badly wounded soldier and was caught by machine gun fire. She died instantly. Morag was quite distraught but pulled herself together and went back to work in the infirmary." They stood in silence for a few seconds, then Jericho said simply; "Brave girls." Everyone muttered their agreement with that.

Alex took a long swig from Wilson's flask and looked at their faces; "What's wrong?" She said slowly. Owen ran a hand over his face; "The papers are fake - made around the 1780's - but very good fakes." Alex stared at the floor and whispered with real emotion in her voice; "So young Rosie died for a bloody fake." She sighed deeply and sat slowly on a nearby chair; "For a bloody fake." She repeated; angrily.

"I wonder if McIves knows the papers are fakes." Owen asked and sipped some brandy. Jericho grunted; "Our friend has been fighting other people's wars for centuries; I don't suppose he would care either way." Alex looked up from her chair and ran a hand through her long dark hair; "Thanks for reminding me about mercenaries; Young Colin told me that the Colonel intends to hold the castle, until a certain General Munroe arrives with the Scottish Northern Army." Alex shifted in her seat and added; "Apparently in a couple of days, the army has many American volunteers, American descendants of Scots or Irish settlers. A lot of them have apparently served in the US forces and so they're professional soldiers; that could make a big difference to the rebellion."

Jericho nodded at that and eased himself onto a wobbly chair; "Now I understand why the English haven't used their heavy weapons on the Scots - planes and tanks -because of public opinion back in the states, which has large populations descended from Scotland and Ireland. Their President is a staunch supporter of the current Prime Minister; Mrs. Thatcher. But I bet, he has made it plain that such tactics would not be acceptable. The English are fighting a civil war with both arms tied behind their backs; Interesting that."

"You were always too clever for your own good." Colonel McIves stood in the doorway, unsmiling, with his arms folded. He placed a whisky bottle on an empty chair, with several decent looking glasses. He smiled at Alex; "A young, but very loyal trooper, has told me about your little visit to the archives and your promise. I'll be quite envious when he comes to collect his prize."

Alex smiled and shrugged her shoulders but said nothing. McIves chuckled; "I've given him a couple of hours off to spruce himself up and the keys to a VERY SPECIAL and lovely state bedroom. You should be undisturbed there. He'll be here shortly, so that you can keep your end of the bargain." He slowly unscrewed the whisky bottle and spoke directly to Jericho; "May I ask what you discovered by allowing our Alex to offer sexual favours to young men? Tut-Tut; very naughty!" He grinned and handed the bottle to Jericho.

Jericho accepted the open bottle and a glass from McIves and slowly poured whisky out. He sipped and spoke softly; "That this rebellion is based on lies - very well made lies - but lies, nevertheless." He raised the glass in salute. "Where does 'Black Sword' stand, now he knows he's fighting for a lie? A lie that's killing people who should never have died and plunging his beloved adopted country into useless bloodshed?"

6. 'BLACK SWORD' SURPRISES JERICHO.

McIves said nothing but indicated to the doorway; "May I introduce Monsignor Francis de Ville to you all." He said loudly and stood to one side. The little dark-haired Frenchman sauntered in and bowed; "So I finally meet the famed Temporal Detective Jericho Tibbs and his loyal foot soldiers." He bowed again to Alex; "You are as beautiful as I imagined. The young soldier is much privileged to be pleasured by you."

"Did the little shit run an advert on the TV about the archives visit?" Alex groaned, adding; "Does everyone bloody know?" She folded her arms and reminded herself about young men and their sexual boasts. "Big mouthed little shit; he's getting sod all off me." She was about to tell the Frenchman when she saw the look on Wilson's face.

Wilson shook his head and quietly showed Alex the little glass orb: it had turned red; completely. They exchanged looks, but said nothing; they were in the presence of a very powerful minion of the 'Dark Prince'. Wilson caught Jericho pushing his orb back into the folds of his long coat. The group stood in silence as the Frenchman lifted a glass and sipped some whisky, he grinned at Jericho and pulled a small black jewel - no bigger that a thumb - from his jacket pocket. "You will discover, my friends that your mirrors will not work anymore. You now have no more power that a mortal human and completely at my command." Jericho stared at the gem and said quietly; "A Judas Stone." That's when three armed soldiers appeared in the doorway, including an excited looking young Colin from Aberdeen.

Owen pulled out his mirror and stared at the blank screen, each of the team checked their mirrors with the same result; they were offline. Jericho slowly pushed the mirror into the folds of his coat; he didn't smile but folded his arms and spoke quietly; "Only certain minions of the 'Dark Prince' can temporally close down a mirror."

Monsignor Francis de Ville smiled; "And so I am; you may know me as Kiri." He whispered. Jericho's face did not betray the fear building inside; Kiri was a Tier 1 Demon - the only person, who could tackle him - in the human world of the living, would be a Knight of God.

Monsignor Francis de Ville pointed to Alex; "Young Colin, this lady will keep her promise to you - take her and enjoy yourself." Wilson and Owen jumped forward, but Alex shouted for them to stop. She took a heavy breath and said with no emotion in her voice; "He could easily kill you without breaking into a sweat. Stand down. Stand down I say." She walked to the doorway and didn't look back. She heard Wilson calling the Minion something very unpleasant and she half smiled; until Colin gripped her arm and walked her to a nearby staircase.

"The Colonel gave me the keys to the Old Queen's state bedroom, we'll be OK there." He sounded quite excited and took hold of her hand; "Best thing I ever did, letting you see the parchments. I've been told I can take all the time I need.

So, I want to do it a couple of times, understand?" Alex forced a smile at the boy; she could almost sense a change in his demeanour and it wasn't a pleasant one. But then McIves words passed through her mind; 'to spruce himself up and the keys to a

VERY SPECIAL and lovely state bedroom'. Was there a message there? Was the infamous 'Black Sword' throwing her a lifeline? Can he really be trusted? Alex was quite distracted by Colonel McIves words and walked with 'Colin from Aberdeen' slowly.

They arrived at the room in the old quarter of the castle and Colin nervously unlocked the door. Alex stepped in and stared about the room; it was quite stunning with a huge four poster bed covered with thick curtain in bright colours. There were many portraits and tapestries hanging on the walls.

"Well, the room is absolutely stunning. I wouldn't mind this as my bedroom." Alex was impressed and then she realised she had 'young Colin from Aberdeen' to disappoint. "Women can change their mind at any time." She spoke quietly and turned around to speak to Colin about this 'agreement'. He was stark naked; holding his erection with both hands.

Alex sighed and folded her arms; "Colin, about this...." But she never finished her sentence. Colin walked straight up to her; grinning broadly and pushed his hand up her short skirt. His groping hand grabbed through her panties and touched her crotch. She slapped him so hard that he actually fell on the bed.

He lay stunned and slowly rose, cursing. "You don't grab a woman like that - ever." She shouted at him and stared about the room. He was trying apologising and pleading with her to forgive him; when she spotted the mirror against the wall, opposite the window.

"A Jerusalem Mirror!" She exclaimed and walked over and shook her head in relief; "You clever, cunning bugger McIves." She whispered and realised that 'Black Sword' must have decided previously, whose side he was on. With the bloody demon hanging about, he had to be really careful and clever.

Colin crept over and took hold of Alex by the waist from behind. forcing a hand into her blouse, taking a fierce hold on her left breast - it hurt. "You will keep your fucking promise!" He shouted, Colin was bloody angry and frustrated - he was losing control - and now tried to kiss her.

Well, Alex knew that the time for pleasantries was over. She turned slowly, with a lovely smile on her face and gently pulled his hand from her breast. "I think this should visit a better place." She guided it back up her skirt, staring into his eyes. He grinned and turned her to him; which she wanted; "That's more fucking like it; I'm going to fuck you like a fucking dog you bitch!" He spoke angrily, with a contorted smile, pushing his hand down into her panties and between her legs. He tried to push his tongue into her mouth, whispering; "So you fucking like it rough. Well, I'm gonna fuck your arse so hard; you won't sit straight for a week." He actually giggled and started to force his fingers into her. Alex was utterly calm and smiled. He never saw it coming.

'Young Colin from Aberdeen' was in such pain after Alex had smashed her knee straight into his testicles that he slid to the floor. He was suffering excruciating pain - he could not even cry - but just lay whimpering on the carpet, unable to breathe properly or speak.

"You turned out; not to be a very nice young man. But one of us, has certainly been fucked now" She muttered and straightened her blouse and adjusted her panties, then stared at the young man curled upon the floor - now sobbing. "By the way, the agreement is off," she said quietly and strode over to the mirror and stepped through.

She was in the Queen's bedchamber; in 1568. Luckily the place was empty, and she peered through the thick glass window, to the late medieval streets of old Edinburgh. "Some better views here than where I just came from." Chuckling with a little relief, she quickly pulled out her mirror and with some delight; saw it was online. Alex disappeared, before the Queen's Ladies-in-waiting arrived to prepare the bed for Her Majesty.

"It was the perfect decade for rebellion. Margret Thatcher was unpopular with her Poll Tax here, her attempts at smashing the Miners and selling state industries that were actually owned by the people. There were riots and strikes and Scotland had just been cheated out of Independence by a crooked referendum; so the people thought. It was the best opportunity for a successful rebellion in over two hundred years." Monsignor Francis de Ville smiled and sipped his whisky.

"But for success, it had to start way back in 1780. With two old friends of mine and a very famous forger - at the time – who could recreate historically accurate documents. By the way, the ring is actually genuine. I took it from the Kings dead body just hours after his death." Monsignor Francis de Ville sighed and walked to the door; "Goodbye Mister Jericho Tibbs. I will now take the place of that lucky young soldier. But I'm sure, that I will not be as pleasant with Lady Alex as the boy would have been. But he is quite a devoted follower of my Master; that's why I choose him to guard the door. I told the boy it was McIves idea." Laughing, he departed, and the door was slammed and bolted. The three sat in silence, Jericho checked his mirror again; it was still offline.

A 'Judas Stone' was a powerful weapon in the armoury of the 'Dark Prince's' 'minions. It basically disrupted communication between the forces of light and prevented travel between the dimensions of Time. They sat waiting in the darkness - the two miserable candles had long since died - All with one real concern on their minds: Alex.

A little stream of light started to appear through the doorway, and they jumped up, as the old door swung slowly open. McIves stood in the doorway and gestured for them to come. "Quick lads, the fucking demon has gone after Alex." Wilson shouted something about ripping off a certain male appendage and stuffing it somewhere unpleasant. That's when they all stood still at the sight, standing in the corridor.

"Oh fucking shit." Whispered McIves very slowly pulling his famous black sword, from the scabbard that hung upon his back. Jericho checked his mirror; it was still offline.

Monsignor Francis de Ville had reverted to his true form as the demon Kiri; a senior Minion of the 'Dark Prince' and it wasn't happy. "Where is the bitch?" It hissed and rolled dark eyes about and licked its sharp teeth. "Where's the bitch?" It repeated and crashed its tail against the corridor ceiling, bringing down plaster and age-old dirt. Jericho whispered to McIves; "Alexandra must have escaped." McIves smiled and lifted his sword slowly; "I knew she was clever enough to de-code my message about the 'Jerusalem Mirror'. She's jumped!"

"Not quite, I'm still here actually and I've brought an old friend." Everyone turned behind them and saw Alex standing in the doorway, hands on hips and not looking happy. "You see, you scaly bastard, you don't need working mirrors when you have one of these." She stepped aside and James - Knight of God – stood in the doorway, gripping his sword, he dropped his visor and said softly; "I think its best, you people wait in the Great Hall." Everyone disappeared at his command; you certainly didn't need a mirror with him around!

Jericho and his team surprised several sleeping soldiers; who jumped from chairs, sofas and tables as the group appeared in the middle of them. McIves slowly sheaved his sword and grinned broadly at Alex; "I hope you didn't hurt that horny young twat too much." He chuckled and started to speak to the amazed soldiers, who gathered around him.

Alex walked up to McIves and placed a smacker of a kiss upon his lips and stayed there for some time. Finally, she broke the kiss and smiled; "That's a little thank you for being a really clever git and staying true to who you really are - Gracias Rodrigo, eres verdaderamente un hombre de gran honor." 'Black Sword' nodded and stared into her eyes; "So you know."

Alex whispered; "Yes we know." There was silence between the two, until one of the young soldiers asked if he could have one as well and received it for sheer cheek alone!

"They're back on!" Owen exclaimed and held up his mirror and received a little admonishment from Jericho about showing a mirror near living humans. Wilson tapped Alex on the shoulder; "Glad to have you back with us, how's your new boyfriend?" Alex stuck up a single finger; but smiled.

7. McIVES & ALEX.

That evening, with the team dozing in their chairs in the rooms they had been given. Alex and McIves made their way up the old servant's stairs - hand in hand - to the old Queen's bedroom. Alex whispered to the smiling big man; "A proper lady should thank her gallant Knight properly for saving her from a fate worse than death; particularly from a bloody horny demon."

McIves stopped and pulled her close, running in hands over hair and face. He shook his head and didn't smile. "No Alex, you should only do this if you really want me and not as some kind of thank you." Alex grinned and touched his lips with her fingers; "I really want this. So don't try and talk me out of it. But I adore you for trying." McIves chuckled and opened the door with the keys he still had on him.

The pair almost ran in and McIves locked the door behind them and handed the keys to Alex. She sighed with real happiness; this man could actually turn out to be a real man who knows how to treat a real woman. With their arms wrapped around each other; they both stared at the huge bed. McIves kissed her face and lips, he whispered; "Shall we make some real noise?" Alex smiled and nodded, the pair shuffled to the bed and fell on it; giggling together.

He lay on top of her and brushed the hair from her face; "Now, your majesty, what would you like?" Alex kissed him and said quietly; "Everything." McIves chuckled; "Your wish is my command your majesty." They stripped each other naked in less than a minute. They both knelt on the bed holding hands and Alex noticed the scars on his powerful torso. She gently touched them with her fingers. McIves kissed those fingers and said quietly; "Battle scars, three sword cuts and one musket ball."

Alex nodded and ran her hand down his taunt chest and abdomen, to grip his big erection with her gentle fingers. He kissed her slowly and looked a little perplexed. Alex asked if anything was wrong with real concern in her voice. He just smiled; "We both have the same damn first name. We can't call each other Alex. What do you think?"

Alex laughed and stoked his cock, which moved in her grasp. "I'll call you stud, and you can call me the Tart." She lowered her head, pushing him onto the heap of pillows. As her mouth enclosed his cock, 'The Stud' muttered; "I don't really care what you call me, but I will never call you the tart. I'll refer to you as Alex. My Alex if you let me."

Alex just nodded and set to work. 'The Stud' was about to get a first class job done on his big deserving cock. Within minutes the pair was in the sixty-nine positions and enjoying each other's talents immensely. Both had noisy climax's and neither one needed to clean themselves up afterwards. The love making started just minutes afterwards. McIves had erected quickly and the pair started really passionate sex, rolling about the huge bed; groaning, laughing, panting and sweating.

They changed position several times and both decided that simple old fashioned 'Missionary' was what both wanted. Alex really wanted him to dominate her, and she didn't have to ask twice. They made love for a couple of hours until both were totally exhausted and fell asleep curled up in each other's arms. Alex's mirror buzzing woke her up from a very peaceful sleep and she stared at the window; dawn was breaking. McIves kissed her and whispered; "Your bloody mirror is buzzing." What Sir David had done flashed through her head and she returned his kiss saying, "It can wait."

But McIves smiled and reached over and picked the mirror up and handed it to her. "You best answer it sweetheart you're a working woman; it may be important." He then chuckled; "I didn't mean 'working woman' in that awful way. You work for a living." Alex just laughed and took the phone; it was Jericho. He told her get downstairs - the team would be jumping as soon as possible. They would return to the lighthouse and then jump back to Scotland in the 1780's. Supplies had already organised their costumes and horses.

Alex spoke for a couple of minutes, saying she needed a bath and other things a woman needs to do, in the morning. Jericho was having none of that and told her to get downstairs. They needed to jump straight away. Alex sighed and agreed. McIves ran his hands over her face and said, "You best get going before they come looking." She nodded and slipped from his embrace - very reluctantly - and started to dress. McIves sat up and watched her. In fact, the pair never took their eyes off each other until Alex headed for the door. "Sweet heaven, I smell like some French whore who's had a very busy night." She giggled and unlocked the door, throwing the keys - wrapped in her panties - to McIves.

He lifted the little frilly panties up and almost smiled. Alex grinned; "Keep them until you can put them back on me." and disappeared from the room. She walked down the stairs carefully, especially when she passed some soldiers coming up them. She held her short skirt down. She wasn't about to flash some very young and probably horny men. She headed for the large Reception room and stood waiting, arms folded and deep in thought. What had passed between the pair had really stirred something in Alex. She smiled to herself and shook her head; she really didn't want to admit it to herself - or anyone else, for now;

but she was in love. That revelation rolled around her mind and it shocked her deeply.

Jericho and Owen came into the room. Alex sighed; Owen was scoffing down a large sandwich. Wilson followed holding two plastic cup, he handed one to Alex; it was warm coffee. "Sorry, that's the best on offer. That and bloody really old cheese sandwiches." He rolled his eyes and nodded towards Owen. Alex chuckled and thanked him; she was so thirsty; she would have drunk dirty water from someone's old boot. She stepped back a little, knowing she probably smelt of lovemaking; that also made her smile. She had said 'lovemaking' not sex.

Wilson looked about; "Have we just missed mad McIves? I can smell that really expensive French aftershave he always wears" Alex actually felt the blush come to her cheeks and turned towards the doors. "Yes, I think he just left with some men; to check the bloody castle walls or something." That's when she saw Jericho smile at her, pulling out his mirror. "Let's go people. Supplies are waiting to kit us out."

 The team jumped back to the lighthouse in relative silence, except for Owen who moaned that he could still smell bloody McIves pungent aftershave. For some reason that made Jericho chuckle and smile again at Alex. This time she blushed fully and was glad that Wilson and Owen didn't notice. But Jericho did.

Alex lay in the hot bath and splashed her face and shoulders with water. She smiled as she remembered sitting in McIves big strong arms. They were talking quietly and kissing, both naked and tired from the lovemaking. He constantly ran his hands over her body and she found that she had trembled a little. Finally, she kissed his lips and whispered something she thought she would never say again to a man - any man - and mean it. McIves nodded and gently turned her face to him and kissed her with unbridled passion. He said softly; "Ditto." It was all she wanted to hear.

8. HIGHLANDS OF SCOTLAND (1780)

Jericho lowered the small brass telescope and rubbed his face. Large snow flurries slapped against his coat and hat, as they rose and fell with the wind. "There's a small farm about two miles south of our position, that's where we will head." He turned and spoke to his team, waiting behind him in single file along the rugged little ridge. Wilson muttered something; he just wanted off this damn horse, even for half hour.

Owen grinned; "Thighs playing up big man?" and received a two-finger salute in return; he knew that Wilson did not care for horses or horse riding. Alex shifted on her mount; happy she didn't have to ride side saddle. But she was showing a lot of her boots - considered a little bit shocking for a lady of quality - in this year 1780. She had a black and white, fur trimmed coat, which covered down to her ankles. But this was now cast behind her, covering the flanks of her horse. She had pulled the white fur hood, over her head and stared at the gathering snow clouds.

"Does it always snow in bloody Scotland?" She asked no-on in particular. Owen wiped snow from his face and pulled his bonnet down a little; "It does, if it's winter in the Highlands." Jericho waved the little group forward and they started to head out of the shallow valley, towards the thin column of grey smoke, coming from the house's chimney.

"At least they must have a bleedin' fire on." Wilson commented, bundling his dark riding coat around his large frame. "And some whisky." Owen grunted, shaking his hipflask which was empty of brandy. "I might be able to get this refilled." He added, smiling a little at that thought. Wilson was chuckling to himself, and he turned to Alex, who was now aside of him. "Is that really true what our little pervert asked you?"

He certainly wasn't going to let the subject drop - it was too good an opportunity; to take the rise out of his young colleague. Alex smiled at Owen and nodded. That made Wilson's day and he laughed out loud; drawing a strange look from Jericho, who was consulting his mirror. But he didn't comment.

"I only meant that..." Owen said softly, but was interrupted by Wilson; "You asked our lovely colleague and friend to show you her fanny because you've never seen one?" He laughed again, adding; "My God, I wish I had been there to hear that request."

Alex stopped brushing snow from her arms and gloves; "Don't be mean Wilson, if poor young Owen has never seen a woman properly and then he's bound to be curious. Especially since that father of his dumped him in that bloody Monastery at such a young age; he never got the chance to find out about girls or women." She grinned and spoke to Owen but winked at Wilson; "I'm still thinking about your request. I bet you couldn't ask anyone at Moorland Monastery."

Owen sat bolt upright in his saddle and smiled broadly; "Christ Alex, are you really considering my request - I mean that would really help me cope." Wilson shook his head and smiled; "You're not serious Alex?" She spurred her horse forward and glanced over her shoulder at the pair. "If it really helps poor Owen to cope with his feelings, I just may have to do so." Then joined a very amused Jericho at the front, adding; "After all, what are friends for?"

"Now that's a real friend." Owen said to Wilson; "Not like some." Wilson just grunted and slapped his horse gently. "Come on you mangy beast." He didn't notice the big smile that passed between Owen and Alex; their charade was working. They liked their little secrets kept secret, even from such a good friend.

The team made the farmhouse, just as night was dropping and the temperature was following it down. Jericho dismounted and pointed to the barn; "The horses will be alright in there. I'll speak to the owners about us staying the night. I'm sure they will like some coins in payment. Times are hard around here after the rebellion was defeated in 1746."

Owen pointed his mirror down and activated its light. In the bright glow everyone could see the three bodies, half buried by the falling snow. Everyone drew their pistols and Alex dismounted and knelt down by the bodies.

"Three men; all shot apparently." She lifted one arm of the nearest corpse and nodded; "They haven't been dead long and if I had to guess; I would say they were lined up and shot - by the way they fell - executed." Owen joined her and pushed about in the snow; "No weapons; if they had any." He then stood up and raised his hands nodding towards the barn.

Several British 'redcoat' soldiers were pointing their muskets at them; having emerged quietly from the barn. The Officer lifted his hat and bowed a little; "Please place your weapons upon the ground. You know that carrying weapons in Scotland is an offence and I would be most reluctant to shoot such a pretty lady and one that clearly is not squeamish about examining dead bodies. I find that fact alone intriguing." He replaced his pistol and pointed to the ground; "Very slowly now; no quick movements please."

Jericho, with raised hands, smiled and indicated to his coat pocket; "Lieutenant, I applaud you for your diligence to duty and your application of our laws, but please read the papers that I carry. Then we can all get inside out of this damn weather and have some whisky." The officer glanced at his sergeant; "They are English; fetch whatever is in his pocket." The sergeant walked slowly over and with his pistol still pointing at Jericho, reached in and pulled out - tied and sealed. - A rolled parchment. He walked back to the officer and handed it over.

A lamp was produced, and the young lieutenant slowly opened the document and read it with great interest for some minutes. "You recognise the signature and seal of the Lord Advocate Sir?" Jericho said softly, adding; "May we please lower our arms and replace our pistols?"

The lieutenant nodded; this strange little group were carrying a very powerful document signed by the Lord Advocate Henry Dundas, 1st Viscount Melville and de-facto ruler of Scotland.

"We're all his men - well, except the lady of course - she works for me." Jericho smiled as the soldiers shouldered their muskets at the sergeant's command. "Let's get inside and have some damn whisky." he added and smiled broadly. The officer wiped his face and stared at Alex, then looked back at Jericho.

Jericho produced a black bottle of single malt and gestured to the door, adding; "May I have my instructions returned please - if all our officers are as diligent as you - we may need it more than once!"

Owen, with the help of a couple of soldiers, stabled the horses in the barn, where the 'redcoats' had made their beds; the officer's black mare was tied up with a pack mule. Jericho and the officer, with Alex and Wilson following pushed into the farmhouse, the Sergeant came too, unloading his pack upon the floor and pulled a small pipe from his pocket and started to fill the bowl.

The officer pulled a chair close to the fire and indicated for Alex to sit and warm herself. She unbuttoned her coat and gracefully eased herself into the seat. Alex was wearing a low-cut bodice and her magnificent breasts were almost showing. She smiled at the young lieutenant, as she accepted a glass of whisky from him.

"Another moth to the bloody flame." Muttered Wilson and smiled, gripping his glass and sipping a most welcome drop of whisky.

Jericho and the officer sat at the table, drinking and talking. Owen had returned and was placing more coal on the fire. He downed his whisky in one throw and refilled his - and the sergeants - glasses. The sergeant was from Yorkshire and he and Owen got on like a house on fire. He was veteran of the war in the American Colonies and liked his whisky. He was fascinated by Wilson's story; how he had served the crown in the America's [he was a free born man] and being loyal to the King; had been driven from his home by the American rebels. He now worked for the Lord Advocate here in Scotland.

The sergeant admitted to Owen, that the lady travelling with them, was the best 'piece of skirt' he had seen in years and wondered about what services she performed for Mr. Tibbs, on behalf of the Lord Advocate. Owen just smiled and re-filled his glass. Alex leaned back in her seat and sipped her whisky, she had already noticed that the lieutenant kept throwing glances at her - despite his ongoing conversation with Jericho - she sighed and leaned forward, tapping an escaped piece of coal back into the fire with her boot; unintentionally giving the young man a real show of her magnificent breasts, barely constrained by her bodice.

The look on his face priceless and he coughed a little, as he gulped down his whisky. He had a very uncomfortable erection in his tight trousers.

Alex was given the sole bedroom of the house, whilst Jericho's team and the officer [with the sergeant] bedded down in the living room. The night passed without further incident and over a breakfast of tea, bread, cheese and apples, Jericho briefed his team. It appears that Willy McKenzie and Daniel Brown were known to the British authorities and had been incarcerated at Scone Castle on suspicion of treason to the crown. But they had produced a smart talking lawyer from Edinburgh and it looked like they would walk from the charges, free men. So the decision was made; Jericho and his team would accompany the English patrol to Scone castle.

Finally, Alex asked the lieutenant about the three dead men and would they receive a decent Christian burial. He shrugged his shoulders - it appears they were caught with a old broadsword and a pistol that had seen better days. The youngest had the outlawed Scottish flag wrapped around his chest. The lieutenant's orders were clear and concise; they were shot where they stood as traitors to the crown. But just to salve Alex's conscious, he would have them buried and a prayer read over them; he didn't even know their names.

But he was intrigued how Alex knew about medicine and accepted her explanation about her father being a surgeon, who pandered to his daughter's strange fascination with all things medical. The lieutenant was greatly amused by Alex's comments regarding the future, where women would be allowed to practise as Licensed Doctors. "A wonderful dream Alex; but who would trust their health to a woman?" He chuckled and re-filled her glass with a big smile.

They set out for Castle Scone in light snow, but the fallen snow was quite deep - it had snowed all night - but the infantry seemed to cope well enough. Owen overheard a few ripe comments about Wilson riding a horse, when 'decent white men' had to 'fucking' walk. He didn't pass them onto Wilson; the big man was unhappy enough, having to ride the bloody horse in the first place!

The journey would take three days slogging through the snow and the highlight of the trek was finding a small village with a tavern. That made Alex very happy because the owner's wife was genuinely delighted to have a 'Lady of quality' under her roof. She even arranged for a hot bath to be provided and had Alex's travelling clothes cleaned. The hot water wasn't wasted on just bathing Alex; when she had soaked long enough and dressed properly, the tavern's serving girl was allowed to bath - apparently, she needed it after servicing four of the soldiers in the small back room - kept aside for such fornication.

When the group left the next day, Jericho paid the tavern owner with silver coin and arranged for the soldiers to have beer and a hot breakfast taken to the stables where they were billeted. They actually gave their benefactor three cheers for that act of kindness; orchestrated by the happy sergeant. Alex gave the tavern owner's wife some silver coin too and they parted like old friends. The officer smiled and spoke quietly to Owen; "Working for the Lord Advocate must pay really well?" Owen nodded; "Mr. TIbbs is his best servant; he ALWAYS gets the job done - regardless of what the task entails - he gets it done." The officer said nothing further, and the convoy headed out into the snow-covered hills.

Late the following afternoon, Castle Scone came into view across the river. Jericho saw through his telescope that several villages were clustered around its imposing walls. As they passed through its grand entrance, everyone saw the two decomposing men hanging from a wooden gibbet; both had small boards hung around their necks, which said simply: Traitor.

Owen whispered to Alex; "There seems to be a lot of them around here - still."

Alex nodded and stared at the pitiful sight, slowing her mount to take a good look. She turned to Owen and said quietly; "The big man with the tattoo's; have we seen him before?" Owen stared at the bodies hanging before the gates, which were being pulled open by several grunting soldiers and nodded slowly; "I think your right. Where have we met a tall, well-built man like that with a full beard before here?"

Alex sighed; "Well, whoever he was he's gone now." The little convoy passed into the courtyard of the castle and the great gates were closed behind them.

9. CASTLE SCONE.

The garrison Commander; Captain Edward Sackville watched the patrol return with their 'guests' in tow, from the bay window of his office. He adjusted his wig and placed his large hat upon his head and checked his appearance in the long mirror that stood by the door. Sir Edward was in his late thirties and was a professional soldier: he had served now for almost twenty years and never advanced beyond the rank of Captain.

The reason was simple; he was a bad soldier and an even worse officer. Captain Sackville simply steered away from decision making; any decision making. His soldier servant often repeated the story about the captain and breakfast; he actually took several minutes to decide if he wanted one egg or two!

He carefully positioned himself at the desk and moved his chair about, to achieve the best position to portray the air of authority; he needn't bothered; none of his officers or men really had any respect for him. He sat drumming his fingers upon the desk and sat bolt upright when there was a knock at his door. "Enter." He spoke, attempting to inject some authority into his weedy voice. His clerk: Sergeant Robertson stuck his head around the door and informed him that Lt. Dunbar and those servants of the Lord Advocate were here.

Captain Sackville straightened himself and adjusted his hat; yet again. Lt. Dunbar entered, saluted and sat down without even being asked. Sackville said nothing about that slight to his rank. "The one called Mr. Tibbs is carrying the Token and Warrant of the Lord Advocate; he certainly seems to know what he's doing. They in pursuit of William McKenzie and Daniel Brown; that pair of fuckers, have apparently, been forging stuff they should have left well alone."

Sackville nodded and ensured that his jacket was fastened properly; he glanced enviously at the mirror, but his attention was drawn back to Lt. Dunbar when he mentioned the woman travelling with the Tibbs party. A real beauty according to his Lieutenant and being a vain man, he believed he could seduce the lady easily; he smiled so much that Lt. Dunbar actually asked him, if anything was wrong.

He snapped back; "No." Sackville stood and paced by the fireplace for a minute or so and he did not reproach the lieutenant about remaining seated when he rose from his chair. Whilst it made it him a little angry, he said nothing; "Did you say William McKenzie and Daniel Brown?" The captain asked; almost smiling.

The Lieutenant nodded; "That's the pair we have sitting in our cells; Mr. Tibbs has a warrant for them. It appears the dumb bastards have tried their hand at forgery. He needs to speak to them before we hang them for treason." The Lieutenant shifted in his seat: "The Lord Advocate has authorised their pardon, if they co-operate with Mr. Tibbs. The finding of the forger and the document is paramount apparently. Its recovery is critically important for the future of English rule in Scotland."

The captain grinned broadly and clasped his hands like a child at Christmas: "Well, the Lord Advocate will be impressed with the Garrison Commander of Scone Castle because the very same pair are sitting in its dungeon." Lt. Dunbar stood and placed his hat on; "I'll inform our guests that their prey waits in our dungeon." He bowed a little and made for the South corridor, where the 'guests' had been given rooms.

Wilson and Owen held aloft two lamps as the small group - with Lt. Dunbar - passed down the old stone steps towards the dungeons. Alex actually covered her face with a scented hankie; "What is that bloody awful smell?" She asked Owen, who smiled and waved a hand across his face; "Welcome to eighteenth century prison care. There are no showers, baths or toilets down here, just a big bucket." Alex groaned and held the hankie close. She caught Lt. Dunbar smiling at her; yet again.

"He's real keen Alex and his father is loaded; a mill owner near Manchester I believe, the sergeant told me." Owen whispered and grinned at her breasts protruding from that tight bodice; "He's seen some of the goods on offer and wants the rest I expect." Alex didn't answer; they had arrived at the cell containing McKenzie and Brown.

The old jailer rose from his rough wooden stall and tipped his hat to Alex and the Lieutenant; "Quiet pair these two, they hardly talk. They just sit there staring at nothing." He scratched his chest under a ragged shirt and then his crotch.

"But they eat anything given to them." He added, with a toothless grin and then stared straight at Alex's breasts - licking his lips - he was quite repulsive, and Alex turned from him and peered into the cell.

William McKenzie and Daniel Brown sat upon some filthy straw, both chained to the wall with leg irons. They didn't look up as the cell door was pulled open. "On your feet you dogs!" The jailer shouted and kicked Brown, who was nearest to him, adding; "These are the Lord Advocates men and you'll be dancing a jig on the wooden lady sooner than later if you disrespect them."

Brown and McKenzie rose slowly, and both stared at Alex, who pulled her cloak about herself.

Brown smiled; "I don't give a fuck about the Lord Advocates men, but the Lord Advocates woman I would fuck." He and McKenzie chuckled and sat back down. The Lieutenant gestured towards them and the jailer suddenly produced a wooden stick from somewhere and struck Brown full across the face. He lay in silence upon the floor, a little blood around his mouth and chin.

"You will show both the Lord Advocates men and women respect." Lt. Dunbar said quietly, as the jailer lifted the stick again. Jericho stepped in, smiling. "Thank you, Lieutenant, we'll take it from here, if you could just post a guard outside while Mister Brown and McKenzie have some words with us." Lt. Dunbar was most reluctant to leave Alex in the room, but she persuaded him with a big smile and some quiet words. There was silence until the Lieutenant and the jailer left, slamming the heavy cell door behind them.

Jericho knelt a few feet from the pair and held up a lamp; "Well gentleman, you seem to have got yourself into some trouble here. If you co-operate with me, I can guarantee that your necks won't be stretched and all I ask is for one name; just one little name and you will walk away from here and not carried out in canvas to a dark hole and a nameless grave." Brown and McKenzie exchanged a glance but said nothing. Brown wiped his bloody face and coughed.

Alex produced a small flask of brandy from her skirts and threw it to Brown; "That will ease the pain a little." Brown took the bottle and pulled the stopper out, he spat a loose tooth from his mouth and took a swig, passing it to McKenzie.

"Thank you, Ma'am." He said quietly and spat more blood out.

"We know who the Mastermind behind the forged Scottish Accession document was and he has already been dealt with. All we ask is the name of the forger or failing that, where the document is now. Either one given to us will ensure you walk from here free men." Jericho gestured around the room; "Unless you find the King's hospitality too good to forsake?"

McKenzie stared at Wilson and spat upon the floor; "How can a

Black men support this bastard King; your people are slaves and all we want is the same freedom your people cry for?" Wilson shrugged his shoulders; "I'm a freeman here in Scotland, at the King's kindness and mercy. But in the land of the so called free, those rebellious bastards that now call them self 'Americans' would have me in chains. It was a very easy choice for me, my friend and now you have a similar choice."

Alex had to smile at the supposed sincerity in Wilson's voice; he had always been a diehard American patriot whilst still breathing and she believed that hadn't changed since he died!

McKenzie just shook his head and said nothing more. Brown threw the empty flask back to Alex with a crooked grin; "Thanks Ma'am, now if those English bastards are going to hang me, I would like to ask one last thing." Alex folded her arms and said quietly; "And what would that be?" Brown chuckled, then groaned and held his chin; "Just lift those skirts of yours and show me your cunt and I'll swing a happy man or better still, let me kiss heaven's slit!"

McKenzie laughed at his friends words and then turned angry; snarling, he shouted; "Fuck off; you'll get nothing from us; you fucking stinking little lap dogs!" Both men slumped against the stone wall and stared up at the ceiling.

Jericho sighed; "When you're ready to talk, let us know; the offer still stands." He then rose and banged upon the cell door and the Jailer opened it slowly and the group left in silence.

The jailer stood in the doorway and chuckled; "I have news for you two fools, that fancy lawyer from Edinburgh has been sent away with his tail between his legs and the Garrison Commander has signed your death warrants for high treason. You'll swing in the morning, so sleep well tonight." He slammed and locked the door, laughing loudly.

Both men sat in the dark, damp cell and contemplated what the morning would bring. Softly at first, they sang and then standing, sung as loud as their voices would allow. The old jailer, perched upon his rough stool, sighed to himself and slowly drank from his tankard. "Stupid brave bastards." was all he muttered and sighed loudly.

10. THE LIEUTENANT GETS IT WRONG.

Alex pulled her bed coat about herself, after she finished drying. Her hot bath had been excellent, and she had enjoyed soaking for some minutes. She sat by the big fireplace and roaring fire, bushing her long dark hair. There was a couple of soft knocks at her door and Alex rose and opened it a little, standing behind and smiling a little at Lt. Dunbar, who stood with a silver tray that contained a brandy decanter and two superb Chrystal glasses. "You asked for some decent brandy, so I thought I would serve you myself." He raised the tray and smiled. Alex just nodded. He was a good-looking young man and well built; so why not. She needed some relaxation.

She opened the door, and he walked in and placed the tray on the small table by the fireplace, whilst Alex slowly closed the door. "Just had a bath?" He asked by way of small talk and Alex again, nodded. She joined him by the table, and he poured two glasses. "You will love this, it's French. What will we drink to Miss Alex?" and raised his glass. Alex took a glass and smiled; "To what all women desire; love and affection." Lt, Dunbar smiled, and they tapped the glasses to together and sipped their brandies with some relish; Alex was impressed, she had drunk enough brandy in her time, to know a real decent one. She gestured for him to sit in the armchair by the fire and he did; not once taking his deep brown eyes off her. She slowly eased herself down on the armchair opposite him and held her bed coat tightly; she was stark naked underneath, and she knew that he knew it.

"It must be interesting working for the Lord Advocate, I mean for a woman." He said softy and Alex just smiled; "I work for Mr. Tibb's who works for the Lord Advocate. He uses me on missions for the Crown, when only a woman would get the results wanted. It makes for an interesting life."

She slowly crossed her legs, revealing a little too much of them. He watched her with growing fascination and anticipation; he was hooked. They sat in silence and finished the good brandy. He rose from the chair and walked over to her and ran a hand over her hair and face, muttering; "Beautiful, quite beautiful." Alex took his hand and gently kissed each finger and rose from the chair. He took hold of her, and the pair kissed with some passion. He was an excellent kisser and soon their tongues were saying hello. He ran both hands beneath her bed coat and gripped her arse really firmly. Alex pulled the chord and pushed back the coat, revealing her naked body to the young man, dropping it to the floor. He gasped with utter pleasure and one hand gripped a big breast and the other pushed between her legs. They continued to kiss, as he gently pushed her to the floor. Alex was a little bemused that he didn't undress, but hurriedly pulled out his erect cock.

She smiled, it wasn't the biggest she had ever seen, but it certainly looked adequate and up to the task. He pulled down his trousers and mounted Alex in the Missionary Position. "So, foreplay not popular around here then?" She whispered as he pushed into her vagina, which needed a little lubricant. He had no idea what 'foreplay' was and so just grinned.

He thrust hard and fast - really fast - and Alex gripped his jacket sleeves and groaned; not with pleasure, without proper lubricate, it was hurting a little. She was about to ask for some bloody butter - unsalted - to dampen her cunt, when the good Lieutenant shot his load, quite unexpectedly, into her. She was very surprised by that, but at least she was now lubricated properly. He grinned and kissed her mouth, pulling his cock from her and standing.

Alex lay on the floor, propped up on her elbow, still with her legs open and his cum tricking from her slightly tender vagina. She watched - with real surprise and some shook - as the young officer pulled up his trousers and buttoned them up. He pushed a hand through his hair and nodded to Alex.

"Thank you, Madame. That was excellent. How much do I owe you? I really should have agreed a price before we started." He fumbled in his jacket pockets and produced some silver coin. "Is five shillings adequate for you? It's all I have on me." Well, Alex rose slowly and pulled her bed coat around her and simply exploded. Young Lt. Dunbar fled from the room; the coins hitting his back and legs as he dived through the door and slammed it behind him.

Alex was shouting and now picked up the tray with the brandy and glasses on and threw it at the door. Brandy and glass flew everywhere. Lt. Dunbar was apologising behind the safety of the big oak door, but Alex wasn't listening. He cringed at her foul language and especially the names she called him.

He walked quickly away - looking around - and ran down the stairs and made for the Officer's Mess. He would pretend that this hadn't happened; he would fawn over her at dinner and be absolutely charming. She would soon forgive him and accept that he was excellent marriage material. He nodded to himself; utterly convinced he could still win the feisty - but beautiful - woman over. He had made a slight error; but that could soon be rectified; so, he thought.

Sergeant Robertson watched his hurried departure and sighed. He knocked on Alex's door and Alex pulled it open and stared at the strapping young man who smiled and gestured to the debris around the door. "Don't you worry Miss; I'll clear that up. You just sit down and get yourself together. I'm afraid the young Lieutenant is bit of a twat when it comes to women. Frankly, he hasn't a bloody clue!" He reached behind him and pulled out his hip flask and handed it to Alex. "Have a drop of that stuff Miss. It leaves any French brandy way behind."

Alex took the cap off and sniffed it; "What is it?" She asked?" It smelt wonderful. The young Sergeant smiled; "Old family receipt Miss. Slow gin. Gin made with Sloe berries. My family has made it for over a century. Try it." Alex took a swig and grinned; she certainly knew good alcohol when she tasted it.

Alex took another sip and looked the young Sergeant up and down; "You say the lieutenant doesn't know about women, so, do you?" The Sergeant really did smile; "Well Miss, I never had any complaints. Well, none in writing." That made Alex laugh and she handed back his flask. As he took it, she gripped his big rough hand and pulled him gently into her room, muttering; "Well, I'll soon find out if you do know about women."

11. THE SERGEANT GET'S IT RIGHT.

The young sergeant lay naked on the floor with an equally naked Alex - in front of the fireplace - and Alex held his cock in her hands and just sighed with amazement. She turned to the young man and gestured to his enormous, erect cock with her head, she spoke with some wonderment in her voice; "Do you have a bloody licence or something for this? Sweet Jesus, you could beat a grizzly bear to death with it."

James just chuckled, hands behind head and was quite relaxed. "Some prossie's [prostitutes] either tell me to fuck off or they want to charge me double. Are you alright with it? I'd be really grateful if you could manage it." Alex stared back at the throbbing monster and ran a hand over her face. "Well, it's going nowhere near my arse, that's for certain. But I will give it a go. Thank God there's some butter left on the dish. I'm going to need every drop to squeeze this in."

Alex stood and pulled the young man up and they walked to the bed. "I not trying to cope with that bloody big thing on the floor." She said and jumped on the bed. James climbed on and Alex sighed, as she slowly pushed the monster into her mouth. Lying partially across his belly, she sucked and caressed the cock with some passion. James stroked her back and pushed a hand between her legs and rubbed her fanny gently, fingers carefully probing her damp cunt. "Let me get a taste of you Miss." He said and Alex nodded, popping the big cock from her stretched mouth. "Sweet Jesus James, you could satisfy a whale with this."

James chuckled and sat up, gesturing for her to come to him. She knew what to do and squatted over his smiling face. His mouth fixed on her fanny and clit - he knew his way around them; that's for certain - and set to work. Alex had both hands on the headboard and was groaning loudly. He worked her cunt for some minutes and Alex squirted twice, leaving her legs trembling and her stomach tight. He rolled her on her back and thoughtfully, pulled pillows under head and backside. He started to mount and had to laugh, as she crossed herself and whispered; "For what we're about to receive...." and receive it, she did.

Alex actually cried and sobbed a little as the huge cock filled her up, thrusting gently and carefully in her dripping fanny. She lost count of her orgasms under the sergeant's very skilled hands. He fucked her for some minutes, and they changed position several times; but his big cock never left her trembling fanny at any time. He had told Alex that it had better remain in her until he came. It would be too painful for her to have him keep pulling the damn thing out and then shoving it back in.

Alex agreed - between sobs and screams of ecstasy - and James also mentioned, as he happily thrusted his cock in and out of her, that when he came, he really came. "Apparently, I been told, I could bottle the damn stuff and sell it by the pint. I must also warn you that I've fucked several women and everyone one has ended up carrying my baby. So do you want me still to finish in your honeypot?"

Alex thanked him for his honesty and consideration in the matter of coming inside of her - between gritted teeth, it should be noted - and told him to go ahead and fill her up with his baby juice. He really did smile at that and after a few more minutes of burying his monster in her, young James emptied his load. Alex gripped his shoulders and called him every name she could think of. She felt like someone had emptied a bucket into her.

But the pair kissed and lay together, with James telling her about his father's farm in Kent. Alex stroked his face and hair, but the pair struggled to pull the huge cock from Alex's fanny - it appeared not to want the cock to go - but they finally pulled the damn thing out and Alex watched in utter amazement as a huge trickle of cum, oozed from her gaping cunt. "I need to pee." she whispered and realised that the only toilet nearby, was the chamber pot under the damn bed!

Alex politely asked young James, who was wiping his cock with a hankie, if he minded about her pissing in front of him. He shook his head and said, "Be just like home. My two young sisters' would squat over the pot and just let it go, even if me and dad were sitting there. We didn't mind, but when gran did it, we always disappeared." He chuckled. Alex smiled and pulled out the pot and squatted down; she was bursting, and she pissed hard and fast.

James nodded his approval; "You piss like a horse Miss." He held his cock with both hands and asked - politely - if Alex was up to another go!

She watched in amazement and a little horror, as the monster stiffened and swelled. He was ready to go again. She walked with her legs open, back to the bed [her fanny was well gaped and hadn't recovered yet] grabbing the butter dish as she went. James really grinned; "You're a great sport Miss, I'd marry you tomorrow if I could afford a wife." Alex climbed on top of him and buttered her fanny really well and threw the dish away. "May God have mercy...."Was all she said and inserted the big cock back into her.

Alex rode the young sergeant with some passion; she could feel him buried inside her and she loved that feeling. He thrusted upwards as she pushed down; their timing was perfect - like they had spent a lifetime fucking each other - and they clasped hands, both groaning and encouraging each other to fuck harder. She pulled up her legs and gripped his thighs with both hands. Back arched, she pushed herself down and had one hell of an organism. Her spurts crashed down on his chest and arms, as he held her hips tightly. She collapsed on him, and they rolled over and her fucked her hard and fast on her back; her hands all over his strong back and neck. She was actually screaming and had to push a hand over her mouth.

He pulled her hand away and their mouths found each other. The bed was now groaning and creaking under their frenzied love making, and the pair rolled about, locked in a passionate embrace. Alex couldn't believe the young man's stamina and they fucked for some time before he came inside her with some gasping and eye rolling. She pulled him down to her and they kissed carefully and slowly; they didn't say anything because their bodies had done all the talking necessary.

They lay quietly together, and Alex pulled up on her elbows and kissed his mouth. She whispered - with a huge smile - that his efforts were some of the best she had encountered; ever. He just smiled and stroked her hair. They lay talking softly together for some time, then Alex realised she had to dress for dinner - after a real hot bath - and the pair reluctantly; would have to part; for now.

She watched the young man dress and walked back to the bed and kissed her forehead, she turned over and touched his face. He smiled at her breasts and very open and pink fanny, that was presented to him. He leaned over and kissed her belly and nipples. "Please let me know what you have Miss, a boy or a girl." He grinned and added; "Until next time my lady."

Alex smiled; "Fucking amen to that." and giggled; she was still trembling, and her stomach felt full. Now that was proper, top notch fucking sex, she told herself and curled up on the bed, wrapping her arms around her breasts and back.

She was happy. He walked to the door and Alex called after him, pointing to the table by the fireplace. She smiled; "There's five shillings there that the lieutenant insulted me with. You can have it, if you want." The sergeant nodded and scooped the coins up; "Thanks Miss," He stopped by the door and asked if they could fuck again - soon - he hoped. "I'll send this money to my father to help with the farm costs. That's all I really want; to go home and farm with my family instead of being an unwelcome guest in someone's county."

Alex groaned in mock despair and sat up on her elbows and just stared at him, then smiled. She nodded; "Yes, we'll 'fuck' again soon. I'll let you know when and where. I hope you get enough money to go home." She collapsed back on the bed and chuckled as the door closed quietly. Life was full of up's and down's, good and bad. She thought about young James and simply had to grin and laugh to herself; despite her aching, stretched fanny.

"What was that bloody Lieutenant's name?" She giggled to herself and dozed on the bed, still quite naked.

12. SCOTLAND THE BRAVE.

The dining room had been laid out for the Garrison Commander and his guests; Lt. Dunbar was joined by Lt. Fairfax, a quiet, chubby young man who seemed uninterested in Alex, but enjoyed Owens's company and conversation at the table. Wilson watched the lieutenant with a growing smile; he certainly did like Owens's company; a lot.

Lt. Dunbar appeared totally engrossed with Alex who sat opposite him and paid little attention to anyone else; mush to the apparent annoyance of Captain Sackville, who couldn't get a word in with Alex.

Jericho and Wilson exchanged amused looks, but the meal was excellent and enjoyed by all. The captain lead the toasts to the King and the Ladies present; there was only one; Alex, who gracefully received them with apparent pleasure and modesty. The after-dinner conversation turned to Brown and McKenzie; they would be hung at nine o'clock the next morning, unless they decided to co-operate with the Lord Advocates men. Owen cleverly steered the conversation around to the dead man already hanging on the gibbet. Lt. Dunbar managed to pull away from Alex and joined the conversation about one of the corpses. It appears he was hung last week after a very short trial for treason. The man gave his name as Mark Bolland; "A very odd fellow actually and he died quite miserably, kicking, screaming and shamefully: crying! He had to be dragged to the scaffold by force. He died disgracefully, not like a man at all. There was a good crowd and his behaviour ruined a grand day out for everyone." Lt. Dunbar sipped his brandy and gestured to the grand window, adding; "With all this snow coming down, Brown and McKenzie will be lucky if Father Stephen bothers to turn up."

"I think they will be happier if the hangman's doesn't show up, rather than Father Stephen." Alex muttered and emptied her brandy glass. Everyone at the table chuckled and Lt. Dunbar seemed quite amazed that a woman could make such a joke - he was impressed - very impressed. Later, he pulled Jericho to one side and asked about Alex; was she married? Promised? Who were her parents? He went on so much that Jericho actually held up his hand to cut the conversation and promised they would talk more tomorrow.

Owen discovered more about Mark Bolland from Lt. Fairfax; he had been discovered with various letters and documents that must have been treasonous in nature. They appeared to show a future Independent Scotland and good King George was to be replaced with a King called William who was – obviously - some pretender to the throne. He really couldn't believe he was to hang and screamed and shouted right up to his neck being snapped.

"A real strange fellow, I think he was from the rebel colonies, here to stir up support and trouble no doubt." Lt. Fairfax then wondered if Owen wished to see his drawings of Highland people and places that he kept in his bedroom; Owen politely declined. The following morning, Jericho again attempted to convince Brown and McKenzie to talk; without success and thus a small group gathered below the gibbet just before nine o'clock; it was still snowing and bitterly cold. Wilson passed a flask of brandy amongst the team and Lt. Dunbar again, tried to persuade Alex not to watch the execution and like Owen before, she politely declined the request. But he walked away with a real smile on his face; 'what a fucking woman', he muttered to himself, as he finished organising the hanging to his satisfaction.

McKenzie and Brown were marched out just before nine o'clock; hands tied behind them and still wearing their leg irons; neither had a coat or hat on in the bitter cold. The two-hangman half frog marched and half dragged them to the gibbet, the nooses were slung causally about their necks and they were stood by the edge. McKenzie started to shout something, but Brown remained silent; his face had swollen up overnight following the blow from the jailer the previous evening.

Without further ceremony, the two hangmen simply pushed the pair from the floor of the gibbet, and they dangled in the air: kicking and choking. It took a couple of minutes for both men to die; the hangman had fucked up somewhat, but no-one was really bothered about that.

Alex discretely pointed to a small hill about half a mile away in the snow flurries; standing upon it was a lone piper. The team could just hear the sad lament being played through the wind and snow. Lt. Dunbar shouted for horses and he, with several men, mounted up to go after the lone piper.

Jericho explained; that by the playing the pipe at a traitor's hanging; they were guilty of treason themselves. Alex watched Lt. Dunbar disappear through the grand gates with his mounted infantry following. They all stared at the small hill; the piper was gone. They turned back to the hung men and saw the strange figure in a nice black suit standing in the snow, just below the dangling pair.

Only Jericho and his team could see the collector standing by the gibbet, soul ledger in hand, he was soon joined by Brown and McKenzie and without a word said; the three walked to the bright light and disappeared.

A soldier swung each body back onto the platform and fixed a little wooden sign about their necks; 'Traitor' it sated in chalk. He let them swing back out and there, they hung for several days, until replaced by two fresh 'traitors' the following Monday.

The team assembled in the castle's drawing room and sipped warming brandies in relative silence. A young soldier appeared carrying a bucket of coal and built the fire up until it roared and crackled. Alex slumped in a comfortable chair by the fire and was joined by Wilson; "Well, that's made the mission come to an abrupt end." He said quietly and sipped his brandy. "How so?" A puzzled Alex asked; the document had not been found and they still didn't know who the forger was.

Wilson chuckled; "That dumb pair were hung the week before they originally delivered the pouch to that damn solicitor. They actually knew nothing about what Jericho was talking about because they had not met with our not so friendly demon Monsignor Francis de Ville, which means it never happened; none of it!" He slumped back into his chair and continued; "Don't need to find the forger now or recover the document; the current Human Time-Line has been restored."

A frustrated Lt. Dunbar returned from his fruitless hunt for the lone piper, cursing his bad luck and the worsening snowstorm; but he cheered up whilst sitting and chatting with Alex. She was totally amazed by this; especially after what she called him!

Alex admitted to her friends that young Lt. Dunbar had spoken about marriage despite what she had called him and she really needed to exit this mission!

After consulting his mirror, that very afternoon, Jericho called the team together in his rooms and they jumped back to the lighthouse together.

John Cordless walked slowly through the snow towards his little office, pulling his heavy coat around and adjusting his scarf and hat. He had money on his mind; if only he could get enough to marry Mary and maybe hire another clerk, his fortunes could rise. He kicked snow from his boots and hung his coat, scarf and hat upon the back of the door, then threw some coal upon the small fire and read the paper with little interest.

Yet another two old Highland warriors had been hung for being traitors; he didn't recognise either of their names and so he turned the page and then an advertisement in the 'Personal' column caught his eye. A Scottish clan leader in the Highland required a Lawyer for his estates and they could be newly qualified and in-experienced. The pay looked good and a modest house would be provided with two servants included.

John Cordless opened the desk drawer and pulled some sheets of paper from it and dipped his quill pen into the ink pot, working for an ignorant, smelly Scottish Chieftain would be better than going bankrupt and ending up in the street. That's when there was a knock at his door, and he said quietly; "Enter." He lowered his pen and smiled as the young lady swept into his office and brushed snow from her fur hat and coat. She smiled broadly and asked; "Are you John Cordless the solicitor?" He nodded; she was beautiful and full figured as she unbuttoned her coat. He asked her to sit and pushed his letter away. "How can I help madam?" he said quietly, and she sat and smiled again; he was hooked and clasped his hands together on the desk. She placed a small bag upon the desk and tapped it; "I want you to ensure this gift reaches a certain British Army sergeant without my identity being revealed; can you do that Sir?" John nodded slowly and asked quietly for details of the lucky sergeant.

The lady handed him a little folded note; "That's the address where he is currently stationed. The gift will allow him to leave the army and return to his father's farm. He really doesn't like his present situation; being the oppressor in someone else's country. You do understand that Sir?" John Cordless nodded and sat back. "With such a delicate mission I would recommend that we do not draw up a contract as that would mean revealing your identity in law, which I feel is something that you do not desire?"

The lady nodded; "Quite so good sir, I do not wish any written papers to exist of this transaction. But without a written contract how could I pay you so that the British taxman doesn't discover and question the payment? I want no written records to exist now and in the future."

John Cordless stood and walked to the old cabinet; "Would you like a whisky to warm you up madam whilst we discuss the payment for this most difficult and private mission?" He smiled broadly and thanked the almighty for his mercy and this little gift.

The woman smiled, removing her hat; "I think we certainly can come to an agreement where no money changes hands Sir."

 And they did.

Bent over the desk, John pulled up her skirt and petticoats and pulled down her smooth silk knickers and ran both hands over her gorgeous peach shaped arse. He groaned in anticipation; he was already fully erect. The lady tided her clothes as John pulled his cock out and spat on it. He pushed a hand between her legs and realised she was already wet. "You came well prepared to pay my girl." He whispered and pushed his cock into her fanny with some force. "Sweet Jesus! Heaven on earth!" he said with a hoarse voice and started to thrust with some determination.

The woman gripped the edge of the desk with one hand and said nothing. Her other hand gripped the hem of her skirt and petticoats. John's legs were trembling slightly as he pushed her down on the desk, thrusting hard and cussing under his breath. He would have paid nearly a guinea for such a woman in old Ma Tyler's top-class brothel near Prince's Street. The lady asked when he would carry out his mission because she would return and pay him the second half of the fees owed.

John groaned; "Tomorrow afternoon, I'll set out tomorrow afternoon and be back in four days and what is the manner you intend to employ in payment?" The woman was happy with that and leaned back and pulled open the cheeks of her arse and took his hand, pushing a finger into her little brown bum hole. "That's the second part of the payment Sir. I'm sure you will carry out the assignment to my full satisfaction." That was too much for John and he came in her with some real cussing and groaning. The thought of fucking that little bum hole had been too much. He now couldn't wait to get back from Scone castle already!

John sat on his chair gripping his flaccid dick and watched the lady smooth down her skirt and petticoats; "I can go again if you help raise this fucker with your mouth." He groaned and jerked at his cock with some desperation, but the woman just pulled on her coat and hat. She leaned over him and placed a kiss on his cheek. "Until your return I bid you goodbye and good luck with your mission. I do feel I can trust you and your anticipated enjoyment of my little bum hole will spur you on in this happy endeavour." She strode from his office without another word and John realised that he hadn't taken her name!

He started to chuckle and wondered if his luck was changing. "I'll make a fucking success of this business if it kills me." He whispered to himself and thought about Mary; he really wanted to fuck her now, more than the mystery woman. Well, just a little bit more! He dropped his floppy cock and reached for the whisky bottle and glass. He poured himself a large one and took a sip. He picked up the small bag and tipped the contents out; it was several gold sovereigns. He wiped his face and smiled, gathering up the coins and pushing them into his pocket. "It's not like we have a signed and sealed legal contract. Who's going to believe the word of a whore who pays for services with her honey pot?" he laughed and pushed his cock away and decided a drink in the 'Crown' tavern was in order. "Stupid trusting trollop." He quietly muttered to himself and with a spring in his step headed for the tavern. He needed to make plans for his anticipated move to the Highlands.

EPISODE 10. "ALEXANDRA'S MIDNIGHT(S) AT GETTYSBURG."

EPISODE PROLOGUE: "Someone or something is trying to change the outcome of the American Civil War and Mr. Tibbs must prevent the Time-Line from being altered; so it's back to 1863 and the forthcoming Battle of Gettysburg. Jericho must discover the plot and who's behind it and quickly, for he also knows that someone is about to betray the temporal detectives. Is it a spy, time-traveler or something more sinister? Alex has her moments at Midnight; twice and persuades the local Sheriff not to lock her up!"

75 Minutes approx. **Episode Warnings:** Smoking – Alcohol – Strong language [including racial slurs] – Violence [including racial violence and references to combat deaths] – Strong graphic sexual references – Mild horror.

NOTES: The original version of this story is published and appears in the **TEMPORAL DETECTIVES:** Book Series 1– Episode 6 entitled: **"BETRAYAL AT GETTYSBURG. "** This is a special EXTENDED episode of the original story.

CAUTION: Recommended for 18+ only.

Please note: "This Episode contains language that was common for the time; but is now considered racist and offensive; it's included because it reflects the reality of the period and the past cannot and must not be sanitized; it can only be studied and the future improved upon." **SJW.**

1. THE SECRET LOST AT GETTYSBURG.

The rebel picket found the body slumped against a small tree; the young man had been stabbed through the stomach and still clutched his pistol in a dirty, gloved hand. The old sergeant prodded the corpse with his rifle and wiped his face with his free hand. "Fresh, only could have been dead a couple of hours."

The young corporal coughed and pointed to the body; "His been run through with a fuckin' sword I'd say, look at the gap on that cut." A couple of other soldiers stared down at the dead man and one scratched his head; "He's got a cocked pistol in his hand ready to shoot, yet someone got so close that he could run a fuckin' sword through him: that don't make sense!"

The sergeant examined the pistol; it had not been fired. One name came to mind: 'Black sword'.

That's when the old man noticed the dead man's other hand; the remains of a torn piece of paper were still tightly held in his fingers. He pulled it gently from the dead fingers and pushed on his spectacles to read.

"Looks like a piece from some map." He turned the fragment about in his hand and could make out just one place name: 'Gettysburg - 1863'. He stared down at the young dead man and told his Corporal to search the body thoroughly. "I think he could 'ave been riding for the damn Yankee's." The corporal grunted and started through the man's pockets and even searched his hat and boots.

The old sergeant looked about; whoever killed him had probably taken his horse; you couldn't get far around these parts without a horse. Far in the distance he could make out a figure on horseback. He pulled a small brass telescope from his canvas sack and focused on the figure. "God damn it, he's lookin' back at me with a damn scope!" He exclaimed and lowered the small telescope; "Some fella in a yellow dust coat, but he has only one horse with him."

"Look sees Sergeant; this was stashed in a hidden pocket, sewn into his shirt." The young corporal held out a small silver, rectangular box with a black glass front and the sergeant took it carefully, turning it in his hands. "Ain't never seen anythin' like this before." He muttered and struggled to open it. He stared at the inside, as the box was now in a couple of pieces. "What fuckin' useless shit is this?" He laughed and threw the broken box onto the mud and grass.

"Yankee Calvary coming' fast up the road!" One of the pickets waved his hat from the thick bushes on the opposite side of the road and everyone dashed into the relative safety of the woods, to watch the Yankee Calvary patrol ride past.

"Whoever killed that young fella must 'ave robbed him sarge, didn't have a plugged nickel on him." The young corporal shouldered his rifle and fell in behind his colleagues, for the long walk back to the rebel encampment.

The old sergeant nodded and rubbed the fragment of paper between his fingers; he had never seen paper like it and he had spent seventeen years working the presses for the main newspaper at Richmond before joining the colours and fighting in the army of North Virginia under General Robert E. Lee.

"Bloody strange paper and even stranger little useless box." He muttered to himself and wondered why the notorious character' Black sword' had killed the young fella; but then, he didn't have another horse when spotted by the picket; strange stuff indeed. He had heard a couple of rumours about the fella in the yellow dust coat from some boys in the 22nd. Apparently, he had killed two men over Greenbrier way with a fucking sword - a fucking black sword - before they even managed to pull their God damn pistols out!

He chuckled to himself and pushed the paper fragment into his pocket. He would report all that his picket had found to Captain Joe 'Shamrock' Delaney and so he headed for the captains tent. He stared about the growing city of tents, horses, wagons and men. If many more arrive; then a great big battle is in the offering here. He spat and wiped his mouth and beard and told his men to rest and get some grub on. The old sergeant made his way to Captain Delaney's tent, clutching the fragment of strange paper. He passed the two strangers leaving the good captain's tent; they nodded and raised their hats and started to talk quietly with each other. The sergeant laughed; the men called the pair 'Too tall and way too short.'

They were apparently 'whisky drummers' trying to sell their stuff to the officers in the army; probably to both God damn sides! Still, they claimed to be English and so they were 'neutrals' in this bloody war and could visit any side they wanted and sell their whisky to whoever they wanted. It was a very good war for some people, the sergeant mused as he arrived at the captains tent.

He shouted out his name and stood outside until Captain Delaney called him in. The captain was a big, powerful Irish man who came from Virginia and sported a black beard to match his hair and eyes. He was sitting on a rough wooden chair with his boots off, rubbing his feet with whisky and cold water. He took a couple of swigs from the same bottle that he had applied to his feet and coughed.

The sergeant pulled open the tent flap and stepped in; he saluted and stood in silence. Delaney looked up and didn't smile; "What you got for me Frank?" The old sergeant recounted the events of the patrol; the dead body, the piece of strange paper, a Yankee cavalry patrol and that strange fellow who carried an old black sword. Captain Delaney stood and leaned upon the small desk that was cluttered with personal objects and maps.

The sergeant actually jumped when the captain swept everything from the table with one hand - except the whisky bottle and cussed loudly. He grabbed up the bottle and took a long hard swig and cursed some more. Finally, he composed himself and straightened his open tunic. "The bastard in the yellow dust coat killed the boy?" he asked the old soldier with clear anger in his voice. The sergeant nodded that 'Black Sword' must have done so; who else around here carries a fucking black sword?

The captain stared at the fragment of paper and cursed again. "Was any money found on him?" The sergeant said the boy had probably been robbed by whoever killed him. Delaney stared at the old sergeant with some suspicion, but then dismissed him and sent for young Lieutenant Tom Harvey - who he could trust - to inform the local Sheriff; he would pay the man a visit later, to discuss the death.

Alone in his tent, Captain Delaney sat nursing the whisky bottle and then slowly placed the whisky bottle upon the empty table and pulled his officer's truck from the rear of the tent and slowly opened the chest. He rummaged inside for a few seconds and pulled out a dark canvas bag and placed it on the table. Slowly he unwrapped the bundle and ran a hand across the strange object that lay before him.

His thoughts were interrupted by a shout outside his tent; "Sir, the scout Mister Sage is here!" Delaney covered the object up and slumped in his chair. The scout pushed his way in and unbuttoned his long dark dust coat, the two white pearl handled pistols, hanging from each hip were immediately noticeable. The scout folded his arms and stared at the whisky bottle - he said nothing.

"That bastard McIves has killed young Benny and probably has the map." He held up the fragment and then handed Mister Sage the whisky bottle. "Sorry to hear that Joe, I know you liked the boy." Sage took a swig and wiped his mouth, then slapped his dust covered hat against his leg. "It's gonna break his mothers heart when I tell her." Delaney muttered and accepted the bottle back.

"Those two fuckwits I hired with that money you gave me, to kill McIves let him get too close despite all what I told them." Sage grunted and added; "They won't make that mistake again; he killed the pair without getting a scratch." Delaney sighed and placed a hand upon the hilt of his sabre; "If I ever catch up with that bastard, we'll see how good he is with a sword."

Sage nodded and pulled a half-smoked cigar from his coat and placed it in his mouth. Delaney tossed him a large match and Sage struck it against his boot and lit his cigar. "Worse news I'm afraid; that other bastard Jericho Tibbs is on his way here." Delaney groaned and ran several fingers through his beard. "Can you get another copy of that damn map before the fight starts?"

Sage blew smoke from his mouth and nodded; "Yep, but how do we get it here in secret, under that fucker's Tibbs nose; his bound to know about me if McIves is on the scene." Delaney leaned back on his wobbly chair and half smiled; "Just get the map to her and she'll do the rest."

Sage actually chuckled, then picked up the whisky bottle again; "Don't leave this around Joe; those other two retards don't have a clue. You won't be able to buy a bottle like this for another couple of years here in the States." Delaney nodded and accepted the bottle back and placed it in his officer's chest. "No money was found on his body, so McIves must have the money we arranged to pay that slimy little rat for his information. See that he gets what's due to him."

The scout pushed his hat back on and said softly; "That will be a pleasure." He turned and left the captain alone. Sage would make sure that the little rat and his dirty whore of a girlfriend would get what's coming to them. He chuckled and glanced back at the tent, then walked over to Major Canter's HQ located in a small seed barn, by the little stream. Sage chuckled; the Major was a known misogynist and a terrible racist - he also didn't mind killing off the battlefield - a perfect choice.

2. MRS. PHILADELPHIA HAZZARD.

The four riders skirted the little ridge and headed into the quiet green valley; ahead lay a small farmhouse and outbuildings with a solitary horse tied outside. "That's Clem Hazzard's place." Jericho said simply and spurred his mount forward. Wilson looked awkward on his horse - riding horse's wasn't his strong point. "We could have hired a carriage in Gettysburg for the price of these four beasts." He muttered, holding tightly onto the reins.

Jericho smiled at the big man; "Didn't have many horses in the NYPD then?"

Wilson nodded; "Not near me. Damn beasts, all hair and teeth - reminds me of my damn Mother-in-law!" That made Jericho laugh and the little group headed for the farmstead that stood out against the small mountains which made up the background.

Owen was a natural horseman and guided his mount with a light touch and clear skill. "I first rode a pony when I was five. Riding was the one real thing that I missed about home when Father sent me to the Monastery." He spoke to Alex who was riding 'side-saddle' with equal skill and balance.

"I really have difficulty envisioning you as a Monk Owen; you definitely don't have a Monk's attributes." Alex said softly and then saw the woman's figure standing upon the farmhouse's wooden porch, arms folded across her clean white apron, she raised a hand in greeting and Jericho waved back; "That's Philadelphia – Clem's wife."

The little group pulled up at the farmhouse and dismounted, well Wilson didn't quite dismount, he sort of slid from the horse and managed to land on both feet. He growled at Owen, when he gave the big man a little applause.

Owen helped Alex from her saddle whilst Jericho dropped from his mount and handed his reins to Owen, who tied the horses together at the hitch post and then joined the others in the farmhouse. Mrs. Philadelphia Hazzard welcomed her visitors with fresh brewed coffee, biscuits and gravy. They sat at the large dining table, eating and chatting. Philadelphia had been a Temporal Agent for Jericho for some years, joining her husband Clement after they married, who had been working for Mr. Tibbs since his teen years.

Wilson was mopping up his breakfast with gusto and thanked Philadelphia, he had not tasted such good biscuits and gravy since he was a boy and stayed at his grandmother's a couple of times a week. He sat back and grinned; "That makes the damn horse-ride worthwhile!"

Everyone laughed and then the door swung open, and Philadelphia's other guest sauntered into the Dining Room. Jericho and Alex recognized him at once; it was 'Strange-ways Stevens' a well-known train and bank robber who had worked for Jericho on a casual basis over the years. "My guts are giving me gripes and that's the second damn visit to the thunder box in an hour." He moaned and slowly sat down; Philadelphia handed him a black coffee, stirring a large spoonful of sugar into the cup.

"You're not gonna like what I'm about to say Jericho, but you need to know about a strange pair hanging around that blue-belly Army of the Potomac, the one under that General Meade. They stick out like tits on a bull. Apparently, they are English Whisky Drummers, looking to sell their wares. But they isn't right, as I was telling Phil here, they talk real strange and don't know shit about anything. But it's what I caught a glimpse of that will scratch your interest." Strange ways leaned back in the chair and sipped his coffee.

"It was a small, dark rectangular box with a class front that had tiny pictures or drawings on – it fits in your hand and Strange-ways says the little fat one of the pair was whispering into it. The tall skinny one kept looking about while he did it." Philadelphia topped up Owen and Wilson's coffee cups and sat down. Jericho rubbed his chin and sat back; thinking.

Owen looked quite puzzled by that; "How could they use a mobile phone here; there's no satellites or towers to carry the signals and who the hell would they call?" Wilson nodded his agreement at that statement, but Jericho made no comment and only Alex caught the strange look upon his face.

"I take it you know that the Reb army under 'Granny Lee' is about thirty miles south of us, heading north. The Blue-bellies are about the same distance south heading north in pursuit. The Reb's have been using the Mountains to screen their movements. The pair should meet up tomorrow somewhere near Gettysburg and that is gonna be a dandy of a fight!" Strange-ways laughed to himself and drained his coffee cup – looking for a refill.

Jericho turned to his team; "About six weeks ago in this time, there was a breach of the Timeline, and it wasn't a natural hit. Two humans' crossed over from the year 2018. Doc Underhill and his team investigated and found nothing. There have been no changes to the current Timeline, so the pair have kept a very efficient 'Low Profile' here – until now, I suspect. But just a few months ago a breech occurred, and someone crossed over from 2016 - why are time travelers arriving here in force, at this time and place? "

"The battle." Alex said quietly, adding "They were going to try and change the outcome of the most important battle of the American Civil war; but how?"

"Don't forget your old friend - McIves was reported in this year some months ago - is that another coincidence?" Wilson sat back and sipped his coffee, but Jericho just nodded and finished his breakfast. He already knew that McIves was creeping around the place, and he wondered what the odd fellow was up to?

"I ain't told you the best bit yet, Jericho." Strange ways accepted more coffee from Philadelphia and some fruit cake to help ease his growling stomach; "Them strange pair have been seen hanging around with an actor, who we know works for General Longstreet; he commands the Reb's First Corps under old 'Granny Lee'. The actor was the bugger that warned the Reb's about the Yankee's movements; he has the ear and confidence of Jim Longstreet. So, what if them pair from the hereafter, get the damn actor to rat out the Yankee's plan's and change what the South intend to do here?"

Jericho nodded and smiled; but said nothing in reply. He glanced across at Alex and she took up the conversation.

Alex sipped her coffee; "Where's Clem, Philly?"

Philadelphia sat back down and gripped her cup with both hands; "He's over at the Mercy Hospital; old Doc Hogan is down with the fever again, so he has to help out." Alex placed her cup upon the table and smiled; Clem Hazzard could never turn his back on a cry for help!

Jericho considered what he had heard and pushed his hands through his dark wavy hair and sat back in the rough chair; Doctor Clement Hazzard was a man of principle – that's what Jericho liked and admired about the man – and that hospital will surely need all the Doctors and Surgeons it can get hold of, in the next few days.

"I'll catch up with Clem when we ride to Gettysburg; is there anything you want us to deliver Philly?" Jericho leaned forward and drained his cup. The others knew that was a signal to finish their late breakfasts and get ready to saddle up again. Wilson groaned to himself, his arse and thighs were already feeling the effects of the short ride from their 'Jump Point' and he really didn't relish another couple of hours on the back of that damn horse.

Philadelphia smiled and rose up quickly from her chair and smoothed down her apron; "There is indeed Jericho; I'll fetch them from the kitchen." Philly had prepared two apple pies; one for her husband who adored apple pie and another for Jericho's team. The thought of her apple pie produced a smile on Wilson's face, and he volunteered to look after the pies. Owen commented that he would also look after the pies, particularly from Wilson!

3. THE BOARDING HOUSE.

Old Strange-way's muttered that he was never given pies; by anyone, never mind Philadelphia. But cheered up when Philly told him he could finish up the biscuits and gravy. Then Jericho took strange ways to one side and gave him some instructions and several silver Dollars, which put an even bigger smile upon his face. The foursome stated their goodbyes and mounted up, heading down the rough road to Gettysburg.

"We'll get rooms at old Ma Crabb's boarding house, just on the outside of the town, The Rebel army will occupy the town tomorrow and we'll be away from it there." Jericho informed Alex as the group rode towards the North Gettysburg turnpike with some determination.

It was Wilson's sharp eye that caught the figure trailing some miles behind them, a lone horseman with a distinctive bright yellow dust coat. "He's been behind us since we left the Hazzard's place." Wilson told Jericho, but the group didn't slow or change course and reached the boarding house a couple of hours later. They could see the figure in the distance, and it vanished beyond small woodland – heading south.

"Heading towards blue or grey?" Wilson grinned and they dismounted; Owen walked the horses towards the Boarding House's Livery stable, tossing a silver dollar in the air that Jericho had given him to pay the stable boy. They walked into the lobby of the house and were sourly greeted by old Ma Crabb's eldest daughter, Victoria. A sour faced spinster in her late thirties with dark greasy hair and missing teeth – she didn't smile when she looked up from her paperwork on the front desk; "You'll have to keep your n****er outside; Negro servants sleep in the stables loft room." She said simply and gestured towards the door; "We only charge two bits for that." She added and again pointed towards the door; "Go on boy, just follow the damn horses." Before Wilson could comment, Jericho tugged gently on his sleeve and nodded towards the door; "You knew to expect this type of crap. Remember, we need to keep a low profile."

But Alex was having none of 'this type of crap': "Mister Wilson is a free man and entitled to respect and proper treatment when he's paying for a room here!" She tapped the desk gently with her hand and added quietly; "He's name is MISTER Wilson Franklyn for your register."

Miss Victoria Crabb actually smiled and folded her arms, nodding her head she muttered; "You don't say Missy!" Standing in the doorway to the kitchen was another woman; tall and thin, wearing a drab grey dress and watching the row develop between Victoria and the beautiful young lady. Smiling, she was clutching a handful of old books that Ma Crabb had given her for the school.

Miss Lillian then noticed the young man standing next to the lovely lady and her smile vanished; "Fucking Jericho Tibbs." She whispered to herself and wondered where young Benny was. Samuel, Ma Crabb's grandson ran past her and through the kitchen door towards the yard, all excited. His aunt (Victoria) had sent him to fetch Sheriff Rook, to the full-blown argument happening in Reception.

Miss Lillian sighed and followed the boy through the kitchen and into the street. Young Samuel was already pushing through the doors of the Sheriff's office, shouting. Miss Lillian stood quietly in the street, as several Union Troopers rode past the dry goods store behind her. She knew that the battle was only a day away now and nothing must interfere with the plan. She would tell Rook to tread carefully in his dealings with that bastard Tibbs.

It was with some relief to her that Jacob 'pudding' Davis wandered from the Jail with Samuel next to him. Sheriff Rook's deputy was fat, useless, and avoided any kind of confrontations - if he could; she would be able to manipulate him easily. Miss Lillian called Jacob and Samuel over and spoke quietly to the sweating deputy who constantly wiped his face and neck in the late sunshine.

Apparently the good Sheriff was in the Mayor's Office, being briefed about the two enormous armies that were converging on the town, along with the entire town council. They were clearly trying to avoid any panic setting in. Most hoped that the Union army would occupy the town before the rebels and confine the fighting to the fields and roads around Gettysburg. Miss Lillian chuckled at that; some hope! Suitably 'advised' by Miss Lillian, the reluctant Jacob headed for the reception area, hitching up his wide trousers and nervously adjusting the badge that hung from his dirty white shirt; stained with sweat and food debris. She watched him go and headed for the rear of the undertaker's, where Troy and Dauphin would be waiting with the wagon and for her instructions. But all she could think of was Benny.

The loft above the barn was quite large and packed with hay; Wilson and Jericho were still chuckling to themselves as they laid blankets out and prepared to settle in for the night. "Well, you told old sour face straight baby girl!" Wilson smiled broadly and eased his sore back down upon the hay and laughed to himself – again. "Fancy not knowing what 'racist' means." He turned to Jericho and whispered; "But she certainly knew what 'white trash' meant!"

Jericho grinned and sighed, pulling the blanket about his shoulders. Old Ma Crabb had intervened before the row at the front desk actually required the local Sheriff being called. His useless deputy: Jacob had done nothing really - except stare at Alex and wipe his fat face – It could have been the worst outcome possible for a team of temporal Detectives trying to keep a low profile.

But old Ma Crabb settled the matter: for a dollar they could all sleep in the hay loft. "Sorry boy's, I sort of lost my head a little there." Alex explained and pulled bits of straw from her hair and skirts. But the rest of the team rejected her apology with some humour; "I think the best bits were frustrated old spinster and pea-brained." Owen said quietly and chuckled loudly.

"Let's get some sleep people; we have a long day tomorrow." Jericho said and still smiling, curled up in his rough blanket. "White trash was my favourite part." He softly added and drifted off to sleep.

In the street below the loft's big window, a lone horseman pulled his bright yellow dust coat off and watched the lamp light flickering through the glass and also smiled. He rattled the little black drawstring bag which contained ten silver Yankee dollars – apparently a down payment for some murder.

4. BEFORE MIDNIGHT IN THE STABLES.

Alex slipped away very quietly and crept down the back stairs of the stable and found the horseman by the rear doors. He smiled broadly and the pair embraced with some passion. Alex kissed him and whispered; "we don't have long darling. The boys and I are sleeping in the hay loft, thanks to my big mouth."

McIves just chuckled and kissed that 'big mouth' gently. Alex grabbed his hand and they disappeared into a vacant horse box and McIves tossed down his saddle blanket. There was plenty of moon light streaming through the big window for the lovers to enjoy each other in the shadows. They didn't undress fully; McIves pulled down his trousers and 'long John's', gripping hold of his big erection, whilst Alex tugged down her big bloomers with some difficultly and put them to one side. She looked relieved to get the bloody things off.

McIves gestured to her tight bodice; "Get them out for me darling. You know how nuts I am about your big titties and especially, those bloody nipples of yours." Alex sighed but pulled open the bodice and her magnificent big tits popped out; nipples erect. McIves grunted his satisfaction with that and told Alex to use her bag as a pillow; he would fuck her in the good old fashioned 'Missionary Position'. Then they would swap to doggy style because he wanted to fuck her arse.

Alex shook her head; "I'm not letting that bloody thing of yours up my bum without proper lubricant." She folded her arms and didn't smile. McIves simply grinned and produced a small jar of Vaseline from his pocket. "Came prepared my darling. Now open your bloody legs!" He climbed on top of her without further comment. She held onto his shoulders, as he pushed his big cock into her wet vagina - after slapping a little Vaseline on the tip and stem - and started to thrust with a growing smile on his face. Leaning on one hand, he gripped a big tit and stuck his mouth over the nipple. He sucked and squeezed hard. Alex was really trying to keep herself from moaning loudly; sounds would carry far at night, especially in a quiet town with two bloody big armies facing each other on the outskirts. People would tend to shoot first and find out later who they shot.

Alexander McIves was thoroughly enjoying Alex. She was taking his big cock really well and keeping the damn noise down. He fucked her hard in the straw and simply didn't hear or see the man behind him. He heard the safety come off the rifle and felt the cold end of its barrel on the back of his neck. "Easy there boy, just pull your cock from the slut and get on your back. No quick moves or I'll blow you both to hell."

McIves stared into Alex's eyes, and she whispered; "Do as he says, the bloody rifle is pointed straight at your head." McIves nodded and slowly pulled from Alex and rolled onto his back. He slowly tucked his cock away and stared at the man with the gun, who smiled at Alex's open legs and fanny. He grunted; "Fucking McIves! I might have known; poking a dam whore in the back of a stable at midnight with two fucking big armies about to kick shit out of each other. Only you my old friend, could be that brazen!"

Sage Columbine snapped on the safety and swung his rifle onto his shoulder and eased onto a large harness and tackle box. He pulled out a half-smoked cigar and stuck it in his mouth. He gestured to Alex, who was pulling down her skirt and petticoats. She sat in the straw and pushed her heaving breasts back into her bodice. "Who's the bloody great looking whore? Can you afford a tart like that?" He slapped his coat pocket and some coins jingled; "Shit man, how much is she? I bet she's a fucking five-dollar whore."

McIves rose from the straw and shook his head. "Thanks for the warning about those two idiots Delaney sent after me. I owe you one. Her name is Alex; she's a good friend of mine." Sage nodded and gestured back to Alex who was staring at the big rough man with deep blue eyes and big shoulders. "I really wish I had a good friend like that; even if she charged me full price."

"You two know each then?" She said quietly. Sage chuckled; "Yes my girl. We sure do." McIves helped Alex up and smiled; "Sage and I have worked together since we met up at the battle of Bull Run. He's from 1925 originally." Alex sighed: another bloody time traveller, the bloody place was full of them.

"Ah, she's that bloody time cop your always on about. Man, she could arrest me any day." McIves grunted and then stared into the stable; there was a man's figure lying in the dirt.

"Who's that?" He asked Sage who chuckled; "Some fucker who was about to shoot first and ask about you later. I think they were about to off you and take turns with the girl. You have quite

a few enemies my friend." McIves slapped Sage on the arm;
"Another one I owe you." Sage chuckled again; "Forget about it
man, you pulled me out the shit as many times." He rose from
the box and tipped his hat at Alex, adding; "The other bastard
got away. So, watch your back. Keep your rifle in one hand, fuck
your friend doggy style and keep an eye out. No one is going to
shoot that piece of honey."

He disappeared out the door and the pair walked into the stable
and stared at the body. McIves turned it over and grunted;
"Don't know him." Alex grabbed her bag and pulled out her
mirror. "His name is Joseph Bell from 1971; No wonder a
Collector didn't appear when your friend killed him." Alex sighed;
this was getting ridiculous; there were sodding time travelers
everywhere. "Still don't know him and never will." was all McIves
said, and they left the stables. They kissed in the moonlight and
parted; McIves disappearing into the darkness, walking his horse.

Alex sighed and then realised she needed to pee; her fanny was
still full of bloody Vaseline from their unfinished lovemaking. She
walked back around the stables and found a quiet spot, in a small
woodshed and squatted down. She groaned a little with relief as
she pissed hard on the floor. She almost jumped and pissed on
her damn shoes, as she heard the soft voice chuckle; "Alex, your
one hell of a woman!"

5. AFTER MIDNIGHT IN THE WOODSHED.

She saw Sage sitting on some uncut wood, smoking the cigar
stub. He smiled and tipped his hat back, adding; "Something real
sexy and arousing about a woman with her skirt up, fanny open
and pissing in front of a man. God dam, it's some turn on." Alex
couldn't stop and had to finish. She stood up and didn't pull her
dress down. She said quietly; "I should really thank you for
saving me from those two. I should also thank you for saving
McIves. They two would have had us easily."

Sage nodded and rose from the wood and walked up to her. He
simply took hold of her and pushed her against the wall. His
hands pulled open her bodice and grabbed her heaving breasts.
His mouth was on her nipples, and he was squeezing hard. Her
hands ran down and pulled open the button on his trousers and
her eager hands grabbed his cock. She was still sexually aroused
from the failed love making with McIves; she needed cock, and

she needed it now! "Sweet Lord, you certainly could make a girl happy with this." She whispered as the big cock came alive in her hands. As it grew, she thanked heaven for the Vaseline, that was still smeared around and in her vagina; she would need it, to take this monster. Sage's mouth and tongue found hers and they crashed together. His hands gripped her hips and she pulled herself into his big strong arms. His cock found her vagina like a ferret down a rabbit hole. Alex wrapped her long legs around his waist and her arms around his big shoulders. He drove his cock into her hard and deep. Her groans were subdued by his tongue buried in her mouth. He fucked her hard against the shaking wall for some minutes, then lowered her onto the floor and continued to fuck her hard in the missionary position.

They rolled about on the dirt floor. Like desperate animals. She managed a couple of squirts and gripped his shirt and trousers. He said nothing but thrusted hard and quick, gasping a little and feasting on her big shaking tits. Quite brutally, he held her down and started to fuck her harder; then roughly pulled his cock from her and rolled Alex onto her stomach. He pulled her dress up and threw it over her head. She felt those big rough hands, pull apart the cheeks of her arse and she couldn't help groaning quite loudly as he pushed his cock into her anus. She thanked heaven for that bloody Vaseline that now covered his cock. He fucked her quivering bum hole hard, and Alex covered her mouth with both hands and squirted again; her cum splashing into the dirt.

Sage gave no quarter to her arse and fucked it hard. Finally, he pulled out his dirty cock and dragged Alex's head around to him and shoved it into her mouth; she sucked for about a minute before he exploded onto her tongue and down her throat. She swallowed the sour tasting cum in a couple of gulps; she could taste her own arse in the semen. He kept his cock in her mouth for some minutes and so, she continued to suck and lick it with some relish. Finally, he eased it from her mouth and wiped it against her face. He grunted and patted her head like a dog. "I think that's the sort of thanks I really do like." He pulled her up and kissed each breast, then pushed his cock back into his trousers and did the buttons up slowly. Alex was gasping and panting, she wiped her mouth and face with her pulled up petticoats.

Sage picked up his rifle and dust coat, then walked to the door. He turned and smiled; "You're a good girl Alex. McIves deserves a woman like you. Until we meet and fuck again. Goodnight my sweet little lady." He waved and was gone. Alex managed to tidy herself up and brush down her dress. She pushed her breasts back into the bodice and slowly walked out the woodshed. She just managed to stop herself screaming. Young Samuel, Ma Crabb's grandson was standing with an illicit cigarette, smoking, and grinning; "Christ Miss darkie lover, you are just what Aunty Vicki said you were; a fucking whore. How much did you charge him for that fuck up your dirt box? I bet it was at least two dollars worth!"

Alex was about to say something, when the boy held up her bloomers and laughed again; "I'm gonna give these to the Sheriff and tell him about you loving darkies and getting fucked in the shit hole for money." He quickly ran off into the night, leaving Alex really angry and upset. She crept back into the hay loft and laid down, managing to fall asleep. Her arse ached, but the little animal inside of her had been well satisfied by Sage Columbine and his rough sex with her.

6. ASSISTANCE FROM A STRANGE PLACE.

Alex suddenly sat up and rubbed her eyes gently. She looked about the hay loft and wondered why she had woken up - it was still dark.

The lamp was casting a dull yellow light about the place and she could smell something sweet. Jericho also stirred and sat up, as something dropped from his chest into the hay, he pushed about and pulled up a small black drawstring bag, wrapped in a piece of paper, held by a length of green string.

Wilson leaned upon his elbows and nodded to the bag Jericho held up; "That sounds like coins rattling." Jericho opened the handwritten note carefully and held it by the lamp. The look upon his face was priceless; he coughed and shook his head in disbelief. "What does it say?" Owen asked, yawing and stretching - he was used to being aroused from sleep in the middle of night - life in the monastery had seen to that. "I almost started praying again." He chuckled to himself, kneeling in the soft hay.

Everyone looked at Alex as she held the single red rose up for all to see. "Where does anyone get a fresh cut English rose in the middle of America in 1863?" She asked with real bewilderment in her voice, adding; "I found it next to my bag." She was using it as a makeshift pillow.

Jericho tossed the bag a couple of times, and everyone heard the coins it contained; "Ten silver dollars paid to a certain 'Black eyed Benny' for a little murder." He spoke softly and pushed the bag into his coat pocket.

"Murder of who?" Wilson asked and Jericho smiled a little; "Me." He said simply. Alex accepted the note from Jericho and read it aloud;

"Jericho, I believe someone paid 'Black eyed Benny' - a new young killer - ten silver dollars to end your time here. You won't be able to question Benny's soul; he was originally from 2016! When I encountered him, he was a carrying a torn map of Gettysburg and Ma Crabb's boarding house was marked on it. I suspect someone knows you and why your here. Go carefully. McIves."

There was silence for a few seconds and Jericho started to chuckle, taking the note from Alex, and placing it with the money bag. "Bloody McIves!" He muttered and slumped back into the hay and consulted his small fob watch, which was set to local time, it showed 4.45 am.

"The sun will be up in an hour." He looked through the large window and could see the flickering of several blazing torches. Wilson wandered to the window and peered out; "Looks like a couple of Sheriff Deputies are bringing a body slung over a horse." He turned and smiled at Jericho; "Young 'Black eyed Benny' I would assume."

"Why would he help us; McIves I mean?" Owen asked, pulling bits of straw from his hair and jacket. Jericho didn't answer, but sat thoughtfully rubbing his chin, wondering what McIves was doing here in 1863 and more importantly; who else knows that temporal detectives are on scene?

Jericho looked up and could see his three colleagues grouped around the hayloft window, watching Sheriff Theodore Rook's men unloading the body outside the jail, which was directly opposite the stables. "They are telling the Sheriff that rebel troops are camped just a few miles from here. But no rebel cavalry has been seen and that's strange apparently." Owen called back to Jericho, still brushing himself down from the straw.

"No cavalry, did you say no cavalry?" Jericho asked and pulled his mirror from the depths of his frock coat pockets. Own walked back over and helped Alex brush down her coat; "Yeah, they seemed to be fascinated that the rebels have no real cavalry with them." Jericho read, then re-read his mirror and nodded to himself. That could well be the answer to why there were repeated breeches to the timeline, here at this period and place.

A thought crept into his head and Jericho had a very strong feeling he could be on the right line of thinking here - the rebel cavalry arrived too late to really influence the outcome of the battle - a defeat for the rebels. What if someone managed to get the rebel cavalry here nice and early? Would that be enough to change the result? Who could do that? Or was he missing something else?

7. THE PIE THAT CHANGED EVERYTHING.

The team took breakfast at Brady's eating house on South Street and rather strangely - to Jericho and his team - none of the early morning patrons objected to Wilson sitting at the table with his white friends. They had told the owner; Tom Brady, that they were reporters from the Citizens Compiler Newspaper, based in Washington DC, and was covering the exploits of the Union Army.

The large camera, tripod and film cases carried by Wilson and Owen drew attention, with many amazed that a black man could take photographs, but they were truly amazed when told that Alex was a reporter working for that title.

One dissenting patron paid his bill and left muttering; "N****rs and women working together, what the fuck next?" Tom Brady half smiled and almost apologised to them for the man's comments; "That's Billy Logan; he and his family are dirt farmers who fled Carolina at the start of the war - they didn't want to fight for anyone - rebels or union. He's all mouth; don't pay any mind to him."

But one man did pay some attention to the little group of strangers; Sheriff Theodore Rook finished up his plate and sipped his coffee, watching Jericho and his team carefully over his cup. He threw a couple of bits on the table and wiped his face with a napkin. Standing, he looked down at his fat and already sweating deputy; "I'm gonna have words with them strangers from the east; stay here."

He walked slowly to their table, scatter gun slung over his shoulder. Sheriff Rook was in his early forties and a former cattle man who had fallen on hard times before he was elected Sheriff - after he shot dead two outlaws - trying to rob the local post office. He was known as fair, but hard - you didn't mess with Rook unless you were prepared to pull your pistol and use it.

Jericho rose slowly from his chair and held out his hand; "Good morning, Sheriff, my colleagues and I are getting some breakfast before we head to the union camp. We're reporters from..." But Jericho never finished his greeting, Sheriff Rook waved his hand aside; "I heard tell who you people are. Old ma Crabb's grandson painted a pretty picture 'bout what occurred at his grandma's boarding house."

The table went silent, except for Owen deliberately slurping his coffee and Alex stared at the big man, who was wearing a bright red waistcoat with a silver star pinned to it. The sheriff wiped his face with a gaudy yellow hankie and blew his nose. "I hear tell that this pretty little thing told Victoria, in no uncertain terms, what she thought of her."

Jericho coughed slightly and nodded.

"Well, you being reporters and the like, I'm sure old Ma Crabb wouldn't want her name plastered across the Northern papers, so I'll leave it at that. I got damn two huge armies sitting on my porch and a young fella killed with a damn sword to sort. Just keep your noses clean, that's all I ask."

He turned to go, but stopped and spoke to Jericho again; "You reporters like to stick your snouts in people's business, don't you?" he didn't wait for Jericho to reply, adding; "Never mind the Rebels or Yankee's, you should speak to Miss Lillian, the school ma'am. She'll tell you a story to curdle your milk and that's a fact. You'll find her place next to the schoolhouse on the Old Turner's Pike. She ain't been here long, but she knows her stuff alright." He actually chuckled and wandered out the café, with his

Fat deputy in tow. The group finished their breakfast and made their way back to the stables in relative silence. They passed a couple of black labourers, loading a wagon, who stopped and raised their hats to Alex and Wilson.

"Word spreads quickly. We need to be really careful now - especially you and Wilson." Jericho spoke softly to Alex, adding; "Whatever our feelings are about the people of this period, we must complete the mission; can you imagine the future if the South win this battle?" Alex nodded, but said nothing, thinking what on earth the local schoolteacher knew, that would interest reporters, here to cover the union army. But maybe the Sheriff does.

8. SHERIFF ROOK.

Alex made her way to the Sheriff's office and found him alone; in the back room cleaning a rifle. His big deputy had been sent to a family argument at the Barber's. He looked up as she appeared in the doorway and smiled; "Well, I wondered when you would turn up here sweet thing. I didn't want to ruin your standing with your colleagues, speaking to you at Bradley's place. I mean, what would they say, if they knew their respected friend sold her fanny and arse to damn men like McIves, who's wanted for murder and that Rebel scout; Sage, who's killed more people that damn smallpox."

He reached into the desk and pulled out Alex's missing bloomers. "Got the evidence and a witness; I can charge you with being a common prostitute, unlawful and un-natural sex, committing acts of gross indecency in a public place and that's just for starters. My friend Judge Harold Caine will give you five to seven at that woman's prison. Now, big mouth how does that sound?"

Alex smiled broadly and walked up to his desk; "Now come on Sheriff, a good Boston Lawyer would make hay with those charges, you know that." The sheriff grinned, gesturing to the cells; "Yeah, you're probably right, but that would mean the trial wouldn't be held for months. In that little room, you would wait; for months."

Alex stared at the small room, a bed and bucket the only furniture. She knew that this incident would be hard to explain to her colleagues, without revealing what was going on with her and

McIves; A wanted fugitive from Temporal Justice. She turned to the sheriff and smiled, as he pulled the cell keys from his desk; "I'm sure we can work something out here sheriff?"

Sheriff Theodore Rook stared at her and rubbed his chin; "What you got in mind sweet thing?"

Alex was bent over the sheriff's desk, her skirt and petticoats held above her bum, and she was trying to read the reports on his desk; something about missing gunpowder. She yelped and turned her head to the sheriff, who was standing behind her, thrusting his cock deep into her bum hole. "Careful Sheriff, I'm not lubricated properly, and you are in my back passage, for heaven's sake!" He just grunted and continued to bury his hard cock in her arsehole, gripping her wobbling bum cheeks with both hands. "You got a wonderful arse sweet thing." He muttered and leaned over her, getting deep as he could go. Alex held her skirts and petticoats with one hand now; the other gripped the desk.

"Sweet bugger, you shove that any deeper into my back passage and I'll feel your cum hitting the back of my throat." She groaned, bent fully over the desk, both hands gripping it now. The old sheriff was using every inch of her anus and thrusting hard. He gave her little pink bottom a couple of slaps and reached round to her breasts. "Get them big titties of yours out sweet thing. I'll have some of them."

Alex sighed and unbuttoned her dress; His hand was in there in an instant and he wasn't gentle; squeezing her breasts and particularly pinching her nipples between thumb and forefinger. "When I've emptied by baby sauce in your back passage; I'm going to spend some time suckling on them." He said and groaned a little; but didn't stop thrusting his cock in Alex's back side. Alex was staring at the dirty floor, with teeth gritted; she had never suspected that the old sheriff would last this long in her arse; especially after she had sucked his cock so hard - really hard - for almost fifteen minutes. She pulled up on her elbows and groaned a little; "Are you going to cum any time soon?" She asked, but Sheriff Rook just chuckled; "No sweet thing, it'll be while yet. But I do come real quickly, if the lady does a little something special for me."

Alex's bum was already tender enough and she really wanted the old sheriff to cum and get this damn well over, "What little something special is that sheriff?" She asked, wishing to save her backside from more abuse. She was actually starting to get sore now. He whispered in her ear, and she sighed - loudly - and nodded; "Anything to get you to bloody cum."

The old sheriff sat on his chair with Alex on his lap. Her skirt and petticoat pulled right up, and he was carefully peering over her shoulder. He was still quite firm and buried up to his balls in her arse. She was facing the desk, with her legs wide open and pulled up. "Come on sweet thing, get going." The sheriff sounded quite inpatient. Alex shook her head and grimaced; "I can't force it, it'll happen when it does." The sheriff was gripping a loose tit with each hand and squeezing hard.

Alex sighed, then yelped; "I think it's happening!" The sheriff groaned with real pleasure as Alex started to piss. She realised that Sage was right about a woman pissing in front of a man; that it was a big turn on for them. Her stream of piss was hitting the metal bucket on the floor below the chair with some force. Suddenly, Alex gripped her skirt hem as she felt the old sheriff filling her back passage with his cum. "Thank heaven for that," She whispered, then stared at the doorway.

Sour faced Miss Victoria Crabb and her nephew - the nasty, peeping little shit - Samuel were standing there. Samuel waved a fist in the air and shouted; "That's it sheriff, give the dirty darky loving whore a good poking in her dirt box!"

Miss Victoria slapped the boy about the head and told him to go home. He left really reluctantly, and Miss Victoria walked over to the desk and sat on the other chair clutching her handbag with both hands. Alex slowly pulled down her dress and half smiled. The sheriff grunted and not very gently pulled his flaccid cock from Alex's arse; finally. He coughed; "What can I do for you?" "Not in front of the whore Teddy." was all she said, as Alex pushed her tits back into the bodice and slowly lifted from Rook's lap. She felt his cum ooze from her gaped bum hole and run down the back of her legs. She straightened her clothes and turned to sheriff Rook; "Have I sorted that little problem about the charges out now Sheriff?" Rook nodded and slapped her arse hard. "You sure have sweet thing, now get."

Alex walked quite awkwardly to the door and only heard the start of the conversation between Miss Victoria Crabb and Sheriff Theodore Rook; it was about money and a very quick marriage; it appears that Miss Crabb was expecting a happy little event and the Sheriff was involved in it somehow.

Alex chuckled to herself and then realised she needed a proper sit-down toilet. Having cum poured into her bum was like having a bloody enema sometimes. She only just made the 'Thunderbox [toilet] behind the Hotel. She sat - much relieved - and wondered about the sheriff and Miss Crabb. Then realised she hadn't asked him a single damn question about the bloody School Ma'am or recovered her frigging bloomers!

9. THE GUNPOWDER PLOT.

They quickly saddled the horses and that's when Wilson noticed the open saddlebag, he peered inside and shouted to Owen; "Someone has lifted a pie!" Owen and Alex joined him and agreed that one pie had gone. "It's the one with Clem's name on - thankfully." Wilson said with some humour. But Owen pointed down to a large stack of straw and quietly said; "There's a ragged old boot sticking out and I think there's a leg attached to it."

Wilson kicked the boot and told the owner to stand up - he had actually drawn his revolver. But a skinny boy emerged from the bale of hay, armed only with an empty pie dish. He had a well-worn confederate infantry uniform hung about him; at least a couple of sizes too large. Alex sighed; the boy was even younger than Owen; a deserter from the army now camped a few miles away.

He was shaking and Alex slowly took the pie dish from him; "Put it down Wilson, he has no gun and he's just a boy." That's when she saw the piece of paper stuck to the pie dish and prised it from the still sticky bottom.

Jericho quietly accepted the paper from Alex, who was now giving the boy water from her canteen. "Since when did America in 1863 have laminated paper?" Wilson asked with some apparent sarcasm in his voice.

The paper was unfolded in silence and Jericho held it up for his team to see; it was the battle plan showing the first day of fighting at Gettysburg - a laminated photocopy taken from a very famous book of the battle - printed in 1986.

Jericho pushed the map into his coat; "Can you imagine if this map fell into Rebel hands. It would change the outcome of the battle, the war and world history in one foul blow."

"I don't want to state the obvious, but what the fuck was the map doing hidden in Clem Hazzard's apple pie?" Owen gave the boy some biscuits he had saved from breakfast and added; "There's only one person that could have placed it under the pie and why the hell would she do that?"

Jericho pulled the money bag from his coat pocket that McIves had left with him and tossed it in the air a couple of times, the coins rattling together; "These are the same ten silver dollar coins that I gave 'Strangeways's Stevens' yesterday and where did we last see him?"

"At Philadelphia's place." Owen said and sighed; "And that's where the pie came from."

"We've been played for suckers Jericho." Wilson sat on an upturned crate and shook his head with some sadness. The young deserter raised a bandaged hand nervously; "Do you mean doc Hazzard?"

 Alex nodded and the boy waved his injured hand about; "He fixed my hand up, a couple of days ago before I decided that the army wasn't for me. He's two friends gave him whisky for free and said that Captain Delaney would get the prize, when young black eyes turned up."

"Doc Hazzard was drinking with a confederate captain and two whisky drummers, is that what you're saying?" Jericho asked the boy directly, who nodded yes vigorously, adding: "He said the south was about to rise again; I didn't understand that Sir, we ain't down yet!"

Alex saw the expression change on Jericho's face and that puzzled her; "What's up Jericho?" She asked quietly and Jericho pulled her aside and whispered; "Oh yes, we've been played for suckers - but nothing is always what it seems." He actually grinned and tossed the boy a couple of silver dollars; "Get yourself some clothes that won't draw the attention of your Adjutant Generals men. Best you get out of the city on the quick. Go now!"

The boy pocketed the coins and profusely thanking everyone, disappeared through the rear door of the stables. Alex folded her arms and smiled at Jericho; "What have you just worked out; I see it on your face."

Jericho shrugged his shoulders; "We best join that young boy and get out the city too." They left the stables and mounted up, heading out to the foothills.

It was Wilson who spotted the schoolhouse and a shabby timber-built bungalow standing some yards away. There was a single horse wagon tied up outside and Owen pointed out, that the two labourers who raised their hats to Alex and Wilson, had been loading the same wagon back in Gettysburg. "Must have been collecting some supplies for Miss Lillian." He said, and then noticed that the wagon was deep in the dirt. "It's certainly loaded with something heavy."

Jericho waved his group towards the buildings, and they tied their horses outside. "I can hear something; like a woman moaning." Owen lifted his hat and wiped his face. Jericho and Alex walked to the side window of the bungalow and peered through the dirty glass, whilst Owen and Wilson checked the wagon.

Alex actually put her hand over her mouth to stop amazed laughter from blurting out - Jericho just shook his head and smiled a little: Miss Lillian, a skinny forty-year-old 'respectable', white schoolteacher was quite naked apart from her little ankle boots and sandwiched between the two black labourers, who oddly enough, were also stark naked, apart from their boots. Miss Lilly was now moaning loudly and shouting that the boys should fuck her harder; especially the one in her arse.

Alex and Jericho turned away and chuckled, as Wilson and Owen approached - they were both grim faced - Wilson jerked a thumb towards the wagon; "You had better see what's under that canvas sheet Jericho." He asked Alex about what had made her laugh. She pointed to the window; "You best take a look." Alex giggled a little, which intrigued Wilson and Owen further, who both went straight to the window.

Alex and Jericho walked to the wagon and pulled the filthy canvas tarpaulin open a little and peered in. Jericho rubbed his chin and said quietly to Alex; "What the hell would a bloody schoolteacher want with ten barrels of gunpowder; there's enough there to blow up a small town." They were joined by Wilson and Owen; laughing and wiping their faces; "That's one old white spinster that don't mind coloured folk!" Wilson managed to say between chuckles. Owen said nothing; he was apparently still a bit shocked at what he had seen. Finally, he turned to Wilson and asked; "How is it possible....I mean doing it with two men at the same time?" But he smiled Alex who really grinned; he should be on the bloody stage!

Alex patted Wilson on the shoulder and between giggles said, "We'll leave you to explain that one to our resident novice monk." They returned to their horses and rode a small distance from the settlement and dismounted. Jericho and the team concealed themselves in a clump of trees. They passed a brandy bottle amongst themselves and waited. It was about half an hour later that the two men emerged from the bungalow and climbed aboard the wagon.

They headed it south along Old Turner's Pike and their singing could be faintly heard. "There, at the rear of the bungalow." Owen suddenly rose from the trees and pointed down to the settlement. From the rear of the bungalow came a single rider; it was Miss Lillian, and she was following the wagon at a distance.

"In this time and place, a white woman just being seen alone with black men could get them lynched." Jericho said grimly and they mounted up and followed the little convoy. It stopped outside a small grey stone-built farmhouse and the two men jumped from the wagon and pulled back the tarpaulin. That's when Jericho and his team spotted the group of riders coming into the farmyard from the south lane.

Watching from a small ridge, Jericho pulled his mirror and scanned the buildings and yards. "There doesn't appear to be anyone in the building - no wait - there are two men inside with shovels and crowbars!" His team was concealed by the ridge they hid behind but could see down into the small farm.

"What the fuck are they doing?" Whispered Owen and then he gripped Jericho's arm; "Jericho, according to my mirror we're on Seminary Ridge; along the Chambersburg Pike and that's seems an important place during the forthcoming battle - my mirror has called it up - this house belongs to an old widowed lady: Mary Thompson."

Jericho was watching the five riders dismounting and greeting Miss Lillian, who had now joined the group. "Well Sheriff Rook and his large deputy are two of them, who's the other three men?" Alex whispered to Jericho who suddenly sat up and asked Owen to repeat what he had just said - which he did.

Jericho wiped his face and pointed down to the house; "This house belongs to the widow Thompson and during the battle, it was the Headquarters of the Confederate Army of North Virginia. General Robert E. Lee will direct his army from here." Everyone sat in silence as they watched the barrels of gunpowder being unloaded. Large white grain sacks - empty - were also removed from the wagon by the two men and handed over to Sheriff Rook.

Wilson grunted; "Look there, those two men. One is tall and skinny and the other is short and fat. Do you think they are our whisky drummers?" Jericho nodded, he now had a pretty good idea of the plan was and it certainly wasn't about changing the outcome of the battle; the North will still win here.

"They're filling the sacks with powder - very carefully - I must say." Alex spoke softly and realised she needed to pee. Muttering her excuses, headed for a nearby thick clump of bushes to relieve herself.

"Who is that fifth man?" Puzzled Owen and Wilson shook his head; "Dunno, but he's a big lad and carrying two pistols: a gunfighter?" Their thoughts we interrupted by a stifled scream from Alex, who ran back from the bushes in some haste. She was still trying to pull down her dress and petticoats; so, everyone gained a glimpse of her thighs as she struggled with her clothes. "Now that's a pleasant treat." Murmured Wilson; grinning.

"I've just pissed on a dead man!" She yelped and the group made their way to the clump of bushes, moving quickly, but keeping low.

It was the young confederate deserter, laying face up in the wet dirt - half concealed by loose branches and leaves - in one hand was an old, large 'Navy' pistol, the other lay across his open stomach. The intestines had spilled out and lay sprawled down his legs. There were several silver coins scattered about his body.

"He must have been killed only a few hours ago, probably just after he left us." Alex said quietly, now recovered from the shock; her medical training had kicked in. She knelt down and examined the open wound. It was finely sliced, but deep.

She rose slowly; "He was killed with a large knife or maybe...." Wilson interrupted; "or a bloody sword and we know who carries one of those." They exchanged glances with the same thought; why would McIves kill the boy? Owen rubbed his face; "How the fuck does McIves do that?" He waved a hand at the boy; "I mean get so close to someone with a cocked pistol and kill them with a fucking sword, without being shot?"

No-one could answer that; not even Jericho. Alex made a mental note to ask him [McIves] when they met again; in private. Now that delicious thought did make her smile.

"Well it means that McIves has been here; but before the gunpowder turned up and why was he here?" Jericho pointed to the dead boy. "I had suspected that he was a 'plant', to foster suspicion against Clem Hazzard. The scrap piece of paper could easily have been placed in the pie tin after the pie was removed. Apparently eaten by the boy and left for us to find. Then that odd comment for a soldier deserting the Confederate army, do you remember it: "He [Clem Hazzard] said the south was about to rise again. I didn't understand that Sir, we ain't down yet!" Not the talk of someone about to walk away from the cause. I think that someone is playing a very clever game with us."

"Right, let's get to Clem Hazzard's place for now." Jericho added, staring sadly down at the dead boy. He then spoke to Owen; "Call up Dispatches and find which Collector attended this dispatch [death] and find out what he said." They quietly but quickly returned to their horses and set off for Clem Hazzard's place.

10. STUCK IN A BIG BATTLE.

They had crossed a small dirt road, between thin trees and broken fencing, when the first bullet struck a tree next to where Owen was standing; adjusting the girth of his horse. Everyone fell from their horses and crawled into the tree's for cover as bullets started to slap into trees and bushes around them.

Wilson found some large stones to hide his bulk behind and was joined by Alex. "Who the fuck is doing all the shooting!" She shouted and bullets ricocheted off the stones and hit the bushes nearby. "Bloody rebels - lots of them - down by that old died up creek bed and they're coming this way." Wilson flipped onto his back and checked his pistol, then saw Jericho gesturing at them. He and Owen were hunkered down amongst some thick bushes; the ground around them kicked up; as bullets hit the dirt.

Wilson reached into his pocket and pulled out his vibrating mirror; it was Jericho calling; "No arguments - jump now. You really cannot become a prisoner of these people. Get to Clem's place when you jump back. You will need another horse. They seem to have all ran off." Wilson was about to argue about leaving, when Alex slapped his arm; "Get the fuck out of here; you know what these bastards will do to a captured Black man!"

Reluctantly he nodded his agreement and activated the mirror. He was gone in an instant and she snuggled closer to the rocks. Alex could see several armed men approaching the trees where they were sheltering; two carried rebel flags and one was clearly an officer; he carried a sword and was actually wearing a proper grey uniform.

Jericho yelled across to Alex; "Pull your skirts up and use your petticoat as a white flag!" The bullets were now flying thick as flies, so Alex grabbed up her dress and pulled down her frilly white petticoat, exposing her long legs and thighs. Owen groaned and shouted to Jericho; "Wilson won't be happy at missing that treat!" Jericho just shook his head and then noticed the firing had stopped - then he saw why - Alex was waving her white petticoat above her head, with her dress still pulled up!

"Clever boss; No man is going to shoot that." Owen actually grinned and with Jericho, rose from the bushes - hands in air - Alex was soon decent again, when they joined her with the Confederate Officer and a small group of soldiers; all very interested in introducing themselves to Alex!

But the officer waved them away and spoke directly to Jericho; "Miss Alexandra tells me you are reporters from the Citizens Compiler Newspaper, based in Washington DC, covering the fighting here. I had heard tell from the town, that there were some nosey Yankee reporters hanging about the place."

"That's us Sir; we're covering the war for our readers up North. But we appear to have lost our cameraman and our damn horses. You can't miss him sir, a big, coloured man who's a freeman and well spoken." Jericho removed his hat and wiped his brow; "As I say Sir, he's a free born man of colour."

The officer just grunted; "If he's a n****er - then he's a slave. I don't go for any of this 'freeman' shit; he's contraband," The officer pushed his sword back into its scabbard and called over for the sergeant. Jericho was impressed that Alex kept her tongue firmly in her mouth; especially with the look she gave the rebel officer.

"Grab a couple of boys and take these Yankee reporters to Captain Delaney; he'll know what to do with them." The officer lifted his hat to Alex and re-joined his men, who were forming up in the dried Creek Bed. Jericho watched as the officer spoke to two men and they joined the sergeant. The old sergeant shouldered his musket and with the two scruffy men - one had no shoes - ordered the reporters to follow him; with hands on heads.

"That name rings a bell." Whispered Owen to Jericho and Alex; "Wasn't that the name of the rebel captain that the deserter mentioned, I mean the one talking to Clem Hazzard?" Jericho nodded. But was watching the quiet conversation between the two men, one had pulled a coin out and tossed it in the air. Jericho turned to Alex and said quietly; "I don't think they're taking us to their captain. I think we will never make the rebel encampment." She nodded her agreement; "We need to reach our mirrors; how do we do that with our hands up?" She whispered, then clearly heard one of the soldiers laughing about 'going first'.

Jericho and Alex exchanged glances; "Distraction time....and press that button as quickly as you can." Alex sighed and suddenly broke step, groaning and grabbing her ankle; she slid to the dirt, moaning about her ankle. The shoeless soldier pointed his musket - with bayonet attached - straight at her; "Get up you Yankee trollop." He said quietly.

Alex babbled on about her ankle and pointed to it, as she pulled her skirt right up - not forgetting she had removed her petticoat earlier - The soldier was getting a first class, close up look at what was on offer. He lowered the musket a little and smiled. The other soldier pushed him shouting; "I won the fucking toss, she's mine first."

The sergeant pushed between the two but said nothing as the roar of cannon drowned out any thinking or speaking. The ground was moving with shell fire, the dirt thrown up several feet into the air - the noise was unbearable - there was no time to do anything; except find cover.

Jericho grabbed Alex and together they fell down a small incline and scrambled for a horseshoe shaped group of rocks and dived in. "Where's Owen?" Alex shouted above the noise of the bombardment. Jericho didn't know and could now see lines of blue soldiers appearing; thousands of them.

"The bloody battle has started!" He shouted and added; "We appear to be in the middle of a bloody big battle, and I mean a big battle!" He pulled his mirror out and jabbed at the emergency icon; he, Alex and Owen were returned instantly to outside the lighthouse.

"They're all dead. The soldiers that were escorting us, they were caught by the cannon fire. I saw it happen; bloody awful." Owen was brushing dirt from his clothes, and he still looked a little shocked by what he had just witnessed. Alex gave him her hipflask and wiped his face with a hankie. It had little splatters of blood from the three soldiers. "There wasn't much left of them." He whispered to Alex and took a big swig from the hipflask. "Wilson's calling." Jericho muttered and answered his mirror. After a few minutes he looked up; "Well, Wilson has made contact with Clem, and we must return at once."

11. THAT'S NOT HISTORY.

From a small group of trees, Jericho, Alex and Owen sat and watched the sky. It was filled with whistling cannon fire and screaming of shells, as both armies clashed in the fields and roads of Gettysburg. Owen was keeping an eye on the small dirt road which lay behind the trees; "Nothing yet." He wiped sweat from his face with a gaudy red hankie and grinned at Alex; "Poor old Wilson missed the best bit - you'll have to hitch up your skirts again - so that he doesn't feel left out." He chuckled and checked his mirror.

Alex simply ignored him and spoke to Jericho; "I did wonder why old Sheriff Rook took the trouble to tell us about Miss Lillian and her supposed strange story that we would be interested in." Jericho nodded; "Well he couldn't really tell us directly that the lady was involved in a gunpowder plot to blow up the rebel HQ. What intrigues me is who told the conspirators, that the rebels would use the widow Thompson's house during the battle; that type of knowledge could only have come from time-travelers."

Alex had to agree with that and wondered when Wilson would turn up with the wagon; she didn't wait long. "They're here." Said Owen and rose from the damp dirt and brushed his trousers down. Alex did the same with her dress and straightened her bonnet. Jericho gestured towards the approaching wagon and keeping low, they quickly departed the trees for the dirt road.

They were clad to see Wilson and watched with great interest as Jericho and Clem Hazzard stood under a large tree and discussed some matters, for several minutes. Finally, they walked back towards the wagon. Alex whispered to Owen; "I'd love to have been a fly on that tree."

They joined Wilson; climbing aboard the canvas covered wagon, on which someone had painted - in black tar - 'Hospital' on both sides. A single brown horse - with saddle - was tied behind it with bulging saddlebags. Clem helped Alex aboard and she smiled to herself, as Clem Hazzard kissed her hand and asked her about being a female doctor; he was good looking and charming. Philadelphia was a lucky lady; she mused and asked Clem about the full saddlebags. "Medical supplies, I think I may need them." He explained with a smile.

Wilson slapped the reins and the horses pulled away. Owen was impressed; the big man knew how to drive a two-horse wagon. Wilson spoke quietly with Jericho; "Sheriff Rook has no great love for the Yankee's, but he doesn't think much of the Confederates either. He found out about the gunpowder plot from bloody

'Strangeways Stevens', who got drunk one night whilst playing poker with the sheriff and his brother-in-law; he blabbered out every detail. Luckily Sheriff Rook didn't pay any attention to his talk about 'small & tall' being time travelers."

Jericho nodded; "Why Miss Lillian?" Wilson smiled at that comment; "Pillow talk. It appears that the respectable School Ma'am really does like cock. 'Small & Tall' serviced her – together - she became part of their plan to blow up General Lee. It was her that told 'Strangeways' of the plot - he was yet another lover - and introduced him to 'small & tall'. Apparently, it was him who told 'small & tall' about a certain Jericho Tibbs, for money. So, they arranged for one of their number [Black eyed Benny] to knock you off, when you arrived; 'Strangeways' would give them the nod."

"Bastard traitor." muttered Owen and then smiled; "Fancy old Miss Lillian being a sexually liberated woman long before it was invented." Jericho turned round; "Say that again." Owen shrugged his shoulders and repeated what he had said. Alex smiled at Jericho; "You have that annoyingly 'I know' look on your face."

Jericho just smiled and pulled his mirror out.

"Why didn't the Sheriff arrest the fuckers; if he knew about the plot?" Owen asked and passed his hipflask round the little group. Clem Hazzard answered that one; "When the Sheriff had obtained all the details, he wondered who to call; but who could he call? The Northern Army wouldn't be exactly unhappy, if General Robert E. Lee disappeared in a puff of smoke. The Confederates? He doesn't hold with their principles, and he already had a run-in with Captain Delaney over the death of 'Black eyed Benny'. So he did some exemplary police work for an ex-cattleman; he infiltrated the group to find out more."

 Jericho rubbed his chin; "Clem, what was the 'run in' between Captain Delaney and the Sheriff over the dead gunman?" Clem waved away the offered hip-flask - he didn't touch alcohol - and settled back in the jolting wagon; "He wanted the Sheriff to raise a posse and get after McIves, he really wasn't happy about the death of 'Black eyed Benny'. I saw the reason when the Sheriff had me examine the boy's body. The Sheriff refused his request point blank; he wasn't about to take out a group of armed men, when they were surrounded by two enormous trigger-happy armies."

Alex sipped at the hipflask; ""What was the reason you saw?" She asked Clem and passed the hipflask to Wilson. Clem sighed; "It was realised by everyone who saw the body; the family resemblance between the two - Delaney and Benny - was really obvious, two peas' in a pod."

Jericho looked up from his mirror; "Delaney is of this time; he's a known historical figure. But we know that Benny was from 2016, he had to be a descendant of the captain." Jericho looked out the wagon, you could still see cannon fire and hear fighting in the distance; tomorrow would be the second day of battle.

He turned back to his team; "Miss Lillian Scott is the key to all this." and returned to his mirror. Everyone exchanged glances and Alex just had to ask; "How so Jericho?"

Jericho smiled; "Miss Scott hails from Delaware and probably breached the timeline in 2016 with our nasty little friend Benny; Young Benny Scott was on the run for murder in 2016 and Miss Scott knew the best place to hide him and where, he would be useful to her plans. None of them counted on McIves appearing on the scene."

"How did you get onto her?" Wilson sounded a little amazed and Jericho jerked a thumb at Owen; "He told me." Everyone stared at Owen who simply shrugged his shoulders; "What the hell did I say?" he asked. Jericho chuckled; "You said, 'Fancy old Miss Lillian being a sexually liberated woman long before it was invented' - and of course - remember, the Sheriff stated that she hadn't been around here long. I looked her up and found she wasn't from this time." He pushed his mirror back into his coat pocket; "According to Human Records, she was born in 1975, got married, had three children and guess who was the oldest?"

Alex sighed; "Bloody 'Black eyed Benny?"

He smiled at his team; "All three children were not by her estranged husband and that poor sap is a teacher of History and surprise, surprise, he is an indirect descendant of the Confederate General James Longstreet, who, if her plan went right, would be standing next to General Lee, when the bloody house disappears in a big explosion."

"Holy fucking shit, she wanted to bump off her estranged husband before he was even fucking born!" Owen exclaimed, adding;"Now that's one way to get away with murder." Alex smiled; "And it would not affect the outcome of the battle and thus the North would still win the civil war; would it not?"

"What is now of equal importance, to us anyway, is finding how Miss Lillian and her murdering brat managed to jump through time and arrive here." Jericho turned to Clem, adding: "Any ideas on that would be welcome."

Clem leaned back against the side of the wagon and blew his nose into a clean white hankie. "Delaney has a strange object stored in his travelling chest. I heard from his young soldier servant whose hand I fixed up, that he keeps it hidden. But he boy caught sight of it once when cleaning up in his tent. I don't know if this makes sense to any of you, but it was a human skull made of glass; beautiful but strange."

Jericho sighed; "A 'Da Vinci skull'. There were seven originally. I know we have recovered three, but there is still four out there and this must be one of them. They are 'free time portals' and they can take a living human to any place in history, provided you have a key to fix the time you want to visit."

Wilson coughed and waved a hand about; "They are named after the great man himself because it's suspected that he used one. But they have a big drawback; you must have another object from the time you wish to visit, so logically, they can only take you backwards in history. After all, few living humans possess stuff from the future."

"I wonder how Delaney got hold of it? Maybe from Miss Lillian? After all it could be him that she's actually with because of his resemblance to Benny; they may have been involved with each other for some time, with her maybe travelling back regularly to meet him?" Owen offered up his deductions and everyone felt he was certainly onto something; especially about Miss Lillian and Delaney's proposed relationship: the hard evidence being the strong likeness between Delaney and Benny.

"Miss Lillian's husband was well into history and may have

possessed relics from his ancestor from this time. All she had to do was match it with a 'Da Vinci' skull and she's away." Owen reasoned and sipped a little brandy.

Jericho turned again to Clem; "Best tell them about the messenger pies." and chuckled. "When I was called to cover old Doc Hogan, Miss Lillian was the one who conveyed the request. Being a kindly lady - apparently - she stayed with Philly and helped her bake some pies. She placed another copy of the map under the cooked pie that Philly was going to send to me. What she didn't realise was that Philly helped me with my assignments from Jericho and Philly caught on. So, Philly placed a message under your pie; you just didn't eat the damn thing quickly enough!"

Owen folded his arms; "Why put the map in your dish, if you were loyal to Jericho, that doesn't make sense?" Alex had to nod her agreement with that.

Clem chuckled; "Miss Lillian knew that she, Captain Delaney and old Doc Hogan would be enjoying the pie after our dinner together and she would be serving the meal. She could retrieve the new map, without any danger of her being caught with it, and pass it onto Delaney; who was her direct ancestor and whose descendant - according to Jericho's search of Human Records - was her lover and father of her first child; that bastard 'Black eyed Benny'."

He grinned and held up his hands; "She also had the delicious irony, that dumb Temporal Detectives would be responsible for delivering the map that would change their fortunes. It didn't matter if the great general Lee and Longstreet were killed. Any of the other Confederate generals could, following a bloody map like that, turn the battle, if necessary. But there was a huge fly in their pudding, and they had to deal with that." Clem looked at Jericho, who took up the story: "She had to get rid of her husband's ancestor by killing Longstreet, but she still needed the North to win because somehow, Delaney must survive the war and produce descendants; her being one of them. Had the North lost here, the war would have dragged on for another four years with the North still winning in the end. The good Captain Delaney would have had a very, almost certain chance of being killed in the much longer conflict. I checked with the Senior Time Controller about the alternative time-line, that extended war would have produced and there is no Miss Lillian Scott of Delaware." Jericho smiled and accepted the hipflask from Owen." So, she had to ensure that the map never reached Delaney despite promising to deliver it. I can safely assume that she arranged – probably by using sex – for the young deserter to turn up and go through his act. But we saw through part of it. Then of course McIves turned up."

"Now you don't read about this in the bloody history books." Chuckled Owen, but Alex voiced her concerns; "Who are 'small & tall' and what the hell are they trying to achieve? Wilson smiled and coughed; "Never mind them; who was the bloody big fly in their pudding?"

Clem smiled and spoke softly; "'Black eyed Benny' had taken ten silver dollars off Delaney to kill Jericho, but I met up with McIves - he was passing through to Washington on matters that he didn't talk about - and I told him what 'Delaney had arranged with Benny about Jericho's murder and he muttered that he had a debt to pay to Jericho and said he would deal with it, and he did. He became a big fly in their pudding because that could wreck their plans, if Jericho was still around."

"Now for small, tall and Miss Lillian." muttered Jericho, as the widow's Thompson's house came into view; the confederates had not occupied it yet. Union forces were encamped there - for the moment - Doctor Clem Hazzard unfurled the Union flag and it flew from the 'hospital' wagon.

12. ONE MOMENT IN TIME.

The Union picket watched the wagon approach quite carefully; this was a quiet sector of the battle - at the moment - but they wouldn't take any chances. They raised their muskets and shouted for the wagon to stop.

Jericho and Clem jumped from the wagon and walked slowly to the soldiers. Wilson turned to the others and grinned; "Our boss is a clever old bugger; just watch."

Alex and Owen smiled as the soldiers saluted Jericho and called for their officer. "What the fuck!" Owen seemed quite amazed by this turn of events. Alex just shook her head and smiled. The wagon was waved forward, and the picket soldiers raised their hats to Alex with shouts of; "Welcome Ma'am!" They met the officer some way from the farmhouse - just in case. The officer carefully checked the badges and papers shown to him by Jericho and Clem. "I'd heard that General Meade had set up such a group and called it 'Military Intelligence', but never thought I'd meet any of them!" The officer smiled and listened intently, as Jericho outlined the dastardly rebel plan to blow up General Meade, while he stayed at the farmhouse. The officer immediately ordered a search of the farmhouse - a very quiet and careful search - and was absolutely astonished to find the bags of gunpowder beneath the floorboards.

Jericho also advised him to search on the small ridge; because there was the body of brave and committed confederate soldier, who had been hiding, ready to set the explosives off. Clem admitted that one of their operatives had already dealt with him - finishing him quietly - with no shooting to raise the alarm.

A corporal from the Union picket found the body and signalled its finding from the ridge. They watched as the barrels were removed and the officer shook Jericho and Clem's hands vigorously. They celebrated by passing a brandy bottle amongst themselves. The young officer really enjoyed that, and he got to chat with Alex for some minutes; giving her his card and telling her to look him up, next time she was in Boston.

They said their farewells and the wagon passed down The Chambersburg Pike towards the Union Army positions. That's when Wilson spotted the solitary horseman approaching; you couldn't really miss him; he was wearing a vivid yellow dust coat. "McIves." Alex whispered to Owen and the wagon pulled up.

McIves wiped dirt from his face and grinned broadly at Jericho and raised his hat to Alex. "So, you managed to dodge murder, execution and being blown up." McIves spoke to Jericho, who shook his hand. "What do you know of the pair called 'Too Tall and too small'?" Jericho asked.

McIves chuckled; "Sheriff Rook went after them after the explosives were discovered and thus, he now has a free hand to deal with everything. He was a little astonished, that they escaped from him, despite being surrounded in a livery stable. He couldn't believe that they just vanished. All I know about that strange pair is that were from Scotland - originally - and they had some kind of connection with Captain Delaney." McIves rubbed his rough unshaven face and nodded his head; "This bit you definitely won't like; the pair may have given Delaney a bloody Da Vinci Skull."

Jericho sighed; he really wanted to catch up with that pair, but now he would have to check whether Delaney actually possessed one of crystal skulls which permitted unlimited time travel. But he asked about Miss Lillian. McIve's expression changed; "She and 'Strangeways' were caught by rebel troops just north of the town. They were camped down for the night when the rebels surprised them. That bloody idiot 'Strangeways' pulled his pistol and was shot about four times by musket fire. The rebels searched the wagon and found Miss Lillian with two coloured men - unfortunately in a state of undress - The rebels didn't show any mercy; they lynched the two-coloured lads and then shot Miss Lillian, after tying her to a big tree." McIves wiped his face and accepted Alex's hipflask.

He continued; "At least they had the decency to bury them near 'Small Round top'. I heard it from a drunken Confederate soldier that the officer in charge; a certain Major Cantor hated women and coloured people in equal measure. Apparently, he took great pleasure in the killings." He swigged the hipflask and handed it back; thanking Alex.

Wilson interrupted and tapped his mirror; "A collector filed a report about collecting my two 'brothers' souls at the time, but, obviously, not Miss Lillian's. Here's the interesting bit; there was no collection listed for a 'Thomas Louis 'Strangeways' Stevens' at the time; he wasn't dead. Somehow, he survived a multiple shooting! His soul wasn't collected for another year, in August 1864 to be exact."

McIves grunted; "The devil looks after his own." He jerked a thumb behind him, adding; "The rebels are now approaching here fast. I understand that old granny Lee himself is moving his HQ this way; towards the widow Thompson's place."

Alex leaned forward in the wagon and asked Jericho about the Union picket still at the farmhouse. Jericho didn't smile; "The rebels take the place after some fighting. None of the Union picket survives that scrap. That's how come the history books, say nothing of the Gettysburg Gunpowder plot - there was no-one left alive to tell the story - it was just one moment in time that went unrecorded."

"But what about Sheriff Rook; he knew all about it." Owen asked; a little puzzled. Jericho nodded and folded his arms; "The Sheriff and his deputy, who were present at the farmhouse with the gunpowder, never told a soul about their involvement. They really didn't want the occupying Union forces to know that they thwarted a plot to blow up General Lee; they feared reprisals. But it didn't matter; just weeks after the battle, Rook and his over sized deputy were killed by renegade Union deserters, who were raiding the countryside around here. They took the story to their graves."

Wilson leaned back on the wagon seat and rubbed his chin; "What about that gunfighter, we saw with the Sheriff at the unloading of the gunpowder; the fellow with two pistols?" Jericho shook his head; "History doesn't record his involvement; he must have stayed silent about the affair."

McIves had suddenly become interested in Wilson's words and asked him; "Was he a big man, with two white handled pistols; the handles pointing away from him?"

Wilson nodded. McIves sat up in his saddle; "Keep an eye out for him Jericho. Had you searched his travelling bags, you would have found a strange Aztec Statue. He used to be a successful Archaeologist who went by the name of Doctor Sage Columbine. Sometime in the 1920's, he discovered the statute at some dig in Mexico; it's a free travel portal and he's been using it ever since. I've encountered him a couple of times in other eras. He's a strange dark character that swings good and bad in equal measure. But if he's on your side; he's loyal."

Alex hid her smile at the mention of Sage's name and said nothing about how much they enjoyed each other's bodies. She and McIves also shared a couple of 'knowing' glances and small smiles.

McIves expressed his goodbyes and disappeared down the road, heading towards the Union lines. Wilson turned to Alex; "And our friend would know all about objects that carry 'free time portals'. That bloody black sword is cursed with one." Alex agreed with Wilson's deduction; she had suspected it for some time. Then glanced at Jericho - deep in conversation with Clem Hazzard - and wondered why he hadn't dealt with the matter.

Everyone said farewell to Clem, who would take his horse into Gettysburg and offer his assistance to the Union Surgical Unit, now working there; with a wave, he disappeared towards the ever changing Union lines with a lot of caution. Both armies were trigger happy around strangers!

13. THE 'DA VINCI' SKULL.

Jericho told Wilson to head for the rebel lines: the back way and do it extra sneakily!

"You get everything I asked for?" Jericho asked Wilson, who nodded and told Owen to unwrap the canvas bundle under his seat. Owen pulled it through into the wagon and threw it open. Alex just had to smile; "I take it we're going after that damn skull." Jericho chuckled; "Well, we can't leave the bloody thing lying around here, especially since Delaney knows what it's capable of." By the time the 'hospital' wagon reached the rebel encampment, the team had acquired their new identities. Jericho was now a Surgeon in the Confederate Army with the rank of Captain; his uniform even had authentic looking blood stains and he smelt strongly of chloroform!

Owen was wearing an ill-fitting and shabby Confederate uniform complete with old boots and 'medical orderly' armband. Wilson was unchanged; he was the good 'Doctor's' Negro man servant and cook. He didn't have to dress up for that role. Miss Alexandra was now a Southern 'Belle' with blood-stained apron and her hair tied up, she was a certain Captain Joe 'Shamrock' Delaney's sister from Virginia and had a pass from General James Longstreet to prove it!

They were stopped by several rebel soldiers guarding the dirt road into the camp and everyone was immediately impressed by Jericho's accent. He wearily explained to the sergeant, that he had to escort this lady to her brother on Jim Longstreet's order's, then make his way to the field hospital. He produced the pass, and the sergeant examined it closely. But it was the skinny, younger man with pebble glasses that could actually read and agreed that was Longstreet's signature and the stamp was true.

The sergeant called a young officer over to the group and explained about the pass. The young man bowed and lifted his hat to Alex and told her that he would personally escort her to her brother's tent. Owen helped Alex down and volunteered to carry her travelling case for her, which was gracefully received.

Jericho and Wilson would wait with the wagon, near the cookhouse tents for the pair's return. They reached Captain Delaney's tent a few minutes later and the officer said farewell - reluctantly - to Alex, kissing her hand and bowing. Alex and Owen didn't waste any time searching the tent and pulled Delaney's travelling chest from under some horse blankets. Owen carefully opened the trunk and gently pulled the dark cloth back to reveal the eerie glass skull. "It's quite beautiful." Alex softly muttered and Owen carefully placed it into Alex's canvas traveling bag and covered it with a rough army towel.

They both looked up as the big figure appeared through the tent flap, cussing and throwing his hat onto the camp bed. He stared at the pair and rubbed his beard, a little puzzled at a beautiful woman and a young confederate medical orderly standing – smiling – in his bloody tent. Alex was quick off the mark – as she normally is! – With a wonderful curtsey showing her restrained breasts. "My, My, sweet Lord cousin David you have surely grown! The army life must suit like a bear wearing a fur coat!"

Delaney stared at her and shrugged his shoulders, replying in a dour voice; "Ma'am I think you're mistaken, I'm Joseph Francis 'Shamrock' Delaney a captain of Calvary in the glorious army of North Virginia!"

Owen now jumped in, saluting and explaining; "Sir, the lady has a pass signed by General Longstreet to visit her brother, a certain Captain Silas Daniels and several men at the food line pointed out this tent was his!" Owen had done his homework on this mission and captain Daniel's was here today [he wouldn't leave Gettysburg, being killed during Pickett's charge on the last day of fighting] and so Delaney just grunted and gestured to the tent flap; "You'll find old Silas at the end of this row of tents, he has a brown goat tied up outside. You probably know that's he's partial to fresh goat's milk in his coffee."

Alex clasped her hand together apologizing profusely and thanked the captain for his kindness, pushing back the tent flap she then signaled to Owen leave and the pair made for the Cookhouse tents, where several hundred men were starting to queue for their meals. Several cheered and waved at her. She returned a little lady-like wave and received even more cheers. The happy pair met up with Jericho and Wilson, just as the shout when up from Captain Delaney: he was a suspicious man by nature and had checked his footlocker!

Jericho looked about and pressed the Travel App on his mirror and the team found themselves outside the lighthouse on a warm summer night. A three-mast sailing ship could be seen on the horizon. Alex noted that the time was 7.35pm; as it always was.

As they walked to the lighthouse, Owen suddenly remembered the assignment Jericho had given him regarding the dead confederate deserter and he pulled Alex to one side; "Should I bother to give Jericho the story, that the young dead deserter told Little Kate the Collector?" Alex shrugged her shoulders; "Seems a bit pointless now, but what was it?"

Owen sighed; "Well, he said that he was betrayed and the bugger with him pulled out a 'Bowie' knife and gutted him before he could use his pistol. They were on the ridge together; waiting for Miss Lillian and the wagon."

Alex looked puzzled; "So McIves didn't kill him?"

Owen nodded; "Nah, he didn't. it was 'Strangeways' that knifed him, came up from behind and gutted him like a fish - even with the pistol cocked - the boy never suspected that his companion would do such a thing; they were bloody conspirators together. 'Strangeways' dropped his money bag with all those silver dollars in, during the fight. He couldn't stop and pick them up because someone else had appeared." Owen started to walk to the lighthouse; arm in arm with Alex.

Alex remembered the coins scattered about the boy's body and no-one had questioned why they were there! She stopped; "So those coins were from Jericho, he gave 'Strangeways' them at the farmhouse. We should have guessed that 'Strangeways' had done the killing by the presence of those damn coins. We could have known about the two-timing rat earlier."

Owen nodded and continued with the story that the boy had

recounted to the Collector; "The boy - whose name was Jacob Sanderson from Mississippi - had been working for Captain Delaney, posing as a deserter to infiltrate a nest of Union spies; that was us by the way. He was told to acquire the pie at all costs because the little dinner party, arranged for the delivery of the pie, had to be called off because they suspected Rook was on to them; especially after the row between Delaney and Rook over Benny. But hunger got the best of him, and he ate the bloody thing and suddenly, we were onto him."

Jericho turned and gestured for Owen and Alex to catch up; dinner was roast lamb tonight. Alex said quietly; "What was he and 'Strangeways' doing on the ridge and who turned up after he had been killed?"

Owen gripped her arm and smiled, in that dumb manner that infuriated Wilson; "They were going to blow up the house after everyone had set the explosives and gone. Someone [the boy didn't know who] had paid 'Strangeways' to carry it out. He [Jacob] thought it was Captain Delaney because he turned up on the ridge after the boy was murdered. He couldn't see what the captain did because the Collector took his soul then. But the odd thing is the captain didn't set the explosives off because we know that the ill-fated Union picket removed them later; now that's a strange twist eh?"

"Maybe Delaney discovered that Miss Lillian didn't want the map to fall into Confederate hands because she needed him to survive?" Alex said quietly and sighed; "Also, why didn't Delaney pick up the silver dollars and if 'Strangeways' was in collusion with him; why did he run off so fast that he didn't pick up the money? And where did Delaney actually get that dam glass skull?"

She believed that there was more to this mission than had been worked out and should Jericho hear about what Owen had discovered; but would it alter the results achieved by the team?

The captain must have returned to the farmhouse for some reason and why pay Steven's to blow up the damn place before anyone was even in it? Maybe Lillian had told him about the war lasting years longer and the huge chance of him dying in that extended conflict? Not that it mattered now with Lillian being murdered, the time line had changed with her death that lost her soul to the darkness of real death. That in turn meant that none of her children were born, including the murderous 'Black Eyed Benny.' Angel Margret – apparently – was quite happy about the outcome and allowed the minor changes to the current Human Time Line.

They followed Jericho and Wilson into the lighthouse and she smiled to herself; there could be a very lively dinner conversation tonight!

SOME BOOKS AVAILABLE IN THE "TEMPORAL DETECTIVES" SERIES.

[Available from 'Amazon.com' and all good bookshops!]

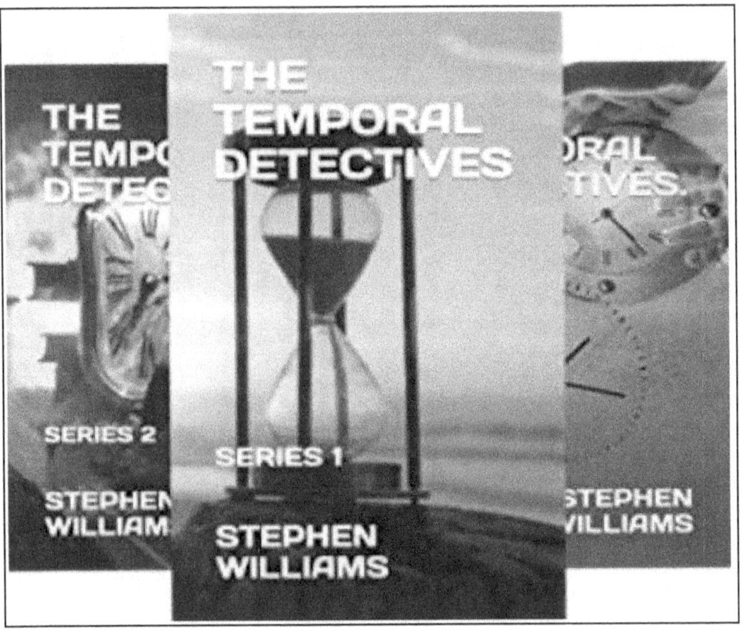

"THE TEMPORAL DETECTIVES!"

"Welcome to the amazing adventures of Mister Jericho Tibbs!" Jericho lives in Stark Island's Lighthouse on Heaven's Edge Bay, in the North of Scotland. A wild and desolate place, the now disused lighthouse is his home and office. You see, Jericho actually works for God - well, his direct Boss is, for now - Angel Margret who is the current Duty Death Angel and runs the Temporal Detectives Department. The Temporal Detectives police the current Timeline of Humanity on the lookout for people who, for whatever reason, have appeared in the wrong time and place in human history. Their mission is protecting the current human Timeline from unwanted changes."

AGE RECOMMENDATION.

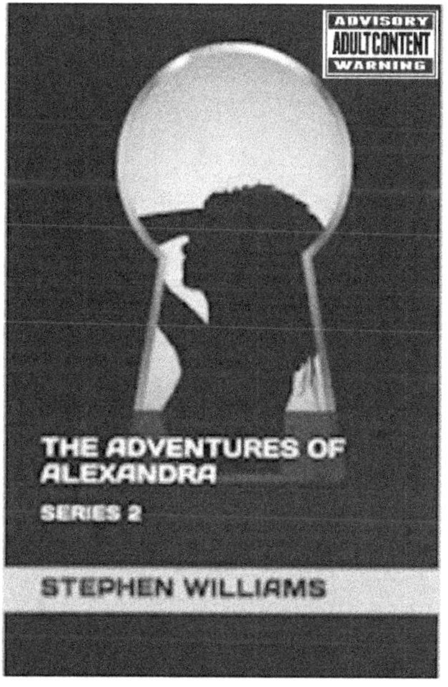

"THE ADVENTURES OF ALEXANDRA: Series 2."

AVAILABLE FROM 'AMAZON.COM' and all good bookshops!

Scan QR code to visit website.

Or type: https://**xxxalexandra.blogspot.com**

AGE RECOMMENDATION:

"These stories contain mild adult erotica which is recommended only suitable for persons aged 18 years and over."